THE SHADOW OF ASHLYDYAT

MRS HENRY WOOD

THE SHADOW OF ASHLYDYAT

ALAN SUTTON PUBLISHING LIMITED

First published in 1863

First published in this edition in the United Kingdom in 1994
Alan Sutton Publishing Limited
Phoenix Mill · Far Thrupp · Stroud · Gloucestershire

First published in this edition in the United States of America in 1994
Alan Sutton Publishing Inc.
83 Washington Street · Dover · NH 03820

Copyright © in this edition
Alan Sutton Publishing Limited, 1994

British Library Cataloguing-in-Publication Data

A catalogue record for this book is available from the British Library.

ISBN 0-7509-0686-3

Library of Congress Cataloging-in-Publication Data applied for

Alan Sutton Publishing Limited.
Printed in Great Britain by
The Guernsey Press Company Limited,
Guernsey, Channel Islands.

"Over him rushed, like a wind that is keen and cold and relentless,
Thoughts of what might have been, and the weight and woe of his
   errand:
All the dreams that had faded, and all the hopes that had vanished,
All his life henceforth a dreary and tenantless mansion,
Haunted by vain regrets, and pallid, sorrowful faces."

LONGFELLOW

CONTENTS

PART THE THIRD

BIOGRAPHICAL NOTE

MRS HENRY WOOD is the married title and pseudonym of Ellen Price who was one of the most popular Sensation novelists of the 1860s–90s. *East Lynne*, her first novel, sold 500,000 copies and subsequent novels achieved sales of nearly two-and-a-half million by 1900. Yet the figure behind the name remained self-effacing and obscure. What was this remarkable woman like? In view of the nature of *East Lynne*, the answer is perhaps rather surprising.

Born in Worcester in 1814, Mrs Henry Wood was the daughter of a glove manufacturer called Thomas Price. Her upbringing was provincial and unexceptional but she was dogged by ill-health and as a very young woman became a virtual invalid. Illness, whether real or psychosomatic, was to be a problem throughout her life but did not prevent her from writing prolifically and profitably. She married a banker called Henry Wood in 1836, and left Worcester to take up residence in France where she lived for twenty years. Both locations appear in her novels; *Johnny Ludlow*, for example (12 vols 1874–89) is set in Worcestershire, and France is used as a land of exile in *East Lynne* (1861).

In 1856 the Woods returned to London and here Mrs Henry Wood spent the rest of her life until she died in 1887. Soon after their move to England Mr Wood's business foundered and it was the urgent need for money that prompted his wife to write for financial gain. She received little support from her husband whom her son described as having 'not a spark of imagination. . . . It was an effort to him to read a novel.' Nevertheless she began writing, starting her career with several short stories which appeared in the *New Monthly Magazine* and *Bentley's Miscellany*. *East Lynne* was published in 1861 and was followed by another forty novels in the ensuing twenty-six years. *The Shadow of Ashlydyat* was published in 1863, and Mrs Wood felt it was her best novel.

In 1867 she assumed the editorship of the *Argosy Magazine*, to which she also contributed. Her authorial appetite was astounding; despite invalidity and being confined to a sofa for much of the time 'she never knew what it was not to be in the humour for writing. It was not only that she could always write, but she ever felt the need to do so – a power urging her, whether she would or no.' (Charles Wood, 1895.) Clearly a woman of considerable business acumen and, as her novels reveal, with a taste for the wildly sensational and outrageous, she was also a paradox. According to those who knew her she appeared to be a perfectly ordinary housewife, interested in the mundane and the domestic. It was as if bearing her husband's name – Henry Wood – provided her with a mask behind which she could indulge in all the literary fantasies that belonged to Ellen Price and which dominate her Sensation fiction.

East Lynne is a truly sensational novel in every sense of the word. While some of her subsequent fiction, such as *The Channings*, reinforced the reputation of Mrs Henry Wood as a chronicler of the everyday English life of the Victorian period, it was the extremism and unorthodoxy of *East Lynne* which established her literary career. The plot alone is breathtakingly lurid and features virtually every aspect of outraged Victorian morality. The sanctity of marriage and the family, female virtue and devoted motherhood are all destroyed by the central character, Lady Isabel Vane. Her 'fall' from grace is total and all the more reprehensible because she comes from the highest social circles. Her seducer is an unscrupulous murderer who abandons his lover and their illegitimate child; he too is of aristocratic stock. No one is safe. Even the solid, respectable, middle-class solicitor Archibald Carlyle who provides the moral backbone of the novel is seen to be hurt and damaged by his adulterous wife.

The harsh message of Victorian morality is clear: 'Never to be redeemed'. In this lies much of the tension in the novel. While Isabel's actions are directly condemned by authorial interjections, and the reader's attention constantly drawn to higher moral standards, Isabel remains a highly attractive and sympathetic character. Perhaps one of the most disturbing elements of the novel is her appeal to the reader for whom she was devised. This is a novel written by a woman, for women. Distributed initially through the circulating libraries which were predominantly supported by prosperous ladies, its immense popularity confirms that it struck a chord within the female population. Isabel represents the repressed frustrations, emotions, boredom and anger of women confined to narrow domestic lives, dependent upon men and expected to achieve fulfilment through others. Of course Isabel receives her come-uppance; the fabric of respectable society must in the end be preserved, but it is the fantasy of her rebellion that proved so attractive, and subversive.

Melodrama and sensationalism abound, but there is more to the novel than this. The intricate plot is sustained and compulsive. Interwoven with Isabel's search for self-fulfilment is a sinister sub-plot in which a murder needs to be solved. It is one of the first tales of detection in Victorian fiction. The power of the novel has long been recognized; it has been repeatedly filmed, dramatized and translated into other languages since its publication. Despite its insistent moralizing and occasional melodrama it remains today as poignant and as forceful as in 1861.

FIONN O'TOOLE

THE SHADOW OF ASHLYDYAT.

CHAPTER I.

THE MEET OF THE HOUNDS.

IT was a bright day in autumn : the scene one of those fair ones rarely witnessed except in England.   The sun, warm and glowing, almost as that of a summer's day, shone on the stubble of the cornfields, whence the golden grain had recently been gathered ; gilded the tops of the trees—so soon to pass into the " sere and yellow leaf ; " illumined the blue hills in the distance, and brought out the nearer features of the landscape in all their light and shade.   A fine landscape, comprising hill and dale, water and green pastures, woods and open plains. Amidst them rose the signs of busy life ; mansions, cottages, hamlets, railways, and churches, whose steeples ascended high, pointing the way to a better Land.

The town of Prior's Ash, lying in a valley, was alive that gay morning with excitement.   It was the day appointed for the first meet of the hounds ; the P. A. hounds, of some importance in the county ; and people from far and near were flocking to see them throw off. Old and young, gentle and simple, lords of the soil and tradesmen, all were wending their way to the meet.   The master, Colonel Max, was wont on this, the first morning of the season, to assemble at his house for breakfast as many as his large dining-room could by any species of crowding contain ; and it was a fine sight, drawing forth its numerous spectators to watch them come out in procession, to the meet.   As many carriages-and-four, with their fair occupants, would come to that first meet, as you could have seen in the old days on a country race-course.   This show was an old-fashioned local custom ; Colonel Max was pleased to keep it up, and he lacked not supporters. The opening this year was unusually early.

The gay crowd was arriving, some from the breakfast, some from their homes.   The rendezvous was a wide, open common, with no space wanting.   The restrained hounds snarled away at a short distance, and their attendants, attired for the hunt, clacked their whips among them.

Riding a noble horse, and advancing from the opposite direction to that of Colonel Max and his guests, came a tall, stately man, getting in years now.   His features were regular as though they had been chiselled from marble : his fine blue eyes could sparkle yet ; and his snow-white hair, wavy as of yore, was worn rather long behind, giving him somewhat the appearance of a patriarch. But the healthy bloom, once characteristic of his face, had left it now: the paleness of ill-health sat there, and he bent his body, as if too weak to bear up on his horse. His approach was discerned; and many started forward, as with one impulse, to greet him. None stood higher in the estima- of his fellow-men than did Sir George Godolphin; no other name was more respected in the county.

"This is good indeed, Sir George! To see you out again!"

"I thought I might venture," said Sir George, essaying to meet a dozen hands at once. "It has been a long confinement; a tedious illness. Six months, and never out of the house; and, for the last fortnight, out only in a garden-chair. My lady wanted to box me up in the carriage this morning; if I must come, she said. But I would not have it: had I been unable to sit my horse, I would have remained at home."

"You fell weak still?" remarked one, after most of the greeters had had their say, and were moving away.

"Ay. Strength, for me, has finally departed, I fear."

"You must not think that, Sir George. Now that you have so far recovered as to go out, you will improve daily."

"And get well all one way, Godolphin," joined in the hearty voice of Colonel Max. "Never lose heart, man."

Sir George turned his eyes upon Colonel Max with a cheerful glance. "Who told you I was losing heart?"

"Yourself. When a man begins to talk of his strength having finally departed, what's that, but a proof of his losing heart? Low spirits never cured any one yet: but they have killed thousands."

"I shall be sixty-six years old to-morrow, colonel: and if, at that age, I can 'lose heart' at the prospect of the great change, my life has served me to little purpose. The young may faint at the near approach of death; the old should not."

"Sixty-six, old!" ejaculated Colonel Max. "I have never kept count of my own age, but I know I am that if I am a day; and I am young yet. I may live these thirty years to come: and shall try for it, too."

"I hope you will, colonel," was the warm answer of Sir George Godolphin. "Prior's Ash could ill spare you."

"I don't know about that," laughed the colonel. "But I do know that I could ill spare life. I wish you could take the run with us this morning!"

"I wish I could. But that you might accuse me of—what was it? —losing heart, I would say that my last run with the hounds has been taken. It has cost me an effort to come so far as this, walking my horse at a snail's pace. Do you see Lady Godolphin? She ought to be here."

Colonel Max, who was a short man, raised himself in his stirrups, and gazed from point to point of the gradually increasing crowd. "In her carriage, I suppose?"

"In her carriage, of course," answered Sir George. "She is no amazon." But he did not avow his reason for inquiring after his wife's carriage—that he felt a giddiness stealing over him, and thought he might be glad of its support. Neither did he explain that he was unable to look round for it himself just then, under fear of falling from his horse.

"I don't think she has come yet," said Colonel Max. "I do not see the livery. As to the ladies, they all look so like one another now, with their furbelows and feathers, that I'll be shot if I should know my own wife—if I had one—at a dozen paces' distance. Here is some one else, however."

Riding up quietly, and reining in at the side of Sir George, was a gentleman of middle height, with dark hair, dark grey eyes, and a quiet, pale countenance. In age he may have wanted some three or four years of forty, and a casual observer might have pronounced him "insignificant," and never have cast on him a second glance. But there was a certain attraction in his face which won its way to hearts; and his voice sounded wonderfully sweet and kind as he grasped the hand of Sir George.

"My dear father! I am so glad to see you here!"

"And surprised too, I conclude, Thomas," returned Sir George, smiling on his son. "Come closer to me, will you, and let me rest my arm upon your shoulder for a minute. I feel somewhat giddy."

"Should you have ventured out on horseback?" inquired Thomas Godolphin, as he hastened to place himself in proximity with his father.

"The air will do me good; and the exertion also. It is nothing to feel a little weak after a confinement such as mine has been. You don't follow the hounds to-day, I see, Thomas," continued Sir George, noting his son's plain costume.

A smile crossed Thomas Godolphin's lips. "No, sir. I rarely do follow them. I leave amusement to George."

"Is he here, that graceless George?" demanded the knight, searching into the crowd with fond and admiring eyes. But the admiring eyes did not see the object they thought to rest on.

"He is sure to be here, sir. I have not seen him."

"And your sisters? Are they here?"

"No. They did not care to come."

"Speak for Janet and Cecil, if you please, Thomas," interrupted a young lady's voice at this juncture. The knight looked down; his son looked down also: there stood the second daughter of the family, Bessy Godolphin. She was a dark, quick, active little woman of thirty, with an ever-ready tongue, and deep grey eyes.

"Bessy!" uttered Sir George, in astonishment. "Have you come here on foot?"

"Yes, papa. Thomas asked us whether we wished to attend the meet; and Janet—who must always be master and mistress, you know—answered that we did not. Cecil dutifully agreed with her. I did care to attend it; so I came alone."

"But, Bessy, why did you not say so?" remonstrated Mr. Godolphin. "You should have ordered the carriage; you should not have come on foot. What will people think?"

"Think!" she echoed, holding up her pleasant face to her brother, in its saucy independence. "They can think anything they please; I

am Bessy Godolphin. I wonder how many scores have come on
foot?"

"None, Bessy, of your degree, who have carriages to sit in or horses
to ride," said Sir George.

"Papa, I like to use my legs better than to have them cramped
under a habit or in a carriage; and you know I never could bend to
form and fashion," she said, laughing. "Dear papa, I am delighted
to see you! I was so thankful when I heard you were here! Janet
will be ready to eat her own head now, for not coming."

"Who told you I was here, Bessy?"

"Old Jekyl. He was leaning on his palings as I came by, and called
out the information to me almost before I could hear him. 'The
master's gone to it, Miss Bessy! he is out once again! But he had
not on his scarlet,' the old fellow added; and his face lost its gladness.
Papa, the whole world is delighted that you should have recovered, and
be once more amongst them."

"Not quite recovered yet, Bessy. Getting better, though; getting
better. Thank you, Thomas; the faintness has passed."

"Is not Lady Godolphin here, papa?"

"She must be here by this time. I wish I could see her carriage:
you must get into it."

"I did not come for that, papa," returned Bessy, with a touch of her
warm temper.

"My dear, I *wish* you to join her. I do not like to see you here on
foot."

"I shall set the fashion, papa," laughed Bessy, again. "At the
great meet next year, you will see half the pretenders of the county
toiling here on foot. I say I am Bessy Godolphin."

The knight ranged his eyes over the motley group, but he could not
discern his wife. Sturdy, bluff old fox-hunters were there in plenty,
and well-got-up young gentlemen, all on horseback, their white cords
and scarlet coats gleaming in the sun. Ladies were chiefly in carriages; a few were mounted, who would ride quietly home again when
the hounds had thrown off; a very few—they might be counted by
units—would follow the field. Prior's Ash and its neighbourhood was
supplied in a very limited degree with what they were pleased to call
masculine women: for the term "fast" had not then come in. Many
a pretty woman, many a pretty girl was present, and the sportsmen
lingered, and were well pleased to linger, in the sunshine of their
charms, ere the business, for which they had come out, began, and
they should throw themselves, heart and energy, into it.

On the outskirts of the crowd, sitting her horse well, was a handsome girl of right regal features and flashing black eyes. Above the
ordinary height of woman, she was finely formed, her waist slender,
her shoulders beautifully modelled. She wore a peculiar dress, and,
from that cause alone, many eyes were on her. A well-fitting habit of
bright grass-green, the corsage ornamented with buttons of silver-gilt;
similar buttons were also at the wrists, but they were partially hidden
by her white gauntlets. A cap, of the same bright green, rested on
the upper part of her forehead, a green-and-gold feather on its left side
glittering as the sun's rays played upon it. It was a style of dress which

had not yet been seen at Prior's Ash, and was regarded with some doubt. But, as you are aware, it is not a dress in itself which is condemned or approved: it depends upon who wears it: and as the young lady wearing this was just now the fashion at Prior's Ash, feather and habit were taken into favour forthwith. She could have worn none more adapted to her peculiar style of beauty.

Bending to his very saddle-bow, as he talked to her—for, though she was tall, he was taller still—was a gentleman of courtly mien. In his fine upright figure, his fair complexion and wavy hair, his chiselled features and dark blue eyes, might be traced a strong resemblance to Sir George Godolphin. But the lips had a more ready smile upon them than Sir George's had ever worn, for his had always been somewhat of the sternest; the blue eyes twinkled with a gayer light when gazing into other eyes, than could ever have been charged upon Sir George. But the bright complexion had been Sir George's once; giving to his face, as it now did to his son's, a delicate beauty, almost as that of woman. "Graceless George," old Sir George was fond of calling him; but it was an appellation given in love, in pride, in admiration. He bent to his saddle-bow, and his gay blue eyes flashed with unmistakable admiration into those black ones as he talked to the lady: and the black eyes most certainly flashed admiration back again. Dangerous eyes were those of Charlotte Pain's! And not altogether lovable.

"Do you always keep your promises as you kept that one yesterday?" she was asking him.

"I did not make a promise yesterday—that I remember. Had I made one to you, I should have kept it."

"Fickle and faithless," she cried. "Men's promises are as words traced upon the sand. When you met me yesterday in the carriage with Mrs. Verrall, and she asked you to take compassion on two forlorn dames, and come to Ashlydyat in the evening and dissipate our ennui, what was your answer?"

"That I would do so, if it were possible."

"Was nothing more explicit implied?"

George Godolphin laughed. Perhaps his conscience told him that he *had* implied more, in a certain pressure he remembered giving to that fair hand, which was resting now, gauntleted, upon her reins. Gay George had meant to dissipate Ashlydyat's ennui, if nothing more tempting offered. But something more tempting did offer: and he had spent the evening in the company of one who was more to him than was Charlotte Pain.

"An unavoidable engagement arose, Miss Pain. Otherwise you may rely upon it I should have been at Ashlydyat."

"Unavoidable!" she replied, her eyes gleaming with something very like anger into those which smiled on her. "I know what your engagement was. You were at Lady Godolphin's Folly."

"Right. Commanded to it by my father."

"Oh!"

"Solicited, if not absolutely commanded," he continued. "And a wish from Sir George now bears its weight: we may not have him very long with us."

A smile of mockery, pretty and fascinating to look upon, played upon her rich red lips. " It is edifying to hear these filial sentiments expressed by Mr. George Godolphin! Take you care, sir, to act up to them."

" Do you think I need the injunction? How shall I make my peace with you?"

" By coming to Ashlydyat some other evening while the present moon lasts. I mean, while it illumines the early part of the evening."

She dropped her voice to a low key, and her tone had changed to seriousness. George Godolphin looked at her in surprise.

" What is the superstition," she continued to whisper, " that attaches to Ashlydyat?"

" Why do you ask me this?" he hastily said.

" Because, yesterday evening, when I was sitting on that seat under the ash-trees, watching the road from Lady Godolphin's Folly—well, watching for you, if you like it better: but I can assure you there is nothing in the avowal that need excite your vanity, as I see it is doing. When a gentleman makes a promise, I expect him to keep it; and, looking upon your coming as a matter of course, I did watch for you; as I might watch for one of Mrs. Verrall's servants, had I sent him on an errand and expected his return."

" Thank you," said George Godolphin, with a laugh. " But suffer my vanity to rest in abeyance for a while, will you, and go on with what you were saying?"

" Are you a convert to the superstition?" she inquired, disregarding the request.

" N—o," replied George Godolphin. But his voice sounded strangely indecisive. " Pray continue, Charlotte."

It was the first time he had ever called her by her Christian name: and though she saw that it was done in the unconscious excitement of the moment, her cheeks flushed to a deeper crimson.

" Did you ever see the Shadow?" she breathed.

He bowed his head.

" What form does it take?"

George Godolphin did not answer. He appeared lost in thought, as he scored his horse's neck with his hunting-whip.

" The form of a bier, on which rests something covered with a pall, that may be supposed to be a coffin; with a mourner at the head and one at the foot?" she whispered.

He bowed his head again: very gravely.

" Then I saw it last night. I did indeed. I was sitting under the ash-trees, and I saw a strange shadow in the moonlight that I had never seen before——"

" Where?" he interrupted.

" In that wild-looking part of the grounds as you look across from the ash-trees. Just in front of the archway, where the ground is bare. It was there. Mr. Verrall says he wonders Sir George does not have those gorse-bushes cleared away, and the ground converted into civilized land, like the rest of it."

" It has been done, but the bushes grow again."

" Well, I was sitting there, and I saw this unusual shadow. It arrested my eye at once. Where did it come from, I wondered: what cast it? I never thought of the Ashlydyat superstition; never for a moment. I only thought what a strange appearance the shadow wore. I thought of a lying-in-state; I thought of a state funeral, where the coffin rests on a bier, and a mourner sits at the head and a mourner at the foot. Shall I tell you," she suddenly broke off, "what the scene altogether looked like?"

"Do so."

"Like a graveyard. They may well call it the Dark Plain! The shadow might be taken for a huge tomb with two images weeping over it, and the bushes around assumed the form of lesser ones. Some, square; some, long; some, high; some, low; but all looking not unlike graves in the moonlight."

"Moonlight shadows are apt to bear fanciful forms to a vivid imagination, Miss Pain," he lightly observed.

"Have not others indulged the same fancy before me? I remember to have heard so."

"As they have said. They never took the form to my sight," he returned, with a half-smile of ridicule. "When I know bushes to be bushes, I cannot by any stretch of imagination magnify them into graves. You must have had this Ashlydyat nonsense in your head."

"I have assured you that I had not," she rejoined in a firm tone. "It was only after I had been regarding it for some time—and the longer I looked, the plainer the shadow seemed to grow—that I thought of the Ashlydyat tale. All in an instant the truth flashed upon me—that it must be the apparition——"

"The *what*, Miss Pain?"

"Does the word offend you? It *is* a foolish one. The Shadow, then. I remembered that the Shadow, so dreaded by the Godolphins, did take the form of a bier, with mourners weeping at its——"

"Was said to take it," he interposed, in a tone of quiet reproof; "that would be the better phrase. And, in speaking of the Shadow being dreaded by the Godolphins, you allude, I presume, to the Godolphins of the past ages. I know of none in the present who dread it: except my superstitious sister, Janet."

"How touchy you are upon the point!" she cried, with a light laugh. "Do you know, George Godolphin, that that very touchiness betrays the fact that you, for one, are not exempt from the dread. And," she added, changing her tone again to one of serious sympathy, "did not the dread help to kill Mrs. Godolphin?"

"No," he gravely answered. "If you give ear to all the stories that the old wives of the neighbourhood love to indulge in, you will collect a valuable stock of fable-lore."

"Let it pass. If I repeated the fable, it was because I had heard it. But now you will understand why I felt vexed last night when you did not come. It was not for your sweet company I was pining, as your vanity has been assuming, but that I wanted you to see the Shadow.— How that girl is fixing her eyes upon us!"

George Godolphin turned at the last sentence, which was uttered abruptly. An open barouche had drawn up, and its occupants, two ladies, were both looking towards them. The one was a young girl, with a pale gentle face and dark eyes, as remarkable for their refined sweetness, as Miss Pain's were for their brilliancy. The other was a little lady of middle age, dressed youthfully, and whose naturally fair complexion was so excessively soft and clear, as to give a suspicion that nature had less hand in it than art. It was Lady Godolphin. She held her eye-glass to her eye, and turned it on the crowd.

"Maria, whatever is that on horseback?" she asked. "It looks green."

"It is Charlotte Pain in a bright-green riding-habit," was the young lady's answer.

"A bright-green riding-habit! And her head seems to glitter! Has she anything in her cap?"

"It appears to be a gold feather."

"She must look beautiful! Very handsome, does she not?"

"For those who admire her style—very," replied Maria Hastings.

Which was certainly not the style of Maria Hastings. Quiet, retiring, gentle, she could only wonder at those who dressed in bright-coloured habits with gold buttons and feathers, and followed the hounds over gates and ditches. Miss Hastings wore a pretty white silk bonnet, and grey cashmere mantle. Nothing could be plainer; but then, she was a clergyman's daughter.

"It is on these occasions that I regret my deficient sight," said Lady Godolphin. "Who is that, in scarlet, talking to her? It resembles the figure of George Godolphin."

"It is he," said Maria. "He is coming towards us."

He was piloting his horse through the throng, returning greetings from every one. A universal favourite was George Godolphin. Charlotte Pain's fine eyes were following him with somewhat dimmed brilliancy: he was not so entirely hers as she could wish to see him.

"How are you this morning, Lady Godolphin?" But it was on the hand of Maria Hastings that his own lingered; and her cheeks took the hue of Charlotte Pain's, as he bent low to whisper words that were all too dear.

"George, do you know that your father is here?" said Lady Godolphin.

George, in his surprise, drew himself upright on his horse. "My father here! Is he, indeed?"

"Yes; and on horseback. Very unwise of him; but he would not be persuaded out of it. It was a sudden resolution that he appeared to take. I suppose the beauty of the morning tempted him. Miss Maria Hastings, what nonsense has George been saying to you? Your face is as red as his coat."

"That is what I was saying to her," laughed George Godolphin. "Asking her where her cheeks had borrowed their roses from."

A parting of the crowd brought Sir George Godolphin within view, and the family drew together in a group. Up went Lady Godolphin's glass again.

"Is that Bessy? My dear, with whom did you come?"

"I came by myself, Lady Godolphin. I walked."

"Oh dear!" uttered Lady Godolphin. "You do do the wildest things, Bessy! And Sir George allows you to do them!"

"Sir George does not," spoke the knight. "Sir George has already desired her to take her place in the carriage. Open the door, James."

Bessy laughed as she stepped into it. She cheerfully obeyed her father; but anything like ceremony, or, as the world may call it, etiquette, she waged war with.

"I expected to meet your sisters here, Bessy," said Lady Godolphin. "I want you all to dine with me to-day. We must celebrate the first reappearance of your father. You will bear the invitation to them."

"Certainly," said Bessy. "We shall be happy to come. I know Janet has no engagement."

"An early dinner, mind: five o'clock. Sir George cannot wait."

"To dine at supper-time," chimed in unfashionable Bessy. "George, do you hear? Lady Godolphin's at five."

A movement; a rush; a whirl. The hounds were preparing to throw off, and the field was gathering. George Godolphin hastily left the side of Miss Hastings, though he found time for a stolen whisper.

"Fare you well, my dearest."

And when she next saw him, after the noise and confusion had cleared away, he was galloping in the wake of the baying pack, side by side with Charlotte Pain.

CHAPTER II.

LADY GODOLPHIN'S FOLLY.

PRIOR'S ASH was not a large town, though of some importance in county estimation. In the days of the monks, when all good people were Roman Catholics, or professed to be, it had been but a handful of houses, which various necessities had caused to spring up round the priory: a flourishing and crowded establishment of religious men then; a place marked but by a few ruins now. In process of time the handful of houses had increased to several handfuls, the handfuls to a village, and the village to a borough town; still retaining the name bestowed on it by the monks—"Prior's Ash."

In the heart of the town was situated the banking-house of Godolphin, Crosse, and Godolphin. It was an old-established and most respected firm, sound and wealthy. The third partner and second Godolphin, mentioned in it, was Thomas Godolphin, Sir George Godolphin's eldest son. Until he joined it, it had been Godolphin and Crosse. It was a matter of arrangement, understood by Mr. Crosse, that when anything happened to Sir George, Thomas would step into his father's place, as head of the firm, and George, whose name at present did not appear, though he had been long in the bank, would represent the last name; so that it would still remain Godolphin, Crosse, and Godolphin. Mr. Crosse, who, like Sir George, was getting in years, was remarkable for nothing but a close attention to business. He was a widower, without children, and Prior's Ash wondered who would be the better for the filling of his garners.

The Godolphins could trace back to the ages of the monks. But of no very high ancestry boasted they; no titles, places, or honours; they ranked among the landed gentry as owners of Ashlydyat, and that was all. It was quite enough for them: to be lords of Ashlydyat was an honour they would not have bartered for a dukedom. They held by Ashlydyat. It was their pride, their stronghold, their boast. Had feudal times been in fashion now, they would have dug a moat around it, and fenced it in with fortifications, and called it their castle. Why did they so love it? It was but a poor place at best; nothing to look at; and, in the matter of space inside, was somewhat straitened. Oak-panelled rooms, dark as mahogany and garnished with cross beams, low ceilings, and mullioned windows, are not the most consonant to modern taste. People thought that the Godolphins loved it from its associations and traditions; from the very fact that certain super-stitions attached to it. Foolish superstitions, you will be inclined to call them, as contrasted with the enlightenment of these matter-of-fact days—I had almost said these days of materialism.

Ashlydyat was not entailed. There was a clause in the old deeds of tenure which prevented it. A wicked Godolphin (by which compli-mentary appellation his descendants distinguished him) had cut off the entail, and gambled the estate away; and though the Godolphins re-covered it again in the course of one or two lives, the entail was not renewed. It was now bequeathed from father to son, and was always the residence of the reigning Godolphin. Thomas Godolphin knew that it would become his on the death of his father, as surely as if he were the heir by entail. The late Mr. Godolphin, Sir George's father, had lived and died in it. Sir George succeeded, and then *he* lived in it—with his wife and children. But he was not Sir George then: therefore, for a few minutes, while speaking of this part of his life, we will call him what he was—Mr. Godolphin. A pensive, thoughtful woman was Mrs. Godolphin, never too strong in health. She was Scotch by birth. Of her children, Thomas and Janet most resembled her; Bessy was like no one but herself: George and Cecilia inherited the beauty of their father. There was considerable difference in the ages of the children, for they had numbered thirteen. Thomas was the eldest, Cecilia the youngest; Janet, Bessy, and George were between them; and the rest, who had also been between them, had died, most of them in infancy. But, a moment yet, to give a word to the descrip-tion of Ashlydyat, before speaking of the death of Mrs. Godolphin.

Passing out of Prior's Ash towards the west, a turning to the left of the high-road took you to Ashlydyat. Built of greystone, and lying somewhat in a hollow, it wore altogether a gloomy appearance. And it was intensely ugly. A low building of two storeys, irregularly built, with gables and nooks and ins-and-outs of corners, and a square turret in the middle, which was good for nothing but the birds to build on. It wore a time-honoured look, though, with all its ugliness, and the moss grew, green and picturesque, on its walls. Perhaps on the prin-ciple, or, let us say, by the subtle instinct of nature, that a mother loves a deformed child with a deeper affection than she feels for her other children, who are fair and sound of limb, did the Godolphins feel pride in their inheritance because it was ugly. But the grounds around it were beautiful, and the landscape, so much of it as could be seen from that unelevated spot, was most grand to look upon. A full view might be obtained from the turret, though it was somewhat of a mount to get to it. Dark groves, and bright undulating lawns, shady spots where the water rippled, pleasant to bask in on a summer's day, sunny parterres of gay flowers scenting the air; charming, indeed, were the environs of Ashlydyat. All, except one spot: and that had charms also for some minds—sombre ones.

In one part of the grounds there grew a great quantity of ash-trees— and it was supposed, though not known, that these trees may originally have suggested the name, Ashlydyat: as they most certainly had that of Prior's Ash, given to the village by the monks. A few people wrote it in accordance with its pronunciation, Ash-*lid*-yat, but the old way of spelling it was retained by the family. As the village had swollen into a town, the ash-trees, growing there, were cleared away as necessity required; but the town was surrounded with them still.

Opposite to the ash-trees on the estate of Ashlydyat there extended a waste plain, totally out of keeping with the high cultivation around. It looked like a piece of rude common. Bushes of furze, broom, and other stunted shrubs grew upon it, none of them rising above the height of a two-year-old child. The description given by Charlotte Pain to George Godolphin was not an inapt one—that the place, with these stunted bushes on it, looked in the moonlight not unlike a graveyard. At the extremity, opposite to the ash-trees, there arose a high archway, a bridge built of greystone. It appeared to have formed part of an ancient fortification, but there was no trace of water having run beneath it. Beyond the archway was a low round building, looking like an isolated windmill without sails. It was built of greystone also, and was called the belfry: though there was as little sign of bells ever having been in it, as there was of water beneath the bridge. The archway had been kept from decay; the belfry had not, but was open in places to the heavens.

Strange to say, the appellation of this waste piece of land, with its wild bushes, was the "Dark Plain." Why? The plain was not dark: it was not shaded: it stood out, broad and open, in the full glare of sunlight. That certain dark tales had been handed down with the appellation, is true: and these may have given rise to the name. Immediately before the archway, for some considerable space, the ground was entirely bare. Not a blade of grass, not a shrub grew on it. Or, as the story went, *would* grow. It was on this spot that the appearance, the Shadow, as mentioned by Charlotte Pain, would be sometimes seen. Whence the Shadow came, whether it was ghostly or earthly, whether those learned in science and philosophy could account for it by Nature's laws, whether it was cast by any gaseous vapour arising in the moonbeams, I am unable to say. If you ask me to explain it, I cannot. If you ask, why then do I write about it, I can only answer, because I have seen it. I have seen it with my own unprejudiced eyes; I have sat and watched it, in its strange stillness; I have looked about and around it, low down, high up, for some substance, ever so infinitesimal, that might cast its shade and enable me to account for it: and I have looked in vain. Had the moon been behind the archway, instead of behind *me*, that might have furnished a loophole of explanation: a very poor and inefficient loophole; a curious one also: for how can an archway in the substance be a bier and two mourners in its shadow? but, still, better than none.

No; there was nothing whatever, so far as human eyes—and I can tell you that keen ones and sceptical ones have looked at it—to cast the shade, or to account for it. There, as you sat and watched, stretched out the plain in the moonlight, with its low, tomb-like bushes, its clear space of bare land, the archway rising behind it. But, on the spot of bare land, before the archway, would rise the Shadow; not looking as if it were a shadow cast on the ground, but a palpable fact: as if a bier, with its two bending mourners, actually stood there in the substance. I say that I cannot explain it, or attempt to explain it; but I do say that there it was to be seen. Not often: sometimes not for years together. It was called the Shadow of Ashlydyat: and superstition told that its appearance foreshadowed the approach of calamity, whether of death or other evil, to the Godolphins. The greater the evil that was coming upon them, the plainer and more distinct would be the appearance of the Shadow—the longer the space of time that it would be observed. Rumour went, that once, on the approach of some terrible misfortune, it had been seen for months and months before, whenever the moon was sufficiently bright. The Godolphins did not care to have the subject mentioned to them: in their scepticism, they (some of them, at least) treated it with ridicule, or else with silence. But, like disbelievers of a different sort, the scepticism was more in profession than in heart. The Godolphins, in their inmost soul, would cower at the appearance of that shadowed bier; as those others have been known to cower, in their anguish, at the approach of the shadow of death.

This was not all the superstition attaching to Ashlydyat: but you will probably deem this quite enough for the present. And we have to return to Mrs. Godolphin.

Five years before the present time, when pretty Cecilia was in her fifteenth year, and most needed the guidance of a mother, Mrs. Godolphin died. Her illness had been of a lingering nature; little hope in it, from the first. It was towards the latter period of her illness that what had been regarded by four-fifths of Prior's Ash as an absurd child's tale, a superstition unworthy the notice of the present-day men and women, grew to be talked of in whispers, as something "strange." For three months antecedent to the death of Mrs. Godolphin, the Shadow of Ashlydyat was to be seen every light night, and all Prior's Ash flocked up to look at it. That they went, is of no consequence: they had their walk and their gaze for their pains: but that Mrs. Godolphin should have been told of it, was. She was in the grounds alone one balmy moonlight night, later than she ought to have been, and she discerned people walking in them, making for the ash-trees.

"What can those people be doing here?" she exclaimed to one of her servants, who was returning to Ashlydyat from executing an errand in the town.

"It is to see the Shadow, ma'am," whispered the girl, in answer, with more direct truth than prudence.

Mrs. Godolphin paused. "The *Shadow!*" she uttered. "Is the Shadow to be seen?"

"It has been there ever since last moon, ma'am. It never was so plain, they say."

Mrs. Godolphin waited her opportunity, and, when the intruders had dispersed, proceeded to the ash-trees. It is as well to observe that these ash-trees, and also the Dark Plain, though very near to the house, were not in the more private portion of the grounds.

Mrs. Godolphin proceeded to the ash-trees. An hour afterwards, her absence from the house was discovered, and they went out to search. It was her husband who found her. She pointed to the shadow, and spoke.

"You will believe that my death is coming on quickly now, George." But Mr. Godolphin turned it off with an attempt at joke, and told her she was old enough to know better.

Mrs. Godolphin died. Two years after, Mr. Godolphin came into contact with a wealthy young widow; young, as compared with himself: Mrs. Campbell. He met her in Scotland, at the residence of his first wife's friends. She was English born, but her husband had been Scotch. Mr. Godolphin married her, and brought her to Ashlydyat. The step did not give pleasure to his children. When sons and daughters are of the age that the Godolphins were, a new wife, brought home to rule, rarely does give pleasure to the first family. Things did not go on very comfortably: there were faults on each side; on that of Mrs. Godolphin, and on that of her step-daughters. After a while, a change was made. Thomas Godolphin and his sisters went to reside in the house attached to the bank, a handsome modern residence hitherto occupied by Mr. Crosse. "You had better come here," that gentleman had said to them: he was no stranger to the unpleasantness at Ashlydyat. "I will take up my abode in the country," he continued. "I would prefer to do so. I am getting to feel older than I did twenty years ago, and country air may renovate me."

The arrangement was carried out. Thomas Godolphin and his three sisters entered upon their residence in Prior's Ash, Janet acting as mistress of the house, and as chaperon to her sisters. She was then past thirty: a sad, thoughtful woman, who lived much in the inward life.

Just about the time of this change, certain doings of local and public importance were enacted in the neighbourhood, in which Mr. Godolphin took a prominent share. There ensued a proposal to knight him. He started from it with aversion. His family started also: they and he alike despised these mushroom honours. Not so Mrs. Godolphin. From the moment that the first word of the suggestion was breathed to her, she determined that it should be carried out; for the appellation, my lady, was as incense in her ears. In vain Mr. Godolphin strove to argue with her: her influence was in the ascendant, and he lay under the spell. At length he yielded; and, though hot war raged in his heart, he bent his haughty knee at the court of St. James's, and rose up Sir George.

"After a storm comes a calm." A proverb pleasant to remember in some of the sharp storms of life. Mrs. Godolphin had carried her point in being too many for her step-daughters; she had triumphed over opposition and become my lady; and now she settled down in calmness at Ashlydyat. But she grew dissatisfied. She was a woman who had no resources within herself, who lived only in excitement, and Ashlydyat's quietness overwhelmed her with ennui. She did not join in the love of the Godolphins for Ashlydyat. Mr. Godolphin, ere he had brought her home to it, a bride, had spoken so warmly of the place, in his attachment to it, that she had believed she was about to step into some modern paradise: instead of which, she found, as she expressed it, a "cranky old house, full of nothing but passages." The dislike she formed for it in that early moment never was overcome.

She would beguile her husband to her own pretty place in Berwickshire; and, just at first, he was willing to be beguiled. But after he became Sir George (not that the title had anything to do with it) public local business grew upon him, and he found it inconvenient to quit Ashlydyat. He explained this to Lady Godolphin: and said their sojourn in Scotland must be confined to an autumn visit. So she perforce dragged out her days at Ashlydyat, idle and listless.

We warn our children that idleness is the root of all evil; that it will infallibly lead into mischief those who indulge in it. It so led Lady Godolphin. One day, as she was looking from her drawing-room windows, wishing all sorts of things. That she lived in her pleasant home in Berwickshire; that she could live amidst the gaieties of London; that Ashlydyat was not such a horrid old place; that it was more modern and less ugly; that its reception-rooms were lofty, and garnished with gilding and glitter, instead of being low, gloomy, and grim; and that it was situated on an eminence, instead of on a flat, so that a better view of the lovely scenery around might be obtained. On that gentle rise, opposite, for instance—what would be more enchanting than to enjoy a constant view from thence? If Ashlydyat could be transported there, as they carry out wooden houses to set up abroad; or, if only that one room, she then stood in, could, with its windows——

Lady Godolphin's thoughts arrested themselves here. An idea had flashed upon her. Why should she not build a pretty summer-house on that hill; a pavilion? The Countess of Cavemore, in this very county, had done such a thing: had built a pavilion on a hill within view of the windows of Cavemore House, and had called it "Lady Cavemore's Folly." Only the week before, she, Lady Godolphin, in driving past it, had thought what a pretty place it looked; what a charming prospect must be obtained from it. Why should she not do the same?

The idea grew into shape and form. It would not leave her again. She had plenty of money of her own, and she would work out her "Folly" to the very top of its bent.

To the top of its bent, indeed! None can tell what a thing will grow into when it is first begun. Lady Godolphin made known her project to Sir George, who, though he saw no particular need for the work, did not object to it. If Lady Godolphin chose to spend money in that way, she might do so. So it was put in hand. Architects, builders, decorators were called together; and the Folly was planned out and begun. Lady Godolphin had done with ennui now; she found employment for her days, in watching the progress of the pavilion.

It is said that the consummation of our schemes generally brings with it a share of disappointment. It did so in this instance to Lady Godolphin. The Folly turned out to be a really pretty place; the views from its windows magnificent; and Lady Godolphin was as enchanted as a child with a new toy. The disappointment arose from the fact that she could not make the Folly her home. After spending a morning in it, or an evening, she must leave it to return to that grey Ashlydyat—the only eyesore to be seen, when gazing from the Folly's windows. If a day turned out wet, she could not walk to the Folly; if she was expecting visitors she must stay at home to receive them; if Sir George felt ill—and his health was then beginning to suffer—she could not leave him for her darling Folly. It was darling because it was new: in six months' time, Lady Godolphin would have grown tired of it; have rarely entered it: but in her present mood, it was all-in-all to her.

Slowly she formed the resolution to enlarge the Folly—slowly for her, for she deliberated upon it for two whole days. She would add "a reception-room or two," "a bedroom or two," "a kitchen," so that she might be enabled, when she chose to do so, to take up her abode in it for a week. And these additions were begun.

But they did not end; did not end as she had intended. As the Folly grew, so grew the ideas of Lady Godolphin: there must be a suite of reception-rooms, there must be several bedrooms, there must be domestic offices in proportion. Sir George told her that she would spend a fortune upon it; my lady answered that, at any rate, she should have something to show for the outlay.

At length it was completed: and Lady Godolphin's Folly—for it retained its appellation—stood out to the view of Prior's Ash, which it overlooked; to the view of Ashlydyat; to the view of the country generally, as a fair, moderate-sized, attractive residence, built in the villa style, its white walls dazzling the eye when the sun shone upon them.

"We will reside there, and let Ashlydyat," said Lady Godolphin to her husband.

"Reside at the Folly! Leave Ashlydyat!" he repeated, in consternation. "It could not be."

"It will be," she added, with a half self-willed, half-caressing laugh. "Why could it not be?"

Sir George fell into a reverie. He admired the modern conveniences of the Folly, greatly admired the lovely scenery, that, look from which room of it he would, charmed his eye. But for one thing, he had been content to do as she wished, and go to live there. That one thing—what was it? Hear the low-breathed, reluctant words he is beginning to say to Lady Godolphin.

"There is an old tradition in our family—a superstition I suppose you will call it—that if the Godolphins leave Ashlydyat, their ruin is at hand."

Lady Godolphin stared at him in amazement. Nothing had surprised her on her arrival at Ashlydyat, like the stories of marvel which she had been obliged to hear. Sir George had cast ridicule on them, if alluded to in his presence; therefore, when the above words dropped from him, she could only wonder. You might search a town through and not find one less prone to superstition than was Lady Godolphin: in all that belonged to it, she was a very heathen. Sir George hastened to explain away his words.

"The tradition is nothing, and I regard it as nothing. That such a one has been handed down is certain, and it may have given rise to the reluctance, which the early Godolphins entertained, to quit Ashlydyat. But that is not our reason: in remaining in it, we only obey a father's behest. You are aware that Ashlydyat is not entailed. It is bequeathed by will from father to son; and to the bequest in each will, so far as I have cognizance of the past wills, there has always been appended a clause—a request—I should best say an injunction—never to quit Ashlydyat. 'When once you shall have come into possession of Ash-lydyat, guard it as your stronghold: resign it neither to your heir nor to a stranger: remain in it until death shall take you.' It was inserted in my father's will, by which Ashlydyat became mine: it is inserted in mine, which devises the estate to Thomas."

"If ever I heard so absurd a story!" uttered Lady Godolphin in her pretty childish manner. "Do I understand you to say that, if you left Ashlydyat to take up your abode elsewhere, it would be no longer yours?"

"Not that, not that," returned Sir George. "Ashlydyat is mine until my death, and no power can take it from me. But a reluctance to leave Ashlydyat has always clung to the Godolphins: in fact, we have looked upon it as a step impossible to be taken."

"What a state of thraldom to live in!"

"Pardon me. We love Ashlydyat. To remain in it is pleasant; to leave it would be pain. I speak of the Godolphins in general; of those who have preceded me."

"I understand now," said Lady Godolphin resentfully. "You hold a superstition that if you were to leave Ashlydyat for the Folly, some dreadful doom would overtake you. Sir George, I thought we lived in the nineteenth century."

A passing flush rose to the face of Sir George Godolphin. To be suspected of leaning to these superstitions chafed his mind unbearably; he had almost rather be accused of dishonour: not to his own heart would he admit that they might have weight with him. "Ashlydyat is our homestead," he said, "and when a man has a homestead, he likes to live and die in it."

"You cannot think Ashlydyat so desirable a residence as the Folly. We *must* remove to the Folly, Sir George; I have set my heart upon it. Let Thomas and his sisters come back to Ashlydyat."

"They would not come."

"Not come! They were inwardly rebellious enough at having to leave it."

"I am sure that Thomas would not take up his residence here, as the master of Ashlydyat, during my lifetime. Another thing: we should not be justified in keeping up two expensive establishments outside the town, leaving the house at the bank to lie idle. People might lose confidence in us, if they saw us launching forth into extravagance."

"Oh, indeed! What did they think of the expense launched upon the Folly?" mockingly smiled my lady.

"They know it is your money which has built that : not mine."

"If Thomas and the rest came to Ashlydyat you might let the house attached to the bank."

"It would take a great deal more money to keep up Ashlydyat than it does the house at the bank. The public might lose confidence in us, I say. Besides, no one but a partner could be allowed to live at the bank."

"You seem to find an answer to all my propositions," said Lady Godolphin, in her softest and sweetest, and least true tone; "but I warn you, Sir George, that I shall win you over to my way of thinking before the paper shall be dry on the Folly's walls. If Thomas cannot, or will not, live at Ashlydyat, you must let it."

In every tittle did Lady Godolphin carry out her words. Almost before the Folly's embellishments were matured to receive them, Sir George was won over to live at it : and Ashlydyat was advertised to be let. Thomas Godolphin would not have become its master in his father's lifetime had Sir George filled its rooms with gold as a bribe. His mother had contrived to imbue him with some of the Ashlydyat superstition—to which *she* had lived a slave—and Thomas, though he did not bow down to it, would not brave it. If ruin was to come—as some religiously believed—when a reigning Godolphin voluntarily abandoned Ashlydyat, Thomas, at least, would not help it on by taking part in the step. So Ashlydyat, to the intense astonishment of Prior's Ash, was put up in the market for hire.

It was taken by a Mr. Verrall; a gentleman from London. Prior's Ash knew nothing of him, except that he was fond of field sports, and appeared to be a man of money : but, the fact of his establishing himself at Ashlydyat, stamped him, in their estimation, as one worthy to be courted. His wife was a pretty, fascinating woman; her sister, Miss Pain, was beautiful : their entertainments were good, their style was dashing, and they became the fashion in the neighbourhood.

But, from the very first day that the step was mooted of Sir George Godolphin's taking up his residence at the Folly, until that of his removal thither, the Shadow had hovered over the Dark Plain at Ashlydyat.

CHAPTER III.

THE DARK PLAIN IN THE MOONLIGHT.

THE beams of the setting sun streamed into the dining-room at Lady Godolphin's Folly. A room of fine proportions; not dull and heavy, as it is much the custom for dining-rooms to be, but light and graceful as could be wished.

Sir George Godolphin, with his fine old beauty, sat at one end of the table; Lady Godolphin, good-looking also in her peculiar style, was opposite to him. She wore a white dress, its make remarkably young, and her hair fell in ringlets, young also. On her right hand sat Thomas Godolphin, courteous and calm, as he ever was ; on her left hand was Bessy, whom you have already seen. On the right of Sir George sat Maria Hastings, singularly attractive in her quiet loveliness, in her white spotted muslin dress with its white ribbons. On his left sat his eldest daughter, Janet. Quiet in manner, plain in features, as was Thomas, her eyes were yet wonderful to behold. Not altogether for their beauty, but for the power they appeared to contain of seeing all things. Large, reflective, strangely-deep eyes, grey, with a circlet of darker grey round them. When they were cast upon you, it was not at you they looked, but at what was within you—at your mind, your thoughts ; at least, such was the impression they conveyed. She and Bessy were dressed alike, in grey watered silk. Cecil sat between Janet and Thomas, a charming girl, with blue ribbons in her hair. George sat between his sister Bessy and Maria Hastings. Thomas was attired much as he had been in the morning : George had exchanged his hunting clothes for dinner dress.

Lady Godolphin was speaking of her visit to Scotland. Sir George's illness had caused it to be put off, or they would have gone in August : it was proposed to proceed thither now. "I have written finally to say that we shall be there on Tuesday," she observed.

"Will papa be able to make the journey in one day?" asked Bessy.

"He says he is quite strong enough to do so now," replied Lady Godolphin. "But I could not think of his running any risk, so we shall stay a night upon the road. Janet, will you believe that I had a battle with Mr. Hastings to-day?"

Janet turned her strange eyes on Lady Godolphin. "Had you, madam?"

"I consider Mr. Hastings the most unreasonable, changeable man I ever met with," complained Lady Godolphin. "But clergymen are apt to be so. So obstinate, if they take up a thing! When Maria was invited to accompany us in August, Mr. Hastings made not a single demur neither he nor Mrs. Hastings : they bought her—oh, all sorts of new things for the visit. New dresses and bonnets ; and— a new cloak, was it not, Maria?"

Maria smiled. "Yes, Lady Godolphin."

"People who have never been in Scotland acquire the notion that in temperature it may be matched with the North Pole, so a warm cloak was provided for Maria for an August visit! I called at the Rectory to-day with Maria, after the hounds had thrown off, to tell them that we should depart next week, and Mr. Hastings wanted to withdraw his consent to her going. "Too late in the season," he urged, or some such plea. I told him she should not be frozen; we should be back before the cold weather set in."

Maria lifted her sweet face, an earnest look upon it. "It was not the cold papa thought of, Lady Godolphin : he knows I am too hardy to fear that. But, as winter approaches, there is so much more to do, both at home and abroad. Mamma has to be out a great deal : and this will be a heavy winter with the poor, after all the sickness."

"The sickness has passed," exclaimed Lady Godolphin, in a tone so sharp, so eager, as to give rise to a suspicion that she might fear, or had feared, the sickness for herself.

"Nearly so," assented Miss Godolphin. "There have been no fresh cases since—— "

"Janet, if you talk of 'fresh cases' at my table, I shall retire from it," interrupted Lady Godolphin in agitation. "Is fever a pleasant or fitting topic of conversation, pray?"

Janet Godolphin bowed her head. "I did not forget your fears, madam. I supposed, however, that, now that the sickness is subsiding, your objection to hearing it spoken of might have subsided also."

"And how did the controversy with Mr. Hastings end?" interposed Bessy, to turn the topic. "Is Maria to go?"

"Of course she is to go," said Lady Godolphin, with a quiet little laugh of power, as she recovered her good-humour. "When I wish a thing, I generally carry my point. I would not stir from his room until he gave his consent, and he had his sermon on the table, and was no doubt wishing me at the antipodes. He thought Maria had already paid me a visit long enough for Sir George to have grown tired of her, he said. I told him that it was not his business: and that whether Sir George or any one else was tired of her, I should take her to Scotland. So he yielded."

Maria Hastings glanced timidly at Sir George. He saw the look. "Not tired of you yet, are we, Miss Hastings?" he said, with, Maria fancied, more gallantry than warmth. But fancy, with Maria, sometimes went a great way.

"It would have been a disappointment to Maria," pursued Lady Godolphin. "Would it not, my dear?"

"Yes," she answered, her face flushing.

"And so very dull for Charlotte Pain. I expressly told her when I invited her that Maria Hastings would be of the party."

"Charlotte Pain!" echoed Bessy Godolphin, in her quick way; "is she going with you? What in the world is that for?"

"I invited her, I say," said Lady Godolphin, with a hard look on her bloom-tinted face: a look that it always wore when her wishes were questioned, her actions reflected on. None brooked interference less than Lady Godolphin.

Sir George bent his head slightly towards his wife. "My dear, I considered that Charlotte Pain invited herself. She fished pretty strongly for the invitation, and you fell into the snare."

"Snare! It is an honour and a pleasure that she should come with us. What do you mean, Sir George?"

"An honour, if you like to call it so; I am sure it will be a pleasure," replied Sir George. "A most attractive young woman is Charlotte Pain: though she did angle for the invitation. George, take care how you play your cards."

"What cards, sir?"

"Look at that graceless George! at his conscious vanity!" exclaimed Sir George to the table generally. "He knows who it is that makes the attraction here to Charlotte Pain. Wear her if you can win her, my boy."

"Would Charlotte Pain be one worthy to be won by George Godolphin?" quietly spoke Janet.

"Rumour says she has thirty thousand charms," nodded Sir George.

"I never would marry for money, if I were George," cried Cecil indignantly. "And, papa, I do not see so much beauty in Charlotte Pain. I do not like her style."

"Cecil, did you ever know one pretty girl like the 'style' of another?" asked George.

"Nonsense! But you can't call Charlotte Pain much of a girl, George. She is as old as you, I know. She's six and twenty, if she's a day."

"Possibly," carelessly replied George Godolphin.

"Did she ride well to-day, George?" inquired his father.

"She always rides well, sir," replied George.

"I wish I had invited her to dinner!" said Lady Godolphin.

"I wish you had," assented Sir George.

Nothing more was said upon the subject; the conversation fell into other channels. But, when the ladies had withdrawn, and Sir George was alone with his sons, he renewed it.

"Mind, George, I was not in jest when speaking of Charlotte Pain. It is getting time that you married."

"Need a man think of marriage on this side thirty, sir?"

"Some men need not think of it on this side forty or on this side fifty, unless they choose to do so: your brother Thomas is one," returned Sir George. "But they are those who know how to sow their wild oats without it."

"I shall sow mine in good time," said George, with a gay, half-conscious smile. "Thomas never had any to sow."

"I wish you would settle the time and keep it, then," was the marked rejoinder. "It might be better for you."

"Settle the time for my marriage, do you mean, sir?"

"You know what I mean. But I suppose you do intend to marry some time, George?"

"I dare say I shall. It is a thing that comes to most of us as a matter of course; as measles or vaccination," spoke irreverent George. "You mentioned Charlotte Pain, sir : I presume you have no urgent wish that my choice should fall upon her?"

"If I had, would you comply with it?"

George raised his blue eyes to his father. "I have never thought of Charlotte Pain as a wife."

"She is a fine girl, a wonderfully fine girl; and if, as is rumoured, she has a fortune, you might go further and fare worse," remarked Sir George. "If you don't like Charlotte Pain, find out some one else that you would like. Only, take care that there's money with her."

"Money is desirable in itself. But it does not invariably bring happiness, sir."

"I never heard that it brought unhappiness, Master George. I cannot have you both marry portionless women. Thomas has chosen one who has nothing: it will not do for you to follow his example. The world is before you : choose wisely."

"If we choose portionless women, we are not portionless ourselves."

"We have a credit to keep up before the public, George. It stands high; it deserves to stand high; I hope it always will do so. But I consider it necessary that one of you should marry a fortune; I should have been glad that both had done so. Take the hint, George; and never expect my consent to your making an undesirable match, for it would not be given."

"But, if my inclination fixed itself upon one who has no money, what then, sir?" asked bold George carelessly.

Sir George pushed from before him a dish of filberts, so hastily as to scatter them on the table. It proved to his sons, who knew him well, that the question had annoyed him.

"Your inclinations are as yet free, George: I say the world is before you, and you may choose wisely. If you do not: if, after this warning, you suffer your choice to rest where it is undesirable that it should rest, you will do it in deliberate defiance of me. In that case I shall disinherit you: partially, if not wholly."

Something appeared to be on the tip of George's tongue, but he checked it, and there ensued a pause.

"Thomas is to be allowed to follow his choice," he presently said.

"I had not warned Thomas with regard to a choice; therefore he has been guilty of no disobedience. It is his having chosen as he has, that reminds me to caution you. Be careful, my boy."

"Well, sir, I have no intention of marrying yet, and I suppose you will not disinherit me for keeping single," concluded George good-humouredly. He rose to leave the room as he spoke, throwing a merry glance towards Thomas as he did so, who had taken no part whatever in the conversation.

The twilight of the evening had passed, but the moon shone bright and clear, rendering the night nearly as light as day. Janet Godolphin stood on the lawn with Miss Hastings, when George stepped out and joined them.

"Moon-gazing, Janet!

"Yes," she answered. "I am going on to the ash-trees."

George paused before he again spoke. "Why are you going thither?"

"Because," whispered Janet, glancing uneasily around, "they say the Shadow is there again."

George himself had heard that it was: had heard it, as you know, from Charlotte Pain. But he chose to make mockery of his sister's words.

"Some say the moon's made of green cheese," quoth he. "Who told you that nonsense?"

"It has been told to me," mysteriously returned Janet. "Margery saw it last night, for one."

"Margery sees double, sometimes. Do not go, Janet."

Janet's only answer was to put the hood of her cloak over her head, and walk away. Bessy Godolphin ran up at this juncture.

"Is Janet going to the ash-trees? She'll turn into a ghost herself some time, believing all the rubbish Margery chooses to dream. I shall go and tell her so."

Bessy followed in the wake of her sister. George turned to Miss Hastings.

"Have you a cloak also, Maria? Draw it round you, then, and let us go after them."

He caught her to him with a fond gesture, and they hastened on, down from the eminence where rose the Folly, to the lower ground nearer Ashlydyat. The Dark Plain lay to the right, and as they struck into a narrow, overhung walk, its gloom contrasted unpleasantly with the late brightness. Maria Hastings drew nearer to her companion with an involuntary shiver.

"Why did you come this dark way, George?"

"It is the most direct way. In the dark or in the light you are safe with me. Did you notice Sir George's joke about Charlotte Pain?"

The question caused her heart to beat wildly. "Was it a joke?" she breathed.

"Of course it was a joke. But he has been giving me a lecture upon —upon——"

"Upon what?" she inquired, helping out his hesitation.

"Upon the expediency of sowing my wild oats and settling down into a respectable man," laughed George. "I promised him it should be done some time. I cannot afford it just yet, Maria," he added, his tone changing to earnestness. "But I did not tell him that."

Meanwhile, Janet Godolphin had gained the ash-trees. She quietly glided before them beneath their shade to reach the bench. It was placed back, quite amidst them, in what might almost be called a recess formed by the trees. Janet paused ere turning in, her sight thrown over the Dark Plain.

"Heavens and earth! how you startled me. Is it you, Miss Godolphin?"

The exclamation came from Charlotte Pain, who was seated there. Miss Godolphin was startled also: and her tone, as she spoke, betrayed considerable vexation.

"*You* here, Miss Pain! A solitary spot, is it not, for a young lady to be sitting in alone at night?"

"I was watching for that strange appearance which you, in this neighbourhood, call the Shadow," she explained. "I saw it last evening."

"Did you?" freezingly replied Janet Godolphin, who had an unconquerable aversion to the supernatural sign being seen or spoken of by strangers.

"Well, pray, and where's the Shadow?" interrupted Bessy Godolphin, coming up. "*I* see nothing, and my eyes are as good as yours, Janet: better, I hope, than Margery's."

"I do not see it to-night," said Charlotte Pain. "Here are more footsteps! Who else is coming?"

"Did you ever know the Shadow come when it was watched for?" cried Janet to Bessy, in a half-sad, half-resentful tone, as her brother and Maria Hastings approached. "Watch for it, and it does not come. It never yet struck upon the sight of any one, but it did so unexpectedly."

"As it did upon me last night," said Charlotte Pain. "It was a strange-looking shadow: but, as to its being supernatural, the very supposition is ridiculous. I beg your pardon, if I offend your prejudices, Miss Godolphin."

"Child! why did you come?" cried Janet Godolphin to Maria.

"I had no idea you did not wish me to come."

"Wish! It is not that. But you are little more than a child, and might be spared these sights."

There appeared to be no particular sight to spare any one. They stood in a group, gazing eagerly. The Dark Plain was stretched out before them, the bare patch of clear ground, the archway behind; all bright in the moonlight. No shadow or shade was to be seen. Charlotte Pain moved to the side of George Godolphin.

"You told me I was fanciful this morning, when I said the Dark Plain put me in mind of a graveyard," she said to him in a half-whisper. "See it now! Those low bushes scattered about look precisely like grave-mounds."

"But we know them to be bushes," returned George.

"That is not the argument. I say they *look* like it. If you brought a stranger here first by moonlight, and asked him what the Plain was, he would say a graveyard."

"Thus it has ever been!" murmured Janet Godolphin to herself. "At the first coming of the Shadow, it will be here capriciously; visible one night, invisible the next: betokening that the evil has not yet arrived, that it is only hovering! You are sure you saw it, Miss Pain?"

"I am quite sure that I saw a shadow, bearing a strange and distinct form, there, in front of the archway. But I am equally sure it is to be accounted for by natural causes. But that my eyes tell me there is no building, or sign of building above the Dark Plain, I should say it was cast from thence. Some fairies, possibly, may be holding up a sheet there," she carelessly added, "playing at magic lantern in the moonlight."

"Standing in the air," sarcastically returned Miss Godolphin. "Archimedes offered to move the world with his lever, if the world would only find him a place, apart from itself, to stand on."

"Are you convinced, Janet?" asked George.

"Of what?"

He pointed over the Plain. "That there is nothing uncanny to be seen to-night. I'll send Margery here when I return."

"I am convinced of one thing—that it is getting uncommonly damp," said practical Bessy. "I never stood under these ash-trees in an evening yet, let the atmosphere be ever so cold and clear, but a dampness might be felt. I wonder if it is the nature of ash-trees to exhale it? Maria, the Rector would not thank us for bringing you here."

"Is Miss Hastings so susceptible to cold?" asked Charlotte Pain.

"Not more so than other people are," was Maria's answer.

"It is her child-like, delicate appearance, I suppose, that makes us fancy it," said Bessy Godolphin. "Come, let us depart. If Lady Godolphin could see us here, she would go crazy: she says, you know, that damp brings fever."

They made a simultaneous movement. Their road lay to the right; Charlotte Pain's to the left. "I envy you four," she said, after wishing them good night. "You are a formidable body, numerous enough to do battle with any assailants you may meet in your way, fairies, or shadows, or fever, or what not. I must encounter them alone."

"Scarcely," replied George Godolphin, as he drew her arm within his, and turned with her in the direction of Ashlydyat.

Arrived at Lady Godolphin's Folly, the Miss Godolphins passed indoors; Maria Hastings lingered a moment behind them. She leaned against a white pillar of the terrace, looking forth on the lovely night. Not altogether was that peaceful scene in accordance with her heart, for, in that, warred passionate jealousy. Who was Charlotte Pain, she asked herself, that she should come between them with her beauty; with her——

Some one was hastening towards her; crossing the green lawn, springing up the steps of the terrace: and the jealous feeling died away into love.

"Were you waiting for me?" whispered George Godolphin. "We met Verrall, so I resigned mademoiselle to his charge. Maria, how your heart is beating!"

"I was startled when you ran up so quickly; I did not think it could be you," was the evasive answer. "Let me go, please."

"My darling, don't be angry with me: I could not well help myself. You know with whom I would rather have been."

He spoke in the softest whisper; he gazed tenderly into her face, so fair and gentle in the moonlight; he clasped her to him with an impassioned gesture. And Maria, as she yielded to his tenderness in her pure love, and felt his stolen kisses on her lips, forgot the jealous trouble that was being wrought by Charlotte Pain.

CHAPTER IV.

ALL SOULS' RECTORY.

AT the eastern end of Prior's Ash was situated the Church and Rectory of All Souls—a valuable living, the Reverend Isaac Hastings its incumbent. The house, enclosed from the high-road by a lofty hedge, was built, like the church, of greystone. It was a commodious residence, but its rooms, excepting one, were small. This one had been added to the house of late years: a long, though somewhat narrow room, its three windows looking on to the flowered lawn. A very pleasant room to sit in on a summer's day; when the grass was green, and the flowers, with their brightness and perfume, gladdened the senses, and the birds were singing, and the bees and butterflies sporting.

Less pleasant to-day. For the skies wore a grey hue; the wind sighed round the house with an ominous sound, telling of the coming winter; and the mossy lawn and the paths were dreary with the yellow leaves, decaying as they lay. Mrs. Hastings, a ladylike woman of middle height and fair complexion, stood at one of these windows, watching the bending of the trees as the wind shook them; watching the falling leaves. She was remarkably susceptible to surrounding influences; seasons and weather held much power over her: but that she was a clergyman's wife, and, as such, obliged to take a very practical part in the duties of life, she might have subsided into a valetudinarian.

A stronger gust sent the leaves rustling up the path, and Mrs. Hastings slightly shivered.

"How I dislike this time of year," she exclaimed. "I wish there were no autumn. I dislike to see the dead leaves."

"I like the autumn: although it heralds in the winter."

The reply came from Mr. Hastings, who was pacing the carpet, thinking over his next day's sermon: for it was Saturday morning. Nature had not intended Mr. Hastings for a parson, and his sermons were the bane of his life. An excellent man; a most efficient pastor of a parish; a gentleman; a scholar, abounding in good practical sense; but *not* a preacher. Sometimes he wrote his sermons, sometimes he tried the extempore plan; but, let him do as he would, there was always a conviction of failure, as to his sermons winning their way to his hearers' hearts. He was under middle height, with keen aquiline features, his dark hair already sprinkled with grey.

"I am glad the wind has changed," remarked the Rector. "We shall say good-bye to the fever. While that warm weather lasted, I always had my fears of its breaking out again. It was only coquetting with us. I wonder—— "

Mr. Hastings stopped, as if lapsing into thought. Mrs. Hastings inquired what his "wonder" might be.

"I was thinking of Sir George Godolphin," he continued. "One thought leads to another and another, until we should find them a strange train, if we traced them back to their origin. Beginning with dead leaves, and ending with—metaphysics."

"What are you talking of, Isaac?" his wife asked in surprise.

A half-smile crossed the thin delicate lips of Mr. Hastings. "You spoke of the dead leaves: that led to the thought of the fever; the fever to the bad drainage; the bad drainage to the declaration of Sir George Godolphin that, if he lived until next year, it should be remedied, even though he had to meet the expense himself. Then the train went on to speculate upon whether Sir George would live; and next upon whether this change of weather may not cause my lady to relinquish her journey; and lastly, to Maria. Cold Scotland, if we are to have a season of bleak winds, cannot be beneficial to Sir George."

"Lady Godolphin has set her mind upon going. She is not likely to relinquish it."

"Mark you, Caroline," said Mr. Hastings, halting in his promenade, and standing opposite his wife; "it is her dread of the fever that is sending her to Scotland. But for that, she would not go, now that it is so late in the year. And for Maria's sake I wish she would not. I do not now wish Maria to go to Scotland."

"Why?" asked Mrs. Hastings.

Mr. Hastings knitted his brow. "It is an objection more easily felt than explained,"

"When the invitation was given in the summer, you were pleased that she should accept it."

"Yes; I acknowledge it: and, had they gone then, I should have felt no repugnance to the visit. But I do feel a repugnance to it now, so far as Maria is concerned; an unaccountable repugnance. If you ask me to explain it, or to tell you what my reason is, I can only answer that I am unable to do so. It is this want of reason, good or bad, which has prevented my entirely withdrawing the consent I gave. I essayed to do so, when Lady Godolphin was here on Thursday; but she pressed me closely, and, having no sound or plausible argument to bring forward against it, my opposition broke down."

Mrs. Hastings wondered. Never was there a man less given to whims and fancies than the Reverend Isaac Hastings. His actions and thoughts were based on the sound principle of plain matter-of-fact sense: he was practical in all things; there was not a grain of ideality in his composition.

At that moment a visitor's knock was heard. Mrs. Hastings glanced across the hall, and saw her second daughter enter. She wore her grey cashmere cloak, soft and fine in texture, delicate in hue; a pretty morning dress, and a straw bonnet trimmed with white. A healthy colour shone on her delicate face, and her eyes were sparkling with inward happiness. Very attractive, very ladylike, was Maria Hastings.

"I was obliged to come this morning, mamma," she said, when greetings had passed. "Some of my things are still here which I wish to take, and I must collect them and send them to the Folly. We start early on Monday morning; everything must be packed to-day."

"One would suppose you were off for a year, Maria," exclaimed Mr. Hastings, "to hear you talk of 'collecting your things.' How many trunk-loads have you already at the Folly?"

"Only two, papa," she replied, laughing, and wondering why Mr. Hastings should speak so sternly. "They are chiefly trifles that I have come for; books, and other things: not clothes."

"Your papa thought it likely that Lady Godolphin would not now go, as the fine weather seems to be leaving us," said Mrs. Hastings.

"Oh yes, she will," replied Maria. "Her mind is fully made up. Did you not know that the orders had already been sent into Berwickshire? And some of the servants went on this morning?"

"Great ladies change their minds sometimes," remarked Mr. Hastings in a cynical tone.

Maria shook her head. She had untied her bonnet-strings, and was unfastening her mantle. "Sir George, who has risen to breakfast since Thursday, asked Lady Godolphin this morning whether it would not be late for Scotland, and she resented the remark. What do you think she said, mamma? That if there was nothing else to take her to Scotland, this absurd rumour, of the Shadow's having come again, would drive her thither."

"What's that, Maria?" demanded the clergyman in a sharp, displeased accent.

"A rumour has arisen, papa, that the Shadow is appearing at Ashlydyat. It was seen on Wednesday night. On Thursday night, some of us went to the ash-trees——"

"*You* went?" interrupted the Rector.

"Yes, papa," she answered, her voice growing timid, for he spoke in a tone of great displeasure. "I, and Miss Godolphin, and Bessy. We were not alone: George Godolphin was with us."

"And what did you see?" eagerly interposed Mrs. Hastings, who possessed more of the organ of marvel in her composition than her husband.

"Mamma, we saw nothing. Only the Dark Plain lying quietly under the moonlight. There appeared to be nothing to see; nothing unusual."

"But that I hear you say this with my own ears, I should not have believed you capable of giving utterance to folly so intense," sternly exclaimed Mr. Hastings to his daughter. "Are you the child of Christian parents? have you received an enlightened education?"

Maria's eyelids fell under the reproof, and the soft colour in her cheeks deepened.

"That a daughter of mine should confess to running after a 'shadow'!" he continued, really with more asperity than the case seemed to need. But the Rector of All Souls' was one who would have deemed it little less heresy to doubt his Bible, than to countenance a tale of superstition. He repudiated such with the greatest contempt: he never, even though proof positive had been brought before his eyes, could accord to it an iota of credence. "An absurd tale of a 'shadow,' worthy only to be told to those who, in their blind credulity, formerly burnt poor creatures as witches; worthy only to amuse the ears of ignorant urchins, whom we put into our fields to frighten away the crows! And *my daughter* has lent herself to it! Can this be the result of your training, madam?"—turning angrily to his wife. "Or of mine?"

"I did not run after it from my own curiosity; I went because the rest went," answered poor Maria in her confusion, all too conscious that the stolen moonlight walk with Mr. George Godolphin had been a far more powerful motive to the expedition than the "Shadow." "Miss Pain saw it on Wednesday night; Margery saw it——"

"Will you cease?" broke forth the Rector. "'Saw it!' If they said they saw it they must have been labouring under a delusion; or else were telling a deliberate untruth. And you do not know better than to repeat such ignorance! What would Sir George think of you?"

"I should not mention it in his presence, papa. Or in Lady Godolphin's."

"Neither shall you in mine. It is not possible"—Mr. Hastings stood before her and fixed his eyes sternly upon hers—"that you can believe in it?"

"I think not, papa," she answered in her strict truth. To truth, at any rate, she had been trained, whether by father or by mother; and she would not violate it even to avoid displeasure. "I think that my feeling upon the point is curiosity; not belief."

"Then that curiosity implies belief," sternly replied the Rector. "If a man came to me and said, 'There's an elephant out there, in the garden,' and I went forth to see, would not that prove my belief in the assertion?"

Maria was no logician; or she had answered, "No, you might go to prove the error of the assertion." "Indeed, papa, if I know anything of myself, I am not a believer in it," she repeated, her cheeks growing hotter and hotter. "If I were once to see the Shadow, why then——"

"Be silent!" he cried, not allowing her to continue. "I shall think next I am talking to that silly dreamer, Janet Godolphin. Is it she who has imbued you with this tone of mind?"

Maria shook her head. There was an undercurrent of consciousness, lying deep in her heart, that if a "tone" upon the point had been insensibly acquired by her, it was caught from one far more precious to her heart, far more essential to her very existence, than was Janet Godolphin. That last Thursday night, in running with George Godolphin after this tale of the Shadow, his arm cast lovingly round her, she had acquired the impression, from a few words he let fall, that he must put faith in it. She was content that his creed should be hers in all things: had she wished to differ from him, it would have been beyond her power to do so. Mr. Hastings appeared to wait for an answer.

"Janet Godolphin does not intrude her superstitious fancies upon the world, papa. Were she to seek to convert me to them, I should not listen to her."

"Dismiss the subject altogether from your thoughts, Maria," commanded the Rector. "If men and women would perform efficiently their allotted part in life, there is enough of hard substance to occupy their minds and their hours, without losing either the one or the other in 'shadows.' Take you note of that."

"Yes, papa," she dutifully answered, scarcely knowing whether she had deserved the lecture or not, but glad that it was at an end. "Mamma, where is Grace?"

"In the study. You can go to her. There's David!" exclaimed Mrs. Hastings, as Maria left the room.

A short, thick-set man had appeared in the garden, giving rise to the concluding remark of Mrs. Hastings. If you have not forgotten the first chapter, you may remember that Bessy Godolphin spoke of a man who had expressed his pleasure at seeing her father out again. She called him "Old Jekyl." Old Jekyl lived in a cottage on the outskirts of Prior's Ash. He had been in his days a working gardener, but rheumatism and age had put him beyond work now. There was a good bit of garden-ground to his cottage, and it was well cultivated. Vegetables and fruit grew in it; and a small board was fastened in front of the laburnum-tree at the gate, with the intimation "Cut flowers sold here." There were also bee-hives. Old Jekyl (Prior's Ash never dignified him by any other title) had no wife: she was dead: but his two sons lived with him, and they followed the occupation that had been his. I could not tell you how many gardens in Prior's Ash and its environs those two men kept in order. Many a family, not going to the expense of keeping a regular gardener, some, perhaps, not able to go to it, entrusted the care of their garden to the Jekyls, paying them a stipulated sum yearly. The plan answered. The gardens were kept in order, and the Jekyls earned a good living; both masters and men were contented.

They had been named Jonathan and David: and were as opposite as men and brothers could well be, both in nature and appearance. Each was worthy in his way. Jonathan stood six feet three if he stood an inch, and was sufficiently slender for a lamp-post: rumour went that he had occasionally been taken for one. An easy-going, obliging, talkative, mild-tempered man, was Jonathan, his opinion agreeing with every one's. Mrs. Hastings was wont to declare that if she were to say to him, "You know, Jonathan, the sun never shone," his answer would be, "Well, ma'am, I don't know as ever it did, over bright like." David had the build of a Dutchman, and was taciturn upon most subjects. In manner he was somewhat surly, and would hold his own opinion, especially if it touched upon his occupation, against the world.

Amongst others who employed them in this way, was the Rector of All Souls'. They were in the habit of coming and going to that or any other garden, as they pleased, at whatever day or time suited their convenience; sometimes one brother, sometimes the other, sometimes one of the two boys they employed, as they might arrange between themselves. Any garden entrusted to their care they were sure to keep in order; therefore their time and manner of doing it was not interfered with. Mrs. Hastings suddenly saw David in the garden. "I will get him to sweep those ugly dead leaves from the paths," she exclaimed, throwing up the window. "David!"

David heard the call, turned and looked. Finding he was wanted, he advanced in a leisurely, independent sort of manner, giving his attention to the beds as he passed them, and stopping to pluck off any dead flower that offended his eye. He gave a nod as he reached Mrs. Hastings, his features not relaxing in the least. The nod was a mark of respect, and *meant* as such; the only demonstration of respect commonly shown by David. His face was not ugly, though too flat and broad; his complexion was fair, and his eyes were blue.

"David, see how the leaves have fallen; how they lie upon the ground!"

David gave a half-glance round, by way of answer, but he did not speak. He knew the leaves were there without looking.

"You must clear them away," continued Mrs. Hastings.

"No," responded David to this. "'Twon't be of no use."

"But, David, you know how very much I dislike to see these withered leaves," rejoined Mrs. Hastings in a voice more of pleading than of command. Command answered little with David.

"Can't help seeing 'em," persisted David. "Leaves will wither; and will fall: it's their natur' to do it. If every one of them lying there now was raked up and swept away, there'd be as many down again to-morrow morning. I can't neglect my beds to fad with the leaves—and bring no good to pass, after all."

"David, I do not think any one ever was so self-willed as you!" said Mrs. Hastings, laughing in spite of her vexation.

"I know my business," was David's answer. "If I gave in at my different places to all the missises' whims, how should I get my work done? The masters would be blowing me up, thinking it was idleness. Look at Jonathan! he lets himself be swayed any way; and a nice time he gets of it, among 'em. His day's work's never done."

"You would not suffer the leaves to lie there until the end of the season!" exclaimed Mrs. Hastings. "They would be up to our ankles as we walked."

"May be they would," composedly returned David. "I have cleared 'em off about six times this fall, and I shall clear 'em again, but not as long as this wind lasts."

"Is it going to last, David?" inquired the Rector, appearing at his wife's side, and laughing inwardly at her diplomatic failure.

David nodded his usual salutation as he answered. He would sometimes relax so far as to say "Sir" to Mr. Hastings, an honour paid exclusively to his pastoral capacity. "No, it won't last, sir. We shall have the warm weather back again."

"You think so!" exclaimed the Rector in an accent of disappointment. Experience had taught him that David, in regard to the weather, was an oracle.

"I am sure so," answered David. "The b'rometer's going fast on to heat, too."

"Is it?" said Mr. Hastings. "You have often told me you put no faith in the barometer."

"No more I don't: unless other signs answer to it," said David. "The very best b'rometer going, is old father's rheumatiz. There was a sharp frost last night, sir."

"I know it," replied Mr. Hastings. "A few nights of that and the fever will be driven away."

"We shan't get a few nights of it," said David. "And the fever has broken out again."

"What!" exclaimed Mr. Hastings. "The fever broken out again?"

"Yes," said David.

The news fell upon the clergyman's heart as a knell. He had fully believed the danger to have passed away, though not yet the sickness. "Are you sure it has broken out again, David?" he asked, after a pause.

"I ain't no surer than I was told, sir," returned phlegmatic David. "I met Cox just now, and he said, as he passed, that fever had shown itself in a fresh place."

"Do you know where?" inquired Mr. Hastings.

"He said, I b'lieve, but I didn't catch it. If I stopped to listen to the talk of fevers, and such-like, where would my work be?"

Taking his hat, one of the very clerical shape, with a broad brim, the Rector left his house. He was scarcely without the gates when he saw Mr. Snow, who was the most popular doctor in Prior's Ash, coming along quickly in his gig. Mr. Hastings threw out his hand, and the groom pulled up.

"Is it true?—this fresh rumour of the fever?"

"Too true, I fear," replied Mr. Snow. "I am on my way thither now; just summoned."

"Who is attacked?

"Sarah Anne Grame."

The name appeared to startle the Rector. "Sarah Anne Grame!" he repeated. "She will never battle through it!" The doctor raised his eyebrows, as if he thought it doubtful himself, and signed to his groom to hasten on.

"Tell Lady Sarah I will call upon her in the course of the day," called out Mr. Hastings, as the gig sped on its way. "I must ask Maria if she has heard news of this," he continued, in soliloquy, as he turned within the Rectory gate.

Maria Hastings had found her way to the study. To dignify a room by the appellation of "study" in a clergyman's house, would at once imply that it must be the private sanctum of its master, consecrated to his sermons and his other clerical studies. Not so, however, in the Rectory of All Souls. The study there was chiefly consecrated to litter, and the master had less to do with it, personally, than with almost any other room in the house. There, the children, boys and girls, played, or learned lessons, or practised; there, Mrs. Hastings would sit to sew when she had any work in hand too plebeian for the eyes of polite visitors.

Grace, the eldest of the family, was twenty years of age, one year older than Maria. She bore a great resemblance to her father; and, like him, was more practical than imaginative. She was very useful in the house, and took much care off Mrs. Hastings's hands. It happened that all the children, five of them besides Maria, were this morning at home. It was holiday that day with the boys. Isaac was next to Maria, but nearly three years younger; one had died between them; Reginald was next; Harry last; and then came a little girl, Rose. They ought to have been preparing their lessons; were supposed to be doing so by Mr. and Mrs. Hastings: in point of fact, they were gathering round Grace, who was seated on a low stool solving some amusing puzzles from a new book. They started up when Maria entered, and went dancing round her.

Maria danced too; she kissed them all; she sang aloud in her joyousness of heart. What was it that made that heart so glad, her life as a very Eden? The ever-constant presence there of George Godolphin.

"Have you come home to stay, Maria?"

"I have come home to *go*," she answered, with a laugh. "We start for Scotland on Monday, and I want to hunt up oceans of things."

"It is fine to be you, Maria," exclaimed Grace, with a sensation very like envy. "You have all the pleasure, and I have to stop at home and do all the work. It is not fair."

"Gracie dear, it will be your turn next. I did not *ask* Lady Godolphin to invite me, instead of you. I never thought of her inviting me, being the younger of the two."

"But she did invite you," grumbled Grace.

"I say, Maria, you are not to go to Scotland," struck in Isaac.

"Who says so?" cried Maria, her heart standing still, as she halted in one corner of the room with at least half a dozen arms round her.

"Mamma said yesterday she thought you were not: that papa would not have it."

" Is that all? " and Maria's pulses coursed on again. " I am to go : I have just been with papa and mamma. They know that I have come to get my things for the journey."

" Maria, who goes? "

" Sir George and my lady, and I and Charlotte Pain."

" Maria, I want to know why Charlotte Pain goes? " cried Grace.

Maria laughed. " You are like Bessy Godolphin, Grace. She asked the same question, and my lady answered, ' Because she chose to invite her.' I can only repeat to you the same reason."

" Does George Godolphin go? "

" No," replied Maria.

" Oh, doesn't he, though! " exclaimed Reginald. " Tell that to the marines, mademoiselle."

" He does not go with us," said Maria. " Regy, you know you will get into hot water if you use those sea phrases."

" Sea phrases! that is just like a girl," retorted Reginald. " What will you lay me that George Godolphin is not in Scotland within a week after you are all there? "

" I will not lay anything," said Maria, who in her inmost heart hoped and believed that George *would* be there.

" Catch him stopping away if Charlotte Pain goes? " went on Reginald. " Yesterday I was at the pastry·cook's, having a tuck-out with that shilling old Crosse gave me, and Mr. George and Miss Charlotte came in. I heard a little."

" What did you hear? " breathed Maria. She could not help the question : any more than she could help the wild beating of her heart at the boy's words.

" I did not catch it all," said Reginald. " It was about Scotland, though, and what they should do when they were there. Mrs. Verrall's carriage came up then, and he put her into it. An out-and-out flirt is George Godolphin! "

Grace Hastings threw her keen dark eyes upon Maria. " Do not let him flirt with *you*," she said in a marked tone. " You like him ; I do not. I never thought George Godolphin worth his salt."

" That's just Grace! " exclaimed Isaac. " Taking her likes and dislikes! and for no cause, or reason, but her own crotchets and prejudices. He is the nicest fellow going, is George Godolphin. Charlotte Pain's is a new face and a beautiful one : let him admire it."

" He admires rather too many," nodded Grace.

" As long as he does not admire yours, you have no right to grumble," rejoined Isaac provokingly : and Grace flung a bundle of work at him, for the laugh turned against her.

" Rose, you naughty child, you have my crayons there! " exclaimed Maria, happening to cast her eyes upon the table, where Rose was seated too quietly to be at anything but mischief.

" Only one or two of your sketching pencils, Maria," said Miss Rose. " I shan't hurt them. I am making a villa with two turrets and some cows."

" I say, Maria, is Charlotte Pain going to take that thoroughbred hunter of hers? " interposed Reginald.

" Of course," scoffed Isaac ; " saddled and bridled. She'll have him with her in the railway carriage; put him in the corner seat opposite Sir George. Regy's brains may do for sea—if he ever gets there; but they are not sharp enough for land."

"They are as sharp as yours, at any rate," flashed Reginald. "Why should she not take him?"

"Be quiet, you boys!" said Grace.

She was interrupted by the appearance of Mr. Hastings. He did not open the door at the most opportune moment. Maria, Isaac, and Harry were executing a dance that probably had no name in the dancing calendar; Reginald was standing on his head; Rose had just upset the contents of the table, by inadvertently drawing off its old cloth cover, and Grace was scolding her in a loud tone.

"What do you call this?" demanded Mr. Hastings, when he had leisurely surveyed the scene. "Studying?"

They subsided into quietness and their places; Reginald with his face red and his hair wild, Maria with a pretty blush, Isaac with a smothered laugh. Mr. Hastings addressed his second daughter.

"Have you heard anything about this fresh outbreak of fever?"

"No, papa," was Maria's reply. "Has it broken out again?"

"I hear that it has attacked Sarah Anne Grame."

"Oh, papa!" exclaimed Grace, clasping her hands in sorrowful consternation. "Will she ever live through it?"

Just the same doubt, you see, that had occurred to the Rector.

CHAPTER V.

THOMAS GODOLPHIN'S LOVE.

FOR nearly a mile beyond All Souls' Rectory, as you went out of Prior's Ash, there were scattered houses and cottages. In one of them lived Lady Sarah Grame. We receive our ideas from association; and, in speaking of the residence of Lady Sarah Grame, or Lady Sarah Anyone, imagination might conjure up some fine old mansion with all its appurtenances, grounds, servants, carriages and grandeur: or, at the very least, a "villa with two turrets and some cows," as Rose Hastings expressed it.

Far more like a humble cottage than a mansion was the abode of Lady Sarah Grame. It was a small, pretty, detached white house, containing eight or nine rooms in all; and, they, not very large ones. A plot of ground before it was crowded with flowers: far too crowded for good taste, as David Jekyl would point out to Lady Sarah. But Lady Sarah loved flowers, and would not part with one of them.

The daughter of one soldier, and the wife of another, Lady Sarah had scrambled through life amidst bustle, perplexity, and poverty. Sometimes quartered in barracks, sometimes following the army abroad; out of one place into another; never settled anywhere for long together. It was an existence not to be envied; although it is the lot of many. She was Mrs. Grame then, and her husband, the captain, was not a very good husband to her. He was rather too fond of

amusing himself, and threw all care upon her shoulders. She passed
her days nursing her sickly children, and endeavouring to make one
sovereign go as far as two. One morning, to her unspeakable embarrassment, she found herself converted from plain, private Mrs. Grame
into the Lady Sarah. Her father boasted a peer in a very remote
relative, and came unexpectedly into the title.

Had he come into money with it, it would have been more welcome;
but, of that, there was only a small supply. It was a very poor Scotch
peerage, with limited estates; and, they, encumbered. Lady Sarah
wished she could drop the honour which had fallen to her share, unless
she could live a little more in accordance with it. She had much
sorrow. She had lost one child after another, until she had only two
left, Sarah Anne and Ethel. Then she lost her husband; and, next,
her father. Chance drove her to Prior's Ash, which was near her
husband's native place; and she settled there, upon her limited income.
All she possessed was her pension as a captain's widow, and the interest
of the sum her father had been enabled to leave her; the whole not
exceeding five hundred a year. She took the white cottage, then just
built, and dignified it with the name of " Grame House : " and the
mansions in the neighbourhood of Prior's Ash were content not to laugh,
but to pay respect to her as an earl's daughter.

Lady Sarah was a partial woman. She had only these two daughters, and her love for them was as different as light is from darkness.
Sarah Anne she loved with an inordinate affection, almost amounting
to passion; for Ethel, she did not care. What could be the reason
of this? What is the reason why parents (many of them may be found)
will love some of their children, and dislike others? They cannot tell
you, any more than Lady Sarah could have told. Ask them, and they
will be unable to give you an answer. It does not lie in the children :
it often happens that those obtaining the least love will be the most
worthy of it. Such was the case here. Sarah Anne Grame was a
pale, sickly, fretful girl; full of whims, full of complaints, giving trouble
to every one about her. Ethel, with her sweet countenance and her
merry heart, made the sunshine of the home. She bore with her
sister's exacting moods, bore with her mother's want of love. *She*
loved them both, and waited on them, and carolled forth her snatches
of song as she moved about the house, and was as happy as the day
was long. The servants—they kept only two—would tell you that
Miss Grame was cross and selfish; but that Miss Ethel was worth her
weight in gold. The gold was soon to be appropriated; transplanted
to a home where it would be appreciated and cherished : for Ethel was
the affianced wife of Thomas Godolphin.

On the morning already mentioned, when you heard it said that
fever had broken out again, Sarah Anne Grame awoke, ill. In her
fretful, impatient way, she called to Ethel, who slept in an adjoining
room. Ethel was asleep: but she was accustomed to be roused at
unseasonable hours by Sarah Anne, and she threw on her dressing-
gown and hastened to her.

" I want some tea," began Sarah Anne. " I am as ill and thirsty as
I can be."

Sarah Anne was really of a sickly constitution, and to hear her complain of being ill and thirsty was nothing unusual. Ethel, in her loving nature, her sweet patience, received the information with as much concern as though she had never heard it before. She bent over Sarah Anne, inquiring tenderly where she felt pain.

"I tell you that I am ill and thirsty, and that's enough," peevishly answered Sarah Anne. "Go and get me some tea."

"As soon as I possibly can," said Ethel soothingly. "There is no fire at present. The maids are not up. I do not think it can be later than six, by the look of the morning."

"Very well!" sobbed Sarah Anne—sobs of temper, not of pain. "You can't call the maids, I suppose! and you can't put yourself the least out of the way to alleviate my suffering! You want to go to bed again and sleep till eight o'clock. When I am dead, you'll wish you had been more like a sister to me. You possess rude health yourself, and you can feel no compassion for any one who does not."

An assertion unjust and untrue: as was many another, made by Sarah Anne Grame. Ethel did not possess "rude health," though she was not, like her sister, always ailing; and she felt far more compassion than Sarah Anne deserved.

"I will see what I can do," she gently said. "You shall soon have some tea."

Passing into her own room, Ethel hastily dressed herself. When Sarah Anne was in one of her exacting moods, there could be no more sleep or rest for Ethel. "I wonder," she thought to herself, "whether I could not light a fire, without calling the servants? They had so hard a day's work yesterday, for mamma kept them both cleaning from morning till night. Yes: if I can only find some wood, I'll try to light one."

She went down to the kitchen, hunted up what was required, laid the fire, and lighted it. It did not burn up well. She thought the wood must be damp, and found the bellows. She was on her knees, blowing away at the wood, and sending the blaze up into the coal, when some one came into the kitchen.

"Miss Ethel!"

It was one of the servants: Elizabeth. She had heard movement in the house, and had risen. Ethel explained that her sister felt ill, and tea was wanted.

"Why did you not call us, Miss Ethel?"

"You went to rest late, Elizabeth. See how I have made the fire burn!"

"It is not ladies' work, miss."

"I certainly think ladies should put on gloves when they attempt it," merrily laughed Ethel. "Look at my black hands."

The tea ready, Ethel carried a cup of it to her sister, with some dry toast that they had made. Sarah Anne drank the tea, but turned with a shiver from the toast. She seemed to be shivering much.

"Who was so stupid as to make that? You might know I should not eat it. I am too ill."

Ethel began to think that she did look unusually ill. Her face was flushed, shivering though she was, her lips were dry, her heavy eyes were unnaturally bright. She gently laid her hands, washed now, upon her sister's brow. It felt burning, and Sarah Anne screamed.

"Do keep your hands away! My head is splitting with pain."

Involuntarily Ethel thought of the fever; the danger from which they had been reckoning had passed away. It was a low sort of typhus which had prevailed; not very extensively, and chiefly amidst the poor: the great fear had been, lest it should turn to a more malignant type. About half a dozen deaths had taken place altogether.

"Would you like me to bathe your forehead with water, Sarah Anne?" asked Ethel kindly. "Or to get you some eau-de-Cologne?"

"I should like you to wait until things are asked for, and not to worry me," retorted Sarah Anne.

Ethel sighed. Not for the temper: Sarah Anne was always fractious in illness: but for the suffering she thought she saw, and the half doubt, half dread, which had arisen within her. "I think I had better call mamma," she deliberated to herself. "Though, if she sees nothing unusually the matter with Sarah Anne, she will only be angry with me."

Proceeding to her mother's chamber, Ethel knocked softly. Lady Sarah slept still, but the entrance aroused her.

"Mamma, I do not like to disturb you; I was unwilling to do so: but Sarah Anne is ill."

"Ill again! And only last week she was in bed three days! Poor dear sufferer! Is it her chest again?"

"Mamma, she seems *unusually* ill. Otherwise I should not have disturbed you. I feared—I thought—you will be angry with me if I say, perhaps?"

"Say what? Don't stand like a statue, Ethel."

Ethel dropped her voice. "Dear mamma, suppose it should be the fever?"

For one startling moment, Lady Sarah felt as if a dagger had pierced her: the next, she turned upon Ethel. Fever for Sarah Anne! how dared she prophesy it? A low, common fever, confined to the poor of the town, and which had subsided; or, all but subsided! Was it likely to return again and come up here to attack her darling child? What did Ethel mean by it?

Ethel, the tears in her eyes, said she hoped it would prove to be only an ordinary headache; it was her love for Sarah Anne which awoke her fears. Lady Sarah proceeded to the sick-room; and Ethel followed. Her ladyship was not in the habit of observing caution, and spoke freely of the "fever" before Sarah Anne; apparently for the purpose of casting blame at Ethel.

Sarah Anne did not imbibe the fear; she ridiculed Ethel as her mother had done. For some hours Lady Sarah did not admit it either. She would have summoned medical advice at first, but that Sarah Anne, in her peevishness, protested she would not have a doctor. Later on she grew worse, and Mr. Snow was sent for. You saw him in his gig hastening to the house.

Lady Sarah came forward to receive him; Ethel, full of anxiety, near her. She was a thin woman, with a shrivelled face and a sharp red nose, her grey hair banded plainly under a close white net cap.

She grasped Mr. Snow's arm. "You must save my child!"

"Higher aid permitting me," the surgeon answered. "Why do you assume it to be fever? For the last six weeks I have been summoned by timid parents to a score of 'fever' cases; and when I have arrived in hot haste, they have turned out to be no fever at all."

"*This* is the fever," replied Lady Sarah. "Had I been more willing to admit that it was, you would have been sent for hours ago. It was Ethel's fault. She suggested at daylight that it might be fever; and it made my darling girl so angry that she forbid my sending for advice. But she is worse now. Come and see her."

Mr. Snow laid his hand upon Ethel's head with a fond gesture, ere he turned to Lady Sarah. All Prior's Ash loved Ethel Grame.

Tossing upon her uneasy bed, her face flushed, her hair floating untidily about it, lay Sarah Anne, shivering still. The doctor gave one glance at her: it was quite enough to satisfy him that Lady Sarah was not mistaken.

"Is it the fever?" impatiently asked Sarah Anne, unclosing her hot eyelids.

"If it is, we must drive it away again," said the doctor cheerily.

"Why should the fever have come to *me*?" she rejoined, her tone rebellious.

"Why was I thrown from my horse last year, and broke my arm?" returned Mr. Snow. "These things come to all of us."

"To break an arm is nothing—people always recover from that," irritably answered Sarah Anne.

"And you will recover from the fever, if you will be quiet and reasonable."

"I am so hot! My head is so heavy!"

Mr. Snow, who had called for water and a glass, was mixing a white powder which he had produced from his pocket. She took it without opposition, and then he lessened the weight of bed-clothes, and afterwards turned his attention to the chamber. It was close and hot; the sun, which had just burst forth brightly from the grey skies, shone full upon it.

"You have that chimney stuffed up!" he exclaimed.

"Sarah Anne will not allow it to be open," said Lady Sarah. "She is sensitive to cold, dear child, and feels the slightest draught."

Mr. Snow walked to the chimney, turned up his coat cuff and wristband, and pulled down a bag filled with shavings. Soot came with it, and covered his hand; but he did not mind that. He was as little given to ceremony as Lady Sarah to caution, and he went leisurely up to the wash-hand-stand to remove it.

"Now, if I catch that bag, or any other bag up there again, obstructing the air, I shall attack the bricks next time, and make a good big hole that the sky can be seen through. Of that I give you notice, my lady."

He next pulled down the window at the top, behind the blind; but the room, at its best, did not find favour with him. "It is not airy; it is not cool," he said. "Is there not a better ventilated room in the house? If so, she should be moved into it."

"My room is cool," interposed Ethel eagerly. "The sun never shines into it, Mr. Snow."

It would appear that Ethel's thus speaking must have reminded Mr. Snow that she was present. In the unceremonious manner that he had laid hands upon the chimney bag, he now laid them upon her shoulders, and marshalled her outside the door.

"You go downstairs, Miss Ethel. And do not come within a mile of this chamber again, until I give you leave to do so."

"I will not be moved into Ethel's room!" interposed Sarah Anne, imperiously and fretfully. "It is not furnished with half the comforts of mine. And it has only a bit of bedside carpet! I will not go there, Mr. Snow."

"Now look you here, Miss Sarah Anne!" said the surgeon firmly. "I am responsible for bringing you well out of this illness; and I shall take my own way to do it. If not; if I am to be contradicted at every suggestion; Lady Sarah may summon some one else to attend you: I will not undertake it."

"My darling, you shall not be moved to Ethel's room," cried my lady coaxingly: "you shall be moved into mine. It is larger than this, you know, Mr. Snow, with a thorough draught through it, if you choose to put the windows and door open."

"Very well," said Mr. Snow. "Let me find her in it when I come up again this evening. And if there's a carpet on the floor, take it up. Carpets were never intended for bedrooms."

He passed into one of the sitting-rooms with Lady Sarah when he descended. "What do you think of the case?" she eagerly asked.

"There will be some difficulty with it," was the candid reply. "Lady Sarah, her hair must come off."

"Her hair come off!" uttered Lady Sarah, aghast. "That it never shall! She has the loveliest hair! What is Ethel's hair, compared with hers?"

"You heard the determination I expressed, Lady Sarah," he quietly said.

"But Sarah Anne will never allow it to be done," she returned, shifting the ground of remonstrance from her own shoulders. "And to do it in opposition to her would be enough to kill her."

"It will not be done in opposition to her," he answered. "She will be unconscious before it is attempted."

Lady Sarah's heart sank. "You anticipate that she will be dangerously ill?"

"In these cases there is always danger, Lady Sarah. But worse cases than—as I believe—hers will be, have recovered from it."

"If I lose her, I shall die myself!" she passionately uttered. "And, if she is to have it badly, she will die! Remember, Mr. Snow, how weak she has always been!"

"We sometimes find that weak constitutions battle best with an epidemic," he replied. "Many a sound one has it struck down and taken off; many a sickly one has struggled through it, and been the stronger for it afterwards."

"Everything shall be done as you wish," said Lady Sarah, speaking meekly in her great fear.

"Very well. There is one caution I would earnestly impress upon you: that of keeping Ethel from the sick-room."

"But there is no one to whom Sarah Anne is so accustomed, as a nurse," objected Lady Sarah.

"Madam!" burst forth the doctor in his heat, "would you subject Ethel to the risk of taking the infection, in deference to Sarah Anne's selfishness, or to yours? Better lose all your house contains than lose Ethel! She is its greatest treasure."

"I know how remarkably prejudiced you have always been in Ethel's favour!" resentfully spoke Lady Sarah.

"If I disliked her as much as I like her, I should be equally solicitous to guard her from the danger of infection," said Mr. Snow. "If you choose to put Ethel out of consideration, you cannot put Thomas Godolphin. In justice to him, she must be taken care of."

Lady Sarah opened her mouth to reply; but closed it again. Strange words had been hovering upon her lips: "If Thomas Godolphin were not blind, his choice would have fallen upon Sarah Anne; not upon Ethel." In her heart that was a sore topic of resentment: for she was quite alive to the advantages of a union with a Godolphin. Those words were suppressed; to give place to others.

"Ethel is in the house; and therefore must be liable to infection, whether she visits the room or not. I cannot fence her round with a wall, so that not a breath of tainted atmosphere shall touch her. I would if I could; but I cannot."

"I would send her from the house, Lady Sarah. At any rate, I forbid her to go near her sister. I don't want two patients on my hands, instead of one," he added in his quaint fashion, as he took his departure.

He was about to get into his gig, when he saw Mr. Godolphin advancing with a quick step. "Which of them is it who is seized?" inquired the latter, as he came up.

"Not Ethel, thank goodness!" responded the surgeon. "It is Sarah Anne. I have been recommending my lady to send Ethel from home. I should send her, were she a daughter of mine."

"Is Sarah Anne likely to have it dangerously?"

"I think so. Is there any necessity for you going to the house just now, Mr. Godolphin?"

Thomas Godolphin smiled. "There is no necessity for my keeping away. I do not fear the fever any more than you do."

He passed into the garden as he spoke, and Mr. Snow drove away. Ethel saw him, and came out to him.

"Oh, Thomas, do not come in! do not come!"

His only answer was to take her on his arm and enter. He threw open the drawing-room window, that as much air might circulate through the house as possible, and stood there with her, holding her before him.

"Ethel! what am I to do with you?"

"To do with me! What should you do with me, Thomas?"

"Do you know, my darling, that I cannot *afford* to let this danger touch you?"

"I am not afraid," she gently whispered.

He knew that: she had a brave, unselfish heart. But he was afraid for her, for he loved her with a jealous love; jealous of any evil that might come too near her,

" I should like to take you out of the house with me now, Ethel. I should like to take you far from this fever-tainted town. Will you come?"

She looked up at him with a smile, the colour rising to her face. " How could I, Thomas!"

Anxious thoughts were passing through the mind of Thomas Godolphin. We cannot put aside the *convenances* of life ; though there are times when they press upon us with an iron weight. He would have given almost his own life to take Ethel from that house : but how was he to do it? No friend would be likely to receive her : not even his own sisters : they would have too much dread of the infection she might bring with her. He would fain have carried her off to some sea-breezed town, and watch over her and guard her there, until the danger should be over. None would have protected her more honourably than Thomas Godolphin. But—those *convenances* that the world has to bow down to! how would the step have agreed with them? Another thought, little less available for common use, passed through his mind.

" Listen, Ethel!" he whispered. " It would be only to procure a license, and half an hour spent at All Souls with Mr. Hastings. It could be all done, and you away with me before nightfall."

She scarcely understood his meaning. Then, as it dawned upon her, she bent her head and her blushing face, laughing at the wild improbability.

" Oh, Thomas! Thomas! you are only joking. What would people say?"

" Would it make any difference to us what they said?"

" It could *not be*, Thomas," she whispered seriously ; "it is as an impossible vision. Were all other things meet, how could I run away from my sister, on her bed of sickness, to marry you?"

Ethel was right : and Thomas Godolphin felt that she was so. Punctilios must be observed, no matter at what cost. He held her fondly to his heart.

" If aught of ill should arise to you from your remaining here, I shall blame myself as long as life shall last. My love! my love!"

Mr. Godolphin could not linger. He must be at the bank, for Saturday was their most busy day of all the week : it was market-day at Prior's Ash : though he had stolen a moment to leave it when the imperfect news reached him. George was in the private room alone when he entered. " Shall you be going to Lady Godolphin's Folly this evening, George? " he inquired.

" The Fates permitting," replied Mr. George, who was buried five fathoms deep in business ; though he would have preferred to be five fathoms deep in pleasure. " Why?"

" You can tell my father that I am sorry not to be able to spend an hour with him, as I had promised. Lady Godolphin will not thank me to be running from Lady Sarah's house to hers just now."

" Thomas," warmly spoke George, in an impulse of kindly feeling : " I do hope it will not extend itself to Ethel!"

" I hope not," fervently breathed Thomas Godolphin.

CHAPTER VI.

CHARLOTTE PAIN.

A FINE old door of oak, a heavy door, standing deep within a portico, into which you might almost have driven a coach-and-six, introduced you to Ashlydyat. The hall was dark and small, the only light admitted to it being from mullioned windows of stained glass. Innumerable passages branched off from the hall. One peculiarity of Ashlydyat was, that you could scarcely enter a single room in it, but you must first go down a passage, short or long, to reach it. Had the house been designed by any architect with a head upon his shoulders and a little common sense with it, he might have made it a handsome mansion with large and noble rooms. As it was, the rooms were cramped and narrow, cornered and confined; and space was lost in these worthless passages.

In the least sombre room of the house, one with a large modern window (put into it by Sir George Godolphin to please my lady, just before that whim came into her head to build the Folly), opening upon a gravel walk, were two ladies, on the evening of this same Saturday. Were they sisters? They did not look like it. Charlotte Pain you have seen. She stood underneath the wax-lights of the chandelier, tall, commanding, dark, handsome; scarlet flowers in her hair, a scarlet bouquet in her corsage; her dress a rich cream-coloured silk interwoven with scarlet sprigs. She had in her hand a small black dog of the King Charles species, holding him up to the lights, and laughing at his anger. He was snarling fractiously, whether at the lights or the position might be best known to his mistress; whilst at her feet barked and yelped an ugly Scotch terrier, probably because *he* was not also held up : for dogs, like men, covet what they cannot obtain.

In a dress of pink gauze, with pretty pink cheeks, smooth features, and hazel eyes, her auburn hair interlaced with pearls, her height scarcely reaching to Miss Pain's shoulder, was Mrs. Verrall. She was younger than her sister : for sisters they were : a lady who passed through life with easy indifference, or appeared to do so, and called her husband "Verrall." She stood before the fire, a delicate white Indian screen in her hand, shading her face from the blaze. The room was hot, and the large window had been thrown open. So calm was the night, that not a breath of air came in to stir the wax-lights : the wind, which you heard moaning round the Rectory of All Souls in the morning, whirling the leaves and displeasing Mrs. Hastings, had dropped at sundown to a dead calm.

"Charlotte, I think I shall make Verrall take me to town with him! The thought has just come into my mind."

Charlotte made no answer. Possibly she did not hear the words, for the dogs were barking and she was laughing louder than ever. Mrs. Verrall stamped her foot petulantly, and her voice rang through the room.

"Charlotte, then, do you hear me? Put that horrible little brute down, or I will ring for both to be taken away! One might as well keep a screaming cockatoo! I say I have a great mind to go up to town with Verrall."

"Verrall would not take you," responded Charlotte, putting her King Charles on to the back of the terrier.

"Why do you think that?"

"He goes up for business only."

"It will be so dull for me, all alone!" complained Mrs. Verrall. "You in Scotland, he in London, and I moping myself to death in this gloomy Ashlydyat! I wish we had never taken it?"

Charlotte Pain bent her dark eyes in surprise upon her sister. "Since when have you found out that you do not like Ashlydyat?"

"Oh, I don't know. It is a gloomy place inside, especially if you contrast it with Lady Godolphin's Folly. And they are beginning to whisper of ghostly things being abroad on the Dark Plain!"

"For shame, Kate!" exclaimed Charlotte Pain. "Ghostly things! Oh, I see—you were laughing."

"Is it not enough to make us all laugh—these tales of the Godolphins? But I shall convert it into a pretext for not being left alone here when you and Verrall are away. Why do you go, Charlotte?" Mrs. Verrall added, in a tone which had changed to marked significance. "It is waste of time."

Charlotte Pain would not notice the innuendo. "I never was in Scotland, and shall like the visit," she said, picking up the King Charles again. "I enjoy fine scenery: you do not care for it."

"Oh," said Mrs. Verrall; "it is scenery that draws you, is it? Take you care, Charlotte."

"Care of what?"

"Shall I tell you? You must not fly into one of your tempers and pull my hair. You are growing too fond of George Godolphin."

Charlotte Pain gave no trace of "flying into a temper;" she remained perfectly cool and calm. "Well?" was all she said, her lip curling.

"If it would bring you any good; if it would end in your becoming Mrs. George Godolphin; I should say *well;* go into it with your whole heart and energy. But it will not so end; and your time and plans are being wasted."

"Has he told you so much?" ironically asked Charlotte.

"Nonsense! There was one in possession of the field before you, Charlotte—if my observation goes for anything. *She* will win the race; you will not even be in at the distance chair. I speak of Maria Hastings."

"You speak of what you know nothing," carelessly answered Charlotte Pain, a self-satisfied smile upon her lips.

"Very well. When it is all over, and you find your time *has* been wasted, do not say I never warned you. George Godolphin may be a prize worth entering the lists for; I do not say he is not: but there is no chance of your winning him."

Charlotte Pain tossed the dog upwards and caught him as he descended, a strange look of triumph on her brow.

"And—Charlotte," went on Mrs. Verrall in a lower tone, "there is a proverb, you know, about two stools. We *may* fall to the ground if we try to sit upon both at once. How would Dolf like this expedition to Scotland, handsome George making one in it?"

Charlotte's eyes flashed now. "I care no more for Dolf than I care for—not half so much as I care for this poor little brute. Don't bring up Dolf to me, Kate!"

"As you please. I would not mix myself up with your private affairs for the world. Only a looker-on sometimes sees more than those engaged in the play."

Crossing the apartment, Mrs. Verrall traversed the passage that led from it, and opened the door of another room. There sat her husband at the dessert-table, taking his wine alone, and smoking a cigar. He was a slight man, twice the age of his wife, his hair and whiskers yellow, and his eyes set deep in his head: rather a good-looking man on the whole, but a very silent one. "I want to go to London with you," said Mrs. Verrall.

"You can't," he answered.

She advanced to the table, and sat down near him. "There's Charlotte going one way, and you another——"

"Don't stop Charlotte," he interrupted, with a meaning nod.

"And I must be left alone in the house; to the ghosts and dreams and shadows they are inventing about that Dark Plain. I *will* go with you, Verrall."

"I should not take you with me to save the ghosts running off with you," was Mr. Verrall's answer, as he pressed the ashes from his cigar on a pretty shell, set in gold. "I go up *incog.* this time."

"Then I'll fill the house with guests," she petulantly said.

"Fill it, and welcome, if you like, Kate," he replied. "But, to go to London, you must wait for another opportunity."

"What a hateful thing business is! I wish it had never been invented!"

"A great many more wish the same. And have more cause to wish it than you," he drily answered. "Is tea ready?"

Mrs. Verrall returned to the room she had left, to order it in. Charlotte Pain was then standing outside the large window, leaning against its frame, the King Charles lying quietly in her arms, and her own ears on the alert, for she thought she heard advancing footsteps; and they seemed to be stealthy ones. The thought—or, perhaps, the wish —that it might be George Godolphin, stealing up to surprise her, flashed into her mind. She bent her head, and stroked the dog, in the prettiest unconsciousness of the approaching footsteps.

A hand was laid upon her shoulder. "Charlotte!"

She cried out—a sharp, genuine cry of dismay—dropped the King Charles, and bounded into the room. The intruder followed her.

"Why, Dolf!" uttered Mrs. Verrall in much astonishment. "Is it you?"

"It is not my ghost," replied the gentleman, holding out his hand. He was a little man, with fair hair, this Mr. Rodolf Pain, cousin to the two ladies. "Did I alarm you, Charlotte?"

"Alarm me!" she angrily rejoined. "You must have sprung from the earth."

"I have sprung from the railway station. Where is Verrall?"

"Why have you come down so unexpectedly?" exclaimed Mrs. Verrall.

"To see Verrall. I return to-morrow."

"Verrall goes up to-morrow night."

"I know he does. And that is why I have come down."

"You might have waited to see him in London," said Charlotte, her equanimity not yet restored.

"It was necessary for me to see him before he reached London. Where shall I find him, Mrs. Verrall?"

"In the dining-room," Mrs. Verrall replied. "What can you want with him so hurriedly?"

"Business," laconically replied Rodolf Pain, as he left the room in search of Mr. Verrall.

It was not the only interruption. Ere two minutes had elapsed, Lady Godolphin was shown in, causing Mrs. Verrall and her sister almost as much surprise as did the last intruder. She had walked over from the Folly, attended by a footman, and some agitation peeped out through her usual courtly suavity of manner, as she asked whether Charlotte Pain could be ready to start for Scotland on the morrow, instead of on Monday.

"To-morrow will be Sunday!" returned Charlotte.

"I do not countenance Sunday travelling, if other days can be made use of," continued Lady Godolphin. "But there are cases where it is not only necessary, but justifiable; when we are glad to feel the value of those Divine words, 'The Sabbath was made for man, and not man for the Sabbath.' Fever has broken out again, and I shall make use of to-morrow to escape from it. We start in the morning."

"I shall be ready and willing to go," replied Charlotte.

"It has appeared at Lady Sarah Grame's," added Lady Godolphin. "one of the most unlikely homes it might have been expected to visit. After this, none of us can feel safe. Were that fever to attack Sir George, his life, in his present reduced state, would not be worth an hour's purchase."

The dread of fever had been strong upon Lady Godolphin from the first; but never had it been so keen as now. Some are given to this dread in an unwonted degree: whilst an epidemic lasts (of whatever nature it may be) they live in a constant state of fear and pain. It is death they fear: being sent violently to the unknown life to come. I know of only one remedy for this: to be at peace with God: death or life are alike then. Lady Godolphin had not found it.

"Will Mr. Hastings permit his daughter to travel on a Sunday?" exclaimed Mrs. Verrall, the idea suddenly occurring to her, as Lady Godolphin was leaving.

"That is my business," was my lady's frigid answer. It has been said that she brooked not interference in the slightest degree.

It certainly could not be called the business of Mr. Hastings. For the travellers were far away from Prior's Ash the next morning before he had received an inkling of the departure.

CHAPTER VII.

BROOMHEAD.

THE contrast between them was great. You could see it most remarkably as they sat together. Both were beautiful, but of a different type of beauty. There are some people—and they bear a very large proportion to the whole—to whom the human countenance is as a sealed book. There are others for whom that book stands open to its every page. The capacity for reading character—what is it? where does it lie? Phrenologists call it, not inaptly, comparison.

There stands a man before you, a stranger; seen now for the first time. As you glance at him you involuntarily shrink within yourself, and trench imaginary walls around you, and say: That man is a bad man. Your eyes fall upon another—equally a stranger until that moment—and your honest heart flows out to him. You could extend to him the hand of confidence there and then, for that man's countenance is an index to his nature, and you *know* that you may trust him to the death. In what part of the face does this index seat itself? In the eyes? the mouth? the features separately? or in the whole?

Certainly in the whole. To judge of temper alone, the eye and mouth—provided you take them in repose—are sure indications; but, to judge of what a man is, you must look to the whole. You don't know precisely where to look for it—any more than do those know who cannot see it at all. You cannot say that it lies in the forehead, the eyebrows, the eyes, or the chin. You see it, and that is the most you can tell. Beauty and ugliness, in themselves, have nothing to do with it. An ugly countenance may, and often does, bear its own innate goodness, as certainly as that one of beauty sometimes bears its own repulsion. Were there certain unerring signs to judge by, the whole human race might become readers of character: but that will never be, so long as the world shall last.

In like manner, as we cannot tell precisely where nature's marks lie, so are we unable to tell where lies the capacity to read them. Is it a faculty? or an instinct? This I do know: that it is one of the great gifts of God. Where the power exists in an eminent degree, rely upon it its possessor is never deceived in his estimation of character. It is born with him into the world. As a little child he has his likes and dislikes to persons: and sometimes may be whipped for expressing them too strongly. As he grows up, the faculty—instinct—call it what you will—is ever in exercise; at rest when he sleeps; never at any other time.

Those who do not possess the gift (no disparagement to them: they may possess others, equally or more valuable) cavil at it—laugh at it—do not believe in it. Read what people are by their face? Nonsense! *they* know better. Others, who admit the fact, have talked of "reducing it to a science," whatever that may mean; of teaching it to the world, as we teach the classics to our boys. It may be done, say they. Possibly. We all acknowledge the wonders of this most wonderful age. Fishes are made to talk; fleas to comport themselves as gentlemen; monkeys are discovered to be men—or men monkeys—which is it? a shirt is advertised to be made in four minutes by a new sewing machine. We send ourselves in photograph to make morning calls. The opposite ends of the world are brought together by electric telegraph. Chloroform has rendered the surgeon's knife something rather agreeable than otherwise. We are made quite at home with "spirits," and ghosts are reduced to a theory. Not to mention other discoveries connected with the air, earth, and water, which would require an F.R.S. to descant upon. Wonderful discoveries of a wonderful age! Compare the last fifty years with the previous fifty years; when people made their wills before going to London, and flocked to the fair to see the learned pig point out the identical young woman who had had the quarrel with her sweetheart the previous Sunday afternoon! It is not my province to dispute these wonders: they may, or may not, be facts; but when you attempt to reduce this great gift to a "science," the result will be failure. Try and do so. Set up a school for it; give lectures; write books; beat it into heads; and then say to your pupils, "Now that you are accomplished, go out into the world and use your eyes and read your fellow-men." And the pupil will, perhaps, think he does read them; but, the first deduction he draws, will be the last—a wrong one. Neither art nor science can teach it; neither man nor woman can make it theirs by any amount of labour; where the faculty is not theirs by divine gift, it cannot be made to exist by human skill.

A reader of character would have noted the contrast between those two young ladies as they stood there: he would have trusted the one; he would not have trusted the other. And yet, Charlotte Pain had her good qualities also. She was kind-hearted in the main, liberal by nature, pleasant tempered, of a spirit firm and resolute, fitted to battle with the world and to make good her own way in it. But she was not truthful; she was not high principled; she was not one, whom I—had I been George Godolphin—would have chosen for my wife, or for my bosom friend.

Maria Hastings was eminent in what Charlotte Pain had not. Of rare integrity; highly principled; gentle, and refined; incapable of deceit; and with a loving nature that could be true unto death! But she was a very child in the ways of the world; timid, irresolute, unfitted to battle with its cares; swayed easily by those she loved; and all too passionately fond of George Godolphin.

Look at them both now—Charlotte, with her marked, brilliant features; her pointed chin, telling of self-will; her somewhat full, red lips; the pose of the head upon her tall, firm form: her large eyes, made to dazzle more than to attract; her perfectly self-possessed, not to say free manners!—All told of power; but not of innate refinement. Maria had too much of this refinement—if such a thing may be said of a young and gentle lady. She was finely and sensitively organized; considerate and gentle. It would be impossible for Maria Hastings to hurt wilfully the feelings of a fellow-creature. To the poorest beggar in the street she would have been courteous, considerate, almost humble. Not so much as a word of scorn could she cast to another, even in her inmost heart. The very formation of her hands would betray how sensitive and refined was her nature. And that is another thing which bears its own character—the hand; if you know how to read it. Her hands were of exceeding beauty; long, slender, taper fingers, of delicate aspect from a physical point of view. Every motion of those hands— and they were ever restless—was a word; every unconscious, nervous movement of the frail, weak-looking fingers had its peculiar character- istic. Maria Hastings had been accused of being vain of her hands; of displaying them more than was necessary: but the accusation, utterly untrue, was made by those who understood her but little, and her hands less. Such hands are rare: and it is as well that they are so: for they indicate a nature far removed from the common; a timid, intellectual, and painfully sensitive nature, which the rude world can neither under- stand, nor, perhaps, love. The gold, too much refined, is not fitted for ordinary uses. Charlotte Pain's hands were widely different: firm, plump, white; not small, and never moving unconsciously of them- selves.

These pretty hands resting upon her knee, sat Maria Hastings, doing nothing. Maria—I grieve to have it to say of her in this very utilita- rian age—was rather addicted to doing nothing. In her home, the Rectory, Maria was reproved on that score more than on any other. It is ever so with those who live much in the inward life. Maria would fall into a train of thought—and be idle.

Master Reginald Hastings would have lost his bet—that George Godolphin would be in Scotland a week after they arrived there—had he found any one to take it. Ten or eleven days had elapsed, and no George had come, and no news of his intention of coming. It was not for *this*, to be moped to death in an old Scotch country-house, that Charlotte Pain had accepted the invitation of Lady Godolphin. Care- less George—careless as to the import any of his words might bear— had said to her when they were talking of Scotland: "I wish you were to be of the party; to help us while away the dull days." Mr. George had spoken in gallantry—he was too much inclined so to speak, not only to Charlotte—without ever dreaming that his wish would be ful- filled literally. But, when Lady Godolphin afterwards gave the invita- tion—Sir George had remarked aloud at the family dinner-table that Miss Pain had fished for it—Charlotte accepted it with undisguised pleasure. In point of fact, Mr. George, had the choice been given him, would have preferred having Maria Hastings to himself there.

But he did not come. Eleven days, and no George Godolphin. Charlotte began to lay mental plans for the arrival of some sudden telegraphic message, demanding her immediate return to Prior's Ash; and Maria could only hope, and look, and long in secret.

It was a gloomy day; not rainy, but enveloped in mist, almost as bad as rain. They had gone out together, after luncheon, these two young ladies, but the weather drove them in again. Charlotte was restless and peevish. She stirred the fire as if she had a spite against it; she dashed off a few bars at the piano, on which instrument she was a skilful player; she cut half the leaves of a new periodical and then flung it from her; she admired herself in the pier-glass; she sat down opposite Maria Hastings and her stillness; and now she jumped up again and violently rang the bell, to order her desk to be brought to her. Maria roused herself from her reverie.

"Charlotte, what is the matter? One would think you had St. Vitus's dance."

"So I have—if to twitch all over with the fidgets is to have it. How you can sit so calm, so unmoved, is a marvel to me. Maria, if I were to be another ten days in this house, I should go mad."

"Why did you come to it?"

"I thought it might be a pleasant change. Ashlydyat grows gloomy sometimes. How was I to know my lady led so quiet a life here? She was always talking of 'Broomhead,' 'Broomhead!' I could not possibly suppose it to be so dull a place as this!"

"It is not dull in itself. The house and grounds are charming."

"Oh dear!" uttered Charlotte. "I wonder what fogs were sent for?"

"So do I," laughed Maria. "I should have finished that sketch, but for this mist."

"No saddle-horses!" went on Charlotte. "I shall forget how to ride. I never heard of such a thing as a country-house without saddle-horses. Where was the use of bringing my new cap and habit? Only to have them crushed!"

Maria seemed to have relapsed into thought. She made no reply. Presently Charlotte began again.

"I wish I had my dogs here! Lady Godolphin would not extend the invitation even to King Charlie. She said she did not like dogs. What a heathen she must be! If I could only see my darling pet, King Charlie! Kate never mentioned him once in her letter this morning!"

The words aroused Maria to animation. "Did you receive a letter this morning from Prior's Ash? You did not tell me."

"Margery brought it to my bedroom. It came last night, I fancy, and lay in the letter-box. I do not think Sir George ought to keep that letter-box entirely under his own control," continued Charlotte. "He grows forgetful. Some evenings I know it is never looked at."

"I have not observed that Sir George is forgetful," dissented Maria.

"You observe nothing. I say that Sir George declines daily: both bodily and mentally. I see a great difference in him, even in the short time that we have been here. He is not the man he was."

"He has his business letters regularly; and answers them."

"Quite a farce to send them," mocked handsome Charlotte. "Thomas Godolphin is ultra-filial."

"What news does Mrs. Verrall give you?" inquired Maria.

"Not much. Sarah Anne Grame is out of immediate danger, and the fever has attacked two or three others."

"In Lady Sarah's house?"

"Nonsense! No. That sickly girl, Sarah Anne, took it because I suppose she could not help it;—but there's not much fear of its spreading to the rest of the house. If they had been going to have it, it would have shown itself ere this. It has crept on to those pests of cottages by the Pollards. The Bonds are down with it."

"The worst spot it could have got to!" exclaimed Maria. "Those cottages are unhealthy at the best of times."

"They had a dinner-party on Saturday," continued Charlotte.

"At the cottages!"

Charlotte laughed. "At Ashlydyat. The Godolphins were there. At least, she mentioned Bessy, and your chosen cavalier, Mr. George."

Maria's cheek flushed crimson. Charlotte Pain was rather fond of this kind of satire. Had she believed there was anything serious between George Godolphin and Maria, she would have bitten her tongue out rather than allude to it. It was not Charlotte's intention to spare him to Maria Hastings.

Charlotte Pain at length settled herself to her desk. Maria drew nearer to the fire, and sat looking into it, her cheek leaning on her hand : sat there until the dusk of the winter's afternoon fell upon the room. She turned to her companion

"Can you see, Charlotte?"

"Scarcely. I have just finished."

A few minutes, and Charlotte folded her letters. Two. The one was directed to Mrs. Verrall; the other to Rodolf Pain, Esquire.

"I shall go up to dress," she said, locking her desk.

"There's plenty of time," returned Maria. "I wonder where Sir George and Lady Godolphin are? They did not intend to stay out so late."

"Oh, when those ancient codgers get together, talking of their past times and doings, they take no more heed how time goes than we do at a ball," carelessly spoke Charlotte.

Maria laughed. "Lucky for you, Charlotte, that Lady Godolphin is not within hearing. 'Ancient codgers!'"

Charlotte left the room, carrying her letters with her. Maria sat on, some time longer—and then it occurred to her to look at her watch. A quarter to five.

A quarter to five! Had she been asleep? No, only dreaming. She started up, threw wide the door, and was passing swiftly into the dark ante-chamber. The house had not been lighted, and the only light came from the fire behind Maria—revealing her clearly enough, but rendering that ante-chamber particularly dark. Little wonder, then, that she gave a scream when she found herself caught in some one's arms, against whom she had nearly run.

"Is it you, Sir George? I beg your pardon."

Not Sir George. Sir George would not have held her to him with that impassioned fervour. Sir George would not have taken those fond kisses from her lips. It was another George, just come in from his long day's journey. He pressed his face, cold from the fresh night air, upon her warm one. "My dearest! I knew you would be the first to welcome me!"

Dark enough around, it was still; but a light as of some sunny Eden, illumined the heart of Maria Hastings. The shock of joy was indeed great. Every vein was throbbing, every pulse tingling, and George Godolphin, had he never before been sure that her deep and entire love was his, must have known it then.

The Shadow of Ashlydyat.   4

A servant was heard approaching with lights. George Godolphin turned to the fire, and Maria turned and stood near him.

"Did any of you expect me?" he inquired.

"Oh no!" impulsively answered Maria. "I can scarcely now believe that it is you in reality."

He looked at her and laughed; his gay laugh : as much as to say that he had given her a tolerable proof of his reality. She stood, in her pretty, timid manner, before the fire, her eyelids drooping, and the flame lighting up her fair face.

"Is my father at home?" he asked, taking off his overcoat. He had walked from the railway station, a mile or two distant.

"He went out with Lady Godolphin this morning to pay a visit to some old friends. I thought they would have returned long before this."

"Is he getting strong, Maria?"

Maria thought of what Charlotte Pain had said, and hesitated. "He appears to me to be better than when we left Prior's Ash. But he is far from strong."

The servant finished lighting the chandelier and retired. George Godolphin watched the door close, and then drew Maria before him, gazing down at her.

"Let me look at you, my darling! Are you glad to see me?"

Glad to see him! The tears nearly welled up with the intensity of her emotion. "I had begun to think you were not coming at all," she said, in a low tone. "Charlotte Pain received a letter from Mrs. Verrall this morning, in which you were mentioned as——"

Charlotte herself interrupted the conclusion of the sentence. She came in, dressed for dinner. George turned to greet her, his manner warm; his hands outstretched.

"Margery said Mr. George was here! I did not believe her!" cried Charlotte, resigning her hands to him. "Did you come on the telegraph-wires?"

"They would not have brought me quickly enough to *your* presence," cried Mr. George.

Charlotte laughed gaily. "I was just prophesying you would not come at all. Mrs. Verrall did not inform me that you were about to start, amidst her other items of intelligence. Besides, I know that you are rather addicted to forgetting your promises."

"What items had Mrs. Verrall to urge against me?" demanded George.

"I forget them now. Nothing I believe. Is Prior's Ash alive still?"

"It was, when I left it."

"And the fever, George?" inquired Maria.

"Fever? Oh, I don't know much about it."

"As if fevers were in his way!" ironically cried Charlotte Pain. "He troubles himself no more about fevers than does Lady Godolphin."

"Than Lady Godolphin would like to do, I suppose you mean, Miss Pain?" he rejoined.

Maria was looking at him wistfully—almost reproachfully. He saw it, and turned to her with a smile. "Has it in truth attacked the cottages down by the Pollards?" she asked.

George nodded. He was not so ignorant as he appeared to be. "Poor Bond had it first; and now two of his children are attacked. I understand Mr. Hastings declares it is a judgment upon the town, for not looking better after the hovels and the drainage."

"Has Bond recovered?" asked Maria.

"No."

"Not recovered?" she exclaimed quickly.

"He is dead, Maria."

She clasped her hands, shocked at the news. "Dead. Leaving that large, helpless family! And Sarah Anne Grame?—is she out of danger?"

"From the violence of the fever. But she is in so dangerously weak a state from its effects, that it will be next to a miracle if she recovers. Lady Sarah is half out of her mind. She had prayers put up for Sarah Anne on Sunday. Pretty Ethel has escaped! to the delight of Prior's Ash in general, and of Thomas in particular. What carriage is that?" suddenly broke off George, as the sound of one approaching was heard.

It proved to be Sir George's, bringing home himself and my lady. George hastened to meet them as they entered the hall, his handsome face glowing, his bright chestnut hair taking a golden tinge in the lamp-light, his hands held out. "My dear father!"

The old knight, with a cry of glad surprise, caught the hands, and pressed them to his heart. My lady advanced with her welcome. She bent her tinted cheek forwards, by way of greeting, and Mr. George touched it with his delicate lips—lightly, as became its softened bloom.

"So you have found your way to us, George! I expected you would have done so before."

"Did you, madam?"

"Did we?" cried the knight, taking up the word. "Listen to that vain George! He pretends to ignore the fact that there was an attraction here. Had a certain young lady remained at Prior's Ash, I expect you would not have given us much of your company at Broomhead. If Miss Charlotte——"

"Did you call me, Sir George?" interrupted Charlotte, tripping forward from the back of the hall, where she and Maria stood, out of sight, but within hearing.

"No, my dear, I did not call you," replied Sir George Godolphin.

CHAPTER VIII.

A SNAKE IN THE GRASS.

SEATED on a camp-stool, amidst a lovely bit of woodland scenery, was Maria Hastings. The day, beautifully bright, was warm as one in September; delightful for the pleasure-seekers at Broomhead, but bad for the fever at Prior's Ash. Maria was putting some finishing touches to a sketch—she had taken many since she came—and Mr. George Godolphin and Charlotte Pain watched her as they pleased, or took sauntering strolls to a distance.

Lady Godolphin was as fond of Broomhead as the Godolphins were of Ashlydyat. Certainly Broomhead was the more attractive home of the two. A fine house of exquisite taste; with modern rooms and modern embellishments; and when she invited the two young ladies to accompany her on a visit to it, she was actuated as much by a sense of exultation at exhibiting the place to them, as by a desire for their companionship, though she did like and desire the companionship. Lady Godolphin, who never read, and never worked; in short, never did anything; was obliged to have friends with her to dissipate her ennui and cheat time. She liked young ladies best; for they did not interfere with her own will, and were rarely exacting visitors.

But she required less of this companionship at Broomhead. There she knew every one, and every one knew her. She was sufficiently familiar with the smallest and poorest cottage to take an interest in its ill-doings and its short-comings; at least, as much interest as it was possible to the nature of Lady Godolphin to take. Old acquaintances dropped in without ceremony and remained the morning with her, gossiping of times past and present: or she dropped into their houses, and remained with them. Of gaiety there was none: Sir George's state of health forbade it: and in this quiet social intercourse—which Charlotte Pain held in especial contempt—the young visitors were not wanted. Altogether they were much at liberty, and went roaming where they would, under the protection of Mr. George Godolphin.

He had now been a week at Broomhead: flirting with Charlotte, giving stolen minutes to Maria. A looker-on might have decided that Miss Pain was the gentleman's chief attraction. for, in public, his attentions were principally given to her. *She* may be pardoned for estimating them at more than they were worth: but she could very well have welcomed any friendly wind that would have wafted away Maria, and have kept her away. They knew, those two girls, that their mutual intercourse was of a hollow nature; their paraded friendship, their politeness, rotten at the core. Each was jealous of the other; and the one subject which filled their minds was never alluded to in conversation. Either might have affirmed to the other, " You are aware that I watch you and George: my jealous eyes are upon your every movement, my jealous ears are ever open." But these avowals are not made in social life, and Charlotte and Maria observed studied courtesy, making believe to be mutually unconscious: knowing all the time that the consciousness existed in a remarkable degree. It was an artificial state of things.

"How dark you are putting in those trees!" exclaimed Charlotte Pain.

Maria paused, pencil in hand; glanced at the trees opposite, and at the trees on paper. "Not too dark," she said. "The grove is a heavy one."

"What's that queer-looking thing in the corner? It is like a half-moon, coming down to pay us a visit."

Maria held out her sketch at arm's distance, laughing merrily. "You do not understand perspective, Charlotte. Look at it now."

"Not I," said Charlotte. "I understand nothing of the work. They tried to teach me when I was a child, but I never could make a straight line without the ruler. After all, where's the use of it? The best-made sketch cannot rival its model—nature."

"But sketches serve to remind us of familiar places, when we are beyond their reach," was Maria's answer. "I love drawing."

"Maria draws well," observed George Godolphin, from his swinging perch on the branch of a neighbouring tree.

She looked up at him, almost gratefully. "This will be one of the best sketches I have taken here," she said. "It is so thoroughly picturesque: and that farm-house, under the hill, gives life to the picture."

Charlotte Pain cast her eyes upon the house in the distance over the green field, to which she had not before vouchsafed a glance. A shade of contempt crossed her face.

"Call *that* a farm-house! I should say it was a tumble-down old cottage."

"It is large for a cottage; and has a barn and a shed round it," returned Maria. "I conclude that it was a farm some time."

"It is not inhabited," said Charlotte.

"Oh, yes it is. There is a woman standing at the door. I have put her into my sketch."

"And her pipe also?" cried George.

"Her pipe!"

George took his own cigar from his mouth, as he answered. "She is smoking, that woman. A short pipe."

Maria shaded her eyes with her hand, and gazed attentively. "I—really—do—think—she—is!" she exclaimed slowly. "What a strange thing!"

"A Welshwoman married to a Scotch husband, possibly," suggested Charlotte. "The Welsh smoke."

"I'll make her a Welshwoman," said Maria gaily, "with a man's coat, and a man's hat. But, there's—there's another now. George, it is Margery!"

"Yes," said Mr. George composedly. "I saw her go in half an hour ago. How smart she is! She must be paying morning calls."

They laughed at this, and watched Margery. A staid woman of middle age, who had been maid to the late Mrs. Godolphin. Margery dressed plainly, but she certainly looked smart to-day, as the sun's rays fell upon her. The sun was unusually bright, and Charlotte Pain remarked it, saying it made her eyes ache.

"Suspiciously bright," observed George Godolphin.

"Suspiciously?"

He flirted the ashes from his cigar with his finger. "Suspicious of a storm," he said. "We shall have it, ere long. See those clouds. They look small and inoffensive; but they mean mischief."

Charlotte Pain strolled away over the meadows towards the side path on which Margery was advancing. George Godolphin leaped from his seat, apparently with the intention of following her. But first of all he approached Maria, and bent to look at her progress.

"Make the farm—as you call it—very conspicuous, Maria, if you are going to keep the sketch as a memento," said he.

"Is it not a farm?"

"It was, once; until idleness suffered it to drop through."

"Why should I make it particularly conspicuous?" she continued.

There was no reply, and she looked quickly up. A peculiar expression, one which she did not understand, sat upon his face.

"If we had a mind to cheat the world, Maria, we might do so, by paying a visit to that house."

"In what way?"

"I might take you in Maria Hastings, and bring you out Mrs. George Godolphin."

"What do you mean?" she inquired, completely puzzled.

Mr. George laughed. "The man who lives there, Sandy Bray, has made more couples one than a rustic parson. Some people call him a public nuisance; others say he is a convenience, as it is three miles to the nearest kirk. He goes by the nickname of Minister Bray. Many a lad and lassie have stolen in there, under cover of the twilight, and in five minutes have come forth again, married, the world being none the wiser."

"Is it the place they call Gretna Green?" inquired Maria in much astonishment.

"No, it is not Gretna Green. Only a place of the same description, and equally serviceable."

"But such marriages cannot be binding!"

"Indeed they are. You have surely heard of the Scotch laws?"

"I have been told that any one can marry people in Scotland. I have heard that the simple declaration of saying you take each other for man and wife constitutes a marriage."

"Yes; if said before a witness. Would you like to try it, Maria?"

The colour mantled to her face as she bent over her drawing. She smiled at the joke, simply shaking her head by way of answer. And Mr. George Godolphin went off laughing, lighting another cigar as he walked. Overtaking Charlotte Pain just as Margery came up, he accosted the latter.

"How grand you are, Margery! What's agate?"

"Grand!" returned Margery. "Who says it? What is there grand about me?"

"That shawl displays as many colours as a kaleidoscope. We

thought it was a rainbow coming along. Did it arrive in an express parcel last night from Paisley?"

"It isn't me that has money to spend upon parcels!" retorted Margery. "I have too many claims dragging my purse at both ends, for that."

A faithful servant was Margery, in spite of her hard features, and her stern speech. Scant of ceremony she had always been, and scant of ceremony she would remain. In fact, she was given to treating the younger branches of the Godolphins, Mr. George included, very much as she had treated them when they were children. They knew her sterling worth, and did not quarrel with her severe manners.

"When you have half a dozen kin pulling at you, 'I want this!' from one, and 'I want that!' from another, and the same cry running through all, it isn't much money you can keep to spend on shawls," resumed Margery. "I was a fool to come here; that's what I was! When the master said to me, 'You had better come with us, Margery,' I ought to have answered, 'No, Sir George, I'm better away.'"

"Well, what is the grievance, Margery?" George asked, while Charlotte Pain turned from one to the other in curiosity.

"Why, they are on at me for money, that's what it is, Mr. George. My lady sent for me this morning to say she intended to call and see Selina to-day. Of course I knew what it meant—that I was to go and give them a hint to have things tidy—for, if there's one thing my lady won't do, it is to put her foot into a pigsty. So I threw on my shawl, that you are laughing at, and went. There was nothing the matter with the place, for a wonder; but there was with them. Selina, she's in bed, ill—and if she frets as she's fretting now, she won't get out of it in a hurry. Why did she marry the fellow? It does make me so vexed!"

"What has she to fret about?" continued George.

"What does she always have to fret about?" retorted Margery. "His laziness, and the children's ill-doings. They go roaming about the country, here, there, and everywhere, after work, as they say, after places; and then they get into trouble and untold worry, and come home or send home for money to help them out of it! One of them, Nick—and a good name for him, say I!—must be off into Wales to those relations of Bray's; and he has been at some mischief there, and is in prison for it, and is now committed for trial. And the old woman has walked all the way here to get funds from them, to pay for his defence. The news has half killed Selina."

"I said she was a Welshwoman," interrupted Charlotte Pain. "She was smoking, was she not, Margery?"

"She's smoking a filthy short pipe," wrathfully returned Margery. "But for that, I should have said she was a decent body—although it's next to impossible to understand her tongue. She puts in ten words of Welsh to two of English. Of course they have no money to furnish for it; it wouldn't be them, if they had; so they are wanting to get it out of me. Fifteen or twenty pounds! My word! They'd like me to end my days in the workhouse."

"You might turn a deaf ear, Margery," said George.

"I know I might; and many a hundred times have I vowed I

would," returned Margery. "But there's she in her bed, poor thing, sobbing and moaning, and asking if Nick is to be quite abandoned. The worse a lad turns out, the more a mother clings to him—as it seems to me. Let me be here, or let me be at Ashlydyat, I have no peace for their wants. By word of mouth or by letter they are on at me for ever."

"If 'Nick' has a father, why can he not supply him?" asked Charlotte.

"It's a sensible question, Miss Pain," said the woman. "Nick's father is one of those stinging-nettles that only encumber the world, doing no good for themselves nor for anybody else. 'Minister' Bray, indeed! it ought to be something else, I think. Many a one has had cause to rue the hour that he 'ministered' for them!"

"How does he minister?—what do you mean?" wondered Charlotte.

"He marries folks; that's his ne'er-do-well occupation, Miss Pain. Give him a five-shilling piece, and he'd marry a boy to his grand-mother. I'm Scotch by birth—though it's not much that I have lived in the land—but, I do say, that to suffer such laws to stand good, is a sin and a shame. Two foolish children—and many of those that go to him are no better—stand before him for a half-minute, and he pronounces them to be man and wife! And man and wife they are, and must remain so, till the grave takes one of them: whatever their repentance may be when they wake up from their folly. It's just one of the blights upon bonny Scotland."

Margery, with no ceremonious leave-taking, turned at the last words, and continued her way. George Godolphin smiled at the blank expression displayed on Charlotte Pain's countenance. Had Margery talked in Welsh, as did the old woman with the pipe, she could not have less understood her.

"You require the key, Charlotte," said he. "Shall I give it to you? Margery was my mother's maid, as you may have heard. Her sister, Selina, was maid to the present Lady Godolphin: not of late years: long and long before she ever knew my father. It appears the girl, Selina, was a favourite with her mistress; but she left her, in spite of opposition from all quarters, to marry Mr. Sandy Bray. And has, there's no doubt, been rueing it ever since. There are several children, of an age now to be out in the world; but you heard Margery's account of them. I fear they do pull unconscionably at poor Margery's purse-strings."

"Why does she let them do so?" asked Charlotte.

Mr. George opened his penknife and ran the point of it through his cigar, ere he answered. "Margery has a soft place in her heart. As I believe most of us have—if our friends could but give us credit for it."

"How strange the two sisters should live, the one with your father's first wife, the other with his second!" exclaimed Charlotte, when she had given a few moments to thought. "Were they acquainted with each other?—the ladies."

"Not in the least. They never saw each other. I believe it was through these women being sisters that my father became acquainted with the present Lady Godolphin. He was in Scotland with Janet, visiting my mother's family; and Margery, who was with them, brought

Janet to that very house, there, to see her sister. Mrs. Campbell—as she was, then—happened to have gone there that day : and that's how the whole thing arose. People say there's a fatality in all things. One would think it must be so. Until that day, Mrs. Campbell had not been in the house for two or three years, and would not be likely to go into it again for two or three more."

"Is Bray a *mauvais sujet ?*"

George lifted his eyebrows. "I don't know that there's much against him, except his incorrigible laziness : that's bad enough when a man has children to keep. Work he will not. Beyond the odds and ends that he gets by the exercise of what he is pleased to call his trade, the fellow earns nothing. Lady Godolphin is charitable to the wife ; and poor Margery, as she says, finds her purse drawn at both ends."

"I wondered why Margery came to Scotland," observed Charlotte, "not being Lady Godolphin's maid. What *is* Margery's capacity in your family? I have never been able to find out."

"It might puzzle herself to tell you what it is, now. After my mother's death, she waited on my sisters : but when they left Ashlydyat, Margery declined to follow them. She would not leave Sir George. She is excessively attached to him, almost as much so as she was to my mother. That quitting Ashlydyat, ourselves first, and then my father, was a blow to Margery," George added in a dreamy tone. "She has never been the same since."

"It was Margery, was it not, who attended upon Sir George in his long illness?"

"I do not know what he would have done without her," spoke George Godolphin in a tone that betrayed its own gratitude. "In sickness she is invaluable : certainly not to be replaced, where she is attached. Lady Godolphin, though in her heart I do not fancy she likes Margery, respects her for her worth."

"I cannot say I like her," said Charlotte Pain. "Her manners are too independent. I have heard her order you about very cavalierly."

"And you will hear her again," said George Godolphin. "She exercised great authority over us when we were children, and she looks upon us as children still. Her years have grown with ours, and there is always the same distance as to age between us. I speak of the younger amongst us : to Thomas and Janet she is ever the respectful servant ; in a measure also to Bessy : of myself and Cecil she considers herself partial mistress."

"If they are so poor as to drain Margery of her money, how is it they can live in that house and pay its rent?" inquired Charlotte, looking towards the building.

"It is Bray's own. The land, belonging to it, has been mortgaged three deep long ago. He might have been in a tolerably good position, had he chosen to make the most of his chances : he was not born a peasant."

"Who is this?" exclaimed Charlotte.

A tall, slouching man, with red hair and heavy shoulders, was advancing towards them from the house. George turned to look.

"That is Bray himself. Look at the lazy fellow! You may tell his temperament from his gait."

George Godolphin was right. The man was not walking along, but sauntering; turning to either side and bending his head as if flowers lay in his path and he wished to look at them: his hands in his pockets, his appearance anything but fresh and neat. They watched him come up. He touched his hat then, and accosted Mr. George Godolphin.

"My service to ye, sir. I didna know you were in these parts."

"So you are still in the land of the living, Bray!" was Mr. George's response. "How is business?"

"Dull as a dyke," returned Bray. "Times are bad. I've hardly took a crown in the last three months, sir. I shall have to emigrate, if this is to go on."

"I fear you would scarcely find another country so tolerant to your peculiar calling, Bray," said George, some mockery in his tone. "And what would the neighbourhood do without you? It must resign itself to single blessedness."

"The neighbourhood dunna come to me. Folk go over to the kirk now: that has come into fashion; and I'm going down. 'Twas different in past times. A man would give a ten-pun note then to have things done neatly and quietly. But there's fresh notions and fresh havers; and, for all the good they have done me, I might as well be out of the world. Is this Miss Cecil?"

The last question was put abruptly, the man turning himself full upon Charlotte Pain, and scanning her face. George Godolphin was surprised out of an answer: had he taken a moment for reflection, he might have deemed the question an impertinence, and passed it by.

"Miss Cecilia is not in Scotland."

"I thought it might be her," said the man; "for Miss Cecil's looks are a country's talk, and I have heard much of them. I see now: there's nought of the Godolphin *there*. But it's a bonny face, young lady: and I dare say there's those that are finding it so."

He shambled on, with a gesture of the hand by way of salutation. Charlotte Pain did not dislike the implied compliment. "How can this man marry people?" she exclaimed. "He is no priest."

"He can, and he does marry them; and is not interfered with, or forbidden," said George Godolphin. "At least, he did do so. By his own account, his patronage seems to be on the decline."

"Did he marry them openly?"

"Well—no; I conclude not. If people found it convenient to marry openly, they would not go to him. And why they should go to him at all, puzzles me, and always has: for, the sort of marriage that he performs can be performed by any one wearing a coat, in Scotland, or by the couple themselves. But he has acquired a name, 'Minister Bray;' and a great deal lies in a name for ladies' ears."

"Ladies!" cried Charlotte scornfully. "Only the peasants went to him, I am sure."

"Others have gone as well as peasants. Bray boasts yet of a fifty-pound note, once put into his hand for pronouncing the benediction. It is a ceremony that we are given to be lavish upon," added George, laughing. "I have heard of money being grudged for a funeral, but I never did for a wedding."

"Were I compelled to be a resident of this place, I should get married myself, out of sheer ennui, or do something else as desperate," she exclaimed.

"You find it dull?"

"It has been more tolerable since you came," she frankly avowed.

George raised his hat, and his blue eyes shot a glance into hers. "Thank you, Charlotte."

"Why were you so long in coming? Do you know what I had done? I had written a letter to desire Mrs. Verrall to recall me. Another week of it would have turned me melancholy. Your advent was better than nobody's."

"Thank you again, mademoiselle. When I promise——"

"Promise," she warmly interrupted. "I have learnt what your promises are worth. Oh, but, George, tell me—What was it that you and Lady Godolphin were saying yesterday? It was about Ethel Grame. I only caught a word here and there."

"Thomas wishes Lady Godolphin would invite Ethel here for the remainder of their stay. He thinks Ethel would be all the better for a change, after being mured up in that fever-tainted house. But, don't talk of it. It was only a little private negotiation that Thomas was endeavouring to carry out upon his own account. He wrote to me, and he wrote to my lady. Ethel knows nothing of it."

"And what does Lady Godolphin say?"

George drew in his lips. "She says No. As I expected. And I believe she is for once sorry to say it, for pretty Ethel is a favourite of hers. But she retains her dread of the fever. Her argument is, that, although Ethel has escaped it in her own person, she might possibly bring it here in her boxes."

"Stuff!" cried Charlotte Pain. "Sarah Anne might do so; but I do not see how Ethel could. I wonder Thomas does not marry, and have done with it! He is old enough."

"And Ethel young enough. It will not be delayed long now. The vexatious question, concerning residence, must be settled in some way."

"What residence? What is vexatious about it?" quickly asked Charlotte, curiously.

"There is some vexation about it, in some way or other," returned George with indifference, not choosing to speak more openly. "It is not my affair; it lies between Thomas and Sir George. When Thomas comes here next week——"

"Is Thomas coming next week?" she interrupted.

"That is the present plan. And I return."

She threw her flashing eyes at him. They said—well, they said a good deal: perhaps Mr. George could read it. "You had better get another letter of recall written, Charlotte," he resumed in a tone which might be taken for jest or earnest, "and give me the honour of your escort."

"How you talk!" returned she peevishly. "As if Lady Godolphin would allow me to go all that way under *your* escort! As if I would go myself!"

"You might have a less safe one, Charlotte mia," cried Mr. George somewhat saucily. "No lion should come near you, to eat you up."

"George," resumed Charlotte, after a pause, "I wish you would tell me whether Mrs. Verrall—— Good Heavens! what's that?"

Sounds of distress were sounding in their ears. They turned hastily. Maria Hastings, her camp-stool overturned, her sketching materials scattered on the ground, was flying towards them, calling upon George Godolphin to save her. There was no mistaking that she was in a state of intense terror.

Charlotte Pain wondered if she had gone mad. She could see nothing to alarm her. George Godolphin cast his rapid glance to the spot where she had sat, and could see nothing, either. He hastened to meet her, and caught her in his arms, into which she literally threw herself.

Entwined round her left wrist was a small snake, or reptile of the species, more than a foot long. It looked like an eel, writhing there. Maria had never come into personal contact with anything of the sort : but she remembered what had been said of the deadly bite of a serpent ; and terror completely overmastered her.

He seized it and flung it from her ; he laid her poor terrified face upon his breast, that she might there sob out her fear ; he cast a greedy glance at her wrist, where the thing had been : and his own face had turned white with emotion.

"My darling, there is no injury," he soothingly whispered. "Be calm! be calm!" And, utterly regardless of the presence of Charlotte Pain, he laid his cheek against hers, as if to reassure her, and kept it there.

Less regardless, possibly, had he seen Charlotte Pain's countenance. It was dark as night. The scales were rudely torn from her eyes : and she saw, in that moment, how fallacious had been her own hopes touching George Godolphin.

CHAPTER IX.

MR. SANDY'S "TRADE."

"WHAT ever is the matter?"

The interruption came from Lady Godolphin. Charlotte Pain had perceived her approach, but had ungraciously refrained from intimating it to her companions. My lady, a coquettish white bonnet shading her delicate face, and her little person enveloped in a purple velvet mantle trimmed with ermine, was on her way to pay a visit to her ex-maid, Selina. She surveyed the group with intense astonishment. Maria Hastings, white, sobbing, clinging to George Godolphin in unmistakable terror; Mr. George soothing her in rather a marked manner; and Charlotte Pain, erect, haughty, her arms folded, her head drawn up, giving no assistance, her countenance about as pleasant as a demon's my lady had once the pleasure of seeing at the play. She called out the above words before she was well up with them.

George Godolphin did not release Maria; he simply lifted his head. "She has been very much terrified, Lady Godolphin; but no harm is done. A reptile of the snake species fastened itself on her wrist. I have flung it off."

He glanced towards the spot where stood Lady Godolphin, as much as to imply that he had flung the offender *there*. My lady shrieked, caught up her petticoats, we won't say how high, and leaped away nimbly.

"I never heard of such a thing!" she exclaimed. "A snake! What should bring snakes about, here?"

"Say a serpent!" broke from the pale lips of Charlotte Pain.

Lady Godolphin did not detect the irony, and felt really alarmed. Maria, growing calmer, and perhaps feeling half ashamed of the emotion which fear had caused her to display, drew away from George Godolphin. He would not suffer that, and made her take his arm. "I am sorry to have alarmed you all so much," she said. "Indeed, I could not help it, Lady Godolphin."

"A serpent in the grass!" repeated her ladyship, unable to get over the surprise. "How did it come to you, Maria? Were you lying down?"

"I was sitting on the camp-stool, there; busy with my drawing," she answered. "My left hand was hanging down, touching, I believe, the grass. I began to feel something cold at my wrist, but at first did not notice it. Then I lifted it and saw that dreadful thing wound round it. I could not shake it off. Oh, Lady Godolphin! I felt—I hardly know how I felt—almost as if I should have died, had there been no one near to run to."

Lady Godolphin, her skirts still lifted, the tips of her toes touching the path gingerly, to which they had now hastened, and her eyes alert, lest the serpent should come trailing forth from any unexpected direction, remarked that it was a mercy Maria had escaped with only fright. "You seem to experience enough of that," she said. "Don't faint, child."

Maria's lips parted with a sickly smile, which she meant should be a brave one. She was both timid and excitable; and, if terror did attack her, she felt it in no common degree. What would have been but a passing fear to another, forgotten almost as soon as felt, was to her agony. Remarkably susceptible, was she, to the extreme of pleasure and the extreme of pain. "There is no fear of my fainting," she answered to Lady Godolphin. "I never fainted in my life."

"I am on my road to see an old servant who lives in that house," said Lady Godolphin, pointing to the tenement, little thinking how far it had formed their theme of discourse. "You shall come with me and rest, and have some water."

"Yes, that is the best thing to be done," said George Godolphin. "I'll take you there, Maria, and then I'll have a hunt after the beast. I ought to have killed him at the time."

Lady Godolphin walked on, Charlotte Pain at her side. Charlotte's lip was curling.

The house door, to which they were bound, stood open. Across its lower portion, as if to prevent the exit of children, was a board, formerly placed there for that express purpose. The children were grown now and scattered, but the board remained; the inmates stepping over it at their will. Sandy Bray, who must have skulked back to his home by some unseen circuit, made a rush to the board at sight of Lady Godolphin, and pulled it out of its grooves, leaving the entrance clear. But for his intense idleness, he, knowing she was coming, would have removed it earlier.

They entered upon a large room, half sitting-room, half kitchen, its boarded floor very clean. The old Welshwoman, a cleanly, well-mannered, honest-faced old woman, was busy knitting then, and came forward, curtseying: no vestige of pipe to be seen or smelt. "Selina was in bed," Bray said, standing humbly before Lady Godolphin. "Selina had heard bad news of one of the brats, and had worried herself sick over it, as my lady knew it was in the stupid nature of Selina to do. Would my lady be pleased to step up to see her?"

Yes; my lady would be pleased to do so by-and-by. But at present she directed a glass of water to be brought to Miss Hastings. Bray brought the water in a cracked yellow cup.

"Eh, but there is some of them things about here," he said, when the cause of alarm was mentioned. "I think there must be a nest of 'em. They are harmless, so far as I know."

"Why don't you find the nest?" asked Mr. George Godolphin.

"And what good, if I did find 'em, sir?" said he.

"Kill the lot," responded George.

He strode out of the house, Bray following in his wake, to look for the reptile which had caused the alarm. Bray was sure nothing would come of it: the thing had had time to get clear away.

In point of fact, nothing did come of it. George Godolphin could not decide upon the precise spot where they had stood when he threw away the reptile; and, to beat over the whole field, which was extensive, would have been endless work. He examined carefully the spot where Maria had sat, both he and Bray, but could see no trace of anything alarming. Gathering up her treasures, including the camp-stool, he set off with them. Bray made a feeble show of offering to bear the stool. "No," said George, "I'll carry it myself: it would be too much trouble for you."

Charlotte Pain stood at the door, watching as they approached, her rich cheek glowing, her eye flashing. Never had she looked more beautiful, and she bent her sweetest smile upon Mr. George, who had the camp-stool swinging on his back. Lady Godolphin had gone up to the invalid. Maria, quite herself again, came forward.

"No luck," said George. "I meant to have secured the fellow and put him under a glass case as a memento; but he has been too cunning. Here's your sketch, Maria; undamaged. And here are the other rattletraps."

She bent over the drawing quite fondly. "I am glad I had finished it," she said. "I can do the filling-in later. I should not have had courage to sit in that place again."

"Well, old lady," cried George in his free-and-easy manner, as he stood by the Welshwoman, and looked down at her nimble fingers, "so you have come all the way from Wales on foot, I hear! You put some of us to shame."

She looked up and smiled pleasantly. She understood English better than she could speak it.

"Not on foot all the way," she managed to explain. "On foot to the great steamer, and then on foot again after the steamer landed her in Scotland. Not less than a hundred miles of land, taking both ways together."

"Oh, I see!" said George, perceiving that Margery had taken up a wrong impression. "But you must have been a good time doing that?"

"She had the time before her," she answered, more by signs than words, "and her legs were used to the roads. In her husband's life-time she had oftentimes accompanied him on foot to different parts of England, when he went there with his droves of cattle. It was in those journeys that she learnt to talk English."

George laughed at her idea of talking English. "Did you learn the use of the pipe also in the journeys, old lady?"

She certainly had; for she nodded fifty times in answer, and looked delighted at his divination. "But she was obliged to put up with cheap tobacco now," she said: "and had a trouble to get that!"

George pulled out a supply of Turkey from some hidden receptacle of his coat. "Did she like that sort?"

She looked at it with the eye of a connoisseur, touched it, smelt it, and finally tasted it. "Ah, yes! that was good; very good; too good for her."

"Not a bit of it," said George. "It's yours, old lady. There! It will keep your pipe going, on the road home."

When fully convinced that he meant it in earnest, she seized his hand, shook it heartily, and plunged into a Welsh oration. It was cut short in the midst. She caught sight of Bray, coming in at the house door, and smuggled the present out of sight amidst her petticoats. Had Mr. Sandy seen it, she might have derived little benefit from it herself.

Time lagged, while they waited for Lady Godolphin. The conversation fell upon Bray's trade—as the man was wont to call it: though who or what led to the topic none of them could remember. He recounted two or three interesting incidents; one, of a gentleman marrying a young wife and being shot dead the next day by her friends. She was an heiress, and they had run away from Ireland. But that occurred years and years ago, he added. Would the ladies like to see the room?

He opened a door at the back of the kitchen, traversed a passage, and entered a small place, which could only be called a room by courtesy. They followed, wonderingly. The walls were whitewashed, the floor was of brick, and the small skylight, by which it was lighted, was of thick coarse glass, embellished with green nobs. What with the lowering sky, and this lowering window, the room wore an appearance of the gloomiest twilight. No furniture was in it, except a table (or something that served for one) covered with a green baize cloth, on which lay a book. The contrast from the kitchen, bright with its fire, with the appliances of household life, to this strange comfortless place made them shiver. "A fit place for the noose to be tied in!" cried irreverent George, surveying it critically.

Bray took the words literally. "Yes," said he. "It's kept for that purpose alone. It is a bit out of the common, and that pleases the women. If I said the words in my kitchen, it might not be so satisfying to them, ye see. It does not take two minutes to do," he added, taking his stand behind the table and opening the book. "I wish I had as many pieces of gold as I have done it, here, in my time."

Charlotte Pain took up the words defiantly. "It is impossible that such a marriage can stand. It is not a marriage."

"'Deed, but it is, young lady."

"It cannot be legal," she haughtily rejoined. "If it stands good for this loose-lawed country, it cannot do so for others."

"Ay, how about that?" interrupted George, still in his light tone of ridicule. "Would it hold good in England?"

Minister Bray craned his long neck towards them, over the table, where they stood in a group. He took the hand of George Godolphin, and that of Charlotte Pain, and put them to together. "Ye have but to say, 'I take you, young lady, to be my lawful wife;' and, 'I take you, sir, to be my husband,' in your right names. I'd then pronounce ye man and wife, and say the blessing on it; and the deed would be done, and hold good all over the world."

Did Mr. Sandy Bray anticipate that he might thus extemporise an impromptu ceremony, which should bring some grist to his empty mill? Not improbably: for he did not release their hands, but kept them joined together, looking at both in silence.

George Godolphin was the first to draw his hand away. Charlotte had only stared with wondering eyes, and she now burst into a laugh of ridicule. "Thank you for your information," said Mr. George. "There's no knowing, Bray, but I may call your services into requisition some time."

"Where are you?" came the soft voice of Lady Godolphin down the passage. "We must all hurry home: it is going to rain. Charlotte, are you there? Where have you all gone to? Charlotte, I say?"

Charlotte hastened out. Lady Godolphin took her arm at once, and walked with a quick step through the kitchen into the open air, nodding adieu to the old Welshwoman. My lady herself, her ermine, her velvets, possibly her delicately-bloomed complexion, all shrank from the violence of a storm. Storms, neither of life nor of weather, had ever come too near Lady Godolphin. She glanced upward at the threatening and angry sky, and urged Charlotte on.

"Can you walk fast? So lovely a morning as it was!"

"Here comes one of the servants," exclaimed Charlotte. "With umbrellas, no doubt. How he runs!"

My lady lifted her eyes. Advancing towards them with fleet foot, as if he were running for a wager, came a man in the Godolphin livery. If umbrellas had been the object of his coming, he must have dropped them on his way, for his arms swung beside him, and his hands were empty.

"My lady," cried the man, almost as much out of breath as Lady Godolphin: "Sir George is taken ill."

My lady stopped then. "Ill!" she repeated. "Ill in what way?"

"Margery has just found him lying on the floor of his room, my lady.

We have got him on to the bed, but he appears to be quite insensible. Andrew has gone for the doctor."

"Hasten to the house there, and acquaint Mr. George Godolphin," said my lady, pointing to Bray's.

But Charlotte had already gone on the errand. She left Lady Godolphin's arm and started back with all speed, calling out that she would inform Mr. George Godolphin. My lady, on her part, had sped on in the direction of Broomhead, with a fleeter foot than before.

Leaving the man standing where he was. "Which of the two am I to follow, I wonder?" he soliloquized. "I suppose I had better keep up with my lady."

When Charlotte Pain had left Mr. Sandy Bray's match-making room, at my lady's call, George Godolphin turned with a rapid, impulsive motion to Maria Hastings, caught her hand, and drew her beside him, as he stood before Bray. "Maria, she will fetter me in spite of myself!" he said in a hoarse whisper. "Let me put it out of her power."

Maria looked at him inquiringly. Well she might!

"Be mine now; here," he rapidly continued, bending his face so that she alone might hear. "I swear that I never will presume upon the act, until it can be more legally solemnized. But it will bind us to each other beyond the power of man or woman to set aside."

Maria turned red, pale, any colour that you will, and quietly drew her hand from that of Mr. George Godolphin. "I do not quite know whether you are in earnest or in jest, George. You will allow me to infer the latter."

Quiet as were the words, calm as was the manner, there was that about her which unmistakably showed Mr. George Godolphin that he might not venture further to forget himself; if, indeed, he had not been in jest. Maria, a true gentlewoman at heart, professed to assume that he had been.

"I beg your pardon," he murmured. "Nay, let me make my peace, Maria." And he took her hand again, and held it in his. Minister Bray leaned towards them with an earnest face. Resigning the hope of doing any little stroke of business on his own account, he sought to obtain some information on a different subject.

"Sir, would ye be pleased to tell me a trifle about your criminal laws, over the border? One of my ne'er-do-weels has been getting into trouble there, and they may make him smart for it."

George Godolphin knew that he alluded to the ill-starred Nick. "What are the circumstances?" he asked. "I will tell you what I can."

Sandy entered upon the story. They stood before him, absorbed in it, for Maria also listened with interest, when an exclamation caused them to turn. Maria drew her hand from George Godolphin's with a quick gesture. There stood Charlotte Pain.

Stood with a white face, and a flashing, haughty eye. "We are coming instantly," said George. "We shall catch you up." For he thought she had reappeared to remind them.

"It is well," she answered. "And it may be as well to haste, Mr. George Godolphin, if you would see your father alive."

The Shadow of Ashlydyat. 5

"What?" he answered. But Charlotte had turned again and was gone like the wind. With all his speed, he could not catch her up until they had left the house some distance behind them.

CHAPTER X.

THE SHADOW.

In the heart of the town of Prior's Ash was situated the banking-house of Godolphin, Crosse, and Godolphin. Built at the corner of a street, it faced two ways. The bank and its doors were in High Street, the principal street of the town; the entrance to the dwelling-house was in Crosse Street, a new, short street, not much frequented, which had been called after Mr. Crosse, who, at the time it was made, lived at the bank. There were only six or eight houses in Crosse Street; detached private dwellings; and the street led to the open country, and to a pathway, not a carriage-way, that would, if you liked to follow it, take you to Ashlydyat.

The house attached to the bank was commodious: its rooms were large and handsome, though few in number. A pillared entrance, gained by steps, led into a small hall. On the right of this hall was the room used as a dining-room, a light and spacious apartment, its large window opening on to a covered terrace, where plants were kept; and that again opened to a sloping lawn, surrounded with shrubs and flowers. This room was hung with fine old pictures, brought from Ashlydyat. Lady Godolphin did not care for pictures; she preferred delicately-papered walls; and very few of the Ashlydyat paintings had been removed to the Folly. On the left of the hall were the rooms belonging to the bank. At the back of the hall, beyond the dining-room, a handsome well-staircase led to the apartments above, one of which was a fine drawing-room. From the upper windows at the back of the house a view of Lady Godolphin's Folly might be obtained, rising high and picturesque; also of the turret of Ashlydyat, grey and grim. Not of Ashlydyat itself: its surrounding trees concealed it.

This dining-room, elegant and airy, and fitted up with exquisite taste, was the favourite sitting-room of the Miss Godolphins. The drawing-room above, larger and grander, less comfortable, and looking on to the High Street, was less used by them. In this lower room there sat one evening Thomas Godolphin and his eldest sister. It was about a month subsequent to that day, at the commencement of this history, when you saw the hounds throw off, and a week or ten days since Sir George Godolphin had been found insensible on the floor of his room at Broomhead. The attack had proved to be nothing but a prolonged fainting-fit; but even that told upon Sir George in his shattered health. It had caused plans to be somewhat changed. Thomas Godolphin's visit to Scotland had been postponed, for Sir George was not strong enough for business consultations, which would have been the chief object of his journey; and George Godolphin had not yet returned to Prior's Ash.

Thomas and Miss Godolphin had been dining alone. Bessy was spending the evening at All Souls' Rectory: she and Mr. Hastings were active workers together in parish matters; and Cecil was dining at Ashlydyat. Mrs. Verrall had called in the afternoon and carried her off. Dessert was on the table, but Thomas had turned from it, and was sitting over the fire. Miss Godolphin sat opposite to him, nearer the table, her fingers busy with her knitting, on which fell the rays of the chandelier. They were discussing plans earnestly and gravely.

"No, Thomas, it would not do," she was saying. "We must go. One of the partners always has resided here at the bank. Let business men be at their place of business."

"But look at the trouble, Janet," remonstrated Thomas Godolphin. "Consider the expense. You may be no sooner out than you may have to come back again."

Janet turned her strangely-deep eyes on her brother. "Do not make too sure of that, Thomas."

"How do you mean, Janet? In my father's precarious state we cannot, unhappily, count upon his life."

"Thomas, I am sure—I seem to see—that he will not be with us long. No: and I am contemplating the time when he shall have left us. It would change many things. Your home would then be Ashlydyat."

Thomas Godolphin smiled. As if any power would keep *him* from inhabiting Ashlydyat when he should be master. "Yes," he answered. "And George would come here."

"There it is!" said Janet. "Would George live here? I do not feel sure that he would."

"Of course he would, Janet. He would live here with you, as I do now. That is a perfectly understood thing."

"Does he so understand it?"

"He understands it, and approves it."

Janet shook her head. "George likes his liberty; he will not be content to settle down to the ways of a sober household."

"Nay, Janet, you must remember one thing. When George shall come to this house, he comes, so to say, as its master. He will not, of course, interfere with your arrangements; he will fall in with them readily; but neither will he, nor must he, be under your control. To attempt anything of the sort again would not do."

Janet knitted on in silence. She had essayed to keep Master George in hand when they first came to the bank to live there: and the result was that he had chosen a separate home, where he could be entirely *en garçon*.

"Eh me!" sighed Janet. "If young men could but see the folly of their ways—as they see them in after-life!"

"Therefore, Janet, I say that it would be exceedingly inadvisable for you to quit the house," continued Thomas Godolphin, leaving her remark unnoticed. "It might be, that before you were well out of it, you must return to it."

"I see the inconvenience also; the uncertainty," she answered. "But there is no help for it."

"Yes there is. Janet, I wish you would let me settle it."

"How would you settle it?"

"By bringing Ethel here. On a visit to you."

Janet laid down her knitting. "What do you mean? That there should be two mistresses in the house, she and I? No, no, Thomas; the daftest old wife in the parish would tell you that does not do."

"Not two mistresses. You would be sole mistress, as you are now: I and Ethel your guests. Janet, indeed it would be the better plan. By the spring we should see how Sir George went on. If he improved, then the question could be definitively settled: and either you or I would take up our residence elsewhere. If he does not improve, I fear, Janet, that spring will have seen the end."

Something in the words appeared particularly to excite Janet's attention. She gazed at Thomas as if she would search him through and through. "By spring!" she repeated. "When, then, do you contemplate marrying Ethel?"

"I should like her to be mine by Christmas," was the low answer.

"Thomas! And December close upon us!"

"If not, some time in January," he continued, paying no attention to her surprise. "It is so decided."

Miss Godolphin drew a long breath. "With whom is it decided?"

"With Ethel."

"You would marry a wife without a home to bring her to? Had thoughtless George told me that he was going to do such a thing, I could have believed it of him. Not of you, Thomas."

"Janet, the home shall no longer be a barrier to us. I wish you would receive Ethel here as your guest."

"It is not likely that she would come. The first thing a married woman looks for is to have a home of her own."

Thomas smiled. "Not come, Janet? Have you yet to learn how unassuming and meek is the character of Ethel? We have spoken of this plan together, and Ethel's only fear is, lest she should 'be in Miss Godolphin's way.' Failing to carry out this project, Janet—for I see you are, as I thought you would be, prejudiced against it—I shall hire a lodging as near to the bank as may be, and there I shall take Ethel."

"Would it be seemly that the heir of Ashlydyat should go into lodgings on his marriage?" asked Janet, grief and sternness in her tone.

"Things are seemly or unseemly, Janet, according to circumstances. It would be more seemly for the heir of Ashlydyat to take temporary lodgings while waiting for Ashlydyat, than to turn his sisters from their home for a month, or a few months, as the case might be. The pleasantest plan would be for me to bring Ethel here: as your guest. It is what she and I should both like. If you object to this, I shall take her elsewhere. Bessy and Cecil would be delighted with the arrangement: they are fond of Ethel."

"And when children begin to come, Thomas?" cried Miss Godolphin in her old-fashioned, steady, Scotch manner. She had a great deal of her mother about her.

Thomas's lips parted with a quaint smile. "Things will be decided, one way or the other, months before children shall have had time to arrive."

Janet knitted a whole row before she spoke again. "I will take a few hours to reflect upon it, Thomas," she said then.

"Do so," he replied, rising and glancing at the timepiece. "Half-past seven! What time will Cecil expect me? I wish to spend half an hour with Ethel. Shall I go for Cecil before, or afterwards?"

"Go for Cecil at once, Thomas. It will be better for her to be home early."

Thomas Godolphin went to the hall-door and looked out upon the night. He was considering whether he need put on an overcoat. It was a bright moonlight night, warm and genial. So he shut the door, and started. "I wish the cold would come!" he exclaimed, half aloud. He was thinking of the fever, which still clung obstinately to Prior's Ash, showing itself fitfully and partially in fresh places about every third or fourth day.

He took the foot-path, down Crosse Street: a lonely way, and at night especially unfrequented. In one part of it, as he ascended near Ashlydyat, the pathway was so narrow that two people could scarcely walk abreast without touching the ash-trees growing on either side and meeting overhead. A murder had been committed on this spot a few years before : a sad tale of barbarity, offered to a girl by one who professed to be her lover. She lay buried in All Souls' churchyard; and he within the walls of the county prison where he had been executed. Of course the rumour went that her ghost "walked" there, the natural sequence to these dark tales ; and, what with that, and what with the loneliness of the place, few could be found in it after dark.

Thomas Godolphin went steadily on, his thoughts running upon the subject of his conversation with Janet. It is probable that but for the difficulty touching a residence, Ethel would have been his in the past autumn. When anything should happen to Sir George, Thomas would be in possession of Ashlydyat three months afterwards; such had been the agreement with Mr. Verrall when he took Ashlydyat. Not in his father's lifetime would Thomas Godolphin (clinging to the fancies and traditions which had descended with the old place) consent to take up his abode as master of Ashlydyat; but no longer than was absolutely necessary would he remain out of it as soon as it was his own. George would then remove to the bank, which would still be his sister's home, as it was now. In the event of George's marrying, the Miss Godolphins would finally leave it : but George Godolphin did not, as far as people saw, give indications that he was likely to marry. In the precarious state of Sir George's health—and it was pretty sure he would soon either get better or worse—these changes might take place any day : therefore it was not desirable that the Miss Godolphins should leave the bank, and that the trouble and expense of setting up and furnishing a house for them should be incurred. Of course *they* could not go into lodgings. Altogether, if Janet could only be brought to see it, Thomas's plan was the best—that his young bride should be Janet's guest for a short time.

It was through the upper part of this dark path, which was called the Ash-tree Walk, that George Godolphin had taken Maria Hastings, the night they had left Lady Godolphin's dinner-table to visit the Dark Plain. Thomas, in due course, arrived at the end of the walk, and passed through the turnstile. Lady Godolphin's Folly lay on the right, high and white and clear in the moonbeams. Ashlydyat lay to the left, dark and grey, and almost hidden by the trees. Grey as it was, Thomas looked at it fondly : his heart yearned to it : and it was to be the future home of himself and Ethel !

"Holloa! who's this? Oh, I beg your pardon, Mr. Godolphin !"

The speaker was Snow, the surgeon. He had come swiftly upon Thomas Godolphin, turning the corner round the ash-trees from the Dark Plain. That he had been to Ashlydyat was certain, for the road led nowhere else. Thomas did not know that illness was in the house.

"Neither did I," said Mr. Snow in answer to the remark, "until an hour ago, when I was sent for in haste."

A thought crossed Thomas Godolphin. "Not a case of fever, I hope!"

"No. I think that's leaving us. There has been an accident at Ashlydyat to Mrs. Verrall. At least, what might have been an accident, I should rather say," added the surgeon, correcting himself. "The injury is so slight as not to be worth the name of one."

"What has happened?" asked Thomas Godolphin.

"She managed to set her sleeve on fire : a white lace or muslin sleeve, falling below the silk sleeve of her gown. In standing near a candle, the flame caught it. But now, look at that young woman's presence of mind! Instead of wasting moments in screams, or running through the house from top to bottom, as most people would have done, she instantly threw herself down upon the rug, and rolled herself in it. That's the sort of woman to go through life."

"Is she much burnt?"

"Pooh! Many a child gets a worse burn a dozen times in its first dozen years. The arm between the elbow and the wrist is slightly scorched. It's nothing. They need not have sent for me. The application of a little cold water will take out all the fire. Your sister Cecilia was ten times more alarmed than Mrs. Verrall."

"I am truly glad it is no worse!" said Thomas Godolphin. "I feared fever might have found its way there."

"That is taking its departure; as I think. And, the sooner it goes, the better. It has been capricious as the smiles of a coquette. How strange it is, that not a soul, down by those Pollard pigsties, should have had it, except the Bonds!"

"It is equally strange that, in many houses, it should have attacked only one inmate, and spared the rest. What do you think now of Sarah Anne Grame?"

Mr. Snow shook his head, and his voice grew insensibly low. "In my opinion she is sinking fast. I found her worse this afternoon; weaker than she has been at all. Lady Sarah said, 'If she could get her to Ventnor?'—'If she could get her to Hastings?' But the removal would kill her : she'd die on the road. It will be a terrible blow to Lady Sarah, if it does come : and—though it may seem harsh to say it —a retort upon her selfishness. Did you know that they used to make Ethel head nurse, while the fever was upon her?"

"No!" exclaimed Thomas Godolphin.

"They did, then. My lady inadvertently let it out to-day. Dear child! If she had caught it, I should never have forgiven her mother, whatever you may have done. Good night. I have a dozen visits now to pay before bedtime."

"Worse!" soliloquized Thomas Godolphin, as he stepped on. "Poor, peevish Sarah Anne! But—I wonder," he hesitated as the thought struck him, "whether, if the worst should come, as Snow seems to anticipate, it would put off Ethel's marriage? What with one delay and another——"

Thomas Godolphin's voice ceased, and his heart stood still. He had turned the corner, to the front of the ash-tree grove, and stretching out before him was the Dark Plain, with its weird-like bushes, so like graves, and—*its Shadow*, lying cold and still in the white moonlight. Yes! there surely lay the Shadow of Ashlydyat. The grey archway rose behind it; the flat plain extended out before it, and the Shadow was between them, all too distinctly visible.

The first shock over, Thomas Godolphin's pulses coursed on again. He had seen that Shadow before in his lifetime, but he halted to gaze at it again. It was very palpable. The bier, as it looked in the middle, a mourner at the head, a mourner at the foot, each—as a spectator could fancy—with bowed heads. In spite of the superstition touching this strange Shadow in which Thomas Godolphin had been brought up, he looked round now for some natural explanation of it. He was a man of intellect, a man of the world, a man who played his full share in the practical business of everyday life: and such men are not given to acknowledging superstitious fancies in this age of enlightenment, no matter what bent may have been given to their minds in childhood.

Therefore Thomas Godolphin ranged his eyes round and round in the air, and could see nothing that would solve the mystery. "I wonder whether it be possible that certain states of the atmosphere should give out these shadows?" he soliloquized. "But—if so—why should it invariably appear in that one precise spot; and in no other? Could Snow have seen it, I wonder?"

He walked on towards Ashlydyat, his head always turned, looking at the Shadow. "I am glad Janet does not see it! It would frighten her into a belief that my father's end was near," came his next thought.

Mrs. Verrall, playing the invalid, lay on a sofa, her auburn hair somewhat ruffled, her pretty pink cheeks flushed, her satin slippers peeping out; altogether challenging admiration. The damaged arm, its silk sleeve pinned up, was stretched out on a cushion, a small delicate cambric handkerchief, saturated with water, resting lightly on the burn. A basin of water stood near, with a similar handkerchief lying in it, and Mrs. Verrall's maid was at hand to change the handkerchiefs as might be required. Thomas Godolphin drew a chair near to Mrs. Verrall, and listened to the account of the accident, giving her his full sympathy, for it might have been a bad one.

"You must possess great presence of mind," he observed. "I think your showing it, as you have done in this instance, has won Mr. Snow's heart."

Mrs. Verrall laughed. "I believe I do possess presence of mind.

And so does Charlotte. Once we were out with some friends in a barouche, and the horses took fright, ran up a bank, turned the carriage over, and nearly kicked it to pieces. While all those with us were fearfully frightened, Charlotte and I remained calm and cool."

"It is a good thing for you," he observed.

"I suppose it is. Better, at any rate, than to go mad with fear, as some do. Cecil"—turning to her—"has had fright enough to last her for a twelvemonth, she says."

"Were you present, Cecil?" asked her brother.

"I was present, but I did not see it," replied Cecil. "It occurred in Mrs. Verrall's bedroom, and I was standing at the dressing-table, with my back to her. The first thing I knew, or saw, was Mrs. Verrall on the floor with the rug rolled round her."

Tea was brought in, and Mrs. Verrall insisted that they should remain for it. Thomas pleaded an engagement, but she would not listen: they could not have the heart, she said, to leave her alone. So Thomas—the very essence of good feeling and politeness—waived his objection and remained. Not the bowing politeness of a *petit maître*, but the genuine consideration that springs from a noble and unselfish heart.

"I am in ecstasy that Verrall was away," she exclaimed. "He would have magnified it into something formidable, and I should not have been allowed to stir for a month."

"When do you expect him home?" asked Thomas Godolphin.

"I never expect him until he comes," replied Mrs. Verrall. "London seems to possess attractions for him. Once up there, he may stay a day, or he may stay fifty. I never know."

Cecil went upstairs to put her things on when tea was over, the maid attending her. Mrs. Verrall turned to see that the door was closed, and then spoke abruptly.

"Mr. Godolphin, can anything be done to prevent the wind whistling as it does in these passages?"

"Does it whistle?" he replied.

"The last few nights it has whistled—oh, I cannot describe it to you! If I were not a good sleeper, it would have kept me awake all night. I wish it could be stopped."

"It cannot be done, I believe, without pulling the house down," he said. "My mother had a great dislike to hear it, and a good deal of expense was incurred in trying to remedy it; but it did little or no good."

"What puzzles me is, that the wind should have been whistling within the house, when there's no wind whistling without. The weather has been quite calm. Sometimes when it is actually blowing great guns we cannot hear it at all."

"Something peculiar in the construction of the passages," he carelessly remarked. "You hear the whistling or not, according to the quarter from which the wind may happen to be blowing."

"The servants tell a tale—these old Ashlydyat retainers who remain in the house—that this strangely-sounding wind is connected with the Ashlydyat superstition, and foretells ill to the Godolphins."

Thomas Godolphin smiled. "I am sure you do not give ear to anything so foolish, Mrs. Verrall."

"No, that I do not," she answered. "It would take a great deal to imbue me with faith in the supernatural. Ghosts! Shadows! As if any one with common sense could believe in such impossibilities! They tell another tale about here, do they not? That a shadow of some sort may occasionally be seen in the moonbeams in front of the archway, on the Dark Plain; a shadow cast by no earthly substance. Charlotte once declared she saw it. I only laughed at her!"

His lips parted as he listened, and he lightly echoed the laugh said to have been given by Charlotte. Considering what his eyes had just seen, the laugh must have been a very conscious one.

"When do you expect your brother home?" asked Mrs. Verrall. "He seems to be making a long stay at Broomhead."

"George is not at Broomhead," replied Thomas Godolphin. "He left it three or four days ago. He has joined a party of friends in the Highlands. I do not suppose he will return here much before Christmas."

Cecil appeared. They wished Mrs. Verrall good night, and a speedy cure to her burns; and departed. Thomas took the open roadway this time, which did not bring them near to the ash-trees or the Dark Plain.

CHAPTER XI.

A TELEGRAPHIC DESPATCH.

"CECIL," asked Thomas Godolphin, as they walked along, "how came you to go alone to Ashlydyat, in this unceremonious manner?"

"There was no harm in it," answered Cecil, who possessed a spice of self-will. "Mrs. Verrall said she was lonely, and it would be a charity if I or Bessy would go home with her. Bessy could not: she was engaged at the Rectory. Where was the harm?"

"My dear, had there been 'harm,' I am sure you would not have wished to go. There was none. Only, I do not care that you should become very intimate with the Verralls. A little visiting on either side cannot be avoided: but let it end there."

"Thomas! you are just like Janet!" impulsively spoke Cecil. "She does not like the Verralls."

"Neither do I. I do not like him. I do not like Charlotte Pain——"

"Janet again!" struck in Cecil. "She and you must be constituted precisely alike, for you are sure to take up the same likes and dislikes. She would not willingly let me go to-day; only she could not refuse without downright rudeness."

"I like Mrs. Verrall the best of them, I was going to say," he continued. "Do not become too intimate with them, Cecil."

"But you know nothing against Mr. Verrall?"

"Nothing whatever. Except that I cannot make him out."

"How do you mean—'make him out?'"

"Well, Cecil, it may be difficult to define my meaning.   Verrall is so impassive; so utterly silent with regard to himself. Who is he? Where did he come from? Did he drop from the moon? Where has he previously lived? What are his family? Where does his property lie?—in the funds, or in land, or in securities, or what? Most men, even though they do come as strangers into a neighbourhood, supply indications of some of these things, either accidentally or purposely."

"They have lived in London," said Cecil.

"London is a wide term," answered Thomas Godolphin.

"And I'm sure they have plenty of money."

"There's where the chief puzzle is. When people possess so much money as Verrall appears to do, they generally make no secret of whence it is derived. Understand, my dear, I cast no suspicion on him in any way: I only say that we know nothing of him: or of the ladies either —— "

"They are very charming ladies," interrupted Cecil again. "Especially Mrs. Verrall."

"Beyond the fact that they are very charming ladies," acquiesced Thomas in a tone that made Cecil think he was laughing at her: "you should let me finish, my dear. But I would prefer that they were rather more open, as to themselves, before they became the too-intimate friends of Miss Cecilia Godolphin."

Cecil dropped the subject. She did not always agree with what she called Thomas's prejudices. "How quaint that old doctor of ours is!" she exclaimed. "When he had looked at Mrs. Verrall's arm, he made a great parade of getting out his spectacles, and putting them on, and looking again. 'What d'ye call it—a burn?' he asked her. 'It is a burn, is it not?' she answered, looking at him. 'No,' said he, 'it's nothing but a scorch.' It made her laugh so. I think she was pleased to have escaped with so little damage."

"That is just like Snow," said Thomas Godolphin.

Arrived at home, Miss Godolphin was in the same place, knitting still. It was turned half-past nine. Too late for Thomas to pay his visit to Lady Sarah's. "Janet, I fear you have waited tea for us!" said Cecil.

"To be sure, child. I expected you home to tea."

Cecil explained why they did not come, relating the accident to Mrs. Verrall. "Eh! but it's like the young!" said Janet, lifting her hands. "Careless! careless! She might have been burned to death."

"What a loud ring!" exclaimed Cecil, as the hall-bell, pealed with no gentle hand, echoed and re-echoed through the house. "If it is Bessy come home, she thinks she will let us know who's there."

It was not Bessy. A servant entered the room with a telegraphic despatch. "The man is waiting, sir," he said, holding out the paper for signature to his master.

Thomas Godolphin affixed his signature, and took up the despatch. It came from Scotland. Janet laid her hand upon it ere it was open: her face looked ghastly pale. "A moment of preparation!" she said. "Thomas, it may have brought us tidings that we have no longer a father."

"Nay, Janet, do not anticipate evil," he answered, though his memory flew unaccountably to that ugly Shadow, and to what he had deemed would be Janet's conclusions respecting it. "It may not be ill news at all."

He glanced his eye rapidly and privately over it, while Cecil came and stood near him with a stifled sob. Then he held it out to Janet, reading it aloud at the same time.

"'Lady Godolphin to Thomas Godolphin, Esquire.

"'Come at once to Broomhead. Sir George wishes it. Take the first train.'"

"He is not dead, at any rate, Janet," said Thomas quietly. "Thank Heaven."

Janet, her extreme fears relieved, took refuge in displeasure. "What does Lady Godolphin mean, by sending so vague a message as that?" she uttered. "Is Sir George worse? Is he ill? Is he in danger? Or has the summons no reference at all to his state of health?"

Thomas had taken it into his hand again, and was studying the words: as we are all apt to do in uncertainty. He could make no more out of them.

"Lady Godolphin should have been more explicit," he resumed.

"Lady Godolphin has no *right* thus to play upon our fears, our suspense," said Janet. "Thomas, I have a great mind to start this very night for Scotland."

"As you please, of course, Janet. It is a long and fatiguing journey for a winter's night."

"And I object to being a guest at Broomhead, unless driven to it, you might add," rejoined Janet. "But our father may be dying."

"I should think not, Janet. Lady Godolphin would certainly have said so. Margery, too, would have taken care that those tidings should be sent to us."

The suggestion reassured Miss Godolphin. She had not thought of it. Margery, devoted to the interests of Sir George and his children (somewhat in contravention to the interests of my lady), would undoubtedly have apprised them were Sir George in danger. "What shall you do?" inquired Janet of her brother.

"I shall do as the despatch desires me—take the first train. That will be at midnight," he added, as he prepared to pay a visit to Lady Sarah's.

Grame House, as you may remember, was situated at the opposite end of the town to Ashlydyat, past All Souls' Church. As Thomas Godolphin walked briskly along, he saw Mr. Hastings leaning over the Rectory gate, the dark trees shading him from the light of the moon.

"You are going this way late," said the Rector.

"It is late for a visit to Lady Sarah's. But I wish particularly to see them."

"I have now come from thence," returned Mr. Hastings.

"Sarah Anne grows weaker, I hear."

"Ay. I have been praying over her."

Thomas Godolphin felt shocked. "Is she so near death as that?" he asked, in a hushed tone.

"So near death as that!" repeated the clergyman in an accent of reproof. "I did not expect to hear a like remark from Mr. Godolphin. My good friend, is it only when death is near that we are to pray?"

"It is chiefly when death is near that prayers are said *over us*," replied Thomas Godolphin.

"True—for those who have not known when and how to pray for themselves. Look at that girl: passing away from amongst us, with all her worldly thoughts, her selfish habits, her evil, peevish temper! But that God's ways are not as our ways, we might be tempted to question why such as these are removed; such as Ethel left. The one child as near akin to an angel as it is well possible to be, here; the other—— In our blind judgment, we may wonder that she, most ripe for heaven, should not be taken to it, and that other one left, to be pruned and dug around; to have, in short, a chance given her of making herself better."

"Is she so very ill?"

"I think her so; as does Snow. It was what he said that sent me up there. Her frame of mind is not a desirable one; and I have been trying to do my part. I shall be with her again to-morrow."

"Have you any message for your daughter?" asked Thomas Godolphin. "I start in two hours' time for Scotland." And then he explained why: telling of their uncertainty.

"When shall you be coming back again?" inquired Mr. Hastings.

"Within a week. Unless my father's state should forbid it. I may be wishing to take a holiday at Christmas time, or thereabouts, so shall not stay away now. George is absent, too."

"Staying at Broomhead?"

"No; he is not at Broomhead now."

"Will you take charge of Maria? We want her home."

"If you wish it, I will. But I should think they would all be returning very shortly. Christmas is intended to be spent here."

"You may depend upon it, Christmas will not see Lady Godolphin at Prior's Ash, unless the fever shall have departed to spend its Christmas in some other place," cried the Rector.

"Well, I shall hear their plans when I get there."

"Bring back Maria with you, Mr. Godolphin. Tell her it is my wish. Unless you find that there's a prospect of her speedy return with Lady Godolphin. In that case, you may leave her."

"Very well," replied Thomas Godolphin.

He continued his way, and Mr. Hastings looked after him in the bright moonlight, till his form disappeared in the shadows cast by the roadside trees.

It was striking ten as Thomas Godolphin opened the iron gates at Lady Sarah Grame's: the heavy clock-bell of All Souls' came sounding upon his ear in the stillness of the night. The house, all except from one window, looked dark: even the hall-lamp was out, and he feared they might all have retired. From that window a dull light shone behind the blind: a stationary light it had been of late, to be seen by any nocturnal wayfarer all night long; for it came from the sick-chamber.

Elizabeth opened the door. " Oh, sir ! " she exclaimed in the surprise of seeing him so late, " I think Miss Ethel has gone up to bed."

Lady Sarah came hastening down the stairs as he stepped into the hall : she also was surprised at the late visit.

" I would not have disturbed you, but that I am about to leave for Broomhead," he explained. " A telegraphic despatch has arrived from Lady Godolphin, calling me thither. I should like to see Ethel, if not inconvenient to her. I know not how long I may be away."

" I sent Ethel to bed : her head ached," said Lady Sarah. " It is not many minutes since she went up. Oh, Mr. Godolphin, this has been such a day of grief ! heads and hearts alike aching."

Thomas Godolphin entered the drawing-room, and Lady Sarah Grame called Ethel down, and then returned to her sick daughter's room. Ethel came instantly. The fire in the drawing-room was still alight, and Elizabeth had been in to stir it up. Thomas Godolphin stood over it with Ethel, telling her of his coming journey and its cause. The red embers threw a glow upon her face : her brow looked heavy, her eyes swollen.

He saw the signs, and laid his hand fondly upon her head. " What has given you this headache, Ethel?"

The ready tears came into her eyes. " It does ache very much," she answered.

" Has crying caused it?"

" Yes," she replied. " It is of no use to deny it, for you would see it by my swollen eyelids. I have wept to-day until it seems that I can weep no longer, and it has made my eyes ache and my head dull and heavy."

" But, my darling, you should not give way to this grief. It may render you seriously ill."

" Oh, Thomas! how can I help it?" she returned, with emotion, as the tears dropped swiftly over her cheeks. " We begin to see that there is no chance of Sarah Anne's recovery. Mr. Snow told mamma so to-day : and he sent up Mr. Hastings."

" Ethel, will your grieving alter it?"

Ethel wept silently. There was full and entire confidence between her and Thomas Godolphin : she could speak out all her thoughts, her troubles to him, as she could have told them to a mother—if she had had a mother who loved her.

" If she were only a little more prepared to go, the pain would seem less," breathed Ethel. " That is, we might feel more reconciled to los- ing her. But you know what she is, Thomas. When I have tried to talk a little bit about heaven, or to read a psalm to her, she would not listen : she said it made her dull, it gave her the horrors. How can she, who has never thought of God, be fit to meet Him ?"

Ethel's tears were deepening into sobs. Thomas Godolphin in- voluntarily thought of what Mr. Hastings had just said to him. His hand still rested on Ethel's head.

" *You* are fit to meet Him?" he exclaimed involuntarily. " Ethel, whence can have arisen the difference between you? You are sisters ; reared in the same home."

" I do not know," said Ethel simply. " I have always thought a great deal about heaven; I suppose it is that. A lady, whom we knew as children, used to buy us a good many story-books, and mine were always stories of heaven. It was that which first got me into the habit of thinking of it."

"And why not Sarah Anne?"

"Sarah Anne would not read them. She liked stories of gaiety and excitement; balls, and things like that."

Thomas smiled; the words were so simple and natural. "Had the fiat gone forth for you, instead of for her, Ethel, it would have brought you no dismay?"

"Only that I must leave all my dear ones behind me," she answered, looking up at him, a bright smile shining through her tears. "I should know that God would not take me, unless it were for the best. Oh, Thomas! if we could only save her!"

"Child, you contradict yourself. If what God does must be for the best—and it *is*—that thought should reconcile you to parting with Sarah Anne."

"Y—es," hesitated Ethel. "Only I fear she has never thought of it herself, or in any way prepared for it."

"Do you know that I have to find fault with you?" resumed Thomas Godolphin, after a pause. "You have not been true to me, Ethel."

She turned her eyes upon him in surprise.

"Did you not promise me—did you not promise Mr. Snow, not to enter your sister's chamber while the fever was upon her? I hear that you were in it often: her head nurse."

A hot colour flushed into Ethel's face. "Forgive me, Thomas," she whispered; "I could not help myself. Sarah Anne—it was on the third morning of her illness, when I was getting up—suddenly began to cry out for me very much, and mamma came to my bedroom and desired me to go to her. I said that Mr. Snow had forbidden me, and that I had promised you. It made mamma angry. She asked if I could be so selfish as to regard a promise before Sarah Anne's life; that she might die if I thwarted her: and she took me by the arm and pulled me in. I would have told you, Thomas, that I had broken my word; I wished to tell you; but mamma forbade me to do so."

Thomas Godolphin stood looking at her. There was nothing to answer: he had *known*, in his deep and trusting love, that the fault had not lain with Ethel. She mistook his silence, thinking he was vexed.

"You know, Thomas, so long as I am here in mamma's home, her child, it is to her that I owe obedience," she gently pleaded. "As soon as I shall be your wife, I shall owe it and give it implicitly to you."

"You are right, my darling."

"And it has produced no ill consequences," she resumed. "I did not catch the fever. Had I found myself growing in the least ill, I should have sent for you and told you the truth."

"Ethel?" he impulsively cried—very impulsively for calm Thomas Godolphin; "had you caught the fever, I should never have forgiven those who led you into danger. I *could* not lose you."

"Hark!" said Ethel. "Mamma is calling."

Lady Sarah had been calling to Mr. Godolphin. Thinking she was not heard, she now came downstairs and entered the room, wringing her hands; her eyes were overflowing, her sharp thin nose was redder than usual. "Oh dear! I don't know what we shall do with her!" she uttered. "She is so ill, and it makes her so fretful. Mr. Godolphin, nothing will satisfy her now but she must see you."

"See me!" repeated he.

"She will, she says. I told her you were departing for Scotland, and she burst out crying, and said if she were to die she should never see you again. Do you mind going in? You are not afraid?"

"No, I am not afraid," said Thomas Godolphin. "Infection cannot have remained all this time. And if it had, I should not fear it."

Lady Sarah Grame led the way upstairs. Thomas followed her. Ethel stole in afterwards. Sarah Anne lay in bed, her thin face, drawn and white, raised upon the pillow; her hollow eyes were strained forward with a fixed look. Ill as he had been led to suppose her, he was scarcely prepared to see her like this; and it shocked him. A cadaverous face, looking ripe for the tomb.

"Why have you never come to see me?" she asked in her hollow voice, as he approached and leaned over her. "You'd never have come till I died. You only care for Ethel."

"I would have come to see you had I known you wished it," he answered. "But you do not look strong enough to receive visitors."

"They might cure me, if they would," she continued, panting for breath. "I want to go away somewhere, and that Snow won't let me. If it were Ethel, he would take care to cure *her*."

"He will let you go as soon as you are equal to it, I am sure," said Thomas Godolphin.

"Why should the fever have come to me at all?—Why couldn't it have gone to Ethel instead? She's strong. She would have got well in no time. It's not fair——"

"My dear child, my dear, dear child, you must not excite yourself," implored Lady Sarah, abruptly interrupting her.

"I shall speak," cried Sarah Anne, with a touch, feeble though it was, of her old peevish vehemence. "Nobody's thought of but Ethel. If you had had your way," looking hard at Mr. Godolphin, "she wouldn't have been allowed to come near me; no, not if I had died."

Her mood changed to tears. Lady Sarah whispered to him to leave the room: it would not do, this excitement. Thomas wondered why he had been brought to it. "I will come and see you again when you are better," he soothingly whispered.

"No you won't," sobbed Sarah Anne. "You are going to Scotland, and I shall be dead when you come back. I don't want to die. Why do they frighten me with their prayers? Good-bye, Thomas Godolphin."

The last words were called after him; when he had taken his leave of her and was quitting the room. Lady Sarah attended him to the threshold: her eyes full, her hands lifted. "You may see that there's no hope of her!" she wailed.

Thomas did not think there was the slightest hope. To his eye—though it was not so practised an eye in sickness as Mr. Snow's, or even as that of the Rector of All Souls'—it appeared that in a very few days, perhaps hours, hope for Sarah Anne Grame would be over for ever.

Ethel waited for him in the hall, and was leading the way back to the drawing-room; but he told her he could not stay longer, and opened the front door. She ran past him into the garden, putting her hand into his as he came out.

"I wish you were not going away," she sadly said, her spirits, that night very unequal, causing her to see things with a gloomy eye.

"I wish you were going with me!" replied Thomas Godolphin. "Do not weep, Ethel. I shall soon be back again."

"Everything seems to make me weep to-night. You may not be back until—until the worst is over. Oh! if she might but be saved!"

He held her face close to him, gazing down at it in the moonlight. And then he took from it his farewell kiss. "God bless you, my darling, for ever and for ever!"

"May He bless you, Thomas!" she answered, with streaming eyes: and, for the first time in her life, his kiss was returned. Then they parted. He watched Ethel indoors, and went back to Prior's Ash.

CHAPTER XII.

DEAD.

"THOMAS, my son, I must go home. I don't want to die away from Ashlydyat!"

A dull pain shot across Thomas Godolphin's heart at the words. Did he think of the old superstitious tradition—that evil was to fall upon the Godolphins when their chief should die, and not at Ashlydyat? At Ashlydyat his father could not die; he had put that out of his power when he let it to strangers: in its neighbourhood, he might.

"The better plan, sir, will be for you to return to the Folly, as you seem to wish it," said Thomas. "You will soon be strong enough to undertake the journey."

The decaying knight was sitting on a sofa in his bedroom. His second fainting-fit had lasted some hours—if that, indeed, was the right name to give to it—and he had recovered, only to be more and more weak. He had grown pretty well after the first attack—when Margery had found him in his chamber on the floor, the day Lady Godolphin had gone to pay her visit to Selina. The next time, he was on the lawn before the house, talking to Charlotte Pain, when he suddenly fell to the ground. He did not recover his consciousness until evening; and nearly the first wish he expressed was a desire to see his son Thomas. "Telegraph for him," he said to Lady Godolphin.

"But you are not seriously ill, Sir George," she had answered.

"No; but I should like him here. Telegraph to him to start by first train."

And Lady Godolphin did so, accordingly, sending the message that angered Miss Godolphin. But, in this case, Lady Godolphin did not deserve so much blame as Janet cast on her: for she did debate the point with herself whether she should say Sir George was ill, or not. Believing that these two fainting-fits had proceeded from want of strength only, that they were but the effect of his long previous illness, and would lead to no bad result, she determined not to speak of it. Hence the imperfect message.

Neither did Thomas Godolphin see much cause for fear when he arrived at Broomhead. Sir George did not look better than when he had left Prior's Ash, but neither did he look much worse. On this, the second day, he had been well enough to converse with Thomas upon business affairs: and, that over, he suddenly broke out with the above wish. Thomas mentioned it when he joined Lady Godolphin afterwards. It did not meet with her approbation.

"You should have opposed it," said she to him in a firm, hard tone.

"But why so, madam?" asked Thomas. "If my father's wish is to return to Prior's Ash, he should return."

"Not while the fever lingers there. Were he to take it—and die—you would never forgive yourself."

Thomas had no fear of the fever on his own score, and did not fear it for his father. He intimated as much. "It is not the fever that will hurt him, Lady Godolphin."

"You have no right to say that. Lady Sarah Grame, a month ago, might have said she did not fear it for Sarah Anne. And now Sarah Anne is dying!"

"Or dead," put in Charlotte Pain, who was leaning listlessly against the window frame devoured with ennui.

"Shall you be afraid to go back to Prior's Ash?" he asked of Maria Hastings.

"Not at all," replied Maria. "I should not mind if I were going to-day, as far as the fever is concerned."

"That is well," he said. "Because I have orders to convey you back with me."

Charlotte Pain lifted her head with a start. The news aroused her. Maria, on the contrary, thought he was speaking in jest.

"No, indeed I am not," said Thomas Godolphin. "Mr. Hastings made a request to me, madam, that I should take charge of his daughter when I returned," continued he to Lady Godolphin. "He wants her at home, he says."

"Mr. Hastings is very polite!" ironically replied my lady. "Maria will go back when I choose to spare her."

"I hope you will allow her to return with me—unless you shall soon be returning yourself," said Thomas Godolphin.

"It is not I that shall be returning to Prior's Ash yet," said my lady. "The sickly old place must give proof of renewed health first. You will not see either me or Sir George there on this side Christmas."

"Then I think, Lady Godolphin, you must offer no objection to my taking charge of Maria," said Thomas courteously, but firmly, leaving the discussion of Sir George's return to another opportunity. "I passed my word to Mr. Hastings."

Charlotte Pain, all animation now, approached Lady Godolphin. She was thoroughly sick and tired of Broomhead: since George Godolplin's departure, she had been projecting how she could get away from it. Here was a solution to her difficulty.

"Dear Lady Godolphin, you must allow me to depart with Mr. Godolphin—whatever you may do with Maria Hastings," she exclaimed. "I said nothing to you—for I really did not see how I was to get back, knowing you would not permit me to travel so far alone—but Mrs. Verrall is very urgent for my return. And now that she is suffering from this burn, as Mr. Godolphin has brought us news, it is the more incumbent upon me to be at home."

Which was a nice little fib of Miss Charlotte's. Her sister had never once hinted that she wished her home again; but a fib or two more or less was nothing to Charlotte.

"You are tired of Broomhead," said Lady Godolphin.

Charlotte's colour never varied, her eye never drooped, as she protested that she should not tire of Broomhead were she its inmate for a twelvemonth; that it was quite a paradise upon earth. Maria kept her head bent while Charlotte said it, half afraid lest unscrupulous Charlotte should call upon her to bear testimony to her truth. Only that very morning she had protested to Maria that the ennui of the place was killing her.

"I don't know," said Lady Godolphin shrewdly. "Unless I am wrong, Charlotte, you have been anxious to leave. What was it that Mr. George hinted at—about escorting you young ladies home—and I stopped him ere it was half spoken? Prior's Ash *would* talk if I sent you home under his convoy."

"Mr. Godolphin is not George," rejoined Charlotte.

"No, he is not," replied my lady significantly.

The subject of departure was settled amicably; both the young ladies were to return to Prior's Ash under the charge of Mr. Godolphin. There are some men, single men though they be, and not men in years, whom society is content to recognize as entirely fit escorts. Thomas Godolphin was one of them. Had my lady despatched the young ladies home under Mr. George's wing, she might never have heard the last of it from Prior's Ash: but the most inveterate scandalmonger in it would not have questioned the trustworthiness of his elder brother. My lady was also brought to give her consent to her own departure for it by Christmas, provided Mr. Snow would assure her that the place was "safe."

In a day or two Thomas Godolphin spoke to his father of his marriage arrangements. He had received a letter from Janet, written the morning after his departure, in which she agreed to the proposal that Ethel should be her temporary guest. This removed all barrier to the immediate union.

"Then you marry directly, if Sarah Anne lives?"

"Directly. In January, at the latest."

"God bless you both!" cried the old knight. "She'll be a wife in a thousand, Thomas."

Thomas thought she would. He did not say it.

"It's the best plan; it's the best plan," continued Sir George in a dreamy tone, gazing into the fire. "No use to turn the girls out of their home. It will not be for long; not for long. Thomas"—turning his haggard, but still fine blue eye upon his son—" I wish I had never left Ashlydyat!"

Thomas was silent. None had more bitterly regretted the departure from it than he.

" I wish I could go back to it to die!"

" My dear father, I hope that you will yet live many years to bless us. If you can get through this winter—and I see no reason whatever why you should not, with care—you may regain your strength and be as well again as any of us."

Sir George shook his head. " It will not be, Thomas ; I shall not long keep you out of Ashlydyat. Mind!" he added, turning upon Thomas with surprising energy, " I *will* go back before Christmas to Prior's Ash. The last Christmas that I see shall be spent with my children."

" Yes, indeed, I think you should come back to us," warmly acquiesced Thomas.

" Therefore, if you find, when Christmas is close upon us, that I am not amongst you, that you hear no tidings of my coming amongst you, you come off at once and fetch me. Do you hear, Thomas ? I enjoin it upon you now with a father's authority; do not forget it, or disobey it. My lady fears the fever, and would keep me here : but I must be at Prior's Ash."

" I will certainly obey you, my father," replied Thomas Godolphin.

Telegraphic despatches seemed to be the order of the day with Thomas Godolphin. They were all sitting together that evening, Sir George having come downstairs, when a servant called Thomas out of the room. A telegraphic message had arrived for him at the station, and a man had brought it over. A conviction of what it contained flashed over Thomas Godolphin's heart as he opened it—the death of Sarah Anne Grame.

From Lady Sarah it proved to be. Not a much more satisfactory message than had been Lady Godolphin's; for if hers had not been explanatory, this was incoherent.

" The breath has just gone out of my dear child's body. I will write by next post. She died at four o'clock. How shall we all bear it ?"

Thomas returned to the room; his mind full. In the midst of his sorrow and regret for Sarah Anne, his compassion for Lady Sarah— and he did feel all that with true sympathy—intruded the thought of his own marriage. It must be postponed now.

" What did Andrew want with you ?" asked Sir George, when he entered.

" A telegraphic message had come for me from Prior's Ash."

" A business message ?"

" No, sir. It is from Lady Sarah."

By the tone of his voice, by the falling of his countenance, they could read instinctively what had occurred. But they kept silence, all, —waiting for him to speak further.

" Poor Sarah Anne is gone. She died at four o'clock."

" This will delay your plans, Thomas," observed Sir George, after some minutes had been given to expressions of regret.

" It will, sir."

The knight leaned over to his son, and spoke in a whisper, meant for his ear alone: "I shall not be very long after her. I feel that I shall not. You may yet take Ethel home at once to Ashlydyat."

Very early indeed did they start in the morning, long before day-break. Prior's Ash they would reach, all things being well, at nine at night. Margery was sent to attend them, a very dragon of a guardian, as particular as Miss Godolphin herself—had a guardian been necessary.

A somewhat weary day; a long one, at any rate; but at last their train steamed into the station at Prior's Ash. It was striking nine. Mr. Hastings was waiting for Maria, and Mrs. Verrall's carriage for Charlotte Pain. A few minutes were spent in collecting the luggage.

"Shall I give you a seat as far as the bank, Mr. Godolphin?" inquired Charlotte, who must pass it on her way to Ashlydyat.

"Thank you, no. I shall just go up for a minute's call upon Lady Sarah Grame."

Mr. Hastings, who had been placing Maria in a fly, heard the words. He turned hastily, caught Thomas Godolphin's hand, and drew him aside.

"Are you aware of what has occurred?"

"Alas, yes!" replied Thomas. "Lady Sarah telegraphed to me last night."

The Rector pressed his hand, and returned to his daughter. Thomas Godolphin struck into a by-path, a short cut from the station, which would take him to Grame House.

Six days ago, exactly, since he had been there before. The house looked precisely as it had looked then, all in darkness, excepting the faint light that burned from Sarah Anne's chamber. It burnt there still. Then it was lighting the living; now——

Thomas Godolphin rang the bell gently.—Does any one like to do otherwise at a house in which death is an inmate? Elizabeth, as usual, opened the door, and burst into tears when she saw who it was. "I said it would bring you back, sir!" she exclaimed.

"Does Lady Sarah bear it pretty well?" he asked, as she showed him into the drawing-room.

"No, sir, not over well," sobbed the girl. "I'll tell my lady that you are here."

He stood over the fire, as he had done the other night: it was low now, as it had been then. Strangely still seemed the house: he could almost have told that one was lying dead in it. He listened, waiting for Ethel's step, hoping she would be the first to come to him.

Elizabeth returned. "My lady says would you be so good as to walk up to her, sir?"

Thomas Godolphin followed her upstairs. She made for the room to which he had been taken the former night—Sarah Anne's chamber. In point of fact, the chamber of Lady Sarah, until it was given up to Sarah Anne for her illness. Elizabeth, with soft and stealthy tread, crossed the corridor to the door, and opened it.

Was she going to show him into the presence of the dead? He thought she must have mistaken Lady Sarah's orders, and he hesitated on the threshold.

"Where is Miss Ethel?" he whispered.

"Who, sir?

"Miss Ethel. Is she well?"

The girl stared, flung the door full open, and with a great cry flew down the staircase.

He looked after her in amazement. Had she gone crazy? Then he turned and walked into the room with a hesitating step.

Lady Sarah was coming forward to meet him. She was convulsed with grief. He took both her hands in his with a soothing gesture, essaying a word of comfort : not of inquiry, as to why she should have brought him to this room. He glanced to the bed, expecting to see the dead upon it. But the bed was empty. And at that moment, his eyes caught something else.

Seated by the fire in an invalid chair, surrounded with pillows, covered with shawls, with a wan, attenuated face, and eyes that seemed to have a glaze over them, was—*who?*

Sarah Anne? It certainly *was* Sarah Anne, and in life still. For she feebly held out her hand in welcome, and the tears suddenly gushed from her eyes. " I am getting better, Mr. Godolphin."

Thomas Godolphin—Thomas Godolphin—how shall I write it? For one happy minute he was utterly blind to what it could all mean : his whole mind was a chaos of wild perplexity. And then, as the dreadful truth burst upon him, he staggered against the wall, with a wailing cry of agony.

It was Ethel who had died.

CHAPTER XIII.

UNAVAILING REGRETS.

YES. It was Ethel who had died.

Thomas Godolphin leaned against the wall in his agony. It was one of those moments that can fall only once in a lifetime ; in many lives never ; when the greatest limit of earthly misery bursts upon the startled spirit, shattering it for all time. Were Thomas Godolphin to live for a hundred years, he never could know another moment like this : the power so to feel would have left him.

It had not left him yet. Nay, it had scarcely come to him in its full realization. At present he was half stunned. Strange as it may seem, the first impression upon his mind, was—that he was so much nearer to the next world. How am I to define this "nearer?" It was not that he was nearer to it by time ; or in goodness : nothing of that sort. *She* had passed within its portals ; and the great gulf, which divides time from eternity, seems to be only a span now to Thomas Godolphin : it was as if he, in spirit, had followed her in. From being a place far, far off, vague, indefinite, indistinct, it had been suddenly brought to him, close and palpable : or he to it. Had Thomas Godolphin been an atheist, denying a hereafter,—Heaven in its compassion have mercy upon all such !—that one moment of suffering would have recalled him to a sense of his mistake. It was as if he looked above with the eye of inspiration and saw the truth; it was as a brief, passing moment of revelation from God. She, with her loving spirit, her gentle heart, her simple trust in God, had been taken from this world to enter upon a better. She was as surely living in it, had entered upon its mysteries, its joys, its rest, as that he was living here : she, he believed, was as surely regarding him now and his great sorrow, as that he was left alone to battle with it. From henceforth Thomas Godolphin possessed a lively, ever-present link with that world; and knew that its gates would, in God's good time, be opened for him.

These feelings, impressions, facts—you may designate them as you please—took up their place in his mind all in that first instant, and seated themselves there for ever. Not yet very consciously. To his stunned senses, in his weight of bitter grief, nothing could be to him very clear : ideas passed through his brain quickly, confusedly ; as the changing scenes in a phantasmagoria. He looked round as one bewildered. The bed, prepared for occupancy, on which, on entering, he had expected to see the dead, but not *her*, was between him and the door. Sarah Anne Grame in her invalid chair by the fire, a table at her right hand, covered with adjuncts of the sick-room—a medicine-bottle with its accompanying wine-glass and tablespoon : jelly, and other delicacies to tempt a faded appetite—Sarah Anne sat there and gazed at him with her dark hollow eyes, from which the tears rolled slowly over her cadaverous cheeks. Lady Sarah stood before him ; sobs choking her voice as she wrung her hands. Ay, both were weeping. But he——it is not in the presence of others that man gives way to grief: neither will tears come to him in the first leaden weight of anguish.

Thomas Godolphin listened mechanically, as one who cannot do otherwise, to the explanations of Lady Sarah. "Why did you not prepare me?—why did you let it come upon me with this startling shock?" was his first remonstrance.

"I did prepare you," sobbed Lady Sarah. "I telegraphed to you last night, as soon as it had happened. I wrote the message with my own hand, and sent it off to the office before I turned my attention to any other thing."

"I received the message. But you did not say—I thought it was," —Thomas Godolphin turned his glance on Sarah Anne. He remembered her state, in the midst of his own anguish, and would not alarm her. "You did not mention Ethel's name," he continued to Lady Sarah. "How could I suppose you alluded to her? How could I suppose that she was ill?"

Sarah Anne divined his motive for hesitation. She was uncommonly keen in penetration : sharp, as the world says ; and she had noted his words on entering, when he began to soothe Lady Sarah for the loss of a child ; she had noticed his startled recoil, when his eyes fell on her. She spoke up with a touch of her old querulousness, the tears arrested, and her eyes glistening.

"You thought it was I who had died! Yes, you did, Mr. Godolphin, and you need not attempt to deny it. You would not have cared, so that it was not Ethel."

Thomas Godolphin had no intention of contradicting her. He

turned from Sarah Anne in silence, to look inquiringly and reproachfully at her mother.

"Mr. Godolphin, I could not prepare you better than I did,"
said Lady Sarah. "When I wrote the letter to you, telling of her
illness——"

"What letter?" interrupted Thomas Godolphin. "I received no
letter."

"But you must have received it," returned Lady Sarah in her
quick, cross manner. Not cross with Thomas Godolphin, but from a
rising doubt whether the letter had miscarried. "I wrote it, and I
know that it was safely posted. You ought to have had it by last
evening's delivery, before you would receive the telegraphic despatch."

"I never had it," said Thomas Godolphin. "When I waited in
your drawing-room now, I was listening for Ethel's footsteps to come
to me."

Thomas Godolphin knew, later, that the letter had arrived duly and
safely at Broomhead, at the time mentioned by Lady Sarah. Sir
George Godolphin either did not open the box that night ; or, if he
opened it, had overlooked the letter for his son. Charlotte Pain's
complaint, that the box ought not to be left to the charge of Sir
George, had reason in it. On the morning of his son's departure with
the young ladies, Sir George had found the letter, and at once despatched it back to Prior's Ash. It was on its road at this same hour
when he was talking with Lady Sarah. But the shock had come.

He took a seat by the table, and covered his eyes with his hand as
Lady Sarah gave him a detailed account of the illness and death. Not
all the account, that she or any one else could give, would take one
iota from the dreadful fact staring him in the face. She was gone ;
gone for ever from this world ; he could never again meet the glance
of her eye, or hear her voice in response to his own. Ah, my readers,
there are griefs that change all our after-life ! rending the heart as
an earthquake will rend the earth : and, all that can be done is, to sit
down under them, and ask of Heaven strength to bear them. To bear
them as we best may, until time shall in a measure bring healing
upon its wings.

On the last night that Thomas Godolphin had seen her, Ethel's brow
and eyes were heavy. She had wept much in the day, and supposed
the pain in her head to arise from that circumstance ; she had given
this explanation to Thomas Godolphin. Neither she, nor he, had had
a thought that it could come from any other source. More than a
month since Sarah Anne was taken with the fever ; fears for Ethel
had died out. And yet those dull eyes, that hot head, that heavy
weight of pain, were only the symptoms of approaching sickness !
A night of tossing and turning, snatches of disturbed sleep, of terrify-
ing dreams, and Ethel awoke to the conviction that the fever was
upon her. About the time that she generally rose, she rang her bell
for Elizabeth.

"I do not feel well," she said. "As soon as mamma is up, will you
ask her to come to me ? Do not disturb her before then."

Elizabeth obeyed her orders. But Lady Sarah, tired and wearied
out with her attendance upon Sarah Anne, with whom she had been

up half the night, did not rise until between nine and ten. Then the maid went to her and delivered the message.

"In bed still! Miss Ethel in bed still!" exclaimed Lady Sarah. She spoke in much anger: for Ethel was wont to be up betimes and in attendance upon Sarah Anne. It was *required* of her to be so.

Throwing on a dressing-gown, Lady Sarah proceeded to Ethel's room. And there she broke into a storm of reproach and anger ; never waiting to ascertain what might be the matter with Ethel, anything or nothing. "Ten o'clock, and that poor child to have lain until now with no one near her but a servant!" she reiterated. "You have no feeling, Ethel."

Ethel drew the clothes from her flushed face, and turned her glisten-ing eyes, dull last night, bright with fever now, upon her mother. "Oh, mamma, I am ill, indeed I am! I can hardly lift my head for the pain. Feel how it is burning! I did not think I ought to get up."

"What is the matter with you?" sharply inquired Lady Sarah.

"I cannot quite tell," answered Ethel. "I only know that I feel ill all over. I feel, mamma, as if I could not get up."

"Very well! There's that dear suffering angel lying alone, and you can think of yourself before you think of her! If you choose to remain in bed you must. But you will reproach yourself for your selfishness when she is gone. Another four and twenty hours and she may be no longer with us. Do as you think proper."

Ethel burst into tears, and caught her mother's robe as she was turning away. "Mamma, do not be angry with me! I trust I am not selfish. Mamma"—and her voice sank to a whisper—"I have been thinking that it may be the fever."

The fever! For one moment Lady Sarah paused in consternation, but the next she decided there was no fear of it. She really believed so.

"The fever!" she reproachfully said. "Heaven help you for a selfish and a fanciful child, Ethel! Did I not send you to bed with headache last night, and what is it but the remains of that headache that you feel this morning? I can see what it is ; you have been fretting after this departure of Thomas Godolphin! Get up and dress yourself, and come in and attend upon your sister. You know she can't bear to be waited on by any one but you. Get up, I say, Ethel."

Will Lady Sarah Grame remember that little episode until death shall take her? I should, in her place. She suppressed all mention of it to Thomas Godolphin. "The dear child told me she did not feel well, but I only thought she had a headache, and that she would perhaps feel better up," were the words in which she related it to him. What sort of a vulture was gnawing at her heart as she spoke them? It was true that, in her blind selfishness for that one undeserving child, she had lost sight of the fact that illness could come to Ethel ; she had not allowed herself to entertain its probability; she, who had accused of selfishness that devoted, generous girl, who was ready at all hours to sacrifice herself to her sister ; who would have sacrificed her very life to save Sarah Anne's.

Ethel got up. Got up as she best could ; her limbs aching, her head burning. She went into Sarah Anne's room, and did for her what she was able, gently, lovingly, anxiously, as of yore. Ah, child! let those, who are left, be thankful that it was so: it is well to be stricken down in the path of duty, working until we can work no more.

She did so. She stayed where she was until the day was half gone; bearing up, it was hard to say how. She could not touch breakfast; she could not take anything. None saw how ill she was. Lady Sarah was wilfully blind; Sarah Anne had eyes and thoughts for herself alone. "What are you shivering for?" Sarah Anne once fretfully asked her. "I feel cold, dear," was Ethel's unselfish answer: not a word said she further of her illness. In the early part of the afternoon, Lady Sarah was away from the room for some time upon domestic affairs; and when she returned to it Mr. Snow was with her. He had been prevented from calling earlier in the day. They found that Sarah Anne had dropped into a doze, and Ethel was stretched on the floor before the fire, moaning. But the moans ceased as they entered.

Mr. Snow, regardless of waking the invalid, strode up to Ethel, and turned her face to the light. "How long has she been like this?" he cried out, his voice shrill with emotion. "Child! child! why did they not send for me?"

Alas! poor Ethel was, even then, growing too ill to reply. Mr. Snow carried her to her room with his own arms, and the servants undressed her and laid her in the bed from which she was never more to rise. The fever attacked her violently: but not more so than it had attacked Sarah Anne; scarcely as badly; and danger, for Ethel, was not imagined. Had Sarah Anne not got over a similar crisis, they would have feared for Ethel: so are we given to judge by collateral circumstances. It was only on the third or fourth day that highly dangerous symptoms declared themselves, and then Lady Sarah wrote to Thomas Godolphin the letter which had not reached him. There was this much of negative consolation to be derived from its miscarriage: that, had it been delivered to him on the instant of its arrival, he could not have been in time to see her.

"You ought to have written to me as soon as she was taken ill," he observed to Lady Sarah.

"I would have done so had I apprehended danger," she repentantly answered. "But I never did apprehend it. Mr. Snow did not do so. I thought how pleasant it would be to get her safe through the danger and the illness, before you should know of it."

"Did she not wish me to be written to?"

The question was put firmly, abruptly, after the manner of one who will not be cheated of his answer. Lady Sarah dared not evade it. How could she equivocate, with her child lying dead in the house.

"It is true. She did wish it. It was on the first day of her illness that she spoke. 'Write, and tell Thomas Godolphin.' She never said it but that once."

"And you did not do so?" he returned, his voice hoarse with pain.

"Do not reproach me! do not reproach me!" cried Lady Sarah, clasping her hands in supplication, while the tears fell in showers from her eyes, "I did it for the best. I never supposed there was danger:

I thought what a pity it was to bring you back, all that long journey: putting you to so much unnecessary trouble and expense."

Trouble and expense, in such a case! She could speak of expense to Thomas Godolphin! But he remembered how she had had to battle both with expense and trouble her whole life long; that for her these must wear a formidable aspect: and he remained silent.

" I wish now I had written," she resumed, in the midst of her choking sobs. "As soon as Mr. Snow said there was danger, I wished it. But "
—as if she would seek to excuse herself—" what with the two upon my hands, she upstairs, Sarah Anne here, I had not a moment for proper reflection."

" Did you tell her you had not written ? " he asked. " Or did you let her lie waiting for me, hour after hour, day after day, blaming me for my careless neglect ? "

" She never blamed any one; you know she did not," wailed Lady Sarah: "and I believe she was too ill to think even of you. She was only sensible at times. Oh, I say, do not reproach me, Mr. Godolphin ! I would give my own life to bring her back again ! I never knew her worth until she was gone. I never loved her as I love her now."

There could be no doubt that Lady Sarah Grame was reproaching herself far more bitterly than any reproach could tell upon her from Thomas Godolphin. An accusing conscience is the worst of all evils. She sat there, her head bent, swaying herself backwards and forwards on her chair, moaning and crying. It was not a time, as Thomas Godolphin felt, to say a word of her past heartless conduct, in forcing Ethel to breathe the infection of Sarah Anne's sick-room. And, all that he could say, all the reproaches, all the remorse and repentance, would not bring Ethel back to life.

" Would you like to see her ? " whispered Lady Sarah, as he rose to leave.

" Yes."

She lighted a candle, and preceded him upstairs. Ethel had died in her own room. At the door, Thomas Godolphin took the candle from Lady Sarah.

" I must go in alone."

He passed on into the chamber, and closed the door. On the bed, laid out in her white night-dress, lay what remained of Ethel Grame. Pale, still, pure, her face was wonderfully like what it had been in life, and a calm smile rested upon it.—But Thomas Godolphin wished to be alone.

Lady Sarah stood outside, leaning against the opposite wall, and weeping silently, the glimmer from the hall-lamp below faintly lighting the corridor. Once she fancied that a sound, as of choking sobs, struck upon her ears, and she caught up a small black shawl that she wore, for grief had chilled her, flung it over her shoulders, and wept the faster.

He came out by-and-by, calm and quiet as he ever was. He did not perceive Lady Sarah standing there in the shade, and went straight down, the wax-light in his hand. Lady Sarah caught him up at the door of Sarah Anne's room, and took the light from him.

" She looks very peaceful, does she not ? " was her whisper.

"She could not look otherwise."

He went on down alone, wishing to let himself out. But Elizabeth had heard his steps, and was already at the door. "Good night, Elizabeth," he said, as he passed her.

The girl did not answer. She slipped out into the garden after him. "Oh, sir! and didn't you know of it?" she whispered.

"No."

"If anybody was ever gone away to be an angel, sir, it's that sweet young lady," continued Elizabeth, letting her tears and sobs come forth as they would. "She was just one here! and she's gone to her own fit place above."

"Ay. It is so."

"You should have been in this house throughout the whole of the illness, to have see the difference between them, sir! Nobody would believe it. Miss Grame, angry and snappish, and not caring who suffered, or who was ill, or who toiled, so that she was served: Miss Ethel, lying like a tender lamb, patient and meek, thankful for all that was done for her. It does seem hard, sir, that we should lose her for ever."

"Not for ever, Elizabeth," he answered.

"And that's true, too! But, sir, the worst is, one can't think of that sort of consolation just when one's troubles are fresh. Good night to you, sir."

"No, no," he murmured to himself; "not for ever."

CHAPTER XIV.

GONE ON BEFORE.

THOMAS GODOLPHIN walked on, leaving the high-road for a less-frequented path, the one by which he had come. About midway between this and the railway station, a path, branching to the right, would take him into Prior's Ash. He went along, musing. In the depth of his great grief, there was no repining. He was one to trace the finger of God in all things. If Mrs. Godolphin had imbued him with superstitious feelings, she had also implanted within him something better: and a more entire trust in God it was perhaps impossible for any one to feel, than was felt by Thomas Godolphin. It was what he lived under. He could not see why Ethel should have been taken; why this great sorrow should fall upon him: but that it must be for the best, he implicitly believed. The best: for God had done it. How he was to live on without her, he knew not. How he could support the lively anguish of the immediate future, he did not care to think about. All his hope in this life gone! all his plans, his projects, uprooted by a single blow! never, any of them, to return. He might still look for the bliss of a hereafter—ay! that remains even for the most heavy-laden, thank God!—but his sun of happiness in this world had set for ever.

Thomas Godolphin might have been all the better for a little sun then—not speaking figuratively. I mean the good sun that illumines our daily world; that would be illumining my pen and paper at this moment, but for an envious fog, which obscures everything but itself. The moon was not shining as it had shone the last night he left Lady Sarah's, when he had left his farewell kiss—oh that he could have known it was the last!—on the gentle lips of Ethel. There was no moon yet; the stars were not showing themselves, for a black cloud enveloped the skies like a pall, fitting accompaniment to his blasted hopes; and his path altogether was dark. Little wonder then, that Thomas Godolphin all but fell over some dark object, crouching in his way: he could only save himself by springing back. By dint of peering, he discovered it to be a woman. She was seated on the bare earth; her hands clasped under her knees, which were raised almost level with her chin which rested on them, and was swaying herself backwards and forwards as one does in grief; as Lady Sarah Grame had done not long before.

"Why do you sit here?" cried Thomas Godolphin. "I nearly fell over you."

"Little matter if ye'd fell over me and killed me," was the woman's response, given without raising her head, or making any change in her position. "'Twould only have been one less in an awful cold world, as seems made for nothing but trouble. If the one half of us was out of it, there'd be room perhaps for them as was left."

"Is it Mrs. Bond?" asked Thomas Godolphin, as he caught a glimpse of her features.

"Didn't you know me, sir? I know'd you by the voice as soon as you spoke. You have got trouble too, I hear. The world's full of nothing else. Why does it come?"

"Get up," said Thomas Godolphin. "Why do you sit there? Why are you here at all at this hour of the night?"

"It's where I'm going to stop till morning," returned the woman, sullenly. "There shall be no getting up for me."

"What is the matter with you?" he resumed.

"Trouble," she shortly answered. "I've been toiling up to the work'us, asking for a loaf, or a bit o' money: anything they'd give to me, just to keep body and soul together for my children. They turned me back again. They'll give me nothing. I may go into the union with the children if I will, but not a stiver of help'll they afford me out of it. Me, with a corpse in the house, and a bare cubbort."

"A corpse!" involuntarily repeated Thomas Godolphin. "Who is dead!"

"John."

Curtly as the word was spoken, the tone yet betrayed its own pain. This John, the eldest son of the Bonds, had been attacked with the fever at the same time as the father and brother. They had succumbed to it: this one had recovered: or, at least, had appeared to be recovering.

"I thought John was getting better," observed Thomas Godolphin.

"He might ha' got better, if he'd had things to make him better! Wine and meat, and all the rest of it. He hadn't got 'em: and he's dead."

Now a subscription had been entered into for the relief of the poor sufferers from the fever, Godolphin, Crosse, and Godolphin having been amongst its most liberal contributors; and to Thomas Godolphin's certain knowledge, a full share, and a very good share, had been handed to the Bonds. Quite sufficient to furnish proper nourishment for John Bond for some time to come. He did not say to the woman, "You have had enough: where has it gone to? it has been wasted in riot." That it had been wasted in riot and improvidence, there was no doubt, for it was in the nature of the Bonds so to waste it; but to cast reproach in the hour of affliction was not the religion of everyday life practised by Thomas Godolphin.

"Yes, they turned me back," she resumed, swaying herself nose and knees together, as before. "They wouldn't give me as much as a bit o' bread. I wasn't going home without taking something to my famished children; and I wasn't going to beg like a common tramp. So I just sat myself down here; and I shan't care if I'm found stark and stiff in the morning!"

"Get up, get up," said Thomas Godolphin. "I will give you something for bread for your children to-night."

In the midst of his own sorrow he could feel for her, improvident old sinner though she was, and though he knew her to be so. He coaxed and soothed, and finally prevailed upon her to rise, but she was in a reckless, sullen mood, and it took him a little effort before it was effected. She burst into tears when she thanked him, and turned off in the direction of the Pollard cottages.

The reflection of Mr. Snow's bald head was conspicuous on the surgery blind: he was standing between the window and the lamp. Thomas Godolphin observed it as he passed. He turned to the surgery door, which was at the side of the house, opened it, and saw that Mr. Snow was alone.

The surgeon turned his head at the interruption, put down a glass jar which he held, and grasped his visitor's hand in silence.

"Snow! why did you not write for me?"

Mr. Snow brought down his hand on a pair of tiny scales, causing them to jangle and rattle. He had been bottling up his anger against Lady Sarah for some days now, and this was his first explosion.

"Because I understood that she had done so. I was present when that poor child asked her to do it. I found her on the floor in Sarah Anne's chamber. On the floor, if you'll believe me! Lying there, because she could not hold her aching head up. My lady had dragged her out of bed in the morning, ill as she was, and forced her to attend as usual upon Sarah Anne. I got it all out of Elizabeth. 'Mamma,' she said, when I pronounced it to be fever, though she was almost beyond speaking then, 'you will write to Thomas Godolphin.' I never supposed but that my lady did it. Your sister, Miss Godolphin, inquired if you had been written for, and I told her yes."

"Snow," came the next sad words, "could you not have saved her?"

The surgeon shook his head and answered in a quiet tone, looking down at the stopper of a phial, which he had taken up and was turning about listlessly in his fingers.

"Neither care nor skill could save her. I gave her the best I had to give. As did Dr. Beale. Godolphin,"—raising his quick dark eyes, flashing then with a peculiar light—"she was ready to go. Let it be your consolation."

Thomas Godolphin made no answer, and there was silence for a time. Mr. Snow resumed. "As to my lady, the best consolation I wish her, is, that she may have her heart wrung with remembrance for years to come! I don't care what people may preach about charity and forgiveness; I do wish it. But she'll be brought to her senses, unless I am mistaken: she has lost her treasure and kept her bane. A year or two more, and that's what Sarah Anne will be."

"She ought to have written for me."

"She ought to do many things that she does not do. She ought to have sent Ethel from the house, as I told her, the instant the disorder appeared in it. Not she. She kept her in her insane selfishness: and now I hope she's satisfied with her work. When alarming symptoms showed themselves in Ethel, on the fourth day of her illness, I think it was, I said to my lady, 'It is strange what can be keeping Mr. Godolphin!' 'Oh,' said she, 'I did not write to him.' 'Not write!' I answered: and I fear I used an ugly word to my lady's face. 'I'll write at once,' returned she humbly. 'Of course,' cried I, 'when the steed's stolen we shut the stable-door.' It's the way of the world."

Another pause. "I would have given anything to take Ethel from the house at the time; to take her from the town," observed Thomas Godolphin in a low tone. "I said so then. But it could not be."

"I should have done it, in your place," said Mr. Snow. "If my lady had said no, I'd have carried her off in the face of it. Not married, you say? Rubbish! Every one knows she'd have been safe with you. And you would have been married as soon as was convenient. What are forms and ceremonies and carping tongues, in comparison with a girl's life? A life, precious as was Ethel's!"

Thomas Godolphin leaned his forehead in his hand, lost in retrospect. Oh, that he *had* taken her! that he had set at nought what he had then bowed to, the *convenances* of society! She might have been by his side now, in health and life, to bless him! Doubting words interrupted the train of thought.

"And yet I don't know," the surgeon was repeating, in a dreamy manner. "What is to be, will be. We look back, all of us, and say, 'If I had acted thus, if I had done the other, so and so would not have happened; events would have turned out differently.' But who is to be sure of it? Had you taken Ethel out of harm's way—as we might have thought it—there's no telling but she'd have had the fever just the same: her blood might have become infected before she left the house. There's no knowing, Mr. Godolphin."

"True. Good evening, Snow."

He turned suddenly and hastily to the outer door, but the surgeon caught him before he passed its threshold, and touched his arm to detain him. They stood there in the obscurity, their faces shaded in the dark night.

"She left you a parting word, Mr. Godolphin."

"Ah?"

"An hour before she died she was calm and sensible, though fearfully weak. Lady Sarah had gone to her favourite, and I was alone with Ethel. 'Has he not come yet?' she asked me, opening her eyes. 'My dear,' I said, 'he could not come; he was never written for.' For I knew she alluded to you, and was determined to tell her the truth, dying though she was. 'What shall I say to him for you?' I continued. She put up her hand to motion my face nearer hers, for her voice was growing faint. 'Tell him, with my dear love, not to grieve,' she whispered, between her panting breath. 'Tell him that I have gone on before.' I think they were almost the last words she spoke."

Thomas Godolphin leaned against the modest post of the surgery door, and eagerly drank in the words. Then he wrung the doctor's hand, and departed, hurrying along the street as one who shrank from observation: for he did not care, just then, to encounter the gaze of his fellow-men.

Coming with a quick step up the side street, in which the entrance to the surgery was situated, was the Reverend Mr. Hastings. He stopped to accost the surgeon.

"Was that Mr. Godolphin?"

"Ay. This is a blow for him."

Mr. Hastings's voice insensibly shrank to a whisper. "Maria tells me that he did not know of Ethel's death or illness. Until they arrived here to-night, they thought it was Sarah Anne who died. He went up to Lady Sarah's after the train came in, thinking so."

"Lady Sarah's a fool," was the complimentary rejoinder of Mr. Snow.

"She is, in some things," warmly assented the Rector. "The telegraphic message she despatched to Scotland, telling of the death, was so obscurely worded as to cause them to assume that it alluded to Sarah Anne."

"Ah well! she's only heaping burdens on her conscience," rejoined Mr. Snow in a philosophic tone. "She has lost Ethel through want of care (as I firmly believe) in not keeping her out of the way of infection; she prevented their last meeting, through not writing to him; she——"

"He could not have saved her, had he been here," interrupted Mr. Hastings.

"No one said he could. There would have been satisfaction in it for him, though. And for her too, poor child."

Mr. Hastings did not contest the point. He was so very practical a man (in contradistinction to an imaginative one) that he saw little use in "last" interviews, unless they produced actual good. Turning away, he walked home at a brisk pace. Maria was alone when he entered. Mrs. Hastings and Grace were out of the room, talking to some late applicant: a clergyman's house, like a parish apothecary's, is never free long together. Divested of her travelling cloaks and seated before the fire in her quiet merino dress, Maria looked as much at home as if she had never left it. The blaze, flickering on her face, betrayed to the keen glance of the Rector that her eyelashes were wet.

"Grieving after Broomhead already, Maria?" asked he, his tone a stern one.

"Oh, papà, no! I am glad to be at home. I was thinking of poor Ethel."

"She is better off. The time may come, Maria—we none of us know what is before us—when some of you young ones who are left may wish you had died as she has. Many a one, battling for very existence with the world's cares, wails out a vain wish that he had been taken early from the evil to come."

"It must be so dreadful for Thomas Godolphin!" Maria resumed, looking straight into the fire, and speaking as if in commune with herself, more than to her father.

"Thomas Godolphin must find another love."

It was one of those phrases, spoken in satire only, to which the Rector of All Souls' was occasionally given. He saw so much to condemn in the world, things which grated harshly on his advanced mind, that his speech had become imbued with a touch of gall, and he would often give utterance to cynical remarks, uncalled for at the moment.

Maria took up the words literally. She turned to Mr. Hastings; her cheek flushed, her hands clasped; altogether betraying vivid emotion. "Oh, papa! another love! You should not say it of Thomas Godolphin. Love, such as his, is not for a week or a year: it is for all time."

The Rector paused a moment in his reply. His penetrating gaze was fixed upon his daughter. "May I inquire whence you have derived your knowledge of 'love,' Miss Maria Hastings?"

Her eyes drooped, her face turned crimson, her manner grew confused. She turned her countenance from that of her father, and stammered forth some lame excuse. "Every one knows, papa, that Thomas Godolphin was fond of Ethel."

"Possibly. But every one does not know that Maria Hastings deems herself qualified to enlarge upon the subject," was the Rector's reply. And Maria shrank into silence.

There came a day, not many days afterwards, when Maria Hastings, her sisters, and two of her brothers, were gathered in sombre silence around the study window of the Rectory. The room was built out at the back of the house, over the kitchen, and its side window commanded a full view of the churchyard of All Souls', and of the church porch. Grace, who constituted herself mistress of the others a great deal more than did Mrs. Hastings herself, allowed the blind to be drawn up about two inches at the bottom of the window; and Maria, Isaac, Harry, and Rose, kneeling down for convenience sake, brought their faces into contact with it, as the mob outside the churchyard gate did there. Human nature is the same everywhere, whether in the carefully-trained children of a Christian gentleman, or in those who know no training but what the streets have given.

The funeral, even now, was inside the church: it had been inside so long that those eager watchers, estimating time by their impatience, began to think it was never coming out again. A sudden movement in the church porch reassured them, and Grace knelt down and made one with the rest.

Slowly—slowly—on it came. The Reverend Mr. Hastings first, in his white robes; the coffin next; Thomas Godolphin last, with a stranger by his side. Nothing more, except some pall-bearers in their white scarfs, and the necessary attendants. It was a perfectly simple funeral : according well with what the dead had been in her simple life.

The appearance of this stranger took the curious gazers by surprise. Who was he? A spare man, past middle age, with a red nose and an unmistakable wig on his head. Rumours circulating in Prior's Ash had said that Thomas Godolphin would be sole mourner. Lady Sarah Grame's relatives—and she could not boast of many— lived far north of Aberdeen. "Who can he be?" murmured Grace Hastings.

"Why, don't you girls know? That's through your having stuck yourselves in the house all the morning, for fear you should lose the funeral. If you had gone out, you'd have heard who he is." The retort came from Harry Hastings. Let it be a funeral or a wedding, that may be taking place under their very eyes, boys must be boys all the world over. And so they ever will be.

"Who is he, then?" asked Grace.

"He is Ethel's uncle," answered Harry. "He arrived by train this morning. The Earl of Macsomething."

"The Earl of Macsomething!" repeated Grace.

Harry nodded. "Mac begins the name, and I forget the rest. Lady Sarah was his sister."

"Is, you mean," said Grace. "It must be Lord Macdoune."

The church porch was opposite the study window. The grave had been dug in a line between the two, very near to the family vault of the Godolphins and to the entrance gate of the churchyard. On it came, crossing the broad churchyard path which wound round·to the road, treading between mounds and graves. The clergyman took his place at the head, the mourners near him, the rest disposing themselves decently around.

"Grace," whispered Isaac, "if we had the window open an inch, we should hear." And Grace was pleased to accord her sanction, and they silently raised it.

"Man that is born of a woman hath but a short time to live, and is full of misery. He cometh up and is cut down like a flower; he fleeth as it were a shadow, and never continueth in one stay."

The children—indeed they were little more—hushed their breath and listened, and looked at Thomas Godolphin. Thomas Godolphin stood there, his head bowed, his face still, the gentle wind stirring his thin dark hair. It was probably a marvel to himself in after-life, how he had contrived, in that closing hour, to retain his calmness before the world.

"The coffin's lowered at last!" broke out Harry, who had been more curious to watch the movements of the men, than the aspect of Thomas Godolphin.

"Hush, sir!" sharply rebuked Grace. And the minister's voice again stole over the silence.

"Forasmuch as it hath pleased Almighty God of his great mercy to take unto himself the soul of our dear sister here departed, we there- fore commit her body to the ground; earth to earth . . . . ashes to ashes . . . . dust to dust . . . . in sure and certain hope of the resurrection to eternal life, through our Lord Jesus Christ; who shall change our vile body, that it may be like unto his glorious body, according to the mighty working, whereby he is able to subdue all things to himself."

Every word came home to Thomas Godolphin's senses; every syllable vibrated upon his heartstrings. That sure and certain hope laid hold of his soul, never again to quit it. It diffused its own holy peace and calm into his troubled mind: and never, until that moment, had he fully realized the worth, the truth, of her dying legacy: "Tell him that I have gone on before." A few years—God, now present with him, alone knew how few or how many—and Thomas Godolphin would have joined her in eternal life.

But why had Mr. Hastings come to a temporary pause? Because his eye had fallen upon one, then gliding up from the entrance of the churchyard to take his place amidst the mourners. One who had evidently arrived in a hurry. He wore neither scarf nor hatband, neither cloak nor hood: nothing but a full suit of plain black clothes.

"Look, Maria," whispered Grace.

It was George Godolphin. He fell quietly in below his brother, his hat carried in his hand, his head bowed, his fair curls waving in the breeze. It was all the work of an instant: and the minister resumed:

"I heard a voice from heaven, saying unto me, Write, From henceforth blessed are the dead which die in the Lord: even so saith the Spirit; for they rest from their labours."

And so went on the service to the end.

The beadle, with much bustle and a liberal use of his staff, scattered and dispersed the mob from the gates, to clear a passage. Two mourning coaches were in waiting. Thomas Godolphin came forth, leaning on his brother's arm, both of them bare-headed still. They entered one; Lord Macdoune stepped into the other.

"Thomas!" cried George Godolphin, leaning forward and seizing his brother's hand impulsively, as the mourning-coach paced slowly on: "I should have been here in good time, but for a delay in the train."

"How did you hear of it? I did not know where to write to you," was Thomas's reply, spoken calmly.

"I heard of it at Broomhead. I went back there, and then I came off at once. Thomas, could they not save her?"

A slight negative movement was all Thomas Godolphin's answer. "How did you find your father, George?"

"Breaking. Breaking fast. Thomas, all his talk is, that he must come home to die."

"To Ashlydyat. I know. How is he to come to it? The Folly is not Ashlydyat. He has desired me to see that he is at Prior's Ash before Christmas, and I shall do so."

George looked surprised. "Desired you to see that he is?"

"If he is not back speedily, I am to go to Broomhead."

"Oh, I see. That your authority, upholding his, may be pitted against my lady's. Take care, Thomas: she may prove stronger than both of you put together."

"I think not," replied Thomas quietly; and he placed his elbow on the window frame, and bent his face upon his hand, as if wishing for silence.

Meanwhile the Reverend Mr. Hastings had passed through the private gate to his own garden; and half a dozen men were shovelling earth upon the coffin, sending it with a rattle upon the bright plate, which told who was mouldering within :

"ETHEL GRAME.   Aged twenty years."

CHAPTER XV.

A MIDNIGHT WALK.

THOMAS GODOLPHIN sat in his place at the bank, opening the morning letters. It was some little time after the interment of Ethel Grame, and the second week in December was already on the wane. In two days more it was his intention to start for Broomhead : for no tidings arrived of the return of Sir George. The very last of the letters he came upon, was one bearing the Scotch post-mark. A poor little note with a scrawled address : no wonder the sorting-clerk had placed it last of all! It looked singularly obscure, in comparison with those large blue letters and their business hands.

Thomas Godolphin knew the writing. It was Margery's. And we may as well read the contents with him, *verbatim :*

"MR. THOMAS SIR,
    "I imbrace this favurible oportunaty of adresing you for I considur it my duty to take up my pen and inform you about my master, *He's not long for this world*, Mr. Thomas I know it by good tokens which I don't write not being an easy writer but they are none the less true, The master's fretting his life away because he is not at home and she is keeping him because she's timorus of the fever. But you saw how it was sir when you were here and it's the same story still. There'd have been a fight for it with my lady but if I'd been you Mr. Thomas I'd have took him also when me and the young ladies went with you to Prior's Ash. When I got back here, sir I saw an awful change in him and Mr. George he saw it but my lady didn't. I pen these lines sir to say you had better come off at once and not wait for it to be nearer Christmas, The poor master is always saying *Thomas is coming for me, Thomas is coming for me* but I'd not answer for it now that he will ever get back alive, Sir it was the worst day's work he ever did to go away at all from Ashlydyat if my lady was dying to live at the new Folly place she might have gone to it but not him, When we do a foolish wrong thing we don't think of the consekences at the time at least not much of em but we think all the more after and fret our hearts out with blame and it have been slowly killing him ever since, I am vexed to disturb you Mr. Thomas with this epistle for I know you must be in enough grief of your own just now,
                    "Your humble servant,
                            "MARGERY."

Thomas Godolphin read it over twice, and then crossed to the opposite side of the private room, where sat a gentleman at another desk. A tall, portly man, with a fresh colour, large, keen dark eyes, and hair white as snow. It was Mr. Crosse.

"Anything particular, Thomas?" he asked, as Thomas Godolphin put the letter into his hand.

"Not in business. Read it, will you?"

Mr. Crosse read the letter through. "Is it my advice you wish for?" asked he, when he came to the last word.

"Not exactly," replied Thomas Godolphin. "I have made up my mind, I believe."

"To go immediately?"

"Yes. Within an hour."

"Right. It is what I should have recommended you to do, had you been undecided. When it comes to letter-writing with Margery, the thing is serious, rely upon it."

And within the hour Thomas Godolphin had started.

The railway station nearest to Broomhead, was three miles distant from it, by the road: but there was a shorter cut across some fields—bearing past the house of that Mr. Sandy Bray, if you are curious to know—which reduced it to less than two. It was one of those rural stations so little frequented that travellers are tempted to ask why they were built at all. Such a thing as a fly, or an omnibus, had never yet been seen at it, at midday: you may therefore judge what chance Thomas Godolphin had of either, getting there, as he did, at midnight. He was the only passenger to alight, and the train went puffing on. The man, who lived in the one-roomed cottage close by, and was called the station-master, appeared to be the only official to receive him. A man who had been drafted thither from one of the English lines.

"For Broomhead, sir?" he questioned, recognizing the traveller.

"Yes. Do you happen to know how Sir George Godolphin is?"

"He looks rare and poorly, sir. He was past here in his carriage to-day. Huddled up in a corner of it, as if he was cold; or else hadn't the strength to sit up. Her ladyship was inside with him."

"There's no porter about, I suppose?"

"He has been gone this two hours, sir. I'd offer to carry your luggage myself, but I shall have the up-express by in half an hour. I shut up for the night then."

"I would not trouble you for so trifling a matter, at this hour, were you at liberty," replied Thomas Godolphin.

He took up his portmanteau himself: a thing not much larger than what the French would call a petit sac-de-nuit, containing little besides a clean shirt and his shaving-tackle: and started, bending his steps not along the road, but across it to the stile.

"I wouldn't take the field way to-night, sir, if I were you," said the man from the station door. "The road is safest."

"Why is it?" asked Thomas Godolphin.

"There's a nasty bit by the field way, a quarter of a mile before you come to Bray's. Anybody, not knowing it well, might take the wrong turning, and go, head first, into the dam."

"But I do know it well," said Thomas Godolphin. "And the night is light enough to distinguish the turnings."

The station-master looked up at the skies—figuratively speaking, for he could see nothing but fog. A light, hazy mist; not a dark one; which seemed likely to turn to rain. He said no more, except a "Good night, sir:" and Thomas Godolphin walked on, hesitating for a moment between the two roads, and then turning decisively to that of the fields, as if some hidden impulse impelled him. Perhaps it did so.

It was not a pleasant night, a pleasant time, or a pleasant way; and Thomas Godolphin began to think he should have done well to have telegraphed his intended journey from Prior's Ash to Broomhead, that they might have sent a conveyance to await him at the station. Regrets were of no use now, and he trudged along, taking two steps forward, and one backward, for the ground in places was wet and slippery. It was a peculiar night. There was no moon; there were no stars; no skies in fact to be seen at all, as you have heard; and yet the night was light.

What were Thomas Godolphin's thoughts bent upon? Need you ask? For some time to come, days and weeks and months, they must run chiefly upon her who had left him. He remembered his last arrival at Broomhead: he remembered his thoughts as he had walked from the station as he was doing now; though then it had been by daylight. His musings had been of Ethel, and his coming marriage; of that farewell kiss which she had pressed upon his lips. Now—now he must only think of her as one of Heaven's angels.

He lifted his hat to wipe his brow, and then changed his load to the other hand. He was coming to the dam now. He could hear its waters. Go carefully, Thomas Godolphin! A few steps down that dark turning, and you might never be heard of more. But he knew his way, and the night was light, and he bore on his course, and the dangerous turn was passed.

A little way farther on, and he could discern the outline of Bray's cottage in the distance. A light burnt in one of the windows, and he wondered who was ill. Probably Margery's sister. It diverted his own sad reflections. Next he became absorbed in thoughts of his father. How should he find him? Ideas, we all know, assume the colouring of surrounding associations, and Thomas Godolphin, in that solitary midnight hour, grew to take a more sombre view of the news contained in Margery's letter than he had hitherto done. It is wonderful how circumstances affect us! In the broad light of day, walking, for instance, as he had done previously to Broomhead, apprehensions would not have come over him. Now he pictured his father (by no will of his own: the scenes rose up unbidden) as lying ill; perhaps dying. Perhaps even then a telegraphic message to him might be on its road to Prior's Ash! Perhaps——

A cry right over his head! And Thomas Godolphin positively started. It proceeded from some night-bird that had dived down upon him, and now flew onwards, flapping its wings. Superstitious Margery would have called it an omen.

Thomas Godolphin followed it with his eyes, speculating upon what bird it could be. It looked like a sea-gull; had screamed like one; but the sea was far off, and, if it was one, it must have come a long distance.

Back it came again, and dived down as before. Thomas Godolphin did not like it, and he wished the portmanteau in his hand had been a gun. "I wonder what good these restless night-birds do," he ejaculated, "except to disturb from sleep any worn-out mortal who may be within hearing?"

Scenes of the recent past rose up before him : the sombre scenes in which he had been an actor. The ominous Shadow of Ashlydyat, striking on his sight as he turned the ash-trees, the night of his previous summons to Broomhead: the dead face of Ethel lying on her bed; the reminiscence of the funeral scene ; of his walking away from it with the dull sound of the earth falling on her coffin smiting his ears! None of them pleasant things to recall at that particular hour. Why should they have come to him?

"What business had they there at such a time?"

Drive them away he could not. But neither did he try to do so. They served to make doubly sad, doubly ominous, his new fears for his father. He knew how precarious was Sir George's life. What if he were then dying! Nay, what if it were the very moment of his departure?—if he were dead? having called upon his children ; upon him, Thomas, in vain?

▸ That odious bird once more! It flew over his head with a shriller cry than the last. Thomas Godolphin was at that moment within a few paces of a stile which lay in his path. He turned his head round to look after the bird, without slackening his pace, putting out his hand before him to feel for the stile. The hand came into contact with it, and Thomas let it rest momentarily. His head was turned, still watching the bird, which was then flying round and round, making fierce circlets in the air.

But he could not stop there all night, staring at the bird, and he turned sharply round to cross the stile. Placing one foot on its lower rail, he——

What made Thomas Godolphin start as if he had been shot? Who and what was that standing on the other side of the stile fixedly gazing at him? A tall, shadowy, upright form, bearing the unmistakable features of Sir George Godolphin.

Will you—strong, practical, unimaginative men of the world—forgive Thomas Godolphin if in that one brief moment the wild superstitions, instilled into his mind in childhood, were allowed their play? Forgive him, or not, it was the fact. In imagination, only the instant before, he had seen his father lying upon his bed, the soul parting from the body: and Thomas Godolphin as much believed what he now saw before him was his father's spirit, as that he, himself, was in existence. The spirit, appearing to him at the moment of its departure. His flesh turned cold, and dew gathered on his brow.

"My son, can it be you?"

Thomas Godolphin came out of his folly, and grasped his father. That it was real flesh and blood which yielded to his arms, he knew now : but perhaps the *surprise* that it should be so, was even greater than the other emotion. Sir George Godolphin there! at that midnight hour! nearly a mile from home! and bareheaded! Was it really Sir George? Thomas Godolphin rubbed his eyes, and thought he, himself, must have taken leave of his senses.

"My father! my dear father! what are you doing here?"

"I thought I'd go to the station, Thomas, and see about a special train. I must go back to Ashlydyat to die."

Thomas climbed over the stile. The tone, the manner, the words, altogether had betrayed to him an unhappy fact—that his father's mind was not in a state of perfect sanity He trembled for his health, too. It was a cold raw night, and here was Sir George in evening dress, without so much as an overcoat thrown on! He, who had only been out since the last fainting-fit in a close carriage: and then well wrapped up.

"Where is your hat, father?"

The old knight lifted his hand to his head, as if he had not known that his hat was not there. "I must have come out without it, Thomas," he said. "What was that noise over there?" he continued, pointing above the stile to the way Thomas had come, his frame shivering with cold as he spoke.

"I think it was a sea-gull. Or some screaming night-bird."

"I could not get over the stile, Thomas. The walk seemed to have taken the strength out of me. How did you come here? I thought you were at Prior's Ash."

Thomas Godolphin was busy. He had taken off his great coat, and was putting it upon his father, buttoning it up carefully. A smaller man than Sir George, it did not fit well : but Sir George had shrunk. The hat fitted better.

"But you have no hat yourself!" said Sir George, surveying his son's head, when he had submitted in patient silence to the dressing.

"I don't want one," replied Thomas. "The night air will not hurt me." Nevertheless, all the way to Broomhead, he was looking on either side, if perchance he might come upon Sir George's hat, lying in the road.

Thomas drew his father close, to support him on his arm, and they commenced their walk to the house. Not until then did Thomas know how very weak his father was. Stooping, shivering, tripping, with every other step, it appeared impossible that he could walk back again : the wonder was, how he had walked there.

Thomas Godolphin halted in dismay. How was he to get his father home? Carry him, he could not : it was of course beyond his strength. The light in Bray's window suggested a thought to him.

"Father, I think you had better go to Bray's and stay there, while I see about your hand-chair. You are not able to walk."

"I won't go to Bray's," returned the knight, with a touch of vehemence. "I don't like Bray, and I will not put my foot inside his threshold. Besides, it's late, and my lady will miss us."

He pressed on somewhat better towards home, and Thomas Godolphin saw nothing else that could be done, except to press on with him, and give him all the help in his power. "My dear father, you should have waited until the morning," he said, "and have gone out then."

"But I wanted to see about a train, Thomas," remonstrated the knight. "And I can't do it in the day. She will not let me. When we drive past the railway station, she won't get out, and won't let me do so. Thomas, I want to go back to Ashlydyat."

"I have come to take you back, my dear father."

"Ay, ay. And mind you are firm when she says I must not go because of the fever. The fever will not hurt me, Thomas. I can't be firm. I have grown feeble, and people take my will from me. You are my first-born son, Thomas."

"Yes."

"Then you must be firm for me, I say."

"I will be, father."

"This is a rough road, Thomas."

"No, it is smooth; and I am glad that it is so. But you are tired."

The old knight bent his head, as if choosing his steps. Presently he lifted his head:

"Thomas, when do they leave Ashlydyat?"

"Who, sir? The Verralls? They have not had notice yet."

Sir George stopped. He drew up his head to its full height, and turned to his son. "Not had notice? When, then, do I go back? I won't go to Lady Godolphin's Folly. I must go to Ashlydyat."

"Yes, sir," said Thomas soothingly. "I will see about it."

The knight, satisfied, resumed his walk. "Of course you will see about it. You are my son and heir, Thomas. I depend upon you."

They pursued their way for some little time in silence, and then Sir George spoke again, his tone hushed. "Thomas, I have put on mourning for her. I mourn her as much as you do. And you did not get there in time to see her alive!"

"Not in time. No," replied Thomas, looking hard into the mist overhead.

"I'd have come to the funeral, Thomas, if she had let me. But she was afraid of the fever. George got there in time for it?"

"Barely."

"When he came back to Broomhead, and heard of it, he was so cut up, poor fellow. Cut up for your sake, Thomas. He said he should be in time to follow her to the grave if he started at once, and he went off then and there. Thomas"—dropping his voice still lower—"whom shall you take to Ashlydyat now?"

"My sisters."

"Nay. But as your wife? You will be replacing Ethel sometime."

"I shall never marry now, father."

At length Broomhead was reached. Thomas held open the gate of the shrubbery to his father, and guided him through it.

"Shall we have two engines, Thomas?"

"Two engines, sir! What for?"

"They'd take us quicker, you know. This is not the station!" broke forth Sir George in a sharp tone of complaint, as they emerged beyond the shrubbery, and the house stood facing them. "Oh, Thomas! you said you were taking me to Ashlydyat! I cannot die away from it!"

Thomas Godolphin stood almost confounded. His father's discourse, the greater part of it, at any rate, had been so rational that he had begun to hope he was mistaken as to his weakness of mind. "My dear father, be at rest," he said : "we will start if you like with to-morrow's dawn. But to go now to the station would not forward us : it is by this time closed for the night."

They found the house in a state of commotion. Sir George had been missed, and servants were out searching for him. Lady Godolphin gazed at Thomas with all the eyes she possessed, thunderstruck at his appearance. "What miracle brought you here?" she exclaimed, wonderingly.

"No miracle, Lady Godolphin. I am thankful that I happened to come. What might have become of Sir George without me, I know not. I expect he would have remained at the stile where I found him until morning; and might have caught his death there."

"He will catch that speedily enough if he is to wander out of the house at midnight in this mad manner," peevishly rejoined my lady.

CHAPTER XVI.

THE LAST JOURNEY.

"I BEG your pardon, Lady Godolphin. That is not the question."

"Not the question!" reiterated Lady Godolphin. "I say that it is the question. The question is, whether Sir George is better and safer here than he would be at Prior's Ash. And of course he is so."

"I think not," replied Thomas Godolphin quietly. "He would be equally well at Prior's Ash : equally safe, as I believe and trust. And the anxiety to be there, which has taken hold of his mind, has grown too strong to be repressed. To detain him here, against his wish, would make him ill, Lady Godolphin. Not returning home."

"Prior's Ash is an unhealthy place just now."

"Its unhealthiness has passed away. The last to be attacked was— was Ethel. And you are aware that time, since then, may be counted by weeks."

"Sir George is partially childish," pursued Lady Godolphin. "You may see for yourself that he is so. It would be most unreasonable, it would be ridiculous to take notice of his whims. Look at his starting out of the house to-night, with nothing on, and roaming a mile or two away in the dark! Is that a proof of sanity?"

"It is a proof how fixedly his mind is bent upon returning home," replied Thomas Godolphin. "He was endeavouring, as I have already informed you, Lady Godolphin, to make his way to the station."

"I shall have him watched in future," said she.

"Lady Godolphin," he resumed, speaking in the calmly quiet tone which characterized him, unmistakably firm now, in spite of its courteousness : "I am here by the desire of my father to accompany him back to Prior's Ash. I may almost say, to convey him back : for I fear he can no longer boast much power of his own, in any way. The last words I said to him, before entering, were, that he should start, if it pleased him, with to-morrow's dawn. I must keep my promise."

"Do you defy me, Thomas Godolphin?"

"I have no wish to do so. I have no wish to abate a particle of the respect and consideration due to you as my father's wife. At the same time, my duty to him is paramount: I hold it more sacred, Lady Godolphin, than any earthly thing. He has charged me, by my duty, to take him back to Ashlyd—to Prior's Ash: and I shall do so."

"You would take him back, I suppose, if Prior's Ash were full of snakes and scorpions?" returned my lady, somewhat losing her temper.

"It is full of neither. Nothing is there, so far as I am aware, that can harm Sir George. Can you urge a single good reason why he should not return to it, Lady Godolphin!"

The delicate bloom on my lady's cheeks was surely heightened—or did Thomas Godolphin fancy it? "But, what if I say he shall *not* return?" she asked, her voice slightly raised.

"I think you will not say it, Lady Godolphin," he replied. "It is Sir George's wish to go to Prior's Ash, and it is my province to see that wish carried out—as he has requested me. Much as I desire to respect your feelings and any plans you may have formed, they cannot weigh with me in this case. There is no necessity whatever for your returning home, Lady Godolphin, unless you choose to do so : but Sir George will leave for it to-morrow."

"And you boast that you do not defy me!" cried Lady Godolphin, with a short laugh. "I would use force to keep him in this house, rather than he should go out of it against my will."

"Force?" repeated Thomas Godolphin, looking at her for an explanation. "What sort of force?"

"Physical force," she answered, assuming a degree of fair suavity. "I would command the servants to bar his exit."

A faint smile crossed Thomas Godolphin's lips. "Do not attempt that, Lady Godolphin," he replied in the respectful manner of one who tenders earnest advice. "I should be sorry indeed to publicly oppose my authority to yours. You know the servants have, most of them, grown old in our service : and that may plead their excuse : but there is not one of them who would not be obedient to the lifting of my finger, in the cause of their master."

Lady Godolphin was foiled. Lady Godolphin had long been aware that she should be foiled, if it ever came to an encounter—strength against strength—between herself and Thomas Godolphin. Easy George she could manage, the Miss Godolphins she could put down, Sir George was, now, as a reed in her hands. But Thomas?—he was different. None of them had been so uniformly respectful and courteous to her as Thomas. And yet she had known that he, of all the rest, would not bend to her authority, were any cause to arise why he should not do so.

She sat biting—as far as she dared—her rose-tinted lips; she lifted one hand and toyed with her perfumed ringlets; she opened a fan which lay at her side, and gently fanned herself; she glanced at the still countenance of Thomas Godolphin : and she knew that she must give up the game. To give it up with a good grace was essential to her future ruling: and she was now making up her mind to do this. It would never do, either, for her to stand in the hall on the morrow, call the servants around her, and say, "It is my pleasure that Sir George does not leave this place for Prior's Ash. Keep him in; hold him in; lock the door; use any necessary means," while Thomas Godolphin was at hand, to lift—as he had phrased it—his finger, and say, "It is my pleasure that my father does go to Prior's Ash. Stand back while he passes." Lady Godolphin was no simpleton, and she could hazard a shrewd guess as to which of the two would be obeyed. So she sat, bringing her mind to make a virtue of necessity, and throw up the plea. In point of fact, she had no cause of objection to Sir George's returning to Prior's Ash, except that she did not care to return to it herself. For two reasons: one, that she liked Broomhead best: the other, that she could not yet subdue her fears of the fever. She bent her head, as if examining the chaste devices on her fan, and spoke indifferently.

"You must be aware that my wish to keep Sir George here arises solely from the state of Prior's Ash. It always has been our custom to spend Christmas there, amongst you all, and I should have had no other thought for this Christmas, but for the illness which arose. Will you guarantee that it is safe for him?"

"Nay, Lady Godolphin. To 'guarantee' an assurance of the sort would be impossible at the best of times. I believe that any fears you may entertain now of the fever will prove only a bugbear."

"The fever has been more than a bugbear to you," she exclaimed, acidity in her tone.

"Yes," he sadly answered.

He drew his chair from the table, where he had been taking some refreshment after his journey, and at that moment the hall clock struck two.

"I am keeping you up very late, Lady Godolphin."

"It is a pleasant change," she answered. "The life here, with Sir George in his delicate state, is so excessively monotonous, that a few nights of sitting up and days of bed, might prove an agreeable variety. Did I understand you rightly—that you intend to start in the morning?"

"If Sir George shall then wish to do so as anxiously as he appeared to wish it to-night. Otherwise, I shall not object to delay it until the following one. I cannot remain longer: business demands my presence at home. And," he added, lowering his voice, "I fear that speed is necessary for my father's sake. If he does not go pretty soon, he may not be able to go at all. It is more than likely that we shall start to-morrow."

"You cannot expect me to be ready in that space of time."

"Certainly not. Just as you please, Lady Godolphin."

Thomas Godolphin was shown to his room. Margery waylaid him in the corridor and entered it with him. "Did you get my epistle, Mr. Thomas?"

"It was that which brought me here now, Margery. Otherwise, I should not have come until the end of the week."

"Then you would have come too late, sir. Yes, Mr. Thomas, I

mean what I say," added the woman, dropping her voice to solemnity. "By dreams and signs and tokens, which I have had——"

"Stay, Margery. You know that I am never very tolerant of your dreams and signs. Let them rest."

"It's true you are not," answered Margery, without the least appearance of discomfiture; "and many's the argument I would have liked to hold with you over it. But you'd never let me. When you were a young man, you'd laugh and joke it down—just as Mr. George might now, were I so foolish as to waste words upon *him*—and since you grew older and steadier you have just put me off as you are doing at this moment. Mr. Thomas, gifts are different in different people. They are not sent upon all alike: and the Scripture says so. One will see what another can't. One will play beautiful music, while another can't tell one tune from another. One man has a head for steam-engines and telegraphs, and will put 'em together as if he had a workshop inside him; and another, his own cousin maybe, can hardly tell an engine when he sees it, and couldn't work one out if he lived to be a hundred years old. And so with other things."

"Well?" responded Thomas Godolphin: for Margery paused, as if waiting for an answer.

"And do you suppose, Mr. Thomas, that it's not the same with signs and warnings? It is not given to all to see or understand them. It is not given, as I take it, for many to see or understand them. But it *is* given to a few. And those few can no more be talked out of knowing that it's truth, than they can be talked out of their own life, or of the skies above 'em. And, Mr. Thomas, it's not only that those who have not the gift can't see or believe for themselves, but they can't be brought to believe that others may do so: and so they laugh at and ridicule it. Many a time, sir, you have laughed at me."

"You see so many, you know, Margery," said Thomas Godolphin, with a slight smile.

Margery looked at him. "Sometimes I have thought, sir, that you are not quite as unbelieving as you seem. But I know it does not do for a gentleman, high and educated and looked up to in his town, to say he puts faith in such. So I'll not trouble you, Mr. Thomas, with the tokens I have had. I'll not tell you that only last night that ever was, I heard the footsteps of——"

"But you are telling me, Margery."

"That's just how you take me up, Mr. Thomas! Well, sir, I say I'll not bring forward these things, but I'll speak of what you may think a surer sign—and that's Sir George's state of health."

"Ay! I can follow you there."

He let her talk on. And she did so, until he was obliged to give her a gentle hint that he should be glad to be alone and get to bed.

The house was awakened before it was yet dawn. Sir George had rung for his servant, had rung for Margery, had rung for the coachman to say the carriage was wanted—in short, had rung for so many, that the whole household was aroused. My lady appeared, in fur slippers and a warm dressing-gown, to know what the commotion could mean. His son Thomas was there, the knight answered. He was sure he had not dreamt it, but that Thomas *had* come the previous night; he met him at the stile; and Thomas had promised that they should go to Ashlydyat in the early morning.

It appeared he was sane enough to remember that. My lady retired, grumbling; and Margery went and called Thomas.

When Thomas reached the room, Sir George was almost in the last stage of dressing. His own trembling, eager fingers had done as much towards it as his servant. He lifted his face with its ashy hue and its strange yearning. "Thomas, my son, I must hasten back to Ashlydyat. You said I should go there to die."

"Do you wish to start immediately, father?"

"You said I should do so!" he wailed in a tone imploringly earnest. "You said I should start with this morning's dawn."

"Yes, yes," acquiesced Thomas. And he forthwith busied himself to advance the preparations.

The best hour that they could leave the station was a little before nine. No train, except one much earlier, stopped at it before. This gave time to get off comfortably: though Sir George, in his impatience, could with difficulty be induced to sit down to breakfast. My lady came in when they were at the table.

"This is really the most extraordinary proceeding!" she exclaimed, speaking chiefly to Thomas Godolphin. "Were such a thing related to me as taking place in another house I should decline to give credence to it. Are the hours of the day so few that you must choose the gloom of a winter's morning for commencing a journey?"

Thomas glanced at Sir George, as if to draw her attention to him. "My father's anxiety will not allow him to wait, Lady Godolphin. I think it well that we should catch the first train."

"I wash my hands of the journey altogether," said Lady Godolphin. "If Sir George does not reach the other end of it alive, you will have the goodness to remember that *I* am not to blame. Far better that he were safely kept in his room wrapped up in his dressing-gown in front of a good fire."

"In that case, my lady, I would not answer for it that he reached the end of the day alive," interposed Margery, who was in and out of the room busier than any of them. "Whether Sir George stays, or whether he goes, he'll not last many days," she added in a lower tone, so that it might not reach her master's ear.

"If I must have gone, I would have started at a Christian hour, Sir George," resumed his wife. "Getting us all out of bed as if we were so many milkmaids?"

Sir George looked round, timidity in his voice and manner. Did he fear that she would detain him even now? "You can come on afterwards, you know, Lady Godolphin; we need not hurry you. Oh, I must, I must be at Ashlydyat!"

Thomas Godolphin came to the rescue. "We shall be in the carriage in five minutes, my dear father, if you will only take your breakfast."

And in a little more than five minutes they were seated in it, on their way to the station, Sir George's own man and Margery attending them. Margery would have deemed it just as possible to cut herself in twain, as to be separated from her master in his present state.

They did not get him that night to Prior's Ash. Thomas feared the long journey for him without a break, so they halted for the night about midway. Singularly to state, Sir George did not utter an impatient word at the delay: from the moment of leaving Broomhead he had become perfectly calm. Whether the fact of his being indisputably on the road had soothed his mind to tranquillity, or whether the strangely eager desire to be home had now left it, certain it was, that he had never mentioned Ashlydyat throughout the day. Of one thing there could be no doubt—that he was fast sinking. Sinking both in mind and body. Margery grew terrified. "Pray Heaven we may get him home!" she aspirated. "Mr. Thomas, as sure as that we are here, he would have been dead before this, had he stopped at Broomhead!"

In the twilight of the second evening, Sir George was at length once more at Prior's Ash. Thomas had telegraphed their arrival, and Janet was at the station with the carriage. But, with the first few words, Janet perceived that he was perfectly childish. Not only childish, but alarmingly changed. Janet grew pale as she turned to Margery.

"Since when?" she murmured.

"Since many days, off and on; but worse since we left Broomhead yesterday morning. He has been sinking hour by hour. Miss Janet, it's death."

They got him to the Folly. And, in half an hour, the whole of his family were gathered round his death-bed. His partner, Mr. Crosse; the surgeon; and the Rector of All Souls' were also there.

He was rambling for the most part in a disconnected manner: but he recognized them all individually, and occasionally gave utterance to rational remarks, as he might have done had he been in full possession of his senses. He fancied himself at Ashlydyat.

"I could not have died away from it, you know, Crosse," he suddenly cried to that gentleman. "Thomas was for bringing me back to the Folly, but I told him I must go to Ashlydyat. If I did let it to strangers, they could not keep me out of it, when I wanted to go there to die. A Godolphin must not die away from Ashlydyat. Where's Cecil?" he added, after a pause.

Poor Cecil, the tears streaming down her cheeks, was close to him; in view then. "I am here, papa."

The knight laid his hand upon her arm—or rather, essayed to do so, but it fell again. His thoughts seemed to pass to another subject.

"Crosse, I have been telling Thomas that I should not allow more than three per cent. on those deposits. Have you seen Mainwaring lately?"

Mr. Snow stepped forward and administered something in a wine-glass. There appeared to be a difficulty in swallowing, and only part of it was taken. "He grows more restless," said the surgeon in an undertone.

Sir George's eyes, as he was slightly raised to take the medicine, had fallen upon some object at the other end of the room, and continued to be strained on it. "Who has changed the position of the cabinet?" he exclaimed, in a stronger tone than he had yet spoken.

It caused them all to turn and look at the spot. A fine old ebony cabinet, inlaid with silver, stood opposite the bed: had stood there ever since they removed to Lady Godolphin's Folly; transplanted thither from Ashlydyat. In the latter house, it had stood on the right of Sir George's bed : and his memory had evidently gone back to that. There could not be a better proof that he was fancying himself at Ashlydyat, lying in his own chamber.

"Janet! why have you placed the cabinet there?"

Janet Godolphin bent her head soothingly over him. "My dear father, it shall be moved, if you wish it."

The knight looked at her, inquiringly for a moment, perhaps not recognizing her. Then he feebly essayed to look beyond her, as if her head interposed between his own view and something behind. "Hush, my dear, I am speaking to your mother. I want to know why she changed the place of the cabinet."

"We thought you'd like it there, Sir George; that you could see it better there," interposed Margery, who knew better than most of them how to deal with the sick. "I'll have it put back before to-morrow morning."

This satisfied him, and he lay still for a few minutes. They thought he would sleep. Presently his eyes opened again, and they rested on George.

"George, where's Charlotte?"

"Who, sir?" demanded George, somewhat taken aback at the question. "Do you mean Charlotte Pain? She is at—she is not here."

"Are you married yet?"

"Oh no," said George hastily, while several pairs of wondering eyes were directed towards him, and those of the Reverend Mr. Hastings were of the number. "Time enough for that, father."

"George!" next came the words, in a hollow whisper this time, "don't let her die, as Ethel did."

"Not if I can help it," replied George, speaking without any serious meaning, except that of humouring his father.

"And don't let Verrall go off the bargain with the money. He is keen that way; but he has no right to touch Charlotte's. If he does— Bessy, is Jekyl dead?"

"Oh no, papa," said Bessy, suppressing her tears as she caressed her father's hand : it was in stooping to do this, that the knight had observed her. "Jekyl is well and hearty yet, and he asked after you to-day. He heard you were coming home."

"Ay! All well and hearty, but me. But it is the will of God to take me, and He knows what's best. Where's Thomas?"

"I am here, father," replied Thomas Godolphin, leaning forward so that his father could see him.

Sir George tried to put up his hand with a beckoning gesture. Thomas understood it : he bent his face close to that pale one, and clasped the nearly inanimate hand in his, listening reverently to the whisper that was breathed so solemnly.

"Thomas, I charge you, never quit Ashlydyat."

"I will not," replied Thomas Godolphin.

"If you bring one home to it, and she would urge you to quit it, urge you until you have no will of your own left, do not yield to it. Do not listen to her. Break with her, let her go forth alone, rather than quit Ashlydyat."

"Father, I will never, of my own free will, leave Ashlydyat. I promise you that, so far as I can hold control over human events, I will live and die in it."

Certainly Sir George understood the promise and its meaning. There could be no mistaking that he did so, by the smile of content which from that moment overspread his countenance, lighting up with satisfaction even his dying eye. He lay for a considerable time still, and then suddenly called for Margery.

"You'll tell your mistress that we can't root up those bushes," he said, as she approached. "It's of no use trying. As fast as they are up from one place they grow in another. They'll not hurt. Tell her I say so."

"I'd get some quicklime, Sir George, and see what that would do," was Margery's response, and the words brought up a smile from one or two of her listeners, solemn moment though it was. Margery's maxim was, never to contradict the dying, but to humour their hallucinations. "Obstinate things, those gorses!" she continued. "But, never you trouble about my mistress, sir: she don't mind them."

The children, standing round his bed, knew quite well that he was alluding to their mother, his first wife. Indeed, Lady Godolphin appeared to have passed entirely from his mind.

Again he lapsed into silence, and remained to all appearance in a stupor, his eyes closed, his breathing ominously slow. Mr. Crosse took his departure, but the Rector and surgeon stayed on yet. The latter saw that the final moment was at hand, and he whispered to Miss Godolphin that she and her sisters might be better from the room. "At any rate," he added, for he saw the dissenting, displeased look which overspread her face, "it might be as well to spare the sight to Cecil."

"No," briefly responded Miss Godolphin. "Our place is here." And they watched on.

With an impulse of strength surprising to see, Sir George suddenly rose up in bed, his eyes fixed with a yearning gaze at the opposite end of the room. Not at the cabinet this time, but at some spot, far, far up, beyond the ceiling, as it appeared. His voice, startling in its clearness, rang through the air, and his arms were outstretched as if he were about to fly.

"Janet!—Janet!—Janet! Oh, my dear Janet, I am coming!"

He fell back and died. Did anything really appear to him, not visible to the mortal eyes around? Were his senses, in that moment of the soul's departure, opened to a glimpse of the world he was about to enter? It cannot be known. Had it been fiction it would not have been written here.

A little later, the bell of All Souls' Church, booming out over the town on the night air, told that Sir George Godolphin had passed away.

It was somewhat remarkable that another funeral, at which Thomas Godolphin was again chief mourner, should follow so closely upon Ethel's. A different sort of ceremony, this: a rare pageant. A pageant which was made up of plumes and trappings and decorated horses, and carriages and mutes and batons, and a line of attendants, and all the other insignia of the illustrious dead.   Ethel could be interred simply and quietly, but Sir George must be attended to the grave as the Godolphin of Ashlydyat.   I don't suppose poor Sir George rested any the better for it.

Sir George made an equitable will, but it proved a vexatious one to his widow.   Thomas had Ashlydyat : George, a fair sum of money ; the Miss Godolphins, each her portion ; and there were certain bequests to servants.   But little was left to Lady Godolphin : indeed, the amount of the bequest was more in accordance with what might be willed to a friend, than to a wife.   But, it was not in that that the grievance lay.   Lady Godolphin had the Folly, she had Broomhead, and she had an ample income of her own.   She was not a particularly covetous woman, and she had never expected or wished that Sir George should greatly take from his family, to add to it.   No, it was not that : but the contents of a certain little codicil which was appended to the will.   This codicil set forth that every article of furniture or property, which had been removed to the Folly from Ashlydyat,' whatever might be its nature, and down to the minutest item, should be returned to Ashlydyat, and become the property of Thomas Godolphin.

It would pretty nearly strip the Folly, and my lady was very wrathful.   Not for the value of the things : she sustained no injury there : for the codicil directed that a specified sum of money (their full value) should be handed over to Lady Godolphin to replace them with new at the Folly.   But it struck upon her in the light of a slight, and she chose to resent it as one.   It was specially enjoined that the things should be placed at Ashlydyat in the old spots where they had formerly stood.

But, be wrathful as she might, grumble as she would, there could be no rebellion to it in action.   And Lady Godolphin had to bow to it.

CHAPTER XVII.

A ROW ON THE WATER.

THE time went on.   Three months glided by ; nay, four, for April had come in : and positions were changed.   Thomas Godolphin was the resident master of Ashlydyat ; Janet its acting mistress ; Bessy and Cecil lived with them.   George had taken up his residence at the bank, with Margery to look after his comforts, never to remove from it, as he supposed, unless Ashlydyat should fall to him.   My lady had left the Folly for a permanency (unless any whim should at any time send her back to it), and the Verralls had taken it.   It may be said that Lady Godolphin gave up the Folly in a fit of pique.   When she found that the things were positively to go out of it, she protested that she would never replace them with others : she would rather throw the money, left for the purpose, into the midst of the sea.   She would let it to any one who would take it, and go back to Broomhead for ever. Mr. Verrall heard of this, and made an application for it ; and my lady, still smarting, let it to him off-hand, accepting him as a yearly tenant. Whether she repented, or not, when the deed was done, and her anger had cooled down, could not be told : she took her farewell and departed for Scotland without betraying signs of it. Many thought that she would return after a while to the place which she had so eagerly and fondly erected. Perhaps she might : she could get rid of the Verralls at any time by giving them due notice.

Thomas had settled down in his father's place : head of the bank, head of all things, as Sir George had been ; Mr. Godolphin, of Ashlydyat. Mr. George was head of himself alone. No one of very particular note was he : but I can tell you that a great many more anxious palpitations were cast to him from gentle bosoms, than were given to unapproachable Thomas. It seemed to be pretty generally conceded that Thomas Godolphin was wedded to the grave of Ethel. Perhaps his establishing his sisters at Ashlydyat, as their home, helped to further the opinion, and dash all hopes ; but, very possible hopes from many quarters were wafted secretly to George. He would be no mean prize : with his good looks, his excellent position, and his presumptive heirdom to Ashlydyat.

April, I say, had come in. A sunny April. And these several changes had taken place, and the respective parties were settled in their new homes. It went forth to the world that the Verralls intended to give a brilliant fête, a sort of house-warming, as they styled it ; and invitations were circulated far and wide. Amongst those favoured with one, were Mr. and the Miss Godolphins.

Janet was indignant. She could scarcely bring herself to decline it civilly. Cecil, who was not less fond of fêtes, and other gay inventions for killing time, than are pretty girls in general, would have given her head to go. It appeared that Mrs. Hastings also declined the invitation : and George Godolphin—who had no intention of declining it on his own score—resolved to know the reason why.

Though not a frequent visitor at the Rectory : for he could not go there much, in the teeth of discouragement so evident as had latterly been shown to him by Mr. Hastings, and depended mostly upon chance meetings in the street for keeping in exercise his love-vows to Maria : George resolved to go boldly down that evening.

Down he accordingly went. And was shown into an empty room. The Rector and Mrs. Hastings were out, the servant said, and the young ladies were in the study with the boys. She would tell them.

Maria came to him. There was no mistaking her start of surprise when she saw him, or the rush of emotion which overspread her face.

"Who did you think it was?" asked George.

"I thought it was your brother. She said 'Mr. Godolphin.' Grace will be down in an instant."

"Will she?" returned George. "You had better go and tell her it's Mr. George, and not Mr. Godolphin, and then she won't hurry herself. I am not a favourite with Miss Grace, I fancy."

Maria coloured. She had no excuse to offer for the fact, and she could not say that it was untrue. George stood with his elbow on the mantel-piece, looking down at her.

"Maria, I hear that Mrs. Hastings has declined to go to the Folly on Thursday. What's that for?"

"I don't know," replied Maria. "We do not go very much amidst those unusually grand scenes," she added, laughing. "Mamma says she always feels as much out of place in them as a fish does out of water. And I think, if papa had his own wish, we should never go within a mile of anything of the sort. He likes quiet social visiting, but not such entertainments as the Verralls give. He and mamma were consulting for a few minutes over the invitation, and then she directed Grace to write and decline it."

"It is an awful shame!" responded George. "I thought I should have had you with me for a few hours that day, at any rate, Maria."

Maria lifted her eyes. "It had nothing to do with me, George. I was not invited."

"Not invited!" repeated George Godolphin.

"Only Grace. 'Mrs. and Miss Hastings.'"

"What was that for?" he exclaimed. "Why were you left out?"

"I do not know," replied Maria, bending her eyelids and speaking with involuntary hesitation. In her heart of hearts, Maria believed that she did know: but the last person she would have hinted it to, was George Godolphin. "Perhaps," she added, "it may have been an omission, an oversight? Or, they may have so many to invite that they can only dispense their cards charily."

"Moonshine!" cried George. "I shall take upon myself to ask Mrs. Verrall why you were left out."

"Oh, George! pray don't," she uttered, feeling an invincible repugnance to have her name brought up in any such way. "Why should you? Had the invitation been sent to me, I should not have gone."

"It is a slight," he persisted. "A little later, and let any dare to show slight to you. They shall be taught better. A slight to you will be a slight to me."

Maria looked at him timidly, and he bent his head with a fond smile. "I shall want somebody to keep house for me at the bank, you know, Maria."

She coloured even to tears. Mr. George was proceeding to erase them after his own gallant fashion, when he was summarily brought-to by the entrance of Grace Hastings.

There was certainly no love lost between them. Grace did not like George, George did not like Grace. She took her seat demurely in her mother's chair of state, with every apparent intention of sitting out his visit. So George cut it short.

"What did he come for?" Grace asked of Maria, when the servant had showed him out.

"He came to call."

"You appeared to be in very close conversation when I came into the room," pursued Grace, searching Maria with her keen eyes. "May I ask its purport?"

"Its purport was nothing wrong," said Maria, her cheeks deepening under the inspection. " You question me, Grace, as if I were a child, and you possessed a right over me."

" Well," said Grace equably. " What was he talking of ? "

Yielding, timid, sensitive Maria was one of the last to resist this sort of importunity. " We had been talking of the Verralls not including me in the invitation. George said it was a slight."

" As of course it was," assented Grace. " And, for that fact alone, I am glad mamma sent them a refusal. It was Charlotte Pain's doings. She does not care that you should be brought too much into contact with George Godolphin, lest her chance should be perilled. Now, Maria, don't pretend to look at me in that incredulous manner ! You know as well as I do that George has a stupid liking for you ; or, at least, acts as though he had. And that naturally is not pleasant to Charlotte Pain."

Maria knew well that Grace had divined the true cause for the slight. She stood for a few minutes looking silent and humble : an intimation, even from Grace, that George " liked her," jarred upon her refined sensitiveness, when openly alluded to. But that feeling was almost lost in the dull pain which the hint touching Charlotte had called up.

" Charlotte Pain is nothing to George Godolphin," she resentfully said.

" Charlotte Pain *is*," responded Grace. " And if your eyes are not yet opened to it, they ought to be. She is to be his wife."

" Oh no, she is not," hastily said Maria.

" Maria, I tell you that she is. I know it."

Now Grace Hastings rarely made an assertion unless she had good grounds for it. Maria knew that. And the dull pain at her heart grew and grew, until it was beating with a sharp agony. She appeared impassive enough, looking down at her thin gold chain, which her fingers were unconsciously wreathing into knots. " You cannot know it, Grace."

" I tell you I do. Mind you, I don't say that they will inevitably be married ; only, that they contemplate being so at present. Charlotte does well not to make too sure of him ! George Godolphin may see half a dozen yet whom he will prefer to Charlotte Pain, in his roving, butterfly nature."

Was Grace right ? Not ten minutes before, Maria had listened to words from his lips which most surely intimated that it was herself George had chosen. Who was Charlotte ?—who was Charlotte Pain, that she should thus thrust herself between them ?

April, as we learn by its reputation, and by our own experience, mocks us with its weather : and not a few envious criticisers had pro- phesied showers, if not snow, for the fête at Lady Godolphin's Folly. The unusually lovely weather which had marked the month, so far as it had gone, had put it into Mrs. Verrall's head to give an outdoor entertainment. Mr. Verrall had himself suggested that the weather might change ; that there was no dependence, at this season of the year, to be placed on it. But she would not give up her project. If the worst came to the worst at the last moment, she said, they must do the best they could with the people indoors.

But, for once, the weather was not fickle. The day rose warm, calm,

beautifully bright, and by three o'clock in the afternoon most of the gay
revellers had gathered at the Folly.

The grounds were dotted with them. These grounds, by the way,
were chiefly the grounds of Ashlydyat; those belonging to the Folly
being exceedingly limited in extent. Janet Godolphin drew down the
blinds of Ashlydyat, that the eyesore might be shut out: but Cecil
stole away to her room, and made herself a peep-hole—as the young
Hastingses had done at Ethel Grame's funeral—and looked out with
covetous eyes. Janet had said something to Thomas about sending a
hint to the Folly that the domains of Ashlydyat would not be open to
the guests: but Thomas, with his quiet good sense, had negatived it.

Graceless George arrived as large as life, one of the first. He was
making himself conspicuous among the many-coloured groups—or,
perhaps it was, that they made him so, by gathering round him—when
two figures in mourning came gliding up to him, one of whom spoke.

"How do you do, Mr. George Godolphin?"

George turned. And—careless and thoughtless as he was, graceless
as he was reported to be—a shock of surprise, not unmixed with indignation, swept over his feelings: for those standing before him were
Lady Sarah and Miss Grame.

She—Sarah Anne—looked like a shadow still; peevish, white, discontented. What brought them there? Was it *thus* that they showed
their regret for the dead Ethel?—Was it seemly that Sarah Anne
should appear at a fête of gaiety in her weak, sickly state; not yet
recovered from the effects of the fever; not yet out of the first deep
mourning·worn for Ethel?

"How do you do, Lady·Sarah?" very gravely responded George
Godolphin.

Lady Sarah may have discerned somewhat of his feeling from the
expression of his face. Not that he intentionally suffered it to rise in
reproof of her: George Godolphin did not set himself up in judgment
against his fellows. He, indeed! Lady Sarah drew him aside with
her, after he had shaken hands with Sarah Anne.

"I am sure it must look strange to you to see us here, Mr. George.
But, poor child, she continues so weak and poorly, that I scarcely
know what to do with her. She set her heart upon coming to this
fête. Since Mrs. Verrall's card arrived, she has talked of nothing else,
and I thought it would not do to cross her. Is Mr. Godolphin here?"

"Oh no," replied George, with more haste than he need have spoken.

"I thought he would not be. I remarked so to Sarah Anne, when
she expressed a hope of seeing him: indeed, I think it was that hope
which chiefly urged her to come. What have we done to him, Mr.
George? He scarcely ever comes near the house."

"I don't know anything about it," returned George. "I can see
that my brother still feels his loss deeply. It may be, Lady Sarah, that
visits to your house remind him too forcibly of Ethel."

Lady Sarah lowered her voice to a confidential whisper: "Will he
ever marry, think you?"

"At present I should be inclined to say he never would," answered
George, wondering what in the world it could matter to Lady Sarah,
and thinking she showed little sorrow or consideration for the memory

of Ethel. "But time works surprising changes," he added: "and time may marry Mr. Godolphin."

Lady Sarah paused. "How do you think she looks—my poor child?"

"Miserable," all but rose to the tip of George's tongue. "She does not look well," he said aloud.

"And she does so regret her dear sister; she's grieving after her always," said Lady Sarah, putting her handkerchief to her eyes.

"I don't believe it," thought George to himself.

"How do you like your new residence?" she resumed, passing with little ceremony to another topic.

"I like it very well. All places are pretty much alike to a bachelor, Lady Sarah."

"Ah, so they are. *You* won't remain a bachelor very long," continued Lady Sarah, with a smile of archness.

"Not so very long, I dare say," frankly acknowledged Mr. George. "It is possible I may put my head in the noose some time in the next ten years."

She would have detained him further, but George did not care to be detained. He went after more attractive companionship.

Chance, or premeditation, led him to Charlotte Pain. Charlotte had all her attractions about her that day. Her bright green silk dress—green was a favourite colour of hers—with its white lace mantle, was frequently to be seen by George Godolphin's side. Once they strayed to the borders of the stream, in a remote part of the grounds. Several were gathered here. A row on the water had been proposed, and a boat stood ready. A small boat, holding very few; but, of those few, George and Charlotte made two.

Could George Godolphin have foreseen what that simple little excursion in the boat was to do for him, he had never entered it. How is it, that no shadow of warning comes over us at these times? How many a day's pleasure, begun as a jubilee, how many a voyage, entered upon in hope, ends but in death! Not a fortnight since; since *now*, the very hour at which I am writing; a fine young lad, fresh from his studies, was going out to one of our colonies, full of youth, of hope, of prospects. Two ships were available for the passage, one as eligible as the other: which should he choose? It seemed not to matter which of them, and the choice was made. Could no warning rise up to his aid, ever so indefinite, and point away from the chosen one and say it must be shunned? The vessel sailed. And she went down—within sight of land—not three days out; and every soul on board, except one, perished. "If we had only chosen the other ship for him!" wail that lad's mourning friends. Ay! if we could only lift the veil, what mistakes might be avoided!

George Godolphin, strong and active, took the oars. And when they had rowed about to their heart's content, and George was in a white heat with exertion, they bethought themselves that they would land for a while on what was called the mock island: a mossy spot, green and tempting to the eye. In stepping ashore, Charlotte Pain tripped, lost her balance, and would have been in the water but for George. He saved her, but he could not save her parasol: a dainty parasol, for which Miss Charlotte had given three guineas only the previous day. She naturally shrieked when it fell into the water : and George Godolphin, in recovering it, nearly lost *his* balance, and went in after the parasol. Nearly ; not quite : he got himself pretty wet, but he made light of it, and sat himself down on the grassy island with the rest.

They were all young. Old people seldom care to venture into these shallow skiffs : but, had any of mature age. been there, experienced in chills and rheumatism, they would certainly have ordered George Godolphin home at his utmost speed, for a change of clothes, and perhaps a glass of brandy.

Charlotte Pain was shaking the wet from her parasol, when some one noticed the, dripping state of George's coat. "It wants shaking also," said they. "Do pray take it off, Mr. George Godolphin !"

George took it off, shook it well, and laid it out in the sun to dry. And down he sat again, in his shirt-sleeves, passing some jokes upon his state of costume, and requesting to know what apology he must make for it.

By-and-by he began to feel rather chilled : in fact, he grew so cold that he put on his coat again, damp as it was. It might have occurred to him that the intense perspiration he had been in had struck inwardly, but it did not. In the evening he was dancing away with the best of them, apparently having escaped all ill effects from the wetting, and thinking no further of it.

Eh, but the young are heedless ! as Janet would have said.

CHAPTER XVIII.

STRAW IN THE STREETS.

ANKLE-DEEP before the banking-house of Godolphin, Crosse, and Godolphin, and for some distance on either side ; ankle-deep down Crosse Street as far as you could see, lay masses of straw. As carriages came up to traverse it, their drivers checked their horses and drove them at a foot-pace, raising their own heads to look up at the windows of the dwelling ; for they knew that one was lying there hovering between life and death.

It was George Godolphin. Imprudent George ! Healthy and strong as he might be, sound as his constitution was, that little episode of the fête-day had told upon him. Few men can do such things with impunity, and come out of them unscathed. "What was a bit of a ducking ; and that only a partial one ? Nothing." As George himself said to some remonstrator on the following day. It is not much, certainly, to those who are used to it : but taken in conjunction with a white heat, and with an hour or two's cooling upon the grass afterwards, in the airy undress of shirt-sleeves, it is a great deal.

It had proved a great deal for George Godolphin. An attack of rheumatic fever supervened, dangerous and violent, and neither Dr. Beale nor Mr. Snow could give a guess as to whether he would live or die. Miss Godolphin had removed to the bank to share with Margery the task of nursing him. Knockers were muffled; bells were tied up; straw, as you hear, was laid in the streets; people passed in and out, even at the swing doors, when they went to transact business, with a softened tread: and as they counted the cash for their cheques, leaned over the counter, and asked the clerks in a whisper whether Mr. George was yet alive. Yes, he was alive, the clerks could always answer, but it was as much as they could say.

It continued to be "as much as they could say" for nearly a month, and then George Godolphin began to improve. But so slowly! day after day seemed to pass without visible sign.

How bore up Maria Hastings? None could know the dread, the grief, that was at work within her, or the deep love she felt for George Godolphin. Her nights were sleepless, her days were restless; she lost her appetite, her energy, almost her health. Mrs. Hastings wondered what was wrong with her, and hoped Maria was not going to be one of those sickly ones who always seem to fade in the spring.

Maria could speak out her sorrow to none. Grace would not have sympathized with any feeling so strong, whose object was George Godolphin. And had Grace sympathized ever so, Maria would not have spoken it. She possessed that shrinking reticence of feeling, that refined sensitiveness, to which betraying its own emotions to another would be little less than death. Maria could not trust her voice to ask after him: when Mr. Hastings or her brothers would come in and say (as they had more than once), "There's a report in the town that George Godolphin's dead," she could not press upon them her eager questions, and ask, "Is it likely to be true? Are there any signs that it is true?" Once, when this rumour came in, Maria made an excuse to go out: some trifle to be purchased in the town, she said to Mrs. Hastings: and went down the street inwardly shivering, too agitated to notice acquaintances whom she met. Opposite the bank, she stole glances up at its private windows, and saw that the blinds were down. In point of fact, this told nothing, for the blinds had been kept down much since George's illness, the servants not troubling themselves to draw them up: but to the fears of Maria Hastings, it spoke volumes. Sick, trembling, she continued her way mechanically: she did not dare to stop, even for a moment, or to show, in her timidity, as much as the anxiety of an indifferent friend. At that moment Mr. Snow came out of the house, and crossed over.

Maria stopped then. Surely she might halt to speak to the surgeon without being suspected of undue interest in Mr. George Godolphin. She even brought out the words, as Mr. Snow shook hands with her: "You have been to the bank?"

"Yes, poor fellow; he is in a critical state," was Mr. Snow's answer. "But I think there's a faint indication of improvement, this afternoon."

In the revulsion of feeling which the words gave, Maria forgot her caution. "He is not dead, then?" she exclaimed, all too eagerly, her face turning to a glowing crimson, her lips apart with emotion.

Mr. Snow gathered in the signs, and a grave expression stole over his lips. But the next minute he was smiling openly. "No, he is not dead yet, Miss Maria; and we must see what we can do towards keeping him alive." Maria turned home again with a beating and a thankful heart.

A weary, weary summer for George Godolphin—a weary, weary illness. It was more than two months before he rose from his bed at all, and it was nearly two more before he went down the stairs of the dwelling-house. A fine, balmy day it was, that one in June, when George left his bed for the first time, and was put in the easy-chair, wrapped up in blankets. The sky was blue, the sun was warm, and bees and butterflies sported in the summer air. George turned his weary eyes, weary with pain and weakness, towards the cheering signs of outdoor life, and wondered whether he should ever be abroad again.

It was August before that time came. Early in that month the close carriage of Ashlydyat waited at the door, to give Mr. George his first airing. A shadowy object he looked, Mr. Snow on one side of him, Margery on the other; Janet, who would be his companion in the drive, following. They got him downstairs between them, and into the carriage. From that time his recovery, though slow, was progressive, and in another week he was removed for change to Ashlydyat. He could walk abroad then with two sticks, or with a stick and somebody's arm. George, who was getting up his spirits wonderfully, declared that he and his sticks should be made into a picture and sent to the next exhibition of native artists.

One morning, he and his sticks were sunning themselves in the porch at Ashlydyat, when a stranger approached and accosted him. A gentlemanly-looking man, in a straw hat, with a light travelling overcoat thrown upon his arm. George looked a gentleman also, in spite of his dilapidated health and his sticks, and the stranger raised his hat with something of foreign urbanity.

"Does Mr. Verrall reside here?"

"No," replied George.

A hard, defiant sort of expression rose immediately to the stranger's face. It almost seemed to imply that George was deceiving him: and his next words bore out the impression. "I have been informed that he does reside here," he said, with a stress upon the "does."

"He did reside here," replied George Godolphin: "but he does so no longer. That is where Mr. Verrall lives," he added, pointing one of his sticks at the white walls of Lady Godolphin's Folly.

The stranger wheeled round on his heel, took a survey of it, and then lifted his hat again, apparently satisfied. "Thank you, sir," he said. "The mistake was mine. Good morning."

George watched him away as he strode with a firm, quick, elastic step towards the Folly. George wondered when he should walk again with the same step. Perhaps the idea, or the desire to do so, impelled him to try it then. He rose from his seat and went tottering out, drawing his sticks with him. It was a tempting morning, and George strolled on in its brightness, resting now on one bench, now on another, and then bearing on again.

"I might get as far as the Folly, if I took my time," he said to himself. "Would it not be a surprise to them!"

So he bore onwards to the Folly, as the stranger had done. He was drawing very near to it, was seated, in fact, on the last bench that he intended to rest on, when Mr. Verrall passed him.

"Have you had a gentleman inquiring for you?" George asked him.

"What gentleman?" demanded Mr. Verrall.

"A stranger. He came to Ashlydyat, supposing you lived there. I sent him to the Folly."

"Describe him, will you?" said Mr. Verrall.

"I noticed nothing much to describe," replied George. "He wore a straw hat, and had a thin tweed coat over his arm. I should fancy he had just come off a journey."

Mr. Verrall left George where he was, and went back to the Folly. George rose and followed more slowly. But when he got beyond the trees, he saw that Mr. Verrall must have plunged into them : as if he would go into the Folly by the servants' entrance. George crossed the lawn, and made straight for the drawing-room windows, which stood open.

Scarcely had he entered, and flung himself into the first easy-chair, when he saw the same stranger approach the house. Where *had* he been, not to have found it before? But George immediately divined that he had taken the wrong turning near the ash-trees, and so had had the pleasure of a round to Prior's Ash and back again. The room was empty, and George sat recovering breath and enjoying the luxury of a rest, when the stranger's knock resounded at the hall-door.

A servant, as he could hear, came forth to open it ; but, before that was effected, flying footsteps followed the man across the hall, and he was called, in the voice of Charlotte Pain.

"James," said she, in a half-whisper, which came distinctly to the ear of George Godolphin, "should that be any one for Mr. Verrall, say nothing, but show him in here."

A second room, a smaller one, stood between the one George had entered, and the hall. It opened both to the drawing-room and the hall ; in fact, it served as a sort of anteroom to the drawing-room. It was into this room that the stranger was shown.

Charlotte, who had taken a seat, and was toying with some embroidery-work, making believe to be busy over it, rose at his entrance, with the prettiest air of surprise imaginable. He could have staked his life, had he been required to do it, that she knew nothing whatever of his approach until that identical moment, when James threw open the door, and announced, "A gentleman, ma'am." James had been unable to announce him in more definite terms. Upon his asking the stranger for a name, the curt answer had been, "Never mind the name. Mr. Verrall knows me."

Charlotte rose. And the gentleman's abruptness changed to courtesy at the sight of her. "I wish to see Mr. Verrall," he said.

"Mr. Verrall is in town," replied Charlotte.

"In town!" was the answer, delivered in an accent of excessive surprise. "Do you mean in London, madam?"

"Certainly," rejoined Charlotte. "In London."

"But he only left London last night to come here!" was the stranger's answer.

It brought Charlotte to a pause. Self-possessed as she was, she had to think a moment before hazarding another assertion. "May I inquire how you know that he left London last night for this?" she asked.

"Because, madam, I had business yesterday of the very last importance with Mr. Verrall. He made the appointment himself, for three o'clock. I went at three: and could not find him. I went at four, and waited an hour, with a like result. I went again at seven, and then I was told that Mr. Verrall had been telegraphed for to his country seat, and had started. I had some difficulty in finding out where his country seat was situated, but I succeeded in doing that: and I followed him in the course of the night."

"How very unfortunate!" exclaimed Charlotte, who had obtained her clue. "He was telegraphed for yesterday, and arrived in answer to it, getting here very late last night. But he could not stay. He said he had business to attend to in London, and he left here this morning by an early train. Will you oblige me with your name?" she added.

"My name, madam, is Appleby. It is possible that you may have heard Mr. Verrall mention it, if, as I presume, I have the honour of speaking to Mrs. Verrall."

Charlotte did not undeceive him. "When did you see Mr. Verrall last?" she suddenly inquired, as if the thought had just struck her.

"The day before yesterday. I saw him three times that day, and he made the appointment for the following one."

"I am so sorry you should have had a useless journey," said Charlotte, with much sympathy.

"I am sorry also," said the stranger. "Sorry for the delay this causes in certain arrangements; a delay I can ill afford. I will wish you good morning, madam, and start back by the first train."

Charlotte touched the bell, and curtsied her adieu. The stranger had the door open, when he turned round, and spoke again.

"I presume I may entirely rely upon what you tell me—that Verrall *has* gone back?"

"Oh, certainly," answered Charlotte.

Now, every syllable of this colloquy had reached the ears of George Godolphin. It puzzled him not a little. Were there *two* Verralls? The Verrall of the Folly, with whom he had so recently exchanged words, had certainly not been in London for a fortnight past, or anywhere else but in that neighbourhood. And what did Charlotte mean, by saying he had gone to town that morning?

Charlotte came in, singing a scrap of a song. She started when she saw George, and then flew to him in a glow of delight, holding out her hands.

What could he do, but take them? What could he do, but draw Charlotte down beside him on the sofa, holding them still? "How pleased I am to see you!" exclaimed Charlotte. "I shall think the dear old times are coming round again."

"Charlotte mia, do you know what I have been obliged to hear? That interesting colloquy you have been taking part in in the next room."

Charlotte burst into a laugh. From the moment when she first caught a glimpse of George, seated there, she had felt sure that he must have heard it. "Did I do it well?" she cried, triumphantly.

" How could you invent such fibs?"

"Verrall came upstairs to me and Kate," said Charlotte, laughing more merrily than before. " He said there was somebody going to call here, he thought with a begging petition, and he did not care to see him. Would I go and put the man off? I asked him how I should put him off, and he answered, ' Any way. Say he had gone to London, if I liked.'"

Was Charlotte telling truth or falsehood? That there was more in all this than met the eye was evident. It was no business, however, of George Godolphin's, neither did he make it his.

"And you have really walked here all the way by yourself!" she resumed. " I am so glad ! You will get well now all one way."

" I don't know about getting well ' all one way,' Charlotte. The doctors have been ordering me away for the winter."

" For the winter!" repeated Charlotte, her tone growing sober. "What for? Where to?"

"To some place where the skies are more genial than in this cold climate of ours," replied George. " If I wish to get thoroughly well, they say, I must start off next month, September, and not return until April."

" But—should you go alone?"

"There's the worst of it. We poor bachelors are like stray sheep— nobody owning us, nobody caring for us."

" Take somebody with you," suggested Charlotte.

" That's easier said than done," said George.

Charlotte threw one of her brilliant glances at him. She had risen, and was standing before him, all her attractions in full play. "There's an old saying, Mr. George Godolphin, that where there's a will, there's a way," quoth she.

George made a gallant answer, and they were progressing in each other's good graces to their own content, when an interruption came to it. The same servant who had opened the door to the stranger entered.

"Miss Pain, if you please, my master says will you go up to him."

" I declare you make me forget everything," cried Charlotte to George, as she left the room. And picking up her King Charley, she threw it at him. " There ! take care of him, Mr. George Godolphin, until I come back again."

A few minutes after, George saw Mr. Verrall leave the house and cross the lawn. A servant behind him was bearing a small portmanteau and an overcoat, similar to the one the stranger had carried on his arm. Was Mr. Verrall also going to London?

CHAPTER XIX.

ONE STICK DISCARDED.

THE morning sun shone on the green lawn, on the clustering flowers, rich in many colours, sweet in their perfume, before the breakfast-room at Ashlydyat. The room itself was in shadow: as it is pleasant in summer for a room to be: but the windows stood open to the delights of outdoor life.

Janet presided at the breakfast-table. She always did preside there. Thomas, Bessy, and Cecil were disposed around her; leaving the side next the windows vacant, that nothing might come between them and the view of the summer's morning. A summer that would soon be on the wane, for September was approaching.

"She ought to be here by four o'clock," observed Bessy, continuing the conversation. "Otherwise, she cannot be here until seven. No train comes in from Farnley between four o'clock and seven, does it, Thomas?"

"I think not," replied Thomas Godolphin. "But I really know very little about their branch lines. Stay. Farnley? No: I remember: I am sure that nothing comes in between four and seven."

"Don't fash yourselves," said Janet with composure, who had been occupied with the urn. "When Mrs. Briscow sends me word she will arrive by the afternoon train, I know she can only mean the one that gets here at four o'clock: and I shall be there at four in the carriage to meet her. She is early in her ideas, and she would have called seven the night train."

Cecil, who appeared to be more engaged in toying with the black ribbons that were flowing from the white sleeves round her pretty wrists, than in taking her breakfast, looked up at her sister. "How long is it since she was here last, Janet?"

"She was here the summer after your mother died."

"All that time!" exclaimed Cecil. "It is very good of her to leave her home at her age, and come amongst us once again."

"It is George who is bringing her here; I am sure of that," returned Janet. "She was so concerned about his illness. She wants to see him now he is getting better. George was always her favourite."

"How is George this morning?" inquired Thomas Godolphin.

"George is alive and pretty well," replied a voice from the door, which had opened. There stood George himself.

Alive decidedly; but weak and wan still. He could walk with the help of one stick now.

"If I don't make an effort—as somebody says, in that bookcase—I may remain a puny invalid for ever, like a woman. I thought I'd try and surprise you."

They made a place for him, and placed a chair, and set good things before him; all in affectionate eagerness. But George Godolphin could not accomplish much breakfast yet. "My appetite is capricious,

Janet," he observed. "I think to-morrow I will try chocolate and milk."

"A cup can be made at once, George, if you would like it."

"No, I don't care about it now. I suppose the doctors are right that I can't get into proper order again, without change. A dull time of it, I shall have, whatever place they may exile me to."

A question had been mooted, bringing somewhat of vexation in its discussion, as to who should accompany George. Whether he should be accompanied at all, in what he was pleased to term his exile : and if so, which of them should be chosen. Janet could not go ; or thought she could not ; Ashlydyat wanted her. Bessy was deep in her schools, her district-visiting, in parish affairs generally, and openly said she did not care to quit them just now. Cecil was perfectly ready and willing. Had George been going to the wilds of Africa, Cecil would have entered on the journey with enthusiasm : the outer world had attractions for Cecil and her inexperience. But Janet did not deem it expedient to trust pretty Cecil to the sole guardianship of thoughtless George, and that was put down ere Cecil had well spoken of it. George's private opinion was—and he spoke it publicly—that he should be better without any of them than with them ; that they would "only be a trouble." On one point, he turned restive. Janet's idea had been to despatch Margery with him ; to see after his comforts, his medicines, his well-aired beds, and his beef-tea. Not if he knew it, George answered. Why not set him up at once with a lady's-maid, and a nurse from the hospitals, in addition to Margery ? And he was pleased to indulge in so much ridicule upon the point, as to anger Janet and offend Margery.

"I wish I knew some fellow who was going yachting for the next six months, and would give me boat-room," observed George, stirring his tea listlessly.

"That *would* be an improvement !" said Janet, speaking in satire. "Six months' sea-sickness and sea-drenching would about do for you what the fever has left undone."

"So it might," said George. "Only that we get over sea-sickness in a couple of days, and sea-drenchings are wholesome. However, don't let it disturb your placidity : the yacht is wanting, and I am not likely to have the opportunity of trying it. No, thank you, Janet "—rejecting a plate she was offering him—" I cannot eat anything."

"Mrs. Briscow comes to-day, George," observed Bessy. "Janet is going to meet her at the station at four. She is coming purposely to see you."

"Very amiable of the old lady !" responded George. "It's a pity I am going out to dinner."

Thomas looked surprised. George was not yet in precisely dinner-visiting condition.

"I have promised Mrs. Verrall to get as far as the Folly this after-noon, and stay and dine with them. *En famille*, you know."

"Mr. Verrall is not at home," said Bessy.

"But she and Charlotte are," responded George.

"You know you must not be out in the night air, George."

"I shall be home by sundown, or thereabouts. Not that the night air would hurt me now."

"You cannot take rich dishes yet," urged Bessy again.

"Bien entendu. Mrs. Verrall has ordered an array of invalid ones: mutton-broth à l'eau, and boiled whiting au naturel," responded George, who appeared to have an answer ready for all dissentient propositions.

Janet interposed, looking and speaking very gravely. "George, it will be a great mark of disrespect to Mrs. Briscow, the lifelong friend of your father and your mother, not to be at home to sit at table with her the first day she is here. Only one thing could excuse your absence— urgent business. And, that, you have not to plead."

George answered tartly. He was weak from his recent illness, and like many others under the same circumstances, did not like being crossed in trifles. "Janet, you are unreasonable. As if it were necessary that I should break a promise, just for the purpose of dining with an old woman! There will be plenty of other days to dine with her. And I shall be at home this evening before you have risen from table."

"I beg you to speak of Mrs. Briscow with more respect, George. It cannot matter whether you dine at the Verralls' to-day or another day," persisted Janet. "I would not say a word against it, were it an engagement of consequence. You can go to the Folly any day."

"But I choose to go to-day," said George.

Janet fixed her deep eyes upon him, her gaze full of sad penetration, her voice changed to one of mourning. "Have those women cast a spell upon you, lad?"

It drove away George's ill-humour. He burst into a laugh, and returned the gaze: openly enough. "Not they, Janet. Mrs. Verrall may have spells to cast, for aught I know: it's Verrall's business, not mine: but they have certainly not been directed to me. And Charlotte——"

"Ay," put in Janet in a lower tone, "what of Charlotte Pain?"

"This, Janet. That I can steer clear of any spells cast by Charlotte Pain. Not but that I admire Charlotte very much," he added in a spirit of mischief. "I assure you I am quite a slave to her fascinations."

"Keep you out of her fascinations, lad," returned Janet in a tone of solemn meaning. "It is my first and best advice to you."

"I will, Janet, when I find them growing dangerous."

Janet said no more. There was that expression on her countenance which they well knew; telling of grievous dissatisfaction.

Rising earlier than his strength was as yet equal to, told upon George Godolphin: and by the middle of the day he felt so full of weariness and lassitude, that he was glad to throw himself on to the sofa in the large drawing-room, quiet and unoccupied then, wheeling the couch first of all with his feeble strength, close to the window, that he might be in the sunshine. Its warmth was grateful to him. He dropped asleep, and only woke considerably later, at the entrance of Cecil.

Cecil was dressed for the day, in a thin, flowing black dress, a jet necklace on her slender neck, jet bracelets on her fair arms. A fair flower was Cecilia Godolphin: none fairer within all the precincts of Prior's Ash. She knelt down by George and kissed him.

"We have been in to glance at you two or three times, George. Margery has prepared something nice for you, and would have aroused you to take it, only she says sleep will do you as much good as food."

"What's the time?" asked George, too indolent to take his own watch from his pocket.

"Half-past three."

"Nonsense!" cried George, partially starting up. "It can't be so late as that."

"It is, indeed. Janet has just driven off to the station. Don't rise this minute: you are hot."

"I wonder Janet let me sleep so long!"

"Why should she not? Janet has been very busy all day, and very——"

"Cross?" put in George.

"I was going to say silent," replied Cecil. "You vexed her this morning, George."

"There was nothing that she need have been vexed at," responded Mr. George.

Cecil remained for a few moments without speaking. "I think Janet is afraid of Charlotte Pain," she presently said.

"Afraid of Charlotte Pain! In what way?"

"George"—lowering her voice, and running her fingers caressingly through his bright hair as he lay—"I wish you would let me ask you something."

"Ask away," replied George.

"Ay, but will you answer me?"

"That depends," he laughed. "Ask away, Cely."

"_Is_ there anything between you and Charlotte Pain?"

"Plenty," returned George in the lightest possible tone. "As there is between me and a dozen more young ladies. Charlotte, happening to be the nearest, gets most of me just now."

"Plenty of what?"

"Talking and laughing and gossip. That's about the extent of it, pretty Cely."

Cecil wished he would be more serious. "Shall you be likely to marry her?" she breathed.

"Just as likely as I shall be to marry you," and he spoke seriously now.

Cecil drew a sigh of relief. "Then, George, I will tell you what it is that has helped to vex Janet. You know our servants get talking to Mrs. Verrall's, and her servants to ours. And the news was brought here that Charlotte Pain has said she should probably be going on a journey: a journey abroad, for six months or so: to some place where she should remain the winter. Margery told Janet: and —and——"

"You construed it, between you, that Charlotte was going to be a partner in my exile! What droll people you must all be!"

"There's no doubt, George, that Charlotte Pain was heard to say it."

"I don't know what she may have been heard to say. It could have borne no reference to my movements. Cecil?"

"Well?"

"Did you ever hear of old Max's hounds losing their scent?"

"No—I don't know. What do you mean?"

And while George Godolphin was laughing at her puzzled look, Margery came in. "Are you almost famished, Mr. George? How could you think of dropping off to sleep till you had had something to sustain you?"

"We often do things that we don't 'think' to do, Margery," quoth he, as he rose from the sofa.

Nothing more true, Mr. George Godolphin.

Ere long he was on his way to Mrs. Verrall's. Notwithstanding Janet's displeasure, he had no idea of foregoing his engagement. The society of two attractive women had more charms for listless George than quiet Ashlydyat. It was a lovely afternoon, less hot than it had been of late, and George really enjoyed it. He was beginning to walk so much better. That long sleep had rested and refreshed him, and he believed that he could walk well into Prior's Ash. "I'll try it to-morrow," thought George.

Up the steps, over the terrace, across to the open windows of the Folly. It was the easiest way in, and George was not given to un-necessary ceremony. He supposed he might find the ladies in the drawing-room, and he stepped over the threshold.

Only one was there. Charlotte. She did not see him enter. She was before a pier-glass, holding up her dog, King Charley, that he might snarl and bark at the imaginary King Charley in the glass. That other dog of hers, the ugly Scotch terrier which you have heard of before, and a third, looking something like a bull-dog, were leaping and howling at her feet. It would appear that nothing pleased Char-lotte better than putting her dogs into a fury. Charlotte wore a dark blue silk dress with shaded flounces, and a lighter blue silk jacket: the latter, ornamented with braidings and buttons of silver, somewhat after the fashion of her green riding-habit, and fitting as tightly to the shape. A well-formed shape!—and George Godolphin thought so, as she stood with her arms lifted, setting the dogs at the glass.

"Hi, King! Seize him, Charley! Go at him!—hiss! Tear him! bite him!—hiss-ss-ss!——"

The noisy reception by the other dogs of Mr. George Godolphin, brought the young lady's words and her pretty employment to a stand-still. She released the imprisoned dog from her arms, letting him drop anywhere, and turned to George Godolphin.

"Have you come at last? I had given you up! I expected you an hour and a half ago."

"And, to while away the time, you set your dogs on to snarl and fight!" returned he, as he took her hand. "I wonder you don't go distracted with the noise, Charlotte!"

"You don't like dogs! I often tell you so."

"Yes, I do—in their proper places."

Charlotte turned from him with a pout. The terrier jumped upon her.

"Down, Pluto, down! A gentleman here thinks I ought to hold you poor dogs at arm's length."

"At the yard's length, if you please, Charlotte," corrected George, who did not feel inclined to compromise his opinion. "Hark at them! they might be heard at Prior's Ash."

"And his name's George Godolphin, good Pluto!" went on Charlotte, doing all she possibly could, in a quiet way, to excite the dogs. "Down, then, Pluto! down!"

"I should muzzle you, Mr. Pluto, if you were mine," cried George, as the dog jumped up at him furiously, and then turned to attack his former adversary. "*Pluto!*" he continued, meaningly: "who gave him that name, Charlotte?"

"I did," avowed Charlotte. "And I named this other one King Charley, after his species. And this one is Deuce. What have you to say against the names?"

"Nothing," said George. "I think them very good, appropriate names," he added, his lips parting.

They were certainly very good dogs—if to make a most excruciating noise constitutes merit. George Godolphin, his nerves still in a shattered condition, lifted his hand wearily to his forehead. It brought Charlotte Pain to her recollection.

"Oh, George, I forgot! I did, really! I forgot you were not as strong yet as the rest of us. Be quiet, then, you three horrid brutes! Be quiet, will you! Go off, and quarrel outside."

Using her pointed toe rather liberally, Charlotte set herself to scatter the dogs. They were not very obedient. As soon as one was got out another sprang in, the noise never ceasing. Charlotte snatched up a basket of macaroons that happened to be on a side-table, and scattered the cakes on the terrace. "There, quarrel and fight over those!"

She put down the empty basket, closed the window to shut out the noise, and turned to George. Spreading out her dress on either side, after the manner once in vogue in ancient ballrooms she dropped him an elaborate curtsey.

"Mr. George Godolphin, what honour do you suppose is thrust upon me to-day?"

"You must tell me, Charlotte, if it's one you wish me to know," he answered. "I can never attempt to guess when I feel tired, as I do now."

"Your walk has tired you?"

"I suppose it has. Though I thought how well I felt as I came along."

"The great honour of entertaining you all by my own self is delegated to me," cried Charlotte gaily, dropping another curtsey. "I hope we shall not quarrel, as those dogs are doing."

"The honour of entertaining me!" he repeated, not grasping her meaning. "Entertaining me for what?"

"For dinner, sir. Mrs. Verrall has gone to London."

"No!" he exclaimed. He did not believe her.

Charlotte nodded. "She went at midday."

"But what took her away so suddenly?" exclaimed George, in surprise. "She had no intention yesterday of going."

"A freak. Or, impulse—if you like the word better. Kate rarely acts upon anything else. She has been expecting Verrall home these last three days; but he has neither come nor written: and this morning, after the post was in, she suddenly declared she'd go to town, and see what was keeping him." ·

"They may cross each other on the road."

"Of course they may: and Kate have her journey for her pains. That's nothing to her ·: she likes travelling. 'What am I to do with Mr. George Godolphin? Entertain him?' I said to her. 'I suppose you can contrive to do it,' she answered. 'I suppose I could,' I said. 'But, what about its being proper?' I asked, with a demure glance at George. "'Oh,' said Kate, 'it's proper enough, poor sick fellow: it would never do to disappoint him.' Therefore, sir, please take care that you behave properly, considering that a young lady is your hostess."

She threw a laughing glance at George; and, sitting down at the table, took a pack of beautifully painted cards from an ivory box, and began that delectable game that the French call "Patience." George watched her from the sofa where he was sitting. A certain thought had darted into his mind. What fit of prudence called it up? Did he think of Charlotte's good?—or of his own? Did the recollection of what Cecil had whispered actuate him? It cannot be told. It was very far indeed from George Godolphin's intention to make a wife of Charlotte Pain, and he may have deemed it well to avoid all situations where he might compromise himself by a hasty word. Such words are more easily dropped than taken up again. Or perhaps George, free and careless though he was, reflected that it was not altogether the thing for Charlotte Pain to entertain him alone. With all his faults, George Godolphin was a gentleman: and Charlotte was not altogether fitted for a gentleman's wife.

"I am glad of it, Charlotte," he remarked. "I shall now have to make excuses to one only, instead of to two. I came to ask Mrs. Verrall to allow me to break through my engagement."

Charlotte had a knave in her hand, pondering where she could place it. She dropped it in her surprise.

"I must dine at home to-day, Charlotte. An old friend of my father and mother's, Mrs. Briscow, is arriving for dinner. I cannot be absent."

The flush deepened on Charlotte's face. "It is unkind of you!" she resentfully said. "But I knew before what your promises are worth."

"Unkind? But, Charlotte, I did not know until this morning that Mrs. Briscow was coming to-day. There's nothing unkind about it."

"It *is* unkind!" flashed Charlotte. "If you were not unkind, you would not leave me here alone, to pass a solitary evening and play at this wretched 'patience.'"

"But I am not going to leave you here. I wish to take you back with me to Ashlydyat to dinner. If you will put on your bonnet, we can be walking thither at once."

"You did not come intending to ask me."

"I did not. I did not know that Mrs. Verrall would be absent. But I ask you now, being alone as you say. And I intend to take you."

"What will Miss Godolphin say?"

"Miss Godolphin will be very happy to see you." Which little assertion Mr. George knew to contain more politeness than truth. "Will you get ready, Charlotte? I must be returning."

Charlotte pushed the cards from her in a heap, and came and stood before George Godolphin, turning herself about for his inspection. "Shall I do without further embellishment?" she asked.

"Admirably," was the gallant answer. "Why dress more for Ashlydyat than you would for home?"

Charlotte marched to the glass and surveyed herself. "Just something in my hair," she said, ringing the bell.

A maid came in by her desire, and fastened some blue and silver flowers in her hair. Charlotte Pain wore her hair capriciously : rarely two days alike. To-day it was all strained back from the face, that most trying of all styles, let the features be ever so pretty. A shawl was thrown over her shoulders, and then she turned to George.

"I am ready now."

"But your bonnet?" returned that gentleman, who had looked on with laughing eyes at the mysteries of the hair-dressing.

"I shall not put on a bonnet," she said. "They can bring it to me to Ashlydyat, for returning at night. People won't meet us : the road's not a public road. And if they should meet us," she added, laughing, "they will rejoice in the opportunity of seeing me abroad like this. It will be food for Prior's Ash."

So they started. Charlotte would not take his arm : she said he must take hers : he needed support and she did not. That, George would not agree to : and they strolled on, side by side, resting on benches occasionally. George found he had not much to boast of yet, in the way of strength.

"Who's this, coming up?" exclaimed Charlotte, when they had almost gained Ashlydyat, and were resting for the last time.

George followed the direction of her eyes. Advancing towards Ashlydyat was a lady, her grey silk dress gleaming in the sun, a light Cashmere shawl folded round her. There was no mistaking the ladylike figure of Mrs. Hastings.

"Is she to be one of your dinner-party?"

"Not that I am aware of."

Mrs. Hastings joined them. She sat down on a bench by George's side, affectionately inquiring into his state of health, speaking kindly and truthfully her pleasure at seeing him, so far, well again. Whatever prejudice may have been taken against George Godolphin by the Rector of All Souls', it did not extend to his wife. She liked him much.

"I am getting on famously," said George, in a merry tone. "I have promoted myself now to one stick : until yesterday I was forced to use two. You are going to Ashlydyat, Mrs. Hastings?"

"I wish to say a few words to Bessy. We have discovered something unpleasant relating to one of the schools, in which the undermistress is mixed up. A good deal of deceit has been going on, in fact. Mr. Hastings says Bessy ought to hear of it at once, for she was as much interested in it as we are. So I came up."

Mrs. Hastings, in speaking, had taken two or three glances at Charlotte's head. That young lady set herself to explain. Mr. George Godolphin had given her an impromptu invitation to go back with him to dine at Ashlydyat.

Then George explained. He had been engaged to dine at the Folly: but found, on arriving, that Mrs. Verrall had departed for London. "My friends are all kind to me, Mrs. Hastings," he observed. "They insist upon it that a change of a few hours must benefit me, and encumber themselves with the trouble of a fanciful invalid."

"I am sure there's nothing like change and amusement for one growing convalescent," said Charlotte.

"Will you let us contribute in some little way to it?" asked Mrs. Hastings of George. "If a few hours' sojourn in our quiet house would be agreeable to you, you know that we should only be too happy for you to try it."

"I should like it of all things," cried George, impulsively. "I cannot walk far yet without resting, and it is pleasant to sit a few hours at my walk's end, before I begin to start back again. I shall soon extend my journeys to Prior's Ash."

"Then come to us the first day that you feel able to get as far. You will always find some of us at home. We will dine at any hour you like, and you shall choose your own dinner."

"A bargain," said George.

They rose to pursue their way to Ashlydyat. Mrs. Hastings offered her arm to George, and he took it with thanks. "He would not take mine!" thought Charlotte, and she flashed an angry glance at him.

The fact was, that for some considerable time Charlotte Pain had put Maria Hastings almost out of her head, as regarded her relations to George Godolphin. Whatever reason she may have seen at Broomhead to believe he was attached to Maria, the impression had since faded away. In the spring, before his illness, George had been much more with her than with Maria. This was not entirely George's fault: the Rectory did not court him : Charlotte Pain and the Folly did. A week had now passed since Mr. Verrall's departure for town, when George and his sticks appeared at the Folly for the first time after his illness; and, not a day of that week since but George and Charlotte had met. Altogether, her hopes of winning the prize had gone up to enthusiastic heat; and Charlotte believed the greatest prize in the world—taking all his advantages collectively—to be George Godolphin. George went at once to his sister Janet's chamber. She was in it, dressing for dinner, after bringing her aged guest, Mrs. Briscow, from the station. He knocked at the door with his stick, and was told to enter.

Janet was before the glass in her black silk dress, trimmed heavily with crape still. She was putting on her sober cap, a white one, with black ribbons. Janet Godolphin had taken to wear caps at thirty years of age : her hair, like Thomas's, was thin; and she was not troubled with cares of making herself appear younger than she was.

"Come in, George," she said, turning to him without any appearance of surprise.

"See how good I am, Janet!" he cried, throwing himself wearily into a chair. "I have come back to dine with you."

"I saw you from the window. You have been walking too far!"

"Only to the Folly and back. But I sauntered about, looking at the flowers, and that tires one far worse than bearing on steadily."

"Ay. Lay yourself down on that couch at full length, lad. Mrs. Hastings is here, I see. And—was that other Charlotte Pain?"

"Yes," replied George, disregarding the injunction to lie down.

"Did she come from the Folly in that guise?—Nothing on her head but those flowers? I could see no bonnet even in her hand."

"It is to be sent after her. Janet"—passing quickly from the other matter—"she has come to dine with us."

Miss Godolphin turned in amazement, and fixed her eyes reproachfully on George. "To dine with us?—to-day? Have you been asking her?"

"Janet, I could not well help myself. When I got to Lady Godolphin's Folly, I found Charlotte alone: Mrs. Verrall has departed for town. To break through my engagement there, I proposed that Charlotte should come here."

"Nay," said Janet, "your engagement was already broken, if Mrs. Verrall was away."

"Not so. Charlotte expected me to remain."

"Herself your sole entertainer?"

"I suppose so."

A severe expression arose to Miss Godolphin's lips, and remained there. "It is most unsuitable, Charlotte Pain's being here to-day," she resumed. "The changes which have taken place render our meeting with Mrs. Briscow a sad one; no stranger ought to be at table. Least of all, Charlotte Pain. Her conversation is at times unfeminine."

"How can you say so, Janet?" he involuntarily exclaimed.

"Should she launch into some of her favourite topics, her horses and her dogs, it will sound unfeminine to Mrs. Briscow's ears. In her young days—in *my* days also, George, for the matter of that—these subjects were deemed more suitable to men's lips than to young women's. George, had your mother lived, it would have been a sore day to her, the one that brought the news that you had fixed your mind on Charlotte Pain."

"It was not so to my father, at any rate," George could not help saying.

"And was it possible that you did not see how Charlotte Pain played her cards before your father?" resumed Janet. "Not a word, that could offend his prejudices as a refined gentleman, did she ever suffer herself to utter. I saw; if you did not."

"You manage to see a great deal that the rest of us don't see, Janet. Or you fancy that you do."

"It is no fancy, lad. I would not like to discourage a thing that you have set your heart upon; I would rather go a mile out of my way than do it: but I stand next door to a mother to you, and I can but warn you that you will repent it, if you ever suffer Charlotte Pain to be more to you than she now is."

George rose. "Set your mind at rest, Janet. It has never been my intention to marry Charlotte Pain: and—so far as I believe at present —it never will be,"

The dinner went off pleasantly. Mrs. Briscow was a charming old lady, although she was of the "antediluvian" school, and Charlotte was on her best behaviour, and half fascinated Mrs. Briscow. George, like a trespassing child, received several hints from Janet that bed might be desirable for him, but he ingeniously ignored them, and sat on. Charlotte's bonnet and an attendant arrived, and Thomas Godolphin put on his hat to see her to the Folly.

"I need not trouble you, Mr. Godolphin. I shall not be run away with."

"I think it will be as well that I should see you do not," said he, smiling.

It was scarcely dark. The clock had not struck ten, and the night was starlight. Thomas Godolphin gave her his arm, and the maid walked behind them. Arrived at Ashlydyat, he left her. Charlotte stood for a few moments, then turned on her heel and entered the hall. The first thing that caught her notice was a hat; next a travelling coat. They had not been there when she left in the afternoon.

"Then Verrall's back!" she mentally exclaimed.

Hastening into the dining-room, she saw, seated at a table, drinking brandy and water, not Mr. Verrall, but Rodolf Pain.

"Good gracious!" exclaimed Charlotte, with more surprise in her tone than satisfaction, "have *you* come?"

"Come to find an empty house," rejoined Mr. Pain. "Where's Mrs. Verrall? They tell me she is gone to London."

"She is," replied Charlotte. "Verrall neither came back nor wrote; she had a restless fit upon her, and started off this morning to him."

"Verrall won't thank her," observed Mr. Pain. "He is up to his eyes in business."

"Good or bad business?" asked Charlotte.

"Both. We have got into a mess, and Verrall's not yet out of it."

"Through what? Through whom?" she questioned.

Rodolf Pain gave his shoulders a jerk, as if he had been a Frenchman. "It need not trouble you, Charlotte."

"Some one came down here from London a week ago; a Mr. Appleby. Is it through him? Verrall seemed strangely put out at his coming."

Mr. Pain nodded his head. "They were such idiots in the office as to give Appleby the address here. I have seen Verrall in a tolerable passion once or twice in my life, but I never saw him in such a one as he went into when me came up. They'll not forget it in a hurry. He lays the blame on me, remotely; says I must have left a letter about with the address on it. I know I have done nothing of the sort."

"But what is it, Rodolf? Anything very bad?"

"Bad enough. But it can be remedied. Let Verrall alone for getting out of pits, however deep they may be. I wish, though, we had never set eyes on that fellow, Appleby!"

"Tell me about it, Rodolf."

Mr. Rodolf declined. "You could do no good," said he, "and business is not fitted for ladies' ears."

"I don't care to know it," said Charlotte. "It's no concern of mine: but, somehow, that man Appleby interested me. As to business not being fitted tor my ears, I should make a better hand at business than some of you men make."

"Upon my word, I think you would, Charlotte. I have often said it. But you are one in a thousand."

"Have you had anything to eat since you came in?"

"They brought me some supper. It has just gone away."

"I had better inquire whether there's a room ready for you?" she remarked, moving towards the bell.

"It's all done, Charlotte. I told them I had come to stay. Just sit down, and let me talk to you."

"Shall you stay long?"

"I can't tell until I hear from Verrall to-morrow. I may be leaving again to-morrow night, or I may be here for interminable weeks. The office is to be clear of Mr. Verrall just now, do you understand?"

Charlotte apparently did understand. She took her seat in a chair listlessly enough. Something in her manner would have told an accurate observer that she could very well have dispensed with the company of Rodolf Pain. He, however, saw nothing of that. He took his cigar-case from his pocket, selected a cigar, and then, by way of sport, held the case out to Charlotte.

"Will you take one?"

For answer, she dashed it out of his hand half way across the room. And she did it in anger, too.

"How uncertain you are!" he exclaimed, as he rose to pick up his property. "There are times when you can take a joke pleasantly, and laugh at it."

He sat down again, lighted his cigar, and smoked a few minutes in silence. Then he turned to her. "Don't you think it is time, Charlotte, that you and I brought ourselves to an anchor?"

"No, I don't," she bluntly answered.

"But I say it is," he resumed. "And I mean it to be done."

"*You* mean!"

Something in the tone roused him, and he gazed at her with surprise. "You are not going from your promise, Charlotte?"

"I don't remember that I made any distinct promise," said she.

Mr. Rodolf Pain grew heated. "You know that you did, Charlotte. You know that you engaged yourself irrevocably to me——"

"Irrevocably!" she slightingly interrupted. "How you misapply words!"

"It was as irrevocable as promise can be. Have you not led me on, this twelvemonth past, believing month after month that you would be my wife the next? And, month after month, you have put me off upon the most frivolous pretexts!"

He rose as he spoke, drew up his little figure to its utmost height in his excitement, and pushed back his light hair from his small, insignificant face. A face that betrayed not too much strength of any sort, physical, moral, or intellectual; but a good-natured face withal. Charlotte retained unbroken calmness.

"Rodolf, I don't think it would do," she said, with an air of candid reasoning. "I have thought it over and over, and that's why I have put you off. It is not well that we should all be so closely connected together. Better get new ties, that will shelter us, in case a—a——"

"A what?" asked Rudolf Pain, his eyes strained on Charlotte through their very light lashes.

"In case a smash comes. That—if we are all in the same boat—would ruin the lot. Better that you and I should form other connections."

"You are talking great nonsense," he angrily said. "A smash!—to us! Can't you trust Verrall better than that?"

"Why, you say that, even at this present moment——"

"You are wrong, Charlotte," he vehemently interrupted; "you entirely misunderstand me. Things go wrong in business temporarily; they must do so in business of all sorts; but they right themselves again. Why! do you know what Verrall made last year?"

"A great deal."

"My little petty share was two thousand pounds: and that is as a drop of water to the ocean compared with his. What has put you upon these foolish fancies?"

"Prudence," returned Charlotte.

"I don't believe it," was the plain answer. "You are trying to blind me. You are laying yourself out for higher game; and to shut my eyes, and gain time to see if you can play it out, you concoct a story of 'prudence' to me. It's one or the other of those Godolphins."

"The Godolphins!" mockingly repeated Charlotte. "You are clever! The one will never marry as long as the world lasts; the other's dead."

"Dead!" echoed Rodolf Pain.

"As good as dead. He's like a ghost, and he is being sent off for an everlasting period to some warmer climate. How ridiculous you are, Rodolf!"

"Charlotte, I'll take care of ways and means. I'll take care of you and your interests. Only fix the time when you will be mine."

"Then I won't, Rodolf. I don't care to marry yet awhile. I'll see about it when the next hunting season shall be over."

Rodolf Pain opened his eyes. "The hunting season!" he cried. "What has that to do with it?"

"Were you my husband, you would be forbidding me to hunt; you don't like my doing it now. So for the present I'll remain mistress of my own actions."

"Another lame excuse," he said, knitting his brow. "You will take very good care always to remain mistress of your own actions, whether married or single."

Charlotte laughed, a ringing laugh of power. It spoke significantly enough to Mr. Rodolf Pain. He would have renewed the discussion, but she peremptorily declined, and shaking hands with him, wished him good night.

CHAPTER XX.

A REVELATION TO ALL SOULS' RECTOR.

GEORGE GODOLPHIN was not long at availing himself of the invitation to All Souls' Rectory. The very day after it was given, he was on his way to it. He started with his stick: made one halt at a shop on his road, and arrived about twelve o'clock.

Not a soul was at home but Maria. Mrs. Hastings, who had not expected him for some days, for she did not suppose his strength would allow him to get so far yet, had gone out with Grace. Mr. Hastings was in the church, and Maria was alone.

She sat in that one pleasant room of the house, the long room looking to the lawn and the flower-beds. She looked so pretty, so refined, so quiet in her simple dress of white muslin, as she pursued her employment, that of drawing, never suspecting how she was going to be interrupted.

The door of the porch stood open, as it often did in summer, and George Godolphin entered without the ceremony of knocking. The hall was well matted, and Maria did not hear him cross it. A slight tap at the room door.

"Come in," said Maria, supposing it to be one of the servants.

He came in and stood in the doorway, smiling down upon her. So shadowy, so thin! his face utterly pale, his dark blue eyes unnaturally large, his wavy hair damp with the exertion of walking. Maria's heart stood still. She rose from her seat, unable to speak, the colour going and coming in her transparent skin; and when she quietly moved forward to welcome him, her heart found its action again, and bounded on in tumultuous beats. The very intensity of her emotion caused her demeanour to be almost unnaturally still.

"Are you glad to see me, Maria?"

It was the first time they had met since his illness; the first time for more than four months. All that time separated; all that time fearing he was about to be removed by death! As he approached Maria, her emotion broke forth—she burst into tears; and surely it may be excused her.

He was scarcely less agitated. He clasped her tenderly to him, and kissed the tears from her face, his own eyelashes glistening. There was no great harm in it after all; for that each looked forward to the hope of being bound together at no great distance of time by nearer and dearer ties, was indisputable. At least no harm would have come of it, if—— Look at the window.

They did. And there they saw the awful face of the Rector glaring in upon them, and by its side, the more awful of the two, that of Charlotte Pain.

Why had she followed George Godolphin to the Rectory? Was she determined not to allow him a single *chance* of escaping her? She, bearing in remembrance the compact with Mrs. Hastings, had watched

George Godolphin's movements that morning from the windows of the Folly; had watched the by-road leading to the Rectory. She saw George and his stick go tottering down it: and by-and-by she put on her things and went out too, imperatively declining the escort of Mr. Rodolf Pain.

Her intention was to make a call at the Rectory—all unconscious of course that she should find Mr. George Godolphin there. By dint of a little by-play with Mrs. Hastings—who was too thoroughly a lady to be given to suspicion—she might receive an invitation to remain also for the day. With these very laudable intentions Charlotte arrived opposite All Souls' Church, where she caught sight of the Reverend Mr. Hastings emerging from the door. She crossed the churchyard, and accosted him.

" Is Mrs. Hastings at home, do you know? I am going to call upon her ? "

Now Charlotte was no great favourite of that gentleman's: nevertheless, being a gentleman, he answered her courteously as he shook hands. He believed Mrs. Hastings and Grace were out, he said, but Maria was at home.

" I am moped to death ! " exclaimed Charlotte, as she and Mr. Hastings entered the private gate to the Rectory garden. " Mrs. Verrall is gone to London, and there am I ! I came out intending to go the round of the town until I could find some good Samaritan or other who would take compassion on me, and let me stay an hour or two with them."

Mr. Hastings gave no particular reply. He did not make for the side door of the house, his usual entrance from the church, but turned towards the front, that he might usher in Charlotte in state. This took them by the windows of the drawing-room : and there they saw —what has been recorded. Mr. Hastings, in his astonishment, halted : Charlotte halted also, as you may be very sure.

George was the first to see them, and a word of anger broke from his lips. Maria hastily raised her head from its resting-place—and felt almost as if she should die. To be seen thus by Charlotte Pain was bad enough : but by her strict father ! Her face grew white.

George Godolphin saw the signs. " My darling, only be calm ! Leave all to me."

That an explanation was forced upon him somewhat prematurely, was undoubted. But it was no unwelcome explanation. Nay, in the second moment, he was deeming it the very best thing that could have happened : for certain visions of taking Maria with him into exile had crossed his brain lately. He would try hard now to get them realized. It is true he would have preferred, all things considered, not to speak before Miss Charlotte Pain : but necessity, as you know, has no law.

The Rector came in at the door : Charlotte following. " Mr. George Godolphin ! " he frigidly began ; but George interrupted what he would have further said.

" I beg your pardon, sir," he said, taking a step forward ; " allow me one word of explanation before you cast blame on me. I was asking your daughter to be my wife. Will you give her to me ? "

Mr. Hastings looked as a man confounded. That he was intensely

surprised at the words was evident: perhaps he half doubted whether
Mr. George Godolphin was playing with him.   He cast a severe glance
at Maria.   George had taken her on his arm, and she stood there
shrinking, her head drooping, her eyelashes resting on her white cheek.
As for Charlotte Pain? well, you should have seen her.

Ah no, there was no deception.   George was in true earnest, and
Mr. Hastings saw that he was.   His eyes were fixed beseechingly on
those of Mr. Hastings, and emotion had brought the hectic to his
wasted cheek.

"Do not blame Maria, sir," he resumed.   "She is innocent of all
offence, and dutiful as innocent.   Were you to interpose your veto
between us, and deny her to me, I know that she would obey you, even
though the struggle killed her.   Mr. Hastings, we have loved each
other for some time past: and I should have spoken to you before, but
for my illness intervening.   Will you give her to me at once, and let
her share my exile!"

Mr. Hastings had no insuperable objection to George Godolphin.
That report had given Mr. George credit for bushels and bushels of
wild oats, which he would have to sow, was certain: but in this respect
he was no worse than many others, and marriage is supposed to be a
cure for youthful follies.   Mr. Hastings had once suspected that Maria
was acquiring more liking for George than was good for her: hence
his repulsion of George, for he believed that he was destined for Charlotte Pain.   Even now he could not comprehend how it was, and the
prominent feeling in his mind was surprised perplexity.

"I love her as my own life, sir.   I will strive to render her happy."

"I cannot understand it," said Mr. Hastings, dropping his tone of
anger.   "I was under the impression—I beg your pardon, Miss Pain,"
turning to her, "but I was under the impression that you were engaged
to Mr. George Godolphin!"

If ever Charlotte Pain had need to fight for composure, she had dire
need then.   Her hopes were suddenly hurled to the ground, and she
had the cruel mortification of hearing him, whom she best loved, reject
and spurn her for a long-hated rival.   If her love for George Godolphin
was not very deep or refined—and it was neither the one nor the other
—she did love him after a fashion; better, at any rate, than she loved
any one else.   The *position* she would take as George Godolphin's wife
was hurled from her; and perhaps Miss Charlotte cared for that more
than she did for George himself.   The Verralls and their appearance of
wealth were all very well in their places—as George had said by the
dogs—but what were they, compared with the ancient Godolphins?
There are moments which drive a woman to the verge of madness,
and Charlotte was so driven now.   Anything like control of temper was
quite beyond her: and malevolence entered her heart.

"I engaged to Mr. George Godolphin!" she echoed, taking up the
Rector's words in a shrieking tone, which she could not have helped
had her life depended on it.   "Engaged to a married man?   Thank
you, Mr. Hastings."

"A married man!" repeated the puzzled Rector.   Whilst George
turned his questioning eyes upon her.

"Yes, a married man," she continued, her throat working, her breath panting. "They may have chosen to hoodwink you, to blind you, Mr. Hastings, but I saw what I saw. When your daughter—innocent Miss Maria there—came home from Scotland, she had been married to George Godolphin. A false priest, a sort of Gretna Green man, had married them : and I saw it done. *I* engaged to George Godolphin!"

Charlotte Pain knew that the words were false : called up to gratify her rage in that angry moment. Scarcely anything else that she could conjure up would so have told upon the Rector. In his straightforward right-doing, to his practical mind, a clandestine marriage appeared one of the cardinal sins. His face turned pale, and his eye flashed as he grasped Maria's shoulder.

"Girl! is this so?"

"Oh, papa, no!" returned Maria, with streaming eyes. "It is a wicked untruth. Charlotte! to tell such an untruth *is* wicked. Papa, I affirm to you——"

"Hush, Maria," interposed George, "let me deal with this. Mr. Hastings, it is a thing that you need scarcely *ask* of your daughter— whether it is true, or untrue. Is she one, think you, to enter into a clandestine marriage? You know better, sir. Nothing has ever passed between myself and Maria more than has passed before you this day. Were I thoughtless enough to solicit her to enter into one—and you need not think of *me* a whit better than you choose—Maria would only repulse me. Miss Pain, will you unsay your words?"

For answer, Miss Pain entered into a scornful account of Sandy Bray and his doings. She reiterated her assertion. She declared that she saw Maria and George standing before him, their hands clasped togethe in the attitude of a couple being married, when she entered suddenly with a message from Lady Godolphin, and she finished up by saying she had always believed since that they were married, only it had been no business of hers to proclaim it. The Rector's brow grew moist again, and George Godolphin looked significantly at Charlotte. He spoke significantly, too.

"No, you have not thought it, Charlotte." And he turned and related to Mr. Hastings as much as he knew of Sandy Bray, emphatically repeating his denial. "If you will take a moment's thought, sir, you may be convinced that the truth lies with me. I am beseeching you to give Maria to me; I crave it of you as the greatest boon that I can ask in life. I know not whether you will yield to my petition : but, what argument could I urge, to induce it, with half the force of the one that she was already secretly my wife? Nay, were she indeed so, why should I care for the ceremony to be repeated? I should only have to confess it, and throw myself and my wife upon your forgiveness. I heartily wish it had been so!"

"You are bold, Mr. George Godolphin!"

"Bold, sir?" returned George, with emotion. "Not more bold than I ought to be. I don't care to defend myself, but I do care to defend Maria. Give her to me, Mr. Hastings! give her to me!" he added, changing his tone to one of tender entreaty. "I will defend her through life with my best blood."

Mr. Hastings looked at him; looked at the tearful, but certainly not guilty countenance of his daughter; turned and looked at the furious one of Charlotte Pain. " Step this way," he said to George Godolphin. " I would speak to you alone."

He took him to another room, and shut the door. " I want the truth," he said, " upon one or two points——"

" Mr. Hastings," said George, drawing himself up, " I have told you nothing but the truth upon all points."

" Were you never engaged to Charlotte Pain?" proceeded Mr. Hastings, taking no notice of the interruption.

" Never. I never sought or wished to be."

" Then what did your good father, Sir George, mean, when he alluded to it the night he was dying? He asked if you and Charlotte were married yet, and you replied, ' Plenty of time for that.' "

" I said it merely in answer to his words : it was not an hour for dissent or explanation. He was not conscious of what he said."

" Had you expressed to him any particular liking for Charlotte Pain?"

" I had not; at any time. Sir George believed Miss Pain had a large fortune, and he recommended me, more than once, to think of her, and it. He said she was a handsome girl, and none the worse for possessing a fortune. He had heard she would have thirty thousand pounds. I used to laugh it off. I cared for Maria too much to cast a thought to Charlotte Pain. That is the whole truth, Mr. Hastings, on my honour."

" Would he have objected to Maria?"

" To Maria I am certain he would not have objected. To her want of fortune he might. But that is a thing that only concerns myself. I do not require fortune with my wife, and I do not seek it. You will give her to me, Mr. Hastings? You will dispense with unnecessary ceremony, and let her go abroad with me?" he urged. " She will do me more good than all else."

" I will give you no promise of any sort, Mr. George Godolphin. As to taking her abroad with you, it is absurd to think of it. And no daughter of mine shall enter a family where she is not sure of a hearty welcome. I must first know the sentiments of yours."

George looked radiant. " Mr. Hastings, if they heartily welcome Maria, will you allow *me* to welcome her?"

" Possibly I may."

" Then it is an affair decided. Janet will be relieved of a nightmare ; and Maria is, I believe, Thomas's prime favourite in all the world, now that Ethel is gone."

" Of what nightmare will it relieve Miss Godolphin?" inquired the Rector.

A smile crossed George's lips. " She, like you, has been fearing that I intended to connect myself with Charlotte Pain. Only yesterday I assured Janet that she was mistaken ; but I scarcely think she placed entire faith in me. She does not like Miss Pain."

" Do you think you have pursued a wise course in giving cause for this talk, regarding Miss Pain?"

" I have not given cause to Miss Pain herself, Mr. Hastings," replied George, warmly. " I am convinced that she has known in her heart of my attachment to Maria. As to whiling away a few hours with her occasionally in idle talk, it is a pastime that Charlotte Pain is given to favour."

"And myself also," Mr. George might have added.

They left the room together. A servant came up to Mr. Hastings as he was crossing the hall, and said an applicant at the door craved speech of him. The Rector turned to it, and George entered the drawing-room alone.

Maria stood, pale, anxious, excited, leaning against a corner of the window, half shrouded by the muslin curtains. She scarcely dared look up when George entered. It was not *his* gaze that she dreaded to meet, but that of Mr. Hastings. To anger or displease her father was wormwood to Maria.

George cast a glance round the room. "Where's Charlotte Pain?" he asked.

"She is gone," was Maria's answer. "Oh, George!" clasping her hands, and lifting to him her streaming eyes : "it was cruel of her to say what she did!"

"I could give it a better name than that, Maria. Never mind : we can afford to be generous to-day."

"Is papa fully convinced that—that I do not deserve blame?"

"He was convinced of that before he left this room. You are to be mine, Maria," he softly added in a whisper. "And very shortly. I must take you abroad with me."

She stood before him, not daring to look up now: shrinking from his ardent gaze, the crimson mantling to her pure cheek.

"Mr. Hastings demurs at the haste ; calls it absurd," continued George; "but, if you will consent to waive ceremony, surely he may do so. Which would be more absurd, Maria? your marrying without the three months' preparation for millinery deemed necessary by fashion, or my going away alone for an indefinite period, perhaps to die."

"Not to die, George!" she involuntarily answered in a tone painfully beseeching—as if he held the fiat of life or death in his own hands. "But—about the haste—I don't know—— I heard you thought of departing soon?"

"I ought to be away in a fortnight's time."

That startled her. "A fortnight's time!" she echoed, in a voice of alarm. "Then it could not be. What would Prior's Ash say?"

"Maria," he gravely answered, "some nine months ago, when Sarah Anne Grame was seized with fever, my brother, alarmed for Ethel's safety, would have married her hastily, so that he might have the right to remove her from danger. Ethel's answer to him was, 'What would Prior's Ash say?'—as you have now answered me. Thomas bowed to it : he suffered the world's notions to reign paramount—and he lost Ethel. What value do you suppose *he* sets now upon the opinions of Prior's Ash? The cases may not be precisely parallel, but they are sufficiently so to decide me. If I go away from home, I take you : if I may not take you, I do not go. And now, my darling, I will say farewell to you for the present."

She was surprised. She thought he had come to stay for some hours.

" Yes," he replied ; " but affairs have changed since I entered. Until they shall be more definitively settled, Mr. Hastings will not care that I remain his guest."

He bent to kiss her.   Not in the stolen manner he had been accustomed to, but—quietly, gravely, turning her shy face to his, as if it were his legal province so to do.   " A little while, young lady," he saucily whispered, " and you will be giving me kiss for kiss."

Mr. Hastings was in the porch still, holding a colloquy with ill-doing and troublesome Mrs. Bond.   George held out his hand as he passed.

" You have not rested yourself," said the Rector.

" I shall get back as far as the bank and rest there," replied George. " I presume, sir, that you intend to see my brother ? "

" And also Miss Godolphin," curtly said the Rector.

His eyes followed George down the path to the gate, as he and his stick moved unsteadily along.   " Marry now ! " mentally cried Mr. Hastings, his brow contracting : " he looks more fit to take to his bed, and keep it.   Now, Mrs. Bond," he added aloud, " let me hear the conclusion of this fine tale."

George took his way to the bank.   He had not passed it in coming, having cut across from Ashlydyat by the nearer way at the back of the town.   He took them by surprise.   Mr. Crosse was out, but the clerks were warm in their congratulations ; they had not believed him yet equal to the exertion.

" You look very tired," said Thomas, when they were alone in the bank parlour.

" I feel fagged to death," was George's answer.   " I must get you to send out for a fly for me, and go home in that.   Thomas," he continued, plunging into his business abruptly, " I expect you will have an application made to you, regarding me."

" In what way ? " quietly asked Thomas.

" Well—it is not exactly a certificate of character that's required," returned George, with a smile.   " I—I am thinking of getting married. Will you approve of it ? "

" I have no right to disapprove," said Thomas, in a kind, grave tone.   " You are your own master ; free to act as you shall judge best. I only hope, George, that you will, in choosing, consider your future happiness."

" Has it never occurred to you that I have chosen ? "

" I used to think at times that you had chosen, or felt inclined to choose, Maria Hastings."

" Right," said George.   " I have been speaking to Mr. Hastings, and it appears to have taken him entirely by surprise.   He would give me no answer until he should have ascertained whether the alliance would be agreeable to you and Janet.   He is a man of crotchets, you know. So I expect he will be coming to you, Thomas."

Thomas Godolphin's eyes lighted up with pleasure.   " He shall receive my hearty approval," he said, warmly.   " George "—changing his tone to sadness—" in the days gone by I thought there were two young beings superior to the rest of the world : Ethel and Maria."

" I said so to Mr. Hastings.   I conclude he fears that Maria's want of fortune would render her unpalatable to my family," remarked George.

"Certainly not to me. Ethel, whom I chose, had even less. If you think well to dispense with fortune in your wife, George, we have no right to object to it. I am *glad* that you have chosen Maria Hastings."

But there was Janet yet to come. George went home in a fly, and threw himself on the first sofa he could find. Janet, full of concern, came to him.

"I said you were attempting too much, George!" she cried. "But you never will listen to me."

"I'm sure, Janet, I listen to you dutifully. I have come home to consult you now," he added, a little spirit of mischief dancing in his gay blue eyes. "It is not fatigue or illness that has brought me. Janet, I am going to be married."

Janet Godolphin's pulses beat more quickly. She sat down and folded her hands with a gesture of pain. "I knew it would be so. You need not have tried to deceive me yesterday, lad."

"But the young lady's friends refuse her to me, unless my family openly sanction and approve of the match," went on George. "You'll be kindly over it, won't you, Janet?"

"No, lad. I cannot forbid it; I have no authority over you: but, sanction it, I never will. What has put it into your head to marry in this haste? You, with one foot in the grave, as may be said, and one out of it?"

"Well, you see, Janet, you won't trust me abroad without some one to look after me," he slowly answered, as if he were arguing some momentous question. "You say you can't go, and Bessy can't go, and Cecil may not, and I say I won't have Margery. What was I to do, but marry? I cannot take a young lady, you know, without first marrying her."

Janet Godolphin's grave eyes were fixed on vacancy, and her thin lips drawn in to pressure. She did not answer.

"Thomas heartily approves," he continued. "I have been with him."

"Thomas must do as he likes," said Janet. "But, unless you have unwittingly misunderstood him, George, you are telling me a deliberate falsehood. He will never approve of your marrying Charlotte Pain."

"Charlotte Pain!" repeated George, with an air of as much surprise as if it were genuine, "who was talking about Charlotte Pain? What put her into your head?"

Janet's face flushed. "Were *you* not talking of Charlotte Pain?"

"Not I," said George. "In spite of the compliments you pay my truthfulness, Janet, I *meant* what I said to you yesterday—that I did not intend to make her my wife. I am speaking of Maria Hastings."

"Eh, lad, but that's good news!"

George burst into a laugh. "What green geese you must all have been, Janet! Had you used your eyes, you might have detected this long time past that my choice was fixed on Maria. But the Rector doubts whether you will approve. He will not promise her to me until he has your sanction."

"I'll put my shawl on and go down at once to the Rectory, and tell him that we all love Maria," said Janet, more impulsively than was common with her: but in truth she had been relieved from a great fear. There was something about Charlotte Pain that frightened sedate Janet. Compared with her, Maria Hastings appeared everything that was desirable as a wife for George. Her want of fortune, her want of position—which was certainly not equal to that of the Godolphins—were lost sight of.

"I could manage to take some broth, Janet," cried George, as she was leaving the room. "I have had nothing since breakfast."

"To be sure. I am growing forgetful. Margery shall wait upon you, my dear. But, to go down to the Rectory without delay, is a courtesy due from me."

So, no impediment was placed upon the marriage. Neither was any impediment placed upon its immediate celebration: the Rector permitting himself to be persuaded into it.

CHAPTER XXI.

CHARLOTTE'S BARGAIN.

THREE weeks after that momentous day at All Souls' Rectory, George Godolphin and Maria stood before the Rector in All Souls' Church. George did not appear very ill now; he was not so shadowy, his fine complexion had returned, and stick the second was discarded. Maria was beautiful. Her soft bridal robes floated around her, her colour went and came as she glanced shyly up at George Godolphin. A handsome couple; a couple seldom seen.

It was quite a private marriage so to say; but few guests being present, and they relatives, or very close friends. Lady Godolphin had responded to the invitation (which Janet had not expected her to do), and was the guest of Ashlydyat. Very superb was she in silks and jewels this day. Old Mrs. Briscow had also remained for it. Mr. Crosse was present, and some relatives of the Hastings family: and Grace and Cecil were bridesmaids. The Rector joined their hands, speaking the necessary words slowly and emphatically; words that bound them to each other until death.

Then came the breakfast at the Rectory, and then the going away. The carriage waited at the gate. The Rector laid his hand upon George Godolphin's arm as he was going out to it, and addressed him in a low tone.

"I have confided her to you in entire trust. You will cherish her in all love and honour?"

"Always!" emphatically pronounced George, grasping the Rector's hand. "You shall never have cause to repent the gift."

Thomas Godolphin was placing Maria in the carriage. She looked out through her tears, nodding her last adieus. George took his place beside her, and the postboy started on the first stage towards Dover.

As they were passing the house of Lady Sarah Grame, by which their route lay, that lady herself sat at the window, as did also Sarah Anne ; both on the tiptoe of curiosity, beyond all doubt. Between them, laughing and talking with a gay air, and looking out, stood Charlotte Pain. Maria gave vent to an involuntary exclamation.

Another moment, and they had whirled by, beyond view. George turned impulsively to Maria and drew her closer to him. "Thank God ! thank God !" he earnestly said.

" For what ? " she murmured.

" That *you* are mine. Maria, I dreamt last night that I had married Charlotte Pain, and that you were dying. The dream has been haunt-ng me all day. I can laugh at it now, thank God !"

In the gayest and lightest room of Lady Godolphin's Folly, its windows open to the green slopes, the gay flowers, the magnificent prospect which swept the horizon in the distance, was Mrs. Verrall. She lay back in a *fauteuil*, in the vain, idle, listless manner favoured by her ; toying with the ribbons of her tasty dress, with the cluster of gleaming trifles on her watch-chain, with her gossamer handkerchief, its lace so fine in texture that unobservant eyes could not tell where the cambric ended and the lace began, with her fan which lay beside her, tapping her pretty foot upon an ottoman in some impatience; there she sat, displaying her conscious charms, and waiting for any callers, idle and vain as herself, who might arrive to admire them.

At a distance, in another *fauteuil*, listless and impatient also, sat Rodolf Pain. Time hung heavily on Mr. Pain's hands just now. He was kept a sort of prisoner at Lady Godolphin's Folly, and it appeared to be the chief business of Charlotte Pain's life to be cross to him. Three weeks had his sojourn there lasted: and though he had hinted to Charlotte on his arrival that he might remain a goodly number of weeks—interminable weeks, was the expression, I think—he had not really expected to do so ; and the delay was chafing him. What particular business might be keeping Mr. Pain at Prior's Ash it is not our province at present to inquire : what his especial motive might be for rather shunning observation than courting it, is no affair of ours. He did not join Mrs. Verrall in her visiting : he had an innate dislike to visitors—to "fine people," as he phrased it. Even now, if any carriage drove up and deposited its freight at the Folly, it would be the signal for Mr. Rodolf Pain to walk out of the drawing-room. He was shy, and had not been accustomed to society. He strolled in and out all day in his restlessness, nearly unnoticed by Mrs. Verrall, fidgeting Charlotte Pain; a cigar in his mouth, and his hands in his pockets; sauntering about the grounds, flinging himself into chairs, one sentence of com-plaint for ever on his lips : " I wish to goodness Verrall would write ! "

But Verrall did not write. Mrs. Verrall had received one or two short notes from him after her return from London—where she had stayed but twenty-four hours—and all the allusion in them to Mr. Pain had been, " Tell Rodolf he shall hear from me as soon as possible." Rodolf could only wait with what patience he might, and feel himself like a caged tiger, without its fierceness. There was no fierceness about Rodolf Pain—timidity rather than that.

A timidity for which Charlotte despised him. Had he been more bold and self-asserting, she might have accorded him greater respect.

What could have possessed Charlotte ever to engage herself to Rodolf Pain, would be a mystery for curious minds to solve, only that such mysteries are enacted every day. Engagements and marriages apparently the most incongruous take place. This much may be said for Charlotte: that let her enter into what engagement she might, she would keep it or break it, just as whim or convenience suited her. Rodolf Pain's thoughts, as he sat in that chair, were probably turned to this very fact, for he broke the silence suddenly by a pertinent question to Mrs. Verrall.

"Does she *never* mean to marry?"

"Who?" languidly asked Mrs. Verrall.

"Charlotte, of course. I have nothing to do with anybody else, that I should ask. She faithfully promised to be my wife: you know she did, Mrs. Verrall—— "

"Don't talk to me, Rodolf," apathetically interrupted Mrs. Verrall. "As if I should interfere between you and Charlotte!"

"I think you are in league together to snub me, Mrs. Verrall, she and you; that's what I think," grumbled Rodolf. "If I only remind her of her promise, she snaps my nose off. Are we to be married, or are we not?"

"It is no affair of mine, I say," said Mrs. Verrall, "and I shall not make it one. I had as soon Charlotte married you, as not; but I am not going to take an active part in urging it—probably only to be blamed afterwards. This is all I can say, and if you tease me more, Rodolf, I shall trouble you to walk into another room."

Thus repulsed, Rodolf Pain held his tongue. He turned about in his chair, stretched out his feet, drew them in again, threw up his arms with a prolonged yawn, and altogether proved that he was going wild for want of something to do. Presently he began again.

"Where's she off to?"

"Charlotte?" cried Mrs. Verrall. "She went into Prior's Ash. She said—yes, I think she said, she should call upon Lady Sarah Grame. Look there!"

Mrs. Verrall rose from her seat, and ran to a farther window, whence she gained a better view of the high-road, leading from Ashlydyat to Prior's Ash. A chariot-and-four was passing slowly towards the town. Its postboys wore white favours, and Margery and a manservant were perched outside. Mrs. Verrall knew that it was the carriage destined to convey away George Godolphin and his bride, who were at that moment seated at the breakfast at All Souls' Rectory, chief amidst the wedding guests.

"Then Margery does go abroad with them!" exclaimed Mrs. Verrall. "The servants had so many conflicting tales, that it was impossible to know which to believe. She goes as Mrs. George's maid, I suppose, and to see after him and his rheumatism."

"His rheumatism's well, isn't it?" returned Rodolf Pain.

"That is well; but *he's* not. He is weak as water, needing care still. Prudent Janet does well to send Margery. What should Maria Hastings know about taking care of the sick? I think they have shown excessively bad manners not to invite me to the breakfast," continued Mrs. Verrall, in a tone of acidity.

"Some one said it was to be quite a private breakfast: confined to relatives."

"I don't care," said Mrs. Verrall; "they might have made an exception in my favour. They know I like such things: and we lived in their house, Ashlydyat, and are now living at Lady Godolphin's Folly."

"That's where Charlotte's gone, I'll lay," cried Mr. Rodolf Pain.

Mrs. Verrall turned her eyes upon him with a slight accession of wonder in them. "Gone *there!* To the Rectory? Nonsense, Rodolf!"

"I didn't say to the Rectory, Mrs. Verrall. She wouldn't be so stupid as to go there without an invitation. She's gone about the town, to stare at the carriages, and look out for what she can see."

"Very possibly," returned Mrs. Verrall, throwing herself into her chair in weariness. "What has become of all the people to-day, that no one comes to call upon me? I should think they are stopping to look at the wedding."

Rodolf, in weariness as great, slowly lifted his body out of the chair, gave himself another stretch, and left the room. The curse of work! Never did work bring a curse half as great as that brought by idleness. Better break stones on the road, better work in galley-chains, than sit through the livelong day, day after day as the year goes round, and be eaten up by lassitude. Rodolf Pain's compulsory idleness was only temporary; he was away from his occupation only for a time: but Mrs. Verrall possessed no occupation from year's end to year's end. Her hands had no duties to perform, no labour to transact: she never touched anything in the shape of ornamental work; she rarely, if ever, opened a book. She was one of those who possess no resources within themselves: and, may Heaven have mercy upon all such!

By-and-by, after Rodolf had smoked two cigars outside, and had lounged in again, pretty nearly done to death with the effort to kill time, Charlotte returned. She came in at the open window, apparently in the highest spirits, her face sparkling.

"Did you hear the bells?" asked she.

"I did," answered Rodolf. "I heard them when I was out just now."

"The town's quite in a commotion," Charlotte resumed. "Half the ragamuffins in the place are collected round the Rectory gates: they had better let the beadle get amongst them!"

"Commotion or no commotion, I know I have not had a soul to call here!" grumbled Mrs. Verrall. "Where have you been, Charlotte?"

"At Lady Sarah's. And I have had the great honour of seeing the bride and bridegroom!" went on Charlotte, in a tone of complaisance so intense as to savour of mockery. "They came driving by in their carriage, and we had full view of them."

This somewhat aroused Mrs. Verrall from her listlessness. "They have started, then! How did she look, Charlotte?"

"Look!" cried Charlotte. "She looked as she usually looks, for all I saw. His cheeks were hectic; I could see that. Mr. George must take care of himself yet, I fancy."

"How was she dressed?" questioned Mrs. Verrall again.

"Could I see?—seated low in the carriage, as she was, and leaning back in it!" retorted Charlotte. "She wore a white bonnet and veil, and that's all I can tell you. Margery and Pearce were with them. Kate, don't you think Lady Sarah must *feel* this day? A few months ago, and it was her daughter who was on the point of marriage with a Godolphin. But she did not seem to think of it. She'd give her head for a daughter of hers to wed a Godolphin still."

Mrs. Verrall raised her eyes to Charlotte's with an expression of simple astonishment. The remark mystified her. Mrs. Verrall could boast little depth of any sort, and never saw half as far as Charlotte did. Charlotte resumed.

"*I* saw; *I* know: I have seen and known ever since Ethel died. My lady would like Sarah Anne to take Ethel's place with Thomas Godolphin."

"I can hardly believe that, Charlotte."

"Disbelieve it then," equally responded Charlotte, as she passed out to the terrace, and began calling to her dogs. They came noisily up in answer, and Charlotte disappeared with them.

And Mr. Rodolf Pain, sitting there in his embroidered chair, with a swelling heart, remarked that Charlotte had not vouchsafed the smallest notice to him. "I wouldn't stop another hour," he murmured to himself, "only that my going back would put up Verrall : and—and it might not do."

Very intense was that gentleman's surprise to see, not two minutes after, Mr. Verrall himself enter the room by the window. Mrs. Verrall gave a little shriek of astonishment; and the new-comer, throwing his summer overcoat upon a chair, shook hands with his wife, and gave her a kiss. Plenty of dust was mingled with his yellow whiskers, and his moustache.

"I came third-class most of the way," explained Mr. Verrall, as an apology for the dust. "The first-class carriage was stuffing hot, and there was no getting a smoke in it. We had a troublesome guard : the fellow excused himself by saying one of the directors was in the train."

"I have been all this time rubbing my eyes to find out whether they are deceiving me," cried Rodolf Pain. "Who was to dream of seeing you here to-day, sir?"

"I should think you expected to see me before, Rodolf," was Mr. Verrall's answer.

"Well, so I did. But it seemed to be put off so long, that I am surprised to see you now. Is—is all straight?"

"Quite straight," replied Mr. Verrall; "after an overwhelming amount of bother. You are going up to-day, Pain."

"And not sorry to hear it, either," cried Rodolf Pain, with emphasis. "I am sick of having nothing to do. Is Appleby settled?" he added, dropping his voice.

Mr. Verrall gave a nod; and, drawing Rodolf Pain to a far window, stood there talking to him for some minutes in an undertone. Mrs. Verrall, who never concerned herself with matters of business, never would listen to them, went out on the terrace, a pale pink parasol with its white fringe, held between her face and the sun. While thus standing, the distant bells of All Souls', which had been ringing occasional peals throughout the day, smote faintly upon her ear. She went in again.

"Verrall," said she, "if you come out, you can hear the bells. Do you know what they are ringing for?"

"What bells? Why should I listen to them?" inquired Mr. Verrall, turning from Rodolf Pain.

"They are ringing for George Godolphin's wedding. He has been married to-day."

The information appeared—as Rodolf Pain would have expressed it, had he given utterance to his sentiments—to strike Mr. Verrall all of a heap. "George Godolphin married to-day!" he repeated, in profound astonishment, remembering the weak state George had been in when he had left Prior's Ash, some weeks before. "Married or buried, do you mean?"

Mrs. Verrall laughed. "Oh, he has got well from his illness: or, nearly so," she said. "The bells would ring muffled peals, if he were buried, Verrall, as they did for Sir George."

"And whom has he married?" continued Mr. Verrall, not in the least getting over his astonishment.

"Maria Hastings."

Mr. Verrall stroked his yellow moustache; a somewhat recent appendage to his beauty. He was by no means a demonstrative man —except on rare occasions—and though the tidings evidently made a marked impression on him, he said nothing. "Is Charlotte at the wedding?" he casually asked.

"No strangers were invited," replied Mrs. Verrall. "Lady Godolphin came for it, and is staying at Ashlydyat. She has put off her weeds for to-day, and appears in colours: glad enough, I know, of the excuse for doing so."

"Where is Charlotte?" resumed Mr. Verrall.

He happened to look at Rodolf Pain as he spoke, and the latter answered, pointing towards some trees on the right.

"She went down there with her dogs. I'll go and find her."

Mr. Verrall watched him away, and then turned to his wife: speaking, however, impassively still.

"You say he has married Maria Hastings? How came Charlotte to let him slip through her fingers?"

"Because she could not help it, I suppose," replied Mrs. Verrall, shrugging her pretty shoulders. "I never thought Charlotte had any chance with George Godolphin, Maria Hastings being in the way. Had Charlotte been first in the field, it might have made all the difference. He had fallen in love with Maria Hastings before he ever saw Charlotte."

Mr. Verrall superciliously drew down his lips at the corners. "Don't talk about a man's 'falling in love,' Kate. Girls fall in love: men know better. Charlotte has played her cards badly," he added, with some emphasis.

"I don't know," said Mrs. Verrall. "That Charlotte would play them to the best of her ability, there's little doubt; but, as I say, she had no chance from the first. I think George did love Maria Hastings.

I'm sure they have been together enough, he and Charlotte, and they have flirted enough: but, as to caring for Charlotte, I don't believe George cared for her any more than he cared for me. They have gone abroad for the winter: will be away six months or more."

"I am sorry for that," quietly remarked Mr. Verrall. "I was in hopes to have made some use of Mr. George Godolphin."

"Use?" cried Mrs. Verrall. "What use?"

"Oh, nothing," carelessly replied Mr. Verrall. "A little matter of business that I was going to propose to him."

"Won't it do when he comes home?"

"I dare say it may," said Mr. Verrall.

Mr. Rodolf Pain had walked to the right, and plunged into the grove of trees in search of Charlotte. He was not long in finding her. The noise made by her dogs was sufficient guide to him. In one respect Charlotte Pain was better off than her sister, Mrs. Verrall: she found more resources for killing time. Charlotte had no greater taste for books than Mrs. Verrall had: if she took one up, it was only to fling it down again: she did not draw, she did not work. For some reasons of her own, Charlotte kept an ornamental piece of work in hand, which never got finished. Once in a way, upon rare occasions, it was taken up, and a couple of stitches done to it; and then, like the book, it was flung down again. Charlotte played well; nay, brilliantly: but she never played to amuse herself, or for the love of music—always for display. The resources which Charlotte possessed above Mrs. Verrall, lay in her horsemanship and her dogs. Mrs. Verrall could ride, and sometimes did so; but it was always in a decorous manner. She did not gallop, helter-skelter, across country, as Charlotte did, with half a dozen cavaliers barely keeping up with her: she took no pleasure in horses for themselves, and she would as soon have entered a pigsty as a stable. With all Mrs. Verrall's vanity, and her not over-strong intellect, she possessed more of the refinement of the gentlewoman than did Charlotte.

Look at Charlotte now: as Rodolf Pain—a cigar, which he had just lighted, between his lips, and his hands in his pockets—approaches her. She is standing on a garden bench, with the King Charley in her arms: the other two dogs she has set on to fight at her feet, their muzzles lying on the bench beside her. What with the natural tempers of these two agreeable animals, and what with Charlotte's frequent pastime of exasperating the one against the other, it had been found necessary to keep them muzzled to prevent quarrels: but Charlotte delighted in removing the muzzles, and setting them on, as she had done now. Charlotte had these resources in addition to any possessed by Mrs. Verrall. Mrs. Verrall would not, of her own free will, have touched a dog with her finger: if compelled to do so, it would have been accomplished in the most gingerly fashion with the extreme tip: and it was a positive source of annoyance to Mrs. Verrall, often of contention between them, Charlotte's admitting these dogs to familiar companionship. Charlotte, when weary from want of pastime, could find it in the stables, or with her dogs. Many an hour did she thus pass: and, so far, she had the advantage of Mrs. Verrall. Mrs. Verrall often told Charlotte that she ought to have been born a man: it cannot be denied that some of her tastes were more appropriate to a man than to a gentlewoman.

Rodolf Pain reached the bench. It was a lovely spot, secluded and shaded by trees; with an opening in front to admit a panoramic view of the enchanting scenery. But, on the mossy turf between that bench and the opening, snarled and fought those awful dogs: neither the noise nor the pastime particularly in accordance with that pleasant spot, so suggestive of peace. Charlotte looked on approvingly, giving a helping word to either side which she might deem required it; while the King Charley barked and struggled in her arms, because he was restrained from joining in the *mêlée*.

"I am going up at last, Charlotte."

"Up where?" asked Charlotte, without turning her eyes on Rodolf Pain.

"To town. Verrall's come back."

Surprise caused her to look at him now. "Verrall back!" she uttered. "He has come suddenly, then; he was not back five minutes ago. When are you going up?"

"I will tell you all about it if you'll muzzle those brutes, and so stop their noise."

"Muzzle them yourself," said Charlotte, kicking the muzzles on to the grass with her foot.

Mr. Pain accomplished his task, though he did not particularly like it; neither was it an easy one; the dogs were ferocious at the moment. He then drove them away, and Charlotte dropped her King Charley that he might run after them; which he did, barking his short squeaking bark. Rodolf held out his hand to help Charlotte down from the bench; but Charlotte chose to remain where she was, and seated herself on one of its arms. Rodolf Pain took a seat on the bench sideways, so as to face her, leaning his back against the other arm.

"When do you go?" repeated Charlotte.

"In an hour from this."

"Quick work," remarked Charlotte. "Verrall gives no time for the grass to grow in anything *he* has to do with."

"The quick departure is mine," said Mr. Pain. "So that I am in town for business to-morrow morning, it's all that Verrall cares about. He suggested that I should go up by a night train."

"*I* should," cried Charlotte, bluntly.

"No you would not," answered Rodolf Pain in a tone of bitterness. "Were you treated by any one as you treat me, you'd be glad enough to get away."

"That's good!" ejaculated Charlotte with a ringing laugh. "I'm sure I treat you beautifully. Many a one would jump at getting the treatment from me that I give you; I can tell you that, Mr. Dolf."

Mr. Dolf smoked on in silence; rather savagely for him.

"What have you to complain of?" pursued Charlotte.

"This," said he, sternly. "That you promised to be my wife; that you have led me on, Heaven knows how long, causing me to believe you meant what you said, that you would keep your promise; and now you coolly turn round and jilt me! That bare fact, is quite enough,

Charlotte, without going into another mortifying fact—your slighting behaviour to me lately."

"Who says I have jilted you—or that I mean to jilt you?" asked Charlotte.

"Who says it?" retorted Rodolf Pain. "Why—are you not doing so?"

"No. I dare say I shall have you some time."

"I am getting tired of it, Charlotte," said he, in a weary tone of pain. "I have cared for nothing but you in the world—in the shape of woman—but I am getting tired; and I have had enough to make me. If you will fix our wedding now, before I go up, and keep to it, I'll bless you for it, and make you a fonder husband than George Godolphin would have made you."

"How dare you mention George Godolphin to me in that way?" cried Charlotte, with flashing eyes, for the sentence had roused all her ire. "You ought to be ashamed of yourself, Dolf Pain! Has not George Godolphin—as it turns out—been engaged to Maria Hastings longer than I have known him, and has now married her? Do you suppose I could have spent that time with them both, in Scotland, at Lady Godolphin's, and not have become acquainted with their secret? That must prove what your senseless jealousy was worth!"

"Charlotte," said he, meekly, "as to George Godolphin, I readily confess I was mistaken, and I am sorry to have been so stupid. You might have set me right with a word, but I suppose you preferred to tease me. However, he is done with now. But, Charlotte, I tell you that altogether I am getting tired of it. Have me, or not, as you feel you can: but, played with any longer, I will not be. If you dismiss me now, you dismiss me for good."

"I have half a mind to say yes," returned Charlotte, in the coolest tone, as if she were deciding a trifling matter—the choice of a bonnet, or the route to be pursued in a walk. "But there's one thing holds me back, Dolf."

"What's that?" asked Dolf, whose cheek had lighted up with eager hope.

Charlotte leaped off the bench and sat down on it, nearer to Dolf, her accent and face as apparently honest as if fibs were unknown to her. "And it is the only thing which has held me back all along," she went on, staring unflinchingly into Dolf's eyes.

"Well, what is it?" cried he.

"The hazard of the step."

"The hazard!" repeated Dolf. "What hazard?"

Charlotte glanced round, as if to convince herself that nothing with human ears was near, and her voice dropped to a whisper. "You and Verrall are not upon the safest course——"

"It's as safe as many others," interrupted Dolf Pain.

"Don't bother about others," testily rebuked Charlotte. "Look to itself. I say that it is hazardous: what little I know of it tells me that. I have heard a word dropped by you and a word dropped by Verrall, and I can put two and two together as well as most people. Is there no danger, no chance," she spoke lower still, and with unmistakable gravity—"that a crisis might come, which—which would carry you to a place where nobody stands willingly—the Criminal Bar?"

"Good gracious, no!" cried Rodolf Pain, flinging his cigar away in his surprise and anger. "What could put that into your head, Charlotte? The—profession—may not be one of the strictest honour, and it has its dark sides as well as its light; but there's no danger of such a thing as you hint at. Where did you pick up the idea?"

"I don't know where. I have caught a word or two, not meant for me; and now and then I see things reported in the newspapers. You can't deny one thing, Dolf: that, if any unpleasantness should drop from the skies, it has been made a matter of arrangement that you should be the sufferer, not Verrall."

Rodolf's light eyes expanded beyond common. "How did you get to know that?" he asked.

"Never mind how I got to know it. Is it so?"

"Yes, it is," acknowledged Mr. Pain, who was by nature more truthful than Charlotte. "But I give you my word of honour, Charlotte, that there's no danger of our falling into such a pit as you have hinted at. We should not be such fools. The worst that could happen to me would be a sojourn, short or long, in some snug place such as this, while Verrall puts things right. As it has been now, for instance, through this business of Appleby's."

"You tell me this to satisfy me," said Charlotte.

"I tell it because it is truth—so far as my belief goes, and as far as I can now foresee."

"Very well. I accept it," returned Charlotte. "But now, Rodolf, mark what I say. If this worst state of things should come to pass——"

"It won't, I tell you," he interrupted. "It can't."

"Will you listen? I choose to put the matter upon a supposition that it may do so. If this state of things should come to pass and you fall, I will never fall with you; and it is only upon that condition that I will become your wife."

The words puzzled Mr. Pain not a little. "I don't understand you, Charlotte. As to 'conditions,' you may make any for yourself that you please—in reason."

"Very well. We will have an understanding with each other, drawn up as elaborately as if it were a marriage settlement," she said, laughing. "Yes, Mr. Rodolf, while you have been ill-naturedly accusing me of designs upon the heart of George Godolphin, I was occupied with precautions touching my married life with you. You don't deserve me; and that's a fact. Let go my hand, will you. One of those dogs has got unmuzzled, I fancy, by the noise, and I must run or there'll be murder committed."

"Charlotte," he cried, feverishly and eagerly, *not* letting go her hand, "when shall it be?"

"As you like," she answered indifferently. "This month, or next month, or the month after: *I* don't care."

The tone both mortified and pained him. His brow knit: and Charlotte saw the impression her words had made. She put on a pretty look of contrition.

"Mind, Rodolf, it shall be an understood thing beforehand that you don't attempt to control me in the smallest particular: that I have my own way in everything."

"You will take care to have that, Charlotte, whether it be an understood thing beforehand, or not," replied he.

Charlotte laughed as she walked away. A ringing laugh of power, which the air echoed: of power, at any rate, over the heart and will of Mr. Rodolf Pain.

CHAPTER XXII.

DANGEROUS AMUSEMENT.

On an April day, sunny and charming, a gentleman with a lady on his arm was strolling down one of the narrowest and dirtiest streets of Homburg. A tall man was he, tall and handsome, with a fair Saxon face, and fair Saxon curls that shimmered like gold in the sunlight. Could it be George Godolphin—who had gone away from Prior's Ash six months before, nothing but a shadowy wreck. It was George safe enough; restored to full strength, to perfect health. Maria, on the contrary, looked thin and delicate, and her face had lost a good deal of its colour. They had wintered chiefly at Pau, but had left it a month past. Since then they had travelled about from place to place, by short stages, taking it easy, as George called it: staying a day or two in one town, a day or two in another, turning to the right or left, as inclination led them, going forward, or backward. So that they were home by the middle of April, it would be time enough. George had received *carte blanche* from Thomas Godolphin to remain out as long as he thought it necessary; and George was not one to decline the privilege. Play before work had always been George's motto.

On the previous evening they had arrived at Homburg from Wiesbaden, and were now taking their survey of the place. Neither liked its appearance so much as they had done many other places, and they were mutually agreeing to leave it again that evening, when a turning in the street brought them in view of another lady and gentleman, arm in arm as they were.

"English, I am sure," remarked Maria, in a low tone.

"I should think so!" replied George, laughing. "Don't you recognize them?"

She had recognized them ere George finished speaking. Mr. and Mrs. Verrall! It took about ten minutes to ask and answer questions. "How strange that we should not have met before!" Mrs. Verrall cried. "We have been here a fortnight. But perhaps you have only just come?"

"Only last night," said George.

"My wife turned ill for a foreign tour, so I indulged her," explained Mr. Verrall. "We have been away a month now."

"And a fortnight of it at Homburg!" exclaimed George in surprise

"What attraction can you find here? Maria and I were just saying that we would leave it to-night."

"It's as good as any other of these German places, for all I see," carelessly remarked Mr. Verrall. "How well you are looking!" he added to George.

"I cannot pay you the same compliment," Mrs. Verrall said to Maria. "What have you done with your roses?"

Maria's "roses" came vividly into her cheeks at the question. "I am not in strong health just now," was all she answered.

George smiled. "There's nothing seriously the matter, Mrs. Verrall," said he. "Maria will find her roses again after a while. Charlotte has—I was going to say, changed her name," broke off George; "but in her case that would be a wrong figure of speech. She is married, we hear."

"Long ago," said Mrs. Verrall. "Charlotte's quite an old married woman by this time. It took place—let me see!—last November. They live in London."

"Mr. Pain is her cousin, is he not?"

"Yes. It was an old engagement," continued Mrs. Verrall, looking at George. "Many a time, when she and you were flirting together, I had to call her to account, and remind her of Mr. Pain."

George could not remember that Mrs. Verrall had ever done such a thing in his presence: and she had been rather remarkable for not interfering: for leaving him and Charlotte to go their own way. But he did not say so.

They turned and continued their walk together. George—he had lost none of his gallantry—taking his place by the side of Mrs. Verrall.

In passing a spot where there was a partial obstruction, some confusion occurred. A house was under repair, and earth and stones lay half-way across the street, barely giving room for any vehicle to pass. Just as they were opposite this, a lumbering coach, containing a gay party with white bows in their caps—probably a christening—came rattling up at a sharp pace. George Godolphin, taking Mrs. Verrall's hand, piloted her to safety. Maria was not so fortunate. Mr. Verrall was a little behind her or before her: at any rate, he was not adroit enough to assist her at the right moment; and Maria, seeing no escape between the coach and the *débris*, jumped upon the latter. The stones moved under her feet, and she slipped off again to the other side. It did not hurt her much, but it shook her greatly. George, who was looking back at the time, had sprung back and caught her before Mr. Verrall well saw what had occurred.

"My darling, how did it happen? Are you hurt? Verrall, could you not have taken better care?" he reiterated, his face flushed with emotion and alarm.

Maria leaned heavily upon him, and drew a long breath before she could speak. "I am not hurt, George."

"Are you sure?" he anxiously cried.

Maria smiled reassuringly. "It is nothing indeed. It has only shaken me. See! I am quite free from the stones. I must have been careless, I think."

George turned to look at the stones. Quite a heap of them, two or

three feet from the ground.   She had alighted on her feet; not quite
falling; but slipping with the lower part of her back against the stones.
Mrs. Verrall shook the dust from her dress, and Mr. Verrall apologized
for his inattention.

George took her upon his arm, with an air that seemed to intimate
he should not trust her to any one again, and they went back to their
hotel, Mrs. Verrall saying she should call upon them in half an hour's
time.

Maria was looking pale; quite white.   George, in much concern, untied
her bonnet-strings.   "Maria, I fear you *are* hurt!"

"Indeed I am not—as I believe," she answered.   "Why do you
think so?"

"Because you are not looking well."

"I was startled at the time; frightened.   I shall get over it directly,
George."

"I think you had better see a doctor.   I suppose there's a decent one
to be found in the town."

"Oh no!" returned Maria, with much emphasis, in her surprise.
"See a doctor because I slipped down a little?   Why, George, that
would be foolish!   I have often jumped from a higher height than that.
Do you remember the old wall at the Rectory?   We children were for
ever jumping from it."

"That was one time, and this is another, Mrs. George Godolphin,"
said he, significantly.

Maria laughed.   "Only fancy the absurdity, George!   Were a
doctor called in, his first question would be, 'Where are you hurt,
madame?'   'Not anywhere, monsieur,' would be my reply.   'Then
what do you want with me?' he would say, and how foolish I should
look!"

George laughed too, and resigned the point.   "You are the better
judge, of course, Maria.   Margery," he continued—for Margery, at
that moment, entered the room—"your mistress has had a fall."

"A fall!" uttered Margery, in her abrupt way, as she turned to
regard Maria.

"It could not be called a fall, Margery," said Maria, slightingly.
"I slipped off some earth and stones.   I did not quite fall."

"Are you hurt, ma'am?"

"It did not hurt me at all.   It only shook me."

"Nasty things, those slips are sometimes!" resumed Margery.   "I
have known pretty good illnesses grow out of 'em."

George did not like the remark.   He deemed it thoughtless of
Margery to make it in the presence of his wife, under the circumstances.   "You must croak, or it would not be you, Margery," said he,
in a vexed tone.

It a little put up Margery.   "I can tell you what, Master George,"
cried she; "your own mother was in her bed for eight weeks, through
nothing on earth but slipping down two stairs.   I say those shakes are
ticklish things—when one is not in a condition to bear them.   Ma'am,
you must just take my advice, and lie down on that sofa, and not get off
it for the rest of the day.   There's not a doctor in the land as knows
anything, but would say the same."

Margery was peremptory; George joined her in being peremptory also; and Maria, with much laughter and protestation, was fain to let them place her on the sofa. "Just as if I were ill, or delicate!" she grumbled.

"And pray, ma'am, what do you call yourself but delicate? You are not one of the strong ones," cried Margery, as she left the room for a shawl.

George drew his wife's face to his in an impulse of affection, and kissed it. "Don't pay any attention to Margery's croaking, my dearest," he fondly said. "But she is quite right in recommending you to lie still. It will rest you."

"I am afraid I shall go to sleep, if I am condemned to lie here," said Maria.

"The best thing you can do," returned George. "Catch me trusting you to any one's care again!"

In a short time Mrs. Verrall came in, and told George that her husband was waiting for him outside. George went out, and Mrs. Verrall sat down by Maria.

"It is Margery's doings, Margery's and George's," said Maria, as if she would apologize for being found on the sofa, covered up like an invalid. "They made me lie down."

"Are you happy?" Mrs. Verrall somewhat abruptly asked.

"Happy?" repeated Maria, at a loss to understand the exact meaning of the words.

"Happy with George Godolphin. Are you and he happy with each other?"

A soft blush overspread Maria's face; a light of love shone in her eyes: "Oh, so happy!" she murmured. "Mrs. Verrall, I wonder sometimes whether any one in the world is as happy as I am!"

"Because it struck me that you were changed; you look ill."

"Oh, that!" returned Maria, with a rosier blush still. "Can't you guess the cause of that, Mrs. Verrall? As George told you, I shall, I hope, look well again, after a time."

Mrs. Verrall shrugged her shoulders with indifference. She had never lost her bloom from any such cause.

Maria found—or Margery did for her—that the fall had shaken her more than was expedient. After all, a medical man had to be called in. Illness supervened. It was not a very serious illness, and not at all dangerous; but it had the effect of detaining them at Homburg. Maria lay in bed, and George spent most of his time with the Verralls.

With Mr. Verrall chiefly. Especially in an evening. George would go out, sometimes before dinner, sometimes after it, and come home so late that he did not venture into Maria's room to say good night to her. Since her illness he had occupied an adjoining chamber. It did Maria no good: she would grow flushed, excited, heated: and when George did come in, he would look flushed and excited also.

"But, George, where do you stay so late?"

"Only with Verrall."

"You look so hot. I am sure you are feverish."

"The rooms were very hot. We have been watching them play. Good night, darling. I wish you were well!"

Watching them play! It is your first deceit to your wife, George Godolphin; and, rely upon it, no good will come of it. Mr. Verrall had introduced George to the dangerous gaming-tables; had contrived to imbue him with a liking for the insidious vice. Did he do so with—as our law terms express it—malice aforethought? Let the response lie with Mr. Verrall.

On the very first evening that they were together, the day of the slight accident to Maria, Mr. Verrall asked George to dine with him; and he afterwards took him to the tables. George did not play that evening; but he grew excited, watching others play. Heavy stakes were lost and won; evil passions were called forth; avarice, hatred, despair. Mr. Verrall played for a small sum; and won. "It whiles away an hour or two," he carelessly remarked to George, as they were leaving. "And one can take care of one's self."

"All can't take care of themselves, apparently," answered George Godolphin. "Did you observe that haggard-looking Englishman, leaning against the wall and biting his nails when his money had gone? The expression of that man's face will haunt me for a week to come. Those are the men who commit suicide."

Mr. Verrall smiled, half-mockingly. "Suicide! Not they," he answered. "The man will be there to-morrow evening, refeathered."

"I never felt more pity for any one in my life," continued George. "There was despair in his face, if I ever saw despair. I could have found in my heart to go up and offer him my purse; only I knew it would be staked the next moment at the table."

"You did not know him, then?"

"No."

Mr. Verrall mentioned the man's name, and George felt momentarily surprised. He was a noted baronet's eldest son.

The next evening came round. Maria was confined to her bed then, and George was a gentleman at large. A gentleman at large to be pounced upon by Mr. Verrall. He came—Verrall—and carried George off again to dinner.

"Let us take a stroll," he said, later in the evening.

Their stroll took them towards the scene of the night before, Mr. Verrall's being the moving *will*. "Shall we see who's there?" he said, with great apparent indifference.

George answered as indifferently: but there was an undercurrent of meaning in his tone, wonderful for careless George Godolphin. "Better keep out of temptation."

Mr. Verrall laughed till the tears came into his eyes: he said George made him laugh. "Come along," cried he, mockingly. "I'll take care of you."

That night George played. A little. "As well put a gold piece down," Mr. Verrall whispered to him; "I shall." George staked more than one gold piece; and won. A fortnight had gone over since then, and George Godolphin had become imbued with the fearful passion of gambling. At any rate, imbued with it temporarily: it is to be hoped that he will leave it behind him when he leaves Homburg.

Just look at him, as he stands over that green cloth, with a flushed face and eager eyes! He is of finer form, of loftier stature than most of those who are crowding round the tables; his features betray higher intellect, greater refinement; but the same passions are just now distorting them. Mr. Verrall is by his side, cool, calm, impassive: somehow, that man, Verrall, always wins. If he did not, he would not lose his coolness: he would only leave the tables.

"*Rouge*," called George.

It was *noir*. George flung his last money on the board, and moved away.

Mr. Verrall followed him. "Tired already?"

Mr. George let slip a furious word. "The luck has been against me all along: almost from the first night I played here. I am cleaned out again."

"I can let you have——"

"Thank you!" hastily interrupted George. "You are very accommodating, Verrall, but it seems we may go on at the same thing for ever: I losing, and you finding me money. How much is it that I owe you altogether?"

"A bagatelle. Never mind that."

"A *bagatelle!*" repeated George. "It's well money is so valueless to you: *I* don't call it one. And I have never been a man given to looking at money before spending it."

"You can pay me when and how you like. This year, next year, the year after: I shan't sue you for it," laughed Mr. Verrall. "There I go and redeem your luck."

He held out a heavy roll of notes to George. The latter's eager fingers clutched them: but, even as they were within his grasp, better thoughts came to him. He pushed them back again.

"I am too deeply in your debt already, Verrall."

"As you please," returned Mr. Verrall, with indifference. "There the notes are, lying idle. As to what you have had, if it's so dreadful a burden on your conscience, you can give me interest for it. You can let the principal lie, I say, though it be for ten years to come. One half-hour's play with these notes may redeem all you have lost."

He left the notes lying by George Godolphin—by hesitating George —with the fierce passion to use them that was burning within him. Mr. Verrall could not have taken a more efficient way of inducing him to play again, than to affect this easy indifference, and to leave the money under his eyes, touching his fingers, fevering his brain. George took up the notes.

"You are sure you will let me pay you interest, Verrall?"

"Of course I will."

And George walked off to the gaming-table.

He went home later that night than he had gone at all, wiping the perspiration from his brow, lifting his face to the quiet stars, and gasping to catch a breath of air. Mr. Verrall found it rather cool, than not; shrugged his shoulders, and said he could do with an overcoat; but George felt stifled. The roll had *gone;* and more to it had gone; and George Godolphin was Mr. Verrall's debtor to a heavy amount.

"Thank goodness the day has already dawned!" involuntarily broke from George.

The Shadow of Ashlydyat.   **11**

Mr. Verrall looked at him for an explanation. He did not understand what particular cause for thankfulness there should be in that.

"We shall get away from the place to-day," said George. "If I stopped in it I should come to the dogs."

"Nothing of the sort," cried Mr. Verrall. "Luck is safe to turn some time. It's like the tide: it has its time for flowing in, and its time for flowing out; once let it turn, and it comes rushing in all one way. But, what do you mean about going? Your wife is not well enough to travel yet."

"Yes she is," was George's answer. "Quite well enough."

"Of course you know best. I think you should consider——"

"Verrall, I should consider my wife's health and safety before any earthly thing," interrupted George. "We might have started to-day, had we liked: I speak of the day that has gone : the doctor said yesterday that she was well enough to travel."

"I was not aware of that. I shall remain here a week longer."

"And I shall be away before to-morrow night."

"Not you," cried Mr. Verrall.

"I shall: if I keep in the mind I am in now."

Mr. Verrall smiled. He knew George was not famous for keeping his resolutions. In the morning, when his smarting should be over, he would stay on, fast enough. They wished each other good night, and George turned into his hotel.

To his great surprise, Margery met him on the stairs. "Are you walking the house as the ghosts do?" cried he, with a renewal of his good-humour. Nothing pleased George better than to give old Margery a joking or a teasing word. "Why are you not in bed?"

"There's enough ghosts in the world, it's my belief, without my personating them, sir," was Margery's answer. "I'm not in bed yet, because my mistress is not in bed."

"Your mistress not in bed!" repeated George. "But that is very wrong."

"So it is," said Margery. "But it has been of no use my telling her so. She took it into her head to sit up for you; and sit up she has. Not there, sir"—for he was turning to their sitting-room—"she is lying back in the big chair in her bedroom."

George entered. Maria, white and wan and tired, was lying back, as Margery expressed it, in the large easy-chair. She was too fatigued, too exhausted to get up · she only held out her hand to her husband.

"My darling, you know this is wrong," he gently said, bending over her. "Good heavens, Maria! how ill and tired you look!"

"I should not have slept had I gone to bed," she said. "George, tell me where you have been : where it is that you go in an evening?"

A misgiving crossed George Godolphin's mind—that she already knew where. She looked painfully distressed, and there was a peculiar significance in her tone, but she spoke with timid deprecation. His conscience told him that the amusement he had been recently pursuing would not show out well in the broad light of day. An unmarried man may send himself to ruin if it pleases him to do it; but not one who has assumed the responsibilities of George Godolphin. Ruin, however, had not yet come to George Godolphin, or fear of ruin. The worst that had happened was, that he had contracted a debt to Mr. Verrall, which he did not at present see his way clear to paying. He could not refund so large a sum out of the bank without the question being put by his partners, Where does it go to? Mr. Verrall had relieved him of the embarrassment by suggesting interest. A very easy settling of the question it appeared to the careless mind of George Godolphin: and he felt obliged to Mr. Verrall.

"Maria!" he exclaimed, "what are you thinking of? What is the matter?"

Maria changed her position. She let her head glide from the chair on to his sheltering arm. "Mrs. Verrall frightened me, George. Will you be angry with me if I tell you? She came in this evening, and she said you and Mr. Verrall were losing all your money at the gaming-table."

George Godolphin's face grew hot and angry, worse than it had been in the gambling-room, and mentally he gave Mrs. Verrall an exceedingly uncomplimentary word. "What possessed her to say that?" he exclaimed. And in truth he wondered what could have possessed her. Verrall, at any rate, was not losing his money. "Were you so foolish as to believe it, Maria?"

"Only a little of it, George. Pray forgive me! I am weak just now, you know, and things startle me. I have heard dreadful tales of these foreign gaming-places: and I knew how much you had been out at night since we came here. It is not so, is it, George?"

George made a show of laughing at her anxiety. "I and Verrall have strolled into the places and watched the play," said he. "We have staked a few coins ourselves—not to be looked upon as two churls who put their British noses into everything and then won't pay for the privilege. I lost what I staked, with a good grace; but as to Verrall, I don't believe he is a halfpenny out of pocket. Mrs. Verrall must have been quarrelling with her husband, and so thought she'd say something to spite him. And my wife must take it for gospel, and begin to fret herself into a fever!"

Maria drew a long, relieved breath. The address was candid, the manner was playful and tender: and she possessed the most implicit faith in her husband. Maria had doubted almost the whole world before she could have doubted George Godolphin. She drew his face down to hers, once more whispering that he was to forgive her for being so silly.

"My dearest, I have been thinking that we may as well go on to-morrow. To-day, that is: I won't tell you the time, if you don't know it; but it's morning."

She knew the time quite well. No anxious wife ever sat up for a husband yet, but knew it. In her impatience to be away—for she was most desirous of being at home again—she could take note of the one sentence only. "Oh, George, yes! Let us go!"

"Will you promise to get a good night's rest first, and not attempt to be out of bed before eleven o'clock to-morrow morning, then?"

"George, I will promise you anything," she cried, with a radiant face. "Only say we shall start for home to-morrow!"

"Yes, we will."

And, somewhat to Mr. Verrall's surprise, they did start. That gentleman made no attempt to detain them. "But it is shabby of you both to go off like this, and leave us among these foreigners, like Babes in the wood," said he, when Maria was already in the carriage, and George was about to step into it.

"There is nothing to prevent you leaving too, is there, Mr. Verrall?" asked Maria, leaning forward. "And what did you and Mrs. Verrall do before we came? You had been ' Babes in the wood ' a fortnight then."

"Fairly put, young lady," returned Mr. Verrall. "I must congratulate you on one thing, Mrs. George Godolphin : that, in spite of your recent indisposition, you are looking more yourself to-day than I have yet seen you."

"That is because I am going home," said Maria.

And home they reached in safety. The land journey, the pleasant sea crossing—for the day and the waters were alike calm—and then the land again, all grew into things of the past, and they were once more at Prior's Ash. As they drove to the Bank from the railway station, Maria looked up at the house when it came into sight, a thrill of joy running through her heart. "What a happy home it will be for me !" was her glad thought.

"What would Thomas and old Crosse say, if they knew I had dipped into it so deeply at Homburg?" was the involuntary thought which flashed across George Godolphin.

Quite a levee had assembled to meet them. Mrs. Hastings and Grace, Bessie and Cecil Godolphin, Thomas Godolphin and Mr. Crosse. Maria threw off her bonnet and shawl, and stood amidst them all in her dark silk travelling dress. There was no mistaking that she was intensely happy : her eye was radiant, her colour softly bright, her fair young face without a cloud. And now walked in the Rector of All Souls', having escaped (nothing loth) from a stormy vestry meeting, to see Maria.

"I have brought her home safely, you see, sir," George said to Mr. Hastings, leading Maria up to him.

"And yourself also," was the Rector's reply. "You are worth two of the shaky man who went away."

"I told you I should be, sir, if you allowed Maria to go with me," cried gallant George. "I do not fancy we are either of us the worse for our sojourn abroad."

"I don't think either of you look as though you were," said the Rector. "Maria is thin. I suppose you are not sorry to come home, Miss Maria?"

"So glad!" she said. "I began to think it very, very long, not to see you all. But, papa, I am not Miss Maria now."

"You saucy child !" exclaimed Mr. Hastings. But the Rector had the laugh against him. Mrs. Hastings drew Maria aside.

"My dear, you have been ill, George wrote me word. How did it happen? We were so sorry to hear it."

"Yes, we were sorry too," replied Maria, her eyelashes resting on her hot cheek. "It could not be helped."

"But how did it happen?"

"It was my own fault: not *intentionally*, you know, mamma. It occurred the day after we reached Homburg. I and George were out walking and we met the Verralls. We turned with them, and then I had not hold of George's arm. Something was amiss in the street, a great heap of stones and earth and rubbish; and, to avoid a carriage that came by, I stepped upon it. And, somehow I slipped off. I did not appear to have hurt myself: but I suppose it shook me."

"You met the Verralls at Homburg?" cried Mrs. Hastings, in surprise.

"Yes. Did George not mention it when he wrote? They are at Homburg still. Unless they have now left it."

"George never puts a superfluous word into his letters," said Mrs. Hastings, with a smile. "He says just what he has to say, and no more. He mentioned that you were not well, and therefore some little delay might take place in the return home; but he said nothing of the Verralls."

Maria laughed. "George never writes a long letter——"

"Who's that, taking George's name in vain?" cried George, looking round.

"It is I, George. You never told mamma, when you wrote, that the Verralls were with us at Homburg."

"I'm sure I don't remember whether I did or not," said George.

"The Verralls are in Wales," observed Mr. Hastings.

"Then they have travelled to it pretty quickly," observed George. "When I and Maria quitted Homburg we left them in it. They had been there a month."

Not one present but looked up with surprise. "The impression in Prior's Ash is, that they are in Wales," observed Thomas Godolphin. "It is the answer given by the servants to all callers at Lady Godolphin's Folly."

"They are certainly at Homburg; whatever the servants may say," persisted George. "The servants are labouring under a mistake."

"It is a curious mistake for the servants to make, though," observed the Rector, in a dry, caustic tone.

"I think the Verralls are curious people altogether," said Bessy Godolphin.

"I don't know but they are," assented George. "But Verrall is a thoroughly good-hearted man, and I shall always speak up for him."

That evening, George and his wife dined alone. George was standing over the fire after dinner, when Maria came and stood near him. He put out his arm and drew her to his side.

"It seems so strange, George—being in this house with you, all alone," she whispered.

"Stranger than being my wife, Maria?"

"Oh, but I have got used to that." And George Godolphin laughed: she spoke so simply and naturally.

"You will get used in time to this being your home, my darling."

PART THE SECOND.

CHAPTER I.

SIXTY POUNDS TO OLD JEKYL.

STANDING on the covered terrace outside the dining-room at the Bank, in all the warm beauty of the late and lovely spring morning, surrounded by the perfume of flowers, the green lawn stretching out before her, the pleasant sitting-room behind her, its large window open and its paintings on the walls conspicuous, was Maria Godolphin. She wore a morning dress, simple and pretty as of yore, and her fair face had lost none of its beauty, scarcely any of its youth. Looking at her you would not think that a month had elapsed since she came there, to her home, after her marriage; and yet the time, since then, would not be counted by months, but by years. Six years and a half, it is, since her marriage took place, and the little girl, whom Maria is holding by the hand, is five years old. Just now Maria's face is all animation. She is talking to the child, and talking also to Jonathan and David Jekyl: but if you saw her at an unoccupied moment, her face in repose, you might detect an expression of settled sadness in it. It arose from the loss of her children. Three had died in succession, one after another; and this one, the eldest, was the only child remaining to her. A wondrously pretty little girl, her bare legs peeping between her frilled drawers and her white socks; with the soft brown eyes of her mother, and the golden Saxon curls of her father. With her mother's eyes the child had inherited her mother's gentle temperament: and Margery—who had found in her heart to leave Ashlydyat and become nurse to George's children—was wont to say that she never had to do with so sweet-tempered a child. She had been named Maria; but the name, for home use, had been corrupted into Meta: not to interfere with Maria's. She held her mother's hand, and, by dint of stretching up on her toes, could just bring here eyes above the marble top of the terrace balustrade.

"Donatan, why don't you get that big ting, to-day?"

Jonathan looked up, a broad smile on his face. He delighted in little children. He liked to hear them call him "Donatan:" and the little lady before him was as backward in the sound of the "th," as if she had been French. "She means the scythe, ma'am," said Jonathan.

"I know she does," said Maria. "The grass does not want mowing to-day, Meta. David, do you not think those rose-trees are very backward?"

David gave his usual grunt. "I should wonder if they were for'ard.

There ain't no rose-trees for miles round but what is back'ard, except them as have been nursed. With the cutting spring we've had, how are the rose-trees to get on, I'd like to know?"

Jonathan looked round, his face quite sunshine compared with David's: his words also. "They'll come on famous now, ma'am, with this lovely weather. Ten days of it, and we shall have them all out in bloom. Little miss shall have a rare posy then, and I'll cut off the thorns first."

"A big one, mind, Donatan," responded the young lady, beginning to dance about in anticipation. The child had an especial liking for roses, which Jonathan remembered. She inherited her mother's great love for flowers.

"David, how is your wife?" asked Maria.

"I've not heard that there's anything the matter with her," was David's phlegmatic answer, without lifting his face from the bed. He and Jonathan were both engaged almost at the same spot: David, it must be confessed, getting through more work than Jonathan.

They had kept that garden in order for Mr. Crosse, when the Bank was his residence. Also for Thomas Godolphin and his sisters, the little time they had lived there: and afterwards for George. George had now a full complement of servants—rather more than a complement, indeed—and one of them might well have attended to that small garden. Janet had suggested as much: but easy George continued to employ the Jekyls. It was not often that the two attended together; as they were doing to-day.

"David," returned Maria, in answer to his remark, "I am sure you must know that your wife is often ailing. She is anything but strong. Only she is always merry and in good spirits, and so people think her better than she is. She is quite a contrast to you, David," Maria added, with a smile. "You don't talk and laugh much."

"Talking and laughing don't get on with a man's work, as ever I heerd on," returned David.

"Is it true that your father slipped yesterday, and sprained his ankle?" continued Maria. "I heard that he did."

"True enough," growled David.

"'Twas all along of his good fortune, ma'am," said sunny Jonathan. "He was so elated with it that he slipped down Gaffer Thorpe's steps, where he was going to tell the news, and fell upon his ankle. The damage ain't of much account. But that's old father all over! Prime him up with a piece of good fortune, and he is all cock-a-hoop about it."

"What is the good fortune?" asked Maria.

"It's that money come to him at last, ma'am, what he had waited for so long. I'm sure we had all given it up for lost; and father stewed and fretted over it, wondering always what was going to become of him in his old age. 'Tain't so very much, neither."

"Sixty pound is sixty pound," grunted David.

"Well, so it is," acquiesced Jonathan. "And father looks to it to make him more comfortable than he could be from his profits; his honey, and his garden, and that. He was like a child last night, ma'am, planning what he'd do with it. I told him he had better take care not to lose it."

"Let him bring it to the Bank," said Maria. "Tell him I say so, Jonathan. It will be safe here. He might be paid interest for it."

"I will, ma'am."

Maria spoke the words in good faith. Her mind had conjured up a vision of old Jekyl keeping his sixty pounds in his house, at the foot of some old stocking: and she thought how easily he might be robbed of it. "Yes, Jonathan, tell him to bring it here: don't let him keep it at home, to lose it."

Maria had another auditor, of whose presence she was unconscious. It was her mother. Mrs. Hastings had been admitted by a servant, and came through the room to the terrace unheard by Maria. The little girl's ears—like all children's—were quick, and she turned, and broke into a joyous cry of "Grandma!" Maria looked round.

"Oh, mamma! I did not know you were here. Are you quite well?" hastily added Maria, fancying that her mother looked dispirited.

"We have had news from Reginald this morning, and the news is not good," was the reply. "He has been getting into some disagreeable scrape over there, and it has taken a hundred pounds or two to clear him. Of course they came upon us for it."

Maria's countenance fell. "Reginald is very unlucky. He seems always to be getting into scrapes."

"He always is," said Mrs. Hastings. "We thought he could not get into mischief at sea: but it appears that he does. The ship was at Calcutta still, but they were expecting daily to sail for home."

"What is it that he has been doing?" asked Maria.

"I do not quite understand," replied Mrs. Hastings. "I saw his letter, but that was not very explanatory. What it chiefly contained were expressions of contrition, and promises of amendment. The captain wrote to your papa: and that letter he would not give me to read. Your papa's motive was a good one, no doubt,—to save me vexation. But, my dear, he forgets that uncertainty causes the imagination to conjure up fears, worse, probably, than the reality."

"As Reginald grows older, he will grow steadier," remarked Maria. "And, mamma, whatever it may be, your grieving over it will not mend it."

"True," replied Mrs. Hastings. "But," she added, with a sad smile, "when your children shall be as old as mine, Maria, you will have learnt how impossible it is to a mother not to grieve. Have you forgotten the old saying? 'When our children are young they tread upon our toes; but when they are older they tread upon our hearts.'"

Little Miss Meta was treading upon her toes, just then. The child's tiny shoes were dancing upon grandmamma's in her eagerness to get close to her, to tell her that Donatan was going to give her a great big handful of roses, as soon as they were out, with the torns cut off.

"Come to me, Meta," said Maria. She saw that her mamma was not in a mood to be troubled with children, and she drew the child on to her own knee. "Mamma, I am going for a drive presently," she continued. "Would it not do you good to accompany me?"

"I don't know that I could spare the time this morning," said Mrs. Hastings. "Are you going far?"

"I can go far or not, as you please," replied Maria. "We have a new carriage, and George told me at breakfast that I had better try it, and see how I liked it."

"A new carriage!" replied Mrs. Hastings, her accent betraying surprise. "Had you not enough carriages already, Maria?"

"In truth, I think we had, mamma. This new one is one that George took a fancy to when he was in London last week; and he bought it."

"Child—though of course it is no business of mine—you surely did not want it. What sort of carriage is it?"

"It is a large one: a sort of barouche. It will do you good to go out with me. I will order it at once, if you will do so, mamma."

Mrs. Hastings did not immediately reply. She appeared to have fallen into thought. Presently she raised her head and looked at Maria.

"My dear, I have long thought of mentioning to you a certain subject; and I think I will do so now. Strictly speaking, it is, as I say, no business of mine, but I cannot help being anxious for your interests."

Maria felt somewhat alarmed. It appeared a formidable preamble.

"I and your papa sometimes talk it over, one with another. And we say"—Mrs. Hastings smiled, as if to disarm her words of their serious import—"that we wish we could put old heads upon young shoulders. Upon yours and your husband's."

"But why?—in what way?" cried Maria.

"My dear, if you and he had old heads, you would, I think, see how very wrong it is—I speak the word only in your interests, Maria—to maintain so great and expensive an establishment. It must cost you and George, here, far more than it costs them at Ashlydyat."

"Yes, I suppose it does," said Maria.

"We do not know what your husband's income is——"

"I do not know, either," spoke Maria, for Mrs. Hastings had paused and looked at her, almost as though she would give opportunity for the information to be supplied. "George never speaks to me upon money matters or business affairs."

"Well, whatever it is," resumed Mrs. Hastings, "we should judge that he must be living up to every farthing of it. How much better it would be if you were to live more moderately, and put something by!"

"I dare say it would," acquiesced Maria. "To tell you the truth, mamma, there are times when I fall into a thoughtful mood, and feel half frightened at our expenditure. But then again I reflect that George knows his own affairs and his own resources far better than I do. The expense is of his instituting: not of mine."

"George is proverbially careless," significantly spoke Mrs. Hastings.

"But, mamma, if at the end of one year, he found his expenses heavier than they ought to be, he would naturally retrench them the next. His not doing it proves that he can afford it."

"I am not saying, or thinking, that he cannot afford it, Maria, in one sense; I do not suppose he outruns his income. But you might live at half your present expense and be quite as comfortable, perhaps more so. Servants, carriages, horses, dress, dinner-parties!—I know you must spend enormously."

"Well, so we do," replied Maria. "But, mamma, you are perhaps unaware that George has an equal share with Thomas. He has indeed. When Mr. Crosse retired, Thomas told George it should be so for the future."

"Did he? There are not many like Thomas Godolphin. Still, Maria, whatever may be your income, I maintain my argument, that you keep up unnecessary style and extravagance. Remember, my dear, that you had no marriage settlement. And, the more you save, the better for your children. You may have many yet."

"I think I will talk to George about it," mused Maria.

Of course the past seven years had not been without their changes. Mr. Crosse had retired from the Bank, and Thomas Godolphin, in his generosity, immediately constituted his brother an equal partner. He had not been so previously. Neither had it been contemplated by Sir George in his lifetime that it was so to be, yet awhile. The state maintained at Ashlydyat took more to keep it up than the quiet way in which it was supposed George would live at the Bank, and Thomas was *the* representative Godolphin. But Thomas Godolphin was incapable of any conduct bordering in the remotest degree upon covetousness or meanness: they were the sons of one father; and though there was the difference in their ages, and he was chief of the Godolphins, he made George's share equal to his own.

It was well perhaps that he did so. Otherwise George might have plunged into shoals and quicksands. He appeared to have no idea of living quietly: had he possessed the purse of Fortunatus, which was always full of gold, we are told, he could not have been much more careless of money. Rumour went, too, that all Mr. George's wild oats (bushels of which, you may remember to have heard, Prior's Ash gave him credit for) were not yet sown; and wild oats run away with a great deal of money. Perhaps the only person in all Prior's Ash who believed George Godolphin to be a saint, or next door to one, was Maria. Best that she should think so! But, extravagant as George was, a suspicion that he lived beyond his income, was never glanced at. Sober people, such as the Rector of All Souls' and Mrs. Hastings, would say in private what a pity it was that George did not think of saving for his family. Ample as the income, present and future, arising from the Bank might be, it could not be undesirable to know that a nest-egg was accumulating. Thomas might have suggested this to George: gossips surmised that he did so, and that George let the suggestion go for nothing. They were wrong. Whatever lectures Janet may have seen well to give him, Thomas gave him none. Thomas was not one to interfere, or play the mentor: and Thomas had a strong silent conviction within him, that ere very long George would come into Ashlydyat. The conviction was born of his suspected state of health. He might be wrong: but he believed he was not. Ashlydyat George's; the double income from the Bank George's—where was the need to tell him to save now?

The Reverend Mr. Hastings had had some trouble with his boys: insomuch as that they had turned their faces against the career he had marked out for them. Isaac, the eldest, destined for the Church, had declined to qualify himself for it when he came to years of discretion. After some uncertainty, and what Mr. Hastings called "knocking about "—which meant that he was doing nothing when he ought to have been at work: and that state of affairs lasted for a year or two —Isaac won Maria over to his side. Maria, in her turn, won over George: and Isaac was admitted into the Bank. He held a good post in it now: the brother of Mrs. George Godolphin was not left to rise by chance or priority. A handsome young man of three and twenty was he; steady; and displaying an aptitude for business beyond his years. Many a one deemed that Isaac Hastings, in a worldly point of view, had done well in quitting the uncertain prospects offered by the Church, for a clerkship in the house of Godolphin. He might rise some time to be a partner in it. Reginald had also declined the career marked out for him. Some government appointment had been promised him: in fact, had been given him: but Reginald would hear of nothing but the sea. It angered Mr. Hastings much. One of the last men, was he, to force a boy into the Church; nay, to allow a boy to enter it, unless he showed a special liking for it; therefore Isaac had, on that score, got off pretty freely; but he was not one of the last men to force a boy to work, who displayed a taste for idleness. Reginald argued that he should lead a far more idle life in a government office, than he should have a chance of doing if he went to sea. He was right, so far. Mrs. Hastings had a special horror of the sea. Mothers, as a general rule, have. She set her face—and Mr. Hastings had also set his—against Reginald's sea visions; which, truth to say, had commenced with his earliest years.

However, Reginald and inclination proved too strong for opposition. The government post had to be declined with thanks; and to sea he went. Not into the navy: the boy had become too old for it: but into the merchant service. A good service, the firm he entered: but an expensive one. The premium was high; the outfit was large; the yearly sum that went in expenses while he was what is called a midshipman was considerable. But he quitted that service in a pique, and had since been trying different ships on his own account. Altogether, Mr. Hastings had trouble with him. Harry was keeping his first term at College. He had chosen the Church of his own free will: and was qualifying for it. Grace was married. And Rose was growing up to be as pretty as Maria.

"Maria," said Mrs. Hastings, "if I am to go out with you to-day, why should we not call upon Mrs. Averil? I have wanted to see her for some time."

"I will call with pleasure," was Maria's answer. "As well take a long drive as a short one. Then we should start at once."

She rang the bell as she spoke. To order the carriage, and for Margery to come for Miss Meta. The latter, who had played the trick before, suddenly broke from Margery, and dashed into the Bank parlour. She had learned to open the door.

George by good luck happened to be alone. He affected great anger, and Margery also scolded sharply. George had been sitting at a table, bending over account books, his spirit weary, his brow knit. His assumed anger was wasted: for he caught up the child the next moment and covered her face with kisses. Then he carried her into the dining-room to Maria.

"What am I to do with this naughty child, mamma? She came bursting in upon me like a great fierce lion. I must buy a real lion and keep him in the closet, and let him loose if she does it again. Meta won't like to be eaten up."

Meta laughed confidentially. "Papa won't let a lion eat Meta."

"You saucy child!" But George's punishment consisted only of more kisses.

"Is Meta going with you?" asked George, when Maria told him of the contemplated visit to Mrs. Averil.

Meta interposed. "Yes, she should go," she said.

"If I take Meta, I must take you also, Margery," observed Maria. "I cannot have the trouble of her in the carriage."

"*I* shan't hinder time," was Margery's response. "My bonnet and shawl's soon put on, ma'am. Come along, child. I'll dress you at once."

She went off with Meta, waiting for no further permission. George stepped out on the terrace, to see what Jonathan and David were about. Maria took the opportunity to tell him of the sixty pounds which had come to old Jekyl, and that she had advised its being brought to the Bank to be taken care of.

"What money is it? Where does it come from?" inquired George of the men.

"It's the money, sir, as was left to father this three years ago, from that dead uncle of ourn," returned Jonathan. "But the lawyers, sir, they couldn't agree, and it was never paid over. Now there has been a trial over it, something about the will; and father has had notice that it's ready for him, all the sixty pound."

"We will take care of it for him, and pay him interest, tell him, if he chooses to leave it here," said George.

"I'll tell him, sure enough, sir. He's safe to bring it."

The carriage was at the door in due course, and they were ready. A handsome carriage; acknowledged to be so by even Mrs. Hastings. George came out to hand them in. Miss Meta, a pretty little dressed-up fairy; Margery, plain and old-fashioned; Mrs. Hastings, quiet and ladylike; Maria, beautiful. Her hand lingered in her husband's.

"I wish you were coming, George," she bent from the carriage to whisper.

"I am too busy to-day, my dearest."

Although nearly seven years a wife, the world still contained no idol for Maria like George Godolphin. She loved, respected, reverenced him. Nothing, as yet, had shaken her faith in her husband. The little tales, making free with Mr. George's name, which would now and then be flying about Prior's Ash, had never reached the ears of Maria.

They had a seven-mile drive. The Honourable Mrs. Averil, who was growing in years, and had become an invalid, was delighted to see them. She kept them for two or three hours, and wanted to keep them for the day. It was late in the afternoon when they returned to Prior's Ash.

They met a cavalcade on entering the town. A riding-party, consisting of several ladies and one or two gentlemen, followed by some grooms. Somewhat apart from the rest, midway between the party and the grooms, rode two abreast, laughing, animated, upon the best of terms with each other. The lady sat her horse unusually well. She was slightly larger, but not a whit less handsome, than on the day you first saw her at the meet of the hounds : Charlotte Pain. He, gay George—for it was no other—was riding carelessly, half turning on his horse, his fair curls bending towards Charlotte.

"Papa ! papa !" shrieked out Meta, joyously.

George turned hastily, but the carriage had then passed. So occupied had he been in making himself agreeable that he had positively not seen it. Charlotte had. Charlotte had bowed. Bowed to Maria with a look of cool assurance, of triumph—as much as to say, You are sitting alone, and your husband is with me. At least, it might have worn that appearance to one given to flights of fancy, which Maria was not ; and she returned the bow with a pleasant smile. She caught George's eye when he turned, and a flush of pleasure lighted her face. George nodded to her cordially, and raised his hat, sending back a smile at the idea of his not having seen her.

"It was papa, was it not, darling !" said Maria, gleefully, bending over to her little girl.

But Maria did not notice that Margery's head had given itself a peculiar toss at sight of George's companion ; or that a severe expression had crossed the face of Mrs. Hastings. An expression which she instantly smoothed away, lest Maria should see it.

The fact was, that gossiping Prior's Ash had for some time coupled together the names of George Godolphin and Charlotte Pain in its usual free manner. No need, one would think, for Mrs. Hastings or Margery to give heed to such tattle : for they knew well what the stories of Prior's Ash were worth.

CHAPTER II.

WHY DID IT ANGER HIM?

THE drawing-rooms at Lady Godolphin's Folly were teeming with light, with noise, with company. The Verralls lived in it still. Lady Godolphin had never given them their dismissal : but they did not spend so much time in it as formerly. London, or elsewhere, appeared to claim them for the greater portion of the year. One year they did not come to it at all. Sometimes only Mrs. Verrall would be sojourning at it ; her husband away : indeed, their residence there was most irregular. Mrs. Verrall was away at present : it was said at the seaside.

A dinner-party had taken place that day. A gentleman's party. It was not often that Mr. Verrall gave one : but when he did so, it was thoroughly well done. George Godolphin did not give better dinners than did Mr. Verrall. The only promised guest who had failed in his attendance was Thomas Godolphin. Very rarely indeed did he accept invitations to the Folly. If there was one man in all the county to whom Mr. Verrall seemed inclined to pay court, to treat with marked consideration and respect, that man was Thomas Godolphin. Thomas almost always declined; declined courteously; in a manner which could not afford the slightest loophole for offence. He was of quiet habits, not strong in health of late, and though he had to give dinner-parties himself, and attended some of George's in the way of business, his friends were nearly all kind enough to excuse his frequenting theirs in return.

This time, however, Thomas Godolphin had yielded to Mr. Verrall's pressing entreaties, made in person, and promised to be present. A promise which was not—as it proved—to be kept. All the rest of the guests had assembled, and they were only waiting the appearance of Mr. Godolphin to sit down, when a hasty note arrived from Janet. Mr. Godolphin had been taken ill in dressing, and was utterly unable to attend. So they dined without him.

Dinner was over now. And the guests, most of them, had gone to the drawing-rooms; teeming, I say, with light, with the hum of many voices—with heat. A few had gone home; a few had taken cigars and were strolling outside the dining-room windows in the moonlight: some were taking coffee; and some were flirting with Charlotte Pain.

Mrs. Pain now, you remember. But Charlotte has worn weeds for her husband since you last saw her, and is free again. About four years after their marriage, the death of Rodolf Pain appeared in the county papers. None of the Verralls were at the Folly at the time; but Charlotte in her widow's dress came to it almost immediately afterwards, to sob out her sorrow in retirement. Charlotte emerged from her widowhood gayer than before. She rode more horses, she kept more dogs, she astonished Prior's Ash with her extraordinary modes of attire, she was altogether "faster" than ever. Charlotte had never once visited the neighbourhood during her married life; but she appeared to be inclined to make up for it now, for she chiefly stayed in it. When the Verralls, one or both, would be away, Charlotte remained at the Folly, its mistress. She held her court; she gave entertainments; she visited on her own score. Rumour went that Mrs. Pain had been left very well off: and that she shared with Mr. Verrall the expense of the Folly.

Charlotte managed to steer tolerably clear of ill-natured tongues. Latterly, indeed, people had got to say that Mr. George Godolphin was at the Folly more than he need be. But, it was certain that George and Mr. Verrall were upon most intimate terms: and Mr. Verrall had been staying at the Folly a good deal of late. George of course would have said that his visits there were paid to Mr. Verrall. Charlotte was popular in the neighbourhood, rather than otherwise; with the ladies as well as with the gentlemen.

Resplendent is Charlotte to-night, in a white silk dress with silver spots upon it. It is a really beautiful dress: but one of a quieter kind would have been more suited to this occasion. Charlotte had not appeared at dinner, and there was not the least necessity for embellishing herself in this manner to receive them in the drawing-room. Charlotte was one, however, who did as she pleased; in the matter of dress, as in other things, setting custom and opinion at defiance. Her hair is taken from her face and wound round and round her head artistically, in conjunction with a white and silver wreath. White and silver ornaments are on her neck and arms, and a choice bouquet of white hot-house flowers serves her to toy with. Just now, however, the bouquet is discarded, and lies on the table near her elbow, for her elbow is resting there as she sits. She is coquetting with a white and silver fan, gently wafting it before her face; her sparkling eyes glancing over its rim at a gentleman, who stands, coffee-cup in hand, bending down to her.

It is not George Godolphin. So do not let your imagination run off to him. For all the world saw, George and Charlotte were as decorous in behaviour with each other as need be: and where Prior's Ash was picking up its ill-natured scandal from, Prior's Ash best knew. Others talked and laughed with Charlotte as much as George did; rode with her, admired her.

The gentleman, bending down to her now, appears to admire her. A tall, handsome man of eight-and-thirty years, with clearly-cut features, and dark luminous eyes. He is the nephew of that Mrs. Averil to whom Maria and Mrs. Hastings went to pay a visit. He has been away from the neighbourhood, until recently, for nearly three years; and this is the first time he has seen Charlotte at Prior's Ash since she was Mrs. Pain.

What does Charlotte promise herself by thus flirting with him— by laying out her charms to attract him?—as she is evidently doing. Is she thinking to make a second marriage? to win him, as she once thought to win George Godolphin? Scarcely. One gentleman in the vicinity, who had thrown himself and his fortune at Charlotte's feet— and, neither fortune nor gentleman could be reckoned despicable—had been rejected with an assurance that she would never marry again; and she spoke it with an earnestness that left no doubt of her sincerity. Charlotte liked her own liberty too well. She was no doubt perfectly aware that every husband would not feel inclined to accord it to her as entirely as had poor Rodolf Pain. He—the one with the coffee-cup in hand, talking to her—is plunging into a sea of blunders. As you may hear, if you listen to what he is saying.

"Yes, I have come back to find many things changed," he was ob-serving; "things and people. Time, though but a three years' flight, leaves its mark behind it, Mrs. Pain. If you will allow me to remark it, I would say that you are almost the only one whom it has not changed—except for the better."

"Your lordship has not lost your talent for flattery, I perceive," was Charlotte's rejoinder.

"Nay, but I speak no flattery; I mean what I say," was the peer's reply, given in an earnest spirit. He was an admirer of beauty; he admired Charlotte's: but to flatter was not one of the failings of Lord Averil. Neither had he any ulterior object in view, save that of passing ten minutes of the evening agreeably with Charlotte's help, ere he took his departure. If Charlotte thought he had, she was mistaken. Lord Averil's affections and hopes were given to one very different from Charlotte Pain.

"But it must be considerably more than three years since I saw you," resumed Lord Averil. "It must be—I should think—nearer seven. You did not return to Prior's Ash—if I remember rightly—after you left it on your marriage."

"I did not return to it," replied Charlotte: "but you have seen me since then, Lord Averil. Ah! your memory is treacherous. Don't you recollect accosting me in Rotten Row? It was soon after you lost your wife."

Did Charlotte intend that as a shaft? Lord Averil's cheek burnt as he endeavoured to recall the reminiscence. "I think I remember it," he slowly said. "It was just before I went abroad. Yes, I do remember it," he added, after a pause. "You were riding with a young, fair man. And—did you not—really I beg your pardon if I am wrong—did you not introduce him to me as Mr. Pain?"

"It was Mr. Pain," replied Charlotte.

"I hope he is well. He is not here probably? I did not see him at table, I think."

Charlotte's face—I mean its complexion—was got up in the fashion. But the crimson that suffused it would have penetrated all the powder and cosmetics extant, let them have been laid on ever so profusely. She was really agitated: could not for the time speak. Another moment, and she turned deadly pale. Let us admire her, at any rate, for this feeling shown to her departed husband.

"My husband is dead, Lord Averil."

Lord Averil felt shocked at his blunder. "You must forgive me," he said in a gentle voice, his tone, his manner, showing the deepest sympathy. "I had no idea of it. No one has mentioned it to me since my return. The loss, I infer, cannot be a very recent one?"

In point of fact, Mr. Pain's demise had occurred immediately after the departure of Lord Averil from England. Charlotte is telling him so. It could not, she thinks, have been more than a week or two subsequent to it.

"Then he could not have been ill long," remarked his lordship. "What was the cause——"

"Oh pray do not make me recall it!" interrupted Charlotte in a tone of pain. "He died suddenly: but—it was altogether very distressing. Distressing to me, and distressing in its attendant circumstances."

An idea flashed over the mind of Lord Averil that the circumstances of the death must have been peculiar: in short, that Mr. Pain might have committed suicide. If he was wrong, Charlotte's manner was to blame. It was from that he gathered the thought. That the subject was a most unwelcome one, there could be no doubt; she palpably shrank from it.

Murmuring again a few clear words of considerate apology, Lord Averil changed the conversation, and presently said adieu to Charlotte.

"You surely are not thinking of going yet?" cried Charlotte, retaining his hand, and recovering all her lightness of manner. "They are setting out the whist-tables."

"I do not play. I have a visit to pay yet to a sick friend," he added, glancing at his watch. "I shall still be in time."

"But I do not think your carriage is here," urged Charlotte, who would fain have detained him.

"I am sure it is not here," was the peer's answer. "I did not order it to come for me. It is a fine night, and I shall walk to Prior's Ash."

He looked round for Mr. Verrall. He could not see him. In at one room, in at another, looked he; out upon the terrace, before the dining-room window, amidst the smokers. But there was no Mr. Verrall: and Lord Averil, impatient to be gone, finally departed without wishing his host good night.

Mr. Verrall had strolled out into the moonlight, and was in low, earnest conversation with George Godolphin. They had got as far as that stream on which you saw George rowing the day of Mrs. Verrall's fête, when he so nearly caught his death. Standing on the arched wooden bridge, which crossed it to the mock island, they leaned forward, their arms on the rails. Mr. Verrall was smoking; George Godolphin appeared to be too ill at ease to smoke. His brow was knit; his face hot with care. As fast as he wiped the drops from his brow they gathered there again.

"Don't worry, lad," said Mr. Verrall. "It always has come right, and it will come right now. Never fear. You will receive news from London to-morrow; there's little doubt of it."

"But it ought to have come to-day, Verrall."

"It will come to-morrow, safe enough. And—you know that you may always count upon me."

"I know I may. But look at the awful cost, Verrall."

"Pooh, pooh! What has put you in this mood to-night?"

"I don't know," said George, wiping the damp from his brow. "Not hearing from town, I think. Verrall!"

"What?"

"Suppose, when I do hear, it should not be favourable? I feel in a fever when I think of it."

"You took too much of that heating port this evening," said Mr. Verrall.

"I dare say I did," returned George. "A man at ease may let the wine pass him: but one worried to death is glad of it to drown care."

"Worried to death!" repeated Mr. Verrall in a reproving tone.

"Next door to it. Look there! They have tracked us and are coming in search."

Two or three dark forms were discerned in the distance, nearer the Folly. Mr. Verrall passed his arm within George Godolphin's and led him towards the house.

"I think I'll go home," said George. "I am not company for a dog to-night."

"Nonsense," said Mr. Verrall. "The tables are ready. I want to give you your revenge."

For once in his life—and it was a notable exception—George Godolphin actually resisted the temptation of the "tables;" the chance of "revenge." He had a heavy trouble upon him; a great fear; perhaps more than Mr. Verrall knew of. Ay, he had! But who would have suspected it of gay, careless George, who had been so brilliant at the dinner-table? He forswore for that one night the attractions of the Folly, including syren Charlotte, and went straight home.

It was not much past ten when he reached the Bank. Maria was

astonished : the Verrall dinner-parties were generally late affairs. She
was sitting alone, reading. In her glad surprise she ran to him with
an exclamation of welcome.

George pressed her tenderly to him, and his manner was gay and
careless again. Whatever scandal Prior's Ash might choose to talk of
George, he had not yet begun to neglect his wife.

"It was rather humdrum, darling, and I got tired," he said in answer
to her questions. "What have you been doing with yourself? Have
you been alone all the evening?"

"Since mamma left. She went home after tea. George, I want to
tell you something mamma has been talking of ; has been suggesting."

George stretched himself on the sofa, as if he were weary. Maria
edged herself on to it, and sat facing him, holding his hand while she
talked.

"It was the new carriage that brought the subject up, George.
Mamma introduced it this morning. She says we are living at too
great an expense ; that we ought not to spend more than half as much
as we do—— "

"What ?" shouted George, starting up from the sofa as if he had
been electrified.

Maria felt electrified ; electrified by the sudden movement, the word,
the tone of anger. Nay, it was not anger alone that it bore, but dismay ; fear—she could hardly tell what sound. "George," she gasped,
"what is the matter?"

"Tell me what it is that Mrs. Hastings has been saying?"

"George, I think you must have mistaken my words," was all that
Maria could reply in the first moment, feeling truly uncomfortable.
"Mamma said this morning that it was a pity we did not live at less
expense, and save money ; that it would be desirable for the sake of
Meta and any other children we may have. I said I thought it would
be desirable, and that I would suggest it to you. That was all."

George gazed at Maria searchingly for the space of a minute or two.
"Has Prior's Ash been saying this?"

"Oh no."

"Good. Tell Mrs. Hastings, Maria, that we are capable of managing our own affairs without interference. I do not desire it, nor will I
admit it."

Maria sat down to the table with her book ; the one she had been
reading when George came in. She put up her hands, as if absorbed
in reading, but her tears were falling. She had never had an ill
word with her husband ; had never had any symptom of estrangement
with him ; and she could not bear this. George lay on the sofa, his
lips compressed. Maria rose, in her loving, affectionate nature, and
stood before him.

"George, I am sure mamma never meant to interfere ; she would
not do such a thing. What she said arose from anxiety for our interests. I am so sorry to have offended you," she added, the tears
falling fast.

A repentant fit had come over him. He drew his wife's face down
on his own and kissed its tears away. "Forgive me, my dearest ; I
was wrong to speak crossly to *you*. A splitting headache has put me

Out of sorts, and I was vexed to hear that people were commenting on our private affairs. Nothing could annoy me half so much."

Maria wondered why. But she fully resolved that it should be the last time she would hint at such a thing as economy. Of course her husband knew his own business best.

CHAPTER III.

CECIL'S ROMANCE.

WE must turn to Ashlydyat, and go back to a little earlier in the evening. Miss Godolphin's note to the Folly had stated that her brother had been taken ill while dressing for Mr. Verrall's dinner-party. It was correct. Thomas Godolphin was alone in his room, ready, when he was attacked by a sharp internal paroxysm of agony. He hastily sat down : a cry escaped his lips, and drops of water gathered on his brow.

Alone he bore it, calling for no aid. In a few minutes the pain had partially passed, and he rang for his servant. An old man now, that servant : he had for years attended on Sir George Godolphin.

"Bexley, I have been ill again," said Thomas, quietly. "Will you ask Miss Godolphin to write a line to Mr. Verrall, saying that I am unable to attend."

Bexley cast a strangely yearning look on the pale, suffering face of his master. He had seen him in these paroxysms once or twice. "I wish you would have Mr. Snow called in, sir!" he cried.

"I think I shall. He may give me some ease, possibly. Take my message to your mistress, Bexley."

The effect of the message was to bring Janet to the room. "Taken ill! a sharp inward pain!" she was repeating, after Bexley. "Thomas, what sort of a pain is it? It seems to me that you have had the same before lately."

"Write a few words the first thing, will you, Janet? I should not like to keep them waiting for me."

Janet, punctilious as Thomas, considerate as he was for others, sat down and wrote the note, despatching it at once by Andrew, one of the serving men. Few might have set about and done it so calmly as Janet, considering that she had a great fear thumping at her heart. A fear which had never penetrated it until this moment. With something very like sickness, had flashed into her memory their mother's pain. A sharp, agonizing pain had occasionally attacked *her*, the symptom of the inward malady of which she had died. Was the same fatal malady attacking Thomas? The doctors had expressed their fears then that it might prove hereditary.

In the corridor, as Janet was going back to Thomas's room, the note despatched, she encountered Bexley. The sad, apprehensive look in the old man's face struck her. She touched his arm, and beckoned him into an empty room.

"What is it that is the matter with your master?"

"I don't know," was the answer: but the words were spoken in a tone which caused Janet to think that the old man was awake to the same fears that she was. "Miss Janet, I am afraid to think what it may be."

"Is he often ill like this?"

"I know but of a time or two, ma'am. But that's a time or two too many."

Janet returned to the room. Thomas was leaning back in his chair, his face ghastly, his hands fallen, prostrate altogether from the effects of the agony. Things were coming into her mind one by one: how much time Thomas had spent in his own room of late; how seldom, comparatively speaking, he went to the Bank; how often he had the brougham, instead of walking, when he did go to it. Once—why, it was only this very last Sunday!—he had not gone near church all day long. Janet's fears grew into certainties.

She took a chair, drawing it nearer to Thomas. Not speaking of her fears, but asking him in a soothing tone how he felt, and what had caused his illness. "Have you had the same pain before?" she continued.

"Several times," he answered. "But it has been worse to-night than I have previously felt it. Janet, I fear it may be the forerunner of my call. I did not think to leave you so soon."

Except that Janet's face went almost as pale as his, and that her fingers entwined themselves together so tightly as to cause pain, there was no outward sign of the grief that laid hold of her heart.

"Thomas, what is the complaint that you are fearing?" she asked, after a pause. "The same that—that——"

"That my mother had," he quietly answered, speaking the words that Janet would not speak.

"It may not be so," gasped Janet.

"True. But I think it is."

"Why have you never spoken of this?"

"Because, until to-night, I have doubted whether it was so, or not. A suspicion, that it might be so, certainly was upon me: but it amounted to no more than suspicion. At times, when I feel quite well, I argue that I must be wrong."

"Have you consulted Mr. Snow?"

"I am going to do so now. I have desired Bexley to send for him."

"It should have been done before, Thomas."

"Why? If it is as I suspect, neither Snow nor all his brethren can save me."

Janet clasped her hands upon her knee, and sat with her head bent. She was feeling the communication in all its bitter force. It seemed that the only one left on earth with whom she could sympathize was Thomas: and now perhaps he was going! Bessy, George, Cecil, all were younger, all had their own pursuits and interests; George had his new ties; but she and Thomas seemed to stand alone. With the deep sorrow for him, the brother whom she dearly loved, came other considerations, impossible not to occur to a practical, foreseeing mind such as Janet's. With Thomas they should lose Ashlydyat. George would come into possession: and George's ways were so different from theirs, that it would seem to be no longer in the family. What would George make of it? A gay, frequented place, as the Verralls—when they were at home—made of Lady Godolphin's Folly? Janet's cheeks flushed at the idea of such degeneracy for stately Ashlydyat. However it might be, whether George turned it into an ever-open house, or shut it up as a nunnery, it would be alike lost to all the rest of them. She and her sisters must turn from it once again and for ever; George, his wife, and his children, would reign there.

Janet Godolphin did not rebel at this; she would not have had it otherwise. Failing Thomas, George was the fit and proper representative of Ashlydyat. But the fact could but strike upon her now with gloom. All things wore a gloomy hue to her in that unhappy moment.

It would cause changes at the Bank, too. At least, Janet thought it probable that it might do so. Could George carry on that extensive concern himself? Would the public be satisfied with gay George for its sole head?—would they accord him the confidence they had given Thomas? These old retainers, too! If she and her sisters quitted Ashlydyat, they must part with them: leave them to serve George.

Such considerations passed rapidly through her imagination. It could not well be otherwise. Would they really come to pass? She looked at Thomas, as if seeking in his face the answer to the doubt.

His elbow on the arm of his chair, and his temples pressed upon his hand, sat Thomas; his mind in as deep a reverie as Janet's. Where was it straying to? To the remembrance of Ethel?—of the day that he had stood over her grave when they were placing her in it? Had the time indeed come, or nearly come, to which he had, from that hour, looked forward?—the time of his joining her? He had never lost the vision: and perhaps the fiat, death, could have come to few who would meet it so serenely as Thomas Godolphin. It would scarcely be right to say *welcome* it; but, certain it was that the prospect was one of pleasantness rather than of pain to him. To one who has lived near to God on earth, the anticipation of the great change can bring no dismay. It brought none to Thomas Godolphin.

But Thomas Godolphin had not done with earth and its cares yet.

Bessy Godolphin was away from home that week. She had gone to spend it with some friends at a few miles' distance. Cecil was alone when Janet returned to the drawing-room. She had no suspicion of the sorrow that was overhanging the house. She had not seen Thomas go to the Folly, and felt surprised at his tardiness.

"How late he will be, Janet!"

"Who? Thomas! He is not going. He is not very well this evening," was the reply.

Cecil thought nothing of it. How should she? Janet buried her fears within her, and said no more.

One was to dine at Lady Godolphin's Folly that night, who absorbed all Cecil's thoughts. Cecil Godolphin had had her romance in life; as so many have it. It had been partially played out years ago. Not quite. Its sequel had still to come. She sat there listlessly; her pretty hands resting inertly on her knee, her beautiful face tinged with the setting sunlight; sat there thinking of him—Lord Averil.

A romance it had really been. Cecil Godolphin had paid a long visit to the Honourable Mrs. Averil, some three or four years ago. She, Mrs. Averil, was in health then, fond of gaiety, and her house had many visitors. Amidst others, staying there, was Lord Averil: and before he and Cecil knew well what they were about, they had learned to love each other. Lord Averil was the first to awake from the pleasant dream: to know what it meant; and he discreetly withdrew himself out of harm's way. Harm only to himself, as he supposed: he never suspected that the same love had won its way to Cecil Godolphin. A strictly honourable man, he would have been ready to kill himself in self-condemnation had he suspected that it had. Not until he had gone, did it come out to Cecil that he was a married man. When only eighteen years of age he had been drawn into one of those unequal and unhappy alliances that can only bring a flush to the brow in after-years. Many a hundred times had it dyed that of Lord Averil. Before he was twenty years of age, he had separated from his wife; when pretty Cecil was yet a child: and the next ten years he had spent abroad, striving to outlive its remembrance. His own family, you may be sure, did not pain him by alluding to it, then, or after his return. He had no residence now in the neighbourhood of Prior's Ash: he had sold it years ago. When he visited the spot, it was chiefly as the guest of Colonel Max, the master of the fox-hounds: and in that way he had made the acquaintance of Charlotte Pain. Thus it happened, when Cecil met him at Mrs. Averil's, that she knew nothing of his being a married man. On Mrs. Averil's part, she never supposed that Cecil did not know it. Lord Averil supposed she knew it: and little enough in his own eyes has he looked in her presence, when the thought would flash over him, "How she must despise me for my mad folly!" He had learned to love her; to love her passionately: never so much as glancing at the thought that it could be reciprocated. He, a married man! But this folly was no less mad than the other had been, and Lord Averil had the sense to withdraw himself from it.

A day or two after his departure, Mrs. Averil received a letter from him. Cecil was in her dressing-room when she read it.

"How strange!" was the comment of Mrs. Averil. "What do you think, Cecil?" she added, lowering her voice. "When he reached town there was a communication waiting for him at his house, saying that his wife was dying, and praying him to go and see her."

"His wife?" echoed Cecil. "Whose wife?"

"Lord Averil's. Have you forgotten that he had a wife? I wish we could all really forget it. It has been the blight of his life."

Cecil had discretion enough left in that unhappy moment not to betray that she had been ignorant of the fact. When her burning cheeks had a little cooled, she turned from the window where she had been hiding them, and escaped to her own room. The revelation had betrayed to her the secret of her own feelings for Lord Averil; and in her pride and rectitude, she thought she should have died.

A day or two more, and Lord Averil was a widower. He suffered some months to elapse, and then came to Prior's Ash, his object being Cecil Godolphin. He stayed at an hotel, and was a frequent visitor at Ashlydyat. Cecil believed that he meant to ask her to be his wife;

and Cecil was not wrong. She could give herself up now to the full joy of loving him.

Busy tongues, belonging to some young ladies who boasted more wit than discretion, hinted something of this to Cecil. Cecil, in her vexation at having her private feelings suspected, spoke slightingly of Lord Averil. "Did they think *she* would stoop to a widower; to one who had made himself so notorious by his first marriage?" she asked. And this, word for word, was repeated to Lord Averil.

It was repeated to him by those false friends, and Cecil's haughty manner, as she spoke it, offensively commented upon. Lord Averil fully believed it. He judged that he had no chance with Cecil Godolphin; and, without speaking to her of what had been his intentions, he again left.

But now, no suspicion of this conversation having been repeated to him, ever reached Cecil. She deemed his behaviour very bad. Whatever restraint he may have placed upon his manner towards her, when at Mrs. Averil's, he had been open enough since: and Cecil could only believe his conduct unjustifiable—the result of fickleness. She resolved to forget him.

But she had not done so yet. All this long time since, nearly three years, had Cecil been trying to do it, and it was not yet accomplished. She had received an offer from a young and handsome earl; it would have been a match in every way desirable: but poor Cecil found that Lord Averil was too deeply seated in her heart for her to admit thought of another. And now Lord Averil was back again at Prior's Ash; and, as Cecil had heard, was to dine that day at Lady Godolphin's Folly. He had called at Ashlydyat since his return, but she was out.

She sat there, thinking of nim: her feeling against him chiefly that of anger. She believed to this hour that he had used her ill; that his behaviour had been unbecoming a gentleman.

Her reflections were disturbed by the appearance of Mr. Snow. It was growing dusk then, and she wondered what brought him there so late: in fact, what brought him there at all. She turned and asked the question of Janet.

"He has come to see Thomas," replied Janet. And Cecil noticed that her sister was sitting in a strangely still attitude, her head bowed down. But she did not connect it with its true cause. It was nothing unusual to see Janet lost in deep thought.

"What is the matter with Thomas, that Mr. Snow should come now?" inquired Cecil.

"He did not feel well, and sent for him."

It was all that Janet answered. And Cecil continued in blissful ignorance of anything being wrong, and resumed her reflections on Lord Averil.

Janet saw Mr. Snow before he went away. Afterwards she went to Thomas's room, and remained in it. Cecil stayed in the drawing-room, buried in her dream. The room was lighted, but the blinds were not drawn: Cecil was at the window, looking out into the bright moonlight.

It must have been growing quite late when she discerned some one approaching Ashlydyat, on the road from Lady Godolphin's Folly.

From the height she fancied at first that it might be George; but as the figure drew nearer, her heart gave a bound, and she saw that it was he upon whom her thoughts had been fixed.

Yes, it was Lord Averil. When he mentioned to Charlotte Pain that he had a visit yet to pay to a sick friend, he had alluded to Thomas Godolphin. Lord Averil, since his return, had been struck with the change in Thomas Godolphin. It was more perceptible to him than to those who saw Thomas habitually. And when the apology came for Mr. Godolphin's absence, Lord Averil determined to call upon him that night. Though, in talking to Mrs. Pain, he almost let the time for it slip by.

Cecil rose up when he entered. In broad daylight he might have seen beyond doubt her changing face, telling of emotion. Was he mistaken, in fancying that she was agitated? His pulses quickened at the thought: for Cecil was as dear to him as she had ever been.

"Will you pardon my intrusion at this hour?" he asked, taking her hand, and bending towards her with his sweet smile. "It is later than I thought it was"—in truth, ten was striking that moment from the hall clock. "I was concerned to hear of Mr. Godolphin's illness, and wished to ascertain how he was, before returning to Prior's Ash."

"He has kept his room this evening," replied Cecil. "My sister is sitting with him. I do not think it is anything serious. But he has not appeared very well of late."

"Indeed I trust it is nothing serious," warmly responded Lord Averil.

Cecil fell into silence. She supposed they had told Janet of the visit, and that she would be coming in. Lord Averil went to the window.

"The same charming scene!" he exclaimed. "I think the moonlight view from this window most beautiful. The dark trees, and the white walls of Lady Godolphin's Folly, rising there, remain on my memory as a painted scene."

He folded his arms and stood there, gazing still. Cecil stole a look up at him: at his pale, attractive face, with its expression of care. She had wondered once why that look of care should be conspicuous there; but not after she became acquainted with his domestic history.

"Have you returned to England to remain, Lord Averil?"

The question awoke him from his reverie. He turned to Cecil, and a sudden impulse prompted him to stake his fate on the die of the moment. It was not a lucky throw.

"I would remain if I could induce one to share my name and home. Forgive me, Cecil, if I anger you by thus hastily speaking. Will you forget the past, and help *me* to forget it?—will you let me make you my dear wife?"

In saying "Will you forget the past," Lord Averil had alluded to his first marriage. In his extreme sensitiveness upon that point, he doubted whether Cecil might not object to succeed the dead Lady Averil: he believed those hasty and ill-natured words, reported to him as having been spoken by her, bore upon that sore point alone. Cecil, on the contrary, assumed that her forgetfulness was asked for his own behaviour to her, in so far as that he had gone away and left her without word or explanation. She grew quite pale with anger. Lord Averil resumed, his manner earnest, his voice low and tender.

"I have loved you, Cecil, from the first day that I saw you at Mrs. Averil's. I dragged myself away from the place, because I loved you, fearing lest you might come to see my folly. It was worse than folly then, for I was not a free man. I have gone on loving you more and more, from that time to this. I went abroad this last time hoping to forget you; striving to forget you. but I cannot do it, and the love has only become stronger. Forgive, I say, my urging it upon you in this moment's impulse."

Poor Cecil was all at sea. "Went abroad, hoping to forget her; striving to forget her!" It was worse and worse. She flung his hand away.

"Oh, Cecil! can you not love me?" he exclaimed in agitation. "Will you not give me hope that you will sometime be my wife?"

"No, I cannot love you. I will not give you hope. I would rather marry any one in the world than you. You ought to be ashamed of yourself, Lord Averil!"

Not a very dignified rejoinder. And Cecil, what with anger, what with *love*, burst into even less dignified tears, and left the room in a passion. Lord Averil bit his lips to pain.

Janet entered, unsuspicious. He turned from the window, and smoothed his brow, gathering what equanimity he could, as he proceeded to inquire after Mr. Godolphin.

CHAPTER IV.

CHARLOTTE PAIN'S "TURN-OUT."

A STYLISH vehicle, high enough for a fire-escape, its green wheels picked out with gleaming red, was dashing up the streets of Pricr's Ash. A lady was seated in it, driving its pair of blood-horses, whose restive mettle appeared more fitted for a man's guidance than a woman's. You need not be told that it was Charlotte Pain; no one else of her sex in Prior's Ash would have driven such a turn-out. Prior's Ash, rather at a loss what name to give it, for the like of it had never been seen in that sober place, christened it "Mrs. Pain's turn-out:" so, if you grumble at the appellation, you must grumble at them, not at me.

Past the Bank it flew; when, as if a sudden thought appeared to take the driver, it suddenly whirled round, to the imminent danger of the street in general, retraced its steps past the Bank, dashed round the corner of Crosse Street, and drew up at the entrance to Mr. George Godolphin's. The servant sprang from the seat behind.

"Inquire if Mrs. George Godolphin is within."

Mrs. George Godolphin was within, and Charlotte entered. Across the hall, up the handsome staircase lined with paintings, to the still more handsome drawing-room, swept she, conducted by a servant. Margery looked out at an opposite door, as Charlotte entered that of the drawing-room, her curious eyes taking in at a glance Charlotte's attire. Charlotte wore a handsome mauve brocaded skirt, trailing the ground at the very least half a yard behind her, and a close habit of mauve velvet. A black hat with a turned-up brim, and a profusion of mauve feathers, adorned her head, and a little bit of gauze, mauve-coloured also, came half-way down her face, fitting tightly round the nose and cheeks. At that period, this style of dress was very uncommon.

Margery retired with a sniff. Had it been any one she approved, any especial friend of her mistress, she would have invited her into her mistress's presence, to the little boudoir, where Maria was seated. A pretty boudoir, tastefully furnished. The bedroom, dressing-room, and this boudoir communicated with each other. Being who it was, Margery allowed the drawing-room the honour of receiving the visitor.

Maria sat at a table, her drawing materials before her. Miss Meta, perched in a high chair, was accommodated with a pencil and paper opposite. "It's Mrs. Pain in a mask," was Margery's salutation.

Maria laid down her pencil. "Mrs. Pain in a mask!" she echoed.

"It looks like nothing else, ma'am," responded Margery. "*I* never saw Christian folks make themselves into such spectacles before. It's to be hoped she won't go in that guise to call at Ashlydyat: Miss Janet would be sending for the mad doctor."

Maria smiled. "You never admire Mrs. Pain's style of dress, Margery."

"It's not taking," rejoined Margery. "Honest faces would as soon see themselves standing out from a brass pan, as with one of them brazen hats stuck upon them."

Apart from her prejudices against Mrs. Pain—whatever those prejudices might be—it was evident that Margery did not admire the fashionable head-gear. Maria moved to the door, and Miss Meta scrambled off her chair to follow her. "Meta go too, mamma."

Margery caught the child up as if she were snatching her from a fiery furnace, smothered her in her arms, and whispered unheard-of visions of immediate cakes and sweetmeats, that were to be had by ascending to the nursery, and bore her away in triumph. Did she fear there was contamination for the child in Mrs. Pain's hat?

Maria, not having observed the bit of by-play, proceeded to the presence of Charlotte. Not a greater contrast had there been between them in those old days at Broomhead, than there was now. Maria was the same quiet, essentially lady-like girl as of yore: she looked but a girl still, in her pretty muslin dress. Charlotte was standing at the window, watching her restless horses, which the servant was driving about in the front street, but could scarcely manage. She put back her hand to Maria.

"How are you to-day, Mrs. George Godolphin? Excuse my apparent rudeness: I am looking at my horses. If the man cannot keep them within bounds, I must go down myself."

Maria took her place by the side of Charlotte. The horses looked terrific animals in her eyes, very much inclined to kick the carriage to pieces and to bolt into the Bank afterwards. "Did *you* drive them here?"

"Nobody else can drive them," replied Charlotte with a laugh. "I should like to seduce Kate behind them some day when she is at Prior's Ash: she would be in a fit with fright before we were home again."

"How can you risk your own life, Mrs. Pain?"

"My life! that is a good joke," said Charlotte. "If I could not manage the horses, I should not drive them. Did you notice the one I was riding yesterday, when you met me with your husband—a party of us together?"

"Not particularly," replied Maria. "It was just at the turn of the road, you know. I think I looked chiefly at George."

"You ought to have noticed my horse. You must see him another time. He is the most splendid animal; down from London only the previous day. I rode him yesterday for the first time."

"I should not detect any of his beauties; I scarcely know one horse from another," acknowledged Maria.

"Ah! You are not particularly observant," returned Charlotte in good-humoured sarcasm. "The horse was a present to me. He cost a hundred and thirty guineas. Those animals below are getting quieter now."

She withdrew from the window, sitting down on a sofa. Maria took a seat near her. "We had been to see Mrs. Averil yesterday when we met you," observed Maria. "She is still a great sufferer."

"So Lord Averil told me," answered Charlotte. "He dined at the Folly yesterday."

"Did he? George did not mention that Lord Averil was of the party. Did you dine with them?"

"Not I," answered Charlotte. "It was bore enough to have them in the drawing-room afterwards. Only a few of them came in. As to your husband, I never set eyes upon him at all."

"He came home early. I think his head ached. He——"

"Oh, he did come home, then!" interrupted Charlotte.

Maria looked surprised. "Of course he came home. Why should he not?"

"How should I know why?" was Charlotte's answer. "This house has the bother of it to-night, I hear. It *is* nothing but a bother, a gentleman's dinner-party!"

"It is a sort of business party to-night, I believe," observed Maria.

"Verrall is coming. He told me so. Do you know how Mr. Godolphin is?"

"He seems as well as usual. He has come to-day, and I saw him for a minute. George told me that he did not appear at dinner yesterday. Margery——"

A commotion in the street. Charlotte flew to one of the windows, opened it, and stretched herself out. But she could not see the carriage, which was then in Crosse Street. A mob was collecting and shouting.

"I suppose I had better go. That stupid man never can keep horses in good humour, if they have any spirit. Good-bye, Mrs. George Godolphin."

She ran down to the hall door, giving no time for a servant to show her out. Maria proceeded to her boudoir, which looked into Crosse Street, to see whether anything was the matter.

Something might have been, but that George Godolphin, hearing the outcry, had flown out to the aid of the servant. The man, in his fear—he was a timid man with horses, and it was a wonder Charlotte kept him—had got *out* of the carriage. George leaped into it, took the reins and the whip, and succeeded in restoring the horses to what Charlotte called good humour. Maria's heart beat when she saw her husband there: she, like the man, was timid. George, however, alighted unharmed, and stood talking with Charlotte. He was without his hat. Then he handed Charlotte in, and stood looking up and talking to her again, the seat being about a mile above his head. Charlotte, at any rate, had no fear; she nodded a final adieu to George, and drove away at a fast pace, George gazing after her.

Intimate as George Godolphin was with Charlotte Pain, no such thought as that of attributing it to a wrong motive ever occurred to Maria. She had been jealous of Charlotte Pain in the old days, when she was Maria Hastings, dreading that George might choose her for his wife: but with their marriage all such feeling ceased. Maria was an English gentlewoman in the best sense of the term; of a refined, retiring nature, simple and modest of speech, innocent of heart: to associate harm now with her husband and Charlotte, was a thing next to impossible for her to glance at. Unbiased by others, she would never be likely to glance at it. She did not like Charlotte: where tastes and qualities are as opposed as they were in her and Charlotte Pain, mutual preference is not easy; but, to suspect any greater cause for dislike, was foreign to Maria's nature. Had Maria even received a hint that the fine saddle-horse, boasted of by Charlotte as worthy of Maria's especial observation, and costing a hundred and thirty guineas, was a present from her husband, she would have attached no motive to the gift, but that of kindness; given him no worse word than a hint at extravagance. Maria could almost as soon have disbelieved in herself, as have disbelieved in the cardinal virtues of George Godolphin.

It was the day of one of George's dinner-parties: as Charlotte has announced for our information. Fourteen were expected to sit down, inclusive of himself and his brother. Most of them county men; men who did business with the Bank; Mr. Verrall and Lord Averil being two of them: but Mr. Verrall did not do business with the Bank, and was not looked upon as a county man. It was not Maria's custom to appear at all at these parties; she did not imitate Charlotte Pain in playing the hostess afterwards in the drawing-room. Sometimes Maria would spend these evenings out: at Ashlydyat, or at the Rectory: sometimes, as was her intention on this evening, she would remain in her pretty boudoir, leaving the house at liberty. She had been busy at her drawing all day, and had not quitted it to stir abroad.

Mr. George had stirred abroad. Mr. George had taken a late afternoon ride with Charlotte Pain. He came home barely in time to dress. The Bank was closed for the day: the clerks had all gone, except one, the old cashier, Mr. Hurde. He sometimes stayed later than the rest.

"Any private letters for me?" inquired George, hastening into the office, whip in hand, and devouring the letter-rack with eager eyes, where the unopened letters were usually placed.

The cashier, a tall man once, but stooping now, with silver spectacles and white whiskers, stretched up his head to look also. "There's one, sir," he cried, before George had quite crossed the office.

George made a grab at the letter. It stuck in the rack, and he gave forth an impatient word. A blank look of disappointment came over his face, when he saw the direction.

"This is not for me. This is for Mr. Hastings. Who sorted the letters?"

"Mr. Hastings, I believe, sir, as usual."

"What made him put his own letter into the rack?" muttered George to himself. He went about the office; went into the private room and searched his own table. No, there was no letter for him. Mr. Hurde remembered that Mr. George Godolphin had been put out in the morning by not receiving an expected letter.

George looked at his watch. "There's no time to go to Verrall's," he thought. "And he would be starting to come here by the time I reached the Folly."

Up to his own room to dress, which was not a long process. He then entered his wife's boudoir.

"Drawing still, Maria?"

She looked up with a bright glance. "I have been so industrious! I have been drawing nearly all day. See! I have nearly finished this."

George stood by the table listlessly, his thoughts preoccupied: not pleasantly preoccupied, either. Presently he began turning over the old sketches in Maria's portfolio. Maria left her seat, and stood by her husband, her arm round his neck. He was now sitting sideways on a chair.

"I put some of these drawings into the portfolio this morning," she observed. "I found them in a box in the lumber-room. They had not been disinterred, I do believe, since they came here from the Rectory. Do you remember that one, George?"

He took up the sketch she pointed to. A few moments, and then recollection flashed over him. "It is a scene near Broomhead. That is Bray's cottage."

"How glad I am that you recognise it!" she cried gleefully. "It proves that I sketched it faithfully. Do you remember the day I did it, George?"

George could not remember that. "Not particularly," he answered.

"Oh, George! It was the day when I was frightened by that snake —or whatever it was. You and I and Charlotte Pain were there. We took refuge in Bray's house."

"Refuge from the snake?" asked George.

Maria laughed. "Lady Godolphin came up, and said I ought to go there and rest, and take some water. How terribly frightened I was! I can recall it still. Bray wanted to marry us afterwards," she continued, laughing more heartily.

"Bray would have married me to both you and Charlotte for a crown a-piece," said George.

"Were you in earnest when you asked me to let him do it?"

she dreamily inquired, after a pause, her thoughts cast back to the past.

"I dare say I was, Maria. We do foolish things sometimes. Had you said yes, I should have thought you a silly girl afterwards for your pains."

"Of course you would. Do you see that old Welshwoman in the doorway?" resumed Maria, pointing to the drawing. "She was a nice old body, in spite of her pipe. I wonder whether she is still alive? Perhaps Margery knows. Margery had a letter from her sister this morning."

"Had she?" carelessly returned George. "I saw there was a letter for her with the Scotch postmark. Has Bray come to grief yet?"

"I fancy they are always in grief, by the frequent appeals to Margery. Lady Godolphin is kind to the wife. She tells Margery if it were not for my lady, she should starve."

An arrival was heard as Maria spoke, and George rang the bell. It was answered by Maria's maid, but George said he wanted the butler. The man appeared.

"Has Mr. Verrall come?"

"No, sir. It is Mr. Godolphin."

"When Mr. Verrall comes, show him into the Bank parlour, and call me. I wish to see him before he goes into the drawing-room."

The man departed with his order. George went into the adjoining bedroom. A few minutes, and some one else was heard to come in, and run up the stairs with eager steps. It was followed by an impatient knock at Maria's door.

It proved to be Isaac Hastings. A fine-looking young man, with a sensible countenance. "Have they gone in to dinner yet, Maria?" he hastily cried.

"No. It is not time. No one has come but Mr. Godolphin."

"I did such a stupid trick! I——"

"Is it you, Isaac?" interrupted George, returning to the room. "I could not think who it was, rushing up."

"I wanted to catch you, sir, before you went in to dinner," replied Isaac, holding out a letter to George. "It came for you this afternoon," he continued, "and I put it, as I thought, into the rack; and one for myself, which also came, I put into my pocket. Just now I found I had brought yours away, and left mine."

"Yours is in the rack now," said George. "I wondered what brought it there."

He took the letter, glanced at its superscription, and retired to the window to read it. There appeared to be but a very few lines. George read it twice over, and then lifted his flushed face: flushed, as it seemed, with pain—with a perplexed, hopeless sort of expression. Maria could see his face reflected in the glass. She turned to him:

"George, what is it? You have had bad news!"

He crushed the letter in his hand. "Bad news! Nothing of the sort. Why should you think that? It is a business letter that I ought to have had yesterday, though, and I am vexed at the delay."

He left the room again. Isaac prepared to depart.

"Will you stay and take tea with me, Isaac?" asked Maria. "I have dined. I am expecting Rose."

"I am taking tea already," answered Isaac, with a laugh. "I was at Grace's. We were beginning tea, when I put my hand into my pocket to take out my letter, and found it was George Godolphin's."

"You were not in haste to read your own letter," returned Maria.

"No. I knew who it was from. There was no hurry. I ran all the way from Grace's here, and now I must run back again. Good-bye, Maria."

Isaac went away. George was in and out of the room, walking about in a restless manner. Several arrivals had been heard, and Maria felt sure that all the guests, or nearly all, must have arrived. "Why don't you go to them, George?" she asked.

The hour for dinner struck as she spoke, and George left the room. He did not enter the drawing-room, but went down and spoke to the butler.

"Has Mr. Verrall not come yet?"

"No, sir. Every one else is here."

George retraced his steps and entered the drawing-room. He was gay George again: handsome George; not a line of perplexity could be traced on his open brow, not a shade of care in his bright blue eye. He shook hands with his guests, offering only a half apology for his tardiness, and saying that he knew his brother was there to replace him.

Some minutes of busy conversation, and then it flagged: another few minutes of it, and a second flag. Thomas Godolphin whispered to his brother. "George, I should not wait. Mr. Verrall cannot be coming."

George went quite red with anger, or some other feeling. "Not be coming? Of course he is coming? Nothing is likely to detain him."

Thomas said no more. But the waiting—— Well, you all know what it is, this awkward waiting for dinner. By-and-by the butler looked into the room. George thought it might be a hint that dinner was spoiling, and he reluctantly gave orders that it should be served.

A knock at the door—a loud knock—resounding through the house. George Godolphin's face lighted up. "There he is!" he exclaimed. "But it is too bad of him to keep us waiting."

There he is *not*, George might have said, could he have seen through the closed door the applicant standing there. It was only Maria's evening visitor, pretty Rose Hastings.

CHAPTER V.

A REVELATION.

THE dinner-table was spacious, consequently the absence of one was conspicuous. Mr. Verrall's chair was still left for him: he would come yet, George said. No clergyman was present, and Thomas Godolphin said grace. He sat at the foot of the table, opposite to his brother.

"We are thirteen!" exclaimed Sir John Pevans, a young baronet,

who had been reared a milksop, and feared consumption for himself.
" I don't much like it. It is the ominous number, you know."

Some of them laughed. "What is that peculiar superstition ?" asked
Colonel Max. " I have never been able to understand it."

" The superstition is, that if thirteen sit down to dinner, one of them
is sure to die before the year is out," replied young Pevans, speaking
with great seriousness.

" Why is thirteen not as good a number to sit down as any other ?"
cried Colonel Max, humouring the baronet. "As good as fourteen,
for instance ?"

" It's the odd number, I suppose."

" *The* odd number. It's no more the odd number, Pevans, than any
other number's odd. What do you say to eleven ?—what do you say
to fifteen ?"

" I can't explain it," returned Sir John. " I only know that the
superstition exists, and that I have noticed, in more instances than one,
that it has been borne out. Three or four parties who have sat down
thirteen to dinner, have lost one of them before the year has come
round. You laugh at me, of course; I have been laughed at before :
but suppose you notice it now ? We are thirteen of us : see if we are
all alive by the end of the year."

Thomas Godolphin, in his inmost heart, thought it not unlikely that
one of them, at any rate, would not be there. Several faces were broad
with amusement : the most serious of them was Lord Averil's.

" *You* don't believe in it, Averil !" muttered Colonel Max in surprise,
as he gazed at him.

" I !" was the answer. " Certainly not. Why should you ask it ?"

" You look so grave over it."

" I never like to joke, though it be only by a smile, on the subject of
death," replied Lord Averil. " I once received a lesson upon the point,
and it will serve me my life."

" Will your lordship tell us what it was !" interposed Sir John, who
had been introduced to Lord Averil to-day for the first time.

" I cannot do so now," replied Lord Averil. " The subject is not
suited to a merry party," he frankly added. " But it would not help
to bear out your superstition, Sir John : you are possibly thinking that
it might do so."

" If I have sat down once thirteen, I have sat down fifty times," cried
Colonel Max, " and we all lived the year out and many a year on to it.
You are a sociable fellow to invite out to dinner, Pevans ! I fancy Mr.
George Godolphin must be thinking so."

Mr. George Godolphin appeared to be thinking of something that
rendered him somewhat distrait. In point of fact, his duties as host
were considerably broken by listening to the door. Above the conversation his ear was strained, hoping for the knock that should announce Mr. Verrall. It was of course strange that he neither appeared
nor sent an excuse. But no knock seemed to come : and George
could only rally his powers and forget Mr. Verrall.

It was a *recherché* repast. George Godolphin's state dinners always
were so. No trouble or expense was spared for them. Luxuries, in
season and out of season, would be there. The turtle would seem

richer at his table than at any other, the venison more delicate; the Moselle of fuller flavour, the sparkling hermitage of rarest vintage.

The evening passed on. Some of the gentlemen were solacing themselves with a cup of coffee, when the butler slipped a note into his master's hand. "The man waits for an answer, sir," he whispered. And George glided out of the room, and opened the note.

"DEAR GODOLPHIN,

"I am ill and lonely, and have halted here midway in my journey for a night's rest before going on again, which I must do at six in the morning. Come in for half an hour—there's a good fellow! I don't know when we may meet again. The regiment embarks to-morrow; and can't embark without me. Come at once, or I shall be gone to bed.

"G. ST. AUBYN."

One burning, almost irrepressible desire had hung over George all the evening—that he could run up to Verrall's and learn the cause of his absence. Mr. Verrall's absence in itself would not in the least have troubled George; but he had a most urgent reason for wishing to see him : hence his anxiety. To leave his guests to themselves would have been scarcely the thing to do : but this note appeared to afford just the excuse wanted. At any rate, George determined to make it an excuse. The note was dated from the principal inn of the place.

"One of the waiters brought this, I suppose, Pierce ?" he said to the butler.

"Yes, sir."

"My compliments, and I will be with Captain St. Aubyn directly."

George went into the room again, and drew his brother aside.

"Thomas, you'll be host for me for half an hour," he whispered. "St. Aubyn has just sent me an urgent summons to go and see him at the Bell. He was passing through Prior's Ash, and is forced to halt and lie up : he's very ill. I'll soon be back again."

Away he went. Thomas felt unusually well that evening, and exerted himself for his brother. Once out of the house, George hesitated. Should he dash up to Lady Godolphin's Folly first, and ease his mind, or should he go first to the Bell ? The Bell was very near, but in the opposite direction to Ashlydyat. He turned first to the Bell, and was soon in the presence of Captain St. Aubyn, an old friend, now bound for Malta.

"I am sorry to have sent for you," exclaimed Captain St. Aubyn, holding out his hand to George. "I hear you have friends this evening."

"It is just the kindest thing you could have done," impulsively answered George. "I would have given a five-pound note out of my pocket for a plea to absent myself; and your letter came and afforded it."

What more he chose to explain was between themselves : it was not much : and in five minutes George was on his way to Lady Godolphin's Folly. On he strode, his eager feet scarcely touching the ground. He lifted his hat and bared his brow, hot with anxiety, to the night air. It was a very light night, the moon high : and, as George pushed on through the dark grove of the Folly, he saw Charlotte Pain emerging from the same at a little distance, a dark shawl, or mantle, thrown completely over her head and figure, apparently for the purpose of disguise or concealment. Her face was turned for a moment towards the moonlight, and there was no mistaking the features of Charlotte Pain. Then she crouched down, and sped along under the friendly cover of the trees. George hastened to overtake her.

But when he got up with her, as he thought, there was no Charlotte there. There was no any one. Where had she crept to? How had she disappeared? She must have plunged into the trees again. But George was in too much haste then to see Mr. Verrall, to puzzle himself about Charlotte. He crossed to the terrace, and rang the bell.

Were the servants making merry? He had to ring again. A tolerable peal this time. Its echoes might have been heard at Ashlydyat.

"Is Mr. Verrall at home?"

"No, sir. Mrs. Pain is."

"Mrs. Pain is not," thought George to himself. But he followed the man to the drawing-room.

To his indescribable astonishment, there sat Charlotte, at work. She was in evening dress, her gown and hair interlaced with jewels. Calmly and quietly sat she, very quietly for her, her King Charley reposing upon a chair at her side, fast asleep. It was next to impossible to fancy, or believe, that she could have been outside a minute or two ago, racing in and out of the trees, as if dodging some one, perhaps himself. And yet, had it been necessary, George thought he could have sworn that the face he saw was the face of Charlotte. So bewildered did he feel, as to be diverted for a moment from the business which had brought him there.

"You may well be surprised!" cried Charlotte, looking at him ; and George noticed as she spoke that there was some peculiar expression in her face not usual to it. "To see me at work is one of the world's wonders. A crochet mat took my fancy to-day in a shop, and I bought it, thinking I would make one like it. Instead of making one, I have managed to unravel the other."

She pointed to the ground as she spoke. There, half covered by her dress, lay a heap of crinkled cotton ; no doubt the unravelled mat. Charlotte was plying her needle again with assiduity, her eyes studying the instructions at her elbow.

"How very quickly you must have come in!" exclaimed George.

"Come in from where?" asked Charlotte.

"As I went up to the door, I saw you stooping near the grove on the left, something dark over your head."

"You dreamt it," said Charlotte. "I have not been out."

"But I certainly did see you," repeated George. "I could not be mistaken. You—were I fanciful, Charlotte, I should say you were in mischief, and wanted to escape observation. You were stooping under the shade of the trees and running along quickly."

Charlotte lifted her face and looked at him with wondering eyes. "Are you joking, or are you in earnest?" asked she.

"I never was more in earnest in my life. I could have staked my existence upon its being you."

"Then I assure you I have not stirred out of this room since I came into it from dinner. What possessed me to try this senseless work, I cannot tell," she added, flinging it across the floor in a momentary accession of temper. "It has given me a headache, and they brought me some tea."

"You are looking very poorly," remarked George.

"Am I? I don't often have such a headache as this. The pain is here, over my left temple. Bathe it for me, will you, George?"

A handkerchief and some eau-de-Cologne were lying on the table beside her. George gallantly undertook the office: but he could not get over his wonder. "I'll tell you what, Charlotte. If it was not yourself, it must have been your—— "

"It must have been my old blind black dog," interrupted Charlotte. "He has a habit of creeping about the trees at night. There! I am sure that's near enough. I don't believe it was anything or any one."

"Your double, I was going to say," persisted George. "I never saw your face if I did not think I saw it then. It proves how mistaken we may be. Where's Verrall? A pretty trick he played me this evening."

"What trick?" repeated Charlotte. "Verrall's gone to London."

"Gone to London!" shouted George, his tone one of painful dismay. "It cannot be."

"It *is*," said Charlotte. "When I came in from our ride I found Verrall going off by train. He had received a telegraphic message, which took him away."

"Why did he not call upon me? He knew—he knew—the necessity there was for me to see him. He ought to have come to me."

"I suppose he was in a hurry to catch the train," said Charlotte.

"Why did he not send?"

"He did send. I heard him send a verbal message by one of the servants, to the effect that he was summoned unexpectedly to London, and could not, therefore, attend your dinner. How early you have broken up!"

"We have not broken up. I left my guests to see after Verrall. No message was brought to me."

"Then I will inquire," began Charlotte, rising. George gently pushed her back.

"It is of little consequence," he said. "It might have saved me some suspense; but I am glad I got dinner over without knowing it. I *must* see Verrall."

Charlotte carried her point, and rang the bell. "If you are glad, George, it is no extenuation for the negligence of the servants. They may be forgetting some message of more importance, if they are left unreproved now."

But forgotten the message had not been. The servant, it appeared, had misunderstood his master, and carried the message to Ashlydyat, instead of to the Bank.

"How very stupid he must have been!" remarked Charlotte to George, when the explanation was given. "I think some people have only half their share of brains."

"Charlotte, I must see Verrall. I received a letter this evening from

London which I ought to have had yesterday, and it has driven me to my wits' end."

"About the old business?" questioned Charlotte.

"Just so. Look here."

He took the letter from his pocket: the letter brought back to him by Isaac Hastings, and which he had assured Maria had not contained bad news: opened it, and handed it to Charlotte for her perusal. Better, possibly, for Mr. George Godolphin that he had made a bosom friend of his wife than of Charlotte Pain! Better for gentlemen in general, it may be, that they should tell their secrets to their wives than to their wives' would-be rivals—however comprehensive the fascinations of these latter ladies may be. George, however, had made his own bed, as we all do; and George would have to lie upon it.

"What am I to do, Charlotte?"

Charlotte sat bending over the note, and pressing her forehead. Her look was one of perplexity; perplexity great as George's.

"It is a dangerous position," she said at length. "If not averted—"

She came to a dead pause, and their eyes met.

"Ay!" he repeated—"if not averted! Nothing would remain for me but—"

"Hush, George," said she, laying her hand upon his lips, and then letting it fall upon his fingers, where it remained.

There they sat, it is hard to say how long, their heads together, talking earnestly. Charlotte was in his full confidence. Whatever may have been the nature, the depth of his perplexities, she fathomed them. At length George sprang up with a start.

"I am forgetting everything. I forgot those people were still at home, waiting for me. Charlotte, I must go."

She rose, put her arm within his, and took a step with him, as if she would herself let him out. Perhaps she was in the habit of letting him out.

"Not there! not that way!" she abruptly said, for George was turning to unclose the shutters of the window. "Come into the next room, and I'll open that."

The next room was in darkness. They opened the window, and stood yet a minute within the room, talking anxiously still. Then he left her, and went forth.

He intended to take the lonely road homewards, as being the nearer; that dark, narrow road you may remember to have heard of, where the ash-trees met overhead, and, as report went, a ghost was in the habit of taking walking exercise by night. George had no thought for ghosts just then: he had a "ghost" within him, frightful enough to scare away a whole lane full of the others. Nevertheless, George Godolphin did take a step backward with a start, when, just within the Ash-tree Walk, after passing the turnstile, there came a dismal groan from some dark figure seated on a broken bench.

It was all dark together there. The ash-trees hid the moon; George had just emerged from where her beams shone bright and open; and not at first did he distinguish who was sitting there. But his eyes grew accustomed to the obscurity.

"Thomas!" he cried, in consternation. "Is it you?"

For answer, Thomas Godolphin caught hold of his brother, bent forward, and laid his forehead upon George's arm, another deep groan breaking from him.

That George Godolphin would rather have been waylaid by a real ghost, than by his brother at that particular time and place, was certain. Better that the whole world should detect any undue anxiety for Mr. Verrall's companionship just then, than that Thomas Godolphin should do so. At least, George thought so: but conscience makes cowards of us all. Nevertheless, he gave his earnest sympathy to his brother.

"Lean on me, Thomas. Let me support you. How have you been taken ill?"

Another minute, and the paroxysm was past. Thomas wiped the dew from his brow, and George sat down on the narrow bench beside him.

"How came you to be here alone, Thomas? Where is your carriage?"

"I ordered the carriage early, and it came just as you had gone out," explained Thomas. "Feeling well, I sent it away as I had to wait, saying I would walk home. The pain overtook me just as I reached this spot, and but for the bench I should have fallen. But, George, what brings *you* here?" was the next very natural question. "You told me you were going to the Bell?"

"So I was; so I did," said George, speaking volubly. "St. Aubyn I found very poorly; I told him he would be best in bed, and came away. It was a nice night; I felt inclined for a run, so I came up here to ask Verrall what had kept him from dinner. He was sent for to London, it seems, and the stupid servant took his apology to Ashlydyat, instead of to the Bank."

Thomas Godolphin might well have rejoined, "If Verrall is away, where have you stopped?" But he made no remark.

"Have they all gone?" asked George, alluding to his guests.

"They have all gone. I made it right with them respecting your absence. My being there was almost the same thing: they appeared to regard it so. George, I believe I must have your arm as far as the house. See what an old man I am getting."

"Will you not rest longer? I am in no hurry, as they have left. What can this pain be, that seems to be attacking you of late?"

"Has it never occurred to you what it may be?" quietly rejoined Thomas.

"No," replied George. But he noticed that Thomas's tone was peculiar, and he began to run over in his own mind all the pharmacopœia of ailments that flesh is heir to. "It cannot be rheumatism, Thomas?"

"It is something worse than rheumatism," said Thomas, in his serene, ever-thoughtful way. "A short time, George, and you will be master of Ashlydyat."

George's heart seemed to stand still, and then bound onwards in a tumult. The words struck upon every chord of feeling he possessed— struck from more causes than one.

"What do you mean, Thomas? What do you fear may be the matter with you?"

"Do you remember what killed our mother?"

There was a painful pause. "Oh, Thomas!"

"It is so," said Thomas, quietly.

"I hope you are mistaken! I *hope* you are mistaken!" reiterated George. "Have you had advice? You must have advice."

"I have had it. Snow confirms my own suspicions. I desired the truth."

"Who's Snow?" returned George, disparagingly. "Go up to London, Thomas; consult the best man there. Or telegraph for one of them to come down to you."

"For the satisfaction of you all, I may do so," he replied. "But it cannot benefit me, George."

"Good Heavens, what a dreadful thing!" returned George, with feeling. "What a blow to fall upon you!"

"You would regard it so, were it to fall upon you; and naturally. You are young, joyous; you have your wife and child. I have none of these attributes: and—if I had them all, we are in the hands of One who knows what is best for us."

George Godolphin did not feel very joyous just then: had not felt particularly joyous for a long time. Somehow, his own inward care was more palpable to him than this news, sad though it was, imparted by his brother. He lifted his right hand to his temples and kept it there. Thomas suffered his right hand to fall upon George's left, which rested on his knee. A more holy contact than that imparted by Mrs. Charlotte Pain's.

"Don't grieve, George. I am more than resigned. I think of it as a happy change. This world, taken at its best, is full of care: if we seem free from it one year, it only falls upon us more unsparingly the next. It is wisely ordered: were earth made too pleasant for us, we might be wishing that it could be permanently our home."

Heaven knew that George had enough care upon him. *He* knew it. But he was not weary of the world. Few so weary of it, whatever may be their care, until they have learned to look for a better.

"In the days gone by, I have felt tempted to wonder why Ethel should have been taken," resumed Thomas Godolphin. "I see now how merciful was the fiat, George. I have been more thoughtful, more observant, perhaps, than many are; and I have learnt to see, to know, how marvellously all these fiats are fraught with mercy; full of gloom as they may seem to us. It would have been a bitter trial to me to leave her here unprotected; in deep sorrow; perhaps with young children. I scarcely think I could have been reconciled to go; and I know what her grief would have been. All's for the best."

Most rare was it for undemonstrative Thomas Godolphin thus to express his hidden sentiments. George never knew him to do so before. Time and place were peculiarly fitted for it: the still, light night, telling of peace; the dark trees around, the blue sky overhead. In these paroxysms of disease, Thomas felt brought almost face to face with death.

"It will be a blow to Janet!" exclaimed George, the thought striking him.

"She will feel it as one."

"Thomas! can *nothing* be done for you?" was the impulsive rejoinder, spoken in all hearty good-feeling.

"Could it be done for my mother, George?"

"I know. But, since then, science has made strides. Diseases, once deemed incurable, yield now to skill and enlightenment. I wish you would go to London!"

"There are some few diseases which bring death with them, in spite of human skill: will bring it to the end of time," rejoined Thomas Godolphin. "This is one of them."

"Well, Thomas, you have given me my pill for to-night: and for a great many more nights, and days too. I *wish* I had not heard it! But that, you will say, is a wish savouring only of selfishness. It is a dreadful affliction for you! Thomas, I must say it—a dreadful affliction."

"The disease, or the ending, do you mean?" Thomas asked, with a smile.

"Both. But I spoke more particularly of the disease. That in itself is a lingering death, and nothing less."

"A lingering death is the most favoured death—as I regard it: a sudden death the most unhappy. See what time is given me to 'set my house in order,'" he added, the sober, pleasant smile deepening. "I must not fail to do it well, must I?"

"And the pain, Thomas; that will be lingering, too."

"I must bear it."

He rose as he spoke, and put his arm within his brother's. George seemed to him then the same powerful protector that he, Thomas, must have seemed to Sir George in that midnight walk at Broomhead. He stood a minute or two, as if gathering strength, and then walked forward, leaning heavily on George. It was the pain, the excessive agony that so unnerved him: a little while, and he would seem in the possession of his usual strength again.

"Ay, George, it will soon be yours. I shall not long keep you out of Ashlydyat. I cannot quite tell how you will manage alone at the Bank when I am gone," he continued, in a more business tone. "I think of it a great deal. Sometimes I fancy it might be better if you took a staid, sober partner; one middle aged. A thorough man of business. Great confidence has been accorded me, you know, George. I suppose people like my steady habits."

"They like you for your integrity," returned George, the words seeming to break from him impulsively. "I shall manage very well, I dare say, when the time comes. I suppose I must settle down to steadiness also; to be more as you have been. I can," he continued, as if in soliloquy. "I can, and I will."

"And, George, you will be a good master," continued Thomas. "Be a kind, considerate master to all who shall then be dependent on you. I have tried to be so: and, now that the end has come, it is, I assure you, a pleasant consciousness to possess—to look back upon. I have a few, very few, poor pensioners who may have been a little the better for me: those I shall take care of, and Janet will sometimes see them. But some of the servants lapse to you with Ashlydyat: I speak of them.

Make them comfortable. Most of them are already in years : take care of them when they shall be too old to work."

"Oh, I'll do that," said George. "I expect Janet—— "

George's words died away. They had rounded the ash-trees, and were fronting the Dark Plain. White enough looked the plain that night ; but dark was the Shadow on it. Yes, it was there ! The dark, portentous, terrific Shadow of Ashlydyat !

They stood still. Perhaps their hearts stood still. Who can know ? A man would rather confess to an unholy deed, than acknowledge his belief in a ghostly superstition.

"How dark it is to-night !" broke from George.

In truth, it had never been darker, never more intensely distinct. If, as the popular belief went, the evil to overtake the Godolphins was foreshadowed to be greater or less, according to the darker or lighter hue of the Shadow, then never did such ill fall on the Godolphins, as was to fall now.

"It is black, not dark," replied Thomas, in answer to George's remark. "I never saw it so black as it is now. Last night it was comparatively light."

George turned his gaze quickly upwards to the moon, searching in the aspect of that luminary a solution to the darker shade of to-night. "There's no difference !" he cried aloud. "The moon was as bright as this, last night, but not brighter. I don't think it could be brighter. You say the Shadow was there last night, Thomas ? "

"Yes. But not so dark as now."

"But, Thomas ! you were ill last night ; you could not see it."

"I came as far as the turnstile here with Lord Averil. He called at Ashlydyat after leaving Lady Godolphin's Folly. I was better then, and strolled out of the house with him."

"Did he see the Shadow ? "

"I don't know. It was there ; but not very distinct. He did not appear to see it. We were passing quickly, and talking about my illness."

"Did you give Averil any hint of what your illness may be ? " asked George hastily.

"Not an indication of it. Janet, Snow, and you, are my only confidants as yet. Bexley is partially so. Were that Shadow to be seen by Prior's Ash, and the fact of my illness transpired, people would say that it was a forewarning of my end," he continued, with a grave smile, as he and George turned to pursue their road to Ashlydyat.

They reached the porch in silence. George shook hands with his brother. "Don't attempt to come to business to-morrow," he said. "I will come up in the evening, and see you."

"Won't you come in now, George ? "

"Not now. Good night, Thomas. I heartily wish you better."

George turned and retraced his steps, past the ash-trees, past the Dark Plain. Intensely black the Shadow certainly looked : darker even than when he had passed it just before—at least so it appeared to George's eyes. He halted a moment, quite struck with the sombre hue. "Thomas said it appeared light last night," he half muttered : "and for *him* death cannot be much of an evil. Superstitious Janet, daft

Margery, would both say that the evil affects me: that I am to bring it!" he added, with a smile of mockery at the words. "Angry enough it certainly looks!"

It did look angry. But George vouchsafed it no further attention. He had too much on his mind to give heed to shadows, even though it were the ominous Shadow of Ashlydyat. George, as he had said to Charlotte Pain, was very nearly at his wits' end. One of his minor perplexities was, how he should get to London. He had urgent necessity for proceeding in search of Mr. Verrall, and equally urgent was it that the expedition should be kept from Thomas Godolphin. What excuse could he invent for his absence?

Rapidly arranging his plans, he proceeded again to the Bell Inn, held a few minutes' confidential conversation with Captain St. Aubyn, waking that gentleman out of his first sleep for it—not that he by any means enlightened *him* as to any trouble that might be running riot in his brain—and then went home. Maria came forward to meet him.

"How is poor Captain St. Aubyn, George? Very ill?"

"Very. How did you know anything about it, Maria?"

"Thomas told me you had been sent for. Thomas came to my sitting-room before he left, after the rest had gone. You have stayed a good while with him."

"Ay. What should you say if I were to go back and stop the night with him?" asked George, half jokingly.

"Is he so ill as that?"

"And also to accompany him a stage or two on his journey to-morrow morning? He starts at six, and is about as fit to travel as an invalid just out of bed after a month's illness."

"Do you really mean that you are going to do all that, George?" she inquired, in surprise.

George nodded. "I do not fancy Thomas will be here to-morrow, Maria. Ask to speak to Isaac when he comes in the morning. Tell him that I shall be home some time in the afternoon, but I have gone out of town a few miles with a sick friend. He can say so if I am particularly inquired for."

George went to his room. Maria followed him. He was changing his coat and waistcoat, and threw an overcoat upon his arm. Then he looked at his watch.

"What is the time?" asked Maria.

"Twenty minutes past eleven. Good night, my darling."

She fondly held his face down to hers while he kissed her, giving him —as George had once saucily told her she would—kiss for kiss. There was no shame in it now; only love. "Oh, George, my dearest, mind you come back safe and well to me!" she murmured, tears filling her eyes.

"Don't I always come back safe and well to you, you foolish child? Take care of yourself, Maria."

Maria's hand rested lingeringly in his. Could she have divined that Mr. George's tender adieux sometimes strayed elsewhere!—that his confidences were given, but not to her! George went out, and the hall door closed upon him.

It was well Maria did not watch him away! Well for her astonishment. Instead of going to the Bell Inn, he turned short round to the
left, and took the by-way which led to the railway station, gaining it
in time to catch the express train, which passed through Prior's Ash at
midnight for London.

CHAPTER VI.

MR. VERRALL'S CHAMBERS.

IN thoroughly handsome chambers towards the west-end of London,
fitted up with costly elegance, more in accordance (one would think)
with a place consecrated to the refinements of life, than to business,
there sat one morning a dark gentleman, of staid and respectable
appearance. To look at his clean, smoothly shaven face, his grey hair,
his gold-rimmed spectacles, his appearance altogether, every item of
which carried respectability with it, you might have trusted the man
at a first glance. In point of fact, he was got up *to be* trusted. A
fire was pleasant on those spring mornings, and a large and clear one
flamed in the burnished grate. Miniature statues, and other articles
possessing, one must suppose, some rare excellence, gave to the room
a refined look; and the venerable gentleman (venerable in sober
respectability, you must understand, more than from age, for his years
were barely fifty) sat enjoying its blaze, and culling choice morsels
from the *Times*. The money article, the price of stock, a large insolvency case, and other news especially acceptable to men of business,
were being eagerly read by him.

An architect might have taken a model of these chambers, so artistically were they arranged. A client could pass into any one of the
three rooms, and not come out by the same door; he might reach
them by the wide, handsome staircase, descend by means of a ladder,
and emerge in a back street. Not absolutely a ladder, but a staircase
so narrow as almost to deserve the name. It did happen, once in
a way, that a gentleman might prefer that means of exit, even if he
did not of entrance. These chambers were, not to keep you longer
in suspense, the offices of the great bill-discounting firm, Trueworthy
and Co.

One peculiar feature in their internal economy was, that no client
ever got to see Mr. Trueworthy. He was too great a man to stoop
to business in his own proper person. He was taking his pleasure in
the East; or he was on a visit to some foreign court, the especial guest
of its imperial head; or sojourning with his bosom friend the Duke of
Dorsetshire at his shooting-box; or reposing at his own country seat;
or ill in bed with gout. From one or other of these contingencies Mr.
Trueworthy was invariably invisible. It happened now and then that
there was a disturbance in these elegant chambers, caused by some ill-
bred and ill-advised gentleman, who persisted in saying that he had
been hardly treated—in point of fact, ruined. One or two had, on these
occasions, broadly asserted their conviction that there was no Mr.

Trueworthy at all: but of course their ravings, whether on the score of their own wrongs, or on the non-existence of that estimable gentleman, whose fashionable movements might have filled a weekly column of the *Court Circular*, were taken for what they were worth.

In the years gone by—only a very few years, though—the firm had owned another head: at any rate, another name. A young, fair man, who had disdained the exclusiveness adopted by his successor, and deemed himself not too great a mortal to be seen of men. This unfortunate principal had managed his affairs badly. In some way or other he came to grief. Perhaps the blame lay in his youth. Some one was so wicked as to prefer against him a charge of swindling; and ill-natured tongues said it would go hard with him—fifteen years at least. What they meant by the last phrase, they best knew. Like many another charge, it never came to anything. The very hour before he would have been captured, he made his escape, and had never since been seen or heard of. Some surmised that he was dead, some that he was in hiding abroad: only one thing was certain—that into this country he could not again enter.

All that, however, was past and gone. The gentleman, Mr. Brompton, sitting at his ease over his newspaper, his legs stretched out to the blaze, was the confidential manager and head of the office. Half the applicants did not know but that he was its principal: strangers, at first, invariably believed that he was so. A lesser satellite, a clerk, or whatever he might be, sat in an outer room, and bowed in the clients, his bow showing far more deference to this gentleman than to the clients themselves. How could the uninitiated suppose that he was anything less than the principal?

On this morning there went up the broad staircase a gentleman whose remarkably good looks drew the eyes of the passers-by towards him, as he got out of the cab which brought him. The clerk took a hasty step forward to arrest his progress, for the gentleman was crossing the office with a bold step: and all steps might not be admitted to that inner room. The gentleman, however, put up his hand, as if to say, Don't you know me? and went on. The clerk, who at the first moment had probably not had time to recognize him, threw open the inner door.

"Mr. George Godolphin, sir."

Mr. George Godolphin strode on. He was evidently not on familiar terms with the gentleman who rose to receive him, for he did not shake hands with him. His tone and manner were courteous.

"Is Mr. Verrall here?"

"He is not here, Mr. Godolphin. I am not sure that he will be here to-day."

"I must see him," said George, firmly. "I have followed him to town to see him. You know that he came up yesterday?"

"Yes. I met him last night."

"I should suppose, as he was sent for unexpectedly—which I hear was the case—that he was sent for on business; and therefore that he would be here to-day," pursued George.

"I am not sure of it. He left it an open question."

George looked uncommonly perplexed. "I must see him, and I must

be back at Prior's Ash during business hours to-day. I must catch
the eleven down-train if possible."

"Can I do for you as well as Mr. Verrall?" asked Mr. Brompton,
after a pause.

"No, you can't. Verrall I must see. It is very strange that you
don't know whether he is to be here or not."

"It happens to-day that I do not know. Mr. Verrall left it last
night, I say, an open question."

"It is the loss of time that I am thinking of," returned George.
"You see if I go down now to his residence, he may have left it to
come up here; and we should just miss each other."

"Very true," asserted Brompton.

George stood for a moment in thought, and then turned on his
heel, and departed. "Do you know whether Mr. Verrall will be up
this morning?" he asked of the clerk, as he passed through the outer
room.

The clerk shook his head. "I am unable to say, sir."

George went down to the cab, and entered it. "Where to, sir?"
asked the driver, as he closed the door.

"The South-Western Railway."

As the echo of George's footsteps died away on the stairs, Mr.
Brompton, first slipping the bolt of the door which led into the clerk's
room, opened the door of another room. A double door, thoroughly
well padded, deadened all sound between the apartments. It was
a larger and more luxurious room still. Two gentlemen were seated
in it by a similarly bright fire: though, to look at the face of the one—
a young man, whose handkerchief, as it lay carelessly on the table
beside him, bore a viscount's coronet—no one would have thought any
fire was needed. His face was glowing, and he was talking in angry
excitement, but with a tone and manner somewhat subdued, as if he
were in the presence of a master, and dared not put forth his metal.
In short, he looked something like a caged lion. Opposite to him,
listening with cold, imperturbable courtesy, his face utterly impassive,
as it ever was, his eyes calm, his yellow hair in perfect order, his
moustache trimmed, his elbows resting on the arms of his chair, and
the tips of his fingers meeting, on one of which fingers shone a monster
diamond of the purest water, was Mr. Verrall. Early as the hour was,
glasses and champagne stood on the table.

Mr. Brompton telegraphed a sign to Mr. Verrall, and he came out,
leaving the viscount to waste his anger upon air. The viscount might
rely on one thing: that it was just as good to bestow it upon air as
upon Mr. Verrall, for all the impression it would make on the latter.

"Godolphin has been here," said Mr. Brompton, keeping the doors
carefully closed.

"He has followed me to town, then! I thought he might do so. It
is of no use my seeing him. If he won't go deeper into the mire, why,
the explosion must come."

"He must go deeper into it," remarked Mr. Brompton.

"He holds out against it, and words seem wasted on him. Where's
he gone now?"

"Down to your house, I expect. He says he must be back home

to-day, but must see you first. I thought you would not care to meet him, so I said I didn't know whether you'd be here or not."

Mr. Verrall mused. "Yes, I'll see him. I can't deal with him altogether as I do with others. And he has been a lucky card to us."

Mr. Verrall went back to his viscount, who by that time was striding explosively up and down the room. Mr. Brompton sat down to his paper again, and his interesting news of the Insolvency Court.

In one of the most charming villas on the banks of the Thames, a villa which literally lacked nothing that money could buy, sat Mrs. Verrall at a late breakfast, on that same morning. She jumped up with a little scream at the sight of George Godolphin crossing the velvet lawn.

"What bad news have you come to tell me? Is Charlotte killed? Or is Lady Godolphin's Folly on fire?"

"Charlotte was well when I left her, and the Folly standing," replied George, throwing care momentarily to the winds, as he was sure to do in the presence of a pretty woman.

"She *will* be killed, you know, some day with those horses of hers," rejoined Mrs. Verrall. "What have you come for, then, at this unexpected hour? When Verrall arrived last night, he said you were giving a dinner at Prior's Ash."

"I want to see Verrall. Is he up yet?"

"Up! He was up and away ages before I awoke. He went up early to the office."

George paused. "I have been to the office, and Mr. Brompton said he did not know whether he would be there to-day at all."

"Oh, well, *I* don't know," returned Mrs. Verrall, believing she might have made an inconvenient admission. "When he goes up to town, I assume he goes to the office; but he may be bound to the wilds of Siberia for anything I can tell."

"When do you expect him home?" asked George.

"I did not ask him," carelessly replied Mrs. Verrall. "It may be to-day, or it may be next month. What will you take for breakfast?"

"I will not take anything," returned George, holding out his hand to depart.

"But you are not going again in this hasty manner! What sort of a visit do you call this?"

"A hasty one," replied George. "I must be at Prior's Ash this afternoon. Any message to Charlotte?"

"Why—yes—I have," said Mrs. Verrall, with some emphasis. "I was about to despatch a small parcel this very next hour to Charlotte, by post. But—when shall you see her? To-night?"

"I can see her to-night if you wish it."

"It would oblige me much. The truth is, it is something I ought to have sent yesterday, and I forgot it. Be sure and let her have it to-night."

Mrs. Verrall rang, and a small packet, no larger than a bulky letter, was brought in. George took it, and was soon being whirled back to London.

He stepped into a cab at the Waterloo Station, telling the man he should have double pay if he drove at double speed : and it conveyed him to Mr. Verrall's chambers.

George went straight to Mr. Brompton's room, as before. That gentleman had finished his *Times*, and was buried deep in a pile of letters. " Is Mr. Verrall in now?" asked George.

" He is here now, Mr. Godolphin. He was here two minutes after you departed : it's a wonder you did not meet."

George knew the way to Mr. Verrall's room, and was allowed to enter. Mr. Verrall, alone then, turned round with a cordial grasp.

" Holloa ! " said he. " We somehow missed this morning. How are you?"

" I say, Verrall, how came you to play me such a trick as to go off in that clandestine manner yesterday?" remonstrated George. " You know the uncertainty I was in : that if I did not get what I hoped for, I should be on my beam ends?"

" My dear fellow, I supposed you had got it. Hearing nothing of you all day, I concluded it had come by the morning's post."

" It had not come then," returned George, crustily. In spite of his blind trust in the unbleached good faith of Mr. Verrall, there were moments when a thought would cross him as to whether that gentleman had been playing a double game. This was one of them.

" I had a hasty summons, and was obliged to come away without delay," explained Mr. Verrall. " I sent you a message."

"Which I never received," retorted George. " But the message is not the question. See here ! A pretty letter, this, for a man to read. It came by the afternoon post."

Mr. Verrall took the letter, and digested the contents deliberately ; in all probability he had known their substance before. " What do you think of it?" demanded George.

" It's unfortunate," said Mr. Verrall.

" It's ruin," returned George.

" Unless averted. But it must be averted."

" How?"

" There is one way, you know," said Mr. Verrall, after a pause. " I have pointed it out to you already."

" And I wish your tongue had been blistered, Verrall, before you ever had pointed it out to me ! " foamed George. " There ! "

Mr. Verrall raised his impassive eyebrows. " You must be aware——"

" Man ! " interrupted George, his voice hoarse with emotion, as he grasped Mr. Verrall's shoulder : " do you know that the temptation, since you suggested it, is ever standing out before me—an *ignis fatuus*, beckoning me on to it ! Though I know that it would prove nothing but a curse to engulf me."

" Here, George, take this," said Mr. Verrall, pouring out a large tumbler of sparkling wine, and forcing it upon him. " The worst of you is, that you get so excited over things ! and then you are sure to look at them in a wrong light. Just hear me for a moment. The pressure is all at this present moment, is it not? If you can lift it, you will recover yourself fast enough. Has it ever struck you," Mr. Verrall added, somewhat abruptly, " that your brother is fading?"

Remembering the scene with his brother the previous night, George looked very conscious. He simply nodded an answer.

"With Ashlydyat yours, you would recover yourself almost immediately. There would positively be no risk."

"*No risk!*" repeated George, with emphasis.

"I cannot see that there would be any. Everything's a risk, if you come to that. We are in risk of earthquakes, of a national bankruptcy, of various other calamities: but the risk that would attend the step I suggested to you is really so slight as not to be called a risk. It never can be known: the chances are a hundred thousand to one."

"But there remains the one," persisted George.

"To let an *exposé* come would be an act of madness, at the worst look out: but it is madness and double madness when you may so soon succeed to Ashlydyat."

"Oblige me by not counting upon that, Verrall," said George. "I hope, ill as my brother appears to be, that he may live yet."

"I don't wish to count upon it," returned Mr. Verrall. "It is for you to count upon it, not me. Were I in your place, I should not blind my eyes to the palpable fact. Look here: your object is to get out of this mess?"

"You know it is," said George.

"Very well. I see but one way for you to do it. The money must be raised, and how is that to be done? Why, by the means I suggest. It will never be known. A little time, and things can be worked round again."

"I have been hoping to work things round this long while," said George. "And they grow worse instead of better."

"Therefore I say that you should not close your eyes to the prospect of Ashlydyat. Sit down. Be yourself again, and let us talk things over quietly."

"You see, Verrall, the risk falls wholly upon me."

"And, upon whom the benefit, for which the risk will be incurred?" pointedly returned Mr. Verrall.

"It seems to me that I don't get the lion's share of these benefits," was George's remark.

"Sit down, I say. Can't you be still? Here, take some more wine. There: now let us talk it over."

And talk it over they did, as may be inferred. For it was a full hour afterwards when George came out. He leaped into the cab, which had waited, telling the man that he must drive as if he were going through fire and water. The man did so: and George arrived at the Paddington station just in time to lose his train.

CHAPTER VII.

BEYOND RECALL.

THE clerks were at a stand-still in the banking-house of Godolphin, Crosse, and Godolphin. A certain iron safe had to be opened, and the key was not to be found. There were duplicate keys to it; one of them was kept by Mr. Godolphin, the other by Mr. George. Mr. Hurde, the cashier, appealed to Isaac Hastings.

"Do you think it has not been left with Mrs. George Godolphin?"

"I'll ask her," replied Isaac, getting off his stool. "I don't think it has: or she would have given it to me when she informed me of Mr. George Godolphin's absence."

He went into the dining-room: that pleasant room, which it was almost a shame to designate by the name. Maria was listlessly standing against the window-frame, plucking mechanically the fading blossoms of a geranium. She turned her head at the opening of the door, and saw her brother.

"Isaac, what time does the first train come in?"

"From what place?" inquired Isaac.

"Oh—from the Portsmouth direction. It was Portsmouth that Captain St. Aubyn was to embark from, was it not?"

"I don't know anything about it," replied Isaac. "Neither can I tell at what hours trains arrive from that direction. Maria, has Mr. George Godolphin left the key of the book-safe with you?"

"No," was Maria's answer. "I suppose he must have forgotten to do so. He has left it with me when he has gone away unexpectedly before, after banking-hours."

Isaac returned to the rest of the clerks. The key was wanted badly, and it was decided that he should go up to Ashlydyat for Mr. Godolphin's.

He took the nearest road to it. Down Crosse Street, and through the Ash-tree Walk. It was a place, as you have heard, especially shunned at night: it was not much frequented by day. Therefore, it was no surprise to Isaac Hastings that he did not, all through it, meet a single thing, either man or ghost. At the very end, however, on that same broken bench where Thomas Godolphin and his bodily agony had come to an anchor the previous night, sat Charlotte Pain.

She was in deep thought: deep perplexity; there was no mistaking that her countenance betrayed both: some might have fancied in deep pain, either bodily or mental. Pale she was not. Charlotte's complexion was made up too fashionably for either red or white, born of emotion, to affect it, unless it might be emotion of a most extraordinary nature. Hands clenched, brow knit, lips drawn from her teeth, eyes staring on vacancy—Isaac Hastings could not avoid reading the signs, and he read them with surprise.

"Good morning, Mrs. Pain!"

Charlotte started from the seat with a half scream. "What's the use of startling one like that!" she fiercely exclaimed.

"I did not startle you intentionally," replied Isaac. "You might have heard my footsteps had you not been so preoccupied. Did you think it was the ghost arriving?" he added, jestingly.

"Of course I did," returned Charlotte, laughing, as she made an effort, and a successful one, to recover herself. "What do you do here this morning? Did you come to look after the ghost, or after me?"

"After neither," replied Isaac, with more truth than gallantry. "Mr. George Godolphin has sent me up here."

Now, in saying this, what Isaac meant to express was nothing more than that his coming up was *caused* by George Godolphin. Alluding of course to George's forgetfulness in carrying off the key. Charlotte, however, took the words literally, and her eyes opened.

"Did George Godolphin not go last night?"

"Yes, he went. He forgot——"

"Then what can have brought him back so soon?" was her vehement interruption, not allowing Isaac time to conclude. "There's no day train in from London yet."

"Is there not?" was Isaac's rejoinder, looking keenly at her.

"Why, of course there's not: as you know, or ought to know. Besides, he could not get through the business he has gone upon and be back yet, unless he came by telegraph. He intended to leave by the eleven o'clock train from Paddington."

She spoke rapidly, thoughtlessly, in her surprise. Her inward thought was, that to have gone to London, and returned again since the hour at which she parted from him the previous night, one way, at least, must have been accomplished on the telegraph wires. Had she taken a moment for reflection, she would not have so spoken. However familiar she might be with the affairs of Mr. George Godolphin, so much the more reason was there for her shunning open allusion to them.

"Who told you Mr. George Godolphin had gone to London, Mrs. Pain?" asked Isaac, after a pause.

"Do you think I did not know it? Better than you, Mr. Isaac, clever and wise as you deem yourself."

"I pretend to be neither one nor the other with regard to the movements of Mr. George Godolphin," was the reply of Isaac. "It is not my place to be so. I heard he had only gone a stage or two towards Portsmouth with a sick friend. Of course if you know he has gone to London, that is a different matter. I can't stay now, Mrs. Pain: I have a message for Mr. Godolphin."

"Then he is not back again?" cried Charlotte, as Isaac was going through the turnstile.

"Not yet."

Charlotte looked after him as he went out of sight, and bit her lips. A doubt was flashing over her—called up by Isaac's last observation—as to whether she had done right to allude to London. When George had been with her, discussing it, he had wondered what excuse he should invent for taking the journey, and Charlotte never supposed

but that it would be known. The bright idea of starting on a bene-
volent excursion towards Portsmouth, had been an after-thought of Mr.
George's as he journeyed home.

"If I have done mischief," Charlotte was beginning slowly to murmur. But she threw back her head defiantly. "Oh, nonsense about
mischief! What does it matter? George can battle it out."

Thomas Godolphin was at breakfast in his own room, his face, pale
and worn, bearing traces of suffering. Isaac Hastings was admitted,
and explained the cause of his appearance. Thomas received the news
of George's absence with considerable surprise.

"He left me late last night—*in* the night, I may say—to return
home. He said nothing then of his intention to be absent. Where do
you say he has gone to?"

"Maria delivered a message to me, sir, from him, to the effect that
he had accompanied a sick friend, Captain St. Aubyn, a few miles on
the Portsmouth line," replied Isaac. "But Mrs. Pain, whom I have
just met, says it is to London that he has gone: she says she knows
it."

Thomas Godolphin made no further comment. It may not have
pleased him to remark upon any information touching his brother furnished by Mrs. Charlotte Pain. He handed the key to Isaac, and said
he should speedily follow him to the Bank. It had not been Thomas
Godolphin's intention to go to the Bank that day, but hearing of
George's absence caused him to proceed thither. He ordered his carriage, and got there almost as soon as Isaac, bearing an invitation to
Maria from Janet.

A quarter of an hour given to business in the manager's room,
George's, and then Thomas Godolphin went to Maria. She was seated
now near the window, in her pretty morning dress, engaged in some
sort of fancy work. In her gentle face, her soft sweet eyes, Thomas
would sometimes fancy he read a resemblance to his lost Ethel.
Thomas greatly loved and esteemed Maria.

She rose to receive him, holding out her hand that he might take it
as she quietly but earnestly made inquiries about his state of health.
Not so well as he was yesterday, Thomas answered. He supposed
George had given her the account of their meeting the previous night,
under the ash-trees, and of his, Thomas's illness.

Maria had not heard it. "How could George have been near the ash-
trees last night?" she, wondering, inquired. "Do you mean *last* night,
Thomas?"

"Yes, last night, after I left you. I was taken ill in going home——"

Miss Meta, who had been fluttering about the terrace, fluttered in to
see who might be talking to her mamma, and interrupted the conclusion of the sentence. "Uncle Thomas! Uncle Thomas!" cried she,
joyously. They were great friends.

Her entrance diverted the channel of their conversation. Thomas
took the child on his knee, fondly stroking her golden curls. Thomas
remembered to have stroked just such golden curls on the head of his
brother George, when he, George, was a little fellow of Meta's age.

"Janet bade me ask if you would go to Ashlydyat for the day, Maria,"
said he. "She——"

"Meta go too," put in the little quick tongue. "Meta go too, Uncle Thomas."

"Will Meta be good?—and not run away from Aunt Janet, and lose herself in the passages, as she did last time?" said Thomas, with a smile.

"Meta very good," was the answer, given with an oracular nod of promise. Thomas turned to Maria.

"Where is it that George has gone?" he asked. "With St. Aubyn? or to London?"

"Not to London," replied Maria. "He has gone with Captain St. Aubyn. What made you think of London?"

"Isaac said Mrs. Pain thought he had gone to London," replied Thomas. "It was some mistake, I suppose. But I wonder he should go out to-day for anything less urgent than necessity. The Bank wants him."

Maria was soon to be convinced that she need not have spoken so surely about George's having gone with Captain St. Aubyn. When she and Meta, with Margery—who would have thought herself grievously wronged had she not been one of the party to Ashlydyat—were starting, Thomas came out of the Bank parlour and accompanied them to the door. While standing there, the porter of the Bell Inn happened to pass, and Maria stopped him to inquire whether Captain St. Aubyn was better when he left.

"He was not at all well, ma'am," was the man's answer: "hardly fit to travel. He had been in a sort of fever all the night."

"And my master, I suppose, must take and sit up with him!" put in Margery, without ceremony, in a resentful tone.

"No, he didn't," said the man, looking at Margery, as if he did not understand her. "It was my turn to be up last night, and I was in and out of his room four or five times: but nobody stayed with him."

"But Mr. George Godolphin went with Captain St. Aubyn this morning?" said Thomas Godolphin to the man.

"Went where, sir?"

"Started with him. On his journey."

"No, sir; not that I know of. I did not see him at the station."

Maria thought the man must be stupid. "Mr. George Godolphin returned to the Bell between eleven and twelve last night," she explained. "And he intended to accompany Captain St. Aubyn this morning on his journey."

"Mr. George was at the Bell for a few minutes just after eleven, ma'am. It was me that let him out. He did not come back again. And I don't think he was at the train this morning. I am sure he was not with Captain St. Aubyn, for I never left the captain till the train started."

Nothing further was said to the porter. He touched his hat, and went his way. Maria's face wore an air of bewilderment. Thomas smiled at her.

"I think it is you who must be mistaken, Maria," said he. "Depend upon it, Mrs. Pain is right: he has gone to London."

"But why should he go to London without telling me?" debated Maria. "Why say he was going with Captain St. Aubyn?"

Thomas could offer no opinion upon the subject. Miss Meta began to stamp her pretty shoes, and to drag her mamma by the hand. She was impatient to depart.

They chose the way by the lonely Ash-tree Walk. It was pleasant on a sunny day: sunshine scares away ghosts: and it was also the nearest. As they were turning into it, they met Charlotte Pain. Maria, simple-hearted and straightforward, never casting a suspicion to—to anything undesirable—spoke at once of the uncertainty she was in, as to her husband.

"Why do you think he has gone to London?" she asked.

"I know he has," replied Charlotte. "He told me he was going there."

"But he told me he was only going with Captain St. Aubyn," returned Maria, a doubtful sound in her voice.

"Oh, my dear, gentlemen do not find it always convenient to keep their wives *au courant* of their little affairs."

Had it been salvation to her, Charlotte could not have helped launching that shaft at Maria Godolphin. No; not even regard for George's secrets stopped her. She had done the mischief by speaking to Isaac, and this opportunity was too glorious to be missed, so she braved it out. Had Charlotte dared—for her own sake—she could have sent forth an unlimited number of poisoned arrows daily at George Godolphin's wife: and she would have relished the sport amazingly. She sailed off: a curiously conspicuous smile of triumph in her eyes as they were bent on Maria, her parting movement being a graciously condescending nod to the child.

Maria was recalled to her senses by Margery. The woman was gazing after Charlotte with a dark, strange look: a look that Maria understood as little as she understood Charlotte's triumphant one. Margery caught the eye of her mistress upon her, and smoothed her face with a short cough.

"I'm just taking the pattern of her jacket, ma'am. It matches so bravely with the hat. I wonder what the world will come to next? The men will take to women's clothes, I suppose, now the women have taken to men's."

Mr. George—as you may remember—missed his train. And Mr. George debated whether he should order a special. Two reasons withheld him. One was, that his arriving at Prior's Ash by a special train might excite comment; the other, that a special train was expensive; and of late Mr. George Godolphin had not had any too much ready money to spare. He waited for the next ordinary train, and that deposited him at Prior's Ash at seven o'clock.

He proceeded home at once. The Bank was closed for the evening. Pierce admitted his master, who went into the dining-room. No sign of dinner; no signs of occupation.

"My mistress is at Ashlydyat, sir. She went up this morning with Miss Meta and Margery. You would like dinner, sir, would you not?"

"I don't much care for it," responded George. "Anything will do. Has Mr. Godolphin been at the Bank to-day?"

"Yes, sir. He has been here all day, I think?"

George went into the Bank parlour, then to other of the business rooms. He was looking about for letters: he was looking at books: altogether he seemed to be busy. Presently he came out and called Pierce.

"I want a light."

Pierce brought it. "I shall be engaged here for half an hour," said his master. "Should any one call, I cannot be disturbed: under any pretence, you understand."

"Very well, sir," replied Pierce, as he withdrew. And George locked the intervening door between the house and the Bank, and took out the key.

He turned into a passage and went diving down a few stairs, the light in his hand; selected one of several keys which he had brought with him, and opened the door of a dry-vaulted room. It was the strong-room of the Bank, secure and fireproof.

"Safe number three, on right," he read, consulting a bit of paper on which he had copied down the words in pencil upstairs. "Number three? Then it must be this one."

Taking another of the keys, he put it into the lock. Turned it, and turned it, and—could not open the lock. George snatched it out, and read the label. "Key of safe number two."

"What an idiot I am! I have brought the wrong key!"

He went up again, grumbling at his stupidity, opened the cupboard where the keys were kept, and looked for the right one. Number three was the one he wanted. And number three was not there.

George stood transfixed. *He* had custody of the keys. No other person had the power of approaching the place they were guarded in: except his brother. Had the Bank itself disappeared, George Godolphin could not have been much more astonished than at the disappearance of this key. Until this moment, this discovery of its absence, he would have been ready to swear that there it was, before all the judges in the land.

He tossed the keys here; he tossed them there; little heeding how he misplaced them. George became convinced that the Fates were dead against him, in spiriting away, just because he wanted it, this particular key. That no one could have touched it except Thomas, he knew: and why he should have done so, George could not imagine. He could not imagine where it was, or could be, at the present moment. Had Thomas required it to visit the safe, he was far too exact, too methodical, not to return it to its place again.

A quarter of an hour given to hunting, to thinking—and the thinking was not entirely agreeable thinking—and George gave it up in despair.

"I must wait until to-morrow," was his conclusion. "If Thomas has carried it away with him, through forgetfulness, he will find it out and replace it then."

He was closing the cupboard door, when something arrested it on its lower shelf, so that it would not close. Bringing the light inside he found—the missing key. George himself must have dropped it there on first opening the cupboard. With a suppressed shout of delight he snatched it up. A shout of delight! Better that George Godolphin had broken into a wail of lamentation! Another moment, and he was going down the stairs to the strong-room, key in hand.

Safe number three, on the right, was unlocked without trouble now. In that safe there were some tin boxes, on one of which was inscribed " Lord Averil." Selecting another and a smaller key from those he held, George opened this.

It was full of papers. George looked them rapidly over with the quick eye of one accustomed to the work, and drew forth one of them. Rather a bulky parcel, some writing upon it. This he thrust into his pocket, and began putting the rest in order. Had a mirror been held before him at that moment, it would have reflected a face utterly colourless. He returned to the office.

Enclosing the packet in a stout envelope, which he directed, he went out, and dropped it into the post-office at the opposite corner of Crosse Street. Very soon he was on his way to Lady Godolphin's Folly, bearing with him the small parcel sent by Mrs. Verrall—a sufficient excuse for calling there, had George required an excuse. Which he did not.

It was a light night; as it had been the previous night, though the moon was not yet very high. He gained the turnstile at the end of the Ash-tree Walk—where he had been startled by the apparition of Thomas, and where Isaac Hastings had seen Charlotte Pain that morning—and turned into the open way to the right. A few paces more, and he struck into the narrow pathway which would lead him through the grove of trees, leaving Ashlydyat and its approaches to the left.

Did George Godolphin love the darkness, that he should choose that way? Last night and again to-night he had preferred it. It was most unusual for any one to approach the Folly by that obscure path. A few paces round, and he would have skirted the thicket, would have gone on to the Folly in the bright, open moonlight. Possibly George scarcely noticed that he chose it: full of thought, was he, just then.

He went along with his head down. What were his reflections? Was he wishing that he could undo the deeds of the last hour—replace in that tin case what he had taken from it? Was he wishing that he could undo the deeds of the last few *years*—be again a man without a cloud on his brow, a heavier cloud on his heart? It was too late: he could recall neither the one nor the other. The deed was already on its way to London; the years had rolled into the awful PAST, with its doings, bad and good, recorded on high.

What was that? George lifted his head and his ears. A murmur of suppressed voices, angry voices, too, sounded near him, in one of which George thought he recognized the tones of Charlotte Pain. He went through to an intersecting path, so narrow that one person could with difficulty walk down it, just as a scream rang out on the night air.

Panting, scared, breathless, her face distorted with fear or passion, as much as George could see of it in the shaded light, her gauze dress torn by every tree with which it came in contact, flying down the narrow pathway, came Charlotte Pain. And—unless George Godolphin was strangely mistaken—some one else was flying in equal terror in the opposite direction, as if they had just parted.

" Charlotte! What is it? Who has alarmed you?"

In the moment's first impulse he caught hold of her to protect her ;

in the second, he loosed his hold, and made after the other fugitive. The impression upon George's mind was, that some one, perhaps a stranger, had met Charlotte, and frightened her with rude words.

But Charlotte was as swift as he. She flung her hands around George, and held him there. Strong hands they always were: doubly strong in that moment of agitation. George could not unclasp them: unless he had used violence.

"Stay where you are! Stay where you are, for the love of Heaven!" she gasped. "You must not go."

"What is all this? What is the matter?" he asked in surprise.

She made no other answer. She clung to him with all her weight of strength, her arms and hands straining with the effort, reiterating wildly, "You must not go! you must not go!"

"Nay, I don't care to go," replied George: "it was for your sake I was following. Be calm, Charlotte: there's no necessity for this agitation."

She went on, down the narrow pathway, drawing him with her. The broader path gained—though that also was but a narrow one—she put her arm within his, and turned towards the house. George could see her white frightened face better now, and all the tricks and cosmetics invented could not hide its ghastliness; he felt her heaving pulses; he heard her beating heart.

Bending down to her, he spoke with a soothing whisper. "Tell me what it was that terrified you."

She would not answer. She only pressed his arm with a tighter pressure, lest he might break from her again in pursuit; she hurried onwards with a quicker step. Skirting round the trees, which before the house made a half circle, Charlotte came to the end, and then darted rapidly across the lawn to the terrace and into the house by one of the windows. He followed her.

Her first movement was to close the shutters and bar them: her next to sit down on the nearest chair. Ill as she looked, George could scarcely forbear a smile at her gauze dress: the bottom of its skirt was in shreds.

"Will you let me get you something, Charlotte? Or ring for it?"

"I don't want anything," she answered. "I shall be all right directly. How could you frighten me so?"

"*I* frighten you!" returned George. "It was not I who frightened you."

"Indeed it was. You and no one else. Did you not hear me scream?"

"I did."

"It was at you, rustling through the trees," persisted Charlotte. "I had gone out to see if the air would relieve this horrid headache, which has been upon me since last night and won't go away. I strolled into the thicket, thinking all sorts of lonely things, never suspecting that you or any one else could be near me. I wonder I did not faint, as well as scream."

"Charlotte, what nonsense! You were whispering angrily with some one; some one who escaped in the opposite direction. Who was it?"

"I saw no one; I heard no one. Neither was I whispering."

He looked at her intently. That she was telling an untruth he believed, for he felt positive that some second person *had* been there. "Why did you stop me, then, when I would have gone in pursuit?"

"It was your fault for attempting to leave me," was Charlotte's answer. "I would not have remained alone for a house full of gold."

"I suppose it is some secret. I think, whatever it may be, Charlotte, you might trust *me*." He spoke significantly, a stress on the last word. Charlotte rose from her seat.

"So I would," she said, "were there anything to confide. Just look at me! My dress is ruined."

"You should take it up if you go amidst clumsy trees, whose rough trunks nearly meet."

"I had it up—until you came," returned Charlotte, jumping upon a chair that she might survey it in one of the side glasses. "You startled me so that I dropped it. I might have it joined, and a lace flounce put upon it," she mused. "It cost a great deal of money, did this dress, I can tell you, Mr. George."

She jumped off the chair again, and George produced the packet confided to him by Mrs. Verrall.

"I promised her that you should have it to-night," he said. "Hence my unfortunate appearance here, which it seems has so startled you."

"Oh, that's over now. When did you get back again?"

"By the seven o'clock train. I saw Verrall."

"Well?"

"It's not well. It's ill. Do you know what I begin to suspect at times?—That Verrall and every one else is playing me false. I am sick of the world."

"No, he is not, George. If I thought he were, I'd tell you so. I would, on my sacred word of honour. It is not likely that he is. When we are in a bilious mood, everything wears to us a jaundiced tinge. You are in one to-night."

CHAPTER VIII.

THE TRADITION OF THE DARK PLAIN.

It is the province of little demoiselles to be naughty: it is their delight to make promises and then break them, all false and fearless—as they may do over other affairs in later life. Miss Meta Godolphin was no exception to the rule. She had gravely promised her uncle Thomas to be a good girl, and not run away to be lost in unfrequented passages; yet no sooner had the young lady arrived at Ashlydyat that morning, and been released of her out-door things by Margery, than with a joyously defiant laugh that would have rejoiced the heart of Charlotte Pain, she flew off to that forbidden spot—the unused passages. Had the little lady's motive been laid bare, it might have been found to consist simply in the enjoyment of a thing forbidden. Truth to say, Miss Meta was very prone to be disobedient to all persons, excepting one. That one was her mother. Maria had never spoken a sharp word to the child in her life, or used a sharp tone: but she had contrived to train the little one to obey, as well as to love. George, Margery, Mrs. Hastings, Miss Meta would openly disobey, and laugh in their faces while she did it: her mother, never. Meta remembered a scolding she received on the last visit she had paid to Ashlydyat, touching the remote passages—she had never found them out until then—and apparently the reminiscence of the scolding was so agreeable that she was longing to have it repeated.

"Now," said Margery, as she concluded the young lady's toilette, "you'll not go up to those old rooms and passages to-day, mind, Miss Meta!"

For answer, Miss Meta shook out her golden curls, laughed triumphantly, and started off to the passages then and there. Maria had never said to her, "You must not go near those passages;" and the commands of the rest of the world went for nothing. Margery remained in blissful ignorance of the disobedience. She supposed the child had run to her mother and the Miss Godolphins. The objection to Meta's being in the passages alone had no mysterious element in it. It proceeded solely from a regard to her personal safety. The staircase leading to the turret was unprotected; the loopholes in the turret were open, and a fall from either might cost the young lady her life. These places, the unfrequented passages at the back of the second storey, and the staircase leading to the square turret above them, were shut in by a door, which separated them from the inhabited part of the house. This door Miss Meta had learned to open: and away she went, as fancy led her.

Maria was in Miss Godolphin's room, talking to that lady and to Bessy, when a sound overhead caused them to pause.

"Where's Meta?" cried Janet, hastening from the room. "She cannot have gone upstairs again! Margery! Where's the child?"

Margery at that moment happened to be putting the finishing touches to her own toilette. She came flying without her cap out of one of the many narrow passages and windings which intersected each other on that floor. "The child went off to you, ma'am, as soon as I had put on her pinafore."

"Then, Margery, she has gone up into the turret. She never came to us."

Up to the turret hastened Janet; up to the turret followed Margery. Bessy and Maria traversed the passage leading to the turret-stairs, and stood there, looking upwards. Maria, had she been alone, could not have told which of the passages *would* lead her to the turret-stairs; and she could not understand why so much commotion need be made, although Meta had run up there. Strange as it may seem, Maria Godolphin, though so many years George's wife, and the presumptive mistress of Ashlydyat, had never passed beyond that separating door. Miss Godolphin had never offered to take her to the unused rooms and the turret; and Maria was of too sensitively refined a nature to ask it of her own accord.

Janet appeared, leading the rebel; Margery, behind, was scolding volubly. " Now," said Janet, when they reached the foot, " tell me, Meta, how it was that you could behave so disobediently, and go where you had been expressly told not to go ? "

Meta shook back her golden curls with a laugh, sprang to Maria, and took refuge in her skirts. " Mamma did not tell me not to go," said she.

Janet looked at Maria : almost as if she would say, Can it be true that you have not done so ?

" It is true," said Maria, answering the look. " I heard something about her running into the turret the last time she was here : I did not know it was of any consequence."

" She might fall through the loopholes," replied Janet. " Nothing could save her from being dashed to pieces."

Maria caught the child to her with an involuntary movement. " Meta, darling, do you hear ? You must never go again."

Meta looked up fondly, serious now. Maria bent her face down on the little upturned one.

" Never again, darling ; do not forget," she murmured. " Does Meta know that if harm came to her, mamma would never look up again ? She would cry always."

Meta bustled out of her mamma's arms, and stood before Miss Godolphin, earnest decision on her little face. " Aunt Janet, Meta won't run away again."

And when the child voluntarily made a promise, they knew that she would keep it. Margery whirled her away, telling her in high tones of a young lady of her own age who would do something that she was bade not to do : the consequence of which act was, that the next time she went out for a walk, she was run at by a bull with brass tips on his horns.

" Is the turret really dangerous ? " inquired Maria.

" It is dangerous for a random child like Meta, who ventures into every hole and corner without reference to dust or danger," was Miss Godolphin's answer. " Would you like to go up, Maria ? "

" Yes, I should. I have heard George speak of the view from it."

" Mind, Maria, the stairs are narrow and winding," interposed Bessy.

Nevertheless, they went up, passing the open loopholes which might be dangerous to Meta. The first thing that Maria's eyes encountered when they had reached the top was a small bow of violet-coloured ribbon. She stooped to pick it up.

" It is a bow off Janet's evening dress," exclaimed Bessy. " Janet "— turning to her sister—" what can have brought it here ? "

" I was up here last night," was the answer of Janet Godolphin, spoken with composure.

" That's just like you, Janet ! " retorted Bessy. " To watch for that foolish Shadow, I suppose."

" Not to watch for it. To see it."

Bessy was afflicted with a taint of heresy. They had never been able to imbue her with the superstition pertaining to the Godolphins. Bessy had seen the Shadow more than once with her own eyes ; but they were practical eyes and not imaginative, and could not be made to see anything mysterious in it. " The shadow is thrown by some tree or other," Bessy would say. And, in spite of its being pointed out to her that there was no tree, which *could* cast a shadow on the spot, Bessy obstinately held to her own opinion.

Maria gazed from two sides of the turret. The view from both was magnificent. The one side overlooked the charming open country; the other, Prior's Ash. On the third side rose Lady Godolphin's Folly, standing out like a white foreground to the lovely expanse of scenery behind it; the fourth side looked upon the Dark Plain.

" There's Charlotte Pain," said Bessy.

Charlotte had returned home, it appeared, since Maria met her, and changed her attire. She was pacing the terrace of the Folly in her riding-habit, a whip in hand, and some dogs surrounding her. Maria turned towards the Dark Plain, and gazed upon it.

" Is it true," she timidly asked, " that the Shadow has been there for the last night or two ? "

Janet answered the question by asking another. " Who told you it was there, Maria ? "

" I heard Margery say so."

" Margery ? " repeated Janet. " That woman appears to know by instinct when the Shadow comes. She dreams it, I think. It is true, Maria, that it has appeared again," she continued, in a tone of un-natural composure. " I never saw it so black as it was last night."

" Do you believe that there can be anything in it—that it foretells ill ? " asked Maria.

" I know that it is the tradition handed down with our house : I know that, in my own experience, the Shadow never came but it brought ill," was the reply of Miss Godolphin.

" What caused the superstition to arise in the first instance ? " asked Maria.

" Has George never told you the tale ? " replied Janet.

" Never. He says he does not remember it clearly enough. Will you not tell it me, Janet ? "

Janet hesitated. " One of the early Godolphins brought a curse upon the house," she at length began, in a low tone. " It was that evil ancestor whose memory we would bury, were it possible; he who earned for himself the title of the Wicked Godolphin. He killed his wife by a course of gradual and long-continued ill-treatment. He wanted her out of the way that another might fill her place. He pretended to have discovered that she was not worthy: than which assertion nothing could be more false and shameless, for she was one of the best ladies ever created. She was a de Commins, daughter of the warrior Richard de Commins, and was brave as she was good. She died; and the Wicked Godolphin turned her coffin out of the house on to the Dark Plain; there "—pointing to the open space before the archway—" to remain until the day of interment. But he did not wait for that day of interment to bring home his second wife."

" Not wait ! " exclaimed Maria, her eager ears drinking in the story.

" The habits in those early days will scarcely admit of allusion to them in these," continued Janet: " they savour of what is worse than barbarism—sin. The father, Richard de Commins, heard of his child's death, and hastened to Ashlydyat, arriving by moonlight. The first sounds he encountered were the revels of the celebration of the second marriage; the first sight he saw was the coffin of his daughter on the open plain, covered by a pall, two of her faithful women bending, the one at the head, the other at the foot, mourning the dead. While he halted there, kneeling in prayer, it was told to the Wicked Godolphin that de Commins had arrived. He—that Wicked Godolphin—rushed madly out, and drew his sword upon him as he knelt. De Commins was wounded, but not mortally, and he rose to defend himself. A combat ensued, de Commins having no resource but to fight, and he was killed; murdered. Weary with his journey, enfeebled by age, weakened by grief, his foot slipped, and the Wicked Godolphin, stung to fury by the few words of reproach de Commins had had time to speak, deliberately ran him through as he lay. In the moment of death, de Commins cursed the Godolphins, and prophesied that the shadow of his daughter's bier, as it appeared then, should remain as a curse upon the Godolphins' house for ever."

"But do you believe the story?" cried Maria, breathlessly.

"How much of it may be true, how much of it addition, I cannot decide," said Janet. "One fact is indisputable: that a shadow, bearing the exact resemblance of a bier, with a mourner at its head and another at its foot, does appear capriciously on that Dark Plain; and that it never yet showed itself, but some grievous ill followed for the Godolphins. It is possible that the Shadow may have partially given rise to the story."

"Janet!" cried Maria, leaning forward, her own tones hushed, "is it *possible* that one, in dying, can curse a whole generation, so that the curse shall take effect in the future?"

"Hush, child!" rebuked Janet. "It does not become us to inquire into these things. Controversy about them is utterly useless, worse than profitless; for there will be believers and unbelievers to the end of time. You wished me to tell you the story, Maria, and I have done so. I do no more. I do not tell you it is to be believed, or it is not to be believed. Let every one decide for himself, according as his reason, his instinct, or his judgment shall prompt him. People accuse me of being foolishly superstitious touching this Shadow and these old traditions. I can only say the superstition has been forced upon me by experience. When the Shadow appears, I cannot close my eyes to it and say, 'It is not there.' It *is* there: and all I do is to look at it, and speculate. When the evil, which *invariably* follows the appearance of the Shadow, falls, I cannot close my heart to it, and say, in the teeth of facts, 'No evil has happened.' The Shadow never appeared, Maria, but it brought ill in its wake. It is appearing again now: and I am as certain that some great ill is in store for us, as that I am talking to you at this moment. On this point I *am* superstitious."

"It is a long time, is it not, since the Shadow last appeared?"

"It is years. But I have not quite finished the story," resumed Janet. "The Wicked Godolphin killed Richard de Commins, and buried him that night on the Dark Plain. In his fury and passion he called his servants around him, ordered a grave to be dug, and assisted

with his own hands.   ᴅe Commins was put into it without the rites of
burial.   Tradition runs that so long as the bones remain unfound, the
place will retain the appearance of a graveyard.   They have been often
searched for.   That tragedy, no doubt, gave its name to the place—
'The Dark Plain.'   It cannot be denied that the place does wear much
the appearance of a graveyard: especially by moonlight."

"It is only the effect of the low gorse bushes," said Bessy.   "They
grow in a peculiar form.   I know I would have those bushes rooted up,
were I master of Ashlydyat!"

"Your father had it done, Bessy, and they sprang up again," replied
Janet.   "You must remember it."

"It could not have been done effectually," was Bessy's answer.
"Papa must have had lazy men at work, who left the roots in.   I would
dig it all up and make a ploughed field of it."

"Did he do any other harm—that Wicked Godolphin?" asked
Maria.

"He!   Other harm!" reiterated Janet, something like indignation at
Maria's question mingling with surprise in her tone.   "Don't you know
that it was he who gambled away Ashlydyat?   After that second
marriage of his, he took to worse and worse courses.   It was said that
his second wife proved a match for him, and they lived together like
two evil demons.   All things considered, it was perhaps a natural
sequence that they should so live," added Janet, severely.   "And in
the end he cut off the entail and gambled away the estate.   Many years
elapsed before the Godolphins could recover it."

Maria was longing to put a question.   She had heard that there
were other superstitious marvels attaching to Ashlydyat, but she
scarcely liked to mention them to the Miss Godolphins.   George
never would explain anything: he always turned it off with laughing
raillery.

"You—think—that Ashlydyat will pass away from the Godolphins,
Janet?"

Janet shook her head.   "We have been reared in the belief," she
answered.   "That the estate is to pass finally away from them, the
Godolphins have been taught to fear ever since that unhappy time.
Each generation, as they have come into possession, have accepted it
as an uncertain tenure: as a thing that might last them for their time,
or might pass away from them ere their earthly sojourn was completed.
The belief was; nay, the tradition was; that so long as a reigning
Godolphin held by Ashlydyat, Ashlydyat would hold by him and his.
My father was the first to break it."

Janet had taken up her dress, and sat down on a dusty, faded bench,
the only article of furniture of any description that the square room
contained.   That strangely speculative look—it was scarcely an earthly
one—had come into her eyes: and though she answered when spoken
to, she appeared to be lost in sad, inward thought.   Maria, somewhat awed with the turn the conversation had taken, with the words
altogether, stood against the opposite window, her delicate hands
clasped before her, her face slightly bent forward, pale and grave.

"Then, do you fear that the end for the Godolphins is at hand?"

"I seem to *see* that it is," replied Janet.   "I have looked for it ever since my father left Ashlydyat. I might say—but that I should be laughed at more than I am for an idealist—that the strangers to whom he resigned it in his place, would have some bearing upon our fall, would in some way conduce to it. I think of these things ever," continued Janet, almost as if she would apologize for the wildness of the confession. "They seem to unfold themselves to me, to become clear and more clear : to be no longer fanciful fears darting across the brain, but realities of life."

Maria's lips slightly parted as she listened. "But the Verralls have left Ashlydyat a long while?" she presently said.

"I know they have. But they were usurpers here for the time. Better—as I believe—that my father had shut it up : better, far better, that he had never left it ! He knew it also : and it preyed upon him on his death-bed."

"Oh, Janet! the ill may not come in our time !"

"It may not. I am anxious to believe it may not, in defiance of the unalterable conviction that has seated itself within me. Let it pass, Maria ; talking of it will not avert it : indeed, I do not know how I came to be betrayed into speaking of it openly."

"But you have not told me about the sounds in the passages?" urged Maria, as Janet rose from her dusty seat.

"There is nothing more to tell. Peculiar sounds, as if caused by the wind, are heard. Moaning, sighing, rushing—the passages at times seem alive with them. It is said to come as a reminder to the Godolphins of a worse sound that will sometime be heard, when Ashlydyat shall be passing away from them."

"But you don't believe that?" uttered Maria.

"Child, I can scarcely tell you what I believe," was Janet's answer. "I can only pray that the one-half of what my heart prompts me to fear, may never take place in reality. That the noise does come, and without any apparent cause, is not a matter of belief, or disbelief : it is a fact, patent to all who have inhabited Ashlydyat. The Verralls can tell you so : they have had their rest broken by it."

"And it is not caused by the wind?"

Janet shook her head in dissent. "It has come on the calmest and stillest night, when there has not been a breath of air to move the leaves of the ash-trees."

Bessy turned from her pastime of watching Charlotte Pain : she had taken little part in the conversation.

"I wonder at you, Janet. You will be setting Maria against Ashlydyat. She will be frightened to come into it, should it lapse to George."

Maria looked at her with a smile. "I should have no fear with him, superstitious or otherwise. If George took me to live in the catacombs, I could be brave with him."·

Ever the same blind faith : the unchanged love for her husband. Better, far better, that it should be so !

"For my part, I am content to take life and its good as I find it, and not waste my time in unprofitable dreams," was the practical remark of Bessy. "If any ill is to come, it must come ; but there's no need to look out for it beforehand."

"There must be dreamers and there must be workers," answered Janet, picking her way down the winding stairs. "We were not all born into the world with minds similarly constituted, or to fulfil the same parts in life."

The day passed on. Thomas Godolphin came home in the evening to dinner, and said George had not returned. Maria wondered. It grew later. Margery went home with Meta: who thought she was very hardly used at having to go home before her mamma.

"I had rather you would stay, Maria," Thomas said to her. "I particularly wish to say a word to George to-night on business matters: if he finds you are here when he returns, he will come up."

George did find so—as you already know. And when he left Mrs. Charlotte Pain, her torn dress and her other attractions, he bent his steps towards Ashlydyat. But, instead of going the most direct road to it, he took his way through the thicket where he had had the encounter an hour ago with Charlotte. There was a little spice of mystery about it which excited Mr. George's curiosity. That some one had parted from her he felt convinced, in spite of her denial. And that she was in a state of excitement, of agitation, far beyond anything he had ever witnessed in Charlotte Pain, was indisputable. George's thoughts went back, naturally, to the previous night: to the figure he had seen, and whom his eyes, his conviction, had told him was Charlotte. She had positively denied it, had said she had not quitted the drawing-room: and George had found her there, apparently composed and stationary. Nevertheless, though he had then yielded to her word, he began now to suspect that his own conviction had been correct: that the dark and partially disguised figure had been no other than Charlotte herself. It is probable that, however powerful was the hold Charlotte's fascinations may have taken upon the senses of Mr. George Godolphin, his *trust* in her, in her truth and single-heartedness, was not of the most perfect nature. What mystery was connected with Charlotte,. or whom she met in the thicket, or whether she met any one or no one, she best knew. George's curiosity was sufficiently excited upon the point to induce him to walk with a slow step and searching eyes, lest haply he might come upon some one or something which should explain the puzzle.

How runs the old proverb? "A watched-for visitor never comes." In vain George halted and listened; in vain he peered into every part of the thicket within view. Not a step was to be heard, not a creature to be seen: and he emerged from the trees ungratified. Crossing the open grass by the turnstile he turned round by the ash-trees, to the Dark Plain.

Turned and started. George Godolphin's thoughts had been on other things than the Shadow. The Shadow lay there, so pre-eminently dark, so menacing, that George positively started. Somehow—fond as he was of ignoring the superstition—George Godolphin did not like its look to-night.

Upon entering Ashlydyat, his first interview was with Thomas. They remained for a few minutes alone. Thomas had business affairs to speak of: and George—it is more than probable—made some good

excuse for his day's absence.   That it would be useless to deny he had
been to London, he knew.   Charlotte had put him on his guard.   Janet
and Bessy asked innumerable questions of him when he joined them, on
the score of his absence; but he treated it in his usual light manner,
contriving to tell them nothing.   Maria did not say a word then: she
left it till they should be alone.

"You will tell *me*, George, will you not?" she gently said, as they
were walking home together.

"Tell you what, Maria?"

"Oh, George, you know what"—and her tone, as Mr. George's ears
detected, bore its sound of pain.   "If you were going to London when
you left me; why did you deceive me by saying you were going elsewhere?"

"You goose!   Do you suppose I said it to deceive you?"

There was a lightness, an untruthfulness in his words, in his whole
air and manner, which struck with the utmost pain upon Maria's heart.
"Why did you say it?" was all she answered.

"Maria, I'll tell you the truth," said he, becoming serious and confidential.   "I wanted to run up to town on a little pressing matter of
business, and I did not care that it should become known in the Bank.
Had I known that I should be away for the day, of course I should
have told Thomas: but I fully intended to be home in the afternoon:
therefore I said nothing about it.   I missed the train, or I should have
been home in due time."

"You might have told me," she sighed.   "I would have kept your
counsel."

"So I would, had I thought you deemed it of any consequence,"
replied George.

Consequence!   Maria walked on a few minutes in silence, her arm
lying very spiritless within her husband's.   "If you did not tell me,"
she resumed, in a low tone, "why did you tell Mrs. Pain?"

"Mrs. Pain's a donkey," was George's rejoinder.   And it is probable
Mr. George at that moment was thinking her one: for his tone in its
vexation, was real enough.   "My business was connected with Verrall,
and I dropped a hint, in the hearing of Mrs. Pain, that I might probably follow him to town.   At any rate, I am safe home again, Maria, so
no great harm has come of my visit to London," he concluded, in a
gayer tone.

"What time did you get in?" she asked.

"By the seven o'clock train."

"The seven o'clock train!" she repeated in surprise.   "And have
only now come up to Ashlydyat!"

"I found a good many things to do after I got home," was the
rejoinder.

"Did you see Meta?   Margery took her home at eight o'clock."

Mr. George Godolphin had not seen Meta.   Mr. George could have
answered, had it so pleased him, that before the child reached home,
he had departed on his evening visit to Lady Godolphin's Folly.

CHAPTER IX.

THE DEAD ALIVE AGAIN.

SATURDAY was a busy day at Prior's Ash; it was a busy day at the banking-house of Godolphin, Crosse, and Godolphin. Country towns and country banks are always more busy on a market-day.

George Godolphin sat in the manager's room, full of business. Not much more than a week had elapsed since that visit of his to London; and it was now Thomas's turn to be away. Thomas had gone to town. His errand there was to consult one of the first surgeons of the day, on the subject of his own health. Not so much that *he* had hope from the visit, as that it would be a satisfaction to his family to have made it.

George Godolphin was full of business. Full of talking also. A hearty country client, one who farmed a large number of acres, and generally kept a good round sum in the Bank's coffers, was with him. What little point of business he had had occasion to see one of the partners upon, was concluded, and he and George were making merry together, enjoying a gossip as to the state of affairs in general and in particular, out of doors and in. Never a man more free from care (if appearances might be trusted) than George Godolphin! When that hearty, honest farmer went forth, he would have been willing to testify that, of carking care, George possessed none.

As he went on, George sat down and bent over some account-books. His face had changed. Lines, of what looked worse than care, grew out upon it, and he lifted his hand to his brow with a weary gesture. Another minute, and he was interrupted again. He had very little peace on a market-day.

"Lord Averil wishes to see you, sir," said one of the clerks. It was Isaac Hastings.

To any other announced name, George Godolphin's ready answer would have been, "Show him in." To that of Lord Averil he evidently hesitated, and a sudden flush dyed his face. Isaac, keen in observation as was his father, as was his sister Grace, noticed it. To him, it looked like a flush of shrinking fear

"Did he ask for me?"

"He asked for Mr. Godolphin, sir. He says it will be the same thing if he sees you. Shall I show him in?"

"Of course," replied George. "What do you stop for?" he angrily added.

He rose from his seat; he put a chair or two in place; he turned to the table, and laid rapidly some of its papers one upon another—all in a fuss and bustle not in the least characteristic of George Godolphin. Isaac thought he must have lost his usual presence of mind. As to the reproach addressed to himself, "What do you stop for?"—it had never been the custom to show clients into the presence of the partners without first asking for permission.

The Shadow of Ashlydyat. **15**

Lord Averil came in. George, only in that short time, had become himself again. They chatted a minute on passing topics, and Lord Averil mentioned that he had not known, until then, that Mr. Godolphin was in London.

"He went up on Thursday," observed George. "I expect he will be back early in the week."

"I intend to be in London myself next week," said Lord Averil. "Will it be convenient for me to have those bonds of mine to-day?" he continued.

A sudden coursing on of all George's pulses; a whirling rush in his brain. "Bonds?" he mechanically answered.

"The bonds of that stock which your father bought for me years ago," explained Lord Averil. "They were deposited here for security. Don't you know it?"—looking at George's countenance, which seemed to speak only of perplexity. "Mr. Godolphin would know."

"Oh yes, yes," replied George, regaining his breath and his courage. "It is all right: I did not remember for the moment. Of course—the deposited bonds."

"I am thinking of selling out," said Lord Averil. "Indeed, I have been for some time thinking of it, but have idly put it off. If it would be quite convenient to give me the bonds, I would take them to town with me. I shall go up on Monday or Tuesday."

Now, George Godolphin, rally your wits! What are you to answer? George did rally them, in a lame manner. Confused words, which neither he nor Lord Averil precisely understood—to the effect that in Thomas Godolphin's absence, he, George, did not know exactly where to put his hand upon the securities—came forth. So Lord Averil courteously begged him not to take any trouble about it. He would leave them until another opportunity.

He shook hands cordially with George, and went out, with a mental comment, "Not half the man of business that his brother is, and his father was: but wondrously like Cecil!" George watched the door close. He wiped the dewdrops which had gathered on his face; he looked round with the beseeching air of one seeking relief from some intense pain. Had Lord Averil persisted in his demand, what would have remained for him? *Those* are the moments in which man has been tempted to resort to the one irredeemable sin.

The door opened again, and George gave a gasp as one in agony. It was only Isaac Hastings. "Mr. Hurde wishes to know, sir, whether those bills are to go up to Glyn's to-day or Monday?"

"They had better go to-day," replied George. "Has Mr. Barnaby been in to-day?" he added, as Isaac was departing.

"Not yet."

"If he does not come soon, some one must go down to the corn market to him. He is sure to be there. That is, if he is in town to-day."

"I know he is in town," replied Isaac. "I saw him as I was coming back from dinner. He was talking to Mr. Verrall."

"To Mr. Verrall!" almost shouted George, looking up as if electrified into life. "Is *he* back again?"

"He is back again, sir. I think he had only then arrived. He was coming from towards the railway station."

"You are *sure* it was Mr. Verrall?" reiterated George.

Isaac Hastings smiled. What could make Mr. George Godolphin so eager? "I am sure it was Mr. Verrall."

George felt as if a whole ton weight of care had been lifted from him. He had been so long in the habit of flying to Mr. Verrall in his difficulties, that it seemed to him he would only have to go to him, to remedy the one hanging over him now. Mr. Verrall had generally accomplished the task as men of his profession do accomplish such tasks—by laying up an awful day of reckoning for the future. That day was not now far off for George Godolphin.

The Bank closed later on Saturdays, and George remained at his post to the end. Then he dined. Then, at the dusk hour—nay, at the hour of darkness, he went out to Lady Godolphin's Folly. Why was it that he rarely went to the Folly now, except under the covert shades of night? Did he fear people might comment on his intimacy with Mr. Verrall, and seek a clue to its cause? Or did he fear the world's gossip on another score?

George arrived at Lady Godolphin's Folly, and was admitted to an empty room. "Mr. Verrall had returned, and had dined with Mrs. Pain, but had gone out after dinner," the servant said. He had believed Mrs. Pain to be in the drawing-room. Mrs. Pain was evidently not there, in spite of the man's searching eyes. He looked into the next room, with similar result.

"Perhaps, sir, she has stepped out on the terrace with her dogs?" observed the man.

George—ungallant as he was!—cared not where Mrs. Pain might have stepped at that present moment: his anxiety was for Mr. Verrall. "Have you any idea when your master will be in?" he inquired of the servant.

"I don't think he'll be long, sir. I heard him say he was tired, and should go to bed early. He may have gone to Ashlydyat. He told Mrs. Pain that he had met Mr. Godolphin in town yesterday, and he should call and tell Miss Godolphin that he was better in London than he felt here. I don't know, sir, though, that he meant he should call to-night."

The man left the room, and George remained alone. He drummed on the table; he tried several seats in succession; he got up and looked at his face in the glass. A haggard face then. Where was Verrall? Where was Charlotte? She might be able to tell him where Verrall had gone, and when he would be in. Altogether George was in a state of restlessness little better than torture.

He impatiently opened the glass doors, which were only closed, not fastened, and stood a few moments looking out upon the night. He gazed in all directions, but could see nothing of Charlotte; and Mr. Verrall did not appear to be coming. "I'll see," suddenly exclaimed George, starting off, "whether he is at Ashlydyat."

He did well. Action is better than inertness at these moments. Standing outside the porch at Ashlydyat, talking to a friend, was Andrew, one of their servants. When he saw George, he drew back to hold open the door for him.

"Are my sisters alone, Andrew?"

"Yes, sir."

George scarcely expected the answer, and it disappointed him. "Quite alone?" he reiterated. "Has no one called on them to-night?"

The man shook his head, wondering probably who Mr. George might be expecting to call. "They are all alone, sir. Miss Janet has one of her bad headaches."

George did not want to go in, Mr. Verrall not being there, and this last item afforded him an excuse for retreating without doing so. "Then I'll not disturb her to-night," said he. "You need not say that I came up, Andrew."

"Very well, sir."

He quitted Andrew, and turned off to the left, deep in thought, striking into a sheltered path. It was by no means the direct road back to the Folly, neither was it to Prior's Ash. In point of fact, it led to nothing but the Dark Plain and its superstition. Not a woman-servant of Ashlydyat, perhaps not one of its men, would have gone down that path at night : for at the other end it brought them out to the archway, before which the Shadow was wont to show itself.

Why did George take it? He could not have told. Had he been asked why, he might have said that one way, to a man bowed under a sharp weight of trouble, is the same as another. True. But the path led him to no part where he could wish to go : and he would have to make his way to Lady Godolphin's Folly through the gorse bushes of the Dark Plain, over the very Shadow itself. These apparently chance steps, which seem to be taken without premeditation or guidance of ours, sometimes lead to strange results.

George went along moodily, his hands in his pockets, his footfalls slow and light. But for the latter fact, he might not have had the pleasure of disturbing a certain scene that was taking place under cover of the archway.

Were they ghosts, enacting it? Scarcely. Two forms, ghostly or human, were there. One of them looked like a woman's. It was dressed in dark clothes, and a dark shawl was folded over the head, not, however, concealing the features—and they were those of Charlotte Pain. She, at any rate, was not ghostly. The other, George took to be Mr. Verrall. He was leaning against the brickwork, in apparently as hopeless a mood as George himself.

They were enjoying a quarrel. Strange that they should leave the house and come to this lonely spot in the grounds of Ashlydyat to hold it! Charlotte was evidently in one of her tempers. She paced to and fro under the archway, something like a restrained tiger, pouring forth a torrent of sharp words and reproaches, all in a suppressed tone.

"I'll tell you what it is," were the first distinct words of anger George caught. But her companion interrupted her, his tone one of sadness and humility.

"I'll tell *you* what it is, Charlotte—— "

The start made by George Godolphin at the tones of the voice, the involuntary sound of utter astonishment that escaped him, disturbed them. Charlotte, with a cry of terror, darted one way, her companion another.

But the latter was not quick enough to elude George Godolphin. Springing forward, George caught him in his powerful grasp, really to assure himself that it was no ghost, but genuine flesh and blood. Then George turned the face to the starlight, and recognized the features of the dead-and-gone Mr. Rodolf Pain.

The return of a husband, popularly supposed to be dead and out of the way for good, may be regarded by the wife as a blessing from some special providence, or as a source of annoying embarrassment, according to the lady's own feeling on the subject. Undoubtedly, Charlotte Pain looked upon it, and most unmistakably so, in the latter light. Charlotte knew, better than the world, that Mr. Rodolf Pain was not dead; but she had believed him to be as surely out of her way as though death and some safe metropolitan cemetery had irrevocably claimed him. Whatever trifling accident might have happened to put Mr. Rodolf Pain and the British criminal law at issue, Charlotte, at any rate, had assumed it one not to be easily got over, except by the perpetual exile of the gentleman from the British shores. When the little affair had occurred, and Mr. Rodolf had saved himself and his liberty by only a hair's-breadth, choosing a foreign exile and a false name in preference to some notoriety at a certain court (a court which does not bear a pleasant sound, and rises ominous and dark and gloomy in the heart of the city), it had pleased Charlotte and those connected with her to give out that Mr. Rodolf Pain had died. In Mr. Rodolf Pain's going out of the world by death, there was certainly no disgrace, provided that he went out naturally; that is, without what may be called malice prepense on his own part. But, for Mr. Rodolf Pain to be compelled to make his exit from London society after another fashion, was quite a different affair—an affair which could never have been quite tolerated by Charlotte: not on his score, but on her own. Any superfluous consideration for him, Charlotte had never been troubled with. Before her marriage she had regarded him in the light of a nonentity; since that ceremony, as an incumbrance. Therefore, on the whole, Charlotte was tolerably pleased to get rid of him, and she played her *rôle* of widow to perfection. No inconvenient disclosure, as to the facts of his hasty exit, had come out to the public, for it had fortunately happened that the transaction, or transactions, which led to it, had not been done in his own name. To describe Charlotte's dismay when he returned, and she found her fond assumption of his perpetual exile to have been a false security, would take a cleverer pen than mine. No other misfortune known to earth, could have been looked upon by Charlotte as so dire a calamity. Had Prior's Ash been blown up, herself included, by some sprung mine, or swallowed down by an earthquake, it would have been little, in comparison.

It certainly was not pleasant to be startled by a faint tap at the unscreened window, while she sat under the chandelier, busy at what she so rarely attempted, some useless fancy-work. Yet that was the unceremonious manner in which her husband made his return known to her. Charlotte was expecting no visitors that night. It was the night of George Godolphin's dinner-party, at which Mr. Verrall had *not* appeared, having started for London instead. When the tapping came, Charlotte turned her head towards the window in surprise. No one was in the habit of entering that way, save free-and-easy George Godolphin; he would now and then do so; sometimes Mr. Verrall. But Charlotte knew of George's dinner party, and Mr. Verrall was away. She could see nothing of the intruder: the room was ablaze with light; outside, it was, comparatively speaking, dark; and the window was also partially shaded by its lace curtains. Charlotte thought she must have been mistaken, and went on unravelling her crochet mat.

The tapping came again. "Very odd!" thought Charlotte. "Come in," she called out.

No one came in. There was no response at all for a minute or two. Then there came another timid tapping.

Charlotte's dress was half covered with cotton. She rose, shook it, let the cotton and the mat (what remained of it) fall to the ground, walked to the window, and opened it.

At the first moment she could see nothing. It was bright moonlight, and she had come from the blazing light within, beside which that outer light was so cold and pure. Not for that reason could she see nothing, but because there appeared to be nothing to see. She ranged her eyes in vain over the terrace, over the still landscape beyond.

"Charlotte!"

It was the faintest possible voice, and close to her. Faint as it was though, there was that in its tone which struck on every fibre of Charlotte's frame with dismay. Gathered against the walls of the Folly, making a pretence to shelter himself beyond a brilliant cape-jessamine which was trained there, was the slight figure of a man. A mere shred of a man, with a shrinking, attenuated frame: the frame of one who has lived in some long agony, bodily or mental: and a white face that shivered as he stood.

Not more white, not more shivering than Charlotte's. Her complexion—well, you have heard of it, as one too much studied to allow vulgar changes to come upon it, in a general way. But there are moments in a lifetime when Nature asserts herself, and Art retires before her. Charlotte's face turned to the hue of the dead, and Charlotte's dismay broke forth in a low passionate wail. It was Rodolf Pain.

A moment of terrified bewilderment; a torrent of rapid words; not of sympathy, or greeting, but of anger; and Charlotte was pushing him away with her hands, she neither knew nor cared whither. It was dangerous for him to be there, she said. He must go.

"I'll go into the thicket, Charlotte," he answered, pointing to the trees on the left. "Come to me there."

He glided off as he spoke, under cover of the walls. Charlotte, feeling that she should like to decline the invitation had she dared, enveloped her head and shoulders in a black shawl, and followed him. Nothing satisfactory came of the interview — except recrimination. Charlotte was in a towering passion that he should have ventured back at all; Rodolf complained that between them all he had been made the scapegoat. In returning home, she caught sight of George Godolphin approaching the house, just as she was about to steal across the lawn. Keeping under cover of the trees, she got in by a back entrance, and sat down to her work in the drawing-room, protesting to George, when he was admitted, that she had not been out. No wonder her face looked strange in spite of its embellishments!

Her interviews with Rodolf Pain appeared to be ill chosen. On the following night she met him in the same place: he had insisted upon it, and she did not dare refuse. More recrimination, more anger; in the midst of which George Godolphin again broke upon them. Charlotte screamed aloud in her terror, and Rodolf ran away. But that Charlotte laid detaining hands upon George, the returned man might have been discovered then, and that would not have suited Charlotte.

A few more days and that climax was to arrive. The plantation appearing unsafe, Rodolf Pain proposed the archway. There they should surely be unmolested: the ghostly fears of the neighbourhood and of Ashlydyat kept every one away from the spot. And there, two or three times, had Charlotte met him, quarrelling always, when they were again intruded upon, and again by George. This time to some purpose.

George Godolphin's astonishment was excessive. In his wildest flights of fancy he had never given a thought to the suspicion that Rodolf Pain could be alive. Charlotte had not been more confidential with George than with the rest of the world. Making a merit of what could not well be avoided, she now gave him a few particulars.

For when she looked back in her flight and saw that Rodolf Pain was fairly caught, that there was no further possibility of the farce of his death being kept up to George, she deemed it well to turn back again. Better bring *her* managing brains to the explanation, than leave it to that simple calf, whom she had the honour of calling husband. The fact was, Rodolf Pain had never been half cunning enough, half rogue enough, for the work assigned him by Mr. Verrall. He—Mr. Verrall—had always said that Rodolf had brought the trouble upon himself, in consequence of trying to exercise a little honesty. Charlotte agreed with the opinion: and every contemptuous epithet cast by Mr. Verrall on the unfortunate exile, Charlotte had fully echoed.

George was some little time before he could understand as much as was vouchsafed him of the explanation. They stood in the shadow of the archway, Charlotte keeping her black shawl well over her head and round her face; Rodolf, his arms folded, leaning against the inner circle of the stonework.

" *What*, do you say? sent you abroad?" questioned George, somewhat bewildered.

" It was that wretched business of Appleby's," replied Rodolf Pain. " You must have heard of it. The world heard enough of it."

" Appleby—Appleby? Yes, I remember," remarked George. " A nice swindle it was. But what had you to do with it?"

" In point of fact, I only had to do with it at second-hand," said Rodolf Pain, his tone one of bitter meaning. " It was Verrall's affair—as everything else is. I only executed his orders."

" But surely neither you nor Verrall had anything to do with that swindling business of Appleby's?" cried George, his voice as full of amazement as the other's was of bitterness.

Charlotte interposed, her manner so eager, so flurried, as to impart the suspicion that she must have some personal interest in it. " Rodolf, hold your tongue! Where's the use of bringing up this old speculative nonsense to Mr. George Godolphin? He does not care to hear about it."

"I would bring it up to all the world if I could," was Rodolf's answer, ringing with its own sense of injury. "Verrall told me in the most solemn manner that if things ever cleared, through Appleby's death, or in any other way, so as to make it safe for me to return, that that hour he would send for me. Well. Appleby has been dead these six months; and yet he leaves me on, on, on, in the New World, without so much as a notice of it. Now, it's of no use growing fierce again, Charlotte! I'll tell Mr. George Godolphin if I please. I am not the patient slave you helped to drive abroad: the trodden worm turns at last. Do you happen to know, sir, that Appleby's dead?"

"I don't know anything about Appleby," replied George. "I remember the name, as being owned by a gentleman who was subjected to some bad treatment in the shape of swindling, by one Rustin. But what had you or Verrall to do with it?"

"Psha!" said Rodolf Pain. "Verrall was Rustin."

George Godolphin opened his eyes to their utmost width. "N—o!" he said, very slowly, certain curious ideas beginning to crowd into his mind. Certain remembrances also.

"He was.—Charlotte, I tell you it is of no use; I *will* speak. What does it matter, Mr. George Godolphin's knowing it? Verrall was the real principal—Rustin, in fact; I, the ostensible one. And I had to suffer."

"Did Appleby think you were Rustin?" inquired George, thoroughly bewildered.

"Appleby at one time thought I was Verrall. Oh, I assure you there were wheels within wheels at work there. Of course there had to be, to carry on such a concern as that. It is so still. Verrall, you know, could not be made the scapegoat; he takes care of that—besides, it would blow the whole thing to pieces, if any evil fell upon him. It fell upon me, and I had to suffer for it, and abroad I went. I did not grumble; it would have been of no use: had I stayed at home and braved it out, I should have been *sent* abroad, I suppose, at her Majesty's cost——"

Charlotte interrupted, in a terrible passion. "Have you no sense of humiliation, Rodolf Pain, that you tell these strange stories? Mr. George Godolphin, I pray you do not listen to him!"

"I am safe," replied George. "Pain can say what he pleases. It is safe with me."

"As to humiliation, that does not fall so much to my share as it does to another's, in the light I look at it. I was not the principal; I was only the scapegoat; principals rarely are made the scapegoats in that sort of business. Let it go, I say. I took the punishment without a word. But, now that the man's dead, and I can come home with safety, I want to know why I was not sent for?"

"I don't believe the man's dead," observed Charlotte.

"I am quite sure that he is dead," said Rodolf Pain. "I was told it from a sure and certain source, some one who came out there, and who used to know Appleby. He said the death was in the *Times*, and he knew it for a fact besides."

"Appleby? Appleby?" mused George, his thoughts going back to a long-past morning, when he had been an unseen witness to Charlotte's interview with a gentleman giving that name—who had previously accosted him in the porch at Ashlydyat, mistaking it for the residence of Mr. Verrall. "I remember his coming down here once."

"I remember it too," said Rodolf Pain, significantly, "and the passion it put Verrall into. Verrall thought his address, down here, had oozed out through my carelessness. The trouble that we had with that Appleby, first and last! It went on for years. The bother was patched up at times, but only to break out again; and to send me into exile at last."

"Does Verrall know of his death?" inquired George of Rodolf.

"There's not a doubt that he must know of it. And Charlotte says she won't ask Verrall, and won't tell him I am here! My belief is that she knows Appleby's dead."

Charlotte had resumed her walk under the archway: pacing there— as was remarked before—like a restrained tiger. She took no notice of Rodolf's last speech.

"Why not tell Verrall yourself that you are here?" was George's sensible question.

"Well—you see, Mr. George Godolphin, I'd rather not, as long as there's the least doubt as to Appleby's death. *I* feel none myself: but if it should turn out to be a mistake, my appearance here would do good neither to me nor to Verrall. And Verrall's a dangerous man to cross. He might kill me in his passion. It takes a good deal to put him into one, but when it does come, it's like a tornado."

"You acknowledge that there is a doubt as to Appleby's death, then!" sarcastically cried Charlotte.

"I say that it's just possible. It was not being fully certain that brought me back in this clandestine way. What I want you to do is to ask Verrall if Appleby's dead. I believe he will answer 'Yes.' 'Very well,' then you can say, 'Rodolf Pain's home again.' And if——"

"And if he says, 'No, he is not dead,' what then?" fiercely interrupted Charlotte.

"Then you can tell me privately, and I must depart the way I came. But I don't depart without being *satisfied* of the fact," pointedly added Mr. Pain, as if he had not entire and implicit reliance upon Charlotte's word. "My firm belief is that he is dead, and that Verrall will tell you he is dead. In that case I am a free man to-morrow."

Charlotte turned her head towards him, terrible anger in her tone, and in her face. "And how is your reappearance to be accounted for to those who look upon *you* as dead?"

"I don't care how," indifferently answered Rodolf. "I did not spread the report of my own death. If you did, you can contradict it."

"If I did do it, it was to save your reputation," returned Charlotte, scarcely able to speak in her passion.

"*I* know," said Rodolf Pain. "You feared something or other might come out about your husband, and so you thought you'd kill me off-hand. Two for yourself and one for me, Charlotte."

She did not answer.

"If my coming back is so annoying to you, we can live apart," he resumed. "You pretty well gave me a sickener before I went away. As you know."

"This must be an amusing dialogue to Mr. George Godolphin!" fumed Charlotte.

"May-be," replied Rodolf Pain, his tone sad and weary. "I have been so hardly treated between you and Verrall, Charlotte, that I don't care who knows it."

"Where are you staying?" asked George, wondering whether the shady spots about Ashlydyat sheltered him by day as well as by night.

"Not far away, sir: at a roadside inn," was the answer. "No one knew me much, about here, in the old days; but, to make assurance doubly sure, I only come out in the evening. Look here, Charlotte. If you refuse to ask Verrall, or to help me, I shall go to London, and obtain the information there. I am not quite without friends in the great city: they would receive me better than you have received me."

"I wonder you did not go there at once," said Charlotte, sharply.

"It was natural that I should go first where my wife was," returned Rodolf Pain; "even though she had not been the most affectionate of wives to me."

Charlotte was certainly not showing herself particularly affectionate then, whether she had, or had not, in the past days. Truth to say, whatever may have been her personal predilection or the opposite for the gentleman, his return had brought all her fears to the surface. His personal safety was imperilled; and, with that, disgrace loomed in ominous attendance; a disgrace which would be reflected upon Charlotte. Could she have sent Rodolf Pain flying on electric wires to the remotest region of the known or unknown globe, she would have done it then.

Leaving them to battle out their dispute alone, George Godolphin bent his steps to Lady Godolphin's Folly, walking over the very Shadow, black as jet, treading in and out amid the dwarf bushes, which, when regarded from a distance, looked so like graves. He gained the Folly, and rang.

The servant admitted him to the drawing-room. It was empty as before. "Has Mr. Verrall not come in?" asked George.

"He has come in, sir. I thought he was here. I will look for him."

George sat on alone. Presently the man returned. "My master has retired for the night, sir."

"What! Gone to bed?" cried George.

"Yes, sir."

"Did you tell him I had been here when he came in?"

"I told him you had been here, sir. In fact, I thought you were here still. I did not know you had left."

"Did Mr. Verrall tell you now that he could see me?"

"He told me to say that he had retired for the night, sir."

"Is he in bed?" questioned George.

The servant hesitated. "He spoke to me through the door, sir. He did not open it."

George caught up his hat, the very movement of his hand showing displeasure. " Tell your master that I shall be here the first thing in the morning. I want to see him."

He passed out, a conviction upon his mind—though he could scarcely tell why it should have arisen—that Mr. Verrall had not retired for the night, but that he had gone upstairs merely to avoid him. The thought angered him excessively. When he had gone some little distance beyond the terrace, he turned and looked at the upper windows of the house. There shone a light in Mr. Verrall's chamber. " Not in bed, at any rate," thought George. " He might have seen me if he would. I shall tell him—— "

A touch upon George's arm. Some one had glided silently up. He turned and saw Charlotte.

" You will not betray the secret that you have learnt to-night ? " she passionately whispered.

" Is it likely ? " he asked.

" He is only a fool, you know, at the best," was her next complimentary remark. " But fools give more trouble sometimes than wise people."

" You may depend upon me," was George's rejoinder. " Where is he ? "

" Got rid of for the night," said Charlotte, in a terrible tone. " Are you going in to see Verrall ? "

" No. Verrall declines to see me. I am going home. Good night."

" Declines to see you ? He is tired, I suppose. Good night, George ! "

George Godolphin walked away at a sober pace, reflecting on the events of the day—of the evening. That he had been intensely surprised by the resuscitation of Rodolf Pain was indisputable ; but George had too much care upon him to give it more than a passing thought, now that the surprise was over. Rodolf Pain occupied a very small space in the estimation of George Godolphin. Charlotte had just said he was a fool : probably George shared in the opinion.

But, however much he felt inclined to dismiss the gentleman from his mind, he could not so readily dismiss a certain revelation made by him. That Rustin was Verrall. Whoever " Rustin " may have been, or what had been his influence on the fortunes, good or ill, of Mr. George Godolphin, it concerns us not very closely to inquire. That George had had dealings with this " Rustin "—dealings which did not bear for him any pleasant reminiscence—and that George had never in his life got to see this Rustin, are sufficient facts for us to know. Rustin was one of those who had contrived to ease George of a good deal of superfluous money at odd times, leaving only trouble in its place. Many a time had George prayed Verrall's good offices with his friend Rustin, to hold over this bill ; to renew that acceptance. Verrall had never refused, and his sympathy with George and abuse of Rustin were great, when his mediation proved—as was sometimes the case—unsuccessful. To hear that this Rustin was Verrall himself, opened out a whole field of suggestive speculation to George. Not pleasant speculation, you may be sure.

He sat himself down, in his deep thought, on that same spot where

Thomas Godolphin had sat the evening of George's dinner-party; the broken bench, near the turnstile. Should he be able to weather the storm that was gathering so ominously above his head? Was that demand of Lord Averil's to-day the first rain-drop of the darkening clouds? In sanguine moments—and most moments are sanguine to men of the light temperament of George Godolphin—he felt not a doubt that he should weather it. There are some men who systematically fling care and gloom from them. They cannot look trouble steadily in the face: they glance aside from it; they do not see it if it comes: they clothe it with the rose-hues of hope: but look at it, they do not. Shallow and careless by nature, they cannot feel deep sorrow themselves, or be too cautious of any wrong they inflict on others. They may bring ruin upon the world, but they go jauntily on their way. George had gone on in his way, in an easy, gentlemanly sort of manner, denying himself no gratification, and giving little heed to the day of reckoning that might come.

But on this night his mood had changed. Affairs generally were wearing to him an aspect of gloom: of gloom so preternaturally dark and hopeless, that his spirits were weighed down by it. For one thing, this doubt of Verrall irritated him. If the man had played him false, had been holding the cards of a double game, why, what an utter fool he, George, had been! How long he sat on that lonely seat he never knew: as long as his brother had, that past night. The one had been ruminating on his forthcoming fate—death; the other was lost in the anticipation of a worse fate—disgrace and ruin. As he rose to pursue his way down the narrow and ghostly Ash-tree Walk, a low cry burst from his lips, sharp as the one that had been wrung from Thomas in his physical agony.

CHAPTER X.

NINE THOUSAND AND FORTY-FIVE POUNDS.

A SHORT time elapsed. Summer weather began to show itself in Prior's Ash, and all things, so far as any one saw or suspected, were going on smoothly. Not a breath of wind had yet stirred up the dangerous current; not the faintest cloud had yet come in the fair sky, to indicate that a storm might be gathering. One rumour however had gone forth, and Prior's Ash mourned sincerely and trusted it was not true—the state of health of Thomas Godolphin. *He* attacked with an incurable complaint, as his mother had been? Prior's Ash believed it not.

He had returned from his visit to town with all his own suspicions confirmed. But the medical men had seemed to think that the fatal result might not overtake him yet; probably not for years. They enjoined tranquillity upon him, both of mind and body, and recommended him to leave the cares of business, so far as was practicable, to other people. Thomas smiled when he recited this piece of advice to George. " I had better retire upon my fortune," he laughed.

"Do so," cried George, impulsively. "That is"—for a disagreeable consciousness came upon him, as he spoke, that Thomas's "fortune," if looked into, might be found more easy to talk of than to realize—"you can virtually retire, by remaining quietly at Ashlydyat. Don't come down to the Bank. I can manage quite well without you."

Thomas shook his head. "So long as I am at all capable, George, I shall not give up. I believe it is my duty not to do so. If what the doctors say is correct—that I may live on in my present state, or nearly in my present state, for years—you may be an older and a wiser man by the time you are left alone. When you shall have gained grey hair, George, and a stoop in the shoulders, Prior's Ash will be thinking you a stronger and a better man than I have ever been."

George made no reply. He knew which had been the better man, himself or his brother.

Everything, I say, seemed to go on in its old routine. Thomas Godolphin came to business; not every day, but frequently. George gave his dinner-parties, and rode as much as ever with Charlotte Pain. What Charlotte had done with her husband, was her affair. He no longer disturbed the night stillness of the Dark Plain, or of Lady Godolphin's Folly ; and not a suspicion of his unwelcome revival from the dead had transpired beyond George Godolphin. Charlotte casually said one day to George that Rodolf was in London. Perhaps he was.

Yes, gay as ever, in the day, was George Godolphin. If he had care, he kept it to himself, and no one saw or suspected it. George was persuadable as a child ; seeing little farther than his own nose; and Mr. Verrall had contrived to lull the suspicions awakened by the words of Rodolf Pain. Mr. Verrall had not remained long at Lady Godolphin's Folly : he was soon away again, and Charlotte had it to herself, queen regnant. George had not forgotten to pay his evening visits there. There or elsewhere, he was out most evenings. And when he came in, he would go into the Bank, and remain alone in the manager's room, often for hours.

One evening—it was the greatest wonder in the world—he had not gone out. At eight o'clock he had gone into the Bank and shut himself in. An hour afterwards Maria knocked, and he admitted her.

George was at a large table; it was covered with account-books. Hard at work he appeared to be, making entries with his pen, by the light of his shaded lamp. "How busy you are, George!" she cried.

"Ay," said he, pleasantly. "Let no one call me idle again."

"But why need you do it, George? You used not to work at night."

"More work falls to my score, now Thomas does not take his full share of it," observed George.

"Does it? I fancied neither you nor Thomas had much actual work to do. I thought you left it to the clerks. Isaac laughed at me one day, a long time ago, when I said something about your keeping the bank accounts. He asked me what I thought clerks were paid for."

"Never mind Isaac. What have you come in for? To tell me you are dull?—as you did last night."

"No. But I do get to feel very dull in an evening. You are scarcely ever with me now, George."

"Business must be attended to," responded George. "You should get some visitors in."

"They would not be you," was Maria's answer, simply spoken. "I came to tell you now that papa is here. Have you time to come and see him?"

George knitted his brow. The prospect of entertaining the Reverend Mr. Hastings did not appear to have charms for him. Not that he allowed Maria to see the frown. She continued:

"Papa has been talking about the Chisholm property. The money is paid over, and he has brought it here for safety."

"Brought it to-night?" echoed George.

"Yes. He said it might be an unprofessional mode of doing business, but he supposed you would receive it," she added, laughing.

"How much is it?" cried George—all too eagerly, had Maria not been unsuspicious.

"Nine—let me see—yes, I think he said nine thousand pounds."

George Godolphin closed the books before him, more than one of which was open, locked them up, put out the lamp, and accompanied his wife to the dining-room.

"Will you let me lodge some money here to-night?" asked Mr. Hastings, as he shook hands.

"As much as you like," replied George, gaily. "We can accommodate an unlimited amount."

The Rector took out a large pocket-book, and counted down some bank-notes upon the table. "Brierly, the agent, brought it to me an hour ago," he observed, "and I had rather your Bank had charge of it than my house. Nine thousand and forty-five pounds, Mr. George."

George counted the notes after Mr. Hastings. "I wonder Brierly did not give a cheque for it," he observed. "Did he bring the money over from Binham?"

"He came over in his gig. He said it had been paid to him in money, and he brought it just as it was. I'll trouble you for a receipt, George."

George carried the money away and came back with the receipt. "It must be placed to your account, I suppose, sir?" he observed.

"Of course," answered Mr. Hastings. "You can't place it to the credit of the little Chisholms. It is the first time I was ever left trustee," he remarked, "and I hope it will be the last."

"Why so?" asked George.

"Why so? Because I like neither the trouble nor the responsibility. As soon as my co-trustee returns, the money is to be placed out on approved security: until then, you must take charge of it. It is a small sum after all, compared with what was expected."

"Very small," assented George. "Is it all that the property has realized?"

"Every shilling—except the expenses. And lawyers, and agents, and auctioneers, take care that they shall never be slight," added Mr. Hastings, his lip curling with the cynical expression that was sometimes seen on it.

"It's their trade, sir."

"Ay. What a cutting up of property it is, this forced selling of an

estate, through death!" he exclaimed. "Many a time has poor
Chisholm said to me, in his last illness: 'There'll be hard upon twenty
thousand to divide amongst them, when it's all sold.' And there is not
ten!"

"I suppose everything was sold?" said George.

"Everything. House, land, ricks as they stood, farming stock,
cattle, and furniture: everything, even to the plate and the books.
The will so expressed it. I suppose Chisholm thought it best."

"Where are the children, papa?" asked Maria.

"The two girls are at school, the little boy is with his granamother.
I saw the girls last week when I was at Binham."

"The boy is to be a clergyman, is he not, papa?"

The Rector answered the question in a tone of rebuke. "When he
shall be of an age to choose, should he evince liking and fitness for the
Church, then he is to be allowed to enter it. Not otherwise, Maria."

"How is the property left?" asked George.

"It is to be invested, and the interest devoted to the education and
maintenance of the three, the boy being allowed a larger share of the
interest than the girls. When the youngest, the boy, shall be of age,
the principal is to be divided equally between them. Such are the
terms of the will."

"What is it to be invested in?"

"The funds, I suppose. It is left to the discretion of myself and Mr.
Harknar. I shall let him decide: he is more of a man of business
than I am."

So they talked on. When Mr. Hastings, a short while before, had
found himself left guardian and co-trustee to the children of a friend
just deceased, his first impulse had been to decline the trust. Even-
tually he had accepted it. The other gentleman named, Mr. Harknar,
had gone on business to one of the Ionian Islands, but he was now
shortly expected home.

An hour the Rector sat with them, talking of the orphaned Chisholms,
and of other matters. When he took his departure, George went again
into the Bank, and sat down to work at his books by the light of the
shaded lamp. He was certainly more attentive to business by night
than by day.

CHAPTER XI.

THOSE BONDS AGAIN!

ONCE more—it was the afternoon of the day following that evening
visit of All Souls' Rector to the Bank—Isaac Hastings entered the
manager's room to announce a visitor to Mr. George Godolphin. Lord
Averil.

George looked up: a startled expression crossing his face. It was
instantly suppressed: but, not for his very life could he have helped its
appearance in the first moment.

"When did *he* come to Prior's Ash?"

"I don't know," replied Isaac. "I told him I was not sure but you were engaged, sir. I had thought Mr. Arkwright was with you. Lord Averil asked me to come and see: he particularly wishes to see you, he says."

"I am engaged," replied George, catching at the excuse as a drowning man catching at a straw. "That is"—taking out his watch—"I have not time now to see him. Tell Lord Averil I am particularly engaged."

"Very well, sir."

Isaac went out with the message, and Lord Averil departed, merely saying that he would call again. The reappearance of Charlotte Pain's husband could not have brought more dire dismay to that lady, than did this reappearance of Lord Averil's at Prior's Ash, bring to George Godolphin.

Did he think Lord Averil would never favour Prior's Ash with his presence again? It is hard to say what foolish thing he thought. Lord Averil had been in town for the last month. Once during that time, he had written to have those deposited deeds sent up to him, about which he had spoken to Mr. George Godolphin. George had answered the letter with some well-framed excuse. But now here was Lord Averil again at Prior's Ash—and at the Bank! Doubtless once more in quest of his deeds.

George Godolphin put his hand to his weary brow. His ever-constant belief was, that he should get straight in time. In time. To his sanguine temperament, time would prove the panacea for all his ills. If he could only avert present difficulties, time would do the rest. That terrible difficulties were upon him, none knew better than he: but the worst difficulty of all would be this of Lord Averil's, should exposure come. Short as George was of ready cash—it may seem a paradox to say it of a banker, but so it was—he would have scraped together every shilling from every available corner and parted with it, to have ensured the absence of Lord Averil from Prior's Ash for an indefinite period.

He pressed his hand upon his weary brow, his brain within working tumultuously. If he must see Lord Averil—and there could be no escape—what should be his plea for the non-production of those deeds? It must be a plausible one. His thoughts were interrupted by a rap at the door.

"Come in," cried George, in a sadly hopeless tone. Was it Lord Averil again?

It was only a note. A three-cornered miniature thing fastened with a silver wafer. No business communication that. George knew the writing well.

"DEAR MR. GEORGE,
          "Will you ride with me to-day at half-past three instead of four? I will tell you my reason then. Lord A. is back again.
                                        "Yours,
                                                "C. P."

George tore the note into fragments and flung them into the paper-basket. It was ten minutes past three. Glad of any excuse to be out of business and its cares, he hastened things away in his room, and left it. There were moments when George was tempted heartily to wish himself out of it for good, safe in some unapproachable island, too remote from civilization to be visited by the world. But he did not see his way clear to get there.

Look at him as he rides through the town, Charlotte by his side, and the two grooms behind them! Look at his fine bay horse, his gentle-manly figure!—look at his laughing blue eyes, his wavy golden hair, at the gay smiles on his lips as he turns to Charlotte! Can you fancy *care* an inmate of that man's breast? Prior's Ash did not. They were only content to admire and to envy their handsome and most attractive banker, George Godolphin.

They rode by the Bank. It was not often—indeed it was very rarely —that they passed it in their rides. There were plenty of other ways, without choosing that one. George never would have chosen it: per-haps he had the grace to think that his frequent rides with Mrs. Charlotte Pain need not be paraded so conspicuously before the windows of his wife. Charlotte, however, had a will of her own, and sometimes she chose to exercise it.

As good luck had it, or ill luck, or no luck at all, Maria hap-pened to be at the drawing-room window to-day. Some ladies were paying her a visit, and Meta—who was sometimes indulged, as an only child is indulged—made one in the drawing-room. She caught sight of her papa, forthwith climbed upon a chair to see him better, and leaned from the open window, clapping her hands. "Papa! papa!"

Maria sprang to hold her in. She was a child who had little sense of danger. Had George held out his arms then, and said, "Jump out to me, Meta," she would have taken the leap fearlessly. Maria caught her round the waist, and the visitors came forward to see.

Charlotte threw up a triumphant glance. One of those curiously triumphant glances that she was rather fond of giving Mrs. George Godolphin. Maria bowed gravely. An idea—a faint idea, glancing at no ill—had been growing over her lately that her husband passed more time with Charlotte Pain than was absolutely necessary. George smiled at his wife, lifted his hat to the ladies at her side, and waved a kiss to Meta.

The red blood had mantled to his cheek. At what? At Charlotte's triumphantly saucy look—which he had not failed to catch—or at his wife's grave one? Or at the sight of a gentleman who stood on the pavement, saluting them as they passed? It was the Viscount Averil. George saluted again, and rode on with a smooth brow and a face bright as day.

Considerably later; just before five, in fact, when the Bank closed, Lord Averil presented himself at it again. Had Mr. George Godolphin returned? If so, could he see him?

Mr. George had not come in. Mr. Hurde came forward and inquired if it was anything that he could do for his lordship.

Lord Averil had known Mr. Hurde a long while. He had seen him in his place there as long as he had banked with Godolphin, Crosse, and Godolphin. He supposed he was a confidential clerk: and, in point of fact, Mr. Hurde was so to a great extent.

"You hold some bonds of mine," said Lord Averil. "Bonds of some stock which Sir George Godolphin purchased for me. Did you know anything of it?"

"I remember the transaction quite well, my lord," replied Mr. Hurde.

"I want the bonds delivered up to me. Can I have them?"

"Certainly. Your lordship can have them whenever you please. They are in your case, in the strong-room."

"I should have liked them to-day, if possible," replied Lord Averil.

"There will be no difficulty at all, my lord. Mr. George Godolphin can deliver them to you as soon as he comes in."

"Will he be in soon, think you?"

"He is sure not to be very long, my lord. I have to see him before I leave."

"Then I think I'll wait," said Lord Averil.

He was shown into the Bank parlour, and left there. At five the clerks quitted the Bank: it was usual for them to do so. Mr. Hurde waited. In about a quarter of an hour George entered.

A few minutes given to the business for which Mr. Hurde had remained, and then he spoke. "Lord Averil is waiting to see you, sir."

"Lord Averil?" cried George, in a hasty tone. "Waiting now?"

"He is in the parlour, sir. He asked if he could have his bonds given up to him. I said I thought he could, and he replied that he would wait."

"Then you had no business to say anything of the sort," burst forth George, in so vehement a tone as to astonish the sober cashier. "It may not be convenient to lay one's hands upon the bonds at a minute's notice, Hurde," he more quietly added, as if he would soothe down or atone for his anger.

"They are in Lord Averil's box in the strong-room, sir," said the old clerk, supposing his master must have temporarily forgotten where the said bonds were placed. "Mr. Godolphin was speaking to me about those bonds the other day."

"What about them?" inquired George, striving to put the question easily.

"It was nothing particular, sir. He was only mentioning their increased value: how they had gone up in the market."

George said no more. He turned from the office and halted before the door of the parlour. Halted to collect his brains. One hand was on the handle of the door, the other on his brow. Lord Averil rose, and shook hands cordially.

"I have come to bother you again about my bonds, Mr. George. I don't care to keep that stock, and the present is a most favourable opportunity to sell."

"They'll go higher yet," observed George.

"Will they? They tell me differently in London. The opinion there is, that they will begin to fall."

"All rubbish," said George. "A *canard* got up on the Stock Exchange."

"Well, I have made up my mind to sell," observed Lord Averil. "I wrote to you from London to send me the shares up; but you did not seem to be in a hurry to do it. So I have come down for them."

George laughed. "Come down for nothing but the shares? But you will make some stay here?"

"No. I go up again to-morrow. I am not sure whether I shall return here for the summer or not. Some friends of mine are going over to Canada for three or four months. Perhaps I may accompany them."

George devoutly wished his lordship could be off, there and then; and that the sojourn might last years instead of months. "I wish *I* had the time to go there!" cried he, aloud: "I'd start to-morrow."

"Will it be troubling you to give me the bonds, Mr. George?"

George sat a few moments, his head bent as if in thought. "The bonds?" he slowly said. "Your bonds? They were sent—yes, certainly, your bonds were sent to our agents in London."

"My bonds sent to your agents in London!" repeated Lord Averil, in surprise. "What for?"

George coughed. "Some of our deposited deeds are kept there. Let me see?" he continued, again plunging into thought. "Yes—yours were amongst those that went up, I remember."

"But why not have told me this before?" asked Lord Averil. "Had you written me word, it would have saved me the journey down."

"To be sure," acquiesced George. "To tell you the truth, I never thought much about it, or where they were, until now."

"Mr. Hurde told me they were here," said Lord Averil.

"No doubt he thought so. They were here until recently."

"I shall have my journey back again, then!" cried his lordship. "Will the town bankers give them up to me on my simple demand, or must they have your authority?"

"I will write to them," responded George.

The viscount rose. Not a shade of suspicion had crossed his mind. But he could not help thinking that he should have made a better man of business than handsome George. "I wish you had told me!" he involuntarily repeated. "But I suppose," he good-naturedly added, "that my poor bonds are too insignificant to have much place in the thoughts of a man surrounded by hundreds of thousands."

George laughed. He was walking with Lord Averil to the front door. They stood together when it was reached, the street before them. Lord Averil asked after Mr. Godolphin.

"He seems a little better," replied George. "Certainly no worse."

"I am glad to hear it. Very glad indeed. You will not forget to write to town, Mr. George?"

"All right," replied George Godolphin.

CHAPTER XII.

"I SEE IT: BUT I CANNOT EXPLAIN IT."

THE light of the setting sun streamed upon the fair hair of Cecil Godolphin. She had strolled out from the dining-room to enjoy the beauty of the late spring evening, or to indulge her own thoughts, as might be. To the confines of the grounds strayed she, as far as those surrounding Lady Godolphin's Folly; and there she sat down on a garden bench.

Not to remain long alone. She was interrupted by the very man upon whom—if the disclosure must be made—her evening thoughts had centred. He was coming up with a quick step on the road from Prior's Ash. Seeing Cecil, he turned off to accost her, his heart beating.

Beating with the slight ascent, or with the sight of Cecil? He best knew. Many a man's heart has beaten at a less lovely vision. She wore her favourite attire, white, set off with blue ribbons, and her golden hair gleamed in the sunlight. She almost exclaimed with surprise. She had been thinking of him, it is true, but as one who was miles and miles away. In spite of his stormy and not long-past rejection, Lord Averil went straight up to her and held out his hand. Did he notice that her blue eyes dropped beneath his, as she rose to answer his greeting; that the soft colour on her cheeks changed to a glowing damask?

"I fear I have surprised you," said Lord Averil.

"A little," acknowledged Cecil. "I did not know you were at Prior's Ash. Thomas will be glad to see you."

She turned to walk with him to the house, as in courtesy bound. Lord Averil offered her his arm, and Cecil condescended to put the tips of her fingers within it. Neither broke the silence; perhaps neither could break it; and they reached the large porch of Ashlydyat. Cecil spoke then.

"Are you going to make a long stay in the country?"

"A very short one. A party of friends are departing for Canada, and they wish me to make one of them. I think I shall do so."

"To Canada!" echoed Cecil. "So far away!"

Lord Averil smiled. "It sounds farther than it really is. I am an old traveller, you know."

Cecil opened the dining-room door. Thomas was alone. He had left the table, and was seated in his armchair at the window. A glad smile illumined his face when he saw Lord Averil. Lord Averil was one of the very few of whom Thomas Godolphin could make a close friend. These close friends! Not above one or two, can we meet with in a lifetime. Acquaintances many; but friends—those to whom the heart can speak out its inmost thoughts, who may be as our own soul—how few!

Cecil left them alone. She ran off to tell Janet that Lord Averil had come, and would perhaps take tea with them, were he invited to do so. Thomas, with more hospitable ideas, was pressing dinner upon him. It could be brought back at once.

"I have dined at the Bell," replied Lord Averil. "Not any, thank you," he added, as Thomas was turning to the wine. "I have taken all I require."

"Have you come to make a long stay?" inquired Thomas—as Cecil had done.

"I shall go back to town to-morrow. Having nothing to do with myself this evening, I thought I could not spend it better than with you. I am pleased to see that you are looking yourself."

"The warm weather seems to be doing me good," was Thomas Godolphin's reply, a consciousness within him how little better he really was. "Why are you making so short a stay?"

"Well, as it turns out, my journey has been a superfluous one. Those bonds that you hold of mine brought me down," continued Lord Averil, little thinking that he was doing mischief by mentioning the subject to Mr. Godolphin. "I am going to sell out, and came down to get them."

"Why did you not write?" said Thomas. "We could have sent them to you."

"I did write, a week or ten days ago, and your brother wrote me word in answer that the bonds should be sent—or something to that effect. But they never came. Having nothing much to do, I thought I would run down for them. I also wanted to see Max. But he is away."

"I believe he is," replied Thomas. "Have you got the bonds?"

"It has proved a useless journey, I say," replied Lord Averil. "The bonds, I find, are in town, at your agents'."

Thomas Godolphin looked up with surprise. "They are not in town," he said. "What should bring them in town? Who told you that?"

"Your brother George."

"George told you the bonds were in town?" repeated Thomas, as if he could not believe his ears.

"He did indeed: not three hours ago. Why? Are they not in town?"

"Most certainly not. The bonds are in our strong-room, where they were first deposited. They have never been moved from it. What could George have been thinking of?"

"To tell you the truth, I did not fancy he appeared over-certain himself, where they were, whether here or in town," said Lord Averil. "At length he remembered that they were in town: he said they had gone up with other deeds."

"He makes a mistake," said Thomas. "He must be confounding your bonds with some that we sent up the other day of Lord Cavemore's. And yet, I wonder that he should do so! Lord Cavemore's went up for a particular purpose, and George himself took the instructions. Lord Cavemore consulted him upon the business altogether."

"Then—if my bonds are here—can I have them at once?" asked Lord Averil.

"You can have them the instant the Bank opens to-morrow morning. In fact, you might have them to-night if George should happen to be at home. I am sorry you should have had any trouble about it."

Lord Averil smiled. "Speaking frankly, I do not fancy George is so much a man of business as you are. When I first asked for the bonds, nearly a month ago, he appeared to be quite at sea about them; not to know what I meant, or to remember that you held bonds of mine."

"Did you ask for the bonds a month ago?" exclaimed Thomas.

"About that time. It was when you were in London. George at last remembered."

"Did he not give them to you?"

"No. He said—— I almost forget what he said. That he did not know where to put his hands upon them, I think, in your absence."

Thomas felt vexed. He wondered what could have possessed George to behave in so unbusiness-like a way: or how it was possible for him to have blundered so about the bonds. But he would not blame his brother to Lord Averil. "You shall have the bonds the first thing in the morning," he said. "I will drop a note to George, reminding him where they are, in case I am not at the Bank early enough for you."

Unusually well felt Thomas Godolphin that evening. He proceeded with Lord Averil to the drawing-room to his sisters; and a very pleasant hour or two they all spent together. Bessy laughed at Lord Averil a great deal about his proposed Canadian expedition, telling him she did not believe he seriously entertained it.

It was a genial night, soft, warm, and lovely, the moon bright again. The church clocks at Prior's Ash were striking ten when Lord Averil rose to leave Ashlydyat. "If you will wait two minutes for me, I will go a little way with you," said Thomas Godolphin.

He withdrew to another room, penned a line, and despatched it by a servant to the Bank. Then he rejoined Lord Averil, passed his arm within his lordship's, and went out with him.

"Is this Canada project a joke?" asked he.

"Indeed, no. I have not quite made up my mind to go. I think I shall do so. If so, I shall be away in a week from this. Why should I not go? I have no settled home, no ties."

"Should you not—I beg your pardon, Averil—be the happier for a settled home? You might form ties. I think a roving life must be the least desirable one of all."

"It is one I was never fitted for. My inclination would lead me to home, to domestic happiness. But, as you know, I put that out of my power."

"For a time. But that is over. You might marry again."

"I do not suppose I ever shall," returned Lord Averil, feeling half prompted to tell his unsuspicious friend that his own sister was the barrier to his doing so. "*You* have never married," he resumed, allowing the impulse to die away.

Thomas Godolphin shook his head. "The cases are different," he said. "In your wife you lost one whom you could not regret——"

"Don't call her by that name, Godolphin!" burst forth Lord Averil.

"And in Ethel I lost one who was all the world to me; who could never be replaced," Thomas went on, after a pause. "The cases are widely different."

"Ay, widely different," assented Lord Averil.

They walked on in silence, each buried in his own thoughts. At the commencement of the road, Lord Averil stopped and took Thomas Godolphin's hand in his.

"You shall not come any farther with me."

Thomas stopped also. He had not intended to go farther. "You will really start for Canada ? "

"I believe I shall."

"Take my blessing with you then, Averil. We may never meet again in this world."

"What ? " exclaimed Lord Averil.

"The medical men entertain hopes that my life may not be terminated so speedily : *I* believe that a few months will end it. I may not live to welcome you home."

It was the first intimation Lord Averil had received of Thomas Godolphin's fatal malady. Thomas explained it to him. He was overwhelmed.

"Oh, my friend! my friend! Cannot death be defied, or coaxed to spare you ? " he called out in his pain. How many have vainly echoed the same cry!

A few more words, a long grasp of the lingering hands, and they parted. Thomas with a God-speed; Lord Averil with a different prayer—a God-*save*—upon his lips. The peer turned to Prior's Ash; Thomas Godolphin towards home.

Not by the path he had come. He had brought Lord Averil down the broad entrance to Ashlydyat : he turned to go round the path by the ash-trees in front of the Dark Plain. Possibly he had a mind to see whether the Shadow was abroad to-night.

Before he had well turned the corner of the trees, or had given more than a glance to the black Shadow—for there it was—he heard hasty footsteps behind him. Looking round, he beheld Lord Averil. Softened by the parting, by the tidings he had heard, an impulse had taken Lord Averil that he would speak of Cecil : and he turned back to do so.

"Godolphin, I—— What's that ? "

The great black Shadow, stretching out there in the distance, had attracted the attention of Lord Averil. He stood with his forefinger extended, pointed towards it.

"That is what they call the Shadow of Ashlydyat," quietly replied Thomas Godolphin.

Lord Averil had never before seen it. He had heard enough of it. Attentively regarding it, he did not for some time speak.

"Do you believe in it ? " he asked at length.

"Believe in it ? " repeated Thomas Godolphin. "I believe that a Shadow does appear there on occasions. I cannot believe otherwise, with that ocular demonstration before me."

"And how do you account for it ? " asked Lord Averil.

"I have been all my life trying to do so. And have come to the conclusion that it is not to be accounted for."

"But I have always treated the report as the most perfect folly," rejoined Lord Averil.

"Ay. No doubt. As I should do but for *that*"—and Thomas Godolphin nodded towards the Shadow, on which the peer's eyes were fixed with an intense gaze. "You and I are rational beings, Averil, not likely to be led away by superstitious folly; we live in an enlightened age, little tolerant of such things. And yet,˙here we stand, gazing with dispassionate eyes on that Shadow, in full possession of our sober judgment. It is there; we see it: and that is all we can tell about it. The Shadow of Ashlydyat is ridiculed from one end of the county to the other: spoken of—when spoken of at all—as an absurd superstition of the Godolphins. But there the Shadow is: and not all the ridicule extant can do away with the plain fact. I see it: but I cannot explain it."

"What do you do about it?"

Lord Averil asked the question in his bewilderment. A smile crossed Thomas Godolphin's lips as he answered.

"We do nothing. We can do nothing. We cannot prevent its coming; we cannot send it away when it comes; we cannot bring it if it does not come of its own accord. If I reason about it for a month, Averil, I could give you no better explanation than this."

Lord Averil drew a deep breath, as one awaking from a reverie. As Thomas Godolphin said: *there* was the Shadow, visible to his eyes, his senses: but of explanation as to its cause, there was none. The little episode had driven away the impulse to speak of Cecil: and, after another hand pressure, he finally turned away, and pursued his walk to Prior's Ash.

Another was also pursuing his walk to Prior's Ash; indeed, had nearly gained it: and that was Thomas Godolphin's messenger. Approaching the Bank residence, he distinguished some one standing at the entrance, and found that it was Mr. George Godolphin.

"What's this?" asked George. "A letter?"

"My master sent me down with it, sir."

George turned it about in his hand. "Does it require an answer, do you know, Andrew?"

"No, sir. My master said I need not wait."

The man departed, and George carried the note into the dining-room. Maria sat there reading, underneath the chandelier. She looked pleased to see her husband, and closed the book. George had been out all the evening. He stood opposite to Maria, and tore the note open.

"DEAR GEORGE,

"Lord Averil's bonds are in his case in the strong-room. How could you make so great a mistake as to tell him they had gone up to town? I send you word, lest he should call for them in the morning before I reach the Bank.

"Ever yours,
"THOMAS GODOLPHIN."

Then the disclosure must come! With a word, that was very

like a groan, George crushed the paper in his hand. Maria heard the sound.

"What is it, George?"

"Nothing. What? This? Only a note from Thomas."

He began whistling lightly, to cover his real feelings, and took up the book Maria had closed. "Is it entertaining?" asked he, turning over its pages.

"Very. It is a charming book. But that I had it to read, I should have been lying on the sofa. I have a very bad headache to-night."

"Go to bed," responded George.

"I think I must. Perhaps you will not care to come so early?"

"Never mind me. I have an hour or two's work to do in the Bank to-night."

"Oh, George!"

"My dear, it need not keep you up."

"George, I cannot *think* how it is that you have night-work to do!" she impulsively exclaimed, after a pause. "I am sure Thomas would not wish you to do it. I think I shall ask him."

George turned round and grasped her shoulder, quite sharply. "Maria!"

His grasp, I say, was sharp, his look and voice were imperatively stern. Maria felt frightened: she scarcely knew why. "What have I done?" she asked, timidly.

"Understand me, please, once for all. What I choose to do, does not regard my brother Thomas. I will have no tales carried to him."

"Why do you mistake me so?" she answered, when she had a little recovered her surprise. "It cannot be well for you, or pleasant for you, to have so much work to do at night, and I thought Thomas would have told you not to do it. Tales! George, you know I should never tell them of you."

"No, no; I know you would not, Maria. I have been idle of late, and am getting up my work; that's all: but it would not do to let Thomas know it. You—you don't tell Isaac that I sit up at the books?" he cried, almost in an accent of terror.

She looked up at him wonderingly, through her wet eyelashes. "Surely, no! Should I be likely to speak to Isaac of what you do? or to any one?"

George folded her in his arms, kissing the tears from her face. "Go to bed at once, darling, and sleep your headache off," he fondly whispered. "I shall be up soon; as soon as I can."

He lighted her candle and gave it to her. As Maria took it, she remembered something she wished to say to him. "When will it be convenient to you to give me some money, George?"

"What for?"

"Oh, you know. For housekeeping. The bills are getting so heavy, and the tradespeople are beginning to ask for their money. The servants want their wages, too. Would it not be better to pay regularly, as we used to do, instead of letting things run on so long?"

"Ay. I'll see about it," replied George.

George had got into the habit of giving the same answer, when asked by his wife for money. She had asked several times lately: but all the satisfaction she received was, " I'll see about it." Not a suspicion that his means were running short ever crossed her brain.

She went upstairs and retired to rest, soon falling asleep. Her head was heavy. The household went to bed; George shut himself into the Bank—according to his recent custom; and the house was soon wrapped in quiet—as a sober house should be.

Two o'clock was striking from All Souls' clock when Maria awoke. Why should she have done so?—there was no noise to startle her. All she knew—and it is all that a great many of us know—was, that she did awake.

To her astonishment, George was not in bed. Two o'clock!—and he had said that he should soon follow her! A vague feeling of alarm stole over Maria.

All sorts of improbable suggestions crowded on her imagination. Imaginations, you know, are more fantastic in the dark, still night, than in the busy day. Had he been taken ill? Had he fallen asleep at his work? Could he—could he have set the books and himself on fire? Had a crown been offered to Maria, she could not have remained tranquil a moment longer.

Slightly dressing herself, she threw on a warm dressing-gown, and stole down the stairs. Passing through the door that divided the dwelling from the Bank, she softly turned the handle of George's room, and opened it. Secure in the house being at rest, he had not locked the doors against interruption.

The tables seemed strewed with books, but George was not then occupied with them. He was sitting in a chair apart, buried, as it appeared—in thought, his hands and his head alike drooping listlessly. He started up at Maria's entrance.

" I grew alarmed, George," she said, trying to explain her appearance. " I awoke suddenly, and finding you had not come up, I grew frightened, thinking you might be ill. It is two o'clock!"

" What made you come down out of your warm bed?" reiterated George. " You'll catch your death."

" I was frightened, I say. Will you not come up now?"

" I am coming directly," replied George. " Go back at once. You'll be sure to take cold."

Maria turned to obey. Somehow the dark passages struck on her with a nervous dread. She shrank into the room again.

" I don't care to go up alone," she cried. " I have no light."

" How foolish!" he exclaimed. " I declare Meta would be braver!"

Some nervous feeling did certainly appear to be upon her, for she burst into tears. George's tone—a tone of irritation, it had been—was exchanged for one of soothing tenderness, as he bent over her. "What is the matter with you to-night, Maria? I'll light you up."

" I don't know what is the matter with me," she answered, suppressing her sobs. " I have not felt in good spirits of late. George, sometimes I think you are not well. You are a great deal changed in your manner to me. Have I—have I displeased you in any way?"

" *You* displeased me! No, my darling."

He spoke with impulsive fondness. Well had it been for George Godolphin had no heavier care been upon him than any little displeasure his wife could give him. The thought occurred to him with strange bitterness.

"I'll light you up, Maria," he repeated. "I shall not be long after you."

And, taking the heavy lamp from the table, he carried it to the outer passage, and held it while she went up the stairs. Then he returned to the room and to his work—whatever that work might be.

Vain work! vain, delusive, useless work! As you will soon find, Mr. George Godolphin.

Morning came. Whether gnawing care or hopeful joy may lie in the heart's inner dwelling-place, people generally meet at their breakfast-tables as usual.

George Godolphin sat at breakfast with his wife. Maria was in high spirits: her indisposition of the previous evening had passed away. She was telling George an anecdote of Meta, as she poured out the coffee, some little *ruse* the young lady had exercised, to come over Margery; and Maria laughed heartily as she told it. George laughed in echo: as merrily as his wife. There must have been two George Godolphins surely at that moment! The outer, presented to the world, gay, smiling, and careless; the inner, kept for his own private and especial delectation, grim, dark, and ghastly.

Breakfast was nearly over, when there was heard a clattering of little feet, the door burst open, and Miss Meta appeared in a triumphant shout of laughter. She had eluded Margery's vigilance, and eloped from the nursery. Margery speedily followed, scolding loudly, her hands stretched forth to seize the runaway. But Meta had bounded to her papa, and found a refuge.

George caught her up on his knee: his hair—the same shade once, but somewhat darker now—mixing with the light golden locks of the child, as he took from her kiss after kiss. To say that George Godolphin was passionately fond of his child would not be speaking too strongly: few fathers can love a child more ardently than George loved Meta. A pretty little lovable thing she was! Look at her on George's knee! her dainty white frock, its sleeves tied up with blue, her pretty socks and shoes, her sunny face, surrounded by its shower of curls. Margery scolded in the doorway, but Miss Meta, little heeding, was casting her inquisitive eyes on the breakfast-table, to see what there might be especially nice upon it.

"If you'd just please to punish her once for it, sir, she wouldn't do it, maybe, in future!" grumbled Margery. "Naughty girl!"

"I think I must," said George. "Shall I whip you, Meta?"

Meta shouted out a joyous little laugh in answer, turned her face round, and clung to him lovingly. She knew what his "whippings" meant.

"But if Margery says so?"

"Margery nobody," responded Meta, bustling her face round to the table again. "Mamma, may I have some of that?"

Maria hesitated. "That" was some tempting-looking breakfast-dish, very good, no doubt, for George, but very rich for Meta. George, how-ever, drew it towards him, and cut her a little, claiming for his reward as many kisses as Meta's impatience would accord him. Margery went off in a temper.

" No wonder the child despises her bread and milk in the morning!
If I had fed *you* upon those spiced things, Mr. George, when you were
a child, I wonder whether you'd have grown into the strong man you
are!"

"Into a stronger," called out George. He as much liked to give a
word of teasing now and then to Margery as he had in the old days she
referred to. Margery retorted with some answer, which he did not hear,
and George laughed. Laughed loud and merrily, and again bent his
face to Meta's.

But he could not remain all day long in that scene of peace. Oh, if
we only could! those who have to go out to battle with the daily world.
If there were only a means of closing the door on the woes that turn a
man's hair white before its time!

George took Meta a triumphal ride round the room on his shoulder,
and then, having extorted his payment, put her down by Maria. Going
into the Bank to his day's work. His day's work! rather an embar-
rassing one, that day, Mr. George Godolphin!

Taking the keys of the strong-room from the cupboard, also certain
other keys, as he had done once before within the knowledge of the
reader, he proceeded to the strong-room, opened a certain safe in it,
and took out the box inscribed "Lord Averil." This he also opened,
and examined its contents. Mr. George Godolphin was searching for
certain bonds: or, making believe to search for them. Having satisfied
himself that they were not there, he returned the box to its place, made
all safe again, went back, and sat down to open the morning letters.
Presently he called to a clerk.

" Has Mr. Hurde come?"

" Yes, sir."

" Desire him to step here."

The old clerk came, in obedience to the summons, taking off his
spectacles as he entered to rub one of their glasses, which had got
misty. George leaned his elbow on the table, and, resting his chin upon
his hand, looked him full in the face.

"Hurde," said he, plunging midway into his communication, which
he made in a lone tone, "those bonds of Lord Averil's are missing."

The clerk paused, as if scarcely understanding. "How do you
mean, sir? Missing in what way?"

" I can't find them," replied George.

"They are in Lord Averil's box in the strong-room, sir, with his
other papers."

"But they are not there," replied George. "I have searched the
papers through this morning. Hurde, we have had some roguery at
work."

Another pause, devoted by Mr. Hurde to revolving the communication. "Roguery!" he slowly repeated. "Have you missed anything
else, Mr. George?"

"No. I have not looked."

"Oh, sir, there's no fear of anything being wrong," resumed the old
clerk, his good sense repudiating the notion. "Mr. Godolphin must
have moved them."

"That's just what I thought until last night," said George. "The fact is, Lord Averil asked me for these bonds some little time ago, while my brother was in London. I opened the box, and, not seeing them there, came to the conclusion that Mr. Godolphin had moved them. Lord Averil said it was of no consequence then, and departed for London: and the thing slipped from my memory. When you spoke to me about it last evening, of course I felt vexed to have forgotten it, and I put off Lord Averil with the best excuse I could."

"And has Mr. Godolphin not moved them, sir?" demanded the clerk.

"It appears not. He dropped me a line last night, saying I should find the bonds in their place in the box. I suppose Lord Averil was up at Ashlydyat and mentioned it. But I can't find them in the box."

"Sir, you know you are not a very good searcher," observed Mr. Hurde, after some consideration. "Once or twice that you have searched for deeds, Mr. Godolphin has found them afterwards, overlooked by you. Shall I go carefully over the box, sir? I think they must be in it."

"I tell you, Hurde, they are not."

He spoke somewhat fractiously. Fully aware that he had occasionally overlooked deeds, in his haste or carelessness, perhaps the contrast between those times and these, gave a sting to his manner. *Then*, whether the deeds had been found or not, he was innocent: now——

"But, if they are not in the box, where can they be?" resumed Mr. Hurde.

"There it is," said George. "Where can they be? I say, Hurde, that some light fingers must have been at work."

Mr. Hurde considered the point in his mind. It seemed that he could not adopt the conclusion readily. "I should think not, sir. If nothing else is missing, I should say certainly not."

"*They* are missing, at any rate," returned George. "It will put Mr. Godolphin out terribly. I wish there had been any means of keeping it from him: but, now that Lord Averil has mentioned the bonds to him, there are none. I shall get the blame. He will think I have not kept the keys securely."

"But you have, sir, have you not?"

"For all I know I have," replied George, assuming a carelessness as to the point, of which he had not been guilty. "Allowing that I had not, for argument's sake, what dishonest person can we have about us, Hurde, who would use the advantage to his own profit?"

Mr. Hurde began calling over the list of clerks, preparatory to considering whether any one of them could be considered in the least degree doubtful. He was engaged in this mental process, when a clerk interrupted them, to say that a gentleman was asking to see Mr. George Godolphin.

George looked up sharply. The applicant, however, was not Lord Averil, and any one else would be more tolerable to him on that day than his lordship; Mr. Godolphin, perhaps, excepted. As the old clerk was withdrawing to give place to the visitor, George caught sight, through the open door, of Mr. Godolphin entering the office. An im-

pulse to throw the disclosure off his own shoulders, prompted him to
hasten after Mr. Hurde.

"Hurde," he whispered, catching his arm, "you may as well make
the communication to Mr. Godolphin. He ought to know it at once,
and I may be engaged some time."

So George remained shut up, and the old clerk followed Thomas
Godolphin to his private room. Mr. Godolphin felt well that morning,
and had come unusually early : possibly lest there should be any
further blundering over Lord Averil's bonds. He looked somewhat
surprised to see the old clerk approaching him with a long face and
mysterious look.

"Do you want me, Hurde?"

"Mr. George has desired me to speak to you, sir, about those bonds
of Lord Averil's. To make an unpleasant communication, in fact.
He is engaged himself, just now. He says he can't find them."

"They are in the strong-room, in Lord Averil's case," replied Mr.
Godolphin.

"He says they are not there, sir : that he can't find them."

"But they are there," returned Thomas. "They have not been
moved out of the box since they were first placed in it."

He spoke quietly as he ever did, but very firmly, almost as if he were
disputing the point, or had been prepared to dispute it. Mr. Hurde
resumed after some deliberation : he was a deliberate man always, both
in temperament and in speech.

"What Mr. George says, is this, sir : That when you were in London
Lord Averil asked for his bonds. Mr. George looked for them, and
found they were not in the box; and he came to the conclusion that
you had moved them. The affair escaped his memory, he says, until
last night, when he was asked for them again. He has been searching
the box this morning, but cannot find the bonds in it."

"They must be there," observed Thomas Godolphin. "If George
has not moved them, I have not. He has a knack of overlooking
things."

"I said so to him, sir, just now. He——"

"Do you say he is engaged?" interrupted Thomas Godolphin.

"The secretary of the railway company is with him, sir. I suppose
he has come about that loan. I think the bonds can't be anywhere
but in the box, sir. I told Mr. George so."

"Let me know when he is disengaged," said Thomas Godolphin.
And Mr. Hurde went out.

George Godolphin was disengaged then. Mr. Hurde saw the gentleman, whom he had called the railway company's secretary, departing.
The next minute George Godolphin came out of his room.

"Have you mentioned that to my brother?" he asked of Hurde.

"I have, sir. Mr. Godolphin thinks that you must be mistaken."

George went in to his brother, shook hands, and said he was glad to
see him so early. "It is a strange thing about these bonds," he continued, without giving Thomas time to speak.

"You have overlooked them," said Thomas. "Bring me the keys,
and I will go and get them."

"I assure you they are not there."

"They must be there, George. Bring me the keys."

George Godolphin produced the key of the strong-room, and of the safe, and Lord Averil's box was examined by Thomas Godolphin. The bonds in question were *not* in it: and Thomas, had he missed himself, could scarcely have been more completely astonished.

"George, you must have moved them," were the first words he spoke.

"Not I," said George, lightly. "Where should I move them to?"

"But no one has power to get into that room, or to penetrate to the safe and the box after it, except you and myself," urged Mr. Godolphin. "Unless, indeed, you have allowed the keys to stray from your keeping."

"I have not done that," answered George. "This seems to be perfectly unaccountable."

"How came you to tell Averil last night that the bonds had gone to London?"

"Well, the fact is, I did not know what to tell him," replied George. "When I first missed the bonds, when you were in London—— "

"Why did you not let me know then that they were missing?" was the interruption.

"I forgot it when you returned home."

"But you should not have allowed yourself the possibility of forgetting a thing like that," remonstrated Thomas. "Upon missing deeds of that value, or in fact of any value however slight, you should have communicated with me the very same hour. George," he added, after a pause, which George did not break: "I cannot understand how it was that you did not see the necessity of it yourself."

George Godolphin was running his hand through his hair—in an absent manner, lost in thought; in—as might be conjectured—contemplation of the past time referred to. "How was I to think anything but that you had moved the deeds?" he said.

"At all events, you should have ascertained. Why, George, were I to miss deeds that I believed to be in a given place, I could not rest a night without inquiring after them. I might assume—and there might be every probability for it—that you had moved them; but my sleep would be ruined until I ascertained the fact."

George made no reply. I wonder where he was wishing himself? Mr. Godolphin resumed.

"In this instance, I do not see how you could have come to the conclusion that I had touched the bonds. Where did you think I was likely to move them to?"

George could not tell—and said so. It was not impossible, but Thomas might have sent them to town—or have handed them back to Lord Averil, he continued to murmur, in a somewhat confused manner. Thomas looked at him: he could scarcely make him out, but supposed the loss had affected his equanimity.

"Had you regarded it dispassionately, George, I think you would have seen it in a more serious light. I should not be likely to move the bonds to a different place of keeping, without your cognizance: and as to returning them to Lord Averil, the transaction would have appeared in the books."

"I am sorry I forgot to mention it to you," said George.

"That you could have forgotten it, and continued to forget it until now, passes all belief. Has there never been a moment at any time, George, in this last month that it has recurred to your memory?"

"Well, perhaps there may have been; just a casual thought," acknowledged George. "I can't be sure."

"And yet you did not speak to me?"

"In your present state of health, I was willing to spare you unnecessary anxiety——"

"Stay, George. If you really assumed that I had moved the deeds, asking me the question could not have been productive of anxiety. If any fear, such as that the deeds were missing without my agency, only crossed your mind as a suggestion, it was your bounden duty to acquaint me with it."

"I wish I could have dealt with the matter now without acquainting you," returned George. "Did not the London doctors warn you that repose of mind was essential to you?"

"George," was the impressive answer, and Thomas had his hand upon his brother's arm as he spoke it, "so long as I pretend to transact business, to come to this Bank, and sit here, its master, so long do I desire and request to be considered equal to discharging its duties efficiently. When I can no longer do that, I will withdraw from it. Never again suffer my state of health to be a plea for keeping matters from me, however annoying or complicated they may be."

Thomas Godolphin spent half that day in looking into other strong boxes, lest perchance the missing deeds should have got into any—though he did not see how that could be. They could not be found; but, neither did any other paper of consequence, so far as could be discovered, appear to have gone. Thomas could not account for the loss in any way, or conjecture why it should have occurred, or who had taken the bonds. It was made known in the Bank that a packet of deeds was missing; but full particulars were not given.

There was no certain data to go upon as to the time of the loss. George Godolphin stated that he had missed them a month ago; Thomas, when visiting Lord Averil's box for some purpose about four months ago, had seen the deeds there, secure. They must have disappeared between those periods. The mystery was—how? The clerks could not get to the strong-room and to the safes and cases in it, unless by some strange accident; by some most unaccountable neglect. Very great neglect it would have been, to allow them the opportunity of getting to one key; but to obtain three or four, as was necessary before those deeds could have been taken, and to obtain them undiscovered, was next door to an impossibility. The internal arrangements in the house of Godolphin, Crosse, and Godolphin were of a stringent nature: Sir George Godolphin had been a most particular man in business. Conjecture upon conjecture was hazarded: theory after theory discussed. When Mr. Hurde found the deeds were really gone, his amazement was excessive, his trouble great. George, as soon as he could, stole away from the discussion. He had got over his part, better perhaps than he had expected: all that remained now, was to make the best of the loss—and to institute a search for the deeds.

"I can't call to mind a single one of them who would do it, or be likely to do it," remarked Mr. Hurde to his master.

"Of whom?"

"Of the clerks in the house, sir. But, one of them, it must have been."

"A stranger it could not have been," replied Thomas Godolphin. "Had a midnight plunderer got into the Bank, he would not have contented himself with one packet of deeds."

"Whoever took them, sir, took them to make money upon them. There's not a doubt of that. I wonder—I wonder——"

"What?" asked Mr. Godolphin.

"I wonder—I have often wondered, sir—whether Layton does not live above his income. If so——"

"Hurde," said Thomas Godolphin gravely, "I believe Layton to be as honest as you or I."

"Well—I have always thought him so, or I should pretty soon have spoken. But, sir, the deeds must have gone somehow, by somebody's hands: and Layton is the least *un*likely of all. I see him on a Sunday driving his new wife out in a gig. She plays the piano, too!"

How these items in the domestic economy of the clerk, Layton, could bear upon the loss of the deeds, especially the latter item, Mr. Hurde did not further explain. He was of the old school, seeing no good in gigs, still less in pianos; and he determined to look a little after Mr. Layton.

Thomas Godolphin, straightforward and honourable, imparted to Lord Averil the fact of the deeds being missing. Whether he would have revealed it to a less intimate client at this early stage of the affair, might be a matter of speculation. The house would not yet call them lost, he said to Lord Averil: it trusted, by some fortunate accident, to put its hands upon them, in some remote pigeon-hole. Lord Averil received the communication with courteous friendliness: he thought it must prove that they had only been mislaid, and he hoped they would be found. Both gentlemen hoped that sincerely. The value of the deeds was about sixteen thousand pounds: too much for either of them to lose with equanimity.

"George must have known of this when I asked him for the deeds a month ago," observed Lord Averil.

"I think not," replied Thomas Godolphin. "It was your asking for the deeds which caused him to search the box for them, and he then found they were gone."

"Perhaps you are right. But I remember thinking his manner peculiar."

"How 'peculiar'?" inquired Thomas.

"Hesitating: uncertain. He appeared, at first, not to know what I meant in asking for the deeds. Since you spoke to me of the loss, it struck me as accounting for George's manner—that he did not like to tell me of it."

"He could not have known of it then," repeated Thomas Godolphin.

As this concluding part of the conversation took place, they were coming out of the room. Isaac Hastings was passing along the passage, and heard a portion of it.

The Shadow of Ashlydyat.   17

"Are they deeds of Lord Averil's that are missing?" he inquired confidentially of Mr. Hurde, later in the day.

The old clerk nodded an affirmative. "But you need not proclaim it there," he added, by way of caution, glancing sideways at the clerks.

"Do you suppose I should do so?" returned Isaac Hastings.

CHAPTER XIII.

A RED-LETTER DAY FOR MRS. BOND.

THE scent of the new-mown hay was in the atmosphere around Prior's Ash. A backward spring it had been until the middle of April, and wiseacres said the crops would be late. But then the weather had suddenly burst into the warmth of summer, vegetation came on all the more rapidly for its previous tardiness, and the crops turned out to be early, instead of late.

Never a more lovely day gladdened the world than that particular day in June. Maria Godolphin, holding Miss Meta by the hand, walked along under the shady field-hedge, all glorious with its clusters of wild roses. The field was covered with hay, now being piled into cocks by the haymakers, and Meta darted ever and anon from her mother's side, to afford the valuable aid of her tiny hands. Meta would have enjoyed a roll on the hay with the most intense delight; but unfortunately Meta was in the full grandeur of visiting attire; not in simple hay-making undress. Had you asked Meta, she would have told you she had on her "best things." Things too good to be allowed to come to grief in the hay. Maria soothed the disappointment by a promise for the morrow. Meta should come in her brown holland dress with Margery, and roll about as much as she pleased. Children are easily satisfied, and Meta paced on soberly under the promise, only giving covetous glances at the hay. With all her impulsive gaiety, her laughter and defiance of Margery, she was by nature a most gentle child, easily led.

Maria was on her way to call at Lady Godolphin's Folly; and thence at Ashlydyat. Maria was not given to making morning calls: she deemed it a very unsatisfactory waste of time. Very pleasant no doubt for gossips, but a hindrance to the serious business of life. She made them now and then; just enough to save her credit, and that was all. Mrs. Pain had honoured Maria with about fifteen visits, and Maria was now going to return them all in one. No one could say Charlotte went in for ceremony; she would run in and out of people's houses, as the whim took her, every day in the week sometimes, and of Maria's amidst the rest. Of late, she had called more frequently on Maria than usual: and Maria, her conscience weighty with the obligation, at last set out to return it.

But she had not dressed for it—as some people would consider dress; Charlotte herself, for instance. Charlotte would arrive, splendid as the sun; not a colour of the rainbow came amiss to her; a green dress one day, a violet another, a crimson a third, and so on. Dresses with flounces and furbelows; jackets interlaced with gold and silver; brim-less hats surmounted by upright plumes. All that Charlotte wore was *good*, as far as cost went: as far as taste went, opinions differed. Maria had inherited the taste of her mother: she could not have been *fine* had you bribed her with gold. She wore to-day a pale dress of watered silk; a beautiful Cashmere shawl of thin texture, and a white bonnet: all plain and quiet, as befitted a lady. The charming day had induced her to walk; and the faint perfume of the hay, wafting through Prior's Ash, had caused her to choose the field way. The longest way, but infinitely the pleasantest.

It took her past those tenements familiarly called the Pollard cottages: in one of which lived troublesome Mrs. Bond. All the inmates of these cottages were well known to Maria: had been known to her from child-hood: the Rector of All Souls' was wont to say that he had more trouble with the Pollard cottages than with all the rest of his parish. For one thing, sickness was often prevalent in them; sometimes death; and sickness and death give trouble and anxiety to a conscientious pastor.

"Mamma, you going to see old Susan to-day?" chattered Miss Meta, as they approached the cottages.

"Not to-day, Meta. I am going straight on to Mrs. Pain's."

Meta, who was troubled with no qualms on the score of ceremony herself, perceiving one of the doors open, darted suddenly into it. Meta was rather in the habit of darting into any open door that it took her fancy so to do. Maria walked on a few steps, and then turned and waited: but the little truant did not appear to be in a hurry to come out, and she went back and followed her in.

A lady in a rusty black stuff gown covered with snuff, her cap awry and her face somewhat flushed, was seated in state before a round deal table, doing nothing; except contemplating certain articles that were on the table, with a remarkably gratified expression of countenance. The lady was Mrs. Bond: and this, as Maria was soon to hear, had been a decidedly red-letter day with her. On the table— and it was this which appeared to be fascinating the attention of Meta —was a large wicker cage containing a parrot; a small parrot with a plumage as fine as Mrs. Charlotte Pain's, an angry-looking tuft on its head, not at all unlike her hat's tuft of feathers. Mrs. Bond's attention appeared not to be so much absorbed by the parrot and cage, as by a green medicine-bottle, containing some clear-looking liquid, and a tea-cup without a handle. These latter articles were standing immediately before her.

Two or three years ago, Mrs. Bond's eldest daughter, Peggy, a damsel who had not borne the brightest of characters for steadiness, had been taken out to Australia by a family to whom she engaged her-self as nurse-girl. After sundry vicissitudes in that country—which she duly chronicled home to her mother, and that lady was wont to relate in convivial moments, over tea or any other social beverage—Peggy had come to an anchor by marrying. She wrote word that her husband was an industrious young carpenter, who was making his fortune, and they were quite at ease in the world. As a proof of the latter state-ment, she had sent over a parrot to her mother as a keepsake, and a trifle of money; which would be safely delivered by a friend, who was going the home voyage.

The friend was faithful. He had arrived on his mission that very morning at Mrs. Bond's, delivering the parrot uninjured and in rude health—if its capacity for screaming might be taken as an indication. The money turned out to be eleven pounds: a ten-pound note, and a sovereign in gold. Peggy probably knew enough of her mother to be certain that the first outlay made would be for "something comforting," and this may have induced her to add a sovereign, in some faint hope that the note would be preserved intact. Mrs. Bond had the sense to discern Peggy's motive, and openly spoke of it to Maria. She was in an open mood. In point of fact she had gone right off to Prior's Ash and changed the sovereign, bringing home that green bottle full of—comfort. It was three parts empty now, and Mrs. Bond, in consequence, had become rather red in the face, and was slipping some of her long words.

"But you will not think of changing the note, will you?" returned Maria, in answer to what Mrs. Bond disclosed. "How useful it would be to you in the winter for clothing and fire—if you would only keep it until then!"

"So it 'ould," responded Mrs. Bond.

She dived into her pocket, and brought forth the note and a handful of silver, all lying loose, amidst a miscellaneous collection. "Don't it look pretty?" cried she.

"Very," said Maria, not certain whether she alluded to the parrot or the money, for Mrs. Bond's eyes were not remarkably direct in their glances just then. "Too pretty to spend," she added, in reference to the note. "You had better give it to papa, Mrs. Bond, and let him take care of it for you."

Mrs. Bond shook her head at this proposition. "Once the parson gets hold on any little bit of our money to keep, he ain't free to give it up again," she objected. "'Keep it for this,' says he, or 'keep it for that;' and it ends in its being laid out as he likes, not as us do."

"As you please, of course," rejoined Maria. "I only thought it a pity you should not derive some real benefit from this money. If you keep it yourself you may be induced to change it, and then it would dwindle away in trifles, and do you no good."

"That it 'ould!" acknowledged Mrs. Bond. "I've a'most a mind to let it be took care on, after all. If 'twas anybody but the Rector!"

"Shall I keep it for you?" asked Maria.

"Well now, 'ould you, ma'am?"

"Yes, I will. If you please."

Mrs. Bond detached the note from the silver and other articles which she had brought up indiscriminately from her pocket. They lay in her capacious lap, and appeared to afford food for gratification to Meta, who had come round from the parrot to look at them. A brass thimble, a damp blue-bag, some halfpence, a recipe for toothache, a piece of ginger, and the end of a tallow candle, being amongst the items.

"You'll promise to let me have it back if I asks for it?" cried she, clutching the note, and waiting for Maria's promise before she would surrender it.

"Certainly I will. Whenever you wish for it, you shall have it. Only," Maria added, smiling, "if you ask for it too soon, I shall beg you still to let me keep it. Don't you remember how badly off you were last winter? Just think what a ten-pound note would have done for you then, Mrs. Bond!"

"Lawks, ay! It would a got me through the cold beautiful."

"And I hope you will let this get you through next year's cold," returned Maria, putting the note into her purse.

"Ay, sure! But now, ain't it kind o' Peggy?"

"Yes. It is delightful to hear that she is so well settled at last."

"I've been drinking her health, and better luck still," said Mrs. Bond, taking the cork out of the bottle, and pouring out half its remaining contents. "'Ould ye just take a drain, ma'am?"

"No, thank you," replied Maria. "I don't like the smell of it."

"No!" returned Mrs. Bond, who, truth to say, but for the "drains" she had taken herself, and which had tended slightly to muddle her perceptions, would never have thought of proffering the invitation. "Not like the smell! It were tenpence the half-pint."

Maria took the child's hand. Meta gave it reluctantly: the new parrot possessed great attractions for her. "I'll come again and see it to-morrow," said she to Mrs. Bond. "I'll come with Margery. I am coming to play in the hayfield."

"Ay," returned Mrs. Bond, "Ain't it pretty! It's the best Old Tom."

She was evidently getting a little confused in her intellects. Had Maria been a strong-minded district visitor, given to reforming the evils of the parish, she might have read Mrs. Bond a lecture on sobriety, and walked off with the bottle. Mrs. Bond and such medicine-bottles had however been too long and too well acquainted with each other, to admit any hope of their effectually parting now: and the last thing Maria caught, as she glanced back, was a vision of that lady's head thrown back, the inverted tea-cup to her lips.

"The note would have been changed before the week was out!" was Maria's mental comment.

Without further adventure, she reached Lady Godolphin's Folly. Charlotte had visitors. A country squire's wife with her two daughters had come for a few days from their sober residence at a few miles' distance to the attractions of the Folly. Charlotte could make it attractive when she liked; and invitations to it were in demand—which has been previously remarked. If people did think Mrs. Pain somewhat "fast" in her manners, she was no faster than some others.

Charlotte was in one of her pleasantest moods, and Maria had rarely seen her looking so well. She wore a morning-dress of pink muslin, made simply, and confined at the waist by a band. Her hair was dressed simply also, brought rather low on her face and rolled: even Margery could not have found fault with her looks this morning.

Or with her manner, either. She regaled Meta with strawberries; and when they were finished, caught her up in her arms and carried her out by the glass door.

"Do not keep her long, Mrs. Pain," said Maria. "I must be going."

"Where is your hurry?" asked Charlotte.

"I am going on to Ashlydyat."

Charlotte departed with Meta, and Maria continued with the ladies, Charlotte's guests. They had been talking a few minutes, when loud screams of terror from Meta alarmed their ears. Maria hastened out in the direction of the sound, her cheeks and lips alike blanched.

She came upon them—Charlotte and the child—in that secluded, lovely spot amidst the grove of trees, where Charlotte Pain—and you saw her—had held an interview with her future husband, Rodolf, on George Godolphin's wedding-day. Charlotte had now carried the child there, and set her on the mossy turf, and called her dogs around. She had done it thinking to give pleasure to the child. But Meta was of a timid nature; she was not used to dogs; and upon one of them springing on her with a bark, "all for play," as Charlotte said, her fear broke forth in terrified cries. When Maria reached them, Charlotte had caught up Meta in her arms, and was kicking the dogs off.

Meta sprang from Charlotte's arms to her mother's, with a great cry. Maria, not so strongly-framed as Charlotte, could not hold this child of between five and six at her ease, but was fain to stagger with her to a bench. Meta lay in her lap, clinging to her and sobbing convulsively.

"My darling, what is it?" whispered Maria. "What has hurt you?"

"Oh, mamma, send them away! send them away!" cried the little imploring voice.

"Would you be so kind as send the dogs away, Mrs. Pain?" asked Maria. "I think she is frightened at them."

"I know she is, foolish little thing!" answered Charlotte, going off with the dogs. Apparently she disposed of them somewhere, for she returned the next minute without them. Maria was in the same place, holding her child to her heart.

"Mrs. George Godolphin, don't you think you will have to answer sometime for the manner in which you are rearing that child?" began she, gravely.

"In what way?" returned Maria.

"You are bringing her up to be as timid as yourself."

"Am I particularly timid?"

"You! Why, you know you are. You don't ride: you wouldn't drive for the world; you are afraid of dogs."

"I could manage to ride a quiet pony," said Maria. "As to dogs, I confess that I am a little afraid of them, if they are rough."

"If a dog only barks, you call it 'rough,'" retorted Charlotte. "I should just put that child down again, and call the dogs round her, and let her battle it out with them. They would not hurt her; there's no fear of that; and it would teach her to overcome fear."

"Oh, Mrs. Pain!" Maria involuntarily strained her child closer to her, and Meta, who had heard the words, pushed her little hot face of distress nearer to its shelter. "It might throw her into such a state of terror, that she would never forget it. She would be frightened at dogs for her life. *That* is not the way to treat children, indeed, Mrs. Pain!"

Meta could not be coaxed down again. Maria was not strong

enough to carry her to the house, so Charlotte took her up in her arms. But the child would not release her hand from her mother's, and Maria had to walk along, holding it.

"You pretty little timid goose!" cried Charlotte, kissing her. "Whatever would you do if you were to lose your mamma?"

"It would be a calamity, would it not, Meta?" said Maria, speaking half-jokingly; and Charlotte answered in the same light spirit.

"A calamity in one sense, of course. But she might get a chance then of having a little of the rust rubbed out of her. Meta, we must have some more strawberries after this."

But Meta could not be seduced to strawberries. Maria said farewell, and led her away, bending her steps to Ashlydyat. The child was frightened still. Janet gravely assured her that the dogs would not come to Ashlydyat, and Meta allowed herself to be taken possession of by Cecil, introducing the subject of Mrs. Bond's beautiful parrot and its large cage as she was going away.

"We have heard about the parrot," remarked Bessy to Maria. "Susan Satcherly hobbled up here this morning, and mentioned its arrival. Susan hopes it won't scream all night as well as all day: she hears it next door as plainly as though the parrot were present there. A ten-pound note has come also, she says. Which I am almost sorry for," added Bessy: "though I suppose Mrs. Bond would think me terribly ill-natured if she heard me say so. She will change that note to-day, and never rest until the last shilling of it has been spent."

"No, she will not," returned Maria, laughing, holding out the note in triumph. "She has given it to me to keep for her."

"Never!" exclaimed Bessy in surprise. "You must have exercised some sleight-of-hand, Maria, to get that!"

Maria laughed. "She was in an unusually tractable humour, Bessy. The fact is, a sovereign had arrived as well as the bank-note: and that she had changed."

Bessy nodded her head. She knew Mrs. Bond of old. "I understand," said she. "Was she very bad, Maria?"

"No; not then. But I can't say what she may be before the day is over. She brought a handful of silver out of her pocket."

"Now, mind, Maria—don't give her up that note, let her ask for it ever so," advised Bessy. "Keep it until winter."

"If she will allow me," replied Maria. "But she only resigned it on condition that I would return it to her if she asked for it. I promised that I would do so."

"*I* should not: promise or no promise," returned Bessy. "Keeping it would be for her good, you know, Maria."

Maria shook her head. She could not be strong-minded, as Bessy was, acting for people's good against their will; and she could not go from her promise. She returned the note to her purse, knowing that Mrs. Bond would have it, if she chose to demand it.

Maria was easily persuaded to remain for the day at Ashlydyat. She sat at the window in the height of enjoyment. It was enjoyment to Maria Godolphin: sitting there in perfect stillness on a calm summer's day. The lovely flowers of Ashlydyat's garden, its velvet lawns, were stretched out before her: the white walls of Lady Godolphin's Folly rose in the distance; and Maria sat in an easy-chair in luxurious idleness, her fair white hands lying in her lap. Meta was away somewhere, fascinating the household, and all was rest. Rest from exertion, rest from care. The time came when Maria looked back on that day and believed it must have been paradise.

Janet sent a note to the Bank, to desire George to come up to dinner with Thomas. When Thomas arrived, however, he was alone. George was out, therefore the note had not been given to him. They supposed he would be up in the evening, and dined without him.

But the evening passed on, and he did not come. Thomas's private opinion was that George must have remained to search for the missing deeds. Thomas could not be easy under such a misfortune—as it might in truth be called. The sum was by far too weighty to be lost with equanimity. And that was not all: there was the unpleasant uncertainty with regard to the disappearance. Thomas mentioned the matter in confidence amongst them. At least, to Maria and Janet; the other two had gone out with Meta. Janet observed that he appeared absorbed in thought, as if uneasy at something; and he readily acknowledged that he had been rendered uneasy by a circumstance which had occurred during the day: the missing of some deeds that they had believed to be in safe custody.

"What if you cannot find them, Thomas?" asked Janet.

"Then we must make good the loss."

"Is it a heavy amount?"

"Yes."

Janet looked startled. Thomas's grave manner did not tend to reassure her. She gave utterance to some half-spoken words.

"It is a heavy amount as a loss," explained Thomas. "In fact, it is a large sum in itself. It would cost us over sixteen thousand pounds to make it good."

Janet lifted her hands in dismay. "And all from the loss of a single packet of deeds?"

"Even so."

"But how can they have been lost?"

"There it is," said Thomas Godolphin. "It we could tell as much as that, it would be some satisfaction. We cannot imagine how or when they were lost. George missed them a month ago; but——"

"A month ago! Did George miss them a month ago?"

It was Maria who interrupted, eagerness in her voice and manner.

had occurred to her that the fact might account for a certain restlessness, an anxiety in George's manner, which she had not failed to remark of late. The next words of Thomas Godolphin served to dissipate the illusion.

"George looked for the deeds a month ago. Not finding them in the box, he concluded that I had moved them. Therefore we cannot be said to have known of the loss until to-day."

"George ought to have asked you," said Janet.

"Yes, he ought," acquiesced Thomas. But it was all he said.

"It is just like careless George!" exclaimed Janet. "Should the time ever come that he is sole head of the Bank, I do not know how it will get on! To whom did the deeds belong, Thomas?"

"To Lord Averil."

"You are sure you had them?" asked cautious Janet.

A half smile crossed Thomas Godolphin's lips. "Quite sure, Janet. You understand," he added, looking at them both, "we do not care that this should be spoken of. You are safe, I know, Janet; and Maria would most likely hear it from George."

Maria had been buried in a reverie. "I cannot conceive how it is possible for anything to have been lost from the strong-room," she said, lifting her head. "All about us are trustworthy. And, were they not, there would be no possibility of their getting to the safes in the strong-room."

"You are right, Maria," said Thomas. "I have thought of it until I am bewildered."

Maria seemed to be getting bewildered also. She was thinking of it in its every aspect and bearing. Many little past incidents, proving that her husband was ill at ease, had something on his mind, rushed into her memory. She had not thought much of them before: but they grew strangely vivid now. To miss deeds of this value would amply account for it.

"Thomas," said she, speaking out her thoughts, "do you not think George must have feared there was something wrong, when he missed them at first? I do."

"No. Why do you think it?"

"Because——" Maria stopped. It suddenly occurred to her that it might not be quite right to comment upon her husband's manner, what it had, or what it had not been; that he might not like her to do so, although it was only to his brother and sister. So she turned it off: speaking any indifferent words that came uppermost.

"It is curious, missing a packet of deeds of that value from its place, that he should not have feared it might be missing altogether."

"The very fact of his not asking me about it, Maria, proves that no suspicion of wrong crossed his mind," was the comment of Thomas Godolphin. "He supposed I had placed it elsewhere."

"That's just like George!" repeated Janet. "Taking things on trust, as he takes people! A child might deceive him."

"I hope we shall find them yet," said Thomas Godolphin.

"Does Lord Averil——"

What Janet might be about to inquire was never known. The words were stopped by a strange noise, an appalling noise, apparently at the very door of the room they were in. A loud, prolonged, discordant noise, unlike anything they had ever heard. Some might have compared it to the shrieks of a strong giant in his agony; some to the hoarse screams of a bird of prey. But it was unlike either: it was unlike anything earthly.

With one bound, they flew to the hall, on to which the room opened, Maria, white with terror. The servants came rushing from their apartments, and stood in consternation.

What was the noise? What had caused it? The questions were pouring forth from all. The hall was perfectly empty, except for its startled gazers; doors and windows had been closed. Thomas walked to the entrance and looked beyond, beyond the porch, but nothing was there. The space was empty; the evening was calm and still. At a distance, borne on the evening air, could be heard the merry laughter of Meta, playing with Bessy and Cecil. Thomas came in and closed the door again.

" I cannot think what it could have been ! " he observed, speaking generally.

The servants were ready with answering remarks. One had thought this; one had thought that; another something else. Maria had seized upon Janet: glad, perhaps, that it was too dark for her white face to be discerned. It was the *sound* which had so terrified her : no association in her mind was connected with it : and it was the sound which had terrified the servants. They had never heard a sound like unto it in all their lives.

" It must have been a night-bird, shrieking as he flew over the house," observed Mr. Godolphin.

But, in truth, he so spoke only in the absence of any other possible assumption, and against his own belief. No bird of prey, known to ornithology, could have made that noise, even had it been within the hall to do it. A dozen birds of prey could not have made it. Thomas, like the rest, felt bewildered.

The servants began to move away. Nothing more than usual was to be seen in the darkened hall : nothing to be heard. As the last one disappeared, Thomas turned to the drawing-room door, and held it open for his sister and Maria.

At that very moment when they had gone in, and Thomas was following, the noise came again. Loud, prolonged, shrill, unearthly ! WHAT was it ? Were the rafters of the house loosening? the walls rending asunder? Were the skies opening for the crack of doom? They gathered in the hall again : master, ladies, servants; and stood there, motionless, appalled, bewildered, their faces whiter than before.

Its echoes died away in shrieks. Human cries this time, and not unfamiliar. One of the women-servants, excited beyond repression, had fallen into hysterics.

But whence had proceeded that noise? Where had been its centre? Without the house, or within the house?—in its walls, its passages, its hall?—where? Its sound had been everywhere. In short, what had caused it ? what had it been?

They could not tell. It was a problem beyond human philosophy to solve. They could not tell then; they could not tell afterwards. It has been no ideal scene that I have described, as living witnesses could testify. Witnesses who can no more account for those unearthly sounds now, than they could account for them then.

CHAPTER XIV.

ISAAC HASTINGS TURNS TO THINKING.

THE revelation to Isaac Hastings, that the deeds, missing, belonged to Lord Averil, set that young gentleman thinking. Like his father, like his sister Grace, he was an exceedingly accurate observer, given to taking note of passing events. He had keen perception, a retentive memory for trifles, great powers of comparison and concentration. What with one thing and another, he had been a little puzzled lately by Mr. George Godolphin. There had been sundry odds and ends out of the common to be detected in Mr. George's manner: not patent to the generality of people, who are for the most part unobservant, but sufficiently conspicuous to Isaac Hastings. Anxiety about letters; trifles in the everyday ordering of the Bank; one little circumstance, touching a delay in paying out some money, which Isaac, and he alone, had become accidentally cognizant of; all formed food for speculation. There had been the somewhat doubtful affair of George Godolphin's secret journey to London, leaving false word with his wife that he was accompanying Captain St. Aubyn on the road to Portsmouth, which had travelled to the knowledge of Isaac through want of reticence in Charlotte Pain. More than all, making more impression upon Isaac, had been the strange, shrinking fear displayed by George, that Saturday when he had announced Lord Averil: a fear succeeded by a confusion of manner that proved his master must for the moment have lost his presence of mind. Isaac Hastings had announced the names of other gentlemen that day, and the announcement, equally with themselves, had been received with the most perfect equanimity. Isaac had often thought of that little episode since, and wondered; wondered what there could be in Lord Averil's visit to scare Mr. George Godolphin. It recurred to him now with double distinctness. The few words he had overheard, between Lord Averil and Mr. Godolphin, recurred to him—the former saying that George must have known of the loss of the deeds when he had asked for them a month ago, that he judged so by his manner, which was peculiar, hesitating, uncertain, "as though he had known of the loss then, and did not like to tell of it."

To the strange manner Isaac himself could have borne witness. Had this strangeness been caused by the knowledge of the loss of the deeds?—if so, why did not George Godolphin make a stir about them then? Only on the previous day, when Lord Averil had again made his appearance, Isaac had been further struck with George's startled hesitation, and with his refusal to see him. He had sent out word as the excuse, that he was particularly engaged. Isaac had believed at the time that George was no more engaged than he himself was. And now, this morning, when it could not be concealed any longer, came the commotion. The deeds were gone: they had disappeared in the most unaccountable manner, no one knowing how or when.

What did it all mean? Isaac Hastings asked himself the question as he pursued his business in the Bank, amidst the other clerks. *He could not help asking it.* A mind, constituted as was that of Isaac Hastings, thoughtful, foreseeing, penetrating, cannot help entering upon these speculations, when surrounding circumstances call them forth. Could it be that George Godolphin had fallen into secret embarrassment?—that he had abstracted the deeds himself and *used* them? Isaac felt his cheek flush with shame at the thought: with shame that he should allow himself to think such a thing of a Godolphin: and yet, he could not help it. No. Do as he would, he could not drive the thought away: it remained to haunt him. And, the longer it remained, the more vivid it grew.

Ought he to give a hint of this to his father? He did not know. On the one hand there was sober reason, which told him George Godolphin was not likely to be guilty of such a thing on the other lay his fancy, whispering that it *might* be so. Things as strange had been enacted lately; as the public knew. Men, in an equally good position with George Godolphin, were proved to have been living upon fraud for years. Isaac was fond of newspapers, and knew all they could tell him. What if anything came wrong to *this* Bank? Why then, Mr. Hastings would be a ruined man. It was not only the loss of his own life's savings, that were in the hands of Godolphin, Crosse, and Godolphin, but there was the larger sum he had placed there as trustee to the little Chisholms.

Isaac Hastings lingered in the Bank till the last that evening. All had gone, except Mr. Hurde. The latter was preparing to leave, when Isaac went up to him, leaning his arms upon the desk.

"It is a strange thing about those deeds, Mr. Hurde!" cried he, in a low tone.

Mr. Hurde nodded.

"It is troubling me amazingly," went on Isaac.

This seemed to arouse the old clerk, and he looked up, speaking curtly.

"Why should it trouble you? You didn't take them, I suppose?"

"No, I didn't," said Isaac.

"Very well, then. The loss won't fall upon you. There's no need for *your* troubling."

Isaac was silent. In truth, he was unable to give any reason for the "troubling," except on general grounds: he could not say that a doubt was haunting his mind as to the good faith of Mr. George Godolphin.

"It is a loss which I suppose Mr. George will have to make good, as they were in his custody," he resumed. "My sister won't like it, I fear."

The observation recalled Mr. Hurde's memory to the fact that Mrs. George Godolphin was the sister of Isaac Hastings. It afforded a sufficient excuse for the remarks in the mind of the clerk, and somewhat pacified him.

"It is to be hoped they'll be found," said he. "*I* don't see how they could have gone."

"Nor I," returned Isaac. "The worst is, if they *have* gone——"

"What?" asked Mr. Hurde, for Isaac had stopped.

"That perhaps money has been made of them."

Mr. Hurde groaned. "They have not been taken for nothing, you may be sure."

"If they have been taken," persisted Isaac.

"If they have been taken," assented Mr. Hurde. "I don't believe they have. From the sheer impossibility of anybody's getting to them, I don't believe it. And I shan't believe it, until every nook and corner between the four walls have been hunted over."

"How do you account for their disappearance, then?"

"I think they must have been moved inadvertently."

"No one could so move them except Mr. Godolphin or Mr. George," rejoined Isaac.

"Mr. Godolphin has not moved them," returned the clerk in a testy tone of reproof. "Mr. Godolphin is too accurate a man of business to move deeds inadvertently, or to move them and forget it the next moment. Mr. George may have done it. In searching for anything in the strong-room, if he has had more than one case open at once, he may have put these deeds back in their wrong place, or even brought them upstairs."

Isaac considered for a minute, and then shook his head. "I should not think it," he answered.

"Well, it is the only supposition I can come to," was the concluding remark of Mr. Hurde. "It is next to an impossibility, Mr. Godolphin excepted, that any one else can have got to the deeds."

He was drawing on his gloves as he spoke, to depart. Isaac went out with him, but their roads lay different ways. Isaac turned towards All Souls' Rectory, and walked along in deep reverie.

The Rectory hours were early, and he found them at tea: his mother, Rose, and Grace. Grace—Mrs. Akeman by her new name—was spending the evening with them with her baby. The Rector, who had gone out in the afternoon, had not yet returned.

Isaac took his tea and then strolled into the garden. Rose and the baby were making a great noise, and Grace was helping them. It disturbed Isaac in his perplexed thought, and he made a mental vow that if he was ever promoted to a home of his own with babies in it, they should be confined to some top room, out of sight and hearing.

By-and-by, when he was leaning over the gate, looking into the road, Mr. Hastings came up. Isaac told him that tea was over.: but Mr. Hastings said he had taken a cup with one of his parishioners. He had apparently walked home quickly, and he lifted his hat and wiped his brow.

"Glorious weather for the haymaking, Isaac!"

"Is it?" returned Isaac abstractedly.

"*Is it!*" repeated Mr. Hastings. "Where are your senses, boy?"

Isaac laughed and roused himself. "I fear they were buried just then, sir. I was thinking of something that has happened at the Bank to-day. A loss has been discovered."

"A loss?" repeated Mr. Hastings. "A loss of what?"

Isaac explained. He dropped his voice to a low tone, and spoke confidentially. They were leaning over the gate side by side. Mr. Hastings rather liked to take recreative moments there, exchanging a nod and a word with the passers-by. At this hour of the evening, however, the road was generally free.

"How can the deeds have gone?" exclaimed Mr. Hastings. As every one else had said.

"I don't know," replied Isaac, breaking off a spray from the hedge, and beginning to bite the thorns. "I suppose it is all right," he presently added.

"Right in what way?" asked Mr. Hastings.

"I suppose George Godolphin's all right, I mean."

The words were as an unknown tongue to Mr. Hastings. He did not fathom them. "You suppose that George Godolphin is all right!" he exclaimed. "You speak in riddles, Isaac."

"I cannot say I *suspect* anything wrong, sir; but the doubt has crossed me. It never would have done so, but for George Godolphin's manner."

Mr. Hastings turned his penetrating gaze on his son. "Speak out," said he. "Tell me what you mean."

Isaac did so. He related the circumstances of the loss; the confused manner he had observed in Mr. George Godolphin, on the visits of Lord Averil, and his reluctance to receive them. One little matter he suppressed: the stolen visit of George to London, and deceit to Maria, relative to it. Isaac did not see what that could have had to do with the loss of the deeds, and his good feeling told him that it was not a pleasant thing to name to his father. Mr. Hastings did not speak for a few minutes.

"Isaac, I see no reasonable grounds for your doubts," he said at length. "The Bank is too flourishing for that. Perhaps you meant only as to George?"

"I can scarcely tell whether I really meant anything," replied Isaac. "The doubts arose to me, and I thought I would mention them to you. I dare say my fancy is to blame: it does run riot sometimes."

A silence ensued. Mr. Hastings broke it. "With a keen man of business, such as Mr. Thomas Godolphin, at the head of affairs, George could not go far wrong, I should presume. I think he spends enough on his own score, mark you, Isaac; but that has nothing to do with the prosperity of the Bank."

"Of course not. Unless——"

"Unless what? Why don't you speak out?"

"Because I am not sure of my premises, sir," frankly answered Isaac. "Unless he were to have become irretrievably embarrassed, and should be using the Bank's funds for his own purposes, I believe I was about to say."

"Pretty blind moles some of you must be, in that case! Could such a thing be done without the cognizance of the house? Of Mr. Hurde and of Thomas Godolphin?"

"Well—no—I don't much think it could," hesitated Isaac, who was not at all certain upon the point. "At any rate, not to any extent. I suppose one of my old crotchets—as Grace used to call them—has taken possession of me, rendering me absurdly fanciful. I dare say it is all right: except that the deeds are mislaid."

"I dare say it is," acquiesced the Rector. "I should be sorry to think it otherwise—for many reasons. Grace is here, is she not?"

"Grace is here, and Grace's son and heir, making enough noise for ten. I can't think why Grace—— "

"What are you taking my name in vain for?" interrupted Grace's own voice. She had come up to them carrying the very son and heir that Isaac had been complaining of: a young gentleman with a bald head, just beginning to exercise his hands in dumb fights; as well as his lungs. "Papa, mamma says are you not going in to tea?"

Before the Rector could answer, or Isaac extricate his hair from the unconsciously mischievous little hands which had seized upon it by Grace's connivance, there came a gay party of equestrians round the corner of the road. Charlotte Pain, with the two young ladies, her guests; Lady Sarah and Miss Grame, who sometimes hired horses for a ride; and three or four gentlemen. Amongst the latter were George Godolphin and Lord Averil. Lord Averil had met them accidentally and joined their party. He was riding by the side of Charlotte Pain.

"I say, Grace!" hastily exclaimed Isaac, twitching away his head, "take that baby in, out of sight. Look there!"

"Take my baby in!" resentfully spoke Grace. "What for? I am not ashamed to be seen holding it. Keeping only two servants, I must turn nurse sometimes: and people know it. I am not situated as Maria is, with a dozen at her beck and call."

Isaac did not prolong the discussion. He thought if he owned an ugly baby with no hair, he should not be so fond of showing it off. Grace stood her ground, and the baby stood his, and lifted its head and its arms by way of greeting. Isaac wondered that it did not lift its voice as well.

The party exchanged bows as they rode past. George Godolphin— he was riding by the side of Sarah Anne Grame—withdrew his horse from the throng and rode up.

"How are you, Grace? How is the baby?"

"Look at him," returned Grace in answer, holding the gentleman up to him.

"Shall I take him for a ride?" asked George, laughing.

"Not if you paid me his value in gold," answered Grace bluntly.

George's gay blue eyes twinkled. "What may that value be? Your estimation of it, Grace?"

"Never mind," said Grace. "I can tell you that your Bank would not meet it. No, not if all its coffers were filled to the brim."

"I see," observed George: "he is inestimable. Do not set your heart too much upon him, Grace," he continued, his voice changing.

"Why not?" she asked.

"Maria had to lose some, equally dear."

"That is true," said Grace in softened tones. "How is Maria to-day?"

"Quite well, thank you. She went to Ashlydyat this afternoon, and I dare say has remained there. Famous weather for the hay, is it not, sir?" he added to the Rector.

"Couldn't be better," replied Mr. Hastings.

George rode off at a canter. The baby burst into a cry; perhaps that he could not go off at a canter too: and Grace, after a vain attempt to hush him, carried him into the house. The Rector remained, looking over the gate.

"Things going wrong with him!—No! He could not be so easy under it," was his mental conclusion. "It is all right, depend upon it," he added aloud to his son.

"I think it must be, sir," was the reply of Isaac Hastings.

CHAPTER XV.

A NIGHTMARE FOR THE RECTOR OF ALL SOULS'.

THE Reverend Mr. Hastings had audibly expressed a wish never again to be left in the responsible position of trustee, and the Reverend Mr. Hastings echoed it a second time as he ascended a gig which was to convey him to Binham. A vestry meeting at All Souls' had been called for that evening at seven o'clock; but something arose during the day connected with the trust, and at four Mr. Hastings set off in a gig to see Brierly, the late agent to the Chisholm property. "I'll be back by seven if I can, Smith," he observed to his clerk. "If not, the meeting must commence without me."

The way to Binham lay through shady lanes and unfrequented roads: unfrequented as compared with those where the traffic is great. It was a small place about six miles' distance from Prior's Ash, and the Rector enjoyed the drive. The day was warm and fine as the previous one had been—when you saw Maria Godolphin walking through the hay-field. Shady trees in some parts met overhead, the limes gave forth their sweet perfume, the heavy crops of grass gladdened the Rector's eye, some still uncut, some in process of being converted into hay by labourers, who looked off to salute the well-known clergyman as he drove past.

"I might have brought Rose, after all," he soliloquized. "She would have had a pleasant drive. Only she would have been half an hour getting ready."

He found Mr. Brierly at home, and their little matter of business was soon concluded. Mr. Hastings had other places to call at in the town: he had always plenty of people to see when he went to Binham, for he knew every one in it.

"I wish you would take something," said the agent.

"I can't stay," replied Mr. Hastings. "I shall find old Mrs. Chisholm at tea, and can take a cup with her, standing. That won't lose time. You have not heard from Harknar?"

"No: not directly. His brother thinks he will be home next week."

"The sooner the better. I want the affair settled, and the money placed out."

He held out his hand as he spoke. Mr. Brierly, who, in days long gone by, when they were both boys together, had been an old school-fellow of the Rector's, put his own into it. But he did not withdraw it: he appeared to be in some hesitation.

"Mr. Hastings, excuse me," he said, presently, speaking slowly, "have you kept the money, which I paid over to you, in your own possession?"

"Of course not. I took it the same night to the Bank."

"Ay. I guessed you would. Is it safe?" he added, lowering his voice.

"*Safe!*" echoed Mr. Hastings.

"I will tell you why I speak. Rutt the lawyer, over at your place, was here this afternoon, and in the course of conversation he dropped a hint that something was wrong at Godolphins'. It was not known yet, he said, but it would be known very soon."

Mr. Hastings paused. "Did he state his grounds for the assertion?"

"No. From what I could gather, it appeared that he spoke from some vague rumour that was going about."

"I think I can explain it," said Mr. Hastings. "A packet of deeds belonging to one of their clients has been lost—has disappeared at least in some unaccountable manner; and this, I expect, must have given rise to the rumour. But the loss of twenty such packets, all to be made good, would not shake the solvency of Godolphin, Crosse, and Godolphin."

"That must be it, then! What simpletons people are! swallowing any absurd rumour that gets afloat; converting a molehill into a mountain! I thought it strange—for a stable old house like the Godolphins'."

"Let me recommend you, Brierly, not to mention it further. If such a report got about, it might cause a run upon the Bank. Not but that, so far as I believe, the Bank could stand any run that might be made upon it."

"I should not have mentioned it at all, except to you," returned Mr. Brierly. "And only to you, because I expected the Chisholms' money was there. Rutt is not a safe man to speak after, at the best of times. I told him I did not believe him. And I did not. Still—if anything were to happen, and I had bottled up the rumour, without giving you a hint of it, I should never cease to blame myself."

"That is the origin of it, you may be sure; the loss of those deeds," observed the Rector. "I know the clerks were questioned about it yesterday, and some of them must have got talking out of doors. Good day, Brierly."

Mr. Hastings paid the rest of his visits, and drove home. In spite of himself, he could not keep his mind from reverting—and somewhat unpleasantly—to what he had heard. He believed the Bank to be perfectly solvent; to be more than solvent. Until the previous evening, when Isaac had made that communication to him, he had been ready to answer for its flourishing condition on his own responsibility, if required. He fully believed the rumour, spoken of by Rutt the lawyer, to arise from some distorted hints of the missing deeds which had oozed out, and to have no other foundation whatever: and yet he could not keep his mind from reverting to it uneasily.

The ting-tang (it deserved no better name, and Prior's Ash gave it no other) of All Souls' Church was sending forth its last notes as the Rector drove in. Handing over the horse and gig to the waiting servant of the friend from whom it was borrowed—a gig always at the disposal of the Rector—he made his way to the vestry, and had the pleasure of presiding at a stormy meeting. There were divided parties in the parish at that time, touching a rate to be paid, or a non-rate; and opposing eloquence ran high. Personally, the Rector was not an interested party; but he had a somewhat difficult course to steer between the two, to avoid offending either. It was half-past nine when the meeting broke up.

"Any news of the missing deeds, Isaac?" he took an opportunity of asking his son.

"I think not," replied Isaac. "We have heard nothing about it to-day."

"I suppose things have gone on, then, as usual?"

"Quite so. We shall hear no more of it, I dare say, in the Bank. If the bonds can't be found, the firm will have to make them good, and there'll be an end of it."

"A very unsatisfactory ending, I should think, if I had to make them good," observed the Rector. "I don't like things disappearing, nobody knows how or why."

He said no more. He gave no hint to Isaac of the rumour that had been whispered to him, nor questioned him upon its probable foundation. It was the best proof that Mr. Hastings assigned to it no foundation. In sober reason he did not do so.

But things—troubles, cares, annoyances—wear different aspects in the day and in the night. More than all, *suspense* wears a different one. An undefined dread, whatever may be its nature, can be drowned in the daily bustle of life: business, pleasure, occupation. These fill up the mind, and the bugbear is lost sight of. . But at night, when the head lies upon the sleepless pillow, and there is nothing to distract the thoughts; when all around is dark and silent, then, if there *is* an inner, secret dread, it asserts itself in guise worse than reality.

Mr. Hastings was not an imaginative man. Quite the contrary. He was more given to dealing with things, whether pleasant or painful, in a practical manner by daylight, than to racking his brains with them at night. Therefore, the way in which the new doubt troubled him as he lay in bed that night, was something wonderful. Had he been a fanciful woman, he could not have experienced worse treatment from his imagination. It was running riot within him. Could it be that the money entrusted to him was gone?—lost? Had he put it into that Bank for safety, only to find that the Bank would never refund it again? How was he to make it good? He could not make it good, and the little Chisholms, the children of his dead friend, would be beggars! He thought not of his own money, lodged in the charge of Godolphin, Crosse, and Godolphin; that seemed as nothing in comparison with this. Mr. Hastings had had rather an expensive family; he had given money away in his parish—a conscientious clergyman is obliged to give, more or less—and his savings, all told, did not amount to more than two thousand pounds. It was not of that, equally at stake, that he thought, but of this other and larger sum, of which he was but the steward.

Try as he would, he could not get to sleep; try as he would, he could not put these half-insane visions from him. His mind became wrought up to its very highest pitch; he could have found it in his heart to get up, make his way to the Bank, knock up George Godolphin, and demand his money back again. He registered a silent resolve that he would go there with the first glimmer of daylight. Yesterday he was a free man, a man at his ease, it may be said a prosperous man; to-morrow, should that money be beyond his reach, he would be ruined for ever; broken down under his weight of care. What if he were too late!—if he went to the Bank, and was told, " The Bank is in embarrassment, and we cannot refund!" Oh, how supinely careless had he been, to suffer a whole day to slip by since Isaac's warning! Any hour of that past day he might have withdrawn the money; might now have had it securely in the chest by his bedside. When another day dawned, it might be too late.

Torments such as these—and they were all the more intolerable from the fact of his not being used to them—haunted him throughout the night. They have haunted us: they, or similar ones. Towards morning he dropped into a heavy sleep, awaking later than his usual hour. Those dark visions had gone then; but their effect remained sufficient to keep the Rector to his resolve of drawing out the money. "I'll go the first thing after breakfast," said he, as he dressed himself.

But, when breakfast was over, and the business of the day was fairly entered upon, Mr. Hastings felt half ashamed of his resolution. The visions of the night appeared to him to be simply fantastic follies, diseased creations of the brain: should there be really no cause for his withdrawal of the money, how worse than foolish he would look!—nay, how unjustifiable would such a procedure be!

What ought he to do? He leaned over the gate while he took counsel with himself. He had put on his hat and taken his stick, and gone forth; and there he stopped, hesitating. A strange frame of mind for Mr. Hastings, who was not of a vacillating nature. Suddenly he flung the gate open and went through with a decisive step; his determination was taken. He would steer a middle course, present himself to his son-in-law, George Godolphin, and ask him frankly, as a friend and relative, whether the money was safe.

Many a one would have decided that it was a safe and proper course to pursue. Mr. Hastings deemed it to be such, and he proceeded to the Bank. The fresh air, the bright sun, the pleasant bustle of daily life, had well-nigh dissipated any remaining fears before he got there.

"Can I see Mr. George Godolphin?" he inquired.

"Mr. George is engaged at present, sir," replied the clerk to whom he had addressed himself. "He will be at liberty soon. Would you like to take a seat?"

Mr. Hastings sat down on the chair handed him, and waited; watching at his leisure the business of the Bank. Several people were there. Some were paying money in, some drawing it out. There appeared to be no hesitation, either in paying or receiving: all seemed as usual. One man brought a cheque for nine hundred and odd pounds, and it was counted out to him. "I feel sure it is all right," was the conclusion come to by Mr. Hastings.

About ten minutes, and George Godolphin came forward. "Ah! is it you?" said he, with his sunny smile. "You are here early this morning."

"I want to say just a word to you in private, Mr. George."

George led the way to his room, talking gaily. He pushed a chair towards Mr. Hastings, and took his own. Never a face more free from care than his; never an eye less troubled. He asked after Mrs. Hastings; asked after Reginald, who was daily expected home from a voyage —whether he had arrived. "Maria dreamt last night that he had returned," said he, laughing, "and told her he was never going to sea again."

Mr. Hastings remembered *his* dreams—if dreams they could be called. He was beginning to think that he must have had nightmare.

"Mr. George, I have come to you upon a strange errand," he began. "Will you for a few moments regard me as a confidential friend, and treat me as one?"

"I hope it is what I always do, sir," was the reply of George Godolphin.

"Ay; but I want a proof of your friendship this morning. But for my being connected with you by close ties, I should not have so come. Tell me, honestly and confidentially, as between man and man—Is that trust-money safe?"

George looked at Mr. Hastings, his countenance slightly changing. Mr. Hastings thought he was vexed.

"I do not understand you," he said.

"I have heard a rumour—I have heard, in fact, two rumours— that—— The long and the short of it is this," more rapidly continued Mr. Hastings, "I have heard that there's something doubtful arising with the Bank."

"What on earth do you mean?" exclaimed George Godolphin. "*Is* there anything the matter? Or is the Bank as solvent as it ought to be?"

"I should be sorry to think it otherwise," replied George. "I don't understand you. What have you heard?"

"Just what I tell you. A friend spoke to me in private yesterday, when I was at Binham, saying that he had heard a suspicion of something being wrong with the Bank here. You will not be surprised that I thought of the nine thousand pounds I had just paid in."

"Who said it?" asked George. "I'll prosecute him if I can find out."

"I dare say you would. But I have not come here to make mischief. I stopped his repeating it, and I, you know, am safe, so there's no harm done. I have passed an uneasy night, and I have come to ask you to tell me the truth in all good faith."

"The Bank is all right," said George. "I cannot imagine how such a report could by any possibility have arisen," he continued, quitting the one point for the other. "There is no foundation for it."

George Godolphin spoke in all good faith when he said he could not tell how the report could have arisen. He really could not. Nothing had transpired at Prior's Ash to give rise to it. Possibly he deemed, in his sanguine temperament, that he spoke in equally good faith, when assuring Mr. Hastings that the Bank was all right : he may have believed that it would so continue.

" The money is safe, then ? "

" Perfectly safe."

" Otherwise, you must let me have it out now. Were it to be lost, it would be ruin to me, ruin to the little Chisholms."

" But it is safe," returned George, all the more emphatically, because it would have been remarkably inconvenient, for special reasons, to refund it then to Mr. Hastings. I repeat, that he may have thought it *was* safe: safe in so far as that the Bank would get along somehow, and could repay it sometime. Meanwhile, the use of it was convenient —how convenient, none knew, except George.

" A packet of deeds has been mislaid; or is missing in some way," resumed George. " They belong to Lord Averil. It must be some version of that which has got abroad—if anything has got abroad."

" Ay," nodded Mr. Hastings. The opinion coincided precisely with what he had expressed to the agent.

" I know of nothing else wrong with the Bank," spoke George. " Were you to ask my brother, I am sure he would tell you that business was never more flourishing. I wish to goodness people could be compelled to concern themselves with their own affairs instead of inventing falsehoods for their friends ! "

Mr. Hastings rose. " Your assurance is sufficient, Mr. George : I do not require your brother's word to confirm it. I have asked it of you in all good faith, Maria being the link between us."

" To be sure," replied George; and he shook Mr. Hastings's hand as he went out.

George remained alone, biting the end of his quill pen. To hear that any such rumour was abroad vexed and annoyed him beyond measure. He only hoped that it would not spread far. Some wiseacre must have picked up an inkling about the deeds, and converted it into a doubt upon the Bank's solvency. " I wish I could hang the fools ! " muttered George.

His wish was interrupted. Some one came in and said that Mr. Barnaby desired to see him.

" Let him come in," said George.

Mr. Barnaby came in. A simple-looking man of quiet manners, a corn-dealer, who kept an account at the Bank. He had a canvas bag in his hand. George asked him to take a seat.

" I was going to pay in two thousand pounds, sir," said he, slightly lifting the bag to indicate that the money was there. " But I should like, first of all, to be assured that it's all right."

George sat and stared at him. Was Prior's Ash all going mad together? George honestly believed that nothing yet had transpired, or could have transpired, to set these doubts afloat. " Really, Mr. Barnaby, I do not understand you," he said, with some hauteur : just as he had answered Mr. Hastings.

" I called in at Rutt's, sir, as I came along, to know what had been done in that business where I was chiselled out of that load of barley, and I happened to mention that I was coming on here to pay in two thousand pounds. 'Take care that it's all right,' said Rutt. 'I heard the Bank talked about yesterday.' *Is* it all right, sir ? "

"It is as right as the Bank of England," impulsively answered George. "Rutt shall be brought to account for this."

"Well, I thought it was odd if there *was* anything up. Then I may leave it with safety?"

"Yes, you may," replied George. "Have you not always found it safe hitherto?"

"That's just it: I couldn't fancy that anything wrong had come to it all of a sudden. I'll go and pay it in then, sir. It won't be for long, though. I shall be wanting it out, I expect, by the end of next week."

"Whenever you please, Mr. Barnaby," replied George.

The corn-dealer retired to leave his money, and George Godolphin sat on alone, biting his pen as before. Where could these rumours have had their rise? Harmlessly enough they might have fallen, had nothing been rotten at the core of affairs: George alone knew how awfully dangerous they might prove now, if they got wind.

CHAPTER XVI.

MR. LAYTON "LOOKED UP."

IF the mysterious loss of the deeds disturbed Thomas Godolphin, it was also disturbing, in no slight degree, the faithful old clerk, Mr. Hurde. Never, since he had entered the house of Godolphin, Crosse, and Godolphin—so many years ago now, that he had almost lost count of them—had any similarly unsatisfactory incident occurred. Mr. Hurde thought and thought and thought it over: he turned it about in his mind, and looked at it in all its bearings. He came to the conclusion that it must be one of two things: either that George Godolphin had inadvertently misplaced it, or that it had been stolen out and out. George Godolphin said that he had not misplaced it: indeed, George did not acknowledge to any recollection of having visited at all Lord Averil's box, except when he went to make the search: and Mr. Godolphin had now looked in every box that the safe contained, and could not find it. Therefore, after much vacillating between opinions, the head clerk came to the conclusion that the deeds had been taken.

"Who could have done it?" he asked himself over and over again. Some one about them, doubtless. He believed all the clerks were safe; that is, honest; except Layton. Until this happened, he would have said Layton was safe: and it was only in the utter absence of any other quarter for suspicion that he cast a doubt upon Layton. Of the clerks, he felt least sure of Layton: but that was the utmost that could be said: he would not have doubted the man, but that he was seeking for some one to lay it on. The deeds could not have gone without hands, and Mr. Hurde, in his perplexity, could only think that Layton's hands were less unlikely hands than others'.

The previous evening he had gone home thinking of it. And there he pondered the affair over, while he digested his dry toast and his milkless tea. He was a man of spare habits: partly that his health compelled him to be so; partly from a parsimonious nature. While seated at it, composedly enjoying the ungenerous fare near the open window, who should he see go by, but the very man on whom his thoughts were fixed—Layton. This Layton was a young, good-looking man, an inveterate dandy, with curls and a moustache. That moustache, sober, clean-shaved Mr. Hurde had always looked askance upon. That Layton had been given to spend more than was wise, Prior's Ash knew well enough; but for that fact, he would not now have been a banker's clerk. His family were respectable—wealthy in a moderate way; but he had run through too much of their money and tired them out. For the last two or three years he had settled down to sobriety. Thomas Godolphin had admitted him to a clerkship in his house, and Layton had married, and appeared contented to live quietly.

Quietly for him—as compared to what he had been accustomed to: too extensively in the opinion of Mr. Hurde. Mrs. Layton had a piano, and played and sang very much, for the benefit of the passers-by; and Layton hired gigs on a Sunday and drove her out. Great food for Mr. Hurde's censure; and he was thinking of all this when Layton passed. Starting up to look after him, he almost upset his tea-table.

He, Layton, was walking arm in arm with a Mr. Jolly: a great sporting character. Mr. Hurde gave a groan of dissatisfaction. "Much good it will bring him if he gets intimate with *him!*"

In the darkness of the evening, when it had grown quite late and Mr. Hurde had taken his frugal supper, he went out, and bent his steps towards the residence of Layton. In his present uncertain frame of mind, touching Layton, it seemed expedient to Mr. Hurde to take a walk past his place of abode; haply he might come upon something or other to confirm his suspicions.

And he did so. At least, it appeared to Mr. Hurde that he did so. Never a shade of doubt rested upon him that night that the thief was Layton.

On the high-road, going towards Ashlydyat, there had been a good deal of building of late years. Houses and terraces had sprung up, almost as by magic, not only along the road, but branching off on either side of it. Down one of these turnings, a row of dwellings of that class called in the local phraseology " genteel," had been erected by a fanciful architect. He had certainly not displayed any great amount of judgment in building them. They contained eight rooms, had glittering white fronts and green porticos of trellis-work. White houses are very nice, and there's nothing objectionable in green porticos; but they need not abut right upon the public pathway. Walking in front of the terrace, the porticos looked like so many green watch-boxes, and the bow-windows appeared to be constructed on purpose that you should see what was inside them. In the last house of this row dwelt the clerk, Layton. He and his wife had lodgings there: the bow-windowed sitting-room, and the bedroom over it.

Mr. Hurde strolled past, in the deliberate manner that he might have done had he been out for only an evening airing, and obtained full view of the interior of the sitting-room. He obtained the pleasure of a very full view indeed. In fact, there appeared to be so much to look at, that his vision at first could only take it in confusedly.

The Laytons were entertaining a party. Two or three ladies, and two or three gentlemen. A supper-tray was at one end of the table; and at this end next the window, were two decanters of wine, some fruit and biscuits. There was a great deal of talking and laughing, and there was plenty of light. Four wax candles Mr. Hurde counted as he stood there; two on the table, two on the mantelpiece. He, the old clerk, stood there, unseen and unsuspected, and took it all in. The display of glass looked profuse, and he almost groaned aloud when he caught sight of the silver forks: silver or imitation, he did not know which, but it appeared all one to Mr. Hurde. *He* had never overstepped the respectable customs of his forefathers—had never advanced beyond the good old-fashioned two-pronged steel fork. They were sitting with the window open: no houses were as yet built opposite, and the road was not invaded, except by persons coming to these houses, from one hour's end to another. Mr. Hurde could stand there, and enjoy the sight at leisure. If ever a man felt conviction rush to his heart, he did then. Wine, and wax candles, and silver forks, and supper, and visitors!—who but Layton could have taken the deeds?

He stood there a little too long. Falling into a reverie, he did not notice a movement within, and suffered himself to be all but dropped upon. He could have made an excuse, it is true; for Layton was a civil fellow, and had several times asked him to go up there; but he preferred not to make it, and not to be seen. The street door opened, and Mr. Hurde had just time to dart past the portico and take shelter round the corner. From his position he was within hearing of anything that might be said.

The sporting character with whom he had seen Layton walking early in the evening, and who made one of the guests, had come forth to depart. Layton had attended him to the door; and they stood inside the portico talking. In Mr. Hurde's fluster, he did not at first catch the sense of the words: but he soon found it related to horse-racing.

"You back Cannonbar," said the sporting man. "You can't be far out then. He's a first-rate horse: will beat the whole field into next week. You were in luck to draw him."

"I have backed him," replied Layton.

"Back him again: he's a little gold mine. I'd spend a fifty-pound note on him. I really would."

Layton answered with a laugh. They shook hands and the sporting friend, who appeared to be in a hurry, set off rapidly in the direction of Prior's Ash. Mr. Layton went in again, and shut the door.

Then Mr. Hurde came out of his corner. All his suspicions were strengthened. Strengthened? nay; changed into certainties. Plate, glass, wax candles, wines, supper and friends, had been doubtful enough; but they were as trifles compared with this new danger; this betting on the turf. Had he seen Layton take Lord Averil's deeds with his own eyes, he could not have been more certain of his guilt, than he felt now.

Enjoying another quiet survey of the room, during which he had the gratification of hearing Mrs. Layton, who had now seated herself at the piano, plunge into a song, which began something about a "bird on the wing," the old clerk, grievously discomfited, retraced his steps past the terrace, picked his way over some loose land in front of another terrace in process of erection, and turned into the high-road, leading to Prior's Ash. He was going along lost in thought, when he nearly ran against a gentleman turning an angle of the road. It was Mr. Godolphin.

"Oh—I beg your pardon sir. I did not look where I was going."

"Enjoying an evening's stroll, Hurde?" said Mr. Godolphin. He had been spending an hour with Lord Averil, who, in doubt and uncertainty as to his deeds, had not departed from Prior's Ash. "It is a beautiful night : so serene and still."

"No, sir, I can't say that I am enjoying it," was Mr. Hurde's reply. "My mind was not at ease as to Layton. I could not help associating him with the loss of the deeds, and I came out, thinking I'd look about a bit. It must have been instinct sent me, for I have had my suspicions confirmed."

"Confirmed in what way?" asked Thomas Godolphin.

"That Layton has had the deeds. It could have been no other."

Thomas Godolphin listened in surprise, not to say incredulity. "How have you had them confirmed?" he inquired, after a pause.

So then the clerk enlarged upon what he had seen. "It could not all come out of his salary, Mr. Godolphin. It does not stand to reason that it could."

"As a daily extravagance, of course it could not, Hurde," was the reply. "But it may be only a chance entertainment?"

Mr. Hurde passed over the question : possibly he felt that he could not meet it. "And the betting?—risking money upon race-horses, sir?"

"Ah! I like that less," readily acknowledged Thomas Godolphin. "Many a clerk of far higher position than Layton has been ruined by it."

"And sent across the herring-pond to expiate his folly," returned Mr. Hurde, whom the mention of "backing" and other such incentive temptations was wont to exasperate in no measured degree. "I am afraid it looks pretty plain, sir."

"I don't know," said Thomas Godolphin musingly. "I cannot think Layton has become a rogue. I see nothing inconsistent—with all due deference to your opinion, Hurde—I see nothing inconsistent with his position in his entertaining a few friends occasionally. But—without any reference to our loss—if he is turning, or has turned a betting-man, it must be looked after. We will have none such in the Bank."

"No, sir ; it would not do at any price," acquiesced Mr. Hurde. "Are you feeling pretty well, sir, this evening?" he inquired, as Mr. Godolphin was preparing to continue his way.

"Quite well. I have not felt so well for a long time, as I have done the last few days. Good night, Hurde."

It seemed that Mr. Hurde was fated that night to come into contact with his principals. Who should overtake him, just as he had come to the spot where the houses were numerous, but Mr. George Godolphin. George slackened his steps—he had been walking along at a striding pace—and kept by his side. He began speaking of the hay and other indifferent topics: but Mr. Hurde's mind was not attuned to such that night.

"I think I have solved the mystery, Mr. George," began he.

"What mystery?" asked George.

"The stealing of Lord Averil's bonds. I know who took them."

George turned his head sharply and looked at him. "What nonsense are you saying now, Hurde?"

"I wish it was nonsense, sir," was the reply of Mr. Hurde. "I am as sure that I know how it was those bonds went, and who took them, as that I am here."

"And whom do you accuse?" asked George, after a pause, speaking somewhat sarcastically.

"Layton."

"Layton!" shouted George, stopping in his astonishment. "What Layton?"

"What Layton, sir? Why, our clerk Layton. I ought to have had my doubts of him before; but I suppose I had dust in my eyes. There are he and his wife entertaining the world; their room crowded: a dozen people, very nearly, and she, Layton's wife, sitting down to the piano with pink bows in her hair."

"What if she is?" asked George.

"You should see the supper-table, Mr. George," continued Hurde, too much annoyed with his own view of things to answer superfluous questions. "I can't tell what they have not upon it: silver, and glass, and decanters of wine. That's not all out of his salary. And Layton is taking to betting."

"But what about the bonds?" impatiently questioned George.

"Why—are not these so many proofs that Layton must have stolen the bonds and made money of them, sir? Where else could he get the means from? I have imparted my suspicions to Mr. Godolphin, and I expect he will follow them up, and have it fully investigated."

"Then you are a fool for your pains, Hurde!" retorted George in anger. "Layton no more took—I dare say Layton no more took those bonds than you did. You'll get into trouble, if you don't mind."

"WHAT, sir?" uttered Hurde, aghast.

"That," curtly answered George, "if you 'follow up' any chimera that your brain chooses to raise, you must expect to get paid out for it. Let Layton alone. It will be time enough to look him up when suspicious circumstances arise to compromise him. The bonds are gone: but we shall not get them back again by making a stir in wrong quarters. The better plan will be to be quiet over it for a while."

He resumed his quick pace and strode along, calling back a good night to Mr. Hurde. The latter gazed after him in undisguised astonishment.

"Make no stir! let the thing go on quietly!" he articulated to himself. "Who'd say such a thing but easy George Godolphin! Not look up Layton? It's well for you, Mr. George, that you have men of business about you! He'd let himself be robbed under his very nose, and never look out to see who did it. However will things go on, if the worst happens to his brother?"

It seemed that they were all saying the same—how would things go on, if the worst happened to Thomas Godolphin?

For once in his life of service the old clerk chose to ignore the wish —the command if you will—of Mr. George Godolphin. He did *not* let Layton alone. Quite the contrary. No sooner did Layton enter the Bank on the following morning, than Mr. Hurde dropped upon him. He had been watching for his entrance the last ten minutes; for Mr. Layton arrived late, the result possibly of the past night's extensive scene of revelry. He had settled himself in his place behind the counter, when the chief clerk's voice arrested him.

"I want you, Mr. Layton."

Now, the fact was, Mr. Hurde, having slept upon the matter, arose perplexed by sundry doubts. The circumstances against Layton appeared by no means so conclusive to his mind as they had done the previous night. Therefore he deemed it good policy to speak to that suspected gentleman in a temperate spirit, and see whether he could fish anything out, rather than accuse him point-blank of having been the delinquent.

"This is a nasty business," began he, when Layton reached him, in answer to his call.

"What is?" asked Layton.

"What is?" repeated Mr. Hurde, believing that the loss must have affected every one connected with the establishment as it was affecting him, and doubting whether the indifferent answer was not a negative proof of guilt. "What should it be, but this loss that has been spoken of in the Bank?"

"Oh, that," returned Layton. "I dare say they will be found."

"It places us all in a very awkward position, from myself downwards," went on Hurde, who was by no means a conjuror at the task he had undertaken. "There's no knowing what, or whom, Mr. Godolphin's suspicions may be turning to."

"Rubbish!" retorted Layton. "It's not likely that Mr. Godolphin would begin to doubt any of us. There's no cause for doing so."

"I don't know that," said Mr. Hurde significantly. "*I* am not so sure of some of you."

Layton opened his eyes. He supposed Mr. Hurde must be alluding to some one clerk in particular; must have a reason for it; but he did not glance at himself. "Why do you say that?" he asked.

"Well—it has occurred to me that some one or two of you may be living at a rate that your salary would neither pay for nor justify. You for one."

"I?" returned Layton.

"Yes, you. Horses, and gigs, and wine, and company, and pianos! They can't be managed out of a hundred a year."

Layton was rather taken to. Not to make an unnecessary mystery over it, it may as well be mentioned that all these expenses which so troubled old Hurde, the clerk was really paying for honestly, but not out of his salary. An uncle of his wife's was allowing them an addition to their income, and this supplied the additional luxuries. He resented the insinuation.

"Whether they are managed out of it, or whether they are not, is no

business of yours, Mr. Hurde," he said, after a pause. "I shall not
come to you to pay for them, or to the Bank either."

"It is my business," replied the old clerk. "It is Mr. Godolphin's
business, which is the same thing. Pray, how long is it since you became a betting man?"

"I am not a betting man," said Layton.

"Oh, indeed! You have not bet upon Cannonbar, I suppose? You
never put into a sweepstakes in your life?—you are not in one now, are
you?"

Layton could only open his mouth in astonishment. He thought
nothing less than that the spirits—then in the height of fashion—must
have been at work. He was really no betting man; had never been
inclined that way: but latterly, to oblige some friend who bothered
him over it, he had gone into a sweepstakes, and drawn the renowned
horse, Cannonbar. And had followed it up by betting a pound upon
him.

"You see, Mr. Layton, your pursuits are not quite so inexpensively
simple as you would wish to make them appear. These things happen
to have come to my knowledge, and I have thought it my duty to
mention them to Mr. Godolphin."

Layton flew into a passion. Partly in soreness of feeling at finding
he had been so closely looked after; partly in anger that dishonesty
could be associated with him; and chiefly at hearing that he had been
obnoxiously reported to Mr. Godolphin. "Have you told *him*," he
foamed, "that you suspect me of robbing the strong-room?"

"Some one has robbed it," was Mr. Hurde's rejoinder. "And has
no doubt made money of the deeds he stole!"

"I ask if you have told Mr. Godolphin that you cast this suspicion
to me?" reiterated Layton, stamping his foot.

"What if I have? Appearances, in my opinion, would warrant my
casting it to you."

"Then you had better cast it to Mr. George Godolphin. There!"

But that they were completely absorbed in the dispute, their voices
raised—at least, Layton's—they might have seen Mr. Godolphin close
to them. In passing through the Bank from his carriage to his private
room—for, in the untoward state of affairs, touching the loss, he had
come betimes—he was attracted by the angry sounds, and turned
towards them.

"Is anything the matter?"

They looked round, saw Mr. Godolphin, and their voices and
tempers dropped to a calm. Neither appeared inclined to answer the
question, and Mr. Godolphin passed on. Another minute or two, and
a message came from him, commanding the presence of the chief
clerk.

"Hurde," he began, "have you been speaking to Layton of what you
mentioned to me last night?"

"Yes, sir, that's what it was. It put him into a passion."

"He repudiates the suspicion, I suppose?"

"Out-and-out, sir," was the answer of Mr. Hurde. "He says his wife
has an income, independent of himself; and that he put into a sweepstakes lately to oblige a friend, and staked a sovereign on the horse he

drew. He says it is all he ever staked in his life, and all he ever means to stake. He was saying this now, when you sent for me. I don't know what to think. He speaks honestly enough, to listen to him."

"What remark did I hear him making, relative to Mr. George Godolphin?"

"He ought to be punished for that," replied Mr. Hurde. "Better suspect Mr. George than suspect him, was what he said. I don't know what he meant, and I don't think he knew himself, sir."

"Why did he say it?"

"When men are beside themselves with passion, sir, they say anything that comes uppermost. I asked him, after you went, what he meant by it, but he would not say any more."

"I think you must be mistaken in suspecting Layton, Hurde. I thought so last night."

"Well, sir, I may be," acknowledged Hurde. "I don't feel so sure of it as I did. But then comes the old puzzle again as to who could have taken the deeds. Layton would not have been so fierce but that he found the doubt had been mentioned to you," added Mr. Hurde, returning to the subject of the clerk's anger.

"Did you tell him you had mentioned it?"

"Yes, sir, I did. It's not my way to conceal faults in a corner; and that the clerks know."

Mr. Godolphin dropped the subject, and entered upon some general business. The old clerk remained with him about ten minutes, and then was at liberty to withdraw.

"Send Layton to me," was the order as he went out. And the clerk appeared in obedience to it.

Thomas Godolphin received him kindly, his manner and words had all the repose of quiet confidence. He believed Mr. Hurde to be completely mistaken, to have erred through zeal, and he intimated as much to Mr. Layton. He might not have personally entered on the topic with him, but that Layton had heard that he had been accused to him.

Layton's heart opened to his master. He was a well-disposed man when not exasperated. He frankly volunteered to Mr. Godolphin the amount of his wife's income and its source; he stated that he was not living up to one penny more than he could afford; and he distinctly denied being a betting man, either by practice or inclination—except for the one bet of a pound, which he had made incidentally. Altogether, his explanation was perfectly satisfactory to Mr. Godolphin.

"Understand me, Mr. Layton, I did not, myself, cast the slightest doubt upon you. To do so, never occurred to me."

"I hope not, sir," was Layton's reply. "Mr. Hurde has his crotchets, and we, who are under him, must put up with them. His bark is worse than his bite: that much may be said for him."

"Yes," said Thomas Godolphin. "You might fare worse, in that respect, than you do under Mr. Hurde. What was the meaning of the words you spoke relative to Mr. George Godolphin?"

Layton felt that his face was on fire. He muttered, in his confusion, something to the effect that it was a "slip of the tongue."

"But you must be aware that such slips are quite unjustifiable.

Something must have induced you to say it. What may it have been?"

"The truth is, I was in a passion when I said it," replied Layton, compelled to speak. "I am very sorry."

"You are evading my question," quietly replied Thomas Godolphin. "I ask you what could have induced you to say it? There must have been something to lead to the remark."

"I did not mean anything, I declare, sir. Mr. Hurde vexed me by casting suspicion upon me; and in the moment's anger, I retorted that he might as well cast it upon Mr. George Godolphin."

Thomas Godolphin pressed the question. In Layton's voice when he had uttered it, distorted though it was with passion, his ears had detected a strange meaning. "But why upon Mr. George Godolphin? Why more upon him than any other?—upon myself, for instance; or Mr. Hurde?"

Layton was silent. Thomas Godolphin waited, his serene countenance fixed upon the clerk's.

"I suppose I must have had in my head a remark I heard yesterday, sir," he slowly rejoined. "Heaven knows, though, I gave no heed to it; and how I came to forget myself in my anger, I don't know. I am sure I thought nothing of it, afterwards, until Mr. Hurde spoke to me this morning."

"What was the remark?" asked Mr. Godolphin.

"Sir, it was that sporting man, Jolly, who said it. He fastened himself on me last evening in going from here, and I could not get rid of him until ten at night. We were talking about different things: the great discount houses in London and one thing or another; and he said, incidentally, that Mr. George Godolphin had a good deal of paper in the market."

Thomas Godolphin paused. "Did he assert that he knew this?"

"He pretended to assert many things, as of his own knowledge. I asked him how he knew it, and he replied a friend of his had seen it—meaning the paper. It was all he said; and how I came to repeat such a thing after him, I cannot tell. I hope you will excuse it, sir."

"I cannot help excusing it," replied Mr. Godolphin. "You said the thing, and you cannot unsay it. It was very wrong. Take care that you do not give utterance to it again."

Layton withdrew, inwardly vowing that he never would. In point of fact, he had not attached much weight to the information; and could now have bitten his tongue out for repeating it. He wondered whether they could prosecute him for slander: or whether, if it came to the ears of Mr. George, *he* would. Mr. Godolphin had met it with the considerate generosity ever characteristic of him; but Mr. George was different from his brother. If ever a man in this world lived up to the Divine command, "Do as ye would be done by," that man was Thomas Godolphin.

But the words, nevertheless, grated on Thomas Godolphin's ears. That George was needlessly lavish in expenditure, he knew: but not more so than his income allowed, if he chose to spend it all—unless he had secret sources of expense. A change came over Thomas Godolphin's face as the idea suggested itself to his mind. Once in the train of thought he could not stop it. *Had* George private channels for expenditure, of which the world knew nothing? Could he have been using the Bank's money?—could it be he who had taken Lord Averil's deeds? Like unto Isaac Hastings, the red flush of shame dyed Thomas's brow at the thought—shame for his own obtrusive imagination that could conjure up such a fancy against his brother. Thomas had never conjured it up, but for the suggestion gratuitously imparted to him by Layton.

But he could not drive it down. No; like the vision which had been gratuitously presented to the Reverend Mr. Hastings, and which he had been unable to dismiss, Thomas Godolphin could not drive it away. In a sort of panic—a panic caused by his own thoughts—he called for certain of the books to be brought to him.

Some of those wanted were in George Godolphin's room. It was Isaac Hastings who was sent in there for them.

"The books!" exclaimed George, looking at Isaac.

"Mr. Godolphin wants them, sir."

It was quite out of the usual order for these books to come under the inspection (unless at stated times) of Mr. Godolphin. The very asking for them implied a doubt on George—at least, it sounded so to that gentleman's all-conscious ears. He pointed out the books to Isaac in silence, with the end of his pen.

Isaac Hastings carried them to Mr. Godolphin, and left them with him. Mr. Godolphin turned them rapidly over and over: they appeared, so far as he could see at a cursory glance, to be all right; the balance on the credit side weighty, the available funds next door to inexhaustible, the Bank altogether flourishing. Thomas took greater shame to himself for having doubted his brother. While thus engaged, an observation suddenly struck him—that all the entries were in George's handwriting. A few minutes later, George came into the room.

"George," he exclaimed, "how industrious you have become!"

"Industrious!" repeated George, looking round for an explanation. ⁎

"All these entries are yours. Formerly you would not have done as much in a year."

George laughed. "I used to be incorrigibly idle. It was well to turn over a new leaf."

He—George—was going out of the room again, but his brother stopped him. "Stay here, George. I want you."

Mr. Godolphin pointed to a chair as he spoke, and George sat down. George, who seemed rather inclined to have the fidgets, took out his penknife and began cutting at an offending nail.

"Are you in any embarrassment, George?"

"In embarrassment? I! Oh dear, no."

Thomas paused. Dropping his voice, he resumed in a lower tone, only just removed from a whisper:

"Have you paper flying about the discount markets?"

George Godolphin's fair face grew scarlet. Was it with conscious emotion?—or with virtuous indignation? Thomas assumed it to be the latter. How could he give it an opposite meaning from the indignant words which accompanied it. A burst of indignation which Thomas stopped.

"Stay, George. There is no necessity to put yourself out. I never supposed it to be anything but false when a rumour of it reached my ear. Only tell me the truth quietly."

Possibly George would have been glad to tell the truth, and get so much of the burden off his mind. But he did not dare. He might have shrunk from the terrible confession at any time to his kind, his good, his upright brother : but things had become too bad to be told to him now. If the exposé did come, why, it must, and there would be no help for it : tell him voluntarily he could not. By some giant strokes of luck and policy, it might yet be averted : how necessary, then, to keep it from Thomas Godolphin !

"The truth is," said George, "that I don't know what you mean. To what rumour are you alluding ? "

"It has been said that you have a good deal of paper in the market. The report was spoken, and it reached my ears."

"It's not true. It's all an invention," cried George vehemently. "Should I be such a fool? There are some people who live, it's my belief, by trying to work ill to others. Mr. Hastings was with me this morning. He had heard a rumour that something was wrong with the Bank."

"With the Bank ! In what way ? "

"Oh, of course, people must have gathered a version of the loss here, and put their own charitable constructions upon it," replied George, returning to his usual careless mode of speech. "The only thing to do is, to laugh at them."

"As you can laugh at the rumour regarding youself and the bills ? " remarked Thomas.

"As I can and do," answered easy George. Never more easy, more apparently free from care than at that moment. Thomas Godolphin, truthful himself, open as the day, not glancing to the possibility that George could be deliberately otherwise, felt all his confidence return to him. George went out, and Thomas turned to the books again.

Yes. They were all in order, all right. With those flourishing statements before him, how could he have been so foolish as to cast suspicion on George? Thomas had a pen in one hand, and the fore-finger of the other pointed to the page, when his face went white as one in mortal agony, and drops of moisture broke out upon his brow.

The same pain, which had taken him occasionally before, had come to him again. Mortal agony in verity it seemed. He dropped the pen ; he lay back in his chair ; he thought he must have fallen to the ground. How long he so lay he could not quite tell : not very long probably, counted by minutes ; but counted by pain long enough for a lifetime. Isaac Hastings, coming in with a message, found him. Isaac stood aghast.

"I am not very well, Isaac. Give me your arm. I will go and sit for a little time in the dining-room."

"Shall I run over for Mr. Snow, sir ? "

"No. I shall be better soon. In fact, I am better, or I could not talk to you. It was a sudden paroxysm."

He leaned upon Isaac Hastings, and reached the dining-room. It was empty. Isaac left him there, and proceeded, unordered, to acquaint Mr. George Godolphin. He could not find him.

"Mr. George has gone out," said a clerk. "Not two minutes ago."

"I had better tell Maria, then," thought Isaac. "He does not look fit to be left alone."

Speeding up to Maria's sitting-room, he found her there, talking to Margery. Miss Meta, in a cool brown-holland dress and a large straw hat, was dancing about in glee. She danced up to him.

"I am going to the hayfield," said she. "Will you come?"

"Don't I wish I could!" he replied, catching her up in his arms. "It is fine to be Miss Meta Godolphin!: to have nothing to do all day but roll in the hay."

She struggled to get down. Margery was waiting to depart. A terrible thing if Margery should have all the rolling to herself and Meta be left behind! They went out, and he turned to his sister.

"Maria, Mr. Godolphin is in the dining-room, ill. I thought I would come and tell you. He looks too ill to be left alone."

"What is the matter with him?" she asked.

"A sudden pain," he said. "I happened to go into his room with a message, and saw him. I almost thought he was dead at first; he looked so ghastly."

Maria hastened down. Thomas, better then, but looking fearfully ill still, was leaning upon the arm of a couch. Maria went up and took his hand.

"Oh, Thomas, you look very ill! What is it?"

He gazed into her face with a serene countenance, a quiet smile. "It is only another of my warnings, Maria. I have been so much better that I am not sure but I thought they had gone for good."

Maria drew forward a chair and sat down by him. "Warnings?" she repeated.

"Of the end. You must be aware, Maria, that I am attacked with a fatal malady."

Maria was not quite unaware of it, but she had never understood that a fatal termination was inevitable. She did not know but that he might live to be an old man. "Can nothing be done for you?" she breathed.

"Nothing."

Her eyes glistened with the rising tears. "Oh, Thomas! you must not die! We could none of us bear to lose you. George could not do without you; Janet could not; I think I could not."

He gently shook his head. "We may not pick and choose, Maria— who shall be left here, and who be taken. Those go sometimes who, seemingly, can be least spared."

She could scarcely speak; afraid lest her sobs should come, for her heart was aching. "But surely it is not to be speedy?" she murmured. "You may live on a long while yet?"

"The doctors tell me I may live on for years, if I keep myself quiet. I think they are wrong."

"Oh, Thomas, then, you surely will!" she eagerly said, her cheek flushing with emotion. "Who can have tranquillity if you cannot?"

How ignorant they both were of the dark cloud looming overhead, ready even then to burst and send forth its torrent! Tranquillity! Tranquillity henceforth for Thomas Godolphin!

CHAPTER XVII.

GONE!

THE days passed on to a certain Saturday. An ominous Saturday for the Godolphins. Rumours, vague at the best, and therefore all the more dangerous, had been spreading in Prior's Ash and its neighbourhood. Some said the Bank had had a loss; some said the Bank was shaky; some said Mr. George Godolphin had been lending money from the Bank funds; some said their London agents had failed; some actually said that Thomas Godolphin was *dead*. The various turns taken by the rumour were extravagantly marvellous: but the whole, combined, whispered ominously of danger. Only let public fear be thoroughly aroused, and it would be all over. It was as a train of powder laid, which only wants one touch of a lighted match to set it exploding.

Remittances arrived on the Saturday morning, in the ordinary course of business. Valuable remittances. Sufficient for the usual demands of the day: but not sufficient for any unusual demands. On the Friday afternoon a somewhat untoward incident had occurred. A stranger presented himself at the Bank and demanded to see Mr. George Godolphin. The clerk to whom he addressed himself left him standing at the counter and went away: to acquaint, as the stranger supposed, Mr. George Godolphin: but, in point of fact, the clerk was not sure whether Mr. George was in or out. Finding he was out, he told Mr. Hurde, who went forward: and was taken by the stranger for Mr. George Godolphin. Not personally knowing (as it would appear) Mr. George Godolphin, it was a natural enough mistake. A staid old gentleman, in spectacles, might well be supposed by a stranger to be one of the firm.

"I have a claim upon you," said the stranger, drawing a piece of paper out of his pocket. "Will you be so good as to settle it?"

Mr. Hurde took the paper and glanced over it. It was an accepted bill, George Godolphin's name to it.

"I cannot say anything about this," Mr. Hurde was beginning: but the applicant interrupted him.

"I don't want anything *said*. I want it paid."

"You should have heard me out," rejoined Mr. Hurde. "I cannot say or do anything in this myself: you must see Mr. George Godolphin. He is out, but—— "

"Come, none of that gammon!" interposed the stranger again, who appeared to have come prepared to enter upon a contest. "I was warned there'd be a bother over it: that Mr. George Godolphin would deny himself, and say black was white, if necessary. You can't do *me*, Mr. George Godolphin."

"You are not taking me for Mr. George Godolphin?" exclaimed the old clerk, uncertain whether to believe his ears.

"Yes, I am taking you for Mr. George Godolphin," doggedly returned the man. "Will you take up this bill?"

"I am *not* Mr. George Godolphin. Mr. George Godolphin will be in presently, and you can see him."

"It's a do," cried the stranger. "I want this paid. I know the claims there are against Mr. George Godolphin, and I have come all the way from town to enforce mine. *I* don't want to come in with the ruck of his creditors, who'll get a sixpence in the pound, maybe."

A very charming announcement to be made in a banking-house. The clerks pricked up their ears; the two or three customers who were present turned round from the counters and listened for more : for the civil gentleman had not deemed it necessary to speak in a subdued tone. Mr. Hurde, scared out of his propriety, in mortal fear lest anything worse might come, hurried the man to a safe place, and left him there to await the entrance of Mr. George Godolphin.

Whether this incident, mentioned outside (as it was sure to be), put the finishing touch to the rumours already in circulation, cannot be known. Neither was it known to those interested, what Mr. George did with his loud and uncompromising customer, when he at length entered and admitted him to an interview. It is possible that but for this untoward application, the crash might not have come quite so soon.

Saturday morning rose busily, as was usual at Prior's Ash. However stagnant the town might be on other days, Saturday was always full of life and bustle. Prior's Ash was renowned for its grain market; and dealers from all parts of the country flocked in to attend it. But on this morning some unusual excitement appeared to be stirring the town; natives and visitors. People stood about in groups, talking, listening, asking questions, consulting; and as the morning hours wore on, an unwonted stream appeared to be setting in towards the house of Godolphin, Crosse, and Godolphin. Whether the reports might be true or false, there would be no harm just to draw *their* money out and be on the safe side, was the mental remark made by hundreds. Could put it in again when the storm had blown over—if it proved to be only a false alarm.

Under these circumstances, little wonder that the Bank was unusually favoured with visitors. One strange feature in their application was, that they all wanted to draw out money : not a soul came to pay any in. George Godolphin, fully aware of the state of things, alive to the danger, was present in person, his words gracious, his bearing easy, his smile gay as ever. Only to look at him eased some of them of half their doubt.

But it did not arrest their cheques, and old Hurde (whatever George might have done) grew paralyzed with fear.

"For the love of Heaven, send for Mr. Godolphin, sir!" he whispered. "We can't go on long at this rate."

"What good can he do?" returned George.

"Mr. George, he *ought* to be sent for; he ought to know what's going on ; it is an imperative duty," remonstrated the clerk, in a strangely severe tone. " In fact, sir, if you don't send, I must. I am responsible to him."

" Send, then," said George. " I only thought to spare him vexation."

Mr. Hurde beckoned Isaac Hastings. " Fly for your life up to Ash-lydyat, and see Mr. Godolphin," he breathed in his ear. " Tell him there's a run upon the Bank."

Isaac, passing through the Bank with apparent unconcern, easy and careless as if he had taken a leaf from the book of George Godolphin, did not let the grass grow under his feet when he *was* out. But, in-stead of turning towards Ashlydyat, he took the way to All Souls' Rectory.

Arriving panting and breathless, he dashed in, and dashed against his brother Reginald, not five minutes arrived from a two years' absence at sea. Scarcely giving half a moment to a passing greeting, he was hastening from the room again in search of his father.

" Do you call *that* a welcome, Isaac ? " exclaimed Mrs. Hastings, in a surprised and reproving tone. " What's your hurry ? One would think you were upon an errand of life and death."

" So I am : it is little short of it," he replied in agitation. " Regy, don't stop me : you will know all soon. Is my father in his room ? "

" He has gone out," said Mrs. Hastings.

" Gone out ! " The words sounded like a knell. Unless his father hastened to the Bank, he might be a ruined man. " Where's he gone, mother ? "

" My dear, I have not the least idea. What is the matter with you ? "

Isaac took one instant's dismayed counsel with himself : he had not time for more. *He* could not go off in search of him ; he must hasten to Ashlydyat. He looked up : laid summary hands upon his sister Rose, put her outside the door, closed it, and set his back against it.

" Reginald, listen to me. You must go out and find my father. Search for him everywhere. Tell him there's a run upon the Bank, and he must make haste if he would find himself safe. Mother, could you look for him as well? The Chisholms' money is there, you know, and it would be nothing but ruin."

Mrs. Hastings gazed at Isaac with wondering eyes, puzzled with per-plexity.

" Don't you understand, mother?" he urged. " *I* can't look for him : I ought not to have come out of my way as far as this. He must be found, so do your best, Reginald. Of course you will be cautious to say nothing abroad : I put Rose out that she might not hear this."

Opening the door again, passing the indignant Rose without so much as a word, Isaac sped across the road, and dashed through some cross-fields and lanes to Ashlydyat. His *détour* had not hindered him above three or four minutes, for he went at the pace of a steam-engine. He considered it—as Hurde had said by Mr. Godolphin—an impera-tive duty to warn his father. Thomas Godolphin was not up when he reached Ashlydyat. It was only between ten and eleven o'clock.

" I must see him, Miss Godolphin," he said to Janet. " It is abso-lutely necessary."

By words or by actions putting aside obstacles, he stood within Thomas Godolphin's chamber. The latter had passed a night of suffering, its traces remaining on his countenance.

"I shall be down at the Bank some time in the course of the day, Isaac: though I am scarcely equal to it," he observed, as soon as he saw him. "Am I wanted for anything in particular?"

"I—I—am sent up to tell you bad news, sir," replied Isaac, feeling the communication an unpleasant one to make. "There's a run upon the Bank."

"A run upon the Bank!" repeated Thomas Godolphin, scarcely believing the information.

Isaac explained. A complete run. For the last hour, ever since the bank opened, people had been thronging in.

Thomas paused. "I cannot imagine what can have led to it," he resumed. "Is my brother visible?"

"Oh yes, sir."

"That is well. He can assure them all that we are solvent: that there is no fear. Have the remittances come down?"

"Yes, sir. But they will be nothing, Mr. Hurde says, with a run like this."

"Be so kind as to touch that bell for me, Isaac, to bring up my servant. I will be at the Bank immediately."

Isaac rang the bell, left the room, and hastened back again. The Bank was fuller than ever: and its coffers must be getting low.

"Do you happen to know whether my father has been in?" he whispered to Layton, next to whom he stood.

Layton shook his head negatively. "I think not. I have not observed him."

Isaac stood upon thorns. He might not quit his post. Every time the doors swung to and fro—and they were incessantly swinging—he looked for Mr. Hastings. But he looked in vain. By-and-by Mr. Hurde came forward, a note in his hand. "Put on your hat, Layton, and take this round," said he. "Wait for an answer."

"Let me take it," almost shouted Isaac. And, without waiting for assent or dissent, he seized the note from Mr. Hurde's hand, caught up his hat, and was gone. Thomas Godolphin was stepping from his carriage as he passed out.

Isaac had not, this time, to go out of his way. The delivery of the note would necessitate his passing the Rectory. "Rose!" he uttered, out of breath with agitation as he had been before, "is papa not in?"

Rose was sitting there alone. "No," she answered. "Mamma and Reginald went out just after you. Where did you send them to?"

"Then they can't find him!" muttered Isaac to himself, speeding off again, and giving Rose no answer. "It will be nothing but ruin."

A few steps farther, and whom should he see but his father. The Reverend Mr. Hastings was coming leisurely across the fields, from the very direction which Isaac had previously travelled. He had probably been to the Pollard cottages: he did sometimes take that round. Hedges and ditches were nothing to Isaac in the moment's excitement, and he leaped one of each to get to him; it cut off a step or two.

"Where were you going an hour ago?" called out Mr. Hastings before they met. "You were flying as swiftly as the wind."

"Oh, father!" wailed Isaac; "did you see me?"

"What should hinder me? I was at old Satcherley's."

"If you had only come out to me! I would rather have seen you then than—than—heaven," he panted. "There's a run upon the Bank. If you don't make haste and draw out your money, you'll be too late."

Mr. Hastings laid his hand upon Isaac's arm. It may be that he did not understand him; for his utterance was rapid and full of emotion. Isaac, in his eagerness, shook it off.

"There's not a moment to lose, father. I don't fancy they can keep on paying long. Half the town's there."

Without another word of delay, Mr. Hastings turned and sped along with a step nearly as fleet as Isaac's. When he reached the Bank the shutters were being put up.

"The Bank has stopped," said an officious bystander to the Rector.

It was even so. The Bank had stopped. The good old firm of Godolphin, Crosse, and Godolphin had—GONE!

CHAPTER XVIII.

MURMURS; AND CURIOUS DOUBTS.

WE hear now and again of banks breaking, and we give to the sufferers a passing sympathy; but none can realize the calamity in its full and awful meaning, except those who are eye-witnesses of the distress it entails, or who own, unhappily, a personal share in it. When the Reverend Mr. Hastings walked into the Bank of Godolphin, Crosse, and Godolphin, he knew that the closing of the shutters, then in actual process, was the symbol of a fearful misfortune, which would shake to its centre the happy security of Prior's Ash. The thought struck him, even in the midst of his own suspense and perplexity.

One of the first faces he saw was Mr. Hurde's. He made his way to him. "I wish to draw my money out," he said.

The old clerk shook his head. "It's too late, sir."

Mr. Hastings leaned his elbow on the counter, and approached his face nearer to the clerk's. "I don't care (comparatively speaking) for my own money: that which you have held so long; but I must have refunded to me what has been just paid in to my account, but which is none of mine. The nine thousand pounds."

Mr. Hurde paused ere he replied, as if the words puzzled him. "Nine thousand pounds!" he repeated. "There has been no nine thousand pounds paid in to your account."

"There has," was the reply of Mr. Hastings, given in a sharp, distinct tone. "I paid it in myself, and hold the receipt."

"Well, I don't know," said the clerk dubiously; "I had your account under my eye this morning, sir, and saw nothing of it. But there's no fear, Mr. Hastings, as I hope and trust," he added, confidentially.

"We have telegraphed for remittances, and expect a messenger down with them before the day's out."

"You are closing the Bank," remarked Mr. Hastings in answering argument.

"We are obliged to do that. We had not an inexhaustible fountain of funds here: and you see how people have been thronging in. On Monday morning I hope the Bank will be open again; and in a condition to restore full confidence."

Mr. Hastings felt a slight ray of reassurance. But he would have felt a greater had the nine thousand pounds been handed to him, there and then. He said so: in fact, he pressed the matter. How ineffectually, the next words of the clerk told him.

"We have paid away all we had, Mr. Hastings," he whispered. "There's not a farthing left in the coffers."

"You have paid the accounts of applicants in full, I presume?"

"Yes: up to the time that the funds, in hand, lasted to do it."

"Was that just?—to the body of creditors?" asked the Rector in a severe tone.

"Where was the help for it?—unless we had stopped when the run began?"

"It would have been the more equable way—if you were to stop at all," remarked Mr. Hastings.

"But we did not know we should stop. How was it possible to foresee that this panic was about to arise? Sir, all I can say is, I hope that Monday morning will see you, and every other creditor, paid in full."

Mr. Hastings was pushed away from the counter. Panic-stricken creditors were crowding in, demanding to be paid. Mr. Hastings elbowed his way clear of the throng, and stood aside. Stood in the deepest perplexity and care. What if that money, entrusted to his hands, should be *gone?* His brow grew hot at the thought.

Not so hot as other brows there: brows of men gifted with less equable temperaments than that owned by the Rector of All Souls'. One gentleman came in and worked his way to the front, the perspiration pouring off him, as from one in sharp agony.

"I want my money!" he cried. "I shall be a bankrupt next week if I can't get my money."

"I want *my* money!" cried a quieter voice at his elbow; and Mr. Hastings recognized the speaker as Barnaby, the corn-dealer.

They received the same answer; the answer which was being reiterated in so many parts of the large room, in return to the same demand. The Bank had been compelled to suspend its payments for the moment. But remittances were sent for, and would be down, if not that day, by Monday morning.

"When I paid in my two thousand pounds a few days ago, I asked, before I would leave it, whether it was all safe," said Mr. Barnaby, his tone one of wailing distress, though quiet still. But, quiet as it was, it was heard distinctly, for the people hushed their murmurs to listen to it. The general feeling, for the most part, was one of exasperation: and any downright good cause of complaint against the Bank and its management, would have been half as welcome to the unfortunate malcontents as their money. Mr. Barnaby continued:

"I had heard a rumour that the Bank wasn't right. I heard it at Rutt's. And I came down here with the two thousand pounds in my hand, and saw Mr. George Godolphin in his private room. He told me it was all right: there was nothing the matter with the Bank: and I left my money. I am not given to hard words; but, if I don't get it paid back to me, I shall say I have been swindled out of it."

"Mr. George couldn't have told that there'd be this run upon the Bank, sir," replied a clerk, giving the best answer he could, the most plausible excuse: as all the clerks had to exert their wits to do, that day. "The Bank *was* all right then."

"If it was all right then, why isn't it all right now?" roared a chorus of angry voices. "Banks don't get wrong in a day."

"Why did Mr. George Godolphin pass his word to me that it was safe?" repeated Mr. Barnaby, as though he had not heard the refuting arguments. "I should not have left my money here but for that."

The Rector of all Souls' stood his ground, and listened. But that George Godolphin was his daughter's husband, he would have echoed the complaint: that, but for his positive assertion of the Bank's solvency, he should not have left *his* money there—the trust-money of the little Chisholms.

When the Bank had virtually closed, the order gone forth to put up the shutters, Mr. Godolphin had retired to an inner room. These clamorous people had pushed in since, in defiance of the assurance that business for the day was over. Some of them demanded to see Mr. Godolphin. Mr. Hurde declined to introduce them to him. In doing so, he was acting on his own responsibility: perhaps to save that gentleman vexation, perhaps out of consideration to his state of health. He knew that his master, perplexed and astounded with the state of affairs, could only answer them as he did—that on Monday morning, all being well, the Bank would be open for business again. Did any undercurrent of doubt that this would be the case, run in Mr. Hurde's own heart? If so, he kept it down, refusing to admit it even to himself. One thing is certain, until that unpleasant episode of the previous day, when the rough, unknown man had applied so loudly and inopportunely for money, Mr. Hurde would have been ready to answer with his own life for the solvency of the house of Godolphin. He had believed, not only in the ability of the house to meet its demands and liabilities, but to meet them, if needed, twice over. That man's words, reflecting upon Mr. George Godolphin, grated upon Mr. Hurde's ears at the time, and they had grated on his memory ever since. But, so far as he could do so, he had beaten them down.

The crowd were got rid of. They became at length aware that to stay there would not answer their purpose in any way, would not do them good. They were fain to content themselves with that uncertain assurance, touching Monday morning, and went out, the doors being immediately barred upon them. If the catastrophe of the day was unpleasant for the principals, it was not much less unpleasant for the clerks: and they lost no time in closing the entrance when the opportunity occurred. The only man who had remained was the Rector of All Souls'.

"I must see Mr. Godolphin," said he.

"You can see him, sir, of course," was Mr. Hurde's answer. Mr. Hastings was different from the mob just got rid of. He had, so to say, a right of admittance to the presence of the principals in a three-fold sense : as a creditor, as their spiritual pastor, and as a near connexion; a right which Mr. Hurde would not presume to dispute.

"Mr. Godolphin will see you, I am sure, sir," he continued, leading the way from the room towards Thomas Godolphin's. "He would have seen every soul that asked for him, of those now gone out. I knew that, and that's why I wouldn't let messages be taken to him. Of what use, to-day?"

Thomas Godolphin was sitting alone, very busily occupied, as it appeared, with books. Mr. Hastings cast a rapid glance round the room, but George was not in it.

It was not two minutes ago that George had left it, and Mr. Hastings had escaped seeing him by those two minutes. George had stood there, condoling with Thomas upon the untoward event of the day, apparently as perplexed as Thomas was, to account for its cause : and apparently as hopeful; nay, as positive ; that ample funds would be down, ere the day should close, to set all things right.

"Mr. Godolphin, I have been asking Hurde for my money," were the first words uttered by the Rector. "Will you not give it me?"

Thomas Godolphin turned his earnest eyes, terribly sad then, on Mr. Hastings, a strangely yearning look in their light. "I wish I could," he answered. "But, even were it possible for us to do so—to give you a preference over others—it is not in our power. All funds in hand are paid out."

The Rector did not go over the old ground of argument, as he had to Mr. Hurde—that it was unfair to give preference to the earlier comers. It would answer no end now : and he was, besides, aware that he might have been among those earlier applicants, but for some untoward fate, which had taken him out of the way to the Pollard cottages, and restrained him from speaking to Isaac, when he saw him fly past. Whether Mr. Hastings would have had his nine thousand pounds is another matter. More especially if—as had been asserted by Mr. Hurde —the fact of the payment did not appear in the books.

"Where is George?" asked Mr. Hastings.

"He has gone to the telegraph office," replied Thomas Godolphin. "There has been more than time for answers to arrive—to be brought here—since our telegrams went up. George grew impatient, and has gone to the station."

"I wish to ask him how he could so have deceived me," resumed the Rector. "He assured me only yesterday, as it were, that the Bank was perfectly safe."

"As he no doubt thought. Nothing would have been the matter, but for this run upon it. There's quite a panic in Prior's Ash, I am told ; but what can have caused it, I know not. Some deeds of value belonging to Lord Averil have been lost or mislaid, and the report may have got about : but why it should have caused this fear, is to me utterly incomprehensible. I would have assured you myself yesterday, had you asked me, that we were perfectly safe and solvent. That we are so still, will be proved on Monday morning."

Mr. Hastings bent forward his head. "It would be worse than ruin to me, Mr. Godolphin. I should be held responsible for the Chisholms' money; should be called upon to refund it; and I have no means of doing so. I dare not contemplate the position."

"What are you talking of?" asked Thomas Godolphin. "I do not understand. We hold no money belonging to the Chisholms."

"Indeed you do," was the reply. "You had it all. I paid in the proceeds of the sale, nine thousand and forty-five pounds."

Mr. Godolphin paused at the assertion, looking at the Rector somewhat as his head clerk had done. "When did you pay it in?" he inquired.

"A few days ago. I brought it in the evening, after banking hours. Brierly came over from Binham and paid it to me in cash, and I brought it here at once. It was a large sum to keep in the house. As things have turned out, I wish I had kept it," concluded the Rector, speaking plainly.

"Paid it to George?"

"Yes. Maria was present. I have his receipt for it, Mr. Godolphin," added the Rector. "You almost appear to doubt the fact. As Hurde did, when I spoke to him just now. He said it did not appear in the books."

"Neither does it," replied Thomas Godolphin. "But I do not doubt you, now that you tell me of the transaction. George must have omitted to enter it."

That "omission" began to work in the minds of both, more than either cared to tell. Thomas Godolphin was marvelling at his brother's reprehensible carelessness: the Rector of All Souls'_was beginning to wonder whether "carelessness" was the deepest sin about to be laid open in the conduct of George Godolphin. Very unpleasant doubts, he could scarcely tell why, were rising up within him. His keen eye searched the countenance of Thomas Godolphin: but he read nothing there to confirm his doubts. On the contrary, that countenance, save for the great sorrow and vexation upon it, was, as it ever was, clear and open as the day. Not yet, not quite yet, had the honest faith of years, reposed by Thomas Godolphin in his brother, been shaken. Very, very soon was it to come: not the faith to be simply shaken, but rudely destroyed: blasted for ever; as a tree torn up by lightning.

It was useless for Mr. Hastings to remain. All the satisfaction to be obtained was—the confidently-expressed hope that Monday would set things straight. "It would be utter ruin to me, you know," he said, as he rose.

"It would be ruin to numbers," replied Thomas Godolphin. "I pray you, do not glance at anything so terrible. There is no cause for it: there is not indeed: our resources are ample. I can only say that I should wish I had died long ago, rather than have lived to witness such ruin, brought upon others, through us."

Lord Averil was asking to see Thomas Godolphin, and entered his presence as Mr. Hastings left it. He came in, all impulse. It appeared that he had gone out riding that morning after breakfast, and knew nothing of the tragedy then being enacted in the town. Do you think the word too strong a one—tragedy? Wait and see its effects. In passing the Bank on his return, Lord Averil saw the shutters up. In the moment's shock, his fears flew to Thomas Godolphin. He forgot that the death, even of the principal, would not close a Bank for business. Lord Averil, having nothing to do with business and its ways, may have been excused the mistake.

He pulled short up, and sat staring at the Bank, his heart beating, his face growing hot. Only the day before he had seen Thomas Godolphin in health (comparatively speaking) and life; and now, could he be dead? Casting his eyes on the stragglers gathered on the pavement before the banking doors—an unusual number of stragglers, though Lord Averil was too much occupied with other thoughts to notice the fact—he stooped down and addressed one of them. It happened to be Rutt the lawyer, who in passing had stopped to talk with the groups gathered there. Why *did* groups gather there? The Bank was closed for the rest of the day, nothing to be obtained from its aspect but blank walls and a blank door. What good did it do to people to halt there and stare at it? What good does it do them to halt before a house where murder has been committed, and stare at that?

The Viscount Averil bent from his horse to Rutt the lawyer. "What has happened? Is Mr. Godolphin dead?"

"It is not that, my lord. The Bank has stopped."

"The—Bank—has——stopped?" repeated Lord Averil, pausing between each word, in his astonishment, and a greater pause before the last.

"Half an hour ago, my lord. There has been a run upon it this morning; and now they have paid out all their funds, and are obliged to stop."

Lord Averil could not recover his consternation. "What occasioned the run?" he asked.

"Well—your lordship must understand that rumours are abroad. I heard them, days ago. Some say, now, that they have no foundation, and that the Bank will resume business on Monday as usual, when remittances arrive. The telegraph has been at work pretty well for the house the last hour or so," concluded Mr. Rutt.

Lord Averil leaped from his horse, gave it to a lad to hold, and went round to the private door. Thence he was admitted, as you have seen, to the presence of Thomas Godolphin. Not of his own loss had he come to speak—the sixteen thousand pounds involved in the disappearance of the deeds—and which, if the Bank ceased its payments, might never be refunded to him. No. Although he saw the premises closed, and heard that the Bank had stopped, not a doubt crossed Lord Averil of its real stability. That the run upon it had caused its temporary suspension, and that all would be made right on the Monday, as Mr. Rutt had suggested, he fully believed. The Bank held other deeds of Lord Averil's, and a little money: not much; his present account was not great. The deeds were safe; the money might be imperilled.

"I never heard of it until this moment," he impulsively cried, clasping the hand of Thomas Godolphin. "In returning now from a ride, I saw the shutters closed, and learned what had happened. There has been a run upon the Bank, I understand."

"Yes," replied Thomas, in a subdued tone, that told of mental pain. "It is a very untoward thing."

"But what induced it?"

"I cannot imagine. Unless it was the rumour, which has no doubt spread abroad, of the loss of your deeds. I suppose it was that: magnified in telling, possibly, into the loss of half the coffers of the Bank. Panics have arisen from far slighter causes; as those versed in the money market could tell you."

"But how foolish people must be!"

"When a panic arises, people are not themselves," remarked Thomas Godolphin. "One takes up the fear from another, as they take an epidemic. I wish our friends and customers had had more confidence in us. But I cannot blame them."

"They are saying, outside, that business will be resumed."

"Yes. As soon as we can get remittances down. Sunday intervenes, and of course nothing can be done until Monday."

"Well, now, my friend, can I help you?" rejoined Lord Averil. "I am a richer man than the world gives me credit for; owing to the inexpensive life I have led, since that one false step of mine, when I was in my teens. I will give you my signature to any amount. If you can contrive to make it known, it may bring people to their senses."

Thomas Godolphin's generous spirit opened to the proof of confidence: it shone forth from his quiet dark-grey eyes as he gazed at Lord Averil.

"Thank you sincerely for the kindness. I shall gratefully remember it to the last day of my life. An hour or two ago I do not know but I might have availed myself of it: as it is, it is too late. The Bank is closed for the day, and nothing more, good or bad, can be done until Monday morning. Long before that, I expect assistance will have arrived."

"Very well. But if you want further assistance, you know where to come for it," concluded Lord Averil. "I shall be in Prior's Ash. Do you know," he continued, in a musing sort of tone, "since I renounced that proposed sea expedition, I have begun to feel more like a homeless man than I ever yet did. If there were a desirable place for sale in this neighbourhood, I am not sure but I should purchase it, and settle down."

Thomas Godolphin gave only a slight answer. His own business was enough for him to think of, for one day. Lord Averil suddenly remembered this, and said something to the effect, but he did not yet rise to go. Surely he could not, at that moment, contemplate speaking to Mr. Godolphin about Cecil! Another minute, and Mr. Hurde had come into the room, bearing a telegraphic despatch in his hand.

"Has Mr. George brought this?" Thomas inquired, as he took it.

"No, sir. It came by the regular messenger."

"George must have missed him then," was Thomas Godolphin's mental comment.

He opened the paper. He cast his eyes over the contents. It was a short message; only a few words in it, simple and easy to comprehend: but Thomas Godolphin apparently could not understand it. Such at least was the impression conveyed to Lord Averil and Mr.

Hurde. Both were watching him, though without motive. The clerk waited for any orders there might be to give him : Lord Averil sat on, as he had been sitting. Thomas Godolphin read it three times, and then glanced up at Mr. Hurde.

"This cannot be for us," he remarked. "Some mistake must have been made. Some confusion, possibly, in the telegraph office in town ; and the message, intended for us, has gone elsewhere."

"That could hardly be, sir," was Mr. Hurde's reply.

In good truth, Thomas Godolphin himself thought it could "hardly be." But—if the message had come right—what did it mean? Mr. Hurde, racking his brains to conjecture the nature of the message that was so evidently disturbing his master, contrived to catch sight of two or three words at the end : and they seemed to convey an ominous intimation that there were no funds to be forthcoming.

Thomas Godolphin *was* disturbed ; and in no measured degree. His hands grew cold and his brow moist, as he gazed at the despatch in its every corner. According to its address, it was meant for their house, and in answer to one of the despatches he had sent up that morning. But—its contents! Surely *they* could not be addressed to the good old house of Godolphin, Crosse, and Godolphin!

A moment or two of wavering hesitation and then he drew to him a sheet of paper, wrote a few words, and folded it. "Take this yourself with all speed to the telegraph station," he said to Mr. Hurde. "Send the message up at once, and wait there for the answer. It will not be long in coming. And if you meet Mr. George, tell him I wish to see him."

"And now I dare say you will be glad to get rid of me," remarked Lord Averil, as Mr. Hurde hastened out. "This is not a day to intrude upon you for long : and I dare say the fellow to whom I intrusted my horse is thinking something of the sort."

He shook hands cordially and went away, leaving Thomas Godolphin to battle alone with his care. Ah me ! no human aid, henceforth, could help him, by so much as a passing word, with the terrible battle already set in. God alone, who had been with Thomas Godolphin through life, could whisper to him a word of comfort, could shed down a few drops of sustaining strength, so that he might battle through and bear. That God had been with him, in the midst of the deep sorrows He had seen fit to cast upon him, Thomas knew : he knew that He would be with him always, even unto the end.

"You had better accept my offer of assistance," Lord Averil turned back to say.

"No," broke from Thomas Godolphin in a sharp tone of pain, very different from the calm, if grateful, answer he had previously given to the same proposition. "What sort of justice would it be, if I robbed you to pay the claims of others?"

"You can refund me when the panic's over," returned the viscount, somewhat surprised at the nature of the reply.

"Yes. But—but—it might be a risk," was the rejoinder, given with unwonted hesitation. "In a crisis, such as this, it is, I believe, impossible to foresee what the end may be. Thank you greatly, Averil, all the same."

Mr. Hurde was not very long before he returned, bringing with him an answer to the last message. Colder and moister became Thomas Godolphin's brow as he read it; colder and colder grew his hand. It appeared to be only a confirmation of the one received before.

"I cannot understand this," he murmured.

Mr. Hurde stood by. That some ominous fear had arisen, he saw. He was an old and faithful servant of the house, entirely devoted to its interests. His master said a few words of explanation to him.

They aroused Mr. Hurde's fears. Had some deep-laid treachery been at work?—some comprehensive scheme of duplicity been enacting for some time past, making a bankrupt house appear to be still a flourishing concern? If so, it could only have been done by falsifying the books: and that could only have been done by George Godolphin.

Mr. Hurde did not dare to give vent to his thoughts. Indeed, he did not seriously contemplate that they could be realities. But, in the uncertainty created, he deemed himself perfectly justified in mentioning to Mr. Godolphin the untoward occurrence of the previous day ; the rude demand of the man for money, and the unpleasant expressions he had used of the state of Mr. George Godolphin's affairs. He was clearing his throat to begin in his usual slow fashion, when Mr. Godolphin spoke.

"I shall go to town by the first train, Hurde. The express. It will pass through in half an hour."

Then Mr. Hurde told his tale. It did not tend to reassure Thomas Godolphin.

He rang the bell. He caused George to be inquired for. But George was not in the house. He had not returned since that errand of his, ostensibly to the telegraph office.

Thomas could not wait. He wrote a note to George, and sealed it. He then charged a servant with a message for Miss Godolphin at Ashlydyat, gave a few directions to Mr. Hurde, proceeded on foot to the station without further preparations, and started on his journey.

Started on his journey, strange doubts and fears making havoc of his beating heart.

CHAPTER XIX.

BOBBING JOAN.

MARIA GODOLPHIN was in her own pretty sitting-room upstairs. She had been sitting there ever since breakfast: had not yet stirred from it, though noon had passed, for she was very busy. Not fond of sewing in a general way, she was plying her needle quickly now : some work of fine intricate braiding, to be converted into a frock for Miss Meta. Maria worked as if her heart were in it : it was for her child.

The door was closed, the window was open to the summer air. The scent of the flowers ascended from the garden below, the gentle hum of the insects was heard as they sported in the sun, the scene altogether was one of perfect tranquillity. There was an air of repose about the room, about Maria in her cool muslin dress, about the scene altogether. Who, looking at it, would have suspected the commotion that was being enacted—or that had been enacted so recently—in another part of the house?

It is a positive fact that Maria knew nothing yet of the grievous calamity which had fallen—the stoppage of the Bank. The servants knew it fast enough; were more correctly acquainted with its details (to hear them speak) than the Bank itself. They stood about in groups and talked in whispers, letting their work go. But not one of them had presumed to acquaint their unconscious mistress. They knew how ignorant of it all she was: they felt certain that not a suspicion of anything going wrong had ever crossed her. Indeed, it had not crossed their own inquisitive selves, and the blow had burst upon them that morning as a thunder-clap.

As a thunder-clap, it was soon to burst upon Maria. A few minutes' respite yet, ere it should come. She certainly had heard the visitors'-bell ring three or four times, which was somewhat unusual, considering that no message for her had followed upon it. That bell in the day-time generally heralded guests for herself. Once, when Pierce came in, bringing a small parcel for her from the bookseller's, Maria had inquired who it was that had just rung at the hall-door. Pierce answered that it was Lord Averil; his lordship had asked to see Mr. Godolphin. Maria could not remember afterwards, when looking back on the circumstances of the day, whether or not it had occurred to her to wonder why Lord Averil should come to the private door, when his visit was to the Bank and Thomas Godolphin. Pierce ventured not another word. He put down the parcel and hurried off, very much after the manner of one who is afraid of being asked questions.

And yet, the man, in his sober judgment, believed that there was little danger of any troublesome questions being put by his mistress. There was none. Of all people living, none were so completely un-conscious that anything wrong was looming, as Mrs. George Godolphin. If there was one house in the kingdom more safe, more staid, more solid than other houses, she believed it to be theirs. Yes, it was a notable fact, that Maria, sitting there so serenely tranquil, knew nothing of what was stirring Prior's Ash, from one end of it to the other, to the highest point of excitement. Perhaps it would not be too much to say that she was the last person in it whom the news reached.

The work—her work, that she held in her hand—was approaching completion, and she looked at it with fond eyes. She had been two or three weeks over it, sitting steadily to it several of the days. It was very pretty, certainly; a new sort of work just come up, done with a new sort of braid; and would, beyond question, look charming on Miss Meta. Now and then Maria would be visited with doubtful visions as to whether the thing would "wash." That is, wash and look as well afterwards as it did now. She could only hope for the best, and that Miss Meta would be upon her good behaviour when wearing it, and not spoil it beyond redemption the first time it was on.

"I hope I shall have enough braid," deliberated Maria, comparing the small portion of work, yet remaining to do, with the braid in hand.

"I wish I had told Margery to bring me in another piece; she will pass the shop. I must send, if I find it running short. If I am not interrupted to-day, I shall finish it."

One interruption occurred almost as Maria was speaking. The entrance of her husband. With him in the room she was continually looking off to talk, if she did not quite lay the work down; altogether she did not get on as fast as when alone. He had just come in from that excursion to the telegraph office. *Had* he been there? Or had his supposed visit been but a plea set forth, an excuse to get out of his brother's presence, away from that troubled scene, the Bank?

There was no knowing. George never said how it was, then or afterwards. Never said whether his return now was the result of his having accidentally seen his brother at a distance, walking along at a quick pace. He came in by the hall-door (there was no other way open to-day), letting himself in with his latch-key. Mr. Hurde was still there, posting or doing something or other to a pile of books.

"Has Mr. Godolphin gone for the day?" asked George.

"Mr. Godolphin's gone to London, sir."

"To London?" echoed George, in surprise. "What is taking him there?"

"Some queer messages have come down by telegraph," returned Mr. Hurde, pushing his spectacles up, and looking George full in the face. "Mr. Godolphin could not understand them, and he has gone to town."

George did not make any observation for a minute. Was he afraid to make further inquiries? "What were the messages?" he presently asked.

"Mr. Godolphin did not show them to me, sir," was the answer, spoken, or George fancied it, in a curt tone. "He said enough to tell me that there appeared to be some great cause for disquiet—and he has gone to see about it. He left a note in the parlour, sir, for you."

Mr. Hurde buried his face over his books again, a genteel hint, perhaps, that he wished the colloquy to end—if his master would be pleased to take it. George entered the parlour and caught up the note.

"'Be at home to callers; answer all inquiries,'" repeated he, reciting the last words of the note. "I wish Thomas may get it! Now that the explosion has come, Prior's Ash is no place for me."

Many and many a day had there intruded into George Godolphin's mind a vision of this very time, when the "explosion" should have "come." He had never dwelt upon it. He had driven it away from him to the utmost of his power. Perhaps it is not in the nature of those, whose course of conduct is such as to bring down these explosions as a natural sequence, to anticipate with uncomfortable minuteness the period of their arrival, or their particular manner of meeting them. Certainly George Godolphin had not done so: but there had been ever an undercurrent of conviction lying dormant in his heart, that he should not face it in person. When the brunt of the scandal was over, then he might return to home and Prior's Ash: but he would not wait there to be present at its fall.

He crushed Thomas Godolphin's note into his pocket, and stood upright on the hearthrug to *think*. He knew that, if treated according to his deserts, this would be the last friendly note written him by his brother for many a day to come. Thomas was then being whirled on his way to the full knowledge of his, George's, delinquency; or, if not to the full knowledge, which perhaps could only be unfolded by degrees, as we turn the pages of a book, to quite enough of it. It was time for him to be off now. If inquisitive callers must be seen, Hurde could see them.

Conscience makes cowards of us all: a saying, not more trite than true. Very absurd cowards it makes of us now and then. As George Godolphin stood there, revolving the *pros* and *cons* of his getting away, the ways and means of his departure, a thought flashed into his mind as to whether he should be allowed to depart, if an inkling of his exodus got wind. It actually did so; unfounded as was any cause for it. The fear came from his lively conscience; but from nothing else. He might be seen at the railway station, and stopped: he might—— "Tush!" interrupted George angrily, coming out of the foolish fear and returning to his sober senses. "People here know nothing yet, beyond the bare fact that the Bank has suspended payment. They can't arrest a man for that."

But, how about ways and means? Ay, that was a greater necessity for consideration. The money in George's pockets amounted—*I am telling you truth*—to three and sixpence. With all his faults, he was open-hearted, open-handed. He had been weak, imprudent, extravagant; he had enacted a course of deceit to his brother and to the world, forced to it (he would have told you) by his great need and his great dread; he had made use of other men's property: he had, in short, violated those good rules that public lamentation is made for every Sunday—he had left undone those things that he ought to have done, and he had done those things that he ought not to have done; but it was not for himself (in one sense) that he had done this. It was not for himself, selfishly. He had not been laying up in store for the evil day, or put by money to serve his wants when other moneys should fail. As long as he had money he spent it: whether in paying claims, or in making charming presents to Charlotte Pain and similarly esteemed friends—elegant little trifles that of course cost nothing, or next to it; or in new dolls for Meta; or in giving a five-pound note to some poor broken-down tradesman, who wanted to get upon his legs again. In one way or other the money had been spent; not a single shilling had George hoarded up; so, in that sense, though in that alone, he had been neither selfish nor dishonest.

And, now that the crash had come, he was without means. He had not so much as the fare in his pocket that would suffice to convey him away from the troubled scene, which the next week would evidently bring forth. The Bank funds were exhausted: so he had not them to turn to. But, get away he must: and, it seemed to him, the sooner the better.

He came forth through the door separating the Bank from the dwelling, and entered the dining-room. The tray was laid for luncheon, and for Meta's dinner: but no one was in the room. He went upstairs to Maria's sitting-room. She was there, quietly at work: and she looked up at him with a glad smile of welcome. Her attitude of repose, her employment, the expression of calm happiness pervading her countenance, told George that she was as yet in ignorance of what had occurred.

"What money have you in your purse, Maria?" asked he, speaking carelessly.

Maria laughed. "Why, none," she answered quite merrily. "Or as good as none. I have been telling you ever so long, George, that I must have some money; and I must. A good deal, I mean; to pay my housekeeping bills."

"Just see what you have," returned George. "I want to borrow it."

Maria put her hand into her pocket, and then found that her purse was in her desk. She gave the keys to George, and asked him to unlock it.

The purse was in a small compartment, lying on a ten-pound note. In the purse there proved to be a sovereign and seven shillings. George put the money and the purse back again, and took up the note.

"You sly girl!" cried he, pretending to be serious. "To tell me you had no money! What special *cadeau* is this put by for? A gold chain for Meta?"

"That is not mine, George. It is old Dame Bond's. I told you about it, if you remember."

"I'll take this," said George, transferring the note to his pocket.

"Oh no, George; don't take that!" exclaimed Maria. "She may come for it at any hour. I promised to return it to her whenever she asked for it."

"My dear, you shall have it again. She won't come to-day."

"Why can you not get a note from the Bank instead of taking that?"

George made no answer. He turned into his bedroom. Maria thought nothing of the omission: she supposed his mind to be pre-occupied. In point of fact, she thought little of his taking the note. With coffers full (as she supposed) to turn to, borrowing a ten-pound note seemed an affair of no moment.

She sat on about ten minutes, hard at work. George remained in his bedroom, occupied (as it appeared to Maria) in opening and shutting various drawers. Somewhat curious as to what he could be doing, she at length rose from her seat and looked in. He was packing a large portmanteau.

"Are you going out, George?" she exclaimed in surprise.

"For a few days. Business is calling me to town. Look here, Maria. I shall take nothing with me, beyond my small black leather hand-case; but you can send this by one of the men to the station to-night. It must come after me."

"What a very sudden determination, George!" she cried. "You did not say anything about it this morning."

"I did not know then I should have to go. Don't look sad, child. I shan't be long away."

"It seems to me that you are always going away now, George," she observed, her tone as sad as her looks.

"Business must be attended to," responded George, shaking out a coat that he was about to fold. "I don't in the least covet going, I assure you, Maria."

What more she would have said, was interrupted by a noise. Some one had entered the sitting-room with much commotion. Maria returned to it, and saw Meta and Margery.

Meta had been the whole morning long in the hayfield. Not the particular hayfield already mentioned; that one was cleared of hay now; but to some other hayfield, whose cocks were in full bloom—if such an expression may be used in regard to hay. There were few things Miss Meta liked so much as a roll in the hay; and, so long as cocks were to be found in the neighbourhood, Margery would be coaxed over to take her to them. Margery did not particularly dislike it herself. Margery's rolling days were over; but, seated at the foot of one of the cocks, her knitting in hand, and the child in view, Margery found the time pass agreeably enough. As she had found it, this day: and the best proof of it was, that she stayed beyond her time. Miss Meta's dinner was waiting.

Miss Meta was probably aware of the fact by sundry inward warnings. She had gone flying into her mamma's sitting-room, tugging at the strings of her hat, which had got into a knot. Margery had flown in, almost as quickly; certainly in greater excitement.

"Is it true, ma'am?" she gasped out, the moment she saw Maria.

"Is what true?" inquired Maria.

"That the Bank has broke. When I saw the shutters up and the door barred, for all the world as if everybody in the house was dead, you might have knocked me down with a feather. There's quite a crowd round: and one of 'em told me the Bank had broke."

George came out of his bedroom. "Take this child to the nursery, and get her ready for her dinner," said he in the quick, decisive, haughty manner that he now and then used, though rarely to Margery.

Margery withdrew with the child, and George looked at his wife. She was standing in perplexity; half aghast, half in disbelief; and she turned her questioning eyes on George.

But for those words of Margery's, whose sound had penetrated to his bedroom, would he have said anything to Maria before his departure? It must remain a question. *Now* he had no resource left but to tell her.

"The fact is, Maria, we have had a run upon the Bank this morning; have been compelled to suspend payment. For the present," added George, vouchsafing to Maria the hopeful view of the case which his brother, in his ignorance, had taken.

She did not answer. She felt too much dismayed. Perhaps, in her mind's confusion, she could not yet distinctly understand. George placed her in a chair.

"How scared you look, child! There's no cause for that. Such things happen every day."

"George—George!" she reiterated, struggling as it were for utterance: "do you mean that the Bank has failed? I don't think I understand."

"For the present. Some cause or other, that we can none of us get to the bottom of, caused a run upon us to-day."

"A run? You mean that people all came together, wanting to withdraw their money?"

"Yes. We paid as long as our funds held out. And then we closed."

She burst into a distressing flood of tears. The shock, from unclouded prosperity—*she* had not known that that prosperity was fictitious—to ruin, to disgrace, was more than she could bear calmly. George felt vexed. It seemed as if the tears reproached him.

"For goodness' sake, Maria, don't go on like that," he testily cried. "It will blow over; it will be all right."

But he put his arm round her in spite of his hasty words. Maria leaned her face upon his bosom and sobbed out her tears upon it. He did not like the tears at all; he spoke quite crossly; and Maria did her best to hush them.

"What will be done?" she asked, choking down the rebellious sobs that rose in spite of her.

"Don't trouble yourself about that. I have been obliged to tell you, because it is a thing that cannot be concealed; but it will not affect your peace and comfort, I hope. There's no cause for tears."

"Will the Bank go on again?"

"Thomas has gone up to London, expecting to bring funds down. In that case it will open on Monday morning."

How could he tell it her? Knowing as he did know, and he alone, that through his deep-laid machinations, there were no longer funds available for the Bank or for Thomas Godolphin.

"Need you go to London," she asked in a wailing tone, "if Thomas has gone? I shall be left alone."

"I must go. There's no help for it."

"And which day shall you be back again? By Monday?"

"Not perhaps by Monday. Keep up your spirits, Maria. It will be all right."

Meta came bursting in. She was going down to dinner. Was mamma coming to luncheon?

No, mamma did not want any. Margery would attend to her. George picked up the child and carried her into his room. In his drawers he had found some trifling toy; brought home for Meta weeks ago, and forgotten to be given to her. It had lain there since. It was one of those renowned articles, rarer now than they once were, called Bobbing Joan. George had given sixpence for it. A lady, with a black head and neck, a round body, and no visible legs. He put it on the top of the drawers, touched it, and set it bobbing at Meta.

She was all delight; she stretched out her hands for it eagerly. But George, neglecting the toy, sat down on a chair, clasped the child in his arms, and showered upon her more passionately heartfelt embraces than perhaps he had ever given to living mortal, child or woman. He did not keep her: the last long lingering kiss was pressed upon her rosy lips, and he put her down, handed her the toy, and bade her run and show it to mamma.

Away she went; to mamma first, and then in search of Margery.

Maria went into the bedroom to her husband. He was locking his portmanteau.

"That is all, I believe," he said, transferring the keys to his pocket, and taking up the small hand-case. "Remember that it is sent off by to-night's train, Maria. I have addressed it."

"You are not going now, George?" she said, her heart seeming to fail her strangely.

"Yes, I am."

"But—there is no train. The express must have passed this half-hour."

"I shall ride over to Crancomb and take the train there," he answered. "I have some business in the place," added he, by way of stopping any questions as to the why and wherefore. "Listen, Maria. You need not mention that I have gone until you see Thomas on Monday morning. Tell *him*."

"Shall you not see him yourself in London?" she returned. "Are you not going to meet him?"

"I may miss him: it is just possible," was the reply of George, spoken with all the candour in life, just as though his mission to London was the express one of meeting his brother. "If Thomas should return home without having seen me, I mean."

"What am I to tell him?" she asked.

"Only that I am gone. There's no necessity to say anything else. I shall—if I miss seeing him in town—write to him here."

"And when shall you be back again?"

"Soon. Good-bye, my darling."

He held his wife folded in his arms, as he had recently held Meta. The tears were raining down her cheeks.

"Don't grieve, Maria. It will blow over, I say. God bless you. Take care of Meta."

Maria's heart felt as if it were breaking. But in the midst of her own distress, she remembered the claims of others. "That ten-pound note, George? If you are not back in a day or two, how shall I have it? The woman may come for it."

"Oh, I shall be back. Or you can ask Thomas."

In his careless indifference he thought he should be back before long. He was not going to *run away*: only to absent himself from the brunt of the explosion. That his delinquencies would be patent to Thomas and to others by Monday morning, he knew: it would be just as well to let some of their astonishment and anger evaporate without his presence; be far more agreeable to himself, personally. In his careless indifference, too, he had spoken the words, "You can ask Thomas." A moment's consideration would have told him that Thomas would have no ten-pound notes to spare for Maria. George Godolphin was one who never lost heart. He was indulging, now, the most extravagantly sanguine hopes of raising money in London, by some means or other. Perhaps Verrall could help him?

He strained his wife to his heart, kissed her again, and was gone. Maria sat down in the midst of her blinding tears.

Walking round to the stables, he waited there while his horse was got ready, mounted him, the small black case in front, and rode away alone. The groom thought his master was only going out for a ride, as he did on other days: but the man did wonder that Mr. George should go *that* day. Crancomb was a small place about five miles off : it had a railway station, and the ordinary trains stopped there. What motive induced him to go there to take the train, he best knew. Probably, he did not care to excite the observation and comment, which his going off from Prior's Ash on that day would be sure to excite. Seriously to fear being stopped, he did not.

He rode along at a leisurely pace, reaching Crancomb just before the up-train was expected. Evidently the day's great disaster had not yet travelled to Crancomb. George was received with all the tokens of respect, ever accorded to the Godolphins. He charged the landlord of the inn to send his horse back to Prior's Ash on Monday morning, changed Mrs. Bond's ten-pound note, and chatted familiarly to the employés at the station, after taking his ticket.

Up came the train. Two or three solitary passengers, bound for the place, descended, two or three entered. The whistle sounded ; the engine shrieked and puffed : and George Godolphin, nodding familiarly around with his gay smile, was carried on his road to London.

Maria had sat on, her blinding tears falling. What an alteration it was! What a contrast to the happiness of the morning ! That a few minutes should have power to bring forth so awful a change ! The work she had done so eagerly before, lay on the table. Where had its enjoyment gone? She turned from it now with a feeling not far removed from sickness. Nothing could be thought of but the great trouble which had fallen ; there was no further satisfaction to be derived from outward things. The work lay there, untouched ; destined, though she knew it not, never to have another stitch set in it by its mistress ; and she sat on and on, her hands clasped inertly before her, her brain throbbing with its uncertainty and its care.

CHAPTER XX.

MRS. BOND'S VISIT.

IN the old study at All Souls' Rectory—if you have not forgotten that modest room—in the midst of almost as much untidiness as used to characterize it when the little Hastingses were in their untidy ages, sat some of them in the summer's evening. Rose's drawings and fancy-work lay about ; Mrs. Hastings's more substantial sewing lay about ; and a good deal of litter besides out of Reginald's pocket ; not to speak of books belonging to the boys, fishing-tackle, and sundries.

Nothing was being touched, nothing used ; it all lay neglected, as Maria Godolphin's work had done, earlier in the afternoon. Mrs. Hastings sat in a listless attitude, her elbow on the old cloth cover of the table, her face turned to her children. Rose sat at the window ; Isaac and Reginald were standing by the mantel-piece ; and Grace, her bonnet thrown off on to the floor, her shawl unpinned and partially falling from her shoulders, half sat, half knelt at her mother's side, her face upturned to her, asking for particulars of the calamity. Grace had come running in only a few minutes ago, eager, anxious, and impulsive.

"Only think the state I have been in!" she cried. "But one servant in the house, and unable to leave baby to get down here! I——"

"What brings you with only one servant?" interrupted Rose.

"Ann's mother is ill, and I have let her go home until Monday morning. I wish you would not interrupt me with frivolous questions, Rose!" added Grace in her old, quick, sharp manner. "Any other day but Saturday, I would have left baby to Martha, and she might have put off her work, but on Saturdays there's always so much to do. I had half a mind to come and bring the baby myself. What should I care, if Prior's Ash did see me carrying him? But, mamma, you don't tell me—how has this dreadful thing been brought about?"

"*I* tell you, Grace!" returned Mrs. Hastings. "I should be glad to know, myself."

"There's a report going about—Tom picked it up somewhere and brought it home to me—that Mr. George Godolphin had been playing pranks with the Bank's money," continued Grace.

"Grace, my dear, were I you I would not repeat such a report," gravely observed Mrs. Hastings.

Grace shrugged her shoulders. George Godolphin had never been a favourite of hers, and never would be. "It may turn out to be true," said she.

"Then, my dear, it will be time enough for us to talk of it when it does. You are fortunate, Grace; you had no money there."

"I'm sure we had," answered Grace, more bluntly than politely. "We had thirty pounds there. And thirty pounds would be as much of a loss to us as thirty hundred to some."

"Tom Akeman must be getting on—to keep a banking account!" cried free Reginald.

Grace for a wonder, did not detect the irony: though she knew that Reginald had never liked Mr. Akeman: he had always told Grace she lowered herself by marrying an unknown architect.

"Seven hundred pounds were lodged in the Bank to his account when that chapel-of-ease was begun," she said, in answer to Reginald's remark. "He has drawn it all out, for wages and other things, except thirty pounds. And of course, that, if it *is* lost, will be our loss. Had the Bank stood until next week, there would have been another large sum paid in. Will it go on again, Isaac?"

"You may as well ask questions of a stranger, as ask them of me, Grace," was her brother Isaac's answer. "I cannot tell you anything certain."

"You won't, you mean," retorted Grace. "I suppose you clerks may not tell tales out of school. What sum has the Bank gone for, Isaac? That, surely, may be told."

"Not for any sum," was Isaac's answer. "The Bank has not 'gone' yet, in that sense. There was a run upon the Bank this morning, and the calls were so great that we had not enough money in the place to satisfy them, and were obliged to cease paying. It is said that the Bank will open again on Monday, when assistance shall have come; that business will be resumed, as usual. Mr. Godolphin himself said so: and he is not one to say a thing unless it has foundation. I know nothing more than that, Grace, whatever you may choose to infer."

"Do you mean to tell me that there are no suspicions in the Bank that something, more than the public yet knows, is amiss with George Godolphin?" persisted Grace.

Isaac answered lightly and evasively. He was aware that such suspicions were afloat with the clerks. Chiefly led to by that application from the stranger, and his rude and significant charges, made so publicly. Isaac had not been present at that application. It was somewhat curious, perhaps—for a freemasonry runs amidst the clerks of an establishment, and they talk freely one with another—that he never heard of it until after the stoppage of the firm. If he had heard of it, he would certainly have told his father. But whatever suspicions he and his fellow-clerks might be entertaining against George Godolphin, he was not going to speak of them to Grace Akeman.

Grace turned to her mother. "Papa has a thousand pounds or two there, has he not?"

"Ah, child! if that were all!" returned Mrs. Hastings, with a groan.

"Why? What more has he there?" asked Grace, startled by the words and the tone. Rose, startled also, turned round to await the answer.

Mrs. Hastings seemed to hesitate. But only for a moment. "I do not know why I should not tell you," she said, looking at her daughters. "Isaac and Reginald both know it. He had just lodged there the trust-money belonging to the Chisholms: nine thousand and forty-five pounds."

A silence fell upon the room. Grace and her sister were too dismayed to speak immediately. Reginald, who had now seated himself astride on a chair, his face and arms over the back of it, set up a soft lugubrious whistle, the tune of some old sea-song, feeling possibly the silence to be uncomfortable. To disclose a little secret, Mr. Reginald was not in the highest of spirits, having been subjected to some hard scolding that day on the part of his father, and some tears on the part of his mother, touching the non-existence of any personal effects. He had arrived at home, for the fourth time since his first departure for sea, baggageless, his luggage consisting exclusively of what he stood up in. Of everything else belonging to him, he was able to give no account whatever. It is rather a common complaint amongst young sailors. And then he was always changing his ships.

"Is papa responsible for it?" The half-frightened question came from Rose.

"Certainly he is," replied Mrs. Hastings. "If the Bank should *not* go on, why—we are ruined. As well as those poor children, the Chisholms."

"Oh, mamma! why did he not draw it out this morning?" cried Grace in a tone of pain. "Tom told me that many people were paid in full."

"Had he known the state the Bank was in, that there was anything the matter with it, no doubt he would have drawn it out," returned Mrs. Hastings.

"Did Maria know it was paid in?"

"Yes."

Grace's eyes flashed fire. Somehow, she was never inclined to be too considerate to Maria. She never had been from their earliest years. "A dutiful daughter! Not to give her father warning!"

"Maria may not have been able to do it," observed Mrs. Hastings. "Perhaps she did not know that anything was wrong."

"Nonsense, mamma!" was Grace's answer. "We have heard— when a thing like this happens, you know people begin to talk freely, to compare notes, as it were—we have heard that George Godolphin and Maria are owing money all over the town. Maria has not paid her housekeeping bills for ever so long. *Of course* she must have known what was coming!"

Mrs. Hastings did not dispute the point with Grace. The main fact troubled her too greatly for minor considerations to be very prominent with her yet. She had never found Maria other than a considerate and dutiful daughter: and she must be convinced that she had not been so in this instance, before she could believe it.

"She was afraid of compromising George Godolphin," continued Grace in a bitter tone. "He has ever been first and foremost with her."

"She might have given a warning without compromising him," returned Mrs. Hastings; but, in making the remark, she did not intend to cast any reflection on Maria. "When your papa went to pay the money in, it was after banking hours. Maria was alone, and he told her what he had brought. Had she been aware of anything wrong, she might have given a hint to him, then and there. It need never have been known to George Godolphin—even that your papa had any intention of paying money in."

"And this was recently?"

"Only a week or two ago."

Grace pushed her shawl more off her shoulders, and beat her knee up and down as she sat on the low stool. Suddenly she turned to Isaac.

"Had *you* no suspicion that anything was wrong?"

"Yes, a slight one," he incautiously answered. "A doubt, though, more than a suspicion."

Grace took up the admission warmly. "And you could hug the doubt slyly to yourself and never warn your father!" she indignantly uttered. "A fine son you are, Isaac Hastings!"

Isaac was of equable temperament. He did not retort on Grace that he *had* warned him, but that Mr. Hastings had not acted upon the hint; at least not effectually. "When my father blames me, it will be time enough for you to blame me, Grace," was all he said in answer. "And—in my opinion—it might be just as well if you waited to hear whether Maria deserves blame, before you cast so much on her."

"Pshaw!" returned Grace. "The thing speaks for itself."

Had Grace witnessed the bitter sorrow, the prostration, the uncertainty in which her sister was sunk at that moment, she might have been more charitable in her judgment. Practical and straightforward herself, it would have been as impossible for Grace to remain ignorant of her husband's affairs, pecuniary or else, as it was for her to believe that Maria Godolphin had remained so. And, if fully convinced that such had indeed been the fact, Grace would have deemed her state of contented ignorance to be little less than a crime. She and Maria were as essentially different as two people can well be. Pity but she could have seen Maria then!

Maria was in her dining-room. She had made a pretence of going down to dinner, not to excite the observation and remarks of the servants: in her excessive sensitiveness she could not bear that they should even see she was in grief. Grace, in her place, might have spoken openly and angrily before the household of the state of affairs. Not so Maria: she buried it all within her.

She could not eat. Toying with this plate and that plate, she knew not how to swallow a morsel or to make pretence of doing so, before the servants, standing by. But it came to an end, that dinner, and Maria was left alone.

She sat on, musing; her brain racked with busy thoughts. To one of the strangely refined organization of Maria Hastings, a blow, such as the one fallen, appeared more terrible even than it was. Of the *consequences* she as yet knew little, could foresee less; therefore they were not much glanced at by her: but of the disgrace Maria took an exaggerated view. Whether the Bank went on again or not, they seemed to have fallen from their high pedestal; and Maria shrank with a visible shudder at the bare thought of meeting her friends and acquaintances; at the idea of going out to show herself in the town.

Many would not have minded it; some would not have looked upon it in the light of a disgrace at all: minds and feelings, I say, are differently constituted. Take Mrs. Charlotte Pain, for example. Had she enjoyed the honour of being George Godolphin's wife, she would not have shed a tear, or eaten a meal the less, or abstained by so much as a single day from gladdening the eyes of Prior's Ash. Walking, riding, or driving, Charlotte would have shown herself as usual.

Pierce came in. And Maria lifted her head with a start, and made a pretence of looking up quite carelessly, lest the man should see how full of trouble she was.

"Here's that Mrs. Bond at the door, ma'am," he said. "I can't get rid of her. She declares that you gave her leave to call, and said that you would see her."

Maria seemed to grow hot and cold. That the woman had come for her ten-pound note, she felt convinced, induced to it, perhaps, by the misfortune of the day, and—she had it not to give her. Maria would have given a great deal for a ten-pound bank-note then.

"I will see her, Pierce," she said. "Let her come in."

Mrs. Bond, civil and sober to-night, came in, curtseying. Maria— ah, that sensitive heart!—felt quite meek and humbled before her; very different from what she would have felt had she had the money to refund. Mrs. Bond asked for it civilly.

"I am sorry that I cannot give it to you to-night," answered Maria. "I will send it to you in a day or two."

"You promised, ma'am, that I should have it whenever I axed," said she.

"I know I did," replied Maria. "If I had it in the house I would give it you now. You shall have it next week."

"Can I have it on Monday?" asked Mrs. Bond.

"Yes," answered Maria. "Shall I send it to you?"

"I'd not give you the trouble," said Mrs. Bond. "I'll make bold to step up again and get it, ma'am, on Monday."

"Very well," replied Maria. "If Miss Meta was here, she would ask after the parrot."

"It's beautiful," exclaimed Dame Bond. "It's tail's like a lovely green plume o' feathers. But I ain't got used to its screeching yet. Then I'll be here on Monday, ma'am, if you please."

Maria rang the bell, and Pierce escorted her to the door. To return again on Monday.

Maria Godolphin never deemed that she was not safe in making the promise. Thomas Godolphin would be home then, and she could get the note from him.

And she sat on alone, as before; her mind more troubled, her weary head upon her hand.

CHAPTER XXI.

A DREAD FEAR.

CAN you picture the sensations of Maria Godolphin during that night? No: not unless it has been your lot to pass through such. She went up to her bedroom at the usual time, not to excite any gossip in the household; she undressed mechanically; she went to bed. It had been much the custom with herself and George to sleep with the blinds up. They liked a light room; and a large gas-lamp in Crosse Street threw its full light in. Now, she lay with her eyes closed: not courting sleep; she knew that there would be no sleep for her, no continuous sleep, for many and many a night to come: now, she turned on her uneasy couch and lay with her eyes open: anything for a change in the monotonous hours. The dressing-table, its large glass, its costly ornaments, stood between the windows; she could trace its outlines, almost the pattern of its white lace drapery over the pink silk. The white window-curtains were looped up with pink; some of the pretty white chairs were finished off with pink beading. A large cheval-glass swung in a corner. On a console of white marble, its frettings of gilt, stood Maria's Prayer-book and Bible, with "Wilson's Supper and Sacra Privata:" a book she frequently opened for a few minutes in a morning. A small ornamental bookcase was on the opposite side, containing some choice works culled from the literature of the day. On the table, in the centre of the room, lay a small travelling-desk of George's, which he had left there when packing his things. All these familiar objects, with others, were perfectly visible to Maria's eyes; and yet she saw them not. If the thought intruded that this comfortable bedchamber might not much longer be hers, she did not dwell upon it. *That* phase of the misfortune had scarcely come to her. Her chief sensation was one of shivering cold: that nervous coldness which only those who have experienced intense dread or pain of mind, ever have felt. She shivered inwardly and outwardly—and she said perpetually, "When will the night be gone?" It was only the precursor of worse nights, many of them, in store for her.

Morning dawned at last. Maria watched in the daylight; and lay closing her eyes against the light until it was the usual time for rising. She got up, shivering still, and unrefreshed. Many a one might have slept through the night, just as usual, have risen renovated, have been none the worse, in short, in spirit or in health, for the blow which had fallen. Charlotte Pain might have slept all the better. *Il y a des femmes et des femmes.*

It was Sunday morning, and the church bells were giving token of it, as it is customary for them to do at eight o'clock. When Maria went down to breakfast, it was nearly nine. The sun was bright, and the breakfast-table, laid with its usual care in the pleasant dining-room, was bright also with its china and silver.

Something else looked bright. And that was Miss Meta. Miss Meta came in, following on her mamma's steps, and attended by Margery. Very bright in her Sunday attire. An embroidered white frock, its sleeves tied up with blue ribbons, and a blue sash. Careful Margery had put a large white pinafore over the whole, lest the frock should come to grief at breakfast. On Sunday mornings Meta was indulged with a seat at her papa and mamma's breakfast-table.

The child was a little bit of a gourmande, as it is in the nature of many children at that age to be. She liked nice things very much indeed. Bounding to the breakfast-table, she stood on tiptoe, her chin up, regarding what might be on it. Maria drew her to a chair apart, and sat down with the child on her knee, to take her morning kiss.

"Have you been a good girl, Meta? Have you said your prayers?"

"Yes," confidently answered Meta to both questions.

"She has said 'em after a fashion," cried Margery. "It's not much prayers that's got out of her on a Sunday morning, except hurried ones. I had to make her say the Lord's Prayer twice over, she gabbled it so. Her thoughts are fixed on coming down here; afraid breakfast should be eaten, I suppose."

Maria was in no mood for bestowing admonition. She stroked the child's fair golden curls fondly, and kissed her pretty lips.

"Where's papa?" asked Meta.

"He is out, dear. Don't you remember? Papa went out yesterday. He has not come home yet."

Meta drew a long face. Papa indulged her more than mamma did, especially in the matter of breakfast. Mamma was apt to say such and such a dainty was not good for Meta: papa helped her to it, whether good for her or not.

Maria put her down. "Place her at the table, Margery. It is cold this morning, is it not?" she added, as Meta was lifted on to a chair.

"Cold!" returned Margery. "Where can your feelings be, ma'am? It's a hot summer's day."

Maria sat down herself to the breakfast-table. Several letters lay before her. On a Sunday morning the letters were brought into the dining-room, and Pierce was in the habit of laying them before his master's place. To-day, he had laid them before Maria's.

She took them up. All, except three, were addressed to the firm. Two of these bore George's private address; the third was for Margery.

"Here is a letter for you, Margery," she said, putting the others down, that they might be carried into the Bank.

"For me!" returned Margery in surprise. "Are you sure, ma'am?"

Maria handed her the letter, and Margery, searching her pocket for her spectacles, opened it without ceremony, and stood reading it.

"I dare say! what else wouldn't they like!" was her ejaculatory remark.

"Is it from Scotland, Margery?" asked her mistress.

"It wouldn't be from nowhere else," answered Margery in vexation. "I have no other kin to pull and tug at me. They're going on to Wales, she and her son, and she wants me to meet her on the journey to-morrow, just for an hour's talk. Some people have consciences! Ride a matter of forty mile, and spend a sight o' money in doing it!"

"Are you speaking of your sister—Mrs. Bray?"

"More's the pity, I am," answered Margery. "Selina was always one of the weak ones, ma'am. She says she has been ill again, feels likely to die, and is going to Wales for some months to his friends, to try if the air will benefit her. She'd be ever grateful for a five-pound note, she adds, not having a penny-piece beyond what will take her to her journey's end. I wonder how much they have had from me in the whole, if it came to be put down!" wrathfully concluded Margery.

"You can have a day's holiday, you know, Margery, if you wish to meet her on the journey."

"I must take time to consider," shortly answered Margery, who was always considerably put out by these applications. "She has been nothing but a trouble to me, ma'am, ever since she married that ne'er-do-well Bray. Now, Miss Meta! you be a good child, and don't upset the whole cup of coffee over your pinafore, as you did last Sunday morning!"

The parting admonition was addressed to Meta, in conjunction with a slight shake administered to that young lady, under the pretence of resetting her on her chair. Meta was at once the idol and the torment of Margery's life. Margery withdrew, and Maria, casting her spiritless eyes on the breakfast-table, took a modest piece of dry toast, and put a morsel into her mouth.

But she found some difficulty in swallowing it. Throat and bread were alike dry. She drew the butter towards her, thinking it might help her to eat the toast. No; no. She could not swallow it any more than the other. The fault did not lie there.

"Would Meta like a nice piece of toast?" she asked.

Meta liked anything that was good in the shape of eatables. She nodded her head several times, by way of answer. And Maria spread the toast and passed it to her.

Breakfast came to an end. Maria took the child on her knee, read her a pretty Bible story, her daily custom after breakfast, talked to her a little, and then sent her to the nursery. She, Maria, sat on alone. She heard the bells ring out for service, but they did not ring for her. Maria Godolphin could no more have shown her face in church that day, than she could have committed some desperately wrong act.

Under the disgrace which had fallen upon them, it would have seemed, to her sensitive mind, something like an act of unblushing impudence. She gathered her books around her, and strove to make the best of them alone. Perhaps she had scarcely yet realized the great fact that God *can* be a comforter in the very darkest affliction. Maria's experience that way was yet limited.

She had told the servants that she would dine in the middle of the day with the child, as their master was out; and at half-past one she sat down to dinner, and made what pretence she could of eating a little. Better pretence than she had made in the morning, for the servants were present now. She took the wing of a fowl on her plate, and turned it about and managed to eat part of it. Meta made up for her: the young lady partook of the fowl and other things with great .relish, showing no sign that her appetite was failing, if her mamma's was.

Later, she was despatched for a walk with Margery, and Maria was once more alone. She felt to wish to run away from herself : the house seemed too large for her. She wandered from the dining-room to her sitting-room upstairs; from the sitting-room across the vestibule to the drawing-room. She paced its large proportions, her feet sinking into the rich velvet-pile carpet; she glanced at the handsome furniture. But she saw nothing : the sense of her eyes, that day, was buried within her.

She felt indescribably lonely : she felt a sense of desertion. No one called upon her, no one came near her : even her brother Reginald had not been. People were not much in the habit of calling on her on a Sunday; but their absence seemed like neglect, in her deep sorrow. Standing for a minute at one of the windows, and looking out mechanically, she saw Isaac pass.

He looked up, discerned her standing there, and nodded. A sudden impulse prompted Maria to make a sign to him to enter. Her brain was nearly wearied out with incertitude and perplexity. All day, all night, had she been wondering how far the calamity would fall; what would be its limit, what its extent. Isaac might be able to tell her something at present she was in complete ignorance of everything.

He came up the stairs swiftly, and entered. "Alone!" he said, shaking hands with her. " How are you to-day ? "

" Pretty well," answered Maria.

" You were not at church, Maria ? "

" No," she answered. " I did not go this morning."

A sort of constrained silence ensued. If Maria waited for Isaac to speak of yesterday's misfortune, she waited in vain. Of all people in the world, he would be least likely to speak of it to George Godolphin's wife. Maria must do it herself, if she wanted it done.

" Isaac, do you know whether the Bank will be open again to-morrow morning ? " she began, in a low tone.

" No, I do not."

" Do you *think* it will ? I wish you to tell me what you think," she added in a pointedly earnest tone.

" You should ask your husband for information, Maria. He must be far better able to give it to you than I."

She remembered that George had told her she need not mention his having left Prior's Ash until she saw Thomas Godolphin on Monday morning. Therefore she did not reply to Isaac that she could not ask George because he was absent. "Isaac, I wish *you* to tell me," she gravely rejoined. "Anything you know, or may think."

"I really know very little, Maria. Nothing, in fact, for certain. Prior's Ash is saying that the Bank will not open again. The report is that some message of an unfavourable nature was telegraphed down last night by Mr. Godolphin."

"Telegraphed to whom?" she asked eagerly.

"To Hurde. I cannot say whether there's any foundation for it. Old Hurde's as close as wax. No fear of his spreading it, if it has come; unless it lay in his business to do so. I walked out of church with him, but he did not say a syllable about it to me."

Maria sat a few minutes in silence. "If the Bank should not go on, Isaac—what then?"

"Why—then, of course it would not go on," was the very logical answer returned by Mr. Isaac.

"But what would be done, Isaac? How would it end?"

"Well—I suppose there'd be an official winding-up of affairs. Perhaps the Bank might be reopened afterwards on a smaller scale. I don't know."

"An official winding-up," repeated Maria, her sweet face turned earnestly on her brother's. "Do you mean bankruptcy?"

"Something of that sort."

A blank pause. "In bankruptcy, everything is sold, is it not? Would these things have to be sold?"—looking round upon the costly furniture.

"Things generally are sold in such a case," replied Isaac. "I don't know how it would be in this."

Evidently there was not much to be got out of Isaac. He either did not know, or he would not. Sitting a few minutes longer, he departed—afraid, possibly, how far Maria's questions might extend. Not long had he been gone, when boisterous steps were heard leaping up the stairs, and Reginald Hastings—noisy, impetuous Reginald—came in. He threw his arms round Maria, and kissed her heartily. Maria spoke reproachfully.

"At home since yesterday morning, and not have come to see me before!" she exclaimed.

"They wouldn't let me come yesterday," bluntly replied Reginald. "They thought you'd be all down in the mouth with this bother, and would not care to see folks. Another thing, I was in hot water with them."

A faint smile crossed Maria's lips. She could not remember the time when Reginald had *not* come home to plunge into hot water with the ruling powers at the Rectory. "What was the matter?" she asked.

"Well, it was the old grievance about my bringing home no traps. Things do melt on a voyage somehow—and what with one outlet and another for your pay, it's of no use trying to keep square. I left the ship, too, and came back in another. I say, where's Meta? Gone out? I should have come here as soon as dinner was over, only Rose kept me. I am going to Grace's to tea. How is George Godolphin? He is out, too?"

"He is well," replied Maria, passing over the other question. "What stay shall you make at home, Reginald?"

"Not long, if I know it. There's a fellow in London looking out for a ship for me. I thought to go up and pass for second mate, but I don't suppose I shall now. It's as gloomy as ditch-water this time at home. They are all regularly cut up about the business here. Will the Bank go on again, Maria?"

"I don't know anything about it, Reginald. I wish I did know."

"I say, Maria," added the thoughtless fellow, lowering his voice, "there's no truth, I suppose, in what Prior's Ash is saying about George Godolphin?"

"What is Prior's Ash saying?" returned Maria.

"Ugly things," answered Reginald. "I heard something about—about swindling."

"About swindling!"

"Swindling, or forgery, or some queer thing of that sort. I wouldn't listen to it."

Maria grew cold. "Tell me what you heard, Reginald—as well as you can remember," she said, her unnatural calmness deceiving Reginald, and cloaking all too well her mental agony.

"Tales are going about that there's something wrong with George. That he has not been doing things on the square. A bankruptcy's not much, they say, except to the creditors; it can be got over: but if there's anything worse—why, the question is, will he get over it?"

Maria's heart beat on as if it would burst its bounds: her blood was fiercely coursing through her veins. A few moments of struggle, and then she spoke, still with unnatural calmness.

"It is not likely, Reginald, that such a thing could be true."

"Of course it is not," said Reginald, with impetuous indignation. "If I had thought it was true, I should not have asked you about it, Maria. Why, that class of people have to stand in a dock and be tried, and get imprisoned, and transported, and all the rest of it! That's just like Prior's Ash! If it gets hold of the story to-day that I have come home without my sea-chest, to-morrow it will be saying that I have come home without my head. George Godolphin's a jolly good fellow, and I hope he'll turn round on the lot. Many a time he has helped me out of a hole that I didn't dare tell any one else of; and I wish he may come triumphantly out of this!"

Reginald talked on, but Maria heard him not. An awful fear had been aroused within her. Entire as was her trust in her husband's honour, improbable as the uncertain accusation was, the terrible fear that something or other might be wrong took possession of her, and turned her heart to sickness.

"I bought Meta a stuffed monkey out there," continued Reginald, jerking his head to indicate some remote quarter of his travels. "I thought you'd not like me to bring home a live one for her—even if the skipper had allowed it to come in the ship. I came across a stuffed one cheap, and bought it."

Maria roused herself to smile. "Have you brought it to Prior's Ash?"

"Well—no," confessed Reginald, coming down a tone or two. "The fact is, it went with the rest of my things. I'll get her something better next voyage. And now I'm off, Maria, for Grace's tea will be ready. Remember me to George Godolphin. I'll come in and see him to-morrow."

With a commotion, equal to that he had made in ascending, Reginald clattered down, and Maria saw him and his not too good sailor's jacket go swaying up the street towards her sister's. It was the only jacket of any sort Mr. Reginald possessed: and the only one he was likely to possess, until he could learn to keep himself and his clothes in better order.

Maria, with the new fear at her heart—which, strive as she might to thrust it indignantly from her, to ignore it, to reason herself out of it, *would* continue to be a fear, and a very horrible one—remained alone for the rest of the day. Just before bedtime, Margery came to her.

"I have been turning it over in my mind, ma'am, and have come to the conclusion that it might be as well if I do go to meet my sister. She's always on the groan, it's true: but maybe she *is* bad, and we might never have a chance of seeing each other again. So I think I'll go."

"Very well," said Maria. "Harriet can attend to the child. What time in the morning must you be away, Margery?"

"By half-past six out of here," answered Margery. "The train goes five minutes before seven. Could you let me have a little money, please, ma'am? I suppose I must give her a pound or two."

Maria felt startled at the request. How was she to comply with it? "I have no money, Margery," said she, her heart beating. "At least, I have very little. Too little to be of much use to you."

"Then that stops it," returned Margery with her abrupt freedom. "It's of no good for me to think of going without money."

"Have you none by you?" asked Maria. "It is a pity you must be away before the Bank opens in the morning."

Before the Bank opens! Was it spoken in thoughtlessness? Or did she merely mean to indicate the hour of Thomas Godolphin's arrival?

"What I have by me isn't much," said Margery. "A few shillings or so. It might take me there and bring me back again: but Selina will look glum if I don't give her something."

In Maria's purse there remained the sovereign and seven shillings which George had seen there. She gave the sovereign to Margery, who could, if she chose, give it to her sister. Maria suggested that more could be sent to her by post-office order. Margery's savings, what the Brays had spared of them, and a small legacy left her by her former mistress, Mrs. Godolphin, were in George's hands. Would she ever see them? It was a question to be solved.

To her bed again to pass another night such as the last. As the last? Had this night been only as the last, it might have been more calmly borne. The coldness, the sleeplessness, the trouble and pain would have been there; but not the sharp agony, the awful dread she scarcely knew of what, arising from the incautious words of Reginald.

It is only by comparison that we can form a true estimate of what is bad, what good. María Godolphin would have said the night before, that it was impossible for any to be worse than that : *now* she looked back upon it, and envied it by comparison. There had been the sense of the humiliation, the disgrace arising from an unfortunate commercial crisis in their affairs; but the worse dread which had come to her now was not so much as dreamt of. Shivering as one in mortal coldness, lay Maria, her brain alone burning, her mouth dry, her throat parched. When, oh when would the night be gone !

Far more unrefreshed did she arise this morning than on the previous one. The day was beautiful; the morning hot : but Maria seemed to shiver as with ague. Margery had gone on her journey, and Harriet, a maid who waited on Maria, attended to the child. Of course, with Margery away, Miss Meta ran riot in having her own will. She chose to breakfast with her mamma : and her mamma, who saw no particular objection, was not in spirits to oppose it.

She was seated at the table opposite Maria, revelling in coffee and good things, instead of plain bread and milk. A pretty picture, with her golden hair, her soft face, and her flushed cheeks. She wore a delicate pink frock and a white pinafore, the sleeves tied up with a light mauve-coloured ribbon, and her pretty little hands and arms were never still above the table. In the midst of her own enjoyment it appeared that she found leisure to observe that her mamma was taking nothing.

" Mamma, why don't you eat some breakfast ? "

" I am not hungry, Meta."

" There's Uncle Thomas ! " she resumed.

Uncle Thomas ! At half-past eight ? But Meta was right. That was Mr. Godolphin's voice in the hall, speaking to Pierce. A gleam of something like sunshine darted into Maria's heart. His early arrival seemed to whisper of a hope that the Bank would be reopened—though Maria could not have told whence she drew the deduction.

She heard him go into the Bank. But, ere many minutes elapsed, he had come out again, and was knocking at the door of the breakfast-room.

" Come in."

He came in : and a grievous sinking fell upon Maria's heart as she looked at him. In his pale, sad countenance, bearing too evidently the traces of acute mental suffering, she read a death-blow to her hopes. Rising, she held out her hand, without speaking.

" Uncle Thomas, I'm having breakfast here," put in a little intruding voice. " I'm having coffee and egg."

Thomas laid his hand for a moment on the child's head as he passed her. He took a seat a little away from the table, facing Maria, who turned to him.

" Pierce tells me that George is not here."

" He went to London on Saturday afternoon," said Maria. " Did you not see him there ? "

" No," replied Thomas, speaking very gravely.

" He bade me tell you this morning that he had gone—in case he did not see you himself in town."

"Why has he gone? For what purpose?"

"I do not know," answered Maria. "That was all he said to me."

Thomas had his earnest dark-grey eyes fixed upon her. Their expression did not tend to lessen the sickness at Maria's heart. "What address has he left?"

"He gave me none," replied Maria. "I inferred from what he seemed to intimate that he would be very soon home again. I can scarcely remember what it was he really did say, his departure was so hurried. I knew nothing of it until he had packed his trunk. He said he was going to town on business, and that I was to tell you so on Monday morning."

"What trunk did he take?"

"The large one."

"Then he must be thinking of staying some time."

It was the thought which had several times occurred to Maria. "The trunk was addressed to the railway terminus in London, I remember," she said. "He did not take it with him. It was sent up by the night train."

"Then, in point of fact, you can give me no information about him: except this?"

"No," she answered, feeling, she could hardly tell why, rather ashamed of having to make the confession. But it was no fault of hers. Thomas Godolphin rose to retire.

"I'm having breakfast with mamma, Uncle Thomas!" persisted the little busy tongue. "Margery's gone for all day. Perhaps I shall have dinner with mamma."

"Hush, Meta!" said Maria, speaking in a sadly subdued manner, as if the chatter, intruding upon their seriousness, were more than she could bear. "Thomas, is the Bank going on again? Will it be opened to-day?"

"It will never go on again," was Thomas Godolphin's answer: and Maria shrank from the lively pain of the tone in which the words were spoken.

There was a blank pause. Maria became conscious that Thomas had turned, and was looking gravely, it may be said searchingly, at her face.

"You have known nothing, I presume, Maria, of—of the state that affairs were getting into? You were not in George's confidence?"

She returned the gaze with honest openness, something like wonder shining forth from her soft brown eyes. "I have known nothing," she answered. "George never spoke to me upon business matters: he never would speak to me upon them."

No; Thomas felt sure that he had not. He was turning again to leave the room, when Maria, her voice a timid one, a delicate blush rising to her cheeks, asked if she could have some money.

"I have none to give you, Maria."

"I expect Mrs. Bond here for her ten-pound note. I don t know what I shall do, unless I can have it to give her. George told me I could have it from you this morning."

Thomas Godolphin did not understand. Maria explained. About her having taken care of the note, and that George had borrowed it on

Saturday. Thomas shook his head. He was very sorry, he said, but he could do nothing in it.

"It is not like an ordinary debt," Maria ventured to urge. "It was the woman's own money, intrusted to me for safe keeping on the understanding that she should claim it whenever she pleased. I should be so much obliged to you to let me have it."

"You do not understand me, Maria. It is no want of will on my part. I have not the money."

Maria's colour was gradually receding from her face, leaving in its place something that looked like terror. She would have wished to pour forth question after question—Has all our money gone? Are we quite ruined? Has George done anything very wrong?—but she did not. In her refined sensitiveness she had not the courage to put such questions to Thomas Godolphin: perhaps she had not the courage yet to encounter the probable answers.

Thomas left the room, saying no more. He would not pain her by speaking of the utter ruin which had come upon them, the *disgraceful* ruin; of the awful trouble looming upon them, in which she must be a sufferer equally with himself; perhaps she the greatest sufferer. Time enough for it. Maria sat down in her place again, a dull mist before her eyes, sorrow in her heart.

"Mamma, I've eaten my egg. I want some of that."

Meta's finger was stretched towards the ham at the foot of the table. Maria rose mechanically to cut her some. There was no saying this morning, "That is not good for Meta." Her heart was utterly bowed down beyond resistance, or thought of it. She placed some ham on a plate, cut it into small pieces, and laid it before that eager young lady.

"Mamma, I should like some buttered roll."

The roll was supplied also. What would not Maria have supplied, if asked for? All these commonplace trifles appeared so pitiably insignificant beside the dreadful trouble come upon them.

"A little more sugar, please, mamma."

Before any answer could be given to this latter demand, either in word or action, a tremendous summons at the hall-door resounded through the house. Maria shrank from its sound. A fear, she knew not of what, had taken up its abode within her, some strange, undefined dread, connected with her husband.

Her poor heart need not have beaten so; her breath need not have been held, her ears strained to listen. Pierce threw open the dining-room door, and there rushed in a lady, all demonstrative sympathy and eagerness. A lady in a handsome light Cashmere shawl, which spread itself over her dress and nearly covered it, and a straw hat, with an upright scarlet plume.

It was Charlotte Pain. She seized Maria's hand and impulsively asked what she could do for her. "I knew it would be so!" she volubly exclaimed—"that you'd be looking like a ghost. That's the worst of you, Mrs. George Godolphin! You let any trifle worry you. The moment I got the letters in this morning, and found how badly things were turning out for your husband, I said to myself, 'There'll be Mrs. George in the dumps!' And I flung this shawl on to cover my toilette, for I was not *en grande tenue*, and came off to cheer you, and see if I could be of any use."

Charlotte flung her shawl *off* as she spoke, ignoring ceremony. She had taken the chair vacated by Thomas Godolphin, and with a dexterous movement of the hands, the shawl fell behind her, disclosing the "toilette." A washed-out muslin skirt of no particular colour, tumbled, and a little torn; and some strange-looking thing above it, neither jacket nor body, of a bright yellow, the whole dirty and stained.

"You are very kind," answered Maria, with a shrinking spirit and a voice that faltered. Two points in Mrs. Pain's words had struck upon her ominously. The mention of the letters, and the hint conveyed in the expression, things turning out "badly" for George. "Have you heard from him?" she continued.

"Heard from him!—how could I?" returned Charlotte. "London letters don't come in this morning. What should he have to write to me about, either? I have heard from another quarter, and I have heard the rumours in Prior's Ash."

"Will you tell me what you have heard?" rejoined Maria.

"Well," said Charlotte in a friendly tone, as she leaned towards her, "I suppose the docket will be struck to-day—if it is not struck already. The Philistines are down on the house, and mean to declare it bankrupt."

Maria sat in blank dismay. She understood very little of the details of these business matters. Charlotte was quite at home in such things. "What will be the proceedings?" Maria asked, after a pause. "What do they do?"

"Oh, there's a world of bother," returned Charlotte. "It will drive quiet Thomas Godolphin crazy. The books have all to be gone through, and accounts of moneys rendered. The worst is, they'll come here and note down every individual thing in the house, and then put a man in to see that nothing's moved. That agreeable item in the business I dare say you may expect this morning."

Let us give Charlotte her due. She had really come in a sympathizing, friendly spirit to Maria Godolphin, and in no other. It may be, that Charlotte rather despised her for being so simple and childish in the ways of the world, but that was only the more reason why she should help her if she could. Every word of information that Mrs. Pain was giving was as a dagger thrust in Maria's heart. Charlotte had no suspicion of this. Had a similar calamity happened to herself, she would have discussed it freely with all the world: possessing no extreme sensibility of feeling, she did not understand it in another. For Maria to talk of the misfortune, let its aspect be ever so bad, seemed to Charlotte perfectly natural.

Charlotte leaned closer to Maria, and spoke in a whisper. "Is there anything you'd like to put away?"

"To put away?" repeated Maria, not awake to the drift of the argument.

"Because you had better give it to me at once. Spoons, or plate of any sort, or your own jewellery; any little things that you may want to save. I'll carry them away under my shawl. Don't you understand me?" she added, seeing the blank perplexity on Maria's face. "If once those harpies of men come in, you can't move or hide a single article, but you might put the whole house away now, if you could get it out."

"But suppose it were known?" asked Maria.

"Then there'd be a row," was Charlotte's candid answer. "Who's to know it? Look at that greedy little monkey?"

Meaning Miss Meta, who was filling her mouth quickly with the pieces of ham and the buttered roll, seemingly with great relish.

"Is it good, child?" said Charlotte.

For answer, Meta nodded her head, too busy to speak. Maria, as in civility bound, invited her visitor to take some breakfast.

"I don't care if I do," said Charlotte. "I was just going to breakfast when I came off to you. Look here, Mrs. George Godolphin, I'll help myself: you go meanwhile and make up a few parcels for me. Just what you set most value by, you know."

"I should be afraid," answered Maria.

"What is there to be afraid of?" asked Charlotte, opening her eyes. "They'll be safe enough at the Folly. That is Lady Godolphin's : her private property. The bankruptcy can't touch that; as it will this place and Ashlydyat. For the matter of that, I'd swear they were mine with all the pleasure in life, if they did get seen."

"Ashlydyat!" broke from Maria's lips.

"Ashlydyat will have to go of course, and everything in it. At the same time that those harpies walk in here, another set will walk into Ashlydyat. I should like to see Janet's face when they arrive! You make haste, and put up all you can. There may be no time to lose."

"I do not think it would be right," debated Maria.

"Stuff and nonsense about 'right!' such things are done every day. I dare say you have many little valuables that you had rather keep than lose."

"I have many that it would be a great grief to me to lose."

"Well, go and put them together. I will take every care of them, and return them to you when the affair has blown over."

Maria hesitated. To her honourable mind, there appeared to be something like fraud in attempting such a thing. "Will you allow me just to ask Thomas Godolphin if I may do it?" she said.

Charlotte Pain began to think that Maria must be an idiot. "Ask Thomas Godolphin! You *would* get an answer! Why, Mrs. George, you know what Thomas Godolphin is—with his strait-laced principles! He would cut himself in two, rather than save a button, if it was not legally his to save. I believe that if by the stroke of a pen he could make it appear that Ashlydyat could not be touched, he wouldn't make the stroke. Were you to go with such a question to Thomas Godolphin, he'd order you, in his brother's name, not to put aside as much as a ten-and-sixpenny ring. You must do it without the knowledge of Thomas Godolphin."

"Then I think I would rather not do it," said Maria. "Thank you all the same, Mrs. Pain."

Mrs. Pain shrugged her shoulders with a movement of contempt, threw off her hat, and drew her chair to the breakfast-table. Maria poured out some coffee, and helped her to what she chose to take.

"Are you sure—the people you speak of will be in the house to-day?" asked Maria.

"I suppose they will."

"I wish George would come back?" involuntarily broke from Maria's lips.

"He'd be a great simpleton if he did," said Charlotte. "He's safer where he is."

"Safer from what?" quickly asked Maria.

"From bother. I should not come if I were George. I should let them fight the battle out without me. Mrs. George Godolphin," added Charlotte, meaning to be good-natured, "you had better reconsider your resolve and let me save you a few things. Not a stick or stone will be left to you. This will be a dreadful failure, and you won't be spared. They'll take every trinket you possess, leaving you nothing but your wedding-ring."

Maria could not be persuaded. She seemed altogether in a fog, understanding little : but she felt that what Charlotte proposed would not be within the strict rules of right.

"They'll poke their noses into drawers and boxes, into every hole and corner in the house ; and from that time forth the things are not yours, but theirs," persisted Charlotte, for her information.

"I cannot help it," sighed Maria. "I wish George was here!"

"At any rate, you'll do one thing," said Charlotte. "You'll let me carry off the child for the day. It will not be a pleasant sight for her, young as she is, to witness a lot of great hulking men going through the rooms, marking down the furniture. I'll take her back with me."

Maria made no immediate reply. She did not particularly like the companionship of Mrs. Pain for Meta. Charlotte saw her hesitation.

"Are you thinking she will be a trouble? Nothing of the sort. I shall be glad to have her for the day, and it is as well to spare her such sights. I am sure her papa would say so."

Maria thought he would, and she thought how kind Mrs. Pain was. Charlotte turned to Meta.

"Will Meta come and spend the day at Lady Godolphin's Folly?— and have a high swing made between the trees, and go out in the carriage in the afternoon, and buy sugar-plums?"

Meta looked dubious, and honoured Mrs. Pain with a full stare in the face. Notwithstanding the swing and the sugar-plums—both very great attractions indeed to Meta—certain reminiscences of her last visit to the Folly were intruding themselves.

"Are the dogs there?" asked she.

Charlotte gave a most decided shake of the head. "The dogs are gone," she said. "They were naughty dogs to Meta, and they have been shut up in the pit-hole, and can never come out again."

"Never, never?" inquired Meta, her wide-open eyes as earnest as her tone.

"Never," said Charlotte. "The great big pit-hole lid's fastened down with a strong brass chain : a chain as thick as Meta's arm. It is all right," added Charlotte in an aside whisper to Maria, while pretending to reach over the breakfast-table for an egg-spoon. "She shan't as much as hear the dogs. I'll have them shut up in the stable. We'll have such a beautiful swing, Meta!"

Meta finished the remainder of her breakfast and slid off her chair. Reassured upon the subject of the dogs, she was eager to be off at once to the pleasures of the swing. Maria rang the bell for Harriet, and gave orders that she should be dressed.

"Let her come in this frock," said Charlotte. "There's no knowing what damage it may undergo before the day's out."

Meta was taken away by Harriet. Charlotte finished her breakfast, and Maria sat burying her load of care, even from the eyes of friendly Charlotte. "Do you like my Garibaldi shirt?" suddenly asked the latter.

"Like what?" questioned Maria, not catching the name.

"This," replied Charlotte, indicating the yellow article by a touch. "They are new things just come up: Garibaldi shirts they are called. Mrs. Verrall sent me three down from London: a yellow, a scarlet, and a blue. They are all the rage, she says. Do you admire it?"

But for Maria's innate politeness, and perhaps for the sadness beating at her heart, she would have answered that she did not admire it at all: that it looked a shapeless, untidy thing. Charlotte continued, without waiting for a reply.

"You don't see it to advantage. It is soiled, and has lost a button or two. Those dogs make horrid work of my things, with their roughness and their dirty paws. Look at this great rent in my gown which I have pinned up! Pluto did that this morning. He is getting fearfully savage, now he's old."

"You must not allow them to frighten Meta," said Maria somewhat anxiously. "She should not see them."

"I have told you she shall not. Can't you trust me? The dogs——"

Charlotte paused. Meta came running in, ready; in her large straw hat with its flapping brim, and her cool brown-holland outdoor dress. Charlotte rose, drew her shawl about her shoulders, and carried her hat to the glass, to settle it on. Then she took Meta by the hand, said good morning, and sailed out; the effect of her visit having been partly to frighten, partly to perplex, Maria.

Maria sat on with her load of care, and her new apprehensions. These agreeable visitors that Charlotte warned her of—she wondered that Thomas had not mentioned it. Would they take all the clothes she had upstairs, leaving her only what she stood upright in? Would they take Meta's? Would they take her husband's out of his drawers and places? Would they take the keeper off her finger? It was studded with diamonds. Charlotte had said they would only leave her her wedding-ring. These thoughts were troubling and perplexing her; but only in a degree. Compared with that other terrible thought, they were as nothing—the uncertain fear, regarding her husband, which had been whispered to her by the careless sailor, Reginald Hastings.

CHAPTER XXII.

BEARING THE BRUNT.

THOMAS GODOLPHIN sat in the Bank parlour, bearing the brunt of the shock. With his pain upon him, mental and bodily, he was facing all the trouble that George ought to have faced: the murmurs, the questions, the reproaches.

All was known. All was known to Thomas Godolphin. Not alone to him. Could Thomas have kept the terrible facts within his own breast, have shielded his brother's reputation still, he would have done it : but that was impossible. In becoming known to Mr. Godolphin, it had become known to others. The discovery had been made jointly, by Thomas and by certain business gentlemen, when he was in London on the Saturday afternoon. Treachery upon treachery! The long course of deceit on George Godolphin's part had come out. Falsified books ; wrongly-rendered accounts ; good securities replaced by false ; false balance-sheets. Had Thomas Godolphin been less blindly trustful in George's honour and integrity, it could never have been so effectually accomplished. George Godolphin was the acting manager : and Thomas, in his perfect trust, combined with his failing health, had left things latterly almost entirely in George's hands. "What business had he so to leave them ?" People were asking it now. Perhaps Thomas's own conscience was asking the same. But why should he not have left things to him, considering that he placed in him the most implicit confidence? Surely, no unprejudiced man would say Thomas Godolphin had been guilty of imprudence. George was fully equal to the business confided to him, in point of power and capacity ; and it could not certainly matter which of the brothers, equal partners, equal heads of the firm, took its practical management. It would seem not : and yet they were blaming Thomas Godolphin now.

Failures of this nature have been recorded before, where fraud has played its part. We have only to look to the records of our law courts—criminal, bankruptcy, and civil—for examples. To transcribe the precise means by which George Godolphin had contrived to bear on in a course of deceit, to elude the suspicion of the world in general, and the vigilance of his own house, would only be to recapitulate what has often been told in the public records : and told to so much more purpose than I could tell it. It is rather with what may be called the domestic phase of these tragedies that I would deal : the private, home details ; the awful wreck of peace, of happiness, caused *there*. The world knows enough (rather too much, sometimes) of the public part of these affairs ; but what does it know of the part behind the curtain?— the, if it may be so said, inner aspect?

I knew a gentleman, years ago, who was partner in a country banking-house : a sleeping partner ; and the Bank failed. Failed through a long-continued course of treachery on the part of one connected with it—something like the treachery described to you as pur-

sued by Mr. George Godolphin. This gentleman (of whom I tell you)
was to be held responsible for the losses, so the creditors and others
decided: the real delinquent having disappeared, escaped beyond their
reach. They lavished upon this gentleman harsh names; rogue, thief,
swindler, and so on!—while, in point of fact, he was as innocent and
unconscious of what had happened as they were. He gave up all he
had; the bulk of his fortune had gone with the Bank; and he went out
of hearing of his abusers for a while until things should become
smoother; perhaps the bad man be caught. A short time, and he
became ill; and a medical man was called in to him. Again, a short
time, and he was *dead*: and the doctors said—I heard them say it—
that his malady had been brought on by grief; that he had, in fact,
died of a broken heart. He was a kindly gentleman; a good husband,
a good father, a good neighbour; a single-hearted, honest man; the
very soul of honour: but he was misjudged by those who ought to
have known him better; and he died for it. I wonder what the real
rogue felt when he heard of the death? They were relatives. There
are many such cases in the world: where reproach and abuse are
levelled at one whose heart is breaking.

There appeared to be little doubt that George Godolphin's embar-
rassments had commenced years ago. It is more than probable that
the money borrowed from Verrall during that short sojourn in Homburg
had been its precursor. Once in the hands of the clever charlatan, the
crafty, unscrupulous bill-discounter, who grew fat on the folly of others,
his downward course was—perhaps not easy or swift, but at all events
certain. If George Godolphin had but been a little more clear-sighted,
the evil might never have come. Could he but have seen Verrall at
the outset as he was: not the gentleman, the good-hearted man, as
George credulously believed, but the low fellow who traded on the
needs of others, the designing sharper, looking ever after his prey,
George would have flung him off with no other feeling than contempt.
George Godolphin was not born a rogue. George was by nature a
gentleman, and honest and open; but, once in the clutches of Verrall,
he was not able to escape.

Bit by bit, step by step, gradually, imperceptibly, George found himself caught. He awoke to the fact that he could neither stir upwards
nor downwards. He could not extricate himself; he could not go on
without exposure; Verrall, or Verrall's agents, those working in con-
cert with him, though not ostensibly, stopped the supplies, and George
was in a fix. Then began the frauds upon the Bank. Slightly at first.
It was only a choice between that and exposure. Between that and
ruin, it may be said, for George's liabilities were so great, that, if
brought to a climax, they must then have caused the Bank to stop,
involving Thomas in ruin as well as himself. In his sanguine temperament, too, he was always hoping that some lucky turn would redeem
the bad and bring all right again. It was Verrall who urged him on.
It was Verrall who, with Machiavellian craft, made the wrong appear
right; it was Verrall who had filled his pockets at the expense of
George's. That Verrall had been the arch-tempter, and George the
arch-dupe, was clear as the sun at noonday to those who were behind
the scenes. Unfortunately but very few were behind the scenes—they

might be counted by units—and Verrall and Co. could still blazon it before the world.

The wonder was, where the money had gone to. It very often is the wonder in these cases. A wonder too often never solved. An awful amount of money had gone in some way; the mystery was, in what way. George Godolphin had kept up a large establishment; had been personally extravagant, privately as well as publicly; but that did not serve to account for half the money missing; not for a quarter of it; nay, scarcely for a tithe. Had it been to save himself from hanging, George himself could not have told how or where it had gone. When the awful sum total came to be added up, to stare him in the face, he looked at it in blank amazement. And he had no good to show for it; none; the money had melted, and he could not tell how.

Of course it had gone to the discounters. The tide of discounting once set in, it was something like the nails in the horseshoe, doubling, and doubling, and doubling. The money went, and there was nothing to show for it. Little marvel that George Godolphin stood aghast at the sum total, when the amount was raked up—or, as nearly the amount as could be guessed at. When George could no longer furnish legitimate funds on his own account, the Bank was laid under contribution to supply them, and George had to enter upon a system of ingenuity to conceal the outgoings. When those contributions had been levied to the very utmost extent compatible with the avoidance of sudden and immediate discovery, and George was at his wits' end for money, which he *must* have, then Verrall whispered a way which George at first revolted from, but which resulted in taking the deeds of Lord Averil. Had the crash not come as it did, other deeds might have been taken. It is impossible to say. Such a course once entered on is always downhill. Like unto some other downward courses, the only safety lies in not yielding to the first temptation.

Strange to say, George Godolphin could not see the rogue's part played by Verrall: or at best he saw it but very imperfectly. And yet, not strange; for there are many of these cases in the world. George had been on intimate terms of friendship with Verrall; had been *lié*, it may be said, with him and Lady Godolphin's Folly. Mrs. Verrall was pretty. Charlotte had her attractions. Altogether, George believed yet in Verrall. Let the dagger's point only be concealed with flowers, and men will rush blindly on to it.

Thomas Godolphin sat, some books before him, pondering the one weighty question—where could all the money have gone to? Until the present moment, this morning when he had the books before him, and his thoughts were more practically directed to business details, he had been pondering another weighty question—where had George's integrity gone to? Whither had flown his pride in his fair name, the honour of the Godolphins? From the Saturday afternoon when the dreadful truth came to light, Thomas had had little else in his thoughts. It was his companion through the Sunday, through the night journey afterwards down to Prior's Ash. He was more fit for bed than to take that journey: but he must face the exasperated men from whom George had flown.

He was facing them now. People had been coming in since nine o'clock with their reproaches, and Thomas Godolphin bore them patiently and answered them meekly : the tones of his voice low, subdued, as if they came from the sadness of a stricken heart. He felt their wrongs keenly. Could he have paid these injured men by cutting himself to pieces, and satisfied them with the "pound of flesh," he would have done so, oh how willingly ! He would have sacrificed his life and his happiness (his happiness !) and done it cheerfully, if by that means they could have been paid their due.

"It's nothing but a downright swindle. I'll say it, sir, to your face, and I can't help saying it. Here I bring the two thousand pounds in my hand, and I say to Mr. George Godolphin, 'Will it be safe ?' 'Yes,' he answers me, 'it will be safe.' And now the Bank has shut up, and where's my money?"

The speaker was Barnaby, the corn-dealer. What was Thomas Godolphin to answer ?

"You told me, sir, on Saturday, that the Bank would open again to-day for business ; that customers would be paid in full."

"I told you but what I believed," rose the quiet voice of Thomas Godolphin in answer. "Mr. Barnaby, believe me this blow has come upon no one more unexpectedly than it has upon me."

"Well, sir, I don't know what may be your mode of carrying on business, but I should be ashamed to conduct mine so as to let ruin come slap upon me, and not have seen it coming."

Again, what was Thomas Godolphin to answer? Generous to the end, he would not say, "My brother has played us both alike false." "If I find that any care or caution of mine could have averted this, Mr. Barnaby, I shall carry remorse to my grave," was all he replied.

"What sort of a dividend will there be ?" went on the dealer.

"I really cannot tell you yet, Mr. Barnaby. I have no idea. We must have time to go through the books."

"Where *is* Mr. George Godolphin?" resumed the applicant ; and it was a very natural question. "Mr. Hurde says he is away, but it is strange that he should be away at such a time as this. I should like to ask him a question or two."

"He is in London," replied Thomas Godolphin.

"But what's he gone to London for now? And when is he coming back ?"

More puzzling questions. Thomas had to bear the pain of many such that day. He did not say, "My brother is gone, we know not why; in point of fact he has run away." He spoke aloud the faint hopes that rose within his own breast—that some train, ere the day was over, would bring him back to Prior's Ash.

"Don't you care, Mr. Godolphin," came the next wailing plaint, "for the ruin that the loss of this money will bring upon me? I have a wife and children, sir."

"I do care," Thomas answered, his throat husky and a mist before his eyes. "For every pang that this calamity will inflict on others, it inflicts two on me."

Mr. Hurde, who was busy with more books in his own department, in conjunction with some clerks, came in to ask a question, his pen behind his ear ; and Mr. Barnaby, seeing no good to be derived by remaining, went out. Little respite had Thomas Godolphin. The next to come in was the Rector of All Souls'.

"What is to become of me?" was his saluting question, spoken in his clear, decisive tone. "How am I to refund this money to my wards, the Chisholms?"

Thomas Godolphin had no satisfactory reply to make. He missed the friendly hand held out hitherto in greeting. Mr. Hastings did not take a chair, but stood up near the table, firm, stern, and uncompromising.

"I hear George is off," he continued.

"He has gone to London, Maria informs me," replied Thomas Godolphin.

"Mr. Godolphin, can you sit there and tell me that you had no suspicion of the way things were turning? That this ruin has come on, and you ignorant of it?"

"I had no suspicion; none whatever. None can be more utterly surprised than I. There are moments when a feeling comes over me that it cannot be true."

"Could you live in intimate association with your brother, and not see that he was turning out a rogue and a vagabond?" went on the Rector in his keenest and most cynical tone.

"I knew nothing, I suspected nothing," was the quiet reply of Thomas.

"How *dared* he take that money from me the other night, when he knew that he was on the verge of ruin?" asked Mr. Hastings. "He took it from me; he never entered it in the books; he applied it, there's no doubt, to his own infamous purposes. When a suspicion was whispered to me afterwards, that the Bank was wrong, I came here to him. I candidly spoke of what I had heard, and asked him to return me the money, as a friend, a relative. Did he return it? No: his answer was a false, plausible assurance that the money and the Bank were alike safe. What does he call it? Robbery? It is worse: it is deceit; fraud; vile swindling. In the old days, many a man has swung for less, Mr. Godolphin."

Thomas Godolphin could not gainsay it.

"Nine thousand and forty-five pounds!" continued the Rector. "How am I to make it good? How am I to find money only for the education of Chisholm's children? He confided them and their money to me; and how have I repaid the trust?"

Every word he spoke was as a dagger entering the heart of Thomas Godolphin. He could only sit still, and bear. Had the malady that was carrying him to the grave never before shown itself, the days of anguish he had now entered upon would have been sufficient to induce it.

"If I find that Maria knew of this, that she was in league with her husband to deceive me, I shall feel inclined to discard her from my affections from henceforth," resumed the indignant Rector. "It was an unlucky day when I gave my consent to her marrying George Godolphin. I never in my heart liked his addressing her. It must have been instinct warned me against it."

"I am convinced that Maria has known nothing," said Thomas Godolphin. "She——"

Mr. Godolphin stopped. Angry sounds had arisen outside, and presently the door was violently opened, and quite a crowd of clamorous people entered, ready to abuse Thomas Godolphin, George not being there to receive it. There was no question but that that day's work took weeks from his short remaining span of life. Could a man's heart break summarily, Thomas Godolphin's would have broken then. Many men would have retaliated: *he* felt their griefs, their wrongs, as keenly as they did. They told him of their ruin, of the desolation, the misery it would bring to them, to their wives and families; some spoke in a respectful tone of quiet plaint, some were loud, unreasonable, insulting. They demanded what dividend there would be : some asked in a covert tone to have *their* bit of money returned in full; some gave vent to most unorthodox language touching George Godolphin; they openly expressed their opinion that Thomas was conniving at his absence; they hinted that he was as culpable as the other.

None of them appeared to glance at the great fact—that Thomas Godolphin was the greatest sufferer of all. If they had lost part of their means, he had lost all his. Did they remember that this terrible misfortune, which they were blaming him for, would leave him a beggar upon the face of the earth? He, a gentleman born to wealth, to Ashlydyat, to a position of standing in the county, to honour, to respect? It had all been rent away by the blow, to leave him homeless and penniless, sick with an incurable malady. Had they only reflected, they might have found that Thomas Godolphin deserved their condolence rather than their abuse.

But they were in no mood to reflect, or to spare him in their angry feelings; they gave vent to all the soreness within them—and perhaps it was excusable.

The Rector of All Souls' had had his say, and strode forth. Making his way to the dining-room, he knocked sharply with his stick on the door, and then entered. Maria rose and came forward : something very like terror on her face. The knock had frightened her : it had conjured up visions of the visitors suggested by Mrs. Charlotte Pain.

"Where is George Godolphin?"

"He is in London, papa," she answered, her heart sinking at the stern tone, the abrupt greeting.

"When do you expect him home?"

"I do not know. He did not tell me when he went; except that he should be home soon. Will you not sit down, papa?"

"No. When I brought that money here the other night, the nine thousand and forty-five pounds," he continued, touching her arm to command her full attention, "could you not have opened your lips to tell me that it would be safer in my own house than in this?"

Maria was seized with inward trembling. She could not bear to be spoken to in that stern tone by her father. "Papa, I could not tell you. I did not know it."

"Do you mean to tell me that you knew nothing—*nothing*—of the state of your husband's affairs? of the ruin that was impending?"

"I knew nothing," she answered. "Until the Bank closed on Saturday, I was in total ignorance that anything was wrong. I never had the remotest suspicion of it."

"Then, I think, Maria, you ought to have had it. Rumour says that you owe a great deal of money in the town for your personal necessities, housekeeping and the like."

"There is a good deal owing, I fear," she answered. "George has not given me money to pay regularly of late, as he used to do."

"And did *that* not serve to open your eyes?"

"No," she faintly said. "I never gave a thought to anything being wrong."

She spoke meekly, softly, just as Thomas Godolphin had spoken. The Rector looked at her pale, sad face, and perhaps a sensation or pity for his daughter came over him, however bitterly he may have felt towards her husband.

"Well, it is a terrible thing for us all," he said in a more kindly voice, as he turned to move away.

"Will you not wait, and sit down, papa?"

"I have not the time now. Good day, Maria."

As he went out, there stood, gathered close against the wall, waiting to go in, Mrs. Bond. Her face was rather red this morning, and a perfume—certainly not of plain waters—might be detected in her vicinity. That snuffy black gown of hers went down in a reverence as he passed. The Rector of All Souls' strode on. Care was too great at his heart to allow of his paying attention to extraneous things, even though they appeared in the shape of attractive Mrs. Bond.

Maria Godolphin, her face buried on the sofa cushions, was giving way to the full tide of unhappy thought induced by her father's words, when she became aware that she was not alone. A sound, half a groan, half a sob, coming from the door, aroused her. There stood a lady, in a crushed bonnet and unwholesome stuff gown that had once been black, with a red face, and a perfume of strong waters around her.

Maria rose from the sofa, her heart sinking. How should she meet this woman? how find an excuse for the money which she had not to give? "Good morning, Mrs. Bond."

Mrs. Bond took a few steps forward, and held on by the table. Not that she was past the power of keeping herself upright; her face must be redder than it was, by some degrees, ere she lost that; but she had a knack of holding on to things.

"I have come for my ten-pound note, if you please, ma'am."

Few can imagine what this moment was to Maria Godolphin; for few are endowed with the sensitiveness of temperament, the refined consideration for the feelings of others, the acute sense of justice, which characterized her. Maria would willingly have given a hundred pounds to have had ten then. How she made the revelation, she scarcely knew—that she had not the money that morning to give.

Mrs. Bond's face turned rather defiant. "You told me to come down for it, ma'am."

"I thought I could have given it to you. I am very sorry. I must trouble you to come when Mr. George Godolphin shall have returned home."

"Is he going to return?" asked Mrs. Bond in a quick, hard tone. "Folks is saying that he isn't."

Maria's heart beat painfully at the words. *Was* he going to return? She could only say aloud that she hoped he would very soon be home.

"But I want my money," resumed Mrs. Bond, standing her ground. "I must have it, ma'am, if you please."

"I have not got it," said Maria. "The very instant I have it, it shall be returned to you."

"I'd make bold to ask, ma'am, what right you had to spend it? Warn't there enough money in the Bank of other folks's as you might have took, without taking mine—which you had promised to keep faithful for me?" reiterated Mrs. Bond, warming with her subject. "I warn't a deposit in the Bank, as them folks was, and I'd no right to have my money took. I want to pay my rent to-day, and to get in a bit o' food. The house is bare of everything. There's the parrot screeching out for seed."

It is of no use to pursue the interview. Mrs. Bond grew bolder and more abusive. But for having partaken rather freely of that cordial which was giving out its scent upon the atmosphere, she had never so spoken to her clergyman's daughter. Maria received it meekly, her heart aching: she felt very much as did Thomas Godolphin—that she had *earned* the reproaches. But endurance has its limits : she began to feel really ill; and she saw, besides, that Mrs. Bond appeared to have no intention of departing. Escaping out of the room in the midst of a fiery speech, she encountered Pierce, who was crossing the hall.

"Go into the dining-room, Pierce," she whispered, "and try to get rid of Mrs. Bond. She is not quite herself this morning, and—and— she talks too much. But be kind and civil to her, Pierce : let there be no disturbance."

Her pale face, as she spoke, was lifted to the butler almost pleadingly. He thought how wan and ill his mistress looked. "I'll manage it, ma'am," he said, turning to the dining-room.

By what process Pierce did manage it, was best known to himself. There was certainly no disturbance. A little talking, and Maria thought she heard the sound of something liquid being poured into a glass near the sideboard, as she stood out of view behind the turning at the back of the hall. Then Pierce and Mrs. Bond issued forth, the best friends imaginable, the latter talking amiably.

Maria came out of her hiding-place, but only to encounter some one who had pushed in at the hall-door as Mrs. Bond left it. A little man in a white neckcloth. He advanced to Mrs. George Godolphin.

"Can I speak a word to you, ma'am, if you please?" he asked, taking off his hat.

She could only answer in the affirmative, and she led the way to the dining-room. She wondered who he was : his face seemed familiar to her. The first words he spoke told her, and she remembered him as the head assistant at the linendraper's where she chiefly dealt. He had been sent to press for payment of the account. She could only tell him as she had told Mrs. Bond—that she was unable to pay it.

"Mr. Jones would be so very much obliged to you, ma'am," he civilly urged. "It has been standing now some little time, and he hopes you will stretch a point to pay him. If you could only give me part of it, he would be glad."

"I have not got it to give," said Maria, telling the truth in her unhappiness. She could only be candid: she was unable to fence with them, to use subterfuge, as others might have done. She spoke the truth, and she spoke it meekly. When Mr. George Godolphin came home, she hoped she should pay them, she said. The messenger took the answer, losing none of his respectful manner, and departed.

But all were not so civil; and many found their way to her that day. Once a thought came across her to send them into the Bank: but she remembered Thomas Godolphin's failing health, and the battle he had to fight on his own account. Besides, these claims were for personalities—debts owed by herself and George. In the afternoon, Pierce came in and said a lady wished to see her.

"Who is it?" asked Maria.

Pierce did not know. She was not a visitor of the house. She gave in her name as Mrs. Harding.

The applicant came in. Maria recognized her, when she threw back her veil, as the wife of Harding, the undertaker. Pierce closed the door, and they were left together.

"I have taken the liberty of calling, Mrs. George Godolphin, to ask if you will not pay our account," began the applicant in a low, confidential tone. "Do pray let us have it, if you can, ma'am!"

Maria was surprised. There was nothing owing that she was aware of. There could be nothing. "What account are you speaking of?" she asked.

"The account for the interment of the child. Your little one who died last, ma'am."

"But surely that is paid!"

"No, it is not," replied Mrs. Harding. "The other accounts were paid, but that never has been. Mr. George Godolphin has promised it times and again: but he never paid it."

Not paid! The burial of their child! Maria's face flushed. Was it carelessness on George's part, or had he been so long embarrassed for money that to part with it was a trouble to him? Maria could not help thinking that he might have spared some little remnant for just debts, while lavishing so much upon bill-discounters. She could not help feeling another thing—that it was George's place to be meeting and battling with these unhappy claims, rather than hers.

"This must be paid, of course, Mrs. Harding," she said. "I had no idea that it was not paid. When Mr. George Godolphin comes home, I will ask him to see about it instantly."

"Ma'am, can't you pay me *now*?" urged Mrs. Harding. "If it waits till the bankruptcy's declared, it will have to go into it; and they say—they do say that there'll be nothing for anybody. We can't afford to lose it," she added, speaking confidentially. "What with bad debts and long-standing accounts, we are on the eve of a crisis ourselves; though I should not like it to be known. This will help to stave it off, if you will let us have it."

"I wish I could," returned Maria. "I wish I had it to give to you. It ought to have been paid long ago."

"A part of it was money paid out of our pocket," said Mrs. Harding reproachfully. "Mrs. George Godolphin, you don't know the boon it would be to us!"

"I would give it you, indeed I would, if I had it," was all Maria could answer.

She could not say more if Mrs. Harding stopped until night. Mrs. Harding became at last convinced of that truth, and took her departure. Maria sat down with burning eyes; eyes into which the tears would not come.

What with one hint and another, she had grown tolerably conversant with the facts patent to the world. One whisper startled her more than any other. It concerned Lord Averil's bonds. What was amiss with them? That there was something, and something bad, appeared only too evident. In her terrible state of suspense, of uncertainty, she determined to inquire of Thomas Godolphin.

Writing a few words on a slip of paper, she sent it into the Bank parlour. It was a request that he would see her before he left. Thomas sent back a verbal message: "Very well."

It was growing late in the evening before he came to her. What a day he had had! and he had taken no refreshment; nothing to sustain him. Maria thought of that, and spoke.

"Let me get you something," she said. "Will you take some dinner here, instead of waiting to get to Ashlydyat?"

He shook his head in token of refusal. "It is not much dinner that I shall eat anywhere to-day, Maria. Did you wish to speak to me?"

"I want—to—ask——" she seemed to gasp for breath, and waited a moment for greater calmness. "Thomas," she began again, going close to him, and speaking almost in a whisper, "what is it that is being said about Lord Averil's bonds?"

Thomas Godolphin did not immediately reply. He may have been deliberating whether it would be well to tell her; perhaps whether it *could* be kept from her. Maria seemed to answer the thought.

"I must inevitably know it," she said, striving not to tremble outwardly as well as inwardly. "Better that I hear it from you than from others."

He thought she was right—the knowledge must inevitably come to her. "It may be better to tell you, Maria," he said. "George used the bonds for his own purposes."

A dread pause. Maria's throat was working. "Then—it must have been he who took them from the strong-room!"

"It was."

The shivering came on palpably now. "What will be the consequences?" she breathed.

"I do not know. I dread to think. Lord Averil may institute a prosecution."

Their eyes met. Maria controlled her emotion, with the desperate energy of despair. "A—criminal—prosecution?"

"It is in his power to do it. He has not been near me to-day, and that looks unfavourable."

"Does he know it yet—that it was George?"

"He must know it. In fact, I think it likely he may have received official notice of it from town. The report has spread from thence—and that is how it has become known in Prior's Ash."

Maria moistened her dry lips, and swallowed down the lump in her throat ere she could speak. "Would it be safe for him to return here?"

"If he does return, it must be at the risk of consequences."

"Thomas!—Thomas!" she gasped, the thought occurring to her with a sort of shock, "is he in hiding, do you think?"

"I think it likely that he is. He gave you no address, it seems: neither has he sent one to me."

She drew back to the wall by the mantel-piece, and leaned against it. Every hour seemed to bring forth worse and worse. Thomas gazed with compassion on the haggardness that was seating itself on her sweet face. She was less able to cope with this misery than he. He laid his hand upon her shoulder, speaking in low tones.

"It is a fiery trial for both of us, Maria: one hard to encounter. God alone can help us to bear it. Be very sure that He will help!"

He went out, taking his way on foot to Ashlydyat. There was greater grief there, if possible, than at the Bank. The news touching the bonds, unhappily afloat in Prior's Ash, had penetrated an hour ago to Ashlydyat.

Scarcely had he entered the presence of his sisters, when he was told that Lady Sarah Grame wanted him.

Thomas Godolphin proceeded to the room where she had been shown. She was not sitting, but pacing it to and fro; and she turned sharply round and met him as he entered, her face flushed with excitement.

"You were once to have been my son-in-law," she said abruptly. Thomas, astonished at the address, invited her to a seat, but made no immediate reply. She would not take the chair.

"I cannot sit," she said. "Mr. Godolphin, you were to have been my son-in-law: you would have been so now had Ethel lived. Do you consider Ethel to be any link between us still?"

He was quite at a loss what to answer. He did not understand what she meant. Lady Sarah continued.

"If you do; if you retain any fond remembrance of Ethel; you will prove it now. I had seven hundred pounds in your Bank. I have been scraping and saving out of my poor yearly income nearly ever since Ethel went; and I had placed it there. Can you deny it?"

"Dear Lady Sarah, what is the matter?" he asked; for her excitement was something frightful. "I know you had it there. Why should I deny it?"

"Oh, that's right. People have been saying the Bank was going to repudiate all claims. I want you to give it me. Now: privately."

"It is impossible for me to do so, Lady Sarah——"

"I cannot lose it; I have been saving it up for my poor child," she interrupted, in a most excited tone. "She will not have much when I am dead. Would you be so cruel as to rob the widow and the orphan?"

"Not willingly. Never willingly," he answered in his pain. "I had thought, Lady Sarah, that though all the world misjudged me, you would not."

"Could you not, you who were to have married Ethel, have given me a private hint of it when you found the Bank was going wrong? Others may afford to lose their money, but I cannot."

"I did not know it was going wrong," he said. "The blow has fallen upon me as unexpectedly as it has upon others."

Lady Sarah Grame, giving vent to one of the fits of passionate excitement to which she had all her life been subject, suddenly flung herself upon her knees before Thomas Godolphin. She implored him to return the money, to avert "ruin" from Sarah Anne; she reproached him with selfishness, with dishonesty, all in a breath. Can you imagine what it was for Thomas Godolphin to meet this? Upright, gifted with lively conscientiousness, tenderly considerate in rendering strict justice to others, as he had been all his life, these unmerited reproaches were as iron entering his soul.

Which was the more to be pitied, himself or Maria? Thomas had called the calamity by its right name—a fiery trial. It was indeed such: to him and to her. You, who read, cannot picture it. How he got rid of Lady Sarah, he could scarcely tell: he believed it was by her passion spending itself out. She was completely beside herself that night, almost as one who verges on insanity, and Thomas found a moment to ask himself whether that uncontrolled woman could be the mother of gentle Ethel. Her loud voice and its reproaches penetrated to the household—an additional drop of bitterness in the cup of the master of Ashlydyat.

But we must go back to Maria, for it is with her this evening that we have most to do. Between seven and eight o'clock Miss Meta arrived, attended by Charlotte Pain. Meta was in the height of glee. She was laden with toys and sweetmeats; she carried a doll as big as herself: she had been out in the carriage; she had had a ride on Mrs. Pain's brown horse, held on by that lady; she had swung "above the tops of the trees;" and, more than all, a message had come from the keeper of the dogs in the pit-hole, to say that they were never, never coming out again.

Charlotte had been generously kind to the child; that was evident; and Maria thanked her with her eyes and heart. As to saying much in words, that was beyond Maria to-night.

"Where's Margery?" asked Meta, in a hurry to show off her treasures.

Margery had not returned. And there was no other train now from the direction in which she had gone. It was supposed that she had missed it, and would be home in the morning. Meta drew a long face; she wanted Margery to admire the doll.

"You can go and show it to Harriet, dear," said Maria. "She is in the nursery." And Meta flew away, with the doll and as many other encumbrances as she could carry.

"Have those bankruptcy men been here?" asked Charlotte, glancing round the room.

"No. I have seen nothing of them."

"Well now, there's time yet, and do for goodness' sake let me save some few trifles for you; and don't fret yourself into fiddle-strings," heartily returned Charlotte. "I am quite sure you must have some treasures that it would be grief to part with. I have been thinking all day long how foolishly scrupulous you are."

Maria was silent for a minute. "They look into everything, you say?" she asked.

"*Look* into everything!" echoed Charlotte. "I should think they do! That would be little. They take everything."

Maria left the room and came back with a parcel in her hand. It was a very small trunk—dolls' trunks they are sometimes called—covered with red morocco leather, with a miniature lock.

"I would save this," she said in a whisper, "if you would be so kind as to take care of it for me. I should not like them to look into it. It cannot be any fraud," she added, in a sort of apology for what she was doing. "The things inside would not sell for sixpence, so I do not think even Mr. Godolphin would be angry with me."

Charlotte nodded, took up her dress, and contrived to thrust the trunk into a huge pocket under her crinoline. There was another on the other side. "I put them on on purpose," she said, alluding to the pockets. "I thought you might think better of it by this evening. But this is nothing, Mrs. George Godolphin. You may as well give me something else. They'll be in to-morrow morning for certain."

Maria replied that she had nothing else to give, and Charlotte rose, saying she should come or send for Meta again on the morrow. As she went out, and proceeded up Crosse Street on her way home, she tossed her head with a laugh.

"I thought she'd come to! As if she wouldn't like to save her jewels, as other people do! She's only rather more sly over it—saying what she has given me would not fetch sixpence! You may tell that to the geese, Mrs. George Godolphin! I should like to see what's inside. I think I will."

And Charlotte put her wish into action. Upon reaching Lady Godolphin's Folly, she flung off her bonnet and mantle, gathered together all the small keys in the house, and had little difficulty in opening the simple lock. The contents were exposed to view. A lock of hair of each of her children who had died, wrapped in separate pieces of paper, with the age of the child and the date of its death written respectively outside. A golden lock of Meta's; a fair curl of George's; half a dozen of his letters to her, written in the short time that intervened between their engagement and their marriage; and a sort of memorandum of their engagement. "I was this day engaged to George Godolphin. I pray God to render me worthy of him! to be to him a loving and dutiful wife."

Charlotte's eyes opened to their utmost width, but there was nothing else to see; nothing except the printed paper with which the trunk was lined. "*Is* she a fool, that Maria Godolphin?" ejaculated Charlotte. Certainly that was not the class of things Mrs. Pain would have saved from bankruptcy. And she solaced her feelings by reading Mr. George's love-letters.

No, Maria was not a fool. Better that she had come under that denomination just now, for she would have felt her position less keenly.

Charlotte perhaps might have found it difficult to believe that Maria Godolphin was one of those who are sensitively intellectual, to a degree that Mistress Charlotte herself could form little notion of.

It is upon these highly-endowed natures that sorrow tells. And the sorrow must be borne in silence. In the midst of her great misery, so great as to be almost irrepressible, Maria contrived to maintain a calm exterior to the world, even to Charlotte and her outspoken sympathy. The first tears that had been wrung from her she shed that night over Meta. When the child came to her for her good-night kiss, and to say her prayers, Maria was utterly unhinged. She clasped the little thing to her heart and burst into a storm of sobs.

Meta was frightened.

Mamma! mamma! What was the matter with mamma?

Maria was unable to answer. The sobs were choking her. Was the child's inheritance to be that of shame? Maria had grieved bitterly when her other children died: she was now feeling that it might have been a mercy had this dear one also been taken. She covered the little face with kisses as she held it against her beating heart. Presently she grew calm enough to speak.

" Mamma's not well this evening, darling."

Once more, as on the previous nights, Maria had to drag herself up to her weary bed. As she fell upon her knees by the bedside, she seemed to pray almost against faith and hope. " Father! all things are possible to Thee. Be with me in Thy mercy this night, and help me to pass through it! "

She saw not how she could pass through it. " Oh! when will the night be gone?" broke incessantly from her bruised heart. Bitterly cold, as before, was she; a chilly, trembling sensation was in every limb; but her head and brain seemed burning, her lips were dry, and that painful nervous affection, the result of excessive anguish, was attacking her throat. Maria had never yet experienced that, and thought she was about to be visited by same strange malady. It was a dreadful night of pain, of apprehension, of *cold;* inwardly and outwardly she trembled as she lay through it. One terrible word kept beating its sound on the room's stillness—*transportation.* Was her husband in danger of it? Just before daylight she dropped asleep, and for half an hour slept heavily; but with the full dawn of day she was awake again. Not for the first minute was she conscious of reality; but, the next, the full tide of recollection had burst upon her. With a low cry of despair, she leaped from her bed, and began pacing the carpet, all but unable to support the surging waves of mental anguish which rose up one by one and threatened to overmaster her reason. Insanity, had it come on, might have been then more of a relief than a calamity to Maria Godolphin.

" How shall I live through the day? how shall I live through the day?" were the words that broke from her lips. And she fell down by the bedside, and lifted her hands and her heart on high, and wailed out a cry to God to help her to get through it. Of her own strength, she truly believed that she could not.

She would certainly have need of some help, if she were to bear it patiently. At seven o'clock, a peal of muffled bells burst over the town, deafening her ears. Some *mauvais sujets*, discontented sufferers, had gone to the belfry of St. Mark's Church, and set them ringing for the calamity which had overtaken Prior's Ash, in the stoppage of the House of Godolphin.

CHAPTER XXIII.

"AS FINE AS A QUEEN!"

" Is Mrs. George Godolphin within ? "

The inquiry came from Grace Akeman. She put it in a sharp, angry tone, something like the sharp, angry peal she had just rung at the hall-bell. Pierce answered in the affirmative, and showed her in.

The house seemed gloomy and still, as one in a state of bankruptcy does seem. Mrs. Akeman thought so as she crossed the hall. The days had gone on to the Thursday, the bankruptcy had been declared, and those pleasant visitors, foretold by Charlotte Pain, had entered on their duties at the Bank and at Ashlydyat. Fearfully ill looked Maria : dark circles had formed under her eyes, her face had lost its bloom, and an expression as of some ever-present dread had seated itself upon her features. When Pierce opened the door to usher in her sister, she started palpably.

Things, with regard to George Godolphin, remained as they were. He had not made his appearance at Prior's Ash, and Thomas did not know where to write to him. *Maria did.* She had heard from him on the Tuesday morning. His letter was written apparently in the gayest of spirits. The contrast that was presented between his state of mind (if the tone of the letter might be trusted) and Maria's was something marvellous. A curiosity in metaphysics, as pertaining to the spiritual organization of humanity. He sent gay messages to Meta, he sent teasing ones to Margery, he never so much as hinted to Maria that he had a knowledge of anything being wrong. He should soon be home, he said ; but meanwhile Maria was to write him word all news, and address the letter under cover to Mr. Verrall. But she was not to give that address to any one. George Godolphin knew he could rely upon the good faith of his wife. He wrote also to his brother : a letter which Thomas burnt as soon as read. Probably it was intended for his eye alone. But he expressed no wish to hear from Thomas ; neither did he say how a letter might reach him. He may have felt himself in the light of a guilty schoolboy, who knows he merits a lecture, and would escape from it as long as possible. Maria's suspense was almost unbearable—and Lord Averil had given no sign of what his intentions might be.

Seeing it was her sister who entered, she turned to her with a sort of relief. " Oh, Grace ! " she said, " I thought I was never going to see any of you again."

Grace would not meet the offered hand. Never much given to ceremony, she often came in and went out without giving hers. But this time Grace had come in anger. She blamed Maria for what had occurred, almost as much as she blamed George. Not of the highly refined organization that Maria was, Grace possessed far keener penetration. Had her husband been going wrong, Grace would inevitably have discovered it; and she could not believe but that Maria must have suspected George Godolphin. In her angry feeling against George, whom she had never liked, Grace would have deemed it right that Maria should denounce him. Whether she had been wilfully blind, or really blind, Grace alike despised her for it. "I shall not spare her," Grace said to her husband: and she did not mean to spare her, now she had come.

"I have intruded here to ask if you will go to the Rectory and see mamma," Grace began. "She is not well, and cannot come to you."

Grace's manner was strangely cold and stern. And Maria did not like the word "intruded." "I am glad to see you," she replied in a gentle voice. "It is very dull here, now. No one has been near me, except Bessy Godolphin."

"You cannot expect many visitors," said Grace in her hard manner —very hard to-day.

"I do not think I could see them if they came," was Maria's answer. "I was not speaking of visitors. Is mamma ill?"

"Yes, she is; and little wonder," replied Grace. "I almost wish I was not married, now this misfortune has fallen upon us: it would at any rate be another pair of hands at the Rectory, and I am more capable of work than mamma or Rose. But I am married; and of course my place must be my husband's home."

"What do you mean by another pair of hands, Grace?"

"There are going to be changes at the Rectory," returned Grace, staring at the wall behind Maria, apparently to avoid looking at her. "One servant only is to be retained, and the two little Chisholm girls are coming there to be kept and educated. Mamma will have all the care upon her; she and Rose must both work and teach. Papa will keep the little boy at school, and have him home in the holidays, to make more trouble at the Rectory. They, papa and mamma, will have to pinch and screw; they must deprive themselves of every comfort; bare necessaries alone must be theirs; and, all that can be saved from their income will be put by towards paying the trust-money."

"Is this decided?" asked Maria in a low tone.

"It is decided so far as papa can decide anything," sharply rejoined Grace. "If the law is put in force against him, by his co-trustee, for the recovery of the money, he does not know what he would do. Possibly the living would have to be sequestered."

Maria did not speak. What Grace was saying was all too true and terrible. Grace flung up her hand with a passionate movement.

"Had I been the one to bring this upon my father and mother, Maria, I should wish I had been out of the world before it had come to pass."

"I did not bring it upon them, Grace," was Maria's scarcely-breathed answer.

"Yes, you did. Maria, I have come here to speak my mind, and I must speak it. I may seem hard, but I can't help it. How could you, for shame, let papa pay in that money, the nine thousand pounds? If you and George Godolphin must have flaunted your state and your expense in the eyes of the world, and ruined people to do it, you might have spared your father and mother."

"Grace, why do you blame *me*?"

Mrs. Akeman rose from her chair, and began pacing the room. She did not speak in a loud tone; not so much in an angry one, as in a clear, sharp, decisive one. It was just the tone used by the Rector of All Souls' when in his cynical moods.

"He has been a respected man all his life; he has kept up his position——"

"Of whom do you speak?" interrupted Maria, really not sure whether she was applying the words satirically to George Godolphin.

"Of whom do I speak!" retorted Grace. "Of your father and mine. I say he has been respected all his life; has maintained his position as a clergyman and a gentleman, has reared his children suitably, has exercised moderate hospitality at the Rectory, and yet was putting something by that we might have a few pounds each, at his death, to help us on in the world. Not one of his children but wants helping on: except the grand wife of Mr. George Godolphin."

"Grace! Grace!"

"And what have you brought him to?" continued Grace, lifting her hand in token that she would have out her say. "To poverty in his old age—he is getting old, Maria—to trouble, to care, to privation: perhaps to disgrace as a false trustee. *I* would have sacrificed my husband, rather than my father."

Maria lifted her aching head. The reproaches were cruel, and yet they told home. It *was* her husband who had ruined her father: and it may be said, ruined him deliberately. Grace resumed, answering the last thought almost as if she had divined it.

"If ever a shameless fraud was committed upon another, George Godolphin wilfully committed it when he took that nine thousand pounds. Prior's Ash may well be calling him a swindler!"

"Oh, Grace, don't!" she said imploringly. "He could not have known that it was unsafe to take it."

"Could not have known!" indignantly returned Grace. "You are either a fool, Maria, or you are deliberately saying what you know to be untrue. You must be aware that he never entered it in the books —that he appropriated it to his own use. He is a heartless, bad man! He might have chosen somebody else to prey upon, rather than his wife's father. Were I papa, I should prosecute him."

"Grace, you are killing me," wailed Maria. "Don't you think I have enough to bear?"

"I make no doubt you have. I should be sorry to have to bear the half. But you have brought it upon yourself, Maria. What though George Godolphin was your husband, you need not have upheld him in his course. Look at the ruin that has fallen upon Prior's Ash. I can tell you that your name and George Godolphin's will be remembered for many a long day. But it won't be with a blessing!"

"Grace," she said, lifting her streaming eyes, for tears had at length come to her relief, " have you no pity for me ? "

"What pity have you had for others ? " was Grace Akeman's retort. " How many must go down to their graves steeped in poverty, who, but for George Godolphin's treachery, would have passed the rest of their lives in comfort ! You have been a blind simpleton, and nothing else. George Godolphin has lavished his money and his attentions broadcast elsewhere, and you have looked complacently on. Do you think Prior's Ash has had its eyes closed, if you have ? "

"What do you mean, Grace ? "

"Never mind what I mean," was Grace's answer. " *I* am not going to tell you what you might have seen for yourself. It is all of a piece. If people will marry gay and attractive men, they must pay for it."

Maria remained silent. Grace also for a time. Then she ceased her walking, and sat down opposite her sister.

" I came to ask you whether it is not your intention to go down and see mamma. She is in bed. Suffering from a violent cold, she says. *I* know; suffering from anguish of mind. If you would not add ingratitude to what has passed, you will pay her a visit to-day. She wishes to see you."

"I will go," said Maria. But as she spoke the words, the knowledge that it would be a fearful trial—showing herself in the streets of the town—was very present to her. " I will go to-day, Grace."

"Very well," said Grace, rising; " that's all I came for."

"Not quite all, Grace. You came, I think, to make me more unhappy than I was."

" I cannot gloss over facts; it is not in my nature to do so," was the reply of Grace. " If black is black, I must call it black; and white, white. I have not said all I could say, Maria. I have not spoken of our loss; a very paltry one, but a good deal to us. I have not alluded to other and worse rumours, touching your husband. I have spoken of the ruin brought on our father and mother, and I hold you nearly as responsible for it as George Godolphin. Where's Meta ? " she added, after a short pause.

"At Lady Godolphin's Folly. Mrs. Pain has been very kind—— "

Grace turned sharply round. "And you can let her go *there !* "

" Mrs. Pain has been kind, I say, in coming for her. This is a dull house now for Meta. Margery went out on Monday, and has been detained by her sister's illness."

" Let Meta come to me, if you want to get rid of her," returned Grace in a tone more stern than any that had gone before it. " If you knew the comments indulged in by the public, you would not let a child of yours be at Lady Godolphin's Folly, while Charlotte Pain inhabits it."

Somehow, Maria had not the courage to inquire more particularly as to the "comments:" it was a subject that she shrank from, though vague and uncertain at the best. Mrs. Akeman went out; and Maria, the strings of her grief loosened, sat down and cried as if her heart would break.

With quite a sick feeling of dread she dressed herself to go to the Rectory. But not until later in the day. She put it off, and put it off, with some faint wish, foolish and vain, that dusk would forestall its usual hour. The western sun, drawing towards its setting, streamed full on the street of Prior's Ash as she walked down it. Walked down it, almost as a criminal, a black veil over her face, flushed with its sensitive dread. No one but herself knew how she shrank from the eyes of her fellow-creatures.

She might have ordered the close carriage and gone down in it—for the carriages and horses were yet at her disposal. But that, to Maria, would have been worse. To go out in state in her carriage, attended by her men-servants, would have seemed more defiant of public feelings than to appear on foot. Were these feelings ultra-sensitive? absurd? Not altogether. At any rate, I am relating the simple truth—the facts as they occurred—the feelings that actuated her.

"Look at her, walking there! She's as fine as a queen!" The words, in an insolent, sneering tone, caught her ear as she passed a group of low people gathered at the corner of a street. They would not be likely to come from any other. That they were directed to her there was no doubt; and Maria's ears tingled as she hastened on.

Was she so fine? she could not help asking herself. She had put on the plainest things she had. A black silk dress and a black mantle, a white silk bonnet and a black veil. All good things, certainly, but plain, and not new. She began to feel that reproaches were cast upon her which she did *not* deserve: but they were not the less telling upon her heart.

Did she dread going into the Rectory? Did she dread the reproaches she might be met with there?—the coldness? the slights? If so, she did not find them. She was met by the most considerate kindness, and perhaps it wrung her heart all the more.

They had seen her coming, and Rose ran forward to meet her in the hall, and kissed her; Reginald came boisterously out with a welcome; a chart in one hand, parallel-rulers and a pair of compasses in the other: he was making a pretence of work, was pricking off a ship's place in the chart. The Rector and Isaac were not at home.

"Is mamma in bed?" she asked of Rose.

"Yes. But her cold is better this evening. She will be so glad to see you."

Maria went up the stairs and entered the room alone. The anxious look of trouble on Mrs. Hastings's face, its feverish hue, struck her forcibly, as she advanced with timidity, uncertain of her reception. Uncertain of the reception of a mother? With an eagerly fond look, a rapid gesture of love, Mrs. Hastings drew Maria's face down to her for an embrace.

It unhinged Maria. She fell on her knees at the side of the bed, and gave vent to a passionate flood of tears. "Oh mother, mother, I could not help it!" she wailed. "It has been no fault of mine."

Mrs. Hastings did not speak. She put her arm round Maria's neck, and let it rest there. But the sobs were redoubled.

"Don't, child!" she said then. "You will make yourself ill. My poor child!"

"I am ill, mamma; I think I shall never be well again," sobbed

Maria, losing some of her reticence. "I feel sometimes that it would be a relief to die."

"Hush, my love! Keep despair from you, whatever you do."

"I could bear it better but for the thought of you and papa. That is killing me. Indeed, indeed I have not deserved the blame thrown upon me. I knew nothing of what was happening."

"My dear, we have not blamed *you*."

"Oh yes, every one blames me!" wailed Maria. "And I know how sad it is for you all—to suffer by us. It breaks my heart to think of it. Mamma, do you know I dreamt last night that a shower of gold was falling down to me, faster than I could gather it in my hands. I thought I was going to pay every one, and I ran away laughing, oh so glad! and held out some to papa. 'Take them,' I said to him, 'they are slipping through my fingers.' I fell down when I was near him, and awoke. I awoke—and—then"—she could scarcely speak for sobbing—"I remembered. Mamma, but for Meta I *should* have been glad in that moment to die."

The emotion of both was very great, nearly overpowering Maria. Mrs. Hastings could not say much to comfort, she was too prostrated herself. Anxious as she had been to see Maria, for she could not bear the thought of her being left alone and unnoticed in her distress—she almost repented having sent for her. Neither was strong enough to bear this excess of agitation.

Not a word was spoken of George Godolphin. Mrs. Hastings did not mention him; Maria could not. The rest of the interview was chiefly spent in silence, Maria holding her mother's hand and giving way to a rising sob now and then. Into the affairs of the Bank Mrs. Hastings felt that she could not enter. There must be a wall of silence between them on that point, as on the subject of George.

At the foot of the stairs, as she went down, she met her father. "Oh, is it you, Maria?" he said. "How are you?"

His tone was kindly. But Maria's heart was full, and she could not answer. He turned into the room by which they were standing, and she went in after him.

"When is your husband coming back? I suppose you don't know?"

"No," she answered, obliged to confess it.

"My opinion is, it would be better for him to face it, than to remain away," said the Rector. "A more honourable course, at any rate."

Still there was no reply. And Mr. Hastings, looking at his daughter's face in the twilight of the evening, saw that it was working with emotion; that she was striving, almost in vain, to repress her feelings.

"It must be very dull for you at the Bank now, Maria," he resumed in a gentle tone: "dull and unpleasant. Will you come to the Rectory for a week or two, and bring Meta?"

The tears streamed from her eyes then, unrepressed. "Thank you, papa! thank you for all your kindness," she answered, striving not to choke. "But I must stay at home as long as I may."

Reginald put on his cap to see her home, and they departed together, Reginald talking gaily, as if there were not such a thing as care in the world; Maria unable to answer him. The pain in her throat was worse than usual then. In turning out of the Rectory gate, whom should they come upon but old Jekyl, walking slowly along, nearly bent double with rheumatism. Reginald accosted him.

"Why, old Jekyl! it's never you! Are you in the land of the living still?"

"Ay, it is me, sir. Old bones don't get laid so easy; in spite, maybe, of their wishing it. Ma'am," added the old man, turning to Maria, "I'd like to make bold to say a word to you. That sixty pound of mine, what was put in the Bank—you mind it?"

"Yes," said Maria faintly.

"The losing of it'll be just dead ruin to me, ma'am. I lost my bees last summer, as you heard on, and that bit o' money was all, like, I had to look to. One must have a crust o' bread and a sup o' tea as long as it pleases the Almighty to keep one above ground : one can't lie down and clam. Would you be pleased just to say a word to the gentlemen, that that trifle o' money mayn't be lost to me? Mr. Godolphin will listen to *you*."

Maria scarcely knew what to answer. She had not the courage to tell him the money was lost; she did not like to raise delusive hopes by saying that it might be saved.

Old Jekyl wrongly interpreted the hesitation. "It was you yourself, ma'am, as advised my putting it there; for myself, I shouldn't have had a thought on't : surely you won't object to say a word for me, that I mayn't lose it now. My two sons, David and Jonathan, come home one day when they had been working at your house, and told me, both of 'em, that you recommended me to take my money to the Bank; it would be safe and sure. I can't afford to lose it," he added in a pitiful tone ; "it's all my substance on this side the grave."

"Of course she'll speak to them, Jekyl," interposed Reginald, answering for Maria just as freely and lightly as he would have answered for himself. "I'll speak to Mr. George Godolphin for you when he comes home ; I don't mind ; I can say anything to him. It would be too bad for you to lose it. Good evening. Don't go pitch-polling over! you haven't your sea-legs on to-night."

The feeble old man continued his way, a profusion of thanks breaking from him. They fell on Maria's heart as a knell. Old Jekyl's money had as surely gone as had the rest! And, but for her, it might never have been placed with the Godolphins.

When they arrived at the Bank, Reginald gave a loud and flourishing knock, pulled the bell with a peal that alarmed the servants, and then made off with a hasty good-night, leaving Maria standing there alone, in his careless fashion. At the same moment there advanced from the opposite direction a woman carrying a brown-paper parcel.

It was Margery. Detained where she had gone to meet her sister by that sister's sudden illness, she had been unable to return until now. It had put Margery out considerably, and altogether she had come home in anything but a good humour.

"I knew there'd be no luck in the journey," she cried, in reply to Maria's salutation. "The night before I started I was in the midst of a muddy pool all night in my dream, and couldn't get out of it."

"Is your sister better?" asked Maria.

"She's better: and gone on into Wales. But she's the poorest creature I ever saw. Is all well at home, ma'am?"

"All well," replied Maria, her tone subdued, as she thought how different it was in one sense from "well."

"And how has Harriet managed with the child?" continued Margery in a tart tone, meant for the unconscious Harriet.

"Very well indeed," answered Maria. "Quite well."

The door had been opened, and they were then crossing the hall. Maria turned into the dining-room, and Margery continued her way upstairs, grumbling as she did so. To believe that Harriet, or any one else, herself excepted, could do "Quite well" by Meta, was a stretch of credulity utterly inadmissible to Margery's biased mind. In the nursery sat Harriet, a damsel in a smart cap with flying pink ribbons.

"What, is it you?" was her welcome to Margery. "We thought you had taken up your abode yonder for good."

"Did you?" said Margery. "What else did you think?"

"And your sister, poor dear!" continued Harriet, passing over the retort, and speaking sympathizingly, for she generally found it to her interest to keep friends with Margery. "Has she got well?"

"As well as she ever will be, I suppose," was Margery's crusty answer.

She sat down, untied her bonnet and threw it off, and unpinned her shawl. Harriet snuffed the candle and resumed her work, which appeared to be sewing tapes on a pinafore of Meta's.

"Has she torn 'em off again?" asked Margery, her eyes following the progress of the needle.

"She's always tearing 'em off," responded Harriet, biting the end of her thread.

"And how's things going on here?" demanded Margery, her voice assuming a confidential tone, as she drew her chair nearer to Harriet's. "The Bank's not opened again, I find, for I asked so much at the station."

"Things couldn't be worse," said Harriet. "It's all a smash together. The house is bankrupt."

"Lord help us!" ejaculated Margery.

Harriet let her work fall on the table, and leant her head towards Margery's, her voice dropped to a whisper.

"I say! We have a man in here!"

"In here!" breathlessly rejoined Margery.

Harriet nodded. "Since last Tuesday. There's one stopping here, and there's another at Ashlydyat. Margery, I declare to you when they were going through the house, them creatures, I felt that sick, I didn't know how to bear it. If I had dared I'd have upset a bucket of boiling water over the lot as they came up the stairs."

Margery sat, revolving the news, a terribly blank look upon her face. Harriet resumed.

"We shall all have to leave, every soul of us: and soon, too, we expect. I don't know about you, you know. I am so sorry for my mistress!"

"Well!" burst forth Margery, giving vent to her indignation; "*he* has brought matters to a fine pass!"

"Meaning master?" asked Harriet.

"Meaning nobody else," was the tart rejoinder.

"He just has," said Harriet. "Prior's Ash is saying such things that it raises one's hair to hear them. We don't like to repeat them again, only just among ourselves."

"What's the drift of 'em?" inquired Margery.

"All sorts of drifts. About his having took and made away with the money in the tills: and those bonds of my Lord Averil's, that there was so much looking after—it was he took them. Who'd have believed it, Margery, of Mr. George Godolphin, with his gay laugh and his handsome face?"

"Better for him if his laugh had been a bit less gay and his face less handsome," was the sharp remark of Margery. "He might have been steadier then."

"Folks talk of the Verralls, and that set, up at Lady Godolphin's Folly," rejoined Harriet, her voice falling still lower. "Prior's Ash says he has had too much to do with them, and——"

"I don't want that scandal repeated over to me," angrily reprimanded Margery. "Perhaps other people know as much about it as Prior's Ash; they have eyes, I suppose. There's no need for you to bring it up to one's face."

"But they talk chiefly about Mr. Verrall," persisted Harriet, with a stress upon the name. "It's said that he and master have had business dealings together of some sort, and that that's where the money's gone. I was not going to bring up anything else. The man downstairs—and upon my word, Margery, he's a decent man enough, if you can only forget who he is—says that there are thousands and thousands gone into Verrall's pockets, which ought to be in master's."

"They'd ruin a saint, and I have always said it," was Margery's angry remark. "See *her* tearing about with her horses and her carriages, in her feathers and her brass; and master after her! Many's the time I've wondered that Mr. Godolphin has put up with it. *I'd* have given him a word of a sort, if I had been his brother."

"I should if I'd been his wife——" Harriet was beginning, but Margery angrily arrested her. Her own tongue might be guilty of many slips in the heat of argument; but it was high treason for Harriet to lapse into them.

"Hold your sauce, girl! How dare you bring your mistress's name up in any such thing? I don't know what you mean, for my part. When she complains of her husband, it will be time enough then for you to join in the chorus. Could you wish to see a better husband, pray?"

"He is quite a model husband to her face," replied saucy Harriet. "And the old saying's a true one: What the eye don't see, the heart won't grieve. Where's the need for us to quarrel over it?" she added, taking up her work again. "You have your opinion and I have mine, and if they were laid side by side, it's likely they'd not be far apart from each other. But let them be bad or good, it can't change the past. What's done, is done: and the house is broken up."

Margery flung off her shawl just as Charlotte Pain had flung off her hers the previous Monday morning in the breakfast-room, and a silence ensued.

"Perhaps the house may go on again?" said Margery, presently, in a dreamy tone.

"Why, how can it?" returned Harriet, looking up from her work at the pinafore, which she had resumed. "All the money's gone. A bank can't go on without money."

"What does he say to it?" very sharply asked Margery.

"What does who say to it?"

"Master. Does *he* say how the money comes to be gone? How does he like facing the creditors?"

"He is not here," said Harriet. "He has not been home since he left last Saturday. It's said he is in London."

"And Mr. Godolphin?"

"Mr. Godolphin's here. And a nice task he has of it every day with the angry creditors. If we have had one of the bank creditors bothering at the hall-door for Mr. George, we have had fifty. At first, they wouldn't believe he was away, and wouldn't be got rid of. Creditors of the house, too, have come, worrying my mistress out of her life. There's a sight of money owing in the town. Cook says she wouldn't have believed there was a quarter of the amount only just for household things, till it came to be summed up. Some of them downstairs are wondering if they will get their wages. And—I say, Margery, have you heard about Mr. Hastings?"

"What about him?" asked Margery.

"He has lost every shilling he had. It was in the Bank, and—— "

"He couldn't have had so very much to lose," interposed Margery, who was in a humour to contradict everything. "What can a parson save? Not much."

"But it is not that—not *his* money. The week before the Bank went, he had lodged between nine and ten thousand pounds in it for safety. He was left trustee, you know, to dead Mr. Chisholm's children, and their money was paid to him, it turns out, and he brought it to the Bank. It's all gone."

Margery lifted her hands in dismay. "I have heard say that failures are like nothing but a devouring fire, for the money they swallow up," she remarked. "It seems to be true."

"My mistress has looked so ill ever since! And she can eat nothing. Pierce says it would melt the heart of a stone to see her make believe to eat before him, waiting at dinner, trying to get a morsel down her throat, and not able to do it. My belief is, that she's thinking of her father's ruin night and day. Report is, that master took the money from the Rector, knowing it would never be paid back again, and used it for himself."

Margery got up with a jerk. "If I stop here I shall be hearing worse and worse," she remarked. "This will be enough to kill Miss Janet. That awful Shadow hasn't been on the Dark Plain this year for nothing. We might well notice that it never was so dark before!"

Perching her bonnet on her head, and throwing her shawl over her arm, Margery lighted a candle and opened a door leading from the room into a bed-chamber. Her own bed stood opposite to her, and in a corner at the opposite end was Miss Meta's little bed. She laid her shawl and bonnet on the drawers, and advanced on tiptoe, shading the light with her hand.

Intending to take a fond look at her darling. But, like many more of us who advance confidently on some pleasure, Margery found nothing but disappointment. The place where Meta ought to have been was empty. Nothing to be seen but the smooth white bed-clothes, laid ready open for the young lady's reception. Did a fear dart over Margery's mind that she must be lost? She certainly flew back as if some such idea occurred to her.

"Where's the child?" she burst out.

"She has not come home yet," replied Harriet, with composure. "I was waiting here for her."

"Come home from where? Where is she?"

"At Lady Godolphin's Folly. But Mrs. Pain has never kept her so late as this before."

"She's *there!* With Mrs. Pain?" shrieked Margery.

"She has been there every day this week. Mrs. Pain nas either come or sent for her. Look there," added Harriet, pointing to a collection of toys in a corner of the nursery. "She has brought home all those things. Mrs. Pain loads her with them."

Margery answered not a word. She blew out her candle, and went downstairs to the dining-room. Maria, her things never taken off, was sitting just as she had come in, apparently lost in thought. She rose up when Margery entered, and began untying her bonnet.

"Harriet says that the child's at Mrs. Pain's: that she has been there all the week," began Margery, without circumlocution.

"Yes," replied Maria. "I cannot think why she has not come home. Mrs. Pain——"

"And you could let her go there, ma'am!" interrupted Margery's indignant voice, paying little heed or deference to what her mistress might be saying. "*There!* If anybody had come and told it to me before this night, I would not have believed it."

"But, Margery, it has done her no harm. There's a pinafore or two torn, I believe, and that's the worst. Mrs. Pain has been exceedingly kind. She has kept her dogs shut up all the week."

Margery's face was working ominously. It bore the sign of an approaching storm.

"Kind! She!" repeated Margery, almost beside herself. "Why, then, if it's come to this pass, you had better have your eyes opened, ma'am, if nothing else will stop the child's going there. Your child at Mrs. Charlotte Pain's! Prior's Ash will talk more than it has talked before."

"What has Prior's Ash said?" asked Maria, an uncomfortable feeling stealing over her.

"It has wondered whether Mrs. George Godolphin has been wholly blind or only partially so; that's what it has done, ma'am," returned Margery, quite forgetting herself in her irritation. "And the woman coming here continually with her bold face! I'd rather see Meta——"

Margery's eloquence was brought to a summary end. A noise in the hall was followed by the boisterous entrance of the ladies in question, Miss Meta and Mrs. Charlotte Pain. Charlotte—really she was wild at times—had brought Meta home on horseback. Late as it was, she had mounted her horse to give the child pleasure, had mounted the child on the saddle before her, and so they had cantered down, attended by a groom. Charlotte wore her habit, and held her whip in her hand. She came in pretending to beat an imaginary horse, for the delectation of Meta. Meta was furnished with a boy's whip, a whistle at one end, a lash at the other. She was beating an imaginary horse too, varying the play with an occasional whistle. What with the noise, the laughing, the lashes, and the whistle, it was as if Bedlam had broken loose. To crown the whole, Meta's brown-holland dress was wofully torn, and the brim of her straw hat was almost separated from the crown.

Meta caught sight of Margery and flew to her. But not before Margery had made a sort of grab at the child. Clasping her in her arms, she held her there, as if she would protect her from some infection. To be clasped in arms, however, and thus deprived of the delights of whip-smacking and whistling, did not accord with Miss Meta's inclinations, and she struggled to get free.

"You'd best stop here and hide yourself, poor child!" cried Margery in a voice excessively pointed.

"It's not much," said Charlotte, supposing the remark applied to the damages. "The brim is only unsewn, and the blouse is an old one. She did it in swinging."

"Who's talking of that?" fiercely responded Margery to Mrs. Pain. "If folks had to hide their faces for nothing worse than torn clothes, it wouldn't be of much account."

Charlotte did not like the tone. "Perhaps you will wait until your opinion's asked for," said she, turning haughtily on Margery. There had been incipient warfare between those two for years: and they both were innately conscious of it.

A shrill whistle from Meta interrupted the contest. She had escaped and was standing in the middle of the room, her legs astride, her damaged hat set rakishly on the side of her head, her attitude altogether not unlike that of a man standing to see a horse go through his paces. It was precisely what the young lady was imitating: she had been taken by Charlotte to the stable-yard that day, to witness the performance.

Clack, clack! "Lift your feet up, you lazy brute!" Clack, clack, clack! "Mamma, I am making a horse canter."

Charlotte looked on with admiring ecstasy, and clapped her hands. Maria seemed bewildered: Margery stood with dilating eyes and open mouth. There was little doubt that Miss Meta, under the able tuition of Mrs. Pain, might become an exceedingly fast young lady in time.

"You have been teaching her that!" burst forth Margery to Mrs. Pain in her uncontrollable anger. "What else might you have been teaching her? It's fit, it is, for you to be let have the companionship of Miss Meta Godolphin!"

Charlotte laughed in her face defiantly—contemptuously—with a gleeful, merry accent. Margery, perhaps distrustful of what she might be further tempted to say herself, put an end to the scene by catching up Meta and forcibly carrying her off, in spite of rebellious kicks and screams. In her temper, she flung the whip to the other end of the hall as she passed through it. "They'd make you into a boy, and worse, if they had their way. I wish Miss Janet had been here to-night!" .

"What an idiotic old maid she is, that Margery!" exclaimed Charlotte, laughing still. "Good night. I can't stay. I shall come for Meta to-morrow."

"Not to-morrow," dissented Maria, feeling that the struggle with Margery would be too formidable. "I thank you very much for your kindness, Mrs. Pain," she heartily added ; "but now that Margery has returned, she will not like to part with Meta."

"As you will," said Charlotte, with a laugh. "Margery would not let her come, you think. Good night. Dormez bien."

Before the sound of the closing of the hall-door had ceased its echoes through the house, Margery was in the dining-room again, her face white with anger. Her mistress, a thing she very rarely did, ventured on a reproof.

"You forgot yourself, Margery, when you spoke just now to Mrs. Pain. I felt inclined to apologize to her for you."

This was the climax. "Forgot myself!" echoed Margery, her face growing whiter. "No, ma'am, it's because I did not forget myself that she's gone out of the house without her ears tingling. I should have made 'em tingle if I had spoke out. Not that some folk's ears can tingle," added Margery, amending her proposition. "Hers is of the number, so I should have spent my words for nothing. If Mr. George had spent *his* words upon somebody else, it might be the better for us all now."

"Margery!"

"I can't help it, ma'am, I must have my say. Heaven knows I wouldn't have opened my mouth to you ; I'd have kept it closed for ever, though I died for it—and it's not five minutes ago that I pretty well snapped Harriet's nose off for daring to give out hints and to bring up your name—but it's time you did know a little of what has been going on, to the scandal of Prior's Ash. Meta up at Lady Godolphin's Folly with that woman !"

"Margery!" again interrupted her mistress. But Margery's words were as a torrent that bears down all before it.

"It has been the talk of the town ; it has been the talk of the servants here; it has been the talk among the servants at Ashlydyat. If I thought you'd let the child go out with her in public again, I'd pray that I might first follow her to the grave in her little coffin."

Maria's face had turned as white as Margery's. She sat as a statue, gazing at the woman with eyes in which there shone a strange kind of fear.

"I—don't—know—what—it—is—you—mean," she said, the words coming out disjointedly.

"It means, ma'am, that you have lived with a mist before your eyes. You have thought my master a saint and a paragon, and he was neither the one nor the other. And now I hope you'll pardon me for saying to your face what others have been long saying behind your back."

She turned sharply off as she concluded, and quitted the room abruptly as she had entered it, leaving Maria motionless, her breath coming in gasps, and the dewdrops cold on her brow.

The substance of what Margery had spoken out so broadly had sometimes passed through her mind as a dim shadow. But never to rest there.

CHAPTER XXIV.

A VISIT TO LORD AVERIL.

A FEW days progressed onwards, and another week was in. Every hour brought to light more—what are we to call it—imprudence?—of Mr. George Godolphin's. His friends termed it imprudence ; his enemies villainy. Thomas called it nothing: he never cast reproach on George by a single word ; he would have taken the whole odium upon himself, had it been possible to take it. George's conduct was breaking his heart, was driving him to his grave somewhat before his time; but Thomas never said in the hearing of others—He has been a bad brother to me.

George Godolphin was not yet home again. It could not be said that he was in concealment, as he was sometimes met in London by people visiting it. Perhaps he carried his habitual carelessness so far as to the perilling of his own safety ; and his absence from Prior's Ash may have been the result only of his distaste to meet that ill-used community. Had he been sole partner, he must have been there to answer to his bankruptcy ; as it was, Thomas, hitherto, had answered all in his own person.

But there came a day when Thomas could not answer it. Ill or well, he rose now to the early breakfast-table : he had to hasten to the Bank betimes, for there was much work there with the accounts ; and one morning when they were at breakfast, Bexley, his own servant, entered with one or two letters.

They were speaking of Lady Godolphin. My lady was showing herself a true friend. She had announced to them that it was her intention to resume her residence at the Folly, that they "might not be separated from Prior's Ash, the place of their birth and home." Of course it was an intimation, really delicately put, that their future home must be with her. " Never for me," Janet remarked : *her* future residence would not be at Prior's Ash; as far removed from it as possible.

Thomas had risen, and was at a distant table, opening his letters, when a faint moan startled them. He was leaning back in his chair, seemingly unconscious : his hands had fallen, his face was the hue of the grave. . Surely those dews upon it were not the dews of death ?

Cecil screamed ; Bessy flung open the door and called for help ; Janet only turned to them, her hands lifted to enjoin silence, a warning word upon her lips. Bexley came running in, and looked at his master.

" He'll be better presently," he whispered.

"Yes, he will be better presently," assented Janet. "But I should like Mr. Snow to be here."

Bexley was the only man-servant left at Ashlydyat. Short work is generally made of the dispersion of a household when the means come to an end, as they had with the Godolphins : and there had been no difficulty in finding places for the excellent servants of Ashlydyat. Bexley had stoutly refused to go. He didn't want wages, he said, but he was not going to leave his master, so long as—— Bexley did not say so long as what, but they had understood him. So long as his master was in life.

Thomas began to revive. He slowly opened his eyes, and raised his hand to wipe the moisture from his white face. On the table before him lay one of the letters open. Janet recognized the handwriting as that of George.

She spurned the letter from her. With a gesture of grievous vexation, her hand pushed it across the table. "It is that which has affected you!" she cried out, with a wail.

"Not so," breathed Thomas. "It was the pain here."

He touched himself below the chest ; in the place where the pain had come before. *Which* pain had seized upon him?—the mental agony arising from George's conduct, or the physical agony of his disease? Probably somewhat of both.

He stretched out his hand towards the letter, making a motion that it should be folded. Bexley, who could not have read a word without his glasses had it been to save his life, took up the letter, folded it, and placed it in its envelope. Thomas's mind then seemed at rest, and he closed his eyes again.

Mr. Snow soon reached Ashlydyat. "Another attack, I hear," he began, in his unceremonious salutation. "Bothered into it, no doubt. Bexley says it came on when he was reading letters."

With the wan white look upon his face, with the moisture of pain still upon his brow, lay Thomas Godolphin. He was on the sofa now ; but he partially rose from it and assumed a sitting posture when the surgeon entered.

A few professional questions and answers, and then Mr. Snow began to grumble. "Did I not warn you that you must have perfect tranquillity?" cried he. "Rest of body and of mind."

"You did. But how am I to have it? Even now, I ought to be at the Bank, facing the trouble there."

"Where's George?" sharply asked Mr. Snow.

"In London," replied Thomas Godolphin. But he said it in no complaining accent : neither did his tone invite further comment.

Mr. Snow was one who did not wait for an invitation in such a cause ere he spoke. "It is one of two things, Mr. Godolphin. Either George must come back and face this worry, or else you'll die."

"I shall die, however it may be, Snow," was the reply of Thomas Godolphin.

"So will most of us, I expect," returned the doctor. "But there's no necessity for being helped on to it by others, ages before death would come of itself. What's your brother at in London? Amusing himself, I suppose. He must be got here."

Thomas shook his head. The action, as implying a negative, aroused the wrath of Mr. Snow. "Do you want to die?" he asked. "One would think it, by your keeping your brother away."

"There is no person who would more gladly see my brother here than I," returned Thomas Godolphin. "If—if it were expedient that he should come."

"Need concealment be affected between us, Mr. Godolphin?" resumed the surgeon, after a pause. "You must be aware that I have heard the rumours afloat. A doctor hears everything, you know. You are uncertain whether it would be safe for George to come back to Prior's Ash."

"It is something of that sort, Snow."

"But now, what is there against him—it is of no use to mince the matter—besides those bonds of Lord Averil's?"

"There's nothing else against him. At least, in—in—— " He did not go on. He could not bring his lips to say of his brother—"from a criminal point of view."

"Nothing else of which unpleasant legal cognizance can be taken," freely interposed Mr. Snow. "Well, now, it is my opinion that there's not a shadow of fear to be entertained from Lord Averil. He is your old and firm friend, Mr. Godolphin."

"He has been mine ; yes. Not so much George's. Most men in such a case of—of loss, would resent it, without reference to former friendship. I am not at any certainty, you see and therefore I cannot take the responsibility of saying to my brother, ' It is safe for you to return.' Lord Averil has never been near me since. I argue ill from it."

"He has not been with you for the best of all possible reasons—that he has been away from Prior's Ash," explained Mr. Snow.

"Has he been away? I did not know it."

"He has. He was called away unexpectedly by some relative's illness, a day or two after your house was declared bankrupt. He may have refrained from calling on you just at the time that happened, from motives of delicacy."

"True," replied Thomas Godolphin. But his tone was not a hopeful one. "When does he return?"

"He has returned. He came back last night."

There was a pause. Thomas Godolphin broke it. "I wish you could give me something to avert or mitigate these sharp attacks of pain, Snow," he said. "It is agony, in fact ; not pain."

"I know it," replied Mr. Snow. "Where's the use of my attempting to give you anything? You don't take my prescriptions."

Thomas lifted his eyes in some surprise. "I have taken all that you have desired me."

"No, you have not. I prescribe tranquillity of mind and body. You take neither."

Thomas Godolphin leaned a little nearer to the doctor, and paused before he answered. "Tranquillity of mind for me has passed. I can never know it again. Were my life to be prolonged, the great healer of all things, Time, might bring it me in a degree : but, for that, I shall not live. Snow, you must know this to be the case, under the calamity which has fallen upon my head."

"It ought to have fallen upon your brother's head, not upon yours," was the rejoinder of the surgeon, spoken crossly, in his inability to contradict Mr. Godolphin's words. "At any rate, you cannot go on any longer facing this business in person."

"I must indeed. There is no help for it."

"And suppose it kills you?" was the retort.

"If I could help going, I would," said Thomas. "But there is no alternative. One of us must be there; and George cannot be. You are not ignorant of the laws of bankruptcy."

"It is another nail in your coffin," growled Mr. Snow, as he took his leave.

He went straight to the Bank. He asked to see Mrs. George Godolphin. Maria, in her pretty morning dress of muslin, was seated with Meta on her knees. She had been reading the child a Bible story, and was now talking to her in a low voice, her own face, so gentle, so pure, and so sad, bent towards the little one's upturned to it.

"Well, young lady, and how are all the dolls?" was the surgeon's greeting. "Will you send her away to play with them, Mrs. George?"

Meta ran off. She intended to come bustling down again with her arms full. Mr. Snow took his seat opposite Maria.

"Why does your husband not come back?" he abruptly asked.

The question seemed to turn Maria's heart to sickness. She opened her lips to answer, but stopped in hesitation. Mr. Snow resumed:

"His staying away is killing Thomas Godolphin. I prescribe tranquillity for him; total rest: instead of which, he is obliged to come here day after day, and be in a continuous scene of worry. Your husband must return, Mrs. George Godolphin."

"Y—es," she faintly answered, lacking the courage to say that considerations for his personal security might forbid it.

"Murder will not mend these unhappy matters, Mrs. George Godolphin; nor would it be a desirable ending to them. And it will be nothing less than murder if he does not return, for Mr. Godolphin will surely die."

All Maria's pulses seemed to beat the quicker. "Is Mr. Godolphin worse?" she asked.

"He is considerably worse. I have been called in to him this morning. My last orders to him were, not to attempt to come to the Bank. His answer was, that he must come: there was no help for it. I believe there is no help for it, George being away. You must get him home, Mrs. George."

She looked sadly perplexed. Mr. Snow read it correctly.

"My dear, I think there would be no danger. Lord Averil is a personal friend of Mr. Godolphin's. I think there's none for another reason: if the viscount's intention had been to stir unpleasantly in the affair, he would have stirred in it before this."

"Yes—I have thought of that," she answered.

"And now I must go again," he said, rising. "I wish to-day was twenty-four hours long, for the work I have to do in it; but I spared a few minutes to call in and tell you this. Get your husband here, for the sake of his good brother."

The tears were in Maria's eyes. She could scarcely think of Thomas Godolphin and his unmerited troubles without their rising. Mr. Snow saw the wet eyelashes, and laid his hand on the smoothly-parted hair.

"You have your share of sorrow just now, child," he said; "more than you ought to have. It is making you look like a ghost. Why does he leave you to battle it out alone?" added Mr. Snow, his anger mastering him, as he gazed at her pale face, her rising sobs. "Prior's Ash is crying shame upon him. Are you and his brother of less account than he, in his own eyes, that he should abandon you to it?"

She strove to excuse her husband—he *was* her husband, in spite of that cruel calumny divulged by Margery—but Mr. Snow would not listen. He was in a hurry, he said, and went bustling out of the door, almost upsetting Meta, with her dolls, who was bustling in.

Maria sent the child to the nursery again after Mr. Snow's departure, and stood, her head pressed against the frame of the open window, looking unconsciously on to the terrace, revolving the words recently spoken. "It is killing Thomas Godolphin. It will be nothing less than murder, if George does not return"

Every fibre of her frame was thrilling to it in answer : every generous impulse of her heart was stirred to its depths. He *ought* to be back. She had long thought so. For her sake—but she was nothing; for Thomas Godolphin's; for her husband's own reputation. Down deep in her heart she thrust that dreadful revelation of his falsity, and strove to bury it as an English wife and gentlewoman has no resource but to do. Ay! to bury it; and to keep it buried ! though the concealment eat away her life—as that scarlet letter A, you have read of, ate into the bosom of another woman renowned in story. It seemed to Maria that the time was come when she must inquire a little into the actual state of affairs, instead of hiding her head and spending her days in the indulgence of her fear and grief. If the whole world spoke against him,—if the whole world had cause to speak,—she was his wife still, and his interests and welfare were hers. Were it possible that any effort she could make would bring him back, she must make it.

The words of Mr. Snow still rang in her ears. How was she to set about it? A few minutes given to reflection, her aching brow pressed to the cold window-frame, and she turned and rang the bell. When the servant appeared, she sent him into the Bank with a request that Mr. Hurde would come and speak with her for five minutes.

Mr. Hurde was not long in obeying the summons. He appeared with a pen behind his ear, and his spectacles pushed up on his brow.

It was not a pleasant task, and Maria had to swallow a good many lumps in her throat before she could make known precisely what she wanted. "Would Mr. Hurde tell her the exact state of things? What there was, or was not, against her husband."

Mr. Hurde gave no very satisfactory reply. He took off his glasses and wiped them. Maria had invited him to a chair, and sat near him, her elbow leaning on the table, and her face slightly bent. Mr. Hurde did not know what Mrs. George Godolphin had or had not heard, or how far it would be expedient for him to speak. She guessed at his dilemma.

"Tell me all, Mr. Hurde," she said, lifting her face to his with imploring eagerness. "It is well that you should, for nothing can be more cruel than the uncertainty and suspense I am in. I know about Lord Averil's bonds."

"Ay?" he replied. But he said no more.

"I will tell you why I ask," said Maria. "Mr. Snow has been here, and he informs me that coming to the Bank daily and the worry are killing Mr. Godolphin. He says Mr. George ought to be back in his brother's place. I think if he can come, he ought to do so."

"I wish he could," returned Mr. Hurde, more quickly and impressively than he usually spoke. "It *is* killing Mr. Godolphin—that, and the bankruptcy together. But I don't know that it would be safe for him, on account of these very bonds of Lord Averil's."

"What else is there against him?" breathed Maria.

"There's nothing else."

"Nothing else?" she echoed, a shade of hope lighting up her face and her heart.

"Nothing else. That is, nothing that he can be made *criminally* responsible for," added the old clerk, with marked emphasis, as if he thought that there was a great deal more, had the law only taken cognizance of it. "If Lord Averil should decline to prosecute, he might return to-morrow. He must be back soon, whether or not, to answer to his bankruptcy; or else——"

"Or else—what?" asked Maria falteringly, for Mr. Hurde had stopped. "Speak out."

"Or else never come back at all; never be seen, in fact, in England again. That's how it is, ma'am."

"Would it not be well to ascertain Lord Averil's feelings upon the subject, Mr Hurde?" she rejoined, breaking a silence.

"It would be very well, if it could be done. But who is to do it?"

Maria was beginning to think that she would do it. "You are sure there is nothing else against him?" she reiterated.

"Nothing, ma'am, that need prevent his returning to Prior's Ash."

There was no more to be answered, and Mr. Hurde withdrew. Maria lost herself in thought. Could she dare to go to Lord Averil and beseech his clemency? Her brow flushed at the thought. But she had been inured to humiliation of late, and it would be only another drop in the cup of pain. Oh, the relief it would be, could the dreadful suspense, the uncertainty, end! The suspense was awful. Even if it ended in the worst, it would be almost a relief. If Lord Averil should intend to prosecute, who knew but he might forego the intention at her prayers? If so—if so—why, she should ever say that God had sent her to him.

There was the reverse side of the picture. A haughty reception of her—for was she not the wife of the man who had wronged him?—and a cold refusal. How she should bear that, she did not like to think. Should she go? Could she go? Even now her heart was failing her——

What noise was that? A sort of commotion in the hall. She opened

the dining-room door and glanced out.   Thomas Godolphin had come,
and was entering the Bank, leaning on his servant Bexley's arm, there
to go through his day's work, looking more fit for his coffin.   It was
the turning of the scale.

"I *will* go to him!" murmured Maria to herself.   "I will go to
Lord Averil, and hear all there may be to hear.   Let me do it!   Let
me do it!—for the sake of Thomas Godolphin!"   And she prepared
herself for the visit.

This proposed application to Lord Averil may appear but a very
slight affair to the careless and thoughtless : one of those trifling annoyances which must occasionally beset our course through life.   Why
should Maria have shrunk from it with that shiveringly sensitive
dread?—have set about it as a forced duty, with a burning cheek and
failing heart?   Consider what it was that she undertook, you who
would regard it lightly; pause an instant and look at it in all its
bearings.   Her husband, George Godolphin, had robbed Lord Averil
of sixteen thousand pounds.   It is of no use to mince the matter.   He
had shown himself neither more nor less than a thief, a swindler.
He, a man of the same social stamp as Lord Averil, moving in the
same sphere of county society, had fallen from his pedestal by his own
fraudulent act, to a level (in crime) with the very dregs of mankind.
Perhaps no one in the whole world could ever feel it in the same
humiliating degree as did his wife—unless it might be Thomas Godolphin.   Both of them, unfortunately for them—yes, I say it advisedly—
unfortunately for them in this bitter storm of shame—both of them
were of that honourable, upright, ultra-refined nature, on which such
a blow falls far more cruelly than death.   Death! death!   If it does
come, it brings at least one recompense : the humiliation and the
trouble, the bitter pain and the carking care are escaped from, left
behind for ever in the cruel world.   Oh! if these miserable ill-doers
could but bear in their own person all the pain and the shame!—if
George Godolphin could only have stood out on a pinnacle in the face of
Prior's Ash and expiated his folly alone!   But it could not be.   It never
can or will be.   As the sins of the people in the Israelitish camp were
laid upon the innocent and unhappy scape-goat, so the sins which
men commit in the present day are heaped upon unconscious and
guileless heads.   As the poor scape-goat wandered with his hidden
burden into the remote wilderness, away from the haunts of man, so
do these other heavily-laden ones stagger away with their unseen load,
only striving to hide themselves from the eyes of men—anywhere—in
patience and silence—praying to die.

Every humiliation which George Godolphin has brought upon himself,—every harsh word cast on him by the world,—every innate sense
of guilt and shame which must accompany such conduct, was being
expiated by his wife.   Yes, it fell worst upon her : Thomas was but
his brother; she was part and parcel of himself.   But that God's ways
are not as our ways, we might feel tempted to ask why it should be
that these terrible trials are so often brought upon the head of such
women as Maria Godolphin—timid, good, gentle, sensitive—the least
of all able to bear them.   That such is frequently the case, is indisputable.   In no way was Maria fitted to cope with this.   Many might

have felt less this very expedition to Lord Averil : to her it was as the very bitterest humiliation. She had hitherto met Lord Averil as an equal—she had entertained him at her house as such—she had stood before him always in her calm self-possession, with a clear face and a clear conscience ; and now she must go to him a humble petitioner—bow before him in all her self-conscious disgrace—implore him to save her husband from the consequences of his criminal act; standing at the felon's bar, and its sequel—transportation. She must virtually ask Lord Averil to put up quietly with the loss of the sixteen thousand pounds, and to make no sign.

With a cheek flushed with emotion,—with a heart sick unto faintness,—Maria Godolphin stepped out of her house in the full blaze of the midday sun. A gloomy day, showing her less conspicuously to the curious gazers of Prior's Ash, had been more welcome to her. She had gone out so rarely since the crash came—but that once, in fact, when she went to her mother—that her appearance was the signal for a commotion. "There's Mrs. George Godolphin!" and Prior's Ash flocked to its doors and its windows, as if Mrs. George Godolphin had been some unknown curiosity in the animal world, never yet exhibited to the eyes of the public. Maria shielded her burning face from observation as well as she could with her small parasol, and passed on.

Lord Averil, she had found, was staying with Colonel Max, and her way led her past the Rectory of All Souls', past the house of Lady Sarah Grame. Lady Sarah was at the window, and Maria bowed. The bow was not returned. It was not returned ! Lady Sarah turned away with a haughty movement, a cold glance. It told cruelly upon Maria : had anything been wanted to prove to her the estimation in which she was now held by Prior's Ash, that would have done it.

The distance from her own house to that of Colonel Max was about two miles. Rather a long walk for Maria at the present time, for she was not in a condition of health to endure fatigue. It was a square, moderate-sized, red-brick house, standing considerably back from the high-road ; and as Maria turned into its avenue of approach, what with the walk, and what with the dread apprehension of the coming interview, the faintness at her heart had begun to show itself upon her face. The insult offered her (could it be called anything less ?) by Lady Sarah Grame, had somehow seemed an earnest of what she might expect from Lord Averil. Lady Sarah had not a tenth of the grievance against the Bank that the viscount had.

No one ever approached the colonel's house without having their ears saluted with the baying and snarling of his fox-hounds, whose kennels were close by. In happier days—days so recently past, that they might almost be counted as present—when Maria had gone to that house to dinner-parties, she had drawn closer to George in the carriage, and whispered how much she should dislike it if *he* kept a pack of fox-hounds near their dwelling-place. Never, never should she drive to that house in state again, her husband by her side. Oh! the contrast it presented—that time and this ! Now she was approaching it like the criminal that the world thought her, shielding her face with her veil, hiding herself, so far as she might, from observation.

She reached the door, and paused ere she rang : her pulses were throbbing wildly, her heart beat as if it would burst its bounds. The nearer the interview, the more formidable did it appear, the less able herself to face it. The temptation came over her to go back. It assailed her very strongly, and she might have yielded to it, but for the thought of Thomas Godolphin.

She rang at the bell : a timid ring. One of those rings that seem to announce the humble applicant—and who was the wife of George Godolphin now, that she should proclaim herself with pomp and clatter ? A man settling himself into his green livery coat opened the door.

" Is Lord Averil within ? "

" No."

The servant was a stranger, and did not know her. He may have thought it curious that a lady, who spoke in a low tone and scarcely raised her eyes through her veil, should come there alone to inquire after Lord Averil. He resumed, rather pertly :

" His lordship walked out an hour ago with the colonel. It's quite unbeknown what time they may come in."

In her shrinking dread of the interview, it almost seemed a relief. Strange to say, so fully absorbed had she been in the anticipated pain, that the contingency of his being out had not crossed her mind. The man stood with the door in his hand, half open, half closed ; had he invited her to walk in and sit down, she might have done so, for the sake of the rest. But he did not.

Retracing her steps down the path, she branched off into a dark walk, overshadowed by trees, just within the entrance-gate, and sat down upon a bench. Now the reaction was coming ; the disappointment : all that mental agony, all that weary way of fatigue, and not to see him ! It must all be gone over again on the morrow.

She threw back her veil ; she pressed her throbbing forehead against the trunk of the old oak tree : and in that same moment some one entered the gate on his way to the house, saw her, and turned round to approach her. It was Lord Averil.

Had the moment really come ? Every drop of blood in her body seemed to rush to her heart, and send it on with a tumultuous bound ; every sense of the mind seemed to leave her ; every fear that the imagination can conjure up seemed to rise in menace. She rose to her feet and gazed at him, her sight partially leaving her, her face changing to a ghastly whiteness.

But when he hastened forward and caught her hands in the deepest respect and sympathy ; when he bent over her, saying some confused words—confused to *her* ear—of surprise at seeing her, of pity for her apparent illness ; when he addressed her with every token of the old kindness, the consideration of bygone days, then the revulsion of feeling overcame her, and Maria burst into a flood of distressing tears, and sobbed passionately.

" I am fatigued with the walk," she said, with a lame attempt at apology, when her emotion was subsiding. " I came over to speak to you, Lord Averil. I—I have something to ask you."

" But you should not have walked," he answered in a kindly tone of remonstrance. "Why did you not drop me a note? I would have come to you."

She felt as one about to faint. She had taken off her gloves, and her small white hands were unconsciously writhing themselves together in her lap, showing how great was her inward pain; her trembling lips, pale with agitation, refused to bring out their words connectedly.

"I want to ask you to be merciful to my husband. Not to prosecute him."

The words were breathed in a whisper; the rushing tide of shame changed her face to crimson. Lord Averil did not for the moment answer, and the delay, the fear of failure, imparted to her somewhat of courage.

"For Thomas's sake," she said. "I ask it for Thomas's sake."

"My dear Mrs. Godolphin," he was beginning, but she interrupted him, her tone changing to one of desperate energy.

"Oh, be merciful, be merciful! Be merciful to my husband, Lord Averil, for his brother's sake. Nay—for George's own sake; for my sake, for my poor child's sake, Meta's. He can never come back to Prior's Ash, unless you will be merciful to him: he cannot come now, and Thomas has to go through all the worry and the misery, and it is killing him. Mr. Snow came to me this morning and said it was killing him; he said that George must return if he would save his brother's life: and I spoke to Mr. Hurde, and he said there was nothing to prevent his returning, except the danger from Lord Averil. And then I made my mind up to come to you."

"I shall not prosecute him, Mrs. George Godolphin. My long friend-ship with his brother debars it. He may come back to-morrow, in perfect assurance that he has nothing to fear from me."

"Is it true?—I may rely upon you?" she gasped.

"Indeed you may. I have never had a thought of prosecuting. I cannot describe to you the pain that it has been to me; I mean the affair altogether, not my particular loss: but that pain would be greatly increased were I to bring myself to prosecute one bearing the name of Godolphin. I am sorry for George; deeply sorry for him. Report says that he has allowed himself to fall into bad hands, and could not extricate himself."

The worst was over; the best known: and Maria leaned against the friendly tree, untied her bonnet-strings, and wiped the moisture from her now pallid face. Exhaustion was supervening. Lord Averil rose and held out his arm to her.

"Let me take you to the house and give you a glass of sherry."

"I could not take it, thank you. I would rather not go to the house."

"Colonel Max will be very glad to see you. I have only just parted from him. He went round by the stables."

She shook her head. "I do not like to see any one now."

The subdued words, the saddened tone seemed to speak volumes. Lord Averil glanced down at her compassionately. "This has been a grievous trial to you, Mrs. Godolphin."

"Yes," she answered very quietly. Had she spoken but a word of what it had really been to her, emotion might again have broken forth.

"But you must not let it affect you too greatly," he remonstrated. "As I fear it is doing."

"I can't help it," she whispered. "I knew nothing of it, and it came upon me as a thunderbolt. I never had so much as a suspicion that anything was going wrong: had people asked me what Bank was the most stable throughout the kingdom, I should have said ours. I never suspected evil: and yet blame is being cast upon me. Lord Averil, I—I—did not know about those bonds."

"No, no," he warmly answered. "You need not tell me that. I wish you could allow the trouble to pass over you more lightly."

The trouble! She clasped her hands to pain. "Don't speak of it," she wailed. "At times it seems more than I can bear. But for Meta, I should be glad to die."

What was Lord Averil to answer? He could only give her the earnest sympathy of his whole heart. "A man who can bring deliberately this misery upon the wife of his bosom deserves hanging," was his bitter thought.

"What are you going to do?" he asked. "Surely not to attempt to walk back again?"

"I shall take my time over it," she answered. "It is not much of a walk."

"Too much for you at present," he gravely said. "Let me send you home in one of Colonel Max's carriages."

"No, oh no!" she quickly answered. "Indeed I have not miscalculated my strength: I can walk perfectly well, and would prefer to do so."

"Then you will first come into the house and rest."

"I would rather not. Let me sit here a little longer ; it is resting me."

"I will be back immediately," he said, walking from her very quickly, and plunging into a narrow path which was a short cut to the house. When he reappeared he bore a glass of wine and a biscuit on a plate.

She took the wine. The biscuit she put back with a shiver. "I never can eat anything now," she said, lifting her eyes to his to beseech his pardon.

When she at length rose, Lord Averil took her hand and laid it within his arm. She supposed he meant to escort her to the gate.

"I have not said a word of thanks to you," she murmured, when they reached it. "I am very, very grateful to you, very sensible of your kindness; but I cannot speak of it. My heart seems broken."

She had halted and held out her hand in farewell. Lord Averil did not release her, but walked on. "If you will walk home, Mrs. George Godolphin, you must at least allow my arm to help you."

"I could not; indeed I could not," she said, stopping resolutely, though the tears were dropping from her eyes. "I must go back alone: I would rather."

Lord Averil partially yielded. The first part of the road was lonely, and he must see her so far. "I should have called on Thomas Godolphin before this, but I have been away," he remarked, as they went on. "I will go and see him—perhaps this afternoon."

"He will be so thankful to hear this! It will be as a renewed lease of life to him. They have been fearful at Ashlydyat."

An exceedingly vexed expression crossed Lord Averil's lips. "I thought they had known me better at Ashlydyat," he said. "Thomas, at any rate. Feared *me!*"

At length Maria would not allow him to go farther, and Lord Averil clasped her hand in both his. "Promise me to try and keep up your spirits," he said. "You should do so for your husband's sake."

"Yes; as well as I can," she replied in a broken tone. "Thank you! thank you ever, Lord Averil!"

She called in at the Rectory as she passed, and sat for a while with her father and mother; but it was pain to her to do so. The bitter wrong inflicted on them by her husband was making itself heard in her heart in loud reproaches. The bitter wrong of another kind dealt out to herself by him, was all too present then. They knew how she had idolized him; they must have known how blindly misplaced that idolatry was; and the red flush mounted to Maria's brow at the thought.

Oh, if she could only redeem the past, so far as they were concerned! It seemed that that would be enough. If she could only restore peace and comfort to their home, refund to her father what he had lost, how thankful she should be! She would move heaven and earth if that might accomplish it,—she would spend her own days in the workhouse,—pass them by a roadside hedge, and think nothing of it—if by those means she could remove the wrong done. She lifted her eyes to the blue sky, almost asking that a miracle might be wrought, to repair the injury which had been dealt out to her father. Ah me! if Heaven repaired all the injuries inflicted by man upon man, it would surely have no time for other works of mercy!

CHAPTER XXV.

IN THE STREETS OF PRIOR'S ASH.

BARELY had Maria departed and closed the Rectory gate behind her, when she encountered a stylish vehicle dashing along at an alarming pace, with a couple of frantic dogs behind it. It was that "turn-out" you have heard of, belonging to Mrs. Charlotte Pain. Mrs. Charlotte Pain was in it, resplendent as the sun, dazzling the admiring eyes of Prior's Ash in a gown of pink moiré antique, and a head-gear which appeared to be composed of pink and white feathers and a glittering silver aigrette, its form altogether not unlike a French gendarme's hat, if you have the pleasure of being familiar with that awe-imparting article. At the sight of Maria she pulled the horses up with a jerk: on which ensued some skirmishing and scattering abroad of dust, the animals, both horses and dogs, not approving of so summary a check; but Charlotte was resolute, and her whip effective. She then flung the reins to the groom who sat beside her, jumped down, and held out her hand to Maria.

Maria accepted it. The revelation gratuitously bestowed on her by Margery was beating its words upon her memory ; and her brow, face and neck had flushed to a glowing crimson. Some might have flung the offered hand aside, and picked up their skirts with a jerk, and sailed away with an air ; but Maria was a gentlewoman.

"How well you look ! " exclaimed Charlotte, regarding her in some surprise. "Perhaps you are warm? I say, Mrs. George "—dropping her voice to a whisper—"whither do you think I am bound ? "

" I cannot tell."

" To see Lord Averil. He is back again, and stopping at old Max's. I am going to badger him out of a promise not to hurt George Godolphin—about those rubbishing bonds, you know. I won't leave him until I get it."

" Yes," said Maria.

" I will have it. Or—war to the knife, my lord ! I should like to see him, or anybody else, attempt to refuse *me* anything I stood out for," she added, with a triumphant glance, meant for the absent viscount. " Poor George has nobody here to fight his battles for him, and he can't return to enter on them in person ; so it's well that some friend should do it. They are saying in the town this morning, that Averil has returned for the purpose of prosecuting : I mean to cut his prosecuting claws off."

" It is a mistake," said Maria. " Lord Averil has no intention of prosecuting."

" How do you know ? " bluntly asked Charlotte.

" I have just seen him."

" You don't mean to say you have been over to old Max's ? " exclaimed Charlotte, opening her brilliant black eyes very widely.

" Yes, I have."

" You quiet slyboots ! You have never walked there and back ? "

" I don't feel very tired. I have been resting with mamma for half an hour."

" And he's safe—Averil ? " eagerly continued Charlotte.

" Quite safe. Remember his long friendship with Thomas Godolphin."

" Oh, my dear, men forget friendship when their pockets are in question," was the light remark of Charlotte. " You are *sure*, though, Averil's not deceiving you ? I don't much think he is one to do a dirty trick of that sort, but I have lived long enough to learn that you must prove a man before you trust him."

" Lord Averil is not deceiving me," quietly answered Maria. " He has given me a message for my husband."

" Then there's no necessity for my going to him," said Charlotte. " Let me drive you home, Mrs. George Godolphin. I am sure you are fatigued. I never saw any one change countenance as you do. A few minutes ago you looked vulgarly hot, and now you are pale enough for the grave. Step in. James, you must change to the back seat."

Step into that formidably high thing, and sit by Mrs. Charlotte Pain's side, and dash through Prior's Ash ! Maria wondered whether the gossips of Prior's Ash—who, as it seemed, had made so free with gay George's name—or Margery, would stare the most. She declined the invitation.

"You are afraid," cried Charlotte. "Well, it's a great misfortune, these timid temperaments : but I suppose they can't be cured. Kate Verrall's another coward : but she's not as bad as you. Toss me my parasol, James."

James handed his mistress a charming toy of pink moiré antique silk and point lace, mounted on a handle of carved ivory. Charlotte put it up before her face, and turned to accompany Maria.

Maria put her parasol up before *her* face, thankful that it might serve to shield it, if only partially, from the curious eyes of Prior's Ash. Remembering the compliments that Prior's Ash had been kind enough to pass on her "blind simplicity," she would not exactly have chosen her present companion to walk through the streets with. Dame Bond, with her unsteady steps and her snuffy black gown, would have been preferable of the two.

"But," thought Maria in her generosity, striving to thrust that other unpleasant feeling down deep into her heart, and to lose sight of it, "it is really kind of Mrs. Pain to be seen thus publicly with me. Other ladies would be ashamed of me now, I suppose."

They stepped on. Maria with her parasol so close to her face that there was danger of her running against people ; Charlotte turning herself from side to side, flirting the costly little pink toy as one flirts a fan, bowing and scraping to all she met. The dogs snarled and barked behind her ; the carriage pranced and curvetted by their side ; the unhappy James, his hands full with the horses, which refused to recognize any mastership except that of Mrs. Charlotte Pain. Altogether, it was a more conspicuous progress than Maria would have chosen. Thus they arrived at the Bank, and Maria held out her hand to Charlotte. She *could* not be otherwise than courteous, no matter to whom.

"I am coming in," said Charlotte bluntly. "Take care what you are about with the horses, James."

Maria led the way to the dining-room. All was as it used to be in that charming room ; furniture, pictures, elegant trifles for show or for use ; all was the same : except—that those things belonged now not to Maria and her husband, but were noted down as the property of others. Soon, soon to be put up for sale ! Charlotte's rich moiré antique came to an anchor on a sofa, and she untied the string of the gendarme hat, and pushed it back on her head.

"I am going to leave Prior's Ash."

"To leave Prior's Ash !" repeated Maria. "When ?"

"Within a week of this. Lady Godolphin's coming back to the Folly."

"But—Lady Godolphin cannot come back to it without giving you due notice to quit ?" debated Maria.

"It's all arranged," said Charlotte, opening her mouth with a loud yawn. "Lady Godolphin wrote to Verrall, and the arrangements have been agreed upon amicably. Lady Godolphin foregoes a certain portion of rent, and we go out immediately. I am very glad, do you know. I had made my mind up not to stay. As to the Verralls, it may be said that they virtually took leave of the Folly long ago. Uncommonly glad I shall be to leave it," repeated Charlotte with emphasis.

"Why?"

"Who'd care to stay at Prior's Ash, after all this bother? You and George will be leaving it for London, you know—and I hope it won't be long first. You must make me useful up there, Mrs. George. I'll—— "

"Who told you we were going to leave for London?" interrupted Maria in astonishment.

"Nobody told me. But of course you will. Do you suppose George Godolphin will care to stop amongst this set? Not he. He'd see Prior's Ash go promenading first. What tie has he here, now Ashlydyat's gone? Verrall talks of buying a hunting-box in Leicestershire."

"Does he?" replied Maria mechanically, her thoughts buried elsewhere.

"Buying or hiring one. *I* should hire; and then there's no bother if you want to make a flitting. But Verrall is one who takes nobody's counsel but his own. What a worry it will be!" added Charlotte, after a pause.

Maria raised her eyes. She did not understand the remark.

"Packing up the things at the Folly," exclaimed Charlotte. "We begin to-morrow morning. I must be at the head of it, for it's of no use trusting that sort of work entirely to servants. Bon jour, petite coquette! Et les poupées?"

The diversion was caused by the flying entrance of Miss Meta. The young lady was not yet particularly well up in the Gallic language, and only half understood. She went straight up to Mrs. Pain, threw her soft sweet eyes right into that lady's flashing black ones, rested her pretty arms upon the moiré antique, and spoke out with her accustomed boldness.

"Where are the dogs now?"

"Chained down in the pit-hole," responded Mrs. Pain.

"Margery says there is no pit-hole, and the dogs were not chained down," asserted Meta.

"Margery's nothing but an old woman. Don't you believe her. If she tells stories again, we'll chain her down with the dogs."

"Two of the dogs are outside," said Meta.

"Not the same dogs, child," returned Mrs. Pain with cool equanimity. "They are street dogs, those are."

"They are with the carriage," persisted Meta. "They are barking round it."

"Are they barking? They can see Margery's face at the nursery window, and are frightened at it. Dogs always bark at ugly old women's faces. You tell Margery so."

"Margery's not ugly."

"You innocent little simpleton! She's ugly enough to frighten the crows."

How long the colloquy might have continued it is hard to say: certainly Meta would not be the one to give in: but it was interrupted by Margery herself. A note had just been delivered at the house for Mrs. George Godolphin, and Margery, who probably was glad of an excuse for entering, brought it in. She never looked at all towards Mrs. Pain ; she came straight up to her mistress, apparently ignoring Charlotte's presence, but you should have seen the expression of her face. The coronet on the seal imparted a suspicion to Maria that it came from Lord Averil, and her heart sank within her. Could he be withdrawing his promise of clemency ?

"Who brought this ?" she asked in a subdued tone.

"A servant on horseback, ma'am."

Charlotte had started up, catching at her feathers, for Pierce was at the dining-room door now, saying that the horses were alarmingly restive. "Good afternoon, Mrs. George Godolphin," she called out unceremoniously, as she hastened away. " I'll come and spend a quiet hour with you before I leave for town. Adieu, petite diablesse! I'd have you up to-morrow for a farewell visit, but that I'm afraid you might get nailed down with the furniture in some of the packing-cases."

Away she went. Meta was hastening after her, but was caught up by Margery with an angry sob—as if she had been saving her from some imminent danger. Maria opened the letter with trembling fingers.

"My dear Mrs. Godolphin,

"It has occurred to me since I parted from you, that you may wish to have the subject of our conversation confirmed in writing. I hereby assure you that I shall take no legal proceedings whatever against your husband on account of my lost bonds, and you may tell him from me that he need not, on that score, remain away from Prior's Ash.

"I hope you have reached home without too much fatigue.

"Believe me, ever sincerely yours,
"AVERIL."

"How kind he is !" came involuntarily from Maria's lips.

The words were drowned in a noise outside. Charlotte had contrived to ascend to her seat in spite of the prancing horses. She stood up in the high carriage, as George Godolphin had once done at the same door, and by dint of strength and skill, subdued them to control. Turning their fiery heads, scattering the assembled multitude right and left, nodding pleasantly to the applause vouchsafed her, Mrs. Charlotte Pain and the turn-out disappeared with a clatter, amidst the rolling of wheels, the barking of dogs, and the intense admiration of the gaping populace.

On this same evening, Miss Godolphin sat at a window facing the west in their home at Ashlydyat. Soon to be their home no more. Her cheek rested pensively on her fingers, as she thought—oh, with what bitterness !—of the grievous past. She had been universally ridiculed for giving heed to the superstitious traditions attaching to the house, and yet how strangely they appeared to be working themselves out. It had begun—Janet seemed to think the ruin had begun—with the departure of her father, Sir George, from Ashlydyat : and the tradition went that when the head of the Godolphins should voluntarily abandon Ashlydyat, the ruin would follow.

Had Sir George's departure brought on the ruin—been the first link in the chain that led to it? Janet was debating the question in her mind. That she was prone to indulging superstitious fancies to a degree many would pronounce ridiculously absurd cannot be denied : but in striving to solve that particular problem she was relinquishing the by-paths of the supernatural for the broad road of common sense. From the facts that were being brought to light by the bankruptcy, turning up by degrees one after another, it was easy to see that George Godolphin had been seduced into a hornet's nest, and so been eased of his money. Whether the process had been summary or slow—whether he had walked into it head foremost in blind simplicity—or whether he had only succumbed to it under the most refined Machiavellian craft, it was of no consequence to inquire. It is of no consequence to us. He had fallen into the hands of a company of swindlers, who ensnared their victims and transacted their business under the semblance of bill-discounting : and they had brought George to what he was.

Head and chief of this apparently reputable firm was Verrall : and Verrall, there was not a doubt, had been chief agent in George Godolphin's undoing. But for Sir George Godolphin's quitting Ashlydyat and putting it up in the market to let, Verrall might never have come near Prior's Ash; never have met Mr. George Godolphin. In that case the chances are that Mr. George would have been a flourishing banker still. Gay he would have been ; needlessly extravagant ; scattering his wild oats by the bushel—but not a man come to ruin and to beggary.

Janet Godolphin was right : it *was* the quitting Ashlydyat by her father, and the consequent tenancy of Mr. Verrall, which had been the first link in the chain, terminating in George's disgrace, in their ruin.

She sat there, losing herself in regret after regret. " If my father had not left it !—if he had never married Mrs. Campbell !—if my own dear mother had not died ! "—she lost herself, I say, in these regrets, bitter as they were vain.

How many of these useless regrets might embitter the lives of us all ! How many do embitter them ! If I had only done so-and-so !—if I had only taken the left turning when I took the right !—if I had only known what that man was from the first, and shunned his acquaintance !—if I had only chosen that path in life instead of this one !—if I had, in short, only done precisely the opposite to what I did do ! Vain, vain repinings ! —vain, useless, profitless repinings ! The only plan is to keep them as far as possible from our hearts. If we could foresee the end of a thing from its beginning,—if we could buy a stock of experience at the outset of life,—if we could, in point of fact, become endowed with the light of Divine wisdom, what different men and women the world would contain !

But we cannot. We cannot undo the past. It is ours with all its folly, its short-sightedness, perhaps its guilt. Though we stretch out our yearning and pitiful hands to Heaven in their movement of agony —though we wail aloud our bitter cry, Lord, pardon me—heal me—help me !—though we beat on our remorseful bosom and lacerate its flesh in bitter repentance, we cannot undo the past. We cannot undo it. The past remains to us unaltered ; and must remain so for ever.

Janet left the room. Thomas, who had been seated opposite to her, was buried in thought, when Bexley appeared, showing in Lord Averil.

He hastened forward to prevent Thomas Godolphin's rising. Laying one hand upon his shoulder and the other on his hands, he pressed him down and would not let him rise.

" How am I to thank you ? " were the first words spoken by Thomas —in reference to the clemency shown to his brother, as promised that day to Maria.

" Hush ! " said Lord Averil. " My dear friend, you are allowing these things to affect you more than they ought. I see the greatest change in you, even in this short time."

The rays of the declining sun were falling on the face of Thomas Godolphin, lighting up its fading vitality. The cheeks were thinner, the weak hair seemed scantier, the truthful grey eyes had acquired an habitual expression of pain. Lord Averil leaned over him and noted it all.

" Sit down," said Thomas, drawing a chair nearer to him.

Lord Averil accepted the invitation, but did not release the hand. " I understand you have been doubting me," he said. " You might have known me better. We have been friends a long time."

Thomas Godolphin only answered by a pressure of the hand he held. Old and familiar friends though they were, understanding each other's hearts almost, as these close friends should do, it was yet a most painful point to Thomas Godolphin. On the one side there was his brother's crime : on the other there was the loss of that large sum to Lord Averil. Thomas had to do perpetual battle with pain now : but there were moments when the conflict was nearer and sharper than at others. This was one of them.

They subsided into conversation : its theme, as was natural, the bankruptcy and its attendant details. Lord Averil found that Thomas was blaming himself.

" Why should you ? " he asked impulsively. " Is it not enough that the world should do so, without yourself indorsing it ? "

A faint smile crossed Thomas Godolphin's face at the thoughtless admission spoken so openly : but he knew, none better, how great a share of blame was dealt out to him. " It is due," he observed to Lord Averil. " I ought not to have reposed trust so implicit in George. Things could not have come to this pass if I had not done so."

" If we cannot place implicit trust in a brother, in whom can we place it ? "

" True. But in my position as trustee to others, I ought not to have *trusted* that things were going on right. I ought to have *known* that they were so."

They went on to the future. Thomas spoke of the selling up of all things, of their turning out of Ashlydyat. " Is that decree irrevocable?" Lord Averil interrupted. " Must Ashlydyat be sold ? "

Thomas was surprised at the question. It was so superfluous a one. " It will be sold very shortly," he said, " to the highest bidder. Any stranger who bids most will get Ashlydyat. I hope," he added, with a half start, as if the possibility occurred to him then for the first time, "that the man Verrall will not become a bidder for it—and get it! Lady Godolphin turns him out of the Folly."

"Never fear," said Lord Averil. "He will only be too glad to relieve Prior's Ash of his presence. Thomas, can nothing be done to the man? Your brother may have been a willing tool in his hands, but broad whispers are going about that it is Verrall who has reaped the harvest. Can no legal cognizance be taken of it?"

Thomas shook his head. "We may suspect a great deal—in fact, it is more than suspicion—but we can prove nothing. The man will rise triumphantly from it all, and carry his head higher than ever. I hope, I say, that he will not think of Ashlydyat. They were in it once, you know."

"Why could not Ashlydyat be disposed of privately?—by valuation? It might be, if the assignees approved."

"Yes, I suppose it might be."

"I wish you would sell it to me," breathed Lord Averil.

"To you!" repeated Thomas Godolphin. "Ay, indeed. Were you to have Ashlydyat I should the less keenly regret its passing from the Godolphins."

Lord Averil paused. He appeared to want to say something, but to hesitate in doubt.

"Would it please you that one of the Godolphins should still inhabit it?" he asked at length.

"I do not understand you?" replied Thomas. "There is no chance —I had almost said no possibility—of a Godolphin henceforward inhabiting Ashlydyat."

"I hope and trust there is," said Lord Averil with emotion. "If Ashlydyat is ever to be mine, I shall not care for it unless a Godolphin shares it with me. I speak of your sister Cecilia."

Thomas sat in calmness, waiting for more. Nothing could stir him greatly now. Lord Averil gave him the outline of the past. Of his love for Cecilia, and her rejection of him.

"There has been something," he continued, "in her manner of late, which has renewed hope within me—otherwise I should not say this to you now. Quite of late; since her rejection of me; I have observed that—that—— I cannot describe it, Thomas," he broke off. "But I have determined to risk my fate once more. And you—loving Cecil as I do—you thought I could prosecute George!"

"But I did not know that you loved Cecil."

"I suppose not. It has seemed to me, though, that my love must have been patent to the world. You would give her to me, would you not?"

"Ay; thankfully," was the warm answer. "The thought of leaving Cecil unprotected has been one of my cares. Janet and Bessy are older and more experienced. Let me give you one consolation, Averil: if Cecilia has rejected you, she has rejected others. Janet has fancied she had some secret attachment. Can it have been to yourself?"

"If so, why should she have rejected me?"

"In truth I do not know. Cecil has seemed grievously unhappy since these troubles arose : almost as one who has no further hope in life. George's peril has told upon her."

"His peril?"

"From you."

Lord Averil bit his lip. "Cecil, above all others—unless it were yourself—might have known that he was safe."

A silence ensued. Lord Averil resumed : "There is one upon whom I fear these troubles are telling all too greatly, Thomas. And that is your brother's wife."

"May God comfort her!" was the involuntary answer that broke from the lips of Thomas Godolphin.

"Had I been ever so harshly inclined, I think the sight of her to-day would have disarmed me. No, no : had I never owned friendship for you; had I never loved Cecil, there is certainly enough evil, cruel, un-avoidable evil, which must fall with this calamity, without my adding to it."

"When I brought word home this afternoon that you were well dis-posed towards George—that he had nothing to fear from you, Cecil burst into tears."

A glow arose to Lord Averil's face. He looked out on the setting sun in silence. "Has your brother been sent for?" he presently asked.

"Maria and I have both written for him now. I should think he will come. What is it, Bexley?"

"A message from Mrs. Pain, sir, about some of the fixtures at Lady Godolphin's Folly. Mrs. Pain wants to know if you have a list of them. She forgets which belong to the house, and which don't."

Thomas Godolphin said a word of apology to Lord Averil, and left the room. In the hall he met Cecil crossing to it. She went in, quite unconscious who was its inmate. He rose up to welcome her.

A momentary hesitation in her steps · a doubt whether she should not run away again, and then she recalled her senses and went for-ward.

She recalled what he had done that day for her brother; she went forward to thank him. But ere the thanks had well begun, they came to an end, for Cecil had burst into tears.

How it went on, and what was exactly said or done, neither of them could remember afterwards. A very few minutes, and Cecil's head was resting upon his shoulder, all the mistakes of the past cleared up between them.

She might not have confessed to him how long she had loved him—ever since that long past time when they were together at Mrs. Averil's—but for her dread lest he should fear that she was only accepting him now out of gratitude—gratitude for his noble behaviour to her erring brother. And so she told him the truth : that she had loved him, and only him, all through.

"Cecil, my darling, what long misery might have been spared me had I known this!"

Cecil looked down. Perhaps some might also have been spared to her. "It is not right that you should marry me now," she said.

"Why?"

" On account of this dreadful disgrace. George must have forgotten how it would fall upon—— "

" Hush, Cecil! The disgrace, as I look upon it—as I believe all just people must look upon it—is confined to himself. It is indeed. Not an iota of the respect due to Thomas by the world, of the consideration due to the Miss Godolphins, will be lessened. Rely upon it I am right."

" But Thomas is being reflected upon daily : personally abused."

" By a few inconsiderate creditors, smarting just now under their loss. That will all pass away. If you could read my heart and see how happy you have made me, you would know how little cause you have to talk of 'disgrace,' Cecil."

She was happy also, as she rested there against him ; too happy.

" Would you like to live at Ashlydyat, Cecil ? Thomas would rather we had it than it should lapse to strangers. I should wish to buy it."

" Oh yes—if it could be."

" I dare say it can be. Of course it can. Ashlydyat must be sold, and I shall be as welcome a purchaser as any other would be. If it must be put up to auction, I can be its highest bidder ; but I dare say they will be glad to avoid the expense of an auction, and let me purchase it privately. I might purchase the furniture also, Cecil ; all the old relics that Sir George set so much store by—that Janet does still."

" If it could be ! " she murmured.

" Indeed I think it may be. They will be glad to value it as it stands. And Cecil, we will drive away all the ghostly superstitions, and that ominous Shadow—— "

Cecil lifted her face, an eager light upon it. " Janet says that the curse has been worked out with the ruin of the Godolphins. She thinks that the dark Shadow will never come any more."

" So much the better. We will have the Dark Plain dug up and made into a children's playground, and a summer-house for them shall be erected on the very spot which the Shadow has made its own. There may be children here some time, Cecil."

Cecil's eyelashes were bent on her flushed cheeks. She did not raise them.

" If you liked—if you liked, Cecil, we might ask Janet and Bessy to retain their home here," resumed Lord Averil, in thoughtful consideration. " Ashlydyat is large enough for all."

" Their home is decided upon," said Cecil, shaking her head. " Bessy has promised to make hers at Lady Godolphin's Folly. Lady Godolphin exacted her promise to that effect, before she decided to return to it. I was to have gone to it also. Janet goes to Scotland. I am quite sure that this place has become too painful for Janet to remain in. She has an annuity, as perhaps you know ; it was money left her by mamma's sister ; so that she is independent, and can live where she pleases ; but I am sure she will go to Scotland, as soon as— as soon as—— "

" I understand you, Cecil. As soon as Thomas shall have passed away."

The tears were glistening in her eyes. " Do you not see a great change in him ? "

"A very great one. Cecil, I should like him to give you to me. Will you waive ceremony, and be mine at once?"

"I will see," murmured Cecil. "When a little of this bustle, this disgrace shall have passed away. Let it die out first."

A grave expression arose to Lord Averil's face. "It must not be very long first, Cecil: if you would be mine while your brother is in life."

"I will, I will; it shall be as you wish," she answered, her tears falling. And before Lord Averil could make any rejoinder, she had hastily left him, and was standing against the window, stealthily drying her eyes: for the door had opened to admit Thomas Godolphin.

CHAPTER XXVI.

MY LADY WASHES HER HANDS.

THE summer was drawing towards its close; and so was the bankruptcy of Godolphin, Crosse, and Godolphin.—If we adhere to the style of the old firm, we only do as Prior's Ash did. Mr. Crosse, you have heard, was out of it actually and officially, but people, in speaking or writing of the firm, forgot to omit his name. One or two maddened sufferers raised a question of his liability, in their desperation; but they gained nothing by the motion: Mr. Crosse was as legally separated from the Godolphins as if he had never been connected with them.— The labour, the confusion, the doubt, attendant upon most bankruptcies, was nearly over, and creditors knew the best and the worst. The dividend would be, to use a common expression, shamefully small, when all was told: it might have been even smaller (not much, though) but that Lord Averil's claim on the sixteen thousand pounds, the value of the bonds, was not allowed to enter into the accounts. Those bonds and all connected with them were sunk in silence so complete, that at length outsiders began to ask whether they and their reported loss had not been altogether a myth.

Thomas Godolphin had given up everything, even to his watch, and the signet ring upon his finger. The latter was returned to him. The jewellery of the Miss Godolphins was given up. Maria's jewellery also. In short, there was nothing that was not given up. The fortune of the Miss Godolphins, consisting of money and bank shares, had of course gone with the rest. The money had been in the Bank at interest; the shares were now worthless. Janet alone had an annuity of about a hundred a year, rather more, which nothing could deprive her of: the rest of the Godolphins were reduced to beggary. Worse off were they than any of their clamorous creditors, since for them all had gone: houses, lands, money, furniture, personal belongings. But that Thomas Godolphin would not long be in a land where these things are required, it might have been a question how he was for the future to find sufficient to live upon.

The arrangement hinted at by Lord Averil had been carried out, and that nobleman was now the owner of Ashlydyat and all that it contained. It may have been departing a little from the usual order of things in such cases to dispose of it by private arrangement; but it had been done with the full consent of all parties concerned. Even the creditors, who of course showed themselves ready to cavil at anything, were glad that the expense of a sale by auction should be avoided. A price had been put upon Ashlydyat, and Lord Averil gave it without a dissentient word; and the purchase of the furniture, as it stood, was undoubtedly advantageous to the sellers.

Yes, Ashlydyat had gone from the Godolphins. But Thomas and his sisters remained in it. There had been no battle with Thomas on the score of his remaining. Lord Averil had clasped his friend's hands within his own, and in a word or two of emotion had given him to understand that his chief satisfaction in its purchase had been the thought that he, Thomas, would remain in his own home, as long—— Thomas Godolphin understood the broken words: as long as he had need of one. "Nothing would induce me to enter upon it until then," continued Lord Averil. "So be it," said Thomas quietly, for he fully understood the feeling, and the gratification it brought to him who conferred the obligation. "I shall not keep you out of it long, Averil." The same words, almost the very same words that Sir George Godolphin had once spoken to his son: "I shall not keep you and Ethel long out of Ashlydyat."

So Thomas remained at Ashlydyat with his broken health, and the weeks had gone on; and summer was now drawing to an end, and other things also. Thomas Godolphin was beginning to be better understood than he had been at the time of the crash, and people were repenting of the cruel blame they had so freely hurled upon him. The first smart of the blow had faded away, and with it the prejudice which had unjustly, though not unnaturally, distorted their judgment, and buried for the time all kindly impulse. Perhaps there was not a single creditor, whatever might be the extent of the damage he had suffered by the Bank, but would have stretched out his hand, and given him more gold, if by that means he could have saved the life of Thomas Godolphin. They learnt to remember that the fault had not lain with him: they believed that if by the sacrifice of his own life he could have averted the calamity he would have cheerfully laid it down: they knew that his days were as one long mourning, for them individually—and they took shame to themselves for having been so bitter against him, Thomas Godolphin.

Not so in regard to George. *He* did not regain his place in their estimation: and if they could have hoisted Mr. George on a pole in front of the Bank and cast at him a few rotten eggs and other agreeable missiles, it had been a relief to their spleen. Had George been condemned to stand at the bar of a public tribunal by the nobleman he so defrauded, half Prior's Ash would have gone to gratify their feelings by staring at him during the trial, and have made it a day of jubilee. Harsh epithets, exceedingly unpleasant when taken personally, were freely lavished upon him, and would be for a long while to come. He *had* wronged them: and time alone will suffice to wash out the everpresent remembrance of such wrongs.

He had been at Prior's Ash. Gay George still. So far as could be seen, the calamity had not much affected *him*. Not a line showed itself on his fair, smooth brow, not a shade less of colour on his bright cheek, not a grey thread in his luxuriant hair, not a cloud in his dark-blue eye. Handsome, fascinating, attractive as ever, was George Godolphin : and he really seemed to be as gay and light of temperament. When any ill-used creditor attacked him outright—as some did, through a casual meeting in the street, or other lucky chance—George was triumphant George still. No shame did he seem to take to himself— but so sunny, so fascinating was he, as he held the hands of the half-reluctant grumbler, and protested it should all come right some time, that the enemy was won over to conciliation for the passing moment. It was impossible to help admiring George Godolphin ; it was impossible to avoid liking him : it was impossible, when brought face to face with him, not to be taken with his frank plausibility : the crustiest sufferer of them all was in a degree subdued by it. Prior's Ash understood that the officers of the bankruptcy "badgered" George a great deal when under examination ; but George only seemed to come out of it the more triumphantly. Safe on the score of Lord Averil, all the rest was light in comparison ; and easy George never lost his good-humour or his self-possession. He appeared to come scot-free out of every-thing. Those falsified accounts in the bank-books, that many another might have been held responsible for, and punished, he emerged from harmlessly. It was conjectured that the full extent of these false entries never was discovered by the commissioners : Thomas Godolphin and Mr. Hurde alone could have told it : and Thomas preferred to allow the odium of loosely-kept books, of reckless expenditure of money, to fall upon himself rather than betray George. Were the whole thing laid bare and declared, it could not bring a fraction of good to the creditors, so, from that point of view, it was as well to let it rest. Are these careless, sanguine, gay-tempered men always lucky? It has been so asserted ; and I do think there is a great deal of truth in it. Most unequivocally lucky in this instance was George Godolphin.

It was of no earthly use asking him where all the money had gone —to what use this sum had been put, to what use the other—George could not tell. He could not tell any more than they could ; he was as much perplexed about it as they were. He ran his white hand uncon-sciously through his golden hair, hopelessly trying his best to account for a great many items that no one living could have accounted for. All in vain. Heedless, off-handed George Godolphin! He appeared before those inquisitive officials somewhat gayer in attire than was needful. A sober suit, rather of the seedy order, might have been deemed appropriate at such a time; but George Godolphin gave no indication of consulting any such rules of propriety. George Godol-phin's refined taste had kept him from falling into the loose and easy style of dress which some men so strangely favour in the present day, placing a gentleman in outward aspect on a level with the roughs of society. George, though no coxcomb, had always dressed well and expensively ; and George appeared inclined to do so still. They could not take him to task on the score of his fine broadcloth or of his neatly-finished boot; but they did bend their eyes meaningly on the massive gold chain which crossed his white waistcoat : on the costly appendages which dangled from it; on the handsome repeater which he more than once took out, as if weary of the passing hours. Mr. George received a gentle hint that those articles, however ornamental to himself, must be confiscated to the bankruptcy; and he resigned them with a good grace. The news of this little incident travelled abroad, as an interesting anecdote connected with the proceedings, and the next time George saw Charlotte Pain, she told him he was a fool to walk into the camp of the Philistines with pretty things about him. But George was not wilfully dishonest (if you can by any possibility understand that assertion, after what you know of his past doings), and he replied to Charlotte that it was only right the creditors should make spoil of his watch, and anything else he possessed. The truth, were it defined, being, that George was only dishonest when driven so to be. He had made free with the bonds of Lord Averil, but he could not be guilty of the meanness of concealing his personal trinkets.

Three or four times now had George been at Prior's Ash. People wondered why he did not remain; what it was that took him again and again to London. The very instant he found that he could be dispensed with at Prior's Ash, away he flew; not to return to it again until imperatively demanded. The plain fact was that Mr. George did *not* like to face Prior's Ash. For all the easy self-possession, the gay good-humour he displayed to its inhabitants, the place had become utterly distasteful to him, almost unbearable; he shunned it and hated it as a pious Roman Catholic hates and would shun purgatory. For that reason, and for no other, George did his best to escape from it.

He had seen Lord Averil. And his fair face had betrayed its shame as he said a few words of apology for what he had done—of thanks for the clemency shown him—of promises for the future. "If I live, I'll make it good to you," he murmured. "I did not intend to *steal* them, Averil; I did not, on my solemn word of honour. I thought I should have replaced them before anything could be known. Your asking for them immediately—that you should do so seemed a very fatality—upset everything. But for that, I might have weathered it all, and the house would not have gone. It was no light pressure that forced me to touch them—Heaven alone knows the need and the temptation."

And the meeting between the brothers? No eye saw it; no ear heard it. Good Thomas Godolphin was dying from the blow, dying before his time; but not a word of reproach was given to George. How George defended himself—or whether he attempted to defend himself, or whether he let it wholly alone—the outside world never knew.

Lady Godolphin's Folly was no longer in the occupancy of the Verralls or of Mrs. Pain: Lady Godolphin had returned to it. Not a day aged; not a day altered. Time flitted lightly over Lady Godolphin. Her bloom-tinted complexion was delicately fresh as ever; her dress was as becoming, her flaxen locks were as youthful. She came with her servants and her carriages, and she took up her abode at the Folly, in all the splendour of the old days. Her income was large, and the misfortunes which had recently fallen on the family did not affect it. Lady Godolphin washed her hands of these misfortunes. She washed her hands of George. She told the world that she did so. She spoke of them openly to the public in general, to her acquaintances in particular, in a slighting, contemptuous sort of manner, as we are all apt to speak of the ill-doings of other people. They don't concern us, and it's rather a condescension on our part to blame them at all.—This was no concern of Lady Godolphin's. She told every one it was not so. George's disgrace did not reflect itself upon the family, and of him she—washed her hands. No: Lady Godolphin could not see that this break-up caused by George should be any reason whatever why she or the Miss Godolphins should hide their heads and go mourning in sackcloth and ashes. Many of her old acquaintances in the county agreed with Lady Godolphin in her view of things, and helped by their visits to make the Folly gay again.

To wash her hands of Mr. George, was, equitably speaking, no more than that gentleman deserved: but Lady Godolphin also washed her hands of Maria. On her return to Prior's Ash she had felt inclined to espouse Maria's part; to sympathize with and pity her; and she drove down in state one day, and left her carriage with its powdered coachman and footman to pace to and fro in Crosse Street before the Bank, while she went in. She openly avowed to Maria that she considered herself in a remote degree the cause which had led to her union with George Godolphin: she supposed that it was her having had Maria so much at the Folly, and afterwards on the visit at Broomhead, which had led to the attachment. As a matter of course she regretted this, and wished there had been no marriage, now that George had turned out so gracelessly. If she could do anything to repair it she would : and, as a first step, she offered the Folly as a present asylum to Maria. She would be safe there from worry, and—from George.

Maria scarcely at first understood her. And when she did so, her only answer was to thank Lady Godolphin, and to stand out, in her quiet, gentle manner, but untiringly and firmly, for her husband. Not a shade of blame would she acknowledge to be due to him; not a reverence would she render him the less: her place was with him, she said, though the whole world turned against him. It vexed Lady Godolphin.

"Do you know," she asked, "that you must choose between your husband and the world?"

"In what way?" replied Maria.

"In what way! When a man acts as George Godolphin has acted, he places a barrier between himself and society. But there's no necessity for the barrier to extend to you, Maria. If you will come to my house for a while, you will find this to be the case—it will not extend to you."

"You are very kind, Lady Godolphin. My husband is more to me than the world."

"Do you approve of what he has done?"

"No," replied Maria. "But it is not my place to show that I blame him."

"I think it is," said Lady Godolphin in the hard tone she used when her opinion was questioned.

Maria was silent. She never could contend with any one.

"Then you prefer to hold out against the world," resumed Lady Godolphin; "to put yourself beyond its pale! It is a bold step, Maria."

"What can I do?" was Maria's pleading answer. "If the world throws me over because I will not turn against my husband, I cannot help it. I married him for better or for worse, Lady Godolphin."

"The fact is, Maria," retorted my lady sharply, "that you have loved George Godolphin in a ridiculous degree."

"Perhaps I have," was Maria's subdued answer, the colour dyeing her face with various reminiscences. "But surely there was no sin in it, Lady Godolphin: he is my husband."

"And you cling to him still?"

"Oh yes."

Lady Godolphin rose. She shrugged her shoulders as she drew her white lace shawl over them, she glanced at her coquettish blue bonnet in the glass as she passed it, at her blush-rose cheeks. "You have chosen your husband, Maria, in preference to me; in preference to the world; and from this moment I wash my hands of you, as I have already done of him."

It was all the farewell she took: and she went out to her carriage, thinking what a blind, obstinate, hardened woman was Maria Godolphin. She saw not what it had cost that "hardened" woman to bear up before her: that her heart was nigh unto breaking; that the sorrow laid upon her was greater than she well knew how to battle with.

CHAPTER XXVII.

A BROKEN IDOL.

GEORGE GODOLPHIN leaned against a pillar of the terrace opening from the dining-room. They had not left the Bank yet as a residence, but this was their last day in it. It was the last day they could remain in it, and why they should have lingered in it so long was food for gossip in Prior's Ash. On the morrow the house would become public property. Men would walk in and ticket all the things, apportion them their place in the catalogue, their order in the days of sale; and the public would crowd in also, to feast their eyes upon the household gods hitherto sacred to George Godolphin.

How did he feel as he stood there? Was his spirit in heaviness, as was the case under similar misfortune with another man—if the written record he left to us may be trusted—that great poet, ill-fated in death as in life, whose genius has since found no parallel of its kind :-

> "It was a trying moment, that which found him,
> Standing alone beside his desolate hearth,
> While all his household gods lay shivered roun him.

Did George Godolphin find it trying? Was his hearth desolate? Not desolate in the full sense in which that other spoke, for George Godolphin's wife was with him still.

She had stood by him. When he first returned to Prior's Ash, she had greeted him with her kind smile, with words of welcome. She spoke not of what that awful shock had been to her, the discovery of the part he had played in Lord Averil's bonds; she spoke not of another shock, not less awful. Whatever effect that unpleasant scandal, mentioned by Margery, which it seems had formed a staple dish for Prior's Ash, may have been taking upon her in secret and silence, she gave no sign of it to George. He never suspected that any such whisper, touching his worthy self, had been breathed to her. Mr. George best knew what grounds there might be for it: whether it bore any foundation, or whether it was but one of those breezy rumours, false as the wind, which have their rise in ill-nature, and in that alone. But however it may have been, whether true or false, he could not divine that such poison would be dropped into his wife's ear. If he had thought her greeting to him strange, her manner more utterly subdued than there was need for, her grief more violent, he attributed it all to the recent misfortunes: and Maria made no other sign.

The effects had been bought in at Ashlydyat, but these had not: and this was the last day, almost the last hour of his occupancy. One would think his eyes would be cast around in lingering looks of farewell—upon chairs and tables, scattered ornaments, and rich carpets, upon the valuable and familiar pictures. Not a bit of it. George's eyes were bent on his nails, which he was trimming to his satisfaction, and he was carolling in an undertone a strain of a new English opera.

They were to go out that evening. At dusk. At dusk, you may be sure. They were to go forth from their luxurious home, and enter upon obscure lodgings, and go down in the scale of what the world calls society. Not that the lodgings were obscure, taken in the abstract; but obscure indeed, as compared with their home at the Bank, very obscure beside the home they had sometime thought to remove to— Ashlydyat.

He stood there in his careless beauty, his bright face bent downwards, his tall, fine form noble in its calmness. The sun was playing with his hair, bringing out its golden tints, and a smile illumined his face, as he went on with his song. Whatever may have been George Godolphin's shortcomings in some points of view, none could reproach him on the score of his personal attractions. All the old terror, the gnawing care, had gone out of him with the easy bankruptcy—easy in its results to him, compared with what might have been—and gay George, graceless George, was himself again. There may have been something deficient in his moral organization, for he really appeared to take no shame to himself for what had occurred. He stood there calmly self-possessed; the perfect gentleman, so far as appearance and manners could make him one: looking as fit to bend his knee at the proud court of St. James's as ever that stately gentleman his father had looked when her Majesty touched him with the sword-blade and bade him rise up Sir George:

> " Once would my heart with the wildest emotion
> Throb, dearest Eily, when near me wert thou ;
> Now I regard thee with deep—— "

The strain was interrupted, and George, as he ceased it, glanced up.

Meta, looking, it must be confessed, rather black about the hands and pinafore, as if Margery had not had time to attend to her within the last hour, came running in. George shut up his knife and held out his arms.

"Papa, are we to have tea at home, or after we get into the lodgings?"

"Ask mamma," responded George.

"Mamma told me to ask you. She doesn't know, she says. She's too busy to talk to me. She's getting the great box on to the stand."

"She's doing what?" cried George in a quick accent.

"Getting the great box on to the stand," repeated Meta. "She's going to pack it. Papa, will the lodgings be better than this? Will there be a big garden? Margery says there'll be no room for my rocking-horse. Won't there?"

Something in the child's questions may have grated on the fine ear of George Godolphin, had he stayed to listen to them. However lightly the bankruptcy might be passing over George's mind on his own score, he regretted its results most bitterly for his wife and child. To see them turned from their home, condemned to descend to the inconveniences and obscurity of these lodgings, was the worst pill George Godolphin had ever had to swallow. He would have cut off his right arm to retain them in their position; ay, and also his left: he could have struck himself to the earth in his rage for the disgrace he had brought on them.

Hastening up the stairs he entered his bedroom. It was in a litter; boxes and wearing-apparel lying about. Maria, flushed and breathless, was making great efforts to drag a cumbrous trunk on to a stand, or small bench, for the convenience of filling it. No very extensive efforts either; for she knew that such might harm her at present in her feeble strength.

George raised the trunk to its place with one lift of his manly arms, and then forced his wife, with more gentleness, into a chair.

"How could you be so imprudent, Maria?" broke from him in a vexed tone, as he stood before her.

"I was not hurting myself," she answered. "The things must be packed."

"Of course they must. But not by you. Where's Margery?"

"Margery has a great deal to do. She cannot do all."

"Then where's Sarah?" resumed George crossly and sharply.

"Sarah's in the kitchen preparing dinner. We must have some to-day."

"Show me what the things are, and I will pack them."

"Nonsense! As if it would hurt me to put the things into the box! You never interfered with me before, George."

"You never attempted this sort of work before. I won't have it, Maria. Were you in a state of health to be knocking about, you might do it; but you certainly shall not, as it is."

It was his self-reproach that was causing his angry tone; very keenly at that moment was it making itself heard. And Maria's spirits were not that day equal to sharpness of speech. It told upon her, and she burst into tears.

How terribly the signs of distress vexed him, no words could tell. He took them as a tacit reproach to himself. And they were so: however unintentional on her part such reproach might be.

"Maria, I won't have this; I can't bear it," he cried, his voice hoarse with emotion. "If you show this temper, this childish sorrow before me, I shall run away."

He could have cut his tongue out for so speaking—for his stinging words; for their stinging tone. "Temper! Childish sorrow!" George chafed at himself in his self-condemnation: he chafed—he knew how unjustly—at Maria.

Very, very unjustly. She had not annoyed him with reproaches, with complaints, as some wives would have done; she had not, to him, shown symptoms of the grief that was wearing out her heart. She had been considerate to him, bearing up bravely whenever he was at Prior's Ash. Even now, as she dried away the rebellious tears, she would not let him think they were being shed for the lost happiness of the past, but murmured some feeble excuse about a headache.

He saw through the fond deceit; he saw all the generosity; and the red shame mantled in his fair face as he bent down to her, and his voice changed to one of the deepest tenderness.

"If I have lost you this home, Maria, I will get you another," he whispered. "Only give me a little time. Don't grieve before me if you can help it, my darling: it is as though you ran a knife into my very soul. I can bear the loud abuse of the whole world, better than one silent reproach from you."

And the sweet words came to her as a precious balm. However bitter had been the shock of that one rude awaking, she loved him fondly still. It may be that she loved him only the more deeply: for the passions of the human heart are wayward and wilful, utterly unamenable to control.

Margery came into the room with her hands and arms full. George may have been glad of the divertisement, and turned upon her, his voice resuming its anger. "What's the meaning of this, Margery? I come up here and I find your mistress packing and dragging boxes about. Can't you see to these things?"

Margery was as cross as George that day, and her answer in its sharpness rivalled his. Direct reproof Margery had never presumed to offer her master, though she would have liked to do it amazingly, for not one of those who condemned him held a more exaggerated view of Mr. George's past delinquencies than she.

"I can't be in ten places at once. And I can't do the work of ten people. If you know them that can, sir, you'd better get them here instead of me."

"Did I not ask you if you should want assistance in packing, and you told me that you should not?" retorted George.

"No more I don't want it," was the answer. "I can do all the packing that is to be done here, if I am let alone, and allowed to take my own time, and do it in my own way. In all that chaffling and changing of houses when my Lady Godolphin chose to move the Ashlydyat things to the Folly, and when they had to be moved back afterwards in accordance with Sir George's will, who did the best part of the packing and saw to everything, but me? It would be odd if I couldn't put up a few gowns and shirts, but I must be talked to about help!"

Poor Margery was evidently in a temper. Time back George would have put her down with a haughty word of authority or with joking mockery, as the humour might have taken him. He did not to-day. There had been wrong inflicted upon Margery; and it may be that he was feeling it. She had lost the little savings of years—the Brays had not allowed them to be very great; she had lost the money bequeathed to her by Mrs. Godolphin. All had been in the Bank, and all had gone. In addition to this, there were personal discomforts. Margery found the work of a common servant thrown upon her in her old age: an under girl, Sarah, was her only help now at the Bank, and Margery alone would follow their fallen fortunes to these lodgings.

"Do as you please," was all George said. "But your mistress shall not meddle with it."

"If my mistress chooses to set to work behind my back, I can't stop it. She knows there's no need to do it. If you'll be so good, ma'am," turning to her mistress, "as just let things alone and leave 'em to me, you'll find they'll be done. What's a few clothes to pack?" indignantly repeated Margery. "And there's nothing else that we may take. If I put up but a pair of sheets or a tin dish-cover, I should be called a thief, I suppose."

There lay the great grievance of Margery's present mood—that everything, except the "few clothes," must be left behind. Margery, for all her crustiness and her outspoken temper, was a most faithfully attached servant, and it may be questioned if she did not feel the abandonment of their goods more keenly than did even Maria and George. The things were not hers: every article of her own, even to a silver cream-jug which had been the boasted treasure of her life, she had been allowed to retain; even to the little work-box of white satinwood, with its landscape, the trees of which Miss Meta had been permitted to paint red, and the cottage blue. Not an article of Margery's that she could remove but was sacred to her: but in her fidelity she did resent bitterly having to leave the property of her master and mistress, that it might all pass into the hands of strangers.

Maria, debarred from assisting, wandered in her restlessness through some of the more familiar rooms. It was well that she should pay them a farewell visit. From the bedroom where the packing was going on, to George's dressing-room, thence to her own sitting-room, thence to the drawing-room, all on that floor. She lingered in all. A home sanctified by years of happiness cannot be quitted without regret, even when exchanged at pleasure for another; but to turn out of it in humiliation, in poverty, in hopelessness, is a trial of the sharpest and sorest kind. Apart from the pain, the feeling was a strange one. The objects crowding these rooms: the necessary furniture costly and substantial; the elegant ornaments of various shapes and sorts, the chaste works of art, not necessary, but so luxurious and charming, had hitherto been their own—hers in conjunction with her husband's. They might have done what they pleased with them. Had she broken that Wedgwood vase, there was no one to call her to account for it : had she or George chosen to make a present of that rare basket in medallion, with its speaking likenesses of the beauties of the whilom gay French court, there was no one to say them nay; had they felt disposed to change that fine piano for another, the liberty to do so was theirs. They had been the owners of these surroundings, master and mistress of the house and its contents. And now? Not a single article belonged to them : they were but tenants on sufferance : the things remained, but their right in them had passed away. If she dropped and broke only that pretty trifle which her hand was touching now, she must answer for the mishap. The feeling, I say, was a strange one.

She walked through the rooms with dry eyes and a hot brow. Tears seemed long ago to have gone from her. It is true she had been surprised into a few that day, but the lapse was unusual. Why should she make this farewell visit to the rooms, she began asking herself. She needed it not to remember them. Visions of the past came crowding upon her memory ; of this or the other happy day spent in them : of the gay meetings when they had received the world; of the sweet home hours when she had sat there alone with him of whom she had well-nigh made an idol—her husband. Mistaken idolatry, Mrs. George Godolphin! mistaken, useless, vain idolatry. Was there ever an earthly idol yet that did not mock its worshipper? I know of none. We make an idol of our child, and the time comes when it will turn and sting us : we make an idol of the god or goddess of our passionate love, and how does it end?

Maria sat down and leaned her head upon her hand, thinking more of the past than of the future. She was getting to have less hope in the future than was good for her. It is a bad sign when a sort of apathy with regard to it steals over us ; a proof that the mind is not in the healthy state that it ought to be. A time of trial, of danger, was approaching for Maria, and she seemed to contemplate the possibility of her sinking under it with strange calmness. A few months ago, the bare glance at such a fear would have unhinged her : she would have clung to her husband and Meta, and sobbed out her passionate prayer to God in her dire distress, not to be taken from them. Things had changed : the world in which she had been so happy had lost its charm for her; the idol in whose arms she had sheltered herself turned out not to have been of pure gold : and Maria Godolphin began to realize the truth of the words of the wise king of Jerusalem—that the world and its dearest hopes are but vanity.

Meanwhile Mrs. Charlotte Pain, in her looped-up petticoats and nicely-fitting kid boots, was tripping jauntily through the streets of Prior's Ash. Mrs. Pain had been somewhat vacillating in regard to her departure from that long-familiar town ; she had reconsidered her determination of quitting it so abruptly ; and on the day she went out of Lady Godolphin's Folly, she entered on some stylish lodgings in the heart of Prior's Ash. Only for a week or two; just to give her time to take proper leave of her friends she said : but the weeks had gone on and on, and Charlotte was still there.

Society had been glad to keep Charlotte. Society of course shuts its lofty ears to the ill-natured tales spread by low-bred people : that is, when it finds it convenient so to do. Society had been pleased to be deaf to any little obscure tit-bits of scandal which had made vulgarly free with Charlotte's name: and as to the vague rumours connecting Mr. Verrall with George Godolphin's ruin, no one knew whether that was not pure scandal too. But if not, why—Mrs. Pain could not be justly reflected on for the faults of Mr. Verrall. So Charlotte was as popular and dashing in her hired rooms as she had been at Lady Godolphin's Folly, and she had remained in them until now.

But now she was really going. This was the last day of her sojourn at Prior's Ash, and Charlotte was walking about unceremoniously, bestowing her farewells on any one who would receive them. It almost seemed as if she had only waited to witness the removal from the Bank of Mr. and Mrs. George Godolphin.

She walked along in exuberant spirits, nodding her head to everyone: up at windows, in at doorways, to poor people on foot, to rich ones in carriages; her good-natured smile was everywhere. She rushed into shops and chatted familiarly, and won the shopkeepers' hearts by asking if they were not sorry to lose her. She was turning out of one when she came upon the Rector of All Souls'. Charlotte's petticoats went down in a swimming reverence.

"I am paying my farewell visits, Mr. Hastings. Prior's Ash will be rid of me to-morrow."

Not an answering smile crossed the Rector's face: it was cold, impassive, haughtily civil: almost as if he were thinking that Prior's Ash might have been none the worse had it been rid of Mrs. Charlotte Pain before.

"How is Mrs. Hastings to-day?" asked Charlotte.

"She is not well."

"No! I must try and get a minute to call in on her. Adieu for the present. I shall see you again, I hope."

Down sank the skirts once more, and the Rector lifted his hat in silence. In the ultra-politeness, in the spice of sauciness gleaming out from her flashing eyes, the clergyman read incipient defiance. But if Mrs. Pain feared that he might be intending to favour her with a little public clerical censure, she was entirely mistaken. The Rector washed his hands of Mrs. Pain, as Lady Godolphin did of her step-son, Mr. George. He walked on, a flash of scorn lighting his face.

Charlotte walked on: and burst into a laugh as she did so. "Was he afraid to forbid my calling at the Rectory?" she asked herself. "He would have liked to, I know. I'll go there now."

She was not long reaching it. But Isaac was the only one of the family she saw. He came to her charged with Mrs. Hastings's compliments—she felt unequal to seeing Mrs. Pain.

"I hear you are going to London," said Charlotte. "You have found some situation there, George Godolphin tells me."

Isaac threw his eyes—they were just like the Rector's—straight and full into her face. In her present spirit, half mischievous, half defiant, she had expressly paraded the name of George, as her informant, and Isaac thoroughly understood her. Charlotte's eyes were dancing with a variety of expressions, but the chief one was good-humoured malice.

"I am going into a bank in Lombard-street. Mr. Godolphin got me into it."

"You won't like it," said Charlotte.

"I dare say not. But I think myself lucky to get it."

"There will be one advantage," continued Charlotte good-naturedly—"you can come and see us. You know Mrs. Verrall's address. Come as often as you can; every Sunday, if you like; any week-day evening: I'll promise you a welcome beforehand."

"You are very kind," briefly returned Isaac. They were walking slowly to the gate, and he held it open for her.

"What's Reginald doing?" she asked. "Have you heard from him lately?"

"Not very lately. You are aware that he is in London, under a master of navigation, preparatory to passing for second officer. As soon as he has passed, he will go to sea again."

"When you write to him, give him our address, and tell him to come and see me. And now good-bye," added Charlotte heartily. "And mind you don't show yourself a muff, Mr. Isaac, but come and see us. Do you hear?"

"I hear," said Isaac, smiling, as he thawed to her good-humour. "I wish you a pleasant journey, Mrs. Pain."

"Merci bien. Good-bye."

The church clock boomed out five as Charlotte passed it, and she came to a standstill of consideration. It was the hour at which she had ordered dinner to be ready.

"Bother dinner!" decided she. "I can't go home for that. I want to see if they are in their lodgings yet. Is that you, Mrs. Bond?"

Sure enough, Mrs. Bond had come into view, and was halting to bob down to Charlotte. Her face looked pale and pinched. There had been no supply of strong waters to-day.

"I be a'most starving, ma'am. I'm waiting here to catch the parson, for I've been to his house, and they say he's out. I dun know as it's of any good seeing him, either. 'Tain't much he has to give away now."

"I am about to leave, Mrs. Bond," cried Charlotte in her free and communicative humour.

"More's the ill-luck, and I have heered on't," responded Mrs. Bond. "Everybody as is good to us poor goes away, or dies, or fails, or sum'at. There'll some be nought left for us but the work'us. Many's the odd bit o' silver you have given me at times, ma'am."

"So I have," said Charlotte, laughing. "What if I were to give you this, as a farewell remembrance?"

She took a half-sovereign out of her purse, and held it up. Mrs. Bond gasped: the luck seemed too great to be realized.

"Here, you may have it," said Charlotte, dropping it into the trembling hand held out. "But you know you are nothing but an old sinner, Mrs. Bond."

"I knows I be," humbly acquiesced Mrs. Bond. "'Tain't of no good denying of it to you, ma'am: you be up to things."

Charlotte laughed, taking the words, perhaps, rather as a compliment. "You'll go and change this at the nearest gin-shop, and you'll reel into

bed to-night blindfold.   That's the only good you'll do with it.   There.
don't say I left Prior's Ash, forgetting you."

She walked on rapidly, leaving Mrs. Bond in her ecstasy of delight
to waste her thanks on the empty air.   The lodgings George had taken
were at the opposite end of the town, nearer to Ashlydyat, and to them
Charlotte was bound.   They were not on the high-road, but in a quiet
side lane.   The house, low and roomy, and built in the cottage style,
stood in the midst of a flourishing garden.   A small grass-plat and
some flowers were before the front windows, but the rest of the ground
was filled with fruit and vegetables.   Charlotte opened the green gate
and walked up the path, which led to the house.

The front door was open to a small hall, and Charlotte went in,
finding her way, and turned to a room on the left : a cheerful, good-
sized, old-fashioned parlour, with a green carpet, and pink flowers on
its walls.   There stood Margery, laying out tea-cups and bread and
butter.   Her eyes opened at the sight of Mrs. Pain.

" Have they come yet, Margery ? "

" No," was Margery's short answer.   " They'll be here in half an
hour, maybe ; and that'll be before I want 'em—with all the rooms and
everything to see to, and only me to do it."

" Is that all you are going to give them for tea ? " cried Charlotte,
looking contemptuously at the table.   " I should surprise them with
a dainty dish or two on the table.   It would look cheering : and they
might soon be cooked.

" I dare say they might, where there's time and convenience,"
wrathfully returned Margery, who relished Mrs. Pain's interference as
little as she liked her presence.   " The kitchen we are to have is about
as big as a rat-hole, and my hands are full enough this evening without
dancing out to buy meats and dainties."

" Of course you will light a fire here ? " said Charlotte, turning to the
grate.   " I see it is laid."

" It's not cold," grunted Margery.

" But a fire will be a pleasant welcome.   I'll do it myself."

She took up a box of matches which stood on the mantel-piece, and
set light to the wood under the coal.   Margery took no notice one
way or the other.   The fire in a fair way of burning, Charlotte hastened
from the house, and Margery breathed freely again.

Not for very long.   A little time, and Charlotte was back again,
accompanied by a boy, bearing sundry parcels.   There was a renowned
comestible shop in Prior's Ash, and Charlotte had been ransacking it.
She had also been home for a small parcel on her own account ; but
that did not contain eatables.

Taking off her cloak and bonnet, she made herself at home.   Critically surveying the bedrooms ; visiting the kitchen to see that the kettle
boiled ; lighting the lamp on the tea-table, for it was dark then ; demanding an unlimited supply of plates, and driving Margery nearly
wild with her audacity.   But Charlotte was doing it all in good feeling ;
in her desire to render this new asylum bright-looking at the moment
of their taking possession of it ; to cheat the first entrance of some of
its bitterness for Maria.   Whatever may have been Mrs. Charlotte
Pain's faults—and Margery, for one, gave her credit for plenty—she

was capable of generous impulses. It is probable that in the days gone by, a feeling of jealousy, of spite, had rankled in her heart against George Godolphin's wife: but that had worn itself out; had been finally lost in the sorrow felt for Maria since misfortune had fallen. When the fly drove up to the door, and George brought in his wife and Meta, the bright room, the well-laden tea-table greeted their surprised eyes, and Charlotte was advancing with open hands.

"I thought you'd like to see some one here to get things comfortable for you, and I knew that cross-grained Margery would have enough to do between the boxes and her temper," she cried, taking Maria's hands. "How are you, Mr. George?"

George found his tongue. "This is kind of you, Mrs. Pain."

Maria felt that it *was* kind: and in her flow of gratitude, as her hand lay in Charlotte's warm grasp, she almost forgot that cruel calumny. Not quite: it could not be quite forgotten, even momentarily, until earth and its passions should have passed away.

"And mademoiselle?" continued Charlotte. Mademoiselle, little gourmande that she was, was raised on her toes, surveying the table with curious eyes. Charlotte lifted her in her arms, and held up to her view a glass jar, something within it the colour of pale amber. "This is for good children, Meta."

"That's me," responded Meta, smacking her lips. "What is it?"

"It's—let me read the label—it's pine-apple jelly. And that's boned fowl; and that's galantine de veau; and that's pâté de lapereaux aux truffes—if you understand what it all means, petite marmotte. And —there—you can look at everything and find out for yourself," concluded Charlotte. "I am going to show mamma her bedroom."

It opened from the sitting-room: an excellent arrangement, as Charlotte observed, in case of illness. Maria cast her eyes round it, and saw a sufficiently comfortable chamber. It was not their old luxurious chamber at the Bank; but luxuries and they must part company now.

Charlotte reigned at the head of the table that night, triumphantly gay. Margery waited with a stiffened neck and pursed-up lips. Nothing more: there were no other signs of rebellion. Margery had had her say out with that one memorable communication, and from thenceforth her lips were closed for ever. Did the woman repent of having spoken?—did she now think it better to have let doubt be doubt? It is hard to say. She had made no further objection to Mrs. Pain in words: she intended to make none. If that lady filled Miss Meta to illness to-night with pine-apple jelly and boned fowl, and the other things with unpronounceable names, which Margery regarded as rank poison, when regaling Miss Meta, *she* should not interfere. The sin might lie on her master and mistress's head.

It was close upon ten when Charlotte rose to depart, which she persisted in doing alone, in spite of George's remonstrance. Charlotte had no fear of being in the streets alone: she would as soon go through them by night as by day.

As a proof of this, she did not proceed directly homewards, but turned up a road that led to the railway station. She had no objection to a stroll that moonlight night, and she had a fancy for seeing what passengers the ten-o'clock train brought, which was just in.

It brought none. None that Charlotte could see: and she was preparing to turn back on the dull road, when a solitary figure came looming on her sight in the distance. He was better than no one, regarding him from Charlotte's sociable point of view: but he appeared to be advanced in years. She could see so much before he came up.

Charlotte strolled on, gratifying her curiosity by a good stare. A tall, portly man, with a fresh colour and snow-white hair. She was passing him, when he lifted his face, which had been bent, and turned it towards her. The recognition was mutual, and she darted up to him, and gave his hand a hearty shake. It was Mr. Crosse.

"Good gracious me! We thought you never meant to come back again!"

"And I would rather not have come back, Mrs. Pain, than come to hear what I am obliged to hear. I went streaming off from Pau, where I was staying, a confounded, senseless tour into Spain, leaving no orders for letters to be sent to me; and so I heard nothing. What *has* brought about this awful calamity?"

"What calamity?" asked Charlotte—knowing perfectly well all the while.

"What calamity!" repeated Mr. Crosse, who was rapid in speech and hot in temper. "The failure of the Bank—the Godolphins' ruin. What else?"

"Oh, that!" slightingly returned Charlotte. "That's stale news now. Folks are forgetting it. Queen Anne's dead."

"What brought it about?" reiterated Mr. Crosse, neither words nor tone pleasing him.

"What does bring such things about?" rejoined Charlotte. "Want of money, I suppose. Or bad management."

"But there was no want of money; there was no bad management in the Godolphins' house," raved Mr. Crosse, becoming excited. "I wish you'd not play upon my feelings, Mrs. Pain."

"Who is playing upon them?" cried Charlotte. "If it was not want of money, if it was not bad management, I don't know what else it was."

"I was told in London, as I came through it, that George Godolphin had been playing up old Rosemary with everything, and that Verrall has helped him," continued Mr. Crosse.

"Folks will talk," said bold Charlotte. "I was told—it was the current report in Prior's Ash—that the stoppage had occurred through Mr. Crosse withdrawing his money from the concern."

"What an unfounded assertion," exclaimed that gentleman in choler. "Prior's Ash ought to have known better."

"So ought those who tell you rubbish about George Godolphin and Verrall," coolly affirmed Charlotte.

"Where's Thomas Godolphin?"

"At Ashlydyat. He's in luck. My Lord Averil has bought it all in as it stands, and Mr. Godolphin remains in it."

"He is ill, I hear?"

"Pretty near dead, *I* hear," retorted Charlotte. "My lord is to marry Miss Cecilia."

"And where's that wicked George?"

"If you call names, I won't answer you another word, Mr. Crosse."

"I suppose *you* don't like to hear it," he returned in so pointed a manner that Charlotte might have felt it as a lance-shaft. "Well, where is he?"

"Just gone into lodgings with his wife and Margery and Meta. I have been taking tea with them. They left the Bank to-day."

Mr. Crosse stood, nodding his head in the moonlight, and communing aloud with himself. "And so—and so—it is all a smash together! It *is* as bad as was said."

"It couldn't be worse," cried Charlotte. "Prior's Ash won't hold up its head for many a day. It's no longer worth living in. I leave it for good to-morrow."

"Poor Sir George! It's a good thing he was in his grave. Lord Averil could have prosecuted George, I hear."

"Were I to hear to-morrow that I could be prosecuted for standing here and talking to you to-night, it wouldn't surprise me," was the answer.

"What on earth did he do with the money? What went with it?"

"Report runs that he founded a cluster of almhouses with it," said Charlotte demurely. "Ten old women, who were to be found in coals and red cloaks, and half-a-crown a week."

The words angered him beyond everything. Nothing could have been more serious than his mood; nothing could savour of levity, of mockery, more than hers. "Report runs that he has been giving fabulous prices for horses to make presents of," angrily retorted Mr. Crosse, in a tone of pointed significance.

"Not a bit of it," returned undaunted Charlotte. "He only gave bills."

"Good night to you, Mrs. Pain," came the next words, haughtily and abruptly; and Mr. Crosse turned to continue his way.

Leaving Charlotte standing there. No other passengers came down from the station: there were none to come: and she turned to retrace her steps to the town. She walked slowly and moved her head from side to side, as if she would take in all the familiar features of the landscape by way of farewell in anticipation of the morrow; the day that was to close her residence at Prior's Ash for ever.

PART THE THIRD.

<hr/>

CHAPTER I.

A MORNING CALL.

TIME elapsed. Autumn weather had come; and things were going on in their progression at Prior's Ash as things always must go on. Be it slow or fast, marked or unmarked, the stream of life must glide forward; onwards, onwards; never turning from its appointed course that bears us straight towards eternity.

In the events that concern us nothing had been very marked. At least, not outwardly. There were no startling changes to be recorded —unless, indeed, it was that noted change in the heart of the town. The Bank of which you have heard so much was no more; but in its stead flourished an extensive ironmongery establishment—which, it was to be hoped, would not come to the same ignoble end. The house had been divided into two dwellings: the one, accessible by the former private entrance, was let to a quiet widow lady and her son, a young man reading for the Church; the other had been opened in all the grandeur and glory of highly-polished steel and iron. Not one of the Godolphins could pass it without a keen heart-pang, but the general public were content to congregate and admire as long as the novelty lasted.

The great crash, which had so upset the equanimity of Prior's Ash, was beginning to be forgotten as a thing of the past. The bankruptcy was at an end—excepting some remaining formal proceedings which did not at all concern the general public, and not much the creditors. Compassion for those who had been injured by the calamity was dying out: many a home had been rendered needy—many desolate; but outside people do not make these uncomfortable facts any lasting concern of theirs. There were only two who did make them so, in regard to Prior's Ash; and they would make them so as long as their lives should last.

George Godolphin's wife was lying in her poor lodgings, and Thomas was dying at Ashlydyat. Dying so slowly and imperceptibly that the passage to the grave was smoothed, and the town began to say that he might yet recover. The wrong inflicted upon others, however unwillingly on his own part, the distress rife in many a house around, was ever present to him. It was ever present to Maria. Some of those who had lost were able to bear it; but there were others upon whom it had brought privation, poverty, utter ruin. It was for these last that the sting was felt.

A little boy had been born to Maria, and had died at the end of a few days. He was baptized Thomas. " Name him Thomas: it will be a remembrance of my brother," George Godolphin had said. But the young Thomas died before the elder one. The same disorder which had taken off two of Maria's other infants took him off—convulsions. " Best that it should be so," said Maria, with closed eyes and folded hands.

Somehow she could not grow strong again. Lying in bed, sick and weak, she had time to ruminate upon the misfortunes which had befallen them: the bitter, hopeless reminiscence of the past, the trouble and care of the present, the uncertainty of the future. To dwell upon such themes is not good for the strongest frame; but for the weak it is worse than can be described. Whether it was that, or whether it was a tendency to keep ill, which might have arisen without any mental trouble at all, Maria did not grow strong. Mr. Snow sent her no end of tonics; he ordered her all kinds of dainties; he sat and chatted and joked with her by the half-hour together: and it availed not. She was about again, as the saying runs, but she remained lamentably weak. " You don't make an effort to rouse yourself," Mr. Snow would say, rapping his stick in displeasure upon the floor as he spoke. Well, perhaps she did not: the simple fact was, that there was neither health nor spirit within her to make the effort.

Circumstances were cruelly against her. She might have battled with the bankruptcy—with the shock and the disgrace; she might have battled with the discomforts of their fallen position, with the painful consciousness of the distress cast upon many a home, with the humiliation dealt out to herself as her own special portion by the pious pharisees around; she might have battled with the vague prospects of the future, hopeless though they looked: women equally sensitive, good, refined as Maria, have had to contend with all this, and have survived it. But what Maria could not battle with; what had told upon her heart and her spirit more than all the rest, was that dreadful shock touching her husband. She had loved him passionately, she had trusted him wholly; in her blind faith she had never cast as much as a thought to the *possibility* that he could be untrue to his allegiance: and she had been obliged to learn that—infidelity forms part of a man's frail nature. It had dashed to the ground the faith and love of years; it had outraged every feeling of her heart; it seemed to have destroyed her trust in all mankind. Implicit faith! pure love! trust that she had deemed stronger than death!—all had been rent in one moment, and the shock had been greater than was her strength to endure. It was just as when one cuts a cord asunder. Anything, anything but this! She could have borne with George in his crime and disgrace, and clung to him when the world shunned him; had he been sent out to Van Diemen's Land, the felon that he might have been, she could have crept by his side and loved him still. But this was different. To a woman of refined feeling, as was Maria, loving trustingly, it was as the very sharpest point of human agony. It must be so. She had reposed calmly in the belief that she was all in all to him: and she awoke to find that she was no more to him than were others. They had lived, as she fondly thought, in a world of their own, a world of tenderness, of love, of unity; she and he alone; and now she learnt that his world at least had not been so exclusive. Apart from more sacred feelings that were outraged, it brought to her the most bitter humiliation. She seemed to have sunk down to a level she scarcely knew with what. It was not the broad and bare infidelity: at that a gentlewoman scarcely likes to glance; but it was the fading away of all the purity and romance which had enshrined them round, as with a halo, they alone, apart from the world. In one unexpected moment, as a flash of lightning will blast a forest tree and strip it of its foliage, leaving it bare—withered—helpless—so had that blow rent the heart's life of Maria Godolphin. And she did not grow strong.

Yes. Thomas Godolphin was dying at Ashlydyat, Maria was breaking her heart in her lonely lodgings, Prior's Ash was suffering in its homes; but where was the cause of it all—Mr. George? Mr. George was in London. Looking after something to do, he told Maria. Probably he was. He knew that he had his wife and child upon his hands, and that something must be done, and speedily, or the wolf would come to the door. Lord Averil, good and forgiving as was Thomas Godolphin, had promised George to try and get him some post abroad —for George had confessed to him that he did not care to remain in England. But the prospect was a remote one at best: and it was necessary that George should exert himself while it came. So he was in town looking after the something, and meanwhile not by any means breaking *his* heart in regrets, or living as an anchorite up in a garret. Maria heard from him, and of him. Once a week, at least, he wrote to her, sometimes oftener; affectionate and gay letters. Loving words to herself, kisses and stories for Meta, teasings and jokes for Margery. He was friendly with the Verralls—which Prior's Ash wondered at; and would now and then be seen riding in the Park with Mrs. Charlotte Pain—the gossip of which was duly chronicled to Maria by her gossiping acquaintance. Maria was silent on the one subject, but she did write a word of remonstrance to him about his friendship with Mr. Verrall. It was scarcely seemly, she intimated, after what people had said. George wrote her word back that she knew nothing about it; that people had taken up a false notion altogether. Verrall was a good fellow at heart; what had happened was not his fault, but the fault of certain men with whom he, Verrall, had been connected; and Verrall was showing himself a good friend now, and he did not know what he should do without him.

"A warm bright day like this, and I find you moping and stewing on that sofa! I'll tell you what it is, Mrs. George Godolphin, you are trying to make yourself into a chronic invalid."

Mr. Snow's voice, in its serio-comic accent, might be heard at the top of the house as he spoke. It was his way.

"I am better than I was," answered Maria. "I shall get well some time."

"Some time! It's to be hoped you will. But you are not doing much yourself towards it. Have the French left you a cloak and bonnet, pray?"

Maria smiled at his joke. She knew he alluded to the bankruptcy commissioners. When Mr. Snow was a boy, the English and French were at war, and he generally used the word French in a jesting way to designate enemies.

"They left me all," she said.

"Then be so good as to put them on. I don't terminate this visit until I have seen you out of doors."

To contend would be more trouble than to obey. She wrapped herself up and went out with Mr. Snow. Her steps were almost too feeble to walk alone.

"See the lovely day it is! And you, an invalid, suffering from nothing but dumps, not to be out in it! It's nearly as warm as September. Halloa, young lady! are you planting cabbages?"

They had turned an angle and come upon Miss Meta. She was digging away with a child's spade, scattering mould over the path; her woollen shawl, put on for warmth, had turned round, and her hat had fallen back, with the ardour of her labours. David Jekyl, who was digging to more purpose close by, was grumbling at the scattered mould on his clean paths.

"I'll sweep it up, David: I'll sweep it up!" the young lady said.

"Fine sweeping it 'ud be!" grunted David.

"I declare it's as warm as summer in this path!" cried Mr. Snow. "Now mind, Mrs. George, you shall stay here for half an hour; and if you grow tired there's a bench to sit upon. Little damsel, if mamma goes indoors, you tell me the next time I come. She is to stay out."

"I'll not tell of mamma," said Meta, throwing down her spade and turning her earnest eyes, her rosy cheeks, full on Mr. Snow.

He laughed as he walked away. "You are to stay out for the half-hour, mind you, Mrs. George. I insist upon it."

Direct disobedience would not have been expedient, if only in the light of example to Meta; but Maria had rather been out on any other day, or been ordered to any other path. This was the first time she had seen David Jekyl since the Bank had failed, and his father's loss was very present to her.

"How are you, David?" she inquired.

"I'm among the middlins," shortly answered David.

"And your father? I heard he was ill."

"So he is ill. He couldn't be worser."

"I suppose the coming winter is against him?"

"Other things are again him as well as the coming winter," returned David. "Fretting, for one."

Ah, how bitter it all was! But David did not mean to allude in any offensive manner to the past, or to hurt the feelings of George Godolphin's wife. It was his way.

"Is Jonathan better?" she asked.

"He isn't of much account, since he got that hurt," was David's answer. "Doing about three days' work in a week! It's to be hoped times 'll mend."

Maria walked slowly to and fro in the sunny path, saying a word or two to David now and then, but choosing safer subjects; the weather, the flowers under his charge, the vegetables already nipped with frost. She looked very ill. Her face thin and white, her soft sweet eyes larger and darker than was natural. Her hands were wrapped in the cloak for warmth, and her steps were unequal. Crusty David actually ventured on a little bit of civility.

"*You* don't seem to get about over quick, ma'am."

"Not very, David. But I feel better than I did."

She sat down on the bench, and Meta came flying to her, spade in hand. Might she plant a gooseberry-tree, and have all the gooseberries off it next year for herself?

Maria stroked the child's hair from her flushed face as she answered. Meta flew off to find the "tree," and Maria sat on, plunged in a train of thought which the question had led to. Where should they be at the gooseberry season next year? In that same dwelling? Would George's prospects have become more certain then?

"Now then! Is that the way you dig?"

The sharp words came from Margery, who had looked out at the kitchen window and caught sight of Miss Meta rolling in the mould. The child jumped up laughing, and ran into the house for her skipping-rope.

"Have I been out half an hour, do you think, David?" Maria asked by-and-by.

"Near upon 't," said David, without lifting his eyes.

She rose to pursue her way slowly indoors. She was so fatigued—and there had been, so to say, no exertion—that she felt as if she could never stir out again. Merely putting on and taking off her cloak was almost beyond her. She let it fall from her shoulders, took off her bonnet, and sank into an easy-chair.

From this she was aroused by hearing the gate hastily opened. Quick footsteps came up the path, and a manly voice said something to David Jekyl in a free, joking tone. She bounded up, her cheek flushing to hectic, her heart beating. Could it be George?

No; it was her brother, Reginald Hastings. He came in with a great deal of unnecessary noise and clatter. He had arrived from London only that morning, he proceeded to tell Maria, and was going up again by the night train.

"I say, Maria, how ill you look!"

Very ill indeed just then. The excitement of sudden expectation had faded, leaving her whiter than before. Dark circles were round her eyes, and her delicate hands, more feeble, more slender than of yore, moved restlessly on her lap.

"I have been very feverish the last few weeks," she said. "I think I am stronger. But I have been out for a walk and am tired."

"What did the little shaver die of?" asked Reginald.

"Of convulsions," she answered, her bodily weariness too great to speak in anything but tones of apathy. "Why are you going up again so soon? Have you a ship?"

Reginald nodded. "We have orders to join to-morrow at twelve. The *Mary*, bound for China, six hundred tons. I know the mother would never forgive me if I didn't come to say good-bye, so I thought I would have two nights of it in the train."

"Are you going as second officer, Reginald?"

"Second officer!—no. I have not passed."

"Regy!"

"They are a confounded lot, that board!" broke out Mr. Reginald, explosively. "I don't believe they know their own business. And as to passing any one without once turning him, they won't do it. I should like to know who has the money! You pay your guinea, and you don't pass. Come up again next Monday, they say. Well, you do go up again, as you want to pass; and you pay another half-guinea. I did so; and they turned me again; said I didn't know seamanship. The owls! not know seamanship! I! They took me, I expect, for one of those dainty middies in Green's service who walk the deck in kid gloves all day. If there's one thing I have at my fingers' ends it is seamanship. I could navigate a vessel all over the world—and be hanged to the idiots! You can come again next Monday, they said to me. I wish the *Times* would show them up!"

"Did you go again?"

"Did I!—no," fumed Reginald. "Just to add to their pockets by another half-guinea! I hadn't it to give, Maria. I just flung the whole lot over, and went down to the first ship in the docks and engaged myself."

"As what?" she asked.

"As A. B."

"A. B.?" repeated Maria, puzzled. "You don't mean—surely you don't mean before the mast?"

"Yes I do."

"Oh, Reginald!"

"It doesn't make much difference," cried Reginald in slighting tones. "The second mates in some of those ships are not much better off than the seamen. You must work, and the food's pretty much the same, except at the skipper's table. Let a fellow rise to be first mate, and he is in tolerably smooth water; but until then he must rough it. After this voyage I'll go up again."

"But you might have shipped as third mate."

"I might—if I had taken my time to find a berth. But who was to keep me the while? It takes fifteen shillings a week at the Sailors' Home, besides odds and ends for yourself that you can't do without—smoke and things. I couldn't bear to ask them for more at home. Only think how long I've been on shore this time, Maria. I was knocking about London for weeks over my navigation, preparing to pass.—And for the mummies to turn me at last!"

Maria sighed. Poor Reginald's gloomy prospects were bringing her pain.

"There's another thing, Maria," he resumed. "If I had passed for second mate, I don't see how I could go out as such. Where was my outfit to come from? An officer—if he is on anything of a ship—must look spruce, and have proper toggery. I am quite certain that to go out as second mate on a good ship would have cost me twenty pounds, for additional things that I couldn't do without. You can't get a sextant under three pounds, second-hand, if it's worth having. You know I never could have come upon them for twenty pounds at home, under their altered circumstances."

Maria made no reply. Every word was going to her heart.

"Whereas, in shipping as a common seaman, I don't want to take much more than you might tie up in a handkerchief. A fo'castle fellow can shift any way aboard. And there's one advantage," ingenuously added Reginald : "if I take no traps out with me, I can't lose them."

"But the discomfort?" breathed Maria.

"There's enough of that in any way, at sea. A little more or less is not of much account in the long-run. It's all in the voyage. I wish I had never been such a fool as to choose the sea. But I did choose it ; so it's of no use kicking against it now."

"I wish you were not going as you are !" said Maria earnestly. "I wish you had shipped as third mate !"

"When a sailor can't afford the time to ship as he would, he must ship as he can. Many a hundred has done the same before me. To one third mate wanted in the port of London, there are scores and scores of able seamen."

"What does mamma say to it?"

"Well, you know she can't afford to be fastidious now. She cried a bit, but I told her I should be all right. Hard work and fo'castle living won't break bones. The parson told me——"

"Don't, Reginald!"

"Papa, then. He told me it was a move in the right direction, and if I would only go on so, I might make up for past shortcomings. I say, Isaac told me to give you his love."

"Did you see much of him?"

"No. On a Sunday now and then. He doesn't much like his new post. They are dreadfully over-worked, he says. It's quite a different thing from what the Bank was down here."

"Will he stop in it?"

"Oh, he'll stop in it. Glad, too. It won't answer for him to be doing nothing, when they can hardly keep themselves at home with the little money screwed out from what's put aside for the Chisholms."

Reginald never meant to hurt her. He only spoke so in his thoughtlessness. He rattled on.

"I saw George Godolphin last week. It was on the Monday, the day that swindling board first turned me back. I flung the books anywhere, and went out miles, to walk my passion off. I got into the Park, to Rotten Row. It's precious empty at this season, not more than a dozen horses in it ; but who should be coming along but George Godolphin and Mrs. Pain with a groom behind them. She was riding that beautiful horse of hers that she used to cut a dash with here in the summer ; the one that folks said George gave——" Incautious Reginald coughed down the conclusion of his sentence, whistled a bar or two of a sea-song, and then resumed :

"George was well mounted, too."

"Did you speak to them?" asked Maria.

"Of course I did," replied Reginald, with some surprise. "And Mrs. Pain began scolding me for not having been to see her and the Verralls. She made me promise to go the next evening. They live at a pretty place on the banks of the Thames. You take the rail at Waterloo Station."

" Did you go ? "

" Well, I did, as I had promised. But I didn't care much about it. I had been at my books all day again, and in the evening, quite late, I started. When I got there I found it was a tea-fight."

" A tea-fight ! " echoed Maria, rather uncertain what the expression might mean.

" A regular tea-fight," repeated Reginald. " A dozen folks, mostly ladies, dressed up to the nines : and there was I in my worn-out sailor's jacket. Charlotte began blowing me up for not coming to dinner, and she made me go into the dining-room and had it brought up for me. Lots of good things ! I haven't tasted such a dinner since I've been on shore. Verrall gave me some champagne."

" Was George there ? " inquired Maria, putting the question with apparent indifference.

" No, George wasn't there. Charlotte said if she had thought of it she'd have invited Isaac to meet me : but Isaac was shy of them, she added, and had never been down once, though she asked him several times. She's a good-natured one, Maria, is that Charlotte Pain."

" Yes," quietly responded Maria.

" She told me she knew how young sailors get out of money in London, and she shouldn't think of my standing the cost of responding to her invitation ; and she gave me a sovereign."

Maria's cheeks burnt. " You did not take it, Reginald ? "

" Didn't I ! it was quite a godsend. You don't know how scarce money has been with me. Things have altered, you know, Maria. And Mrs. Pain knows it too, and she has no stuck-up nonsense about her. She made me promise to go and see them when I had passed. —But I have not passed," added Reginald, by way of parenthesis. " And she said if I was at fault for a home the next time I was looking out for a ship, she'd give me one, and be happy to see me. And I thought it was very kind of her ; for I am sure she meant it. Oh —by the way—she said she thought you'd let her have Meta up for a few weeks."

Maria involuntarily stretched out her hand—as if Meta were there, and she would clasp her and withhold her from some threatened danger. Reginald rose.

" You are not going yet, Regy ? "

" I must. I only ran in for a few minutes. There's Grace to see and fifty more folks, and they'll expect me home to dinner. I'll say good-bye to Meta as I go through the garden. I saw she was there ; but she did not see me."

He bent to kiss her. Maria held his hand in hers. " I shall be thinking of you always, Reginald. If you were only going under happier circumstances ! "

" Never mind me, Maria. It will be uphill work with most of us, I suppose, for a time. I thought it the best thing I could do. I couldn't bear to come upon them for more money at home."

" Yours will be a hard life."

" A sailor's is that, at best. Don't worry about me. I shall make it out somehow. You make haste, Maria, and get strong. I'm sure you look ill enough to frighten people."

She pressed his hands between hers, and the tears were filling her eyes as she raised them—their expression one wild yearning. "Reginald, try and do your duty," she whispered in an imploring tone. "Think always of heaven, and try and work for it. It may be very near. I have learned to think of it a great deal now."

"It's all right, Maria," was the careless and characteristic answer. "It's a religious ship I'm going in this time. We have had to sign articles for divine service on board at half-past ten every Sunday morning."

He kissed her several times, and the door closed upon him. As Maria lay back in her chair, she heard his voice outside for some time afterwards laughing and talking with Meta, largely promising her a ship-load of monkeys, parrots, and various other live wonders.

In this way or that, she was continually being reminded of the unhappy past and their share in it; she was perpetually having brought before her its disastrous effects upon others. Poor Reginald! entering upon his hard life! This need not have been, had means not grown scarce at home. Maria loved him best of all her brothers, and her very soul seemed to ache with its remorse. And by some means or other, she was, as you see, frequently learning that Mr. George was not breaking *his* heart with remorse. The suffering in all ways fell upon her.

And the time went on, and Maria Godolphin grew no stronger. It went on, and instead of growing stronger she grew weaker. Mr. Snow could do nothing more than he had done; he sent her tonic medicines still, and called upon her now and then, as a friend more than as a doctor. The strain was on the mind, he concluded, and time alone would heal it.

But Maria was worse than Mr. Snow or any one else thought. She had been always so delicate-looking, so gentle, that her wan face, her sunken spirits, attracted less attention than they would have done in one of a more robust nature. No one glanced at the possibility of danger. Margery's expressed opinion, "My mistress only wants rousing," was the one universally adopted: and there may have been truth in it.

All question of Maria's going out of doors was over now. She was really not equal to it. She would lie for hours together on her sofa, the little child Meta gathered in her arms. Meta appeared to have changed her very nature. Instead of dancing about incessantly, running into every mischief, she was content to nestle to her mother's bosom and listen to her whispered words, as if some foreshadowing were on her spirit that she might not long have a mother to nestle to.

You must not think that Maria conformed to the usages of an invalid. She was up before breakfast in the morning, she did not go to bed until the usual hour at night, and she sat down to the customary meals with Meta. She has risen from the breakfast-table now, on this fine morning, not at all cold for late autumn, and Margery has carried away the breakfast-things, and has told Miss Meta that if she will come out as soon as her mamma has read to her, and have her things put on, she may go and play in the garden.

But when the little Bible story was over, her mamma lay down on the sofa, and Meta appeared inclined to do the same. She nestled on to it, and lay down too, and kissed her mamma's face, so pretty still, and began to chatter. It was a charming day, the sun shining on the few late flowers, the sky blue and bright.

"Did you hear Margery say you might go out and play, darling? See how fine it is."

"There's nothing to play with," said Meta.

"There are many things, dear. Your skipping-rope and hoop, and——"

"I'm tired of them," interposed Meta. "Mamma, I wish you'd come out and play at something with me."

"I couldn't run, dear. I am not strong enough."

"When shall you be strong enough? How long will it be before you get well?"

Maria did not answer. She lay with her eyes fixed upon the far-off sky, her arm clasped round the child. "Meta, darling, I—I—am not sure that I shall get well. I begin to think that I shall never go out with you again."

Meta did not answer. She was looking out also, her eyes staring straight at the blue sky.

"Meta, darling," resumed Maria in low tones, "you had two little sisters once, and I cried when they died, but I am glad now that they went. They are in heaven."

Meta looked up more fixedly, and pointed with her finger. "Up in the blue sky?"

"Yes, up in heaven. Meta, I think I am going to them. It is a better world than this."

"And me too," quickly cried Meta.

Maria laid her hand upon her bosom to press down the rising emotion. "Meta, Meta, if I might only take you with me!" she breathed, straining the child to her in an agony. The prospect of parting, which Maria had begun to look at, was indeed hard to bear.

"You can't go and leave me," cried Meta in alarm. "Who'd take care of me, mamma? Mamma, do you mean that you are going to die?"

Meta burst into tears. Maria cried with her. Oh reader, reader! do you know what it is, this parting between mother and child? To lay a child in the grave is bitter grief; but to leave it to the mercy of the world!—there is nothing like unto it in human anguish.

Maria's arms were entwined around the little girl, clasping her nervously, as if that might prevent the future parting; the soft rounded cheek was pressed to hers, the golden curls lay around.

"Only for a little while, Meta. If I go first, it will be only for a little while. You——" Maria stopped; her emotion had to be choked down.

"It is a happier world than this, Meta," she resumed, mastering it. "There will be no pain there; no sickness, no sorrow. This world seems made up of sorrow, Meta. Oh, child! but for God's love in holding out to our view that other one, we could never bear this, when trouble comes. God took your little sisters and brothers from it: and —I think—He is taking me."

Meta turned her face downwards, and held her mother with a frightened movement, her little fingers clasping the thin arms to pain.

" The winter is coming on here, my child, and the trees will soon be bare; the snow will cover the earth, and we must wrap ourselves up from it. But in that other world there will be no winter; no cold to chill us; no summer heat to exhaust us. It will be a pleasant world, Meta; and God will love us."

Meta was crying silently. " Let me go too, mamma."

" In a little while, darling. If God calls me first, it is His will," she continued, the sobs breaking from her aching heart. " I shall ask Him to take care of you after I am gone, and to bring you to me in time; I am asking Him always."

"Who'll be my mamma then?" cried Meta, lifting her head in a bustle, as the thought occurred to her.

More pain. Maria choked it down, and stroked the golden curls.

" You will have no mamma, then, in this world. Only papa."

Meta paused. " Will he take me to London, to Mrs. Pain?"

The startled shock that these simple words brought to Maria cannot well be pictured: her breath stood still, her heart beat wildly. " Why do you ask that?" she said, her tears suddenly dried.

Meta had to collect her childish thoughts to tell why. " When you were in bed ill, and Mrs. Pain wrote me that pretty letter, she said if papa would take me up to London she'd be my mamma for a little while, in place of you."

The spell was broken. The happy visions of heaven, of love, had been displaced for Maria. She lay quite silent, and in the stillness the bells of All Souls' Church were heard ringing out a joyous peal on the morning air. Meta clapped her hands and lifted her face, radiant now with glee. Moods require not time to change in childhood: now sunshine, now rain. Margery opened the door.

" Do you hear them, ma'am? The bells for Miss Cecil. They're as joyous as the day. I said she'd have it fine, last night, when I found the wind had changed. I can't bear to hear wedding-bells ring out on a wet day: the two don't agree. Eh me! Why, here's Miss Rose coming in!"

Rose Hastings was walking up the path with a quick step, nodding at Meta as she came along. That young lady slipped off the sofa, and ran out to meet her, and Maria rose up from her sick position, and strove to look her best.

" I have come for Meta," said Rose, as she entered. " Mamma thinks she would like to see the wedding.—Will you let her come, Maria?"

Maria hesitated. " To the church, do you mean? Suppose she should not be good?"

" I will be good," said Meta, in a high state of delight at the prospect. " Mamma, I'll be very good."

She went with Margery to be dressed. Rose turned to her sister. " Are you pretty well this morning, Maria?"

" Pretty well, Rose. I cannot boast of much strength yet."

" I wish you would return with me and Meta. Mamma told me to try and bring you. To spend the day with us will be a change, and you need not go near the church."

"I don't feel equal to it, Rose. I should not have strength to walk. Tell mamma so, with my dear love."

"Only fancy!—she is to be married in a bonnet!" exclaimed Rose with indignation. "A bonnet and a grey dress. I wonder Lord Averil consented to it! I should hardly call it a wedding. A bonnet!—and no breakfast!—and Bessy Godolphin and Lord Averil's sister, who is older if anything than Bessy, for bridesmaids!"

"And only one clergyman," added Maria, her lips parting with a smile. "Do you think the marriage will stand good, Rose?"

Rose felt inclined to resent the joke, for Maria was laughing at her. But Meta came in, full of bustling excitement, eager to be gone. She kissed her mamma in careless haste, and was impatient because Rose lingered to say a word. Maria watched her down the path; her face and eyes sparkling, her feet dancing with eagerness, her laughter ringing on the air.

"She has forgotten already her tears for the parting that must come," murmured Maria. "How soon, I wonder, after I shall be gone, will she forget me?"

She laid her temples lightly against the window-frame, as she looked dreamily at the blue sky; as she listened dreamily to the sweet bells that rang out so merrily in the ears of Prior's Ash.

CHAPTER II.

NEARER AND NEARER.

PRIOR'S ASH lingered at its doors and windows, curious to witness the outer signs of Cecilia Godolphin's wedding. The arrangements for it were to them more a matter of speculation than of certainty, since various rumours had gone afloat, and were eagerly caught up, although of the most contradictory character. All that appeared certain as yet was—that the day was charming and the bells were ringing.

How the beadle kept the gates that day, he alone knew. That staff of his was brought a great deal more into requisition than was liked by the sea of heads collected there. And when the first carriage came, the excitement in the street was great.

The *first* carriage! There were only two; that and another. Prior's Ash turned up its disappointed nose, and wondered, with Rose Hastings, what the world was coming to.

"It was a chariot drawn by four horses. The livery of the postillions and the coronet on the panels proclaimed it to be Lord Averil's. He sat within it with Thomas Godolphin. The carriage following it was Lady Godolphin's; it appeared to contain only ladies, all wearing bonnets and coloured gowns. The exasperated gazers, who had bargained for something very different, set up a half-groan.

They set up a whole one, those round the gates, when Lord Averil and his friend alighted. But the groan was not one of exasperation, or of anger. It was a low murmur of sorrow and sympathy, and it was called forth by the appearance of Thomas Godolphin. It was some little time now since Thomas Godolphin had been seen in public, and the change in him was startling. He walked forward, leaning on the arm of Lord Averil, lifting his hat to the greeting that was breathed around; a greeting of sorrow meant, as he knew, not for the peer, but for him and his fading life. The few scanty hairs stood out to their view as he uncovered his head, and the ravages of the disease that was killing him were all too conspicuous on his wasted features.

"God bless him! He's very nigh the grave."

Who said it, of the crowd, Thomas Godolphin could not tell, but the words and their accent, full of rude sympathy, came distinctly upon his ear. He quitted the viscount's arm, turned to them, and raised his hands with a solemn meaning.

"God bless you all, my friends. I am indeed near the grave. Should there be any here who have suffered injury through me, let them forgive me for it. It was not intentionally done, and I may almost say that I am expiating it with my life. May God bless you all, here and hereafter!"

Something like a sob burst from the astonished crowd. But that he had hastened on with Lord Averil, they might have fallen on their knees and clung to him in their flood-tide of respect and love.

The Reverend Mr. Hastings stood in his surplice at the altar. He, too, was changed. The keen, vigorous, healthy man had now a grey, worn look. He could not forgive the blow; minister though he was, he could not forgive George Godolphin. He was not quite sure that he forgave Thomas for not having looked more closely after his brother and the Bank generally: had he done so, the calamity might never have occurred. Every hour of the day reminded Mr. Hastings of his loss, in the discomforts which had necessarily fallen upon his home, in the position of his daughter Maria. George Godolphin had never been a favourite of his: he had tried to like him in vain. The Rector of All Souls' was a man of severe judgment, and rumour had made free with gay George's name.

Lord Averil was the first to enter. Cecilia Godolphin came next with Thomas. She wore a light-grey silk robe, and a plain white bonnet, trimmed with orange-blossoms. The Honourable Miss Averil and Bessy Godolphin followed; their silk gowns of a darker shade of grey, and their white bonnets without orange-blossoms. Lady Godolphin came next, more resplendent than any, in a lemon brocaded silk, that stood on end with richness.

Did the recollection of the last wedding service he had performed for a Godolphin cause the Rector of All Souls' voice to be subdued now, as he read? Seven years ago he had stood there as he was standing to-day, George and Maria before him. How had that promising union ended? And for the keeping of his sworn vows?—George best knew what he had kept and what he had broken. The Rector was thinking of that past ceremony now.

This one was soon over. The promises were made, the register signed, and Lord Averil was leading Cecilia from the church, when the Rector stepped before them and took her hand.

"I pray God that your union may be more happy than some other unions have been," he said. "That, in a great degree, rests with you, Lord Averil. Take care of her."

Her eyes filled with tears, but the viscount grasped his hand warmly. " I will ; I will."

The beadle was rapping his stick on sundry heads with great effect, and the excited crowd pushed and danced round that travelling carriage, but they made their way to it. To hand in Cecil and take his place beside her seemed to be but the work of a moment, so quickly did it pass, and Lord Averil, a pleasant smile upon his face, bowed to the shouts on either side as the carriage threaded its way through the throng. The three ladies next stepped into their carriage, and Thomas Godolphin turned into the Rectory. Mrs. Hastings, grey, worn, old— ten years older than she had been six months before—came forward to greet him, commiseration in every line of her countenance.

" I thought I would say good-bye to you," he said, as he held her hands in his. " It will be my only opportunity. I expect this is my last quitting of Ashlydyat."

" Say good-bye ?" she faltered. " Are you—are you—so near——"

" Look at me," quietly said Thomas, answering her unfinished sentence.

But there was an interruption. Bustling little feet and a busy little tongue came upon them. Miss Meta had broken from Rose and run in alone, throwing her straw hat aside as she entered.

" Uncle Thomas ! Uncle Thomas ! I saw you at the wedding, Uncle Thomas."

He sat down and took the child upon his knee. " And I saw Meta," he answered. " How is mamma ? I am going to see her presently."

" Mamma's not well," said Meta, shaking her head. " Mamma cries often. She was crying this morning.. Uncle Thomas "—lowering her voice and speaking slowly—"mamma says she's going to heaven."

There was a startled pause. Thomas broke it by laying his hand upon the golden-haired head.

" I trust we are all going there, Meta. A little earlier or a little later, as God shall will. It will not much matter which."

A few minutes' conversation, and Thomas Godolphin went out to the fly which had been brought for him. Bexley, who was with it, helped him in.

" To Mrs. George Godolphin's."

The attentive old retainer—older by twenty years than Thomas, but younger in health and vigour—carefully assisted his master up the path. Maria saw the approach from the window. Why it was she knew not, but she was feeling unusually ill that day : scarcely able to rise to a sitting position on the sofa. Thomas was shocked at the alteration in her, and involuntarily thought of the child's words, " Mamma says she's going to heaven."

" I thought I should like to say farewell to you, Maria," he said, as he drew a chair near her. " I did not expect to find you looking so ill."

She had burst into tears. Whether it was the unusual depression of her own spirits, or his wan face, emotion overcame her.

" It has been too much for both of us," he murmured, holding her hands. "We must forgive him, Maria. It was done in carelessness, perhaps, but not wilfulness. Why do you not come to Ashlydyat sometimes? You know we should be glad to see you."

She shook her head. "I cannot go out, Thomas. Indeed, I am not strong enough for it now."

"But Maria, you should not give way to this grief; this weakness. You are young; you have no incurable complaint, as I have."

"I don't know," she sighed. "At times I feel as though I should never be well again. I—I—have been so reproached, Thomas; so much blame has been cast on me by all people; it has been as if *I* had made away with their money; and you know that I was as innocent as they were. And there have been other things. If—if—— "

"If what?" asked Thomas, leaning over her.

She was sitting back upon the sofa, her fair young face wan and colourless, her delicate hands clasped together, as in apathy. "If it were not for leaving Meta, I should be glad to die!"

"Hush, Maria! Rather say you are glad to live for her sake. George may by some means or other become prosperous again, and you may once more have a happy home. You are young, I say; you must bear up against this weakness."

"If I could only pay all we owe; our personal debts!" she whispered, unconsciously giving utterance to the vain longing that was ever working in her heart. "Papa's nine thousand pounds—and Mrs. Bond's ten pounds—and the Jekyls—and the tradespeople!"

"If *I* could only have paid!" he rejoined in a voice broken by emotion. "If I could—if I could—I should have gone easier to the grave. Maria, we have a God, remember, who sees all our pangs, all our bitter sorrow: but for Him, and my trust in Him, I should have died long ago of the pain."

Maria covered her face with her hand. Thomas rose.

"You are not going?" she exclaimed.

"Yes, for I must hasten home. This has been a morning of exertion, and I find there's no strength left in me. God bless you, Maria!"

"Are we never to meet again?" she asked, as he held her thin hands in his, and she looked up at him through her blinding tears.

"I hope we shall meet again, Maria, and be together for ever and for ever. The threshold of the next world is opening to me: this is closing. Fare you well, child; fare you well."

Bexley came to him as he opened the parlour door. Thomas asked for Margery: he would have said a kind word to her. But Margery had gone out.

Maria stood at the window, and watched him through her tears as he walked down the path to the fly, supported by Bexley. The old man closed the door on his master and took his seat by the driver. Thomas looked forth as they drove away, and smiled a last farewell.

A farewell in the deepest sense of the word. It was the last look, the last smile, that Maria would receive in this life, from Thomas Godolphin.

CHAPTER III.

FOR THE LAST TIME.

IN the old porch at Ashlydyat, of which you have heard so much, sat Thomas Godolphin. An invalid chair had been placed there, and he lay back on its pillows in the sun of the late autumn afternoon. A warm, sunny autumn had it been; a real " Eté de St. Martin." He was feeling wondrously well; almost, but for his ever-present sensation of weakness, quite well. His fatigue of the previous day—that of Cecil's wedding—had left no permanent effects upon him, and had he not known thoroughly his own hopeless state, he might have fancied this afternoon that he was about to get well all one way.

Not in looks. Pale, wan, ghastly were they; the shadow of the grim, implacable visitor that was so soon to come was already on them; but the face in its stillness told of ineffable peace : the brunt of the storm had passed.

The white walls of Lady Godolphin's Folly glittered brightly in the distance ; the dark-blue sky was seen through the branches of the trees, growing bare and more bare against the coming winter; the warm sun rays fell on Thomas Godolphin. Margery came up, and he held out his hand.

" My mistress told me you'd have said good-bye to me yesterday, Mr. Thomas, and it was just my ill-luck to be out. I had gone to take the child's shoes to be mended—she wears them out fast. But you are not going to leave us yet, sir ? "

" I know not how soon it may be, Margery : very long it cannot be. Sit down."

She stood yet, however, looking at him, disregarding the bench to which he had pointed ; stood with a saddened expression and compressed lips. Margery's was an experienced eye, and it may be that she saw the shadow which had taken up its abode on his face.

" You are going to see my old master and mistress, sir," she burst forth, dashing some rebellious moisture from her eyes. " Mr. Thomas, do you recollect it ?—my poor mistress sat here in this porch the very day she died."

" I remember it well, Margery. I am dying quietly, thank God, as my mother died."

" And what a blessing it is when folks can die quietly, with their conscience and all about 'em at peace ! " ejaculated Margery. " I wonder how Mr. George would have took it, if he'd been called instead of you, sir ? "

There was considerable acidity, not to say sarcasm, in the remark ; perhaps not altogether suited to the scene and interview. Good Thomas Godolphin would not see it or appear to notice it. He took Margery's hands in his.

" I never thought once that I should die leaving you in debt, Margery," he said, his earnest tone bearing its own emotion. " It was always my intention to bequeath you an annuity that would have kept you from want in your old age. But it has been decreed otherwise; and it is of no use to speak of what might have been. Miss Janet will refund to you by degrees what you have lost in the Bank; and so long as you live you will be welcome to a home with her. She has not much, but—— "

" Now never fash yourself about me, Mr. Thomas," interrupted Margery. " I shall do well, I dare say; I'm young enough yet for work, I hope; I shan't starve. Ah, this world's nothing but a pack o' troubles," she added, with a loud sigh. " It has brought its share to you, sir."

" I am on the threshold of a better, Margery," was his quiet answer; " one where troubles cannot enter."

Margery sat for some time on the bench, talking to him. At length she rose to depart, declining the invitation to enter the house or to see the ladies, and Thomas said to her his last farewell.

" My late missis, I remember, looked once or twice during her illness as grey as he does," she cogitated within herself as she went along. " But it strikes me that with him it's death. I've a great mind to ask old Snow what he thinks. If it is so, Mr. George ought to be telegraphed for; they *are* brothers, after all."

Margery's way led her past the turning to the railway station. A train was just in. She cast an eye on the passengers coming from it, and in one of them she saw her master, Mr. George Godolphin.

Margery halted and rubbed her eyes, and almost wondered whether it was a vision. Her mind had been busy with the question, ought he, or ought he not to be telegraphed for? and there he was, before her. Gay, handsome George! with his ever-distinguished *entourage* —I don't know a better word for it in English: his bearing, his attire, his person so essentially the gentleman; his pleasant face and his winning smile.

That smile was directed to Margery as he came up. He bore in his hand a small wicker-work basket, covered with delicate tissue paper. But for the bent of Margery's thoughts at the time, she would not have been particularly surprised at the sight, for Mr. George's visits to Prior's Ash were generally impromptu ones, paid without warning. She met him rather eagerly: speaking of the impulse that had been in her mind—to send a message for him, on account of the state of his brother.

" Is he worse? " asked George eagerly.

" If ever I saw death written in a face, it's written in his, sir," returned Margery.

George considered a moment. " I think I will go up to Ashlydyat without loss of time, then," he said, turning back. But he stopped to give the basket into Margery's hands.

" It is for your mistress, Margery. How is she? "

" *She's* nothing to boast of," replied Margery, in tones and with a stress that might have awakened George's suspicions, had any fears with reference to his wife's state yet penetrated his mind. But they had not. " I wish she could get a little of life into her, and then health might be the next thing to come," concluded Margery.

" Tell her I shall soon be home." And George Godolphin proceeded to Ashlydyat.

It may be that he had not the faculty for distinguishing the different indications that a countenance gives forth, or it may be that to find his brother sitting in the porch disarmed his doubts, but certainly George saw no reason to endorse the fears expressed by Margery. She had entered into no details, and George had pictured Thomas as in bed. To see him therefore sitting out of doors, quietly reading, certainly lulled all George's present fears.

Not that the ravages in the worn form, the grey look in the pale face, did not strike him as that face was lifted to his; struck him almost with awe. For a few minutes their hands were locked together in silence. Generous Thomas Godolphin! Never since the proceedings had terminated, the daily details were over, had he breathed a word of the bankruptcy and its unhappiness to George.

" George, I am glad to see you. I have been wishing for you all day. I think you must have been sent here purposely."

" Margery sent me. I met her as I was coming from the train."

It was not to *Margery* that Thomas Godolphin had alluded—but he let it pass. " Sent purposely," he repeated aloud. " George, I think the end is very near."

" But you are surely better ? " returned George, speaking in impulse. " Unless you were better, would you be sitting here ? "

" Do you remember, George, my mother sat here in the afternoon of the day she died ? A feeling came over me to-day that I should enjoy a breath of the open air; but it was not until after they had brought my chair out and I was installed in it, that I thought of my mother. It struck me as being a curious coincidence; almost an omen. Margery recollected the circumstance, and spoke of it."

The words imparted a strange sensation to George, a shivering dread. " Are you in much pain, Thomas ? " he asked.

" Not much ; a little, at times ; but the great agony that used to come upon me has quite passed. As it did with my mother, you know."

Could George Godolphin help the feeling of bitter contrition that came over him? He had been less than man, lower than human, had he helped it. Perhaps the full self-reproach of his conduct never came home to him as it came now. With all his faults, his lightness, he loved his brother : and it seemed that it was he—he—who had made the face wan, the hair grey, who had broken the already sufficiently stricken heart, and had sent him to his grave before his time.

" It is my fault," he spoke in his emotion. " But for me, Thomas, you might have been with us, at any rate, another year or two. The trouble has told upon you."

" Yes, it has told upon me," Thomas quietly answered. There was nothing else that he could answer.

" Don't think of it, Thomas," was the imploring prayer. " It cannot be helped now."

" No, it cannot be helped," Thomas rejoined. But he did not add that, even now, it was disturbing his death-bed. " George," he said, pressing his brother's hands, " but that it seems so great an improbability, I would ask you to repay to our poor neighbours and friends what they have lost, should it ever be in your power. Who knows but you may be rich some time? You are young and capable, and the world is before you. If so, think of them: it is my last request to you."

"It would be my own wish to do it," gravely answered George. "But do not think of it now, Thomas; do not let it trouble you."

"It does not trouble me much now. The thought of the wrong inflicted on them is ever present with me, but I am content to leave that, and all else, in the care of the all-powerful, ever-merciful God. He can recompense better than I could, even had I my energies and life left to me."

There was a pause. George loosed his brother's hands and took the seat on the bench where Margery had sat; the very seat where he had once sat with his two sticks, in his weakness, years before, when the stranger, Mr. Appleby, came up and inquired for Mr. Verrall. Why or wherefore it should have come, George could not tell, but that day flashed over his memory now. Oh, the bitter remembrance! He had been a lightsome man then, without care, free from that depressing incubus that must, or that ought to, weigh down the soul—cruel wrong inflicted on his fellow-toilers in the great journey of life. And now? He had brought the evil of poverty upon himself, the taint of disgrace upon his name; he had driven his sisters from their home; had sent that fair and proud inheritance of the Godolphins, Ashlydyat, into the market; and had hastened the passage of his brother to the grave. Ay! dash your bright hair from your brow as you will, George Godolphin! —pass your cambric handkerchief over your heated face!—you cannot dash away remembrance. You have done all this, and the consciousness is very present with you.

Thomas Godolphin interrupted his reflections, bending towards George his wasted features. "George, what are your prospects?"

"I have tried to get into something or other in London, but my trying has been useless. All places that are worth having are so soon snapped up. I have been offered a post in Calcutta, and I think I shall accept it. If I find that Maria has no objection to go out, I shall: I came down to-day to talk it over with her."

"Is it through Lord Averil?"

"Yes. He wrote to me yesterday morning before he went to church with Cecil. I received the letter by the evening mail, and came off this morning."

"And what is the appointment? Is it in the civil service?"

"Nothing so grand—in sound, at any rate. It's only mercantile. The situation is at an indigo merchant's, or planter's; I am not sure which. But it's a good appointment; one that a gentleman may accept; and the pay is liberal. Lord Averil urges it upon me. These merchants—they are brothers—are friends of his. If I decline it, he will try for a civil appointment for me; but to obtain one might take a considerable time: and there might be other difficulties in the way."

"Yes," said Thomas shortly. "By the little I can judge, this appears to me to be just what will suit you."

"I think so. If I accept it, I shall have to start with the new year.

I saw the agents of the house in town this morning, and they tell me it is quite a first-class appointment for a mercantile one. I hope Maria will not dislike to go."

They sat there conversing until the sun had set. George pointed out to his brother's notice that the air was growing cold, but Thomas only smiled in answer: it was not the night air, hot or cold, that could any longer affect Thomas Godolphin. But he said that he might as well go in, and took George's arm to support his feeble steps.

"Is no one at home?" inquired George, finding the usual sitting-room empty.

"They are at Lady Godolphin's," replied Thomas, alluding to his sisters. "Bessy goes there for good next week, and certain arrangements have to be made, so they walked over this afternoon just before you came up."

George sat down. To find his sisters absent was a relief. Since the unhappy explosion, George had always felt as a guilty schoolboy in the presence of Janet. He remained a short time, and then rose to depart. "I'll come up and see you in the morning, Thomas."

Was there any prevision of what the night would bring forth in the mind of Thomas Godolphin? It might be. He entwined in his the hands held out to him.

"God bless you, George! God bless you, and keep you always!" And a lump, not at all familiar to George Godolphin's throat, rose in it as he went out from the presence of his brother.

It was one of those charmingly clear evenings that bring a sensation of tranquillity to the senses. Daylight could not be said to have quite faded, but the moon was up, its rays shining brighter and brighter with every departing moment of day. As George passed Lady Godolphin's Folly, Janet was coming from it.

He could not avoid her. I do not say that he wished to do so, but he could not if he had wished it. They stood talking together for some time; of Thomas's state; of this Calcutta prospect of George's, for Janet had heard something of it from Lord Averil; and she questioned him closely on other subjects. It was growing quite night when Janet made a movement homewards, and George could do no less than attend her.

"I thought Bessy was with you," he remarked, as they walked along.

"She is remaining an hour or two longer with Lady Godolphin; but it was time I came home to Thomas. When do you say you must sail, George?"

"The beginning of the year. My salary will commence with the first of January, and I ought to be off that day. I don't know whether that will give Maria sufficient time for preparation."

"Sufficient time!" repeated Miss Godolphin. "Will she want to take out a ship's cargo? I should think she might be ready in a tithe of it. Shall you take the child?"

"Oh yes," he hastily answered; "I could not go without Meta. And I am sure Maria would not consent to be separated from her. I hope Maria will not object to going on her own score."

"Nonsense!" returned Janet. "She will have the sense to see that it is a remarkable piece of good fortune, far better than you had any right to expect. Let me recommend you to put by half your salary, George. It is a very handsome one, and you may do it if you will. Take a lesson from the past."

"Yes," replied George, with a twitch of conscience. "I wonder if the climate will try Maria?"

"I trust that the change will be good for her in all ways," said Janet emphatically. "Depend upon it she will be only too thankful to turn her back on Prior's Ash. She will not get strong as long as she stops in it, or so long as your prospects are uncertain, doing nothing, as you are now. *I* can't make out, for my part, how you live."

"You might easily guess that I have been helped a little, Janet."

"By one that *I* would not be helped by if I were starving," severely rejoined Janet. "You allude, I presume, to Mr. Verrall?"

George did allude to Mr. Verrall; but he avoided a direct answer. "All that I borrow I shall return," he said, "as soon as it is in my power to do so. It is not much: and it is given and received as a loan only. What do you think of Thomas?" he asked, willing to change the subject.

"I think——" Janet stopped. Her voice died away to a whisper, and finally ceased. They had taken the path home round by the ash-trees. The Dark Plain lay stretched before them in the moonlight. In the brightest night the gorse-bushes gave the place a shadowy, weird-like appearance, but never had the moonlight on the plain been clearer, whiter, brighter than it was now. And the Shadow?

The ominous Shadow of Ashlydyat lay there: the Shadow which had clung to the fortunes of the Godolphins, as tradition said, in past ages; which had certainly followed the present race. But the blackness that had characterized it was absent from it now: the Shadow was undoubtedly there, but had eyes been looking on it less accustomed to its form than were Miss Godolphin's, they might have failed to make out distinctly its outlines. It was of a light, faint hue; more as the reflection of the Shadow, if it may be so expressed.

"George! do you notice?" she breathed.

"I see it," he answered.

"But do you notice its peculiarity—its faint appearance? I should say—I should say that it is indeed going from us; that it must be about the last time it will follow the Godolphins. With the wresting from them of Ashlydyat the curse was to die out."

She sat down on the bench under the ash-trees, and was speaking in low, dreamy tones: but George heard every word, and the topic was not particularly palatable to him. He could only remember that it was he and no other who had caused them to lose Ashlydyat.

"Your brother will not be here long," murmured Janet. "That warning is for the last chief of the Godolphins."

"Oh, Janet! I wish you were not so superstitious! Of course we know—it is patent to us all—that Thomas cannot last long: a few days, a few hours even, may close his life. Why should you connect with him that wretched Shadow?"

"I know what I know, and I have seen what I have seen," was the reply of Janet, spoken slowly; nay, solemnly. "It is no wonder that *you* wish to ignore it, to affect to disbelieve in it; but you can do neither the one nor the other, George Godolphin."

George gave no answering argument. It may be that he had felt he had forfeited the right to argue with Janet. She again broke the silence.

"I have watched and watched; but never once, since the day that those horrible misfortunes fell, has that Shadow appeared. I thought it had gone for good; I thought that our ruin, the passing of Ashlydyat into the possession of strangers, was the working out of the curse. But it seems it has come again; for the last time, as I believe. And it is only in accordance with the past, that the type of the curse should come to shadow forth the death of the last Godolphin."

"You are complimentary to me, Janet," cried George good-humouredly. "When poor Thomas shall have gone, I shall be here still, the last of the Godolphins."

"*You!*" returned Janet, and her tone of scornful contempt, unconscious as she might herself be of it, brought a sting to George's mind, a flush to his brow. "You might be worthy of the name of Godolphin once, laddie, but that's over. The last true Godolphin dies out with Thomas."

"How long are you going to sit here?" asked George, after a time, as she gave no signs of moving.

"You need not wait," returned Janet. "I am at home now, as may be said. Don't stay, George: I would rather you did not: your wife must be expecting you."

Glad enough to be released, George went his way, and Janet sat on, alone. With that Shadow before her—though no longer a dark one—it was impossible but that her reflections should turn to the unhappy past: and she lost herself in perplexity.

A great deal of this story, The Shadow of Ashlydyat, is a perfectly true one; it is but the recital of a drama in real life. And the superstition that encompasses it? ten thousand inquisitive tongues will ask. Yes, and the superstition. There are things, as I have just said, which can neither be explained nor accounted for: they are marvels, mysteries, and so they must remain. Many a family has its supernatural skeleton, religiously believed in; many a house has its one dread corner which has never been fully unclosed to the light of day. Say what men will to the contrary, there is a tendency in the human mind to tread upon the confines of superstition. We cannot shut our eyes to things that occur within our view, although we may be, and always shall be, utterly unable to explain them; what they are, what they spring from, why they come. If I were to tell you that I believed there are such things as omens, warnings, which come to us—though seldom are they sufficiently marked at the time to be attended to—I should be called a visionary day-dreamer. I am nothing of the sort. I have my share of plain common sense. I pass my time in working, not in dreaming. I never had the gratification of seeing a ghost yet, and I wish I was as sure of the fruition of my dearest hopes, as I am that I never shall see one. I have not been taken into favour by the spirits, have never been promoted to so much as half a message from them—and never expect to be. But some curious incidents have forced themselves on my life's experience, causing me to echo as a question the assertion of the Prince of Denmark—Are there not more things in heaven and earth than are dreamt of in our philosophy?

Janet Godolphin rose with a deep sigh and her weight of care. She kept her head turned to the Shadow until she had passed from its view, and then continued her way to the house, murmuring: "It's but a small misfortune; the Shadow is scarcely darker than the moonlight itself."

Thomas was in his arm-chair, bending forward towards the fire, as she entered. His face would have been utterly colourless, save for the bluish tinge which had settled there, a tinge distinguishable even in the red blaze. Janet, keen-sighted as Margery, thought the hue had grown more ominous since she quitted him in the afternoon.

"Have you come back alone?" asked Thomas, turning towards her.

"George accompanied me as far as the ash-trees: I met him. Bessy is staying on for an hour with Lady Godolphin."

"It's a fine night," he observed.

"It is," replied Janet. "Thomas," dropping her voice, "the Shadow is abroad."

"Ah!"

The response was spoken in no tone of dread, or dismay; but calmly, pleasantly, with a smile upon his lips.

"It has changed its tone," continued Janet, "and may be called grey now instead of black. I thought it had left us for good, Thomas: I suppose it had to come once more."

"If it cared to keep up its character for consistency," he said, his voice jesting. "If it has been the advance herald of the death of other Godolphins, why should it not herald in mine?"

"I did not expect to hear you joke about the Shadow," observed Janet, after a pause of vexation.

"Nay, there's no harm in it. I have never understood it, you know, Janet; none of us have; so little have we understood, that we have not known whether to believe or disbelieve. A short while, Janet, and things may be made plainer to me."

"How are you feeling to-night?" somewhat abruptly asked Janet, looking askance at his face.

"Never better of late days. It seems as if ease both of mind and body had come to me. I think," he added, after a few moments' reflection, "that what George tells me of a prospect opening for him, has imparted this sense of ease. I have thought of him a great deal, Janet; of his wife and child: of what would become of him and of them. He may live yet to be a comfort to his family; to repair to others some of the injury he has caused. Oh, Janet! I am ready to go."

Janet turned her eyes from the fire, that the rising tears might not be seen. "The Shadow was very light, Thomas," she repeated. "Whatever it may herald forth, will not be much of a misfortune."

"A misfortune!—to be taken to my rest!—to the good God who has so loved and kept me here! No, Janet. A few minutes before you came in, I fell into a doze, and I dreamt that I saw Jesus Christ standing there by the window, waiting for me. He had His hand stretched out to me with a smile. So vivid had been the impression, that when

I awoke I thought it was reality, and was hastening towards the window before I recollected myself."

Janet rang the bell for lights to be brought in. Thomas, his elbow resting on the arm of his chair, bent his head upon his hand, and became lost in imagination in the glories that might so soon open to him. Bright forms were flitting around a wondrous throne, golden harps in their hands; and in one of them, her harp idle, her radiant face turned as if watching for one who might be coming, he seemed to recognize Ethel.

George Godolphin meanwhile had gone home, and was sitting with his wife and child. The room was bright with light and fire, and George's spirits were bright in accordance with it. He had been enlarging upon the prospect offered to him, describing a life in India in vivid colours; had drawn some imaginative pen-and-ink sketches of Miss Meta on a camel's back; in a gorgeous palanquin; in an open terrace gallery, being fanned by about fifty slaves: the young lady herself looking on at the pictures in a high state of excitement, her eyes sparkling, her cheeks flushed. Maria seemed to partake of the general hilarity. Whether she was really better, or the unexpected return of her husband had infused into her artificial strength, unwonted excitement, certain it is that she was not looking very ill that night: her cheeks had borrowed some of Meta's colour, and her lips were parted with a smile. The child's chatter never ceased; it was papa this, papa the other, incessantly. Margery felt rather cross, and when she came in to add some dainty to the substantial tea she had prepared for her master, told him she hoped he would not be for carrying Miss Meta out to the wretched foreign places that were only good for convicts. India and Botany Bay ranked precisely alike in Margery's estimation.

But tea was done with and removed, and the evening went on, and Margery came again to escort Miss Meta to bed. Miss Meta was not in a hurry to be escorted. Her nimble feet were flying everywhere: from papa at the table, to mamma who sat on the sofa near the fire: from mamma to Margery, standing silent and grim, scarcely deigning to look at the pen-and-ink sketches that Meta exhibited to her.

" I don't see no sense in 'em, for my part," slightingly spoke Margery, regarding with dubious eyes one somewhat indistinct representation held up to her. " Those things bain't like Christian animals. An elephant, d'ye call it ? Which is its head and which is its tail ? "

Meta whisked off to her papa, elephant in hand. " Papa, which is its head, and which is its tail ? "

" That's its tail," said George. " You'll know its head from its tail when you come to ride one, Margery," cried he, throwing his laughing glance at the woman.

" Me ride an elephant ! me mount one o' them animals ! " was the indignant response. " I should like to see myself at it ! It might be just as well, sir, if you didn't talk about them to the child : I shall have her starting out of her sleep screaming to-night, fancying that a score of them's eating her up."

George laughed. Meta's busy brain was at work ; very busy, very blithesome just then.

The Shadow of Ashlydyat.   27

"Papa, do we have swings in India?"

"Lots of them," responded George.

"Do they go up to the trees? Are they as good as the one Mrs. Pain made for me at the Folly?"

"Ten times better than that," said George slightingly. "That was a muff of a swing, compared with what the others will be."

Meta considered. "You didn't see it, papa. It went up—up—oh, ever so high."

"Did it?" said George. "We'll send the others higher."

"Who'll swing me?" continued Meta. "Mrs. Pain? She used to swing me before. Will she go to India with us?"

"Not she," said George. "What should she go for? Look here. Here's Meta on an elephant, and Margery on another, in attendance behind."

He had been mischievously sketching it off: Meta sitting at her ease on the elephant, her dainty little legs astride, boy fashion, was rather a pretty sight: but poor Margery grasping the animal's head, her face one picture of horror in her fear of falling, and some half-dozen natives propping her up on either side, was only a ludicrous one.

Margery looked daggers, but nothing could exceed Meta's delight. "Draw mamma upon one, papa; make her elephant alongside mine."

"Draw mamma upon one?" repeated George. "I think we'll have mamma in a palanquin; the elephants shall be reserved for you and Margery."

"Is she coming to bed to-night, or isn't she?" demanded Margery, in uncommonly sharp tones, speaking for the benefit of the company generally, not to any one in particular.

Meta paid little attention; George appeared to pay less. In taking his knife from his waistcoat-pocket to cut the pencil, preparatory to "drawing mamma and the palanquin," he happened to bring forth a ring. Those quick little eyes saw it: they saw most things. "That's Uncle Thomas's!" cried the child.

In his somewhat hasty attempt to return it to his pocket, George let the ring fall to the ground, and it rolled towards Margery. She picked it up, wonderingly—almost fearfully. She had believed that Mr. Godolphin would not part with his signet-ring during life: the ring which he had offered to the bankruptcy commissioners, and they, with every token of respect, had returned to him.

"Oh, sir! Surely he is not dead?"

"Dead!" echoed George, looking at her in surprise. "I left him better than usual, Margery, when I came away."

Margery said no more. Meta was not so scrupulous. "Uncle Thomas always has that on his finger: he seals his letters with it. Why have you brought it away, papa?"

"He does not want it to seal letters with any longer, Meta," George answered, speaking gravely now, and stroking her golden curls. "I shall use it in future for sealing mine."

"Who'll wear it?" asked Meta. "You, or Uncle Thomas?"

"I shall—some time. But it is quite time Meta was in bed; and Margery looks as if she thought so. There! just a few of mamma's grapes, and away to dream of elephants."

Some fine white grapes were heaped on a plate upon the table; they were what George had brought from London for his wife. He broke some off for Meta, and that spoiled young damsel climbed on his knee, while she ate them, chattering incessantly.

" Will there be parrots in India ?   Red ones ? "

" Plenty.   Red and green and blue and yellow," returned George, who was rather magnificent in his promises.   " There'll be monkeys as well—as Margery's fond of them."

Margery flung off in a temper.   But the words had brought a recollection to Meta.   She bustled up on her knees, neglecting her grapes, gazing at her papa in consternation.

" Uncle Reginald was to bring me home some monkeys and some parrots and a Chinese dog that won't bite.   How shall I have them, papa, if I have gone to Cal—what is it ? "   She spoke better than she did, and could sound the " th " now ; but the name of the place was difficult to be remembered.

" Calcutta.   We'll write word to Regy's ship to come round there and leave them," replied ready George.

It satisfied the child.   She finished her grapes, and then George took her in his arms to Maria to be kissed, and afterwards put her down outside the door to offended Margery, after kissing lovingly her pretty lips and her golden curls.

His manner had changed when he returned.   He stood by the fire, near Maria, grave and earnest, and began talking more seriously to her on this new project than he had done in the presence of his child.

" I think I should do wrong were I to refuse it : do not you, Maria ? It is an offer that is not often met with."

" Yes, I think you would do wrong to refuse it.   It is far better than anything I had hoped for."

" And can you be ready to start by New Year's Day ? "

" I—I could be ready, of course," she answered.   " But I—I—don't know whether—— "

She came to a final stop.   George looked at her in surprise : in addition to her hesitation, he detected considerable emotion.

She stood up by him and leaned her arm on the mantel-piece.   She strove to speak quietly, to choke down the rebellious rising in her throat : her breath went and came, her bosom heaved.   " George, I am not sure whether I shall be able to undertake the voyage.   I am not sure that I shall live to go out."

Did his heart beat a shade quicker ?   He looked at her more in surprise still than in any other feeling.   He had not in the least realized this faint suggestion of the future.

" My darling, what do you mean ? "

He passed his arm round her waist, and drew her to him.   Maria let her head fall upon his shoulder, and the tears began to trickle down her wasted cheeks.

" I cannot get strong, George.   I grow weaker instead of stronger ; and I begin to think I shall never be well again.   I begin to know I shall never be well again ! " she added, amending the words.   " I have thought it for some time."

" How do you feel ? " he asked, breaking the silence that had ensued.
" Are you in any pain ? "

" I have had a pain in my throat ever since the—ever since the
summer : and I have a constant inward pain here "—touching her
chest. " Mr. Snow says both arise from the same cause—nervousness !
but I don't know."

" Maria," he said, his voice quite trembling with its tenderness, " shall
I tell you what it is ? The worry of the past summer has had a bad
effect upon you, and brought you into this weak state. Mr. Snow
is right : it is nervousness : and you must have change of scene ere
you can recover. Is he attending you ? "

" He calls every other day or so, and he sends me medicine of different kinds ; tonics, I fancy. I wish I could get strong ! I might—
perhaps—get a little better, that is, I might feel a trifle better, if I were
not always so entirely alone. I wish," she more timidly added, " that
you could be more with me than you are."

" You cannot wish it as heartily as I," returned George. " A little
while, my darling, and things will be bright again. I have been
earnestly and constantly seeking for something to do in London ; I
was obliged to be there. Now that I have this place given me, I must
be there still, chiefly, until we sail, making my preparations. You can
come to me if you like, until we do go," he added, " if you would
rather be there than here. I can change my bachelor lodgings, and
get a place large enough for you and Meta."

She felt that she was not equal to the removal, and she felt that if
she really were to leave Europe she must remain this short intervening
time near her father and mother. But—even as she thought it—the
conviction came upon her, firm and strong, that she never should leave
it ; should not live to leave it. George's voice, eager and hopeful,
interrupted.

" We shall begin life anew in India, Maria : with the old country we
shall leave old sores behind us. As to Margery—I don't know what's
to be done about her. It would half break her heart to drag her to a
new land, and quite break it to carry off Meta from her. Perhaps we
had better not attempt to influence her either way, but let the decision
rest entirely with her."

" She will never face the live elephants," said Maria, her lips smiling
at the joke, as she endeavoured to be gay and hopeful as George was.
But the effort entirely failed. A vision came over her of George there
alone; herself in the cold grave, whither she believed she was surely
hastening ; Meta—ay—what of Meta ?

" Oh, George ! if I might but get strong ! if I might but live to go
with you ! " she cried in a wail of agony.

" Hush, hush ! Maria, hush ! I must not scold you : but indeed it
is not right to give way to these low spirits. That of itself will keep
you back. Shall I take you to town with me when I return to-morrow,
just for a week's change ? I know it would partially bring you round,
and we would make shift in my rooms for the time. Margery will take
care of Meta here."

She knew how worse than useless was the thought of attempting it ;
she saw that George could not be brought to understand her excessive

weakness. A faint hope came across her that, now that the uncertainty of his future prospects was removed, she might grow better. That uncertainty had been distressing her sick heart for months.

She subdued her emotion and sat down in the chair quietly, saying that she was not strong enough to go up with him this time: it would be a change in one sense for her, she added, thinking of the new life; and then she began to talk of other things.

"Did you see Reginald before he sailed?"

"Not immediately before it, I think."

"You are aware that he has gone as a common seaman?"

"Yes. By the way, there's no knowing what I may be able to do for Regy out there, and for Isaac too, perhaps. Once I am in a good position I shall be able to assist them—and I'll do it. Regy hates the sea: I'll get him something more to his taste in Calcutta."

Maria's face flushed with hope, and she clasped her nervous hands together. "If you could, George! how thankful I should be! I think of poor Regy and his hard life night and day."

"Which is not good for you by any means, young lady. I wish you'd get out of that habit of thinking and fretting about others. It has been just poor Thomas's fault."

She answered by a faint smile. "Has Thomas given you his ring?" she asked.

"He gave it me this afternoon," replied George, taking it from his pocket. It was a ring with a bright green stone, on which was engraved the arms of the Godolphins. Sir George had worn it always, and it came to Thomas at his death: now it had come to George.

"You do not wear it, George."

"Not yet. I cannot bear to put it on my finger while Thomas lives. In point of fact, I have no right to do so—at least to use the signet: it belongs exclusively to the head of the Godolphins."

"Do you see Mrs. Pain often?" Maria presently said, with apparent indifference. But George little knew the fluttering emotion that had been working within, or the effort it had taken to subdue that emotion ere the question could be put.

"I see her sometimes; not often. She gets me to ride with her in the Park now and then."

"Does she continue to reside with the Verralls?"

"I suppose so. I have not heard her mention anything about it."

"George, I have wondered where Mrs. Pain's money comes from," Maria resumed in a dreamy tone. "It was said in the old days, you know, that the report of her having thirty thousand pounds was false; that she had nothing."

"I don't believe she had a penny," returned George. "As to her income, I fancy it is drawn from Verrall. Mrs. Pain's husband was connected in some business way with Verrall, and I suppose she still benefits by it. I know nothing whatever, but I have thought it must be so. Listen!"

George raised his hand as he abruptly spoke, for a distinct sound had broken upon his ear. Springing to the window he threw it open. The death-bell of All Souls' was booming out over Prior's Ash.

Before a word was spoken by him or by his wife; before George could still the emotion that was thumping at his heart, Margery came in with a scared face. In her flurry, her sudden grief, she addressed him as she had been accustomed to address him in his boyhood.

"Do you hear it, Master George? That's the passing-bell! It is for *him*. There's nobody else within ten miles they would trouble to have the bell tolled for at nigh ten o'clock at night. The Master of Ashlydyat's gone."

She sat down on a chair, regardless of the presence of her master and mistress, and, flinging her apron up to her face, burst into a storm of sobs.

A voice in the passage aroused her, for she recognized it as Bexley's. George opened the room-door, and the old man came in.

"It is all over, sir," he said, his manner strangely still, his voice unnaturally calm and low, as is sometimes the case where emotion is striven to be suppressed. "Miss Janet bade me come to you with the tidings."

George's bearing was suspiciously quiet too. "It is very sudden, Bexley," he presently rejoined.

Maria had risen and stood with one hand leaning on the table, her eyes strained on Bexley, her white face turned to him. Margery never moved.

"Very sudden, sir : and yet my mistress did not seem unprepared for it. He took his tea with her, and was so cheerful and well over it that I declare I began to hope he had taken a fresh turn. Soon afterwards Miss Bessy came back, and I heard her laughing in the room as she told them some story that had been related to her by Lady Godolphin. Presently my mistress called me in, to give me directions about a little matter she wanted done to-morrow, and while she was speaking to me, Miss Bessy cried out. We turned round and saw her leaning over my master. He had slipped back in his chair powerless, and I hastened to raise and support him. Death was in his face, sir ; there was no mistaking it; but he was quite conscious, quite sensible, and smiled at us. 'I must say farewell to you,' he said, and Miss Bessy burst into a fit of sobs ; but my mistress kneeled down quietly before him, and took his hands in hers, and said, 'Thomas, is the moment come?' 'Yes, it is come,' he answered, and he tried to look round at Miss Bessy, who stood a little behind his chair. 'Don't grieve,' he said; 'I am going on first ·' but she only sobbed the more. 'Good-bye, my dear ones,' he continued ; 'good-bye, Bexley. I shall wait for you all, as I know I am being waited for. Fear?' he went on, for Miss Bessy sobbed out something that sounded like the word : 'fear, when I am going to God!—when Jesus——'"

Bexley fairly broke down with a great burst, and the tears were rolling silently over Maria's cheeks. George wheeled round to the window and stood there with his back to them. Presently Bexley mastered himself and resumed : Margery had come forward then and taken her apron from her eyes.

"It was the last word he spoke—'Jesus.' His voice ceased, his hands fell, and the eyelids dropped. There was no struggle; nothing but a long gentle breath ; and he died with the smile upon his lips."

"He had cause to smile," interjected Margery, the words coming from her brokenly. " If ever a man has gone to his rest in heaven, it is Mr. Godolphin. He had more than his share of sorrow in this world, and God has taken him to a better."

Every feeling in George's heart echoed to the words, every pulse beat in wild sorrow for the death of his good brother,—every sting that remorse could bring pricked him with the consciousness of his own share in it. He thrust his burning face beyond the window into the cool night; he raised his eyes to the blue canopy of heaven, serene and fair in the moonlight, almost as if he saw in imagination the redeemed soul winging its flight thither. He pressed his hands upon his throbbing breast to still its emotion; but for the greatest exercise of self-control he would have burst into sobs, as Bexley had done; and it may be that he—he, careless George Godolphin—breathed forth a yearning cry to heaven to be pardoned his share of the past. If Thomas, in his changed condition, could look down upon him, now, with his loving eyes, his ever-forgiving spirit, he would know how bitter and genuine, how full of anguish were these regrets!

George leaned his head on the side of the window to subdue his emotion, to gather the outward calmness that man likes not to have ruffled before the world; he listened to the strokes of the passing-bell ringing out so sharply in the still night air: and every separate stroke was laden with its weight of pain.

CHAPTER IV.

GATHERED TO HIS FATHERS.

YOU might have taken it to be Sunday in Prior's Ash—except that Sundays in ordinary did not look so gloomy. The shops were closed, a drizzling rain fell, and the heavy bell of All Souls' was booming out at solemn intervals. It was tolling for the funeral of Thomas Godolphin. Morning and night, from eight o'clock to nine, had it so tolled since his death; but on this, the last day, it did not cease with nine o'clock, but tolled on, and would so toll until he should be in his last home. People had closed their shutters with one accord as the clock struck ten; some indeed had never opened them at all: if they had not paid him due respect always in life, they paid it to him in death. Ah, it was only for a time, in the first brunt of the shock, that Prior's Ash mistook Thomas Godolphin. He had gone to his long home; to his last resting-place: he had gone to the merciful God to whom (it may surely be said!) he had belonged in life; and Prior's Ash mourned for him.

You will deem this a sad story; perhaps bring a reproach upon me for recording it. That bell has tolled out all too often in its history; and this is not the first funeral you have seen at All Souls'. If I wrote only according to my own experiences of life, my stories would be always sad ones. Life wears different aspects for us, and its cares and its joys are unequally allotted out. At least they so appear to be. One glances up heavily from the burdens heaped upon him, and sees others without care basking in the sunshine. But I often wonder whether those who seem so gay, whose path seems to be cast on the broad, sunny road of pleasure,—whether they have not a skeleton in *their* closet. I look, I say, and wonder, marvelling what the reality may be. Nothing but gaiety, nothing but lightness, nothing, to all appearance, but freedom from care. Is it really so? Perhaps; with some—a very few. Is it well for those few? The broad road of pleasure, down which so many seem to travel, is not the safest road to a longer home, or the best preparation for it. Oh, if we could only see the truth when the burden upon us is heavy and long!—could only read how good it is!

But we never can. We are but mortal; born with a mortal's keen susceptibility to care and pain. We preach to others, that these things are sent for their benefit; we complaisantly say so to ourselves when not actually suffering; but when the fiery trial is upon us, then we groan out in our sore anguish that it is greater than we can bear.

There is no doubt that, with the many, suffering predominates in life, and if we would paint life as it is, that suffering must form a comprehensive view in the picture. Reverses, sickness, death—they seem to follow some people as surely as the shadow follows the sun at noontide. It is probable; nay, it is certain, that minds are so constituted as to receive them differently. Witness, as a case in point, the contrast between Thomas Godolphin and his brother George. Thomas, looking back, could say that nearly the whole course of his life had been marked by sorrow. Some of its sources have been mentioned here : not all. There was the melancholy death of Ethel; there was the long-felt disease which marked him for its early prey; there was the dreadful crash, the disgrace, which nearly broke his heart. It is to those who feel them keenly that sorrows chiefly come.

And George? Look at him. Gay, light, careless, handsome George. What sorrows had marked *his* path? None. He had revelled in the world's favour, he had made a wife of the woman he loved, he had altogether floated gaily down the sunniest part of the stream of life. The worry which his folly had brought upon himself, and which ended in his own ruin and in the ruin of so many others, *he* had not felt. No, he had scarcely felt it : and once let him turn his back on England and enter upon new scenes, he will barely remember it.

All Souls' clock struck eleven, and the beadle came out of the church and threw wide the gates. It was very punctual, for there came the hearse in sight; punctual as he who was borne within it had in life always liked to be. Prior's Ash peeped through the chinks of its shutters, behind its blinds and its curtains, to see the sight, as it came slowly winding along the street to the sound of the solemn bell. Through the mist of blinding tears, which rolled down many a face, did Prior's Ash look out. They might have attended him to the grave, following unobtrusively, but that it was known to be the wish of the family that such demonstration should not be made : so they contented themselves with shutting up their houses, and observing the day as one of mourning. "Bury me in the plainest and simplest manner possible," had been Thomas Godolphin's directions when the end was drawing near. Under the circumstances, it was only seemly to do so; but so antagonistic were pomp and show of all kinds to the tastes of Thomas Godolphin, in all things that related to himself, that it is more than probable the same orders would have been given had he died as his forefathers had died—the Master of Ashlydyat, the wealthy chief of the Godolphins.

So a hearse and a mourning-coach were all that had been commanded to Ashlydyat. What means, then, this pageantry of carriages that follow? Fine carriages, gay with colours as they file past, one by one, the eyes of Prior's Ash strained on them, some with coronets on their panels, all with closed blinds, a long line of them. Lady Godolphin's is first, taking its place next the mourning-coach. They have come from various parts of the county, near and distant, to show their owners' homage to that good man who had earned their deepest respect during life. Willingly, willingly would those owners have attended and mourned him in person, but for the same reason which kept away the more humble inhabitants of Prior's Ash. Slowly the procession gained the churchyard, and the hearse and the mourning-coach stopped: the rest of the carriages filed off and turned their horses' heads to face the churchyard, and waited still and quiet while the hearse was emptied. Out of the mourning-coach stepped two mourners only: George Godolphin and the Viscount Averil.

The Rector of All Souls' stood at the gate in his surplice, book in hand. He turned, reciting the commencement of the service for the burial of the dead: "I am the resurrection and the life." While they were in the church, the graveyard filled; by ones, by twos, by threes, they came stealing in, regardless of the weather, to see the last of the Master of Ashlydyat: and the beadle was lenient to-day.

The Rector of All Souls' took his place at the head of the grave and read the service, as the coffin was lowered. George stood next to him; close to George, Lord Averil; and the other mourners were clustered beyond. Their faces were bent: the drizzling rain beat upon their bare heads. How did George feel as he stood there, between the two men whom he had so wronged? The Rector glanced at him once, and saw that he had difficulty in suppressing his emotion.

"I heard a voice from heaven, saying unto me, Write, From henceforth blessed are the dead which die in the Lord: even so, saith the Spirit: for they rest from their labours."

So hushed was the silence, that every word, as it fell solemnly from the lips of the minister, might be heard in all parts of the churchyard. If ever that verse could apply to frail humanity, with its unceasing struggle after holiness and its unceasing failure *here*, it most surely applied to him over whom it was being spoken. George Godolphin's head was bowed, his face hidden in his handkerchief; the rain pattered down on his golden hair. He had gone to his grave so early! Bend forward, as so many of those spectators are doing, and read the inscription on the plate. There is a little earth on the coffin, but the plate is visible. "Thomas Godolphin of Ashlydyat: aged forty-five years."

Only forty-five years! A period at which some men think they are only beginning life. So early a grave!—and George had helped to send him to it!

It was over: and the spectators began to draw unobtrusively away, silently and decently. In the general crowd and bustle, for every one seemed to be on the move, George turned suddenly to the Rector and held out his hand. "Will you shake hands with me, Mr. Hastings?"

There was a perceptible hesitation on the Rector's part, not in the least sought to be disguised, ere he responded to it, and then he put his own hand into the one held out. It was the first time they had met since the crash. "I cannot do otherwise over the dead body of your brother," was the answer. "But neither can I be a hypocrite, George Godolphin, and say that I forgive you, for it would not be true. The result of the injury you did me presses daily and hourly upon us in a hundred ways, and my mind as yet has refused to be brought into that charitable frame necessary to entire forgiveness. This is not altogether the fault of my will. I wish to forgive you for your wife's sake and for my own; I pray night and morning that I may be enabled heartily to forgive you before I die. I would not be your enemy; I wish you well, and there's my hand in token of it: but to pronounce forgiveness is not yet in my power. Will you call in and see Mrs. Hastings?"

"I have not time to-day. I must go back to London this evening, but I shall be down again very shortly and will see her then. It was a peaceful ending."

George was gazing down dreamily at the coffin as he spoke the last words. The Rector looked at him.

"A peaceful ending! Yes. It could not be anything else with *him*."

"No, no," murmured George. "Not anything else with him."

"May God in His mercy send us all as happy a one, when our time shall comè!"

As the words left the Rector's lips, the heavy bell boomed out again, giving notice to Prior's Ash that the last rites were over: that the world had closed for ever on Thomas Godolphin.

"Oh, George! *can't* you stay with me?"

The words broke from Maria with a wail of anguish as she rose to bid her husband good-bye. He was hastening away to catch the evening train. It seemed that she had not liked to prefer the request before, had put it off to the last moment. In point of fact, she had seen very little of George all day. After the funeral he had returned in the coach with Lord Averil to Ashlydyat, and only came home late in the afternoon.

Lord and Lady Averil, recalled so suddenly from their wedding tour, had reached Ashlydyat the previous night, and would not leave it again. Janet was to depart from it in a few days; Bessy would be on the morrow with Lady Godolphin.

George would not believe that his wife was in any sort of danger. He had been to Mr. Snow, begged him to take all possible care of her, and asked whether there were really any grounds for alarm. Mr. Snow answered him that he could not say for certain: she was, no doubt, very weak and poorly, but he saw no reason why she should not get out of it; and as for himself, he *was* taking of her all the care he could take. The reply satisfied George, and he became full of the projects and details of his departure, entering into them so warmly with her that Maria caught the spirit of enterprise, and was beguiled into a belief that she might yet go also.

He had come home from the funeral bearing a parcel wrapped in paper for Meta. It had been found amidst Thomas Godolphin's things, directed to the child. George lifted Meta on to his knee—very grave, very subdued was his face to-day—and opened it. It proved to be a Bible, and on the fly-leaf in his own hand was written, " Uncle Thomas's last and best gift to Meta," and it was dated the day he died. Lower down were the words, " My ways are ways of pleasantness, and all my paths are peace."

And the evening had gone on, and it grew time for George to leave. It was as he bent to kiss his wife that she had burst out with that wailing cry. " Oh, George! can't you stay with me ? "

" My darling, I must go. I shall soon be down again."

" Only a little while ! A little longer ! "

The tone in its anguish quite distressed him. " I would stay if it were possible : but it is not so. I came down for a day only, you know, Maria, and I have remained more than a week. It will not be so very long before we sail, and I shall have my hands full with the preparations for our voyage."

" I have been so much alone," she sobbed hysterically. " I get thinking and thinking : it does not give me a chance to recover. George, you have been always away from me since the trouble came."

" I could not help it. Maria, I could not bear Prior's Ash; I *could* not stop in it," he cried with a burst of genuine truth. " But for you and Thomas, I should never have set my foot in the place again, once I was quit of it. Now, however, I am compelled to be in London; there are fifty things to see to. Keep up your courage, my darling ! A little while, and we shall be together and happy as we used to be."

" Sir," said Margery, putting her head in the door, " do you want to catch the nine train ? "

" All right," answered George.

" It may be all right if you run for it, it won't be all right else," grunted Margery.

He flew off, catching up his hand-portmanteau as he went, and waving his adieu to Meta. That young damsel, accustomed to be made a great deal of, could not understand so summary and slight a leave-taking, and she stood quite still in her consternation, staring after her papa : or rather at the door he had gone out of. Margery was right, and George found that he must indeed hasten if he would save the train. Maria, with a storm of hysterical sobs, grievous to witness, caught Meta in her arms, sat down on the sofa, and sobbed over the child, as she strained her to her bosom.

Meta was used to her mamma's grief now, and she lay quite still, her shoes and white socks peeping out beyond the black frock; nay, a considerable view of the straight little legs peeping out as well. Maria bent her head until her aching forehead rested·on the fair plump neck.

"Mamma! Mamma, dear! Mamma's crying for poor Uncle Thomas!"

"No," said Maria in the bitterness of her heart. "If we were but where Uncle Thomas is, we should be happy. I cry for us who are left, Meta!"

"Hey-day! and what on earth's the meaning of this? Do you think this is the way to get strong, Mrs. George Godolphin?"

They had not heard him come in. Meta, always ready for visitors, scuffled off her mamma's lap gleefully, and Mr. Snow drew a chair in front of Maria and watched her trying to dry away her tears. He moved a little to the right, that the light of the lamp which was behind him might fall upon her face.

"Now just you have the goodness to tell me what it is that's the matter."

"I—I am low-spirited, I think," said Maria, her voice subdued and weak now.

"Low-spirited!" echoed Mr. Snow. "Then I'd get high-spirited, if I were you. I wish there never had been such a thing as spirits invented, for my part! A nice excuse it is for you ladies to sigh away half your time instead of being rational and merry, as you ought to be. A woman of your sense ought to be above it, Mrs. George Godolphin."

"Mr. Snow," interrupted a troublesome little voice, "papa's gone back to London. He went without saying good-bye to Meta!"

"Ah! Miss Meta had been naughty, I expect."

Meta shook her head very decisively in the negative, but Mr. Snow had turned to Maria.

"And so you were crying after that roving husband of yours! I guessed as much. He nearly ran over me at the gate. 'Step in and see my wife, will you, Snow?' said he. 'She wants tonics, or something.' You don't want tonics half as much as you want common sense, Mrs. George Godolphin."

"I am so weak," was her feeble excuse. "A little thing upsets me now."

"Well, and what can you expect? If I sat over my surgery fire all day stewing and fretting, a pretty doctor I should soon become for my patients! I wonder you——"

"Have you looked at my new black frock, Mr. Snow?"

She was a young lady who would be attended to, let who would go without attention. She had lifted up her white pinafore and stood in front of him, waiting for the frock to be admired.

"Very smart indeed!" replied Mr. Snow.

"It's not smart," spoke Meta resentfully. "My smart frocks are put away in the drawers. It is for Uncle Thomas, Mr. Snow! Mr. Snow, Uncle Thomas is in heaven now."

"Ay, child, that he is. And it's time that Miss Meta Godolphin was in bed."

That same night Mr. Snow was called up to Mrs. George Godolphin. —Let us call her so to the end; but she is Mrs. Godolphin now. Margery was sleeping quietly, the child in a little bed by her side, when she was aroused by some one standing over her. It was her mistress in her night-dress. Up started the woman, wide awake instantly, crying out to know what was the matter.

"Margery, I shan't be in time. The ship's waiting to sail, and none of my things are ready. I can't go without my things."

Margery, experienced in illness of many kinds, saw what it was. Her mistress had suddenly awakened from some vivid dream, and in her weak state was unable to shake off the delusion. In fact, that species of half-consciousness, half-delirium was upon her, which is apt in the night-time to attack some patients labouring under long-continued and excessive weakness.

She had come up exactly as she got out of bed. No slippers on her feet, nothing upon her shoulders. As Margery threw a warm woollen shawl over those shoulders, she felt the ominous damp of the night-dress. A pair of list-shoes of her own were at the bedside, and she hastily put them upon her mistress's feet.

"There'll be no time, Margery; there'll be no time to get the things ready: they never could be bought and made, you know. Oh, Margery! the ship must not go without me! What will be done?"

"I'll telegraph up to that ship to-morrow morning, and get him to put off starting for a week or two," cried Margery, nodding her head with authority. "Never you trouble yourself, ma'am; it will be all right. You shall go to sleep again comfortably, and we'll see about the things with morning light."

Margery talked as she conveyed her mistress back to bed, and remained talking after she was in it. A stock of this should be got in, a stock of the other: as for linen, it could all be bought ready made—and the best way too, now calico was so cheap. Somewhat surprised that she heard no answer, no further expressed fear, Margery looked close at her mistress by the night-lamp, wondering whether she had gone to sleep again. She had not gone to sleep. She was lying still, cold, white, without sense or motion; and Margery, collected Margery, very nearly screamed.

Maria had fainted away. Margery did not understand it at all, or why she should have fainted when she ought to have gone to sleep. Margery liked it as little as she understood it; and she ran upstairs to their landlady, Mrs. James, and got her to despatch her son for Mr. Snow.

But that was only the beginning. Night after night would these attacks of semi-delirium come upon her, though in the day she seemed pretty well. Mr. Snow came and came, and drew an ominous face and doubled the tonics and changed them, and talked and joked and scolded. But it all seemed unavailing: she certainly did not get better. Weary, weary hours! weary, weary days! as she lay there alone, struggling with her malady. And yet no malady, either, that Mr. Snow could discover; nothing but a weakness which he only half believed.

Janet and Bessy Godolphin were one day sitting with Mrs. George. The time had come for Janet to quit Ashlydyat, and she was paying her farewell visit to Maria. Maria was at the window at work when they arrived; at work with her weak and fevered hands. No very poetical employment, that on which she was engaged, but one which has to be done in most families nevertheless—stocking-darning. She was darning socks for Miss Meta. Miss Meta, her sleeves and white pinafore tied up with black ribbon, her golden curls somewhat in disorder, for the young lady had rebelliously broken from Margery and taken a race round the garden in the blowing wintry wind, her smooth cheeks fresh and rosy, was now roasting her face in front of the fire, her doll and a whole collection of dolls' clothes lying around her on the hearth-rug.

Bessy had come, not so much to accompany Janet, as for a special purpose—to deliver a message from Lady Godolphin. My lady, deeming possibly that her displeasure had lasted long enough, graciously charged Bessy with an invitation to Maria—to spend a day or two at the Folly ere her departure for Calcutta.

Maria gave a sort of sobbing sigh. "She is very kind. Tell Lady Godolphin how kind I think it of her, Bessy, but that I am not strong enough to go from home now."

Bessy looked at her. "But, Maria, if you are not strong enough to go out on a short visit, how shall you be strong enough to undertake a three or four months' voyage?"

Maria paused ere she answered the question. She was gazing out straight before her, as if seeing something at a distance—something in the future. "I think of it and of its uncertainty a great deal," she presently said. "If I can only get away: if I can only keep up sufficiently to get away, I can lie down always in my berth. And if I do die before I reach India, George will be with me."

"Child!" almost sharply interrupted Janet, "what are you saying?"

She seemed scarcely to hear the interruption. She sat, gazing still, her white and trembling hands lying clasped on her black dress, and she resumed, as if pursuing the train of thought.

"My great dread is, lest I should not keep up to get to London, to be taken on board; lest George should, after all, be obliged to sail without me. It is always on my mind, Janet; it makes me dream constantly that the ship has gone and I am left behind. I wish I did not have those dreams."

"Come to Lady Godolphin's Folly, Maria," persuasively spoke Bessy. "It will be the very best thing to cheat you of those fears. They all arise from weakness."

"I have no doubt they do. I had a pleasant dream one night," she added with some animation. "I thought we had arrived in safety, and I and George and Meta were sitting under a tree whose leaves were larger than an umbrella. It was very hot, but these leaves shaded us, and I seemed to be well, for we were all laughing merrily together. It *may* come true, you know, Janet."

"Yes," assented Janet. "Are you preparing much for the voyage?"

"Not yet. Clothes can be had so quickly now. George talked it over with me when he was down, and we decided to send a list to the outfitter's, just before we sailed, so that the things might not come down here, but be packed in London."

"And Margery?" asked Janet.

"I do not know what she means to do," answered Maria, shaking her head. "She protests ten times a day that she will not go; but I see she is carefully mending up all her cotton gowns, and one day I heard her say to Meta that she supposed nothing but cotton was bearable out there. What I should do without Margery on the voyage I don't like to think about. George told her to consider of it, and give us her decision when he next came down. And you, Janet? When shall you be back again at Prior's Ash?"

" I do not suppose I shall ever come back to it," was Janet's answer. " Its reminiscences will not be so pleasing to me that I should seek to renew my acquaintance with it."

" Bexley attends you, I hear."

" Yes. My aunt's old servant has got beyond his work—he has been forty-two years in the family, Maria—and Bexley will replace him."

When Janet rose to leave, she bent over Maria and slipped four sovereigns into her hand. " It is for yourself, my dear," she whispered.

" Oh, thank you! But indeed I have enough, Janet. George left me five pounds when he was at home, and it is not half gone. You don't know what a little keeps us. I eat next to nothing, and Margery, I think, lives chiefly upon porridge : there's only Meta."

" But you ought to eat, child ! "

" I can't eat," said Maria. " I have never lost that pain in my throat."

" What pain? " asked Janet.

" I do not know. It came on with the trouble. I feel—I feel always ill within myself, Janet. I seem to be always shivering inwardly ; and the pain in the throat is sometimes better, sometimes worse, but it never quite goes away."

Janet looked at her searchingly. She heard the meek, resigned tone, she saw the white, wan face, the attenuate hands, the chest rising with every passing emotion, the mournful look in the sweet eyes ; and for the first time a suspicion that another life would shortly have to go, took possession of Miss Godolphin.

" What is George at, that he is not here to see after you?" she asked in a strangely severe accent.

" He cannot bear Prior's Ash, Janet," whispered Maria. " But for me and Thomas, he never would have come back to it. And I suppose he is busy in London : there must be many arrangements to make."

Janet stooped and gravely kissed her ; kissed her twice. " Take care of yourself, my dear, and do all you can to keep your mind tranquil and to get up your strength. You shall hear from me before your departure."

Margery stood in the little hall. Miss Bessy Godolphin was in the garden, in full chase after that rebellious damsel, Meta, who had made a second escape through the opened door, passing angry Margery and the outstretched hand that would have made a prisoner of her, with a laugh of defiance. Miss Godolphin stopped to address Margery.

" Shall you go to India or not, Margery ? "

" I'm just almost torn in two about it, ma'am," was the answer, delivered confidentially. " Without me, that child would never reach the other side alive : she'd be clambering up the sides o' the ship and get drownded ten times over before they got there. Look at her now! And who'd take care of her over there, among those native beasts—those elephants and black people? If I thought she'd ever come to be waited on by a black woman with woolly hair, I should be fit to smother her before she went out. I shall see, Miss Janet."

" Margery, your mistress appears to want the greatest care."

" She has wanted that a long while," was Margery's composed answer.

" She ought to have everything strengthening. Wine and other necessaries required by the sick."

" I suppose she ought," said Margery. " But she won't take them, Miss Janet; she says she can't eat and drink. And for the matter of that, we have nothing of that sort for her to take. There were more good things consumed in the Bank in a day than we should see in a month now."

" Where's your master?" repeated Janet in an accent not less sharp than the one she had used for the same question to Maria.

" He?" cried wrathful Margery, for the subject was sure to put her out uncommonly, in the strong opinion she was pleased to hold touching her master's short-comings. " I suppose he's riding about with his choice friend, Madam Pain. Folks talk of their horses being seen abreast pretty often."

There was no opportunity for further colloquy. Bessy came in, carrying the laughing truant; and Margery, with a tart word to the young lady, attended the Miss Godolphins down the garden path to throw open the gate for them. In her poor way, in her solitary self, Margery strove to make up for the state they had been accustomed to, when the ladies called from Ashlydyat.

Maria, lying motionless on the sofa, where on being left alone she had thrown herself in weariness, heard Margery's gratuitous remark about Mrs. Pain, through the unlatched door, and a contraction arose to her brow. In her hand lay the four sovereigns left there by Janet. She looked at them musingly, and then murmured, " I can afford to give her half." When Margery returned indoors, she called her in, and sent her for Mrs. Bond.

A little while, and Mrs. Bond, on her meekest and civilest behaviour, stood before Maria, her thin shawl and wretched old gown drawn tightly round her, to protect her from the winter's cold. Maria put two sovereigns into her hand.

" It is the first instalment of my debt to you, Mrs. Bond. If I live, I will pay it you all, but it will be by degrees. And perhaps that is the best way that you could receive it. I wish I could have given you some before."

Mrs. Bond burst into tears. Not the crocodile's tears that she was somewhat in the habit of favouring the world with when not quite herself, but real, genuine tears of gratitude. She had given up all hope of the ten pounds, did not expect to see a penny of it; and the joy overcame her. Her conscience pricked her a little also, for she remembered sundry hard words she had at one time liberally regaled her neighbours' ears with, touching Mrs. George Godolphin. In her grateful repentance she could have knelt at Maria's feet: hunger and other ills of poverty had tended to subdue her spirit.

"May the good Lord bless and repay you, ma'am!—and send you a safe journey to the far-off place where I hear you be going!"

"Yes, I shall go, if I am well enough," replied Maria. "It is from thence that I shall send you home some money from time to time if I can do so. Have you been well, lately?"

"As well as pretty nigh clamming will let me be, ma'am. Things has gone hard with me: many a day I've not had as much as a crust to eat. But this 'll set me up again, and, ma'am, I'll never cease to pray for you."

"Don't spend it in—in—you know, Mrs. Bond," Maria ventured timidly to advise, in a lowered voice.

Mrs. Bond shook her head and turned up her eyes by way of expressing a very powerful negative. Probably she did not feel altogether comfortable on the subject, for she hastened to quit it.

"Have you heard the news about old Jekyl, ma'am?"

"No. What news?"

"He's dead. He went off at one o'clock this a'ternoon. He fretted continual after his money, folks says, and it wore him to a skeleton. He couldn't abear to be living upon his sons; and Jonathan don't earn enough for himself now, and the old 'un felt it."

Some one else was feeling it. Fretting continually after his money! —that money which might never have been placed in the Bank but for her! Miss Meta came flying in, went straight up to the visitor, and leaned her pretty arm upon the snuffy black gown.

"When shall I come and see the parrot?"

"The parrot! Lawks bless the child! I haven't got the parrot now, I haven't had him this many a day. I couldn't let *him* clam," she continued, turning to Maria. "I was clamming myself, ma'am, and I sold him, cage and all, just as he stood."

"Where is he?" asked Meta, looking disappointed.

"He's where he went," lucidly explained Mrs. Bond. "It were the lady up at t'other end o' the town, beyond the parson's, what bought him, ma'am. Leastways her daughter did: sister to her what was once to have married Mr. Godolphin. It's a white house."

"Lady Sarah Grame's," said Maria. "Did she buy the parrot?"

"Miss did: that cross-looking daughter of her'n. She see him as she was going by my door one day, ma'am, and she stopped and looked at him, and asked me what I'd sell him for. Well, on the spur o' the moment I said five shilling; for I'd not a halfpenny in the place to buy him food, and for days and days he had had only what the neighbours brought him; but it warn't half his worth. And miss was all wild to buy him, but her mother wasn't. She didn't want screeching birds in her house, she said, and they had a desperate quarrel in my kitchen before they went away. Didn't she call her mother names! She's a vixen that daughter, if ever there were one. But she got her will, for an hour or two after that, a young woman come down for the parrot with the five shilling in her hand. And there's where he is."

"I shall have twenty parrots when I go to India," struck in Meta.

"What a sight of food they'll eat!" ejaculated Mrs. Bond. "That there one o' mine eats his fill now. I made bold one day to go up and ask after him, and the two young women in the kitchen took me to the room to see him, the ladies being out, and he had his tin stuffed full o' seed. He knowed me again, he did, and screeched out to be heerd a mile off. The young women said that what with his screeching and the two ladies quarrelling, the house weren't bearable sometimes."

Meta's large eyes were open in wondering speculation. "Why do they quarrel?" she asked.

"'Cause it's their natur'," returned Mrs. Bond. "The one what had the sweet natur' was took, and the two fretful ones was left. Them young women said that miss a'most drove my lady mad with her temper, and they expect nothing less but there'd be blows some day. A fine disgraceful thing to say of born ladies, ain't it, ma'am?"

Maria, in her delicacy of feeling, would not endorse the remark of Dame Bond. But the state of things at Lady Sarah Grame's was perfectly well known at Prior's Ash. Sarah Anne Grame had become her mother's bane, as Mr. Snow had once said she would be. A very terrible bane; to herself, to her mother, to all about her. And the "screeching" parrot had only added a little more noise to an already too noisy house.

Mrs. Bond curtsied herself out. She met Margery in the passage, and stopped to whisper.

"I say! how ill she do look!"

"Who looks ill?" was the ungracious demand.

Mrs. Bond nodded towards the parlour door. "The missis. Her face looks more as if it had death writ in it, than voyage-going."

"Perhaps you'll walk on your way, Dame Bond, and keep your opinions till they're asked for," was the tart reply of Margery.

But, in point of fact, the words had darted into the faithful servant's heart, piercing it as a poisoned arrow. It seemed so great a confirmation of her own fears.

CHAPTER V.

COMMOTION AT ASHLYDYAT.

A FEW more days went on, and they wrought a further change in Mrs. George Godolphin. She grew weaker and weaker: she grew—it was apparent now to Mr. Snow as it was to Margery—nearer and nearer to that vault in the churchyard of All Souls'. There could no longer be any indecision or uncertainty as to her taking the voyage; the probabilities were, that before the ship was ready to sail, all sailing in this world for Maria would be over. And rumours, faint, doubtful, very much discredited rumours of this state of things, began to circulate in Prior's Ash.

Discredited because people were so unprepared for it. Mrs. George Godolphin had been delicate since the birth of her baby, as was known to every one, but not a soul, relatives, friends, or strangers, had felt a suspicion of danger. On the contrary, it was supposed that she was about to depart on that Indian voyage: and ill-natured spirits tossed their heads and said it was fine to be Mrs. George Godolphin, to be set up again and go out to lead a grand life in India, after ruining half Prior's Ash. How she misjudged! how many more unhappy wives have been, and will be again, misjudged by the world!

One dreary afternoon, as dusk was coming on, Margery, not stopping, or perhaps not caring, to put anything upon herself, but having hastily wrapped up Miss Meta, went quickly down the garden path, leading that excitable and chattering demoiselle by the hand. Curious news had reached the ears of Margery. Their landlady's son had come in, describing the town as being in strange commotion, in consequence of something which had happened at Ashlydyat. Rumour set it down as nothing less than murder; and, according to the boy's account, all Prior's Ash was flocking up to the place to see and to hear.

Margery turned wrathful at the news. Murder at Ashlydyat! The young gentleman was too big to be boxed or shaken for saying it, but he persisted in his story, and Margery in her curiosity went out to see with her own eyes. "The people are running past the top of this road in crowds," he said to her.

For some days past, workmen had been employed digging up the Dark Plain by the orders of Lord Averil. As he had told Cecil weeks before, his intention was to completely renew it; to do away entirely with its past character and send its superstition to the winds. The archway was being taken down, the gorse-bushes were being uprooted, the whole surface, in fact, was being dug up. He intended to build an extensive summer-house where the archway had been, and to make the plain a flower-garden, a playground for children when they should be born to Ashlydyat: and it appeared that in digging that afternoon under the archway, the men had come upon a human skeleton, or rather upon the bones of what had once been a skeleton. This was the whole foundation for the rumour and the "murder."

As Margery stood, about to turn home again, vexed for having been brought out in the cold for nothing more, and intending to give a few complimentary thanks for it to the young man who had been the means of sending her, she was accosted by Mr. Crosse, who had latterly been laid up in his house with gout. Not the slightest notice had he taken of George Godolphin and his wife since his return home, though he had been often with Thomas.

"How d'ye do, Margery?" he said, taking up Meta at the same time to kiss her. "Are you going to Ashlydyat with the rest?"

"Not I, the simpletons!" was Margery's free rejoinder. "There's my poor mistress alone in the house."

"Is she ill?" asked Mr. Crosse.

"Ill!" returned Margery, not at all pleased at the question. "Yes, sir, she is ill. I thought everybody knew that."

"When does she start for India?"

"She don't start at all. She'll be starting soon for a place a little bit nearer. Here! you run on and open the gate," added Margery, whisking Meta from Mr. Crosse's hand and sending her down the lane out of hearing. "She'll soon be where Mr. Thomas Godolphin is, sir, instead of being marched off in a ship to India," continued the woman, turning to Mr. Crosse confidentially.

He felt greatly shocked. In his own mind, he, as many others, had associated Maria with her husband, in regard to the summer's work, in a lofty, scornful sort of way: but it did shock him to hear that she was in fear of death. It is most wonderful how our feelings towards others soften when we find that they and their shortcomings are about to be taken from us to a more merciful Judge.

"But what is the matter with her, Margery?" Mr. Crosse asked; for it happened that he had not heard the ominous rumours that were beginning to circulate in Prior's Ash.

"*I* don't know what's the matter with her," returned Margery. "I don't believe old Snow knows, either. I suppose the worry and misfortunes have been too much for her; as they were for somebody else. Mr. Godolphin is in his grave, and now she's going to hers."

Mr. Crosse walked mechanically by the side of Margery down the lane. It was not his road, and perhaps he was unconscious that he took it; he walked by her side, listening.

"He'll have to go by himself now—and me to have been getting up all my cotton gowns for the start! Serve him right! for ever thinking of taking out that dear little lamb amid elephants and savages!"

Mr. Crosse was perfectly aware that Margery alluded to her master—his own *bête noire* since the explosion. But he did not choose to descant upon his gracelessness to Margery. "Can nothing be done for Mrs. George Godolphin?" he asked.

"I expect not, sir. There's nothing the matter with her that can be laid hold of," resentfully spoke Margery; "no malady to treat. Snow says he can't do anything, and he brought Dr. Beale in the other day: and it seems he can't do nothing, either."

Meta had reached the gate, flung it open in obedience to orders, and now came running back. Mr. Crosse took her hand and went on with her. Was he purposing to pay a visit to George Godolphin's wife? It seemed so.

It was quite dusk when they entered. Maria was lying on the sofa, with a warm woollen wrapper drawn over her. There was no light in the room except that given out by the fire, but its blaze fell directly on her face. Mr. Crosse stood and looked at it, shocked at its ravages; at the tale it told. All kinds of unpleasant pricks were sending their darts through his conscience. He had been holding himself aloof in his assumed superiority, his haughty condemnation, while she had been going to the grave with her breaking heart.

Had she wanted things that money could procure? had she wanted *food?* Mr. Crosse actually began to ask himself the question, as the wan aspect of the white face grew and grew upon him: and in the moment he quite loathed the thought of his well-stored coffers. He remembered what a good, loving gentlewoman this wife of George Godolphin's had always been, this dutiful daughter of All Souls' pastor: and for the first time Mr. Crosse began to separate her from her husband's misdoings, to awaken to the conviction that the burden and sorrow laid upon her had been enough to bear, without the world meting out its harsh measure of blame by way of increase.

He sat down quite humbly, saying "hush" to Meta. Maria had dropped into one of those delirious sleeps: they came on more frequently now, and would visit her at the twilight hour of the evening as well as at night: and the noise of their entrance had failed to arouse her. Margery, however, came bustling in.

"It's Mr. Crosse, ma'am."

Maria, a faint hectic of surprise coming into her cheeks, sat up and let him take her hand. "I am glad to have the opportunity of seeing you once again," she said.

"Why did you not send and tell me how ill you were?" burst forth Mr. Crosse, forgetting how exceedingly ill such a procedure would have accorded with his own line of holding aloof in condemning superiority.

She shook her head. "I might, had things been as they used to be. But people do not care to come near me now."

"I am going in the ship, Mr. Crosse. I am going to ride upon an elephant and to have parrots."

He laid his hand kindly upon the chattering child: but he turned to Maria, his voice dropping to a whisper. "What shall you do with her? Shall you send her out without you?"

The question struck upon the one chord of her heart that for the last day or two, since her own hopeless state grew more palpable, had been strung to the utmost tension. What was to become of Meta—of the cherished child whom she must leave behind her? Her face grew moist, her bosom heaved, and she suddenly pressed her hands upon it as if they could still its wild and painful beating. Mr. Crosse, blaming himself for asking it, blaming himself for many other things, took her hands within his, and said he would come and see her in the morning: she seemed so fatigued then.

But, low as the question had been put, Miss Meta heard it; heard it and understood its purport. She entwined her pretty arms within her mamma's dress as Mr. Crosse went out, and raised her wondering eyes.

"What did he mean? You are coming too, mamma!"

She drew the little upturned face close to hers, she laid her white cheek upon the golden hair. The very excess of pain that was rending her aching heart caused her to speak with unnatural stillness. Not that she could speak at first: a minute or two had to be given to mastering her emotion.

"I am afraid not, Meta. I think God is going to take me."

The child made no reply. Her earnest eyes were kept wide open with the same wondering stare. "What will papa do?" she presently asked.

Maria hastily passed her hand across her brow, as if that recalled another phase of the pain. Meta's little heart began to swell, and the tears burst forth.

"Don't go, mamma! Don't go away from papa and Meta! I shall be afraid of the elephants without you."

She pressed the child closer and closer to her beating heart. Oh the pain, the pain!—the pain of the parting that was so soon to come!

They were interrupted by a noise at the gate. A carriage had bowled down the lane and drawn up at it, almost with the commotion that used to attend the dashing visits to the Bank of Mrs. Charlotte Pain. A more sober equipage this, however, with its mourning appointments, although it bore a coronet on its panels. The footman opened the door, and one lady stepped out of it.

"It is Aunt Cecil," called out Meta.

She rubbed the tears from her pretty cheeks, her grief forgotten, child-like, in the new excitement, and flew out to meet Lady Averil. Maria, trying to look her best, rose from the sofa and tottered forward to receive her. Meta was pounced upon by Margery and carried off to have her tumbled hair smoothed; and Lady Averil came in alone.

She threw back her crape veil to kiss Maria. She had come down from Ashlydyat on purpose to tell her the news of the bones being found: there could be little doubt that they were those of the ill-fated Richard de Commins, which had been so fruitlessly searched for: and Lady Averil was full of excitement. Perhaps it was natural that she should be so, being a Godolphin.

"It is most strange that they should be found just now," she cried; "at the very time that the Dark Plain is being done away with. You know, Maria, the tradition always ran that so long as the bones remained unfound, the Dark Plain would retain the appearance of a graveyard. Is it not a singular coincidence—that they should be discovered just at the moment that the Plain is being dug up? Were Janet here, she would say how startlingly all the old superstition is being worked out."

"I think one thing especially strange—that they should not have been found before," observed Maria. "Have they not been searched for often?"

"I believe so," replied Cecil. "But they were found under the archway; immediately beneath it: and I fancy they had always been searched for in the Dark Plain. When papa had the gorse-bushes rooted up they were looked for then in all parts of the Dark Plain, but not under the archway."

"How came Lord Averil to think of looking under the archway?" asked Maria.

"He did not think of it. They have been found unexpectedly, without being searched for. The archway is taken down, and the men were digging the foundation for the new summer-house, when they came upon them. The grounds of Ashlydyat have been like a fair all the afternoon with people coming up to see and hear," added Cecil. "Lord Averil is going to consult Mr. Hastings about giving them Christian burial."

"It does seem strange," murmured Maria. "Have you written to tell Janet?"

"No, I shall write to her to-morrow. I hastened down to you. Bessy came over from the Folly, but Lady Godolphin would not come. She said she had heard enough in her life of the superstition of Ashlydyat. She never liked it, you know, Maria; never believed in it."

"Yes, I know," Maria answered. "It used to anger her when it was spoken of. As it angered papa."

"As George used to pretend that it angered him. I think it was only pretence, though. Poor Thomas, never. If he did not openly accord it belief, he never ridiculed it. How are your preparations getting on Maria?"

Maria was crossing the room with feeble steps to stir the fire into a blaze. As the light burst forth, she turned her face to Lady Averil with a sort of apology.

"I do not know what Margery is about that she does not bring in the lamp. I am receiving you very badly, Cecil."

Cecil smiled. "I think our topic, the Ashlydyat superstition, is better discussed in such light as this, than in the full glare of lamplight."

But as Lady Averil spoke she was looking earnestly at Maria. The blaze had lighted up her wan face, and Cecil was struck aghast at its aspect. *Was* it real?—or was it only the effect of the firelight? Lady Averil had not heard of the ominous fears that were ripening, and hoped it was the latter.

"Maria! are you looking worse this evening? Or is the light deceiving me?"

"I dare say I am looking worse. I am worse. I am very ill, Cecil."

"You do not look fit to embark on this voyage."

Maria simply shook her head. She was sitting now in an old-fashioned arm-chair, one white hand lying on her black dress, the other supporting her chin, while the firelight played on her wasted features.

"Would the little change to Ashlydyat benefit you, Maria? If so, if it would help to give you strength for your voyage, come to us at once. Now don't refuse! It will give us so much pleasure. You do not know how Lord Averil loves and respects you. I think there is no one he respects as he respects you. Let me take you home with me now."

Maria's eyelashes were wet as she turned them on her. "Thank you, Cecil, for your kindness : and Lord Averil—will you tell him so for me —I am always thanking in my heart. I wish I could go home with you; I wish I could go with any prospect of it doing me good; but that is over. I shall soon be in a narrower home than this."

Lady Averil's heart stood still and then bounded on again. "No, no! Surely you are mistaken! It cannot be."

"I have suspected it long, Cecil! but since the last day or two it has become certainty, and even Mr. Snow acknowledges it. About this time yesterday, he was sitting here in the twilight, and I bade him not conceal the truth from me. I told him that I knew it, and did not shrink from it; and therefore it was the height of folly for him to pretend ignorance to me."

"Oh, Maria! And have you no regret at leaving us? I should think it a dreadful thing if I were going to die."

"I have been battling with my regrets a long while," said Maria, bending her head and speaking in low, subdued tones. "Leaving Meta is the worst. I know not who will take her, who will protect her : she cannot go with George, without—without a mother!"

"Give her to me," feverishly broke from the lips of Lady Averil. "You don't know how dearly I have ever loved that child. Maria, she shall never know the want of the good mother she has lost, as far as I can supply your place, if you will let her come to me. It is well that the only child of the Godolphins—and she is the only one—should be reared at Ashlydyat."

Of all the world, Maria could best have wished Lady Averil to have Meta: and perhaps there had been moments when in her troubled imagination she had hoped it would be so. But she could not close her eyes to its improbabilities.

"You will be having children of your own, Cecil. And there's Lord Averil to be considered!"

"Lord Averil is more than indulgent to me. I believe if I wished to adopt half a dozen children, he would only smile and tell me to prepare a nursery for them. I am quite sure he would like to have Meta."

"Then—if he will—oh, Cecil, I should die with less regret."

"Yes, yes, that is settled. He shall call and tell you so. But—Maria—is your own state so certain? Can nothing be done for you?—nothing be tried?"

"Nothing, as I believe. Mr. Snow cannot find out what is the matter with me. The trouble has been breaking my heart, Cecil: I know of nothing else. And since I grew alarmed about my own state, there has been the thought of Meta. Many a time have I been tempted to wish that I could have her with me in my coffin."

"Aunt Cecil! Aunt Cecil! How many summer-houses are there to be, Aunt Cecil?"

You need not ask whose interrupting voice it was. Lady Averil lifted the child to her knee, and asked whether she would come and pay her a long, long visit at Ashlydyat. Meta replied by inquiring into the prospect of swings and dolls' houses, and Cecil plunged into promises as munificently as George could have done.

"Should George not be with you?" she whispered, as she bent over Maria before leaving.

"Yes, I am beginning to think he ought to be now. I intend to write to him to-night; but I did not like to disturb him in his preparations. It will be a blow to him."

"What! does he not know of it?"

"Not yet. He thinks I am getting ready to go out. I *wish* I could have done so!"

No, not until the unhappy fact was placed beyond all doubt, would Maria disturb her husband. And she did it gently at last. "I have been unwilling to alarm you, George, and I would not do so now, but that I believe it is all too certain. Will you come down and see what you think of me? Even Mr. Snow fears there is no hope for me now. Oh, if I could but have gone with you! have gone with you to be your ever-loving wife still in that new land!"

Lord Averil came in while she was addressing the letter. Greatly shocked, greatly grieved at what his wife told him, he rose from his dinner-table and walked down. Her husband excepted, there was no one whom Maria would have been so pleased to see as Lord Averil. He had not come so much to tell her that he heartily concurred in his wife's offer with regard to the child, though he did say it—say that she should be done by entirely as though she were his own, and his honest honourable nature shone out of his eyes as he spoke it—as to see whether nothing could be done for herself, to entreat her to have further advice called in.

"Dr. Beale has been here twice," was her answer. "He says there is no hope."

Lord Averil held her hand in his, as he had taken it in greeting; his grave eyes of sympathy were bent with deep concern on her face.

"Cecil thinks the trouble has been too much for you," he whispered. "Is it so?"

A streak of hectic came into her cheek. "Yes, I suppose it is that. Turn to which side I would, there was no comfort, no hope. Throughout it all, I never had a friend, save you, Lord Averil: and you know, and God knows, what you did for us. I have not recompensed you: I don't see how I could have recompensed you had I lived: but when I am gone, you will be happy in knowing that you took the greatest weight from one who was stricken by the world."

"You have been writing to George?" he observed, seeing the letter on the table. "But it will not go to-night: it is too late."

"It can go up by to-morrow's day mail, and he will receive it in the evening. Perhaps you will post it for me as you walk home: it will save Margery's going out."

Lord Averil put the letter into his pocket. He stood looking at her as she lay a little back in her easy-chair, his arm resting on the mantel-piece, curious thoughts passing through his mind. Could he do nothing for her?—to avert the fate that was threatening her? He, rich in wealth, happy now in the world's favour; she, going to the grave in sorrow, it might be in privation—*what* could he do to help her?

There are moments when we speak out of our true heart, when the conventionality that surrounds the best of us is thrown aside, all deceit, all form forgotten. Lord Averil was a good and true man, but never better, never truer than now, when he took a step forward and bent to Maria.

"Let me have the satisfaction of doing something for you; let me try to save you!" he implored in low earnest tones. "If that may not be, let me help to lighten your remaining hours. How can I best do it?"

She held out her hand to him: she looked up at him, the gratitude she could not speak shining from her sweet eyes. "Indeed there is nothing now, Lord Averil. I wish I could thank you as you deserve for the past."

He held her hand for some time, but she seemed weak, exhausted, and he said good night. Margery attended him to the outer gate, in spite of his desire that she should not do so, for the night air was cold and seemed to threaten snow.

"Your mistress is very ill, Margery," he gravely said. "She seems to be in danger."

"I'm afraid she is, my lord. Up to the last day or two I thought she might take a turn and get over it; but since then she has grown worse with every hour. Some folks can battle out things, and some folks can't; she's one of the last sort, and she has been tried in all ways."

Lord Averil dropped the letter into the post-office, looking mechanically at its superscription, George Godolphin, Esquire. But that he was preoccupied with his own thoughts, he might have seen by the very writing how weak she was, for it was scarcely recognizable as hers. Very, very ill she looked, as if the end were growing ominously near ; and Lord Averil did not altogether like the tardy summons which the letter would convey. A night and a day yet before George could receive it. A moment's communing with himself, and then he took the path to the telegraph office, and sent off a message :

" Viscount Averil to George Godolphin, Esquire.
" Your wife is very ill.   Come down by first train."

The snow came early. It was nothing like Christmas yet, and here was the ground covered with it. The skies had seemed to threaten it the previous night, but people were not prepared to find everything wearing a white aspect when they rose in the morning.

The Reverend Mr. Hastings was ill. A neglected cold was telling so greatly upon him that his daughter Rose had at length sent for Mr. Snow. Mrs. Hastings was away for a day or two, on a visit to some friends at a distance.

Mr. Hastings sat over the fire, dreamily watching David Jekyl, awaiting the visit of Mr. Snow, and thinking his own thoughts. David was busy in the garden. He had a bit of crape on his old felt hat for his recently-interred father. The crape led the Rector's thoughts to the old man, and thence to the deprivation brought to the old man's years, the loss to the sons, through George Godolphin. How many more, besides poor old Jekyl, had George Godolphin ruined ! himself, that reverend divine, amongst the rest !

" A good thing when the country shall be rid of him !" spoke the Rector in his bitterness. " I would give all the comfort left in my life that Maria, for her own sake, had not linked her fate with his ! But that can't be remedied now. I hope he will make her happier there, in her new home, than he has made her here !"

By which words you will gather that Mr. Hastings had no suspicion of the change in his daughter's state. It was so. Lord and Lady Averil were not alone in learning the tidings suddenly ; at, as it may be said, the eleventh hour. Maria had not sent word to the Rectory that she was worse. She knew that her mother was absent, that her father was ill, that Rose was occupied ; and that the change from bad to worse had come upon herself so imperceptibly, that she saw not its real danger—as was proved by her not writing to her husband. The Rector, as he sits there, has his mind full of Maria's voyage, and its discomfort : of her changed life in India : and he is saying to himself that he shall get out in the afternoon and call to see her.

The room faced the side of the house, but as Mr. Hastings sat he could catch a glimpse of the garden gate, and presently saw the well-known gig stop at it, and the surgeon descend.

" Well, and who's ill now ?" cried Mr. Snow, as he let himself in at the hall-door, and thence to the room, where he took a seat in front of the Rector, examined his ailment, and gossiped at the same time, as was his wont ; gossiped and grumbled.

"Ah, yes; just so: feel worse than you have felt for twenty years. You caught this cold at Thomas Godolphin's funeral, and you have not chosen to pay attention to it."

"I think I did. I felt it coming on the next day. I could not read the service in my hat, Snow, over *him*, and you know that rain was falling. Ah! There was a sufferer! But had it not been for the calamity that fell upon him, he might not have gone to the grave quite so soon."

"He felt it too keenly," remarked Mr. Snow. "And your daughter —there's another sad victim. Ah me! Sometimes I wish I had never been a doctor, when I find all that I can do in the way of treatment comes to nothing."

"If she can only get well through the fatigues of the voyage, she may be better in India. Don't you think so? The very change from this place will put new life into her."

Mr. Snow paused in surprise, and the truth flashed into his mind— that Mr. Hastings was as yet in ignorance of Maria's danger: flashed with pain. Of course it was his duty to enlighten him, and he would rather have been spared the task. "When did you see her last?" he inquired.

"The day Mrs. Hastings left. I have not been well enough to go out much since. And I dare say Maria has been busy."

"I am sorry then to have to tell you that she has not been busy; that she has not been well enough to be busy. She is much worse."

There was a significance in the tone that spoke to the father more effectually than any words could have done. He was silent for a full minute, and then he rose from his chair and walked once up and down the room before he turned to Mr. Snow.

"The full truth, Snow? Tell it me."

"Well—the truth is, that hope is over. That she will not very long be here. I had no suspicion that you knew it not."

"I knew nothing of it. When I and her mother were with her last: it was, I tell you, the day Mrs. Hastings left: Maria was talking of going back to London with her husband the next time he came down to Prior's Ash. I thought her looking better that morning; she had quite a colour; was in good spirits. When did you see her?"

"Now. I went up there before I came down to you. She grows worse and worse every hour. Lord Averil telegraphed for George Godolphin last night."

"And I have not been informed of this!" burst forth the Rector. "My daughter dying—for I infer no less—and I to be left in ignorance of the truth!"

"Understand one thing, Mr. Hastings—that until this morning we saw no fear of *immediate* danger. Lord Averil says he suspected it last night; I did not see her yesterday in the after-part of the day. I have known some few cases precisely similar to Mrs. George Godolphin's; where danger and death seem to have come on suddenly together."

"And what is her disease?"

The surgeon threw up his arms. "*I* don't know—unless the trouble has fretted her into her grave. Were I not a doctor, I might say she had died of a broken heart, but the faculty don't recognize such a thing."

Half an hour afterwards, the Reverend Mr. Hastings was bending over his daughter's dying bed. A dying bed, it too surely looked; and if Mr. Hastings had indulged a gleam of hope, the first glance at Maria's countenance dispelled it. She lay wrapped in a shawl, the lace border of her nightcap shading her delicate face and its smooth brown hair, her eyes larger and softer and sweeter than of yore.

They were alone together. He held her hand in his, he gently laid his other hand on her white and wasted brow. " Child! child! why did you not send to me ? "

" I did not know I was so ill, papa," she panted. " I seem to have grown so much worse this last night. But I am better than I was an hour ago."

" Maria," he gravely said, " are you aware that you are in a state of danger ?—that death may come to you."

" Yes, papa, I know it. I have seen it coming a long while : only I was not quite sure."

" And my dear child, are you—— " Mr. Hastings paused. He paused and bit his lips, gathering firmness to suppress the emotion that was rising. His calling made him familiar with death-bed scenes ; but Maria was his own child, and nature will assert her supremacy. A minute or two and he was himself again . not a man living was more given to reticence in the matter of his own feelings than the Rector of All Souls' : he could not *bear* to betray emotion in the sight of his fellow-men.

" Are you prepared for death, Maria ? Can you look upon it without terror ? "

" I think I am," she murmured. " I feel that I am going to God. Oh, papa, forgive, forgive me ! " she exclaimed, bursting into tears of emotion, as she raised her hands to him in the moment's excitement. " The trouble has been too much for me ; I could not shake it off. All the sorrow that has been brought upon you through us, I think of it always : my heart aches with thinking of it. Oh, papa, forgive me before I die ! It was not my fault ; indeed, I did not know of it. " Papa "—and the sobs became painfully hysterical, and Mr. Hastings strove in vain to check them—" I would have sacrificed my life to bring good to you and my dear mamma : I would have *sold* myself, to keep this ill from you ! "

" Child, hush ! There has been nothing to forgive to *you*. In the first moment of the smart, if I cast an unkind thought to you, it did not last; it was gone almost as soon as it came. My dear child, you have ever been my loving and dutiful daughter. Maria, shall I tell it you ?—I know not why, but I have loved you better than any of my other children."

She had raised herself from the pillow, and was clasping his hand to her bosom, sobbing over it. Few daughters have loved a father as Maria had loved and venerated hers. The Rector's face was preternaturally pale and calm, the effect of his powerfully suppressed emotion.

" It has been too much for me, papa. I have thought of your trouble, of the discomforts of your home, of the blighted prospects of my brothers, feeling that it was our work. I thought of it always, more perhaps than of other things : and I could not battle with the pain it brought, and it has killed me. But, papa, I am resigned to go: I know that I shall be better off. Before these troubles came, I had not learned to think of God, and I should have been afraid to die."

"It is through tribulation that we must enter the Kingdom," interrupted the calm, earnest voice of the clergyman. "It must come to us here in some shape or other, my child; and I do not see that it matters how, or when, or through whom it does come, if it takes us to a better world. You have had your share of it: but God is a just and merciful Judge, and if He has given you a full share of sorrow, He will deal out to you His full recompense."

"Yes," she gently said, "I am going to God. Will you pray for me, papa?—that He will pardon me and take me for Christ's sake. Oh, papa! it seems—it seems when we get near death as if the other world were so very near to this! It seems such a little span of time that I shall have to wait for you all before you come to me. Will you give my dear love to mamma if I should not live to see her, and say how I have loved her: say that I have only gone on first; that I shall be there ready for her. Papa, I dare say God will let me be ever waiting and looking for you."

Mr. Hastings turned to search for a Book of Common Prayer. He saw Maria's on her dressing-table—one which he had given her on her marriage, and written her name in—and he opened it at the "Visitation of the Sick." He looked searchingly at her face as he returned: surely the signs of death were already gathering there!

"The last Sacrament, Maria?" he whispered. "When shall I come?"

"This evening," she answered. "George will be here then."

The Reverend Mr. Hastings bent his eyebrows with a frown, as if he thought—— But no matter. "At eight o'clock, then," he said to Maria, as he laid the book upon the bed and knelt down before it. Maria lay back on her pillow, and clasping her hands upon the shawl which covered her bosom, closed her eyes to listen.

It was strange that even then, as he was in the very act of kneeling, certain words which he had spoken to Maria years ago, should flash vividly into the Rector's mind—words which had referred to the death of Ethel Grame.

"The time may come, Maria—we none of us know what is before us—when some of you young ones who are left, may wish you had died as she has. Many a one, battling for very existence with the world's carking cares, wails out a vain wish that he had been taken from the evil to come."

Had the gift of prevision been on the Rector of All Souls' when he spoke those words to Maria Hastings? Poor child! lying there now on her early death-bed; with her broken heart! The world's carking cares had surely done their work on Maria Godolphin!

CHAPTER VI.

A CROWD OF MEMORIES.

IF it were not for mismanagement, how smoothly things might go on! That telegraphic despatch which Lord Averil had deemed it well to send, and which had not been sent any too soon, did not reach George Godolphin for hours and hours, through mismanagement at his lodgings.

It was afternoon when he reached Prior's Ash. The first person he saw at the station was Lord Averil. That nobleman, wondering at George's non-appearance, believing that Maria was getting nearer to death with every hour, had come to the conclusion that by some mischance his message had miscarried; and he had now gone to the station to send another. Lord Averil linked his arm within George's, and they walked rapidly away through the snow that lay on the path.

Yes, he linked his arm within George Godolphin's who had so very nearly been held up to the virtuous British public as a candidate for a free passage to Australia. Somehow, George had slipped through that danger, and was a gentleman still: moreover, he was Lord Averil's brother-in-law, and it was the earnest wish of that nobleman that society should forget the little mistake in George's life as heartily as he did. He explained as he walked along: Maria had got rapidly worse all at once: it was only within a few hours that immediate danger had shown itself.

George could not understand it. He had left his wife, ill certainly, but not, as he believed, seriously so; he had supposed her to be busy in preparations for the voyage: and now to be told that she was dying! If this was so, why had Maria not sent for him before?

Lord Averil explained. No one seemed to have known of the danger.

"Snow must have known it," remonstrated George.

"I think not. I was talking to him to-day, and he expressed his surprise at the disorder having suddenly increased in this rapid manner."

"What *is* the disorder?" asked George. "My wife had no disorder —except weakness."

"I suppose that is it—weakness."

"But weakness does not kill!"

"Yes, it does, sometimes."

Margery was standing at the door when they reached the gate, possibly looking out for her master, for she knew the hours of the arrival of the trains. The windows of the sitting-room faced that way, and George's eyes naturally turned to them. But there was no sign of busy life, of every-day occupation: the curtains hung in their undisturbed folds, the blinds were partially down.

"I will just ask how your wife is now, and whether Cecil is here," said Lord Averil, following George up the path.

No, Lady Averil and Miss Bessy Godolphin had left about ten minutes before, Margery said. My Lady Godolphin, who had driven up in her carriage and come in for a quarter of an hour, had left; and Miss Rose Hastings, who had been there the best part of the morning, had also left. Mrs. George Godolphin seemed a trifle better; inclined to sleep, tired out, as it were; and she, Margery, didn't wonder at it with such a heap of visitors: she had given them a broad hint herself that her mistress might be all the better for an hour's quiet.

Lord Averil departed. George flung his railway wrapper on to a chair and hung his hat up in the little hall: he turned his face, one of severity then, on Margery.

"Is your mistress so very ill? Why was I not sent for earlier? Is she so very ill?" he continued in an impassioned tone.

"Well, sir, I don't know," answered Margery, willing perhaps to soften the truth to him. "She is certainly better than she was in the morning. She is sitting up."

George Godolphin was of a hopeful nature. Even those few words seemed to speak to his heart with a certainty. "Not there, sir," interposed Margery, as he opened the door of the sitting-room. "But it don't matter," she added: "you can go in that way."

He walked through the room and opened the door of the bed-chamber. Would the scene ever leave his memory? The room was lighted more by the blaze of the fire than by the daylight, for curtains partly covered the windows and the winter's dreary afternoon was already merging into twilight. The bed was at the far end of the room, the dressing-table near it. The fire was on his right as he entered, and on a white-covered sofa, drawn before it, sat Maria. She was partly dressed and wrapped in a light cashmere shawl; her cap was untied, and her face, shaded though it was by its smooth brown hair, was all too visible in the reflection cast by the firelight.

Which was the more colourless—that face, or the white cover of the sofa? George Godolphin's heart stood still as he looked upon it and then bounded on with a rush. Every shadow of hope had gone from him.

Maria had not heard him, did not see him; he went in gently. By her side on the sofa lay Miss Meta, curled up into a ball and fast asleep, her hands and her golden curls on her mamma's knee. With George's first step forward, Maria turned her sad sweet eyes towards him, and a faint cry of emotion escaped her lips.

Before she could stir or speak, George was with her, his protecting arms thrown round her, her face gathered to his breast. What a contrast it was! she so wan and fragile, so near the grave, he in all his manly strength, his fresh beauty. Miss Meta woke up, recognized her papa with a cry and much commotion, but Margery came in and carried her off, shutting the door behind her.

Her fair young face—too fair and young to die—was laid against her husband's; her feeble hand lay carelessly in his. The shock to George was very great; it almost seemed that he had already lost her; and the scalding tears, so rarely wrung from man, coursed down his cheeks, and fell on her face.

"Don't grieve," she whispered, the tears raining from her own eyes.

"Oh, George, my husband, it is a bitter thing to part, but we shall meet again in heaven, and be together for ever. It has been so weary here; the troubles have been so great!"

He steadied his voice to speak. "The troubles have not killed you, have they, Maria?"

"Yes, I suppose it has been so. I did try and struggle against them, but—I don't know—— Oh, George!" she broke out in a wailing tone of pain, "if I could have but got over them and lived!—if I could only have gone with you to your new home!"

George sat down on the sofa where Meta had been, and held her to him in silence. She could hear his heart beating; could feel it bounding against her side.

"It will be a better home in heaven," she resumed, laying her poor pale face upon his shoulder. "You will come to me there, George; I shall only go on first a little while; all the pains and the cares, the heart-burnings of earth will be forgotten, and we shall be together in happiness for ever and ever."

He dropped his face upon her neck, he sobbed aloud in his anguish. Whatever may have been his gracelessness and his faults, he had loved his wife; and now that he was losing her, that love was greater than it had ever been: some pricks of conscience may have been mingled with it, too! Who knows?

"Don't forget me quite when I am gone, George. Think of me sometimes as your poor wife who loved you to the last; who would have stayed with you if God had let her. When first I began to see that it must be, that I should leave you and Meta, my heart nearly broke; but the pain has grown less, and I think God has been reconciling me to it."

"What shall I do?—what will the child do without you?" broke from his quivering lips.

Perhaps the thought crossed Maria that he had done very well without her in the last few months, for his sojourn with her might be counted by hours instead of by days: but she was too generous to allude to it; and the heart-aching had passed. "Cecil and Lord Averil will take Meta," she said. "Let her stay with them, George! It would not be well for her to go to India alone with you."

The words surprised him. He did not speak.

"Cecil proposed it yesterday. They will be *glad* to have her. I dare say Lord Averil will speak to you about it later. It was the one great weight left upon my mind, George—our poor child, and what could be done with her: Cecil's generous proposal removed it."

"Yes," said George hesitatingly. "For a little while; perhaps it will be the best thing. Until I shall get settled in India. But she must come to me then; I cannot part with her for good."

"For good? No. But, George, you may—it is possible—" she seemed to stammer and hesitate—"you may be forming new ties. In that case you would care less for the loss of Meta——"

"Don't talk so!" he passionately interrupted. "How can you glance at such things, Maria, in these our last moments?"

She was silent for a few minutes, weeping softly. "Had this parting come upon me as suddenly as it has upon you, I might have started from the very thought with horror; but, George, I have had nothing else in my own mind for weeks but the parting, and it has made me look at the future as I could not else have looked at it. Do not blame me for saying this: I must allude to it, if I am to speak of Meta. I can understand how full of aversion the thought is to you now: but, George, it *may* come to pass."

"I think not," he said, and his voice and manner had changed to grave deliberation. "If I know anything of myself, Maria, I shall never marry again."

"It is not impossible."

"No," he assented; "it is not impossible."

Her heart beat a shade quicker, and she hid her face upon him so that he could not see it. When she spoke again, it was with difficulty he could catch the whispered words.

"I know how foolish and wrong it is for a dying wife to extract any promise of this nature from her husband: were I to say to you, Do not marry again, it would be little else than a wicked request; and it would prove how my thoughts and passions must still cling to earth. Bear with me while I speak of this, George; *I* am not going to be so wicked; but—but——"

Agitation stopped her voice. Her bosom heaved, her breath almost left her. He saw that this was mental emotion, not bodily weakness; and he waited until it should pass, stroking the hair from her brow with his gentle hand.

"My darling, what is it?"

"But there is one promise that I do wish to beg of you," she resumed, mastering her emotion sufficiently to speak. "If—if you should marry, and your choice falls upon *one*—upon *her*—then, in that case, do not seek to have Meta home; let her remain always with Cecil."

A pause: broken by George. "Of whom do you speak, Maria?"

The same laboured breathing; the same cruel agitation; and they had to be fought with before she could bring out the words.

"Of Charlotte Pain."

"Charlotte Pain!" echoed George, shouting out the name in surprise.

"I could not bear it," she shivered. "George, George! do not make her the second mother of my child! I could not bear it; it seems to me that I could not even in my grave bear it! Should you marry her, promise me that Meta shall not be removed from Ashlydyat."

"Maria," he quietly said, "I shall never marry Charlotte Pain."

"You don't know. You may think now you will not, but you cannot answer for yourself. George! she has helped to kill me. She must not be Meta's second mother."

He raised her face so that he could see it: his dark blue eyes met hers searchingly, and he took her hand in his as he gravely spoke.

"She will never be Meta's second mother: nay, if it will be more satisfactory, I will say she never shall be. By the heaven that perhaps even I may some day attain to, I say it! Charlotte Pain will never be Meta's second mother, or my wife."

She did not answer in words. She only nestled a little nearer to him in gratitude; half in repentance perhaps for having doubted him. George resumed, in the same grave tone:

The Shadow of Ashlydyat. 29

"And now, Maria, tell me what you mean by saying that Charlotte Pain has helped to kill you."

A vivid flush came over her wan face, and she contrived to turn it from him again, so that her eyes were hidden. But she did not speak quite at first.

"It all came upon me together, George," she murmured at length, her tone one of loving tenderness, in token that she was not angry now; that the past, whatever may have been its sins against her, any or none, was forgiven. "At that cruel time when the blow fell, when I had nowhere to turn to for comfort, then I also learnt what Prior's Ash had been saying, about—about Charlotte Pain. George, it seemed to wither my very heart; to take the life out of it. I had so loved you; I had so trusted you: and to find—to find—that you loved her, not me—— "

"Hush!" thundered George, in his emotion. "I never *loved* any one but you, Maria. I swear it!"

"Well—well. It seems that I do not understand. I—I could not get over it," she continued, passing her hand across her brow where the old aching pain had come momentarily again, "and I fear it has helped to kill me. It was so cruel, to have suffered me to know her all the while."

George Godolphin compressed his lips. He never spoke.

"But, George, it is over; it is buried in the past; and I did not intend to mention it. I should not have mentioned it but for speaking of Meta. Oh, let it go; let it pass: it need not disturb our last hour together."

"It appears to have disturbed you a great deal more than it need have done," he said, a shade of anger in his tone.

"Yes, looking back, I see it did. When we come to the closing scenes of life, as I have come, this world closing to our view, the next opening, then we see how foolish in many things we have been; how worse than vain our poor earthly passions. So to have fretted ourselves over this little space of existence with its passing follies, its temporary interests, when we might have been living and looking for that great one that shall last for ever! To gaze back on my life it seems but a span; a passing hour compared with the eternity that I am entering upon. Oh, George, we have all need of God's loving forgiveness! I, as well as you. I did not mean to reproach you: but I *could* not bear—had you made her your second wife—that she should have had the training of Meta."

Did George Godolphin doubt whether the fear was wholly erased from her heart? Perhaps so: or he might not have spoken to her as he was about to speak.

"Let me set your mind further at rest, Maria. Had I ever so great an inclination to marry Mrs. Pain, it is impossible that I could do so. Mrs. Pain has a husband already."

Maria raised her face, a flashing light, as of joy, illuminating it. George saw it: and a sad, dreamy look of self-condemnation settled on his own. *Had* it so stabbed her? "Has she married again?—since she left Prior's Ash?"

"She has never been a widow, Maria," he answered. "Rodolf Pain, her husband, did not die."

" He did not die? "

" As it appears.   He is now back again in England."

" And did you know of this? "

" Only since his return.   I supposed her to be a widow, as every one else supposed it.   One night last summer, in quitting Ashlydyat, I came upon them both in the grounds, Mr. and Mrs. Pain; and I then learned to my great surprise that he, whom his wife had passed off as dead, had in point of fact been hiding abroad.   There is some unpleasant mystery attached to it, the details of which I have not concerned myself to inquire into : he fell into trouble, I expect, and feared his own country was too hot for him.   However it may have been, he is home again, and with her.   I suppose the danger is removed, for I met them together in Piccadilly last week walking openly, and they told me they were looking out for a house."

She breathed a sobbing sigh of relief, as one hears sometimes from a little child.

" But were Mrs. Pain the widow she assumed to be, she would never have been made my wife.   Child! " he added, in momentary irritation, " don't you understand things better?   *She* my wife !—the second mother, the trainer of Meta!   What could you be thinking of?   Men do not marry women such as Charlotte Pain."

" Then you do not care for her so very much? "

" I care for her so much, Maria, that were I never to see her or hear of her again it would not give me one moment's thought," he impulsively cried.   " I would give a great deal now not to have kept up our acquaintance with the woman—if that had saved you one single iota of pain."

When these earthly scenes are closing—when the grave is about to set its seal on one to whom we could have saved pain, and did not,— when heaven's solemn approach is to be seen, and heaven's purity has become all too clear to our own sight, what would *we* give to change inflicted wrongs—to blot out the hideous past !   George Godolphin sat by the side of his dying wife, his best-beloved in life as she would be in death, and bit his lips in his crowd of memories, his unavailing repentance.   Ah, my friends ! these moments of reprisal, prolonged as they may seem, must come to us in the end.   It is convenient no doubt to ignore them in our hot-blooded carelessness, but the time will come when they must find us out.

He, George Godolphin, had leisure to hug them to himself, and make the best and the worst of them.   Maria, exhausted with excitement, as much as by her own weakness, closed her eyes as she lay upon his breast and dropped into a sleep, and he sat watching her face, holding her to him, not daring to move, lest he should disturb her, not daring even to lift a finger and wipe off his own bitter and unavailing tears.

Yes, there could be no doubt of the fact—that the troubles of one kind and another had been too much for her; that she was dying of them; and he felt the truth to his heart's core.   He felt that she, that delicate, refined, sensitive woman had been the very last who should have been treated rudely.   You may remember it was observed at the beginning of her history that she was one unfitted to battle with the world's sharp storms—it had now proved so.   Charlotte Pain would

have braved them, whatever their nature, have weathered them jauntily
on a prancing saddle-horse; Maria had shrunk down, crushed by their
weight. *Il y a*—let me once more repeat it—*il y a des femmes et des
femmes.*

There came one with hurried steps up the path; with hurried steps
and a distressed, anxious countenance. Passing Margery in the
passage, she bore on as if no power on earth should stop her, and
entered the sick-chamber.

It was Grace: Mrs. Akeman. This sudden change in the illness of
Maria had certainly come at an inopportune moment: Mrs. Hastings
was at a distance, Grace had gone for the day with her husband some
miles into the country   A messenger was sent to her, and it brought
her home.

It brought her home with a self-condemning conscience. Maria
dying!—when Grace had only thought of her as flaunting off to India;
when she had that very day remarked to her husband, as they drove
along the snowy road in his four-wheeled chaise, crammed with archi-
tectural plans, that some people had all the luck of it in this world, and
that Mr. and Mrs. George Godolphin, she supposed, would soon be
swaying it in the Bengal presidency, as they had swayed it in Prior's
Ash.   Maria dying! dying of the trouble, the sorrow, the disgrace, the
humiliation, the neglect! dying of a broken heart!   It came flashing
into Grace Akeman's mind that she *might* have taken a different
view of her conduct: have believed in the wrongs of wives, who are
bound to their husbands for worse as well as for better; it came into
her mind that she might have accorded her a little sisterly sympathy
instead of reproach.

She came in now, brimming over with repentance: she came in with
a sort of belief that things could not have gone so very far; that there
must be some remedy still, some hope; and that if she, Grace, exerted
her energies to rouse Maria, health and life would come again.   Maria
had awakened out of her temporary slumber then, and George was
standing with his arm on the mantel-piece.   A half-frown crossed his
brow when he saw Grace enter.   He had never liked her; he was
conscious that she had not been kind to Maria, and he deemed her
severe manner and sharp voice scarcely suited to that dying chamber.
But she was his wife's sister, and he advanced to welcome her.

Grace did not see his welcome; would not see it.   Perhaps in truth
she was wholly absorbed by the sight which met her view in Maria.
Remedy still?—hope yet?   Ah no! death was there, was upon her, and
Grace burst into tears.   Maria held out her hand, a smile lighting up
her wan countenance.

"I thought you were not coming to see me, Grace."

"I was out; I went to Hamlet's Wood this morning with Mr. Akeman," sobbed Grace.   "Whatever is the reason that you have suddenly
grown so ill as this?"

"I have been growing ill a long time," was Maria's answer.

"But there must be hope!" said Grace in her quick way.   "Mr.
George Godolphin"—turning to him and dashing away the tears on her
cheeks, as if she would not betray them to *him*—"surely there must be
hope!   What do the medical men say?"

"There is no hope, Grace," interposed Maria in her feeble voice. "The medical men know there is not. Dr. Beale came with Mr. Snow at midday; but their coming at all is a mere form now."

Grace untied her bonnet and sat down. "I thought," said she, "you were getting well."

Maria made a slight motion or dissent. "I have not thought it myself; not really thought it. I hoped it might be so, and the hope prevented my speaking: but there was always an undercurrent of conviction to the contrary in my heart."

George looked at her, half-reproachfully. She understood the look, and answered it.

"I wish now I had told you, George: but I was not sure. And if I had spoken you would only have laughed at me then in disbelief."

"You speak very calmly, Maria," said Grace with passionate earnestness. "Have you no regret at leaving us?"

A faint hectic shone suddenly in Maria's cheek. "Regret!" she repeated with emotion; "my days have been one long regret; one long, wearying pain. Don't you see it is the pain that has killed me, Grace?"

Grace's temper was sharp: her sense of right and wrong cynically keen: the Rector had had the same sharp temper in his youth, but he had learned to control it; Grace had not. She turned her flashing eyes, her flaming cheeks, on George Godolphin.

"Do you hear?—the pain has killed her. Who brought that pain upon her? Mr. George Godolphin, I wish you joy of your conscience! I almost seemed to foresee it—I almost seemed to foresee this," she passionately cried, "ere ever my sister married you."

"Don't, Grace!" wailed Maria, a faint cry of fear escaping her; a sudden terror taking possession of her raised face. "George, George!" She held out her hands yearningly to him, as if she would shield him, or as if she wanted him to shield her from the sharp words. George crossed over to her with his protecting presence, and bent to catch her whisper, praying him for peace.

"You forget your sister's state when you thus speak, Mrs. Akeman," he gravely said. "Say anything you please to me later; you shall have the opportunity if you desire it; but in my wife's presence there must be peace."

Grace flung off the shawl which she had worn, and stood beating the toe of her foot upon the fender, her throat swelling with the effort to subdue her emotion. What with her anger in the past, her grief in the present, she had well-nigh burst into sobs.

"I think I could drink some tea," said Maria. "Could we not have it together; here; for the last time? You will make it, Grace?"

Poor, weak, timid heart! Perhaps she only so spoke as an incentive to keep that "peace" for which she tremblingly yearned; which was essential to her, as to all, in her dying hour. George rang the bell and Margery came in.

It was done as she seemed to wish. The small round table was drawn to the fire, and Grace sat at it, making the tea. Maria turned her face and asked for Meta: Margery answered that she was coming in by-and-by. Very little was said. George drew a chair near Maria and leaned upon the arm of the sofa. The tea, so far as she went, was a mockery: George put a teaspoonful into her mouth, but she with difficulty swallowed it, and shook her head when he would have given her more. It did not seem to be much else than a mockery for the others: Grace's tears dropped into hers, and George suffered his to grow cold and then swallowed it at a draught, as if it was a relief to get rid of it. Margery was called again to take the things away, and Maria, who was leaning back on the sofa with closed eyes, asked again for Meta to come in.

Then Margery had to confess that Miss Meta was not at home to come in. She had gone out visiting. The facts of the case were these. Lord Averil, after quitting the house, had returned to it to say a word to George which he had forgotten: but finding George had gone into his wife's room, he would not have him disturbed. It was just at the moment that Margery had carried out Meta, and the young lady was rather restive at the proceedings, crying loudly. His lordship proposed to carry her off to Ashlydyat. Margery seized upon the offer. She took down a woollen shawl and the child's garden-hat that were hanging on the pegs, and enveloped her in them without ceremony. "They'll do as well as getting out her best things, my lord, if you won't mind them: and it will be almost dusk by the time you get to Ashlydyat."

It was quite the same to Lord Averil, whether the young lady was bundled up as she was now, or decked out in a lace frock and crinoline. He led her down the path, talking pleasantly; but Meta's breath was caught up incessantly with sobbing sighs. Her heart was full, imperfect as her idea of the calamity overshadowing her necessarily was.

Thus it happened that Miss Meta was not at hand when Maria asked for her. Whether it was from this, or from causes wholly unconnected with it, in a short time Maria grew restless: restless, as it seemed, both in body and mind, and it was deemed advisable that she should not sit up longer.

"Go for Meta while they get me into bed, George," she said to him. "I want her to be near me."

He went out at once. But he did not immediately turn to Ashlydyat: with hasty steps he took the road to Mr. Snow's. There had been a yearning on George Godolphin's mind, ever since he first saw his wife in the afternoon, to put the anxious question to one or both of the medical men: "Can nothing be done to prolong her life, even for the shortest space of time?"

Mr. Snow was out: the surgery boy did not know where: "Paying visits," he supposed, and George turned his steps to Dr. Beale's, who lived now in Prior's Ash, though he used not to live in it. Dr. Beale's house was ablaze with light, and Dr. Beale was at home, the servant said, but he had a dinner-party.

How the words seemed to grate on his ear! A dinner-party!— gaiety, lights, noise, mirth, eating and drinking, when his wife was dying! But the next moment reflection came to him: the approaching death of a patient is not wont to cast its influence on a physician's private life.

He demanded to see Dr. Beale in spite of the dinner-party. George

Godolphin forgot recent occurrences, exacting still the deference paid to him all his life, when Prior's Ash had bowed down to the Godolphins. He was shown into a room, and Dr. Beale came out to him.

But the doctor, though he would willingly have smoothed matters to him, could not give him hope. George asked for the truth, and he had it—that his wife's life now might be counted by hours. He went out and proceeded towards Ashlydyat, taking the near way down Crosse Street, by the Bank—the Bank that once was: it would lead him through the dull Ash-tree Walk with its ghostly story; but what cared George Godolphin?

Did a remembrance of the past come over him as he glanced up at the Bank's well-known windows?—a remembrance that pricked him with its sharp sting? He need never have left that house; but for his own recklessness, folly, wickedness—call it what you will—he might have been in it still, one of the honoured Godolphins, heir to Ashlydyat, his wife well and happy by his side. Now!—he went striding on with wide steps, and he took off his hat and raised his burning brow to the keen night air. You may leave the house behind you, George Godolphin, and so put it out of your sight, but you cannot blot out your memory.

Grace had remained with Maria. She was in bed now, but the restlessness seemed to continue. "I want Meta; bring Meta."

"Dear Maria, your husband has but just gone for her," breathed Grace. "She will soon be here."

It seemed to satisfy her. She lay still, looking upwards, her breath, or Mrs. Akeman fancied it, growing shorter. Grace, hot tears blinding her eyes, bent forward to kiss her wasted cheek.

"Maria, I was very harsh to you," she whispered. "I feel it now. I can only pray God to forgive me. I loved you always, and when that dreadful trouble came, I felt angry for your sake. I said unkind things to you and of you, but in the depth of my heart there lay the pain and the anger because you suffered. Will *you* forgive me?"

She raised her feeble hand and laid it lovingly on the cheek of Grace. "There is nothing to forgive, Grace," she murmured. "What are our poor little offences one against the other? Think how much Heaven has to forgive us all. Oh, Grace, I am going to it! I am going away from care."

Grace stood up to dash away her tears; but they came faster and faster. "I would ask you to let me atone to you, Maria," she sobbed— "I would ask you to let me welcome Meta to our home. We are not rich, but we have enough for comfort, and I will try to bring her up a good woman; I will love her as my own child."

"She goes to Cecil." There was no attempt at thanks in words— Maria was growing beyond it; nothing but the fresh touch of the hand's loving pressure. And that relaxed with the next moment and fell upon the bed.

Grace felt somewhat alarmed. She cleared the mist from her eyes and bent them steadily on Maria's face. It seemed to have changed. "Do you feel worse?" she softly asked.

Maria opened her lips, but no sound came from them. She attempted to point with her finger to the door; she then threw her eyes in the same direction; but why or what she wanted it was impossible to tell.

Grace, her heart beating wildly, flew across the little hall to the kitchen.

"Oh, Margery, I think she is sinking! Come you and see."

Margery hastened in. Her mistress evidently *was* sinking, and was conscious of it. The eager, anxious look upon her face and her raised hand proved that she was wanting something.

"Is it my master?—Is it the child?" cried Margery, bending over her. "They won't be long, ma'am."

It was Margery's habit to soothe the dying, even if she had to do it at some little expense of veracity. She knew that her master could not go to Ashlydyat and be home just yet: she did not know of his visits to the houses of the doctors: but if she had known it she would equally have said, "They won't be long."

But the eager look continued on Maria's face, and it became evident to experienced Margery that her master and Meta were not the anxious point. Maria's lips moved, and Margery bent her ear.

"Papa! Is it time?"

"It's the Sacrament she's thinking of," whispered Margery to Mrs. Akeman: "or else that she wants to take leave of him. The Rector was to come at eight o'clock; he told me so when he called in again this afternoon. What is to be done, ma'am?"

"And it is only half-past six! We must send to him at once."

Margery seemed in some uncertainty. "Shall you be afraid to stay here alone, ma'am, if I go?"

"Why! where is Jean?"

Jean, one of the old servants of Ashlydyat, discharged with the rest when the bankruptcy had come, but now in service there again under Lord and Lady Averil, had been with Margery all day. She had now been sent out by the latter for certain errands wanted in the town.

A tremor came over Mrs. Akeman at Margery's question, as to whether she would be afraid to stay there alone. To one not accustomed to it, it does require peculiar courage to remain with the dying. But Grace could call up a brave spirit at will, and she no longer hesitated, when she saw the continued eager look on her sister's face.

"Make haste, Margery. I shall not mind. Mrs. James is in the house, and I can call her if I see a necessity for doing so. Margery!"— following her outside the door to whisper it—"do you see that strange look in her face? Is it *death?*"

She was trembling all over, as she spoke, in nervous trepidation. It was to be a memorable night, that, what with one emotion and another, in the memory of Grace Akeman. Margery's answer was characteristic. "It does look like it, ma'am; but I have seen them like this, and then rally again. Anyhow, it can't be far off. Mrs. Akeman, it seems to me that all the good ones are leaving the world. First Mr. Godolphin, and now her!"

Margery had scarcely been gone five minutes when Lord Averil came back with Meta. They had not met George. It was not likely that they had, seeing that he was going to Ashlydyat by a different route. In point of fact, at that moment George was about turning into Crosse Street, passing his old house with those enlivening reminiscences of his.

Grace explained why she was alone, and Lord Averil took off his hat and great-coat to remain.

Maria asked for him. He went up to the bed and she smiled at him and moved her hand. Lord Averil took it between his, the tears gathering in his earnest eyes as he saw the change in her.

"She has been as happy as possible with us all the evening," he gently said, alluding to the child. "We will do all we can for her always."

"Tell Cecil—to bring—her up—for God."

She must have revived a little or she could not have spoken the words. By-and-by, Margery was heard to enter, panting with the speed she had made, and Mr. Hastings was not far behind.

As the clergyman approached the gate, he saw a man leaning over it, in the light cast by the white snow of the winter's night. It was David Jekyl.

"I thought I'd ask how the young missis was, sir, as I went home, but it might be disturbing of 'em to go right up to the door," he said, drawing back to make way for the Rector. "It were said in the town, as I come along, that she was worse."

"Yes, David, she is worse; as ill as she can be. I have just had a message."

David twirled his grey felt hat awkwardly round on his hand, stroking its napless surface with his other arm. He did not raise his eyes as he spoke to the Rector.

"Might be, you'd just say a word to her about that money, sir, asking of her not to let it worry her mind. It is said as them things *have* worried her more nor need be. If you could say a word for us, sir, that we don't think of it any more, it might comfort her like."

"The trouble for her has passed, David: to say this to her might bring her thoughts back to it. Heaven is opening to her, earth is closing. Thank you for your thoughtfulness."

The Reverend Mr. Hastings continued his way slowly up the path, whence the snow had been swept away. Illness was upon him, and he could not walk quickly. It was a dull night, and yet there was that peculiar light in the atmosphere, often seen when the earth is covered with snow. The door was held open, awaiting him; and the minister uncovered his head, and stepped in with his solemn greeting:

"PEACE BE TO THIS HOUSE AND TO ALL THAT DWELL IN IT!"

There could be no waiting for George Godolphin: the spirit might be on its wing. They gathered in the room, Grace, Margery, and Viscount Averil: and, the stillness broken only by the hushed sobs of Grace, Mr. Hastings administered the last rite of our religion to his dying child.

CHAPTER VII.

AT REST.

BREATHE softly, tread gently, for it is the chamber of the dying! The spirit is indeed on its wing, hovering on the very isthmus which separates time from eternity.

A small shaded lamp throws its subdued light upon the room, blending with the ruddier hue cast by the fire. The white, wan face of Maria Godolphin lies quietly on the not whiter pillow; her breath comes in short gasps, and may be heard at a distance; otherwise she is calm and still; the sweet soft eyes are open yet, and the world and its interests, so far as cognizance goes, has not closed. Meta, in her black frock, dressed as she had been in the day, is lying on the bed by her mother's side: one weak arm is thrown round the child, as if she could not part with her greatest earthly treasure; and George is sitting in a chair on the other side the bed, his elbow on the pillow, his face turned to catch every shade that may appear on that fading one, so soon to be lost to him for ever.

The silence was interrupted by the striking of the house-clock; twelve: and its strokes came through the doors of the room with preternatural loudness in the hushed stillness of midnight. Margery glided in. Margery and Jean were keeping watch over the fire in the next room, the sitting-room, ready for any services required of them: and they knew that services for the dead as well as for the living might be wanted that night.

The doctors had paid a last visit, superfluous as they knew it to be. Dr. Beale had come with the departure of his dinner guests; Mr. Snow earlier in the evening: she was dying, they said, calmly and peacefully: and those friends who had wished to take their farewell had taken it ere they left the house, leaving her, as she wished, alone with her husband.

Margery came in with a noiseless step. If Margery had come in once upon the same errand which brought her now, she had come in ten times. Maria turned her eyes towards her.

"She would be a sight better in bed. It has gone midnight. It can't do any good, her lying there."

Meta partly stirred her golden curls as she moved nearer to her mother, and Maria's feeble hand tightened its clasp on the little one. George nodded; and Margery went back rather in dudgeon, and gave the fire in the next room a fierce poke.

"It's not *well* to let her see a mortal die. Just you hold your tongue, Jean, about mother and child! Don't I know it's parting them as well as you?—but the parting *must* come, and before another hour is over; and I say it would be better to bring her away now. Master has no more sense than a calf, or he'd send her. Not he! He just gave me one of his looks, as much as to say, 'You be off again; she isn't coming.'"

"How does she seem now?" asked Jean, a tall woman, with a thin, straight figure, and an old-fashioned, large white cap.

"I saw no change. There won't be any till the minute comes."

On the table was a tray of cups and saucers. Margery went up to them and drew two from the rest. "We may as well have a drop o' tea now," she said, taking up a small black tea-pot that was standing on the hob—for the grate was old-fashioned. "Shall I cut you a bit of bread and butter, Jean?"

"No, thank you. I couldn't eat it."

They sat on either side the table, the tea-cups between them. Margery put the tea-pot back on the hob. Jean stirred her tea noiselessly.

"I have known those, as far gone as she, rally for hours," Jean remarked, in a half-whisper.

Margery shook her head. "*She* won't rally. It will be only the working out of my dream. I dreamt last night—— "

"Don't get talking of dreams now, Margery," interrupted Jean, with a shiver. "I never like to bring dreams up when the dead are about."

Margery cast a resentful glance at her. "Jean, woman, if you have laughed at my dreams once you have laughed at them a hundred times when we lived together at Ashlydyat, ridiculing and saying you never could believe in such things. You know you have."

"No more I don't believe in 'em," said Jane, taking little sips of her hot tea. "But it's not a pleasant subject for to-night. The child is to come to the old home, they say, to be brought up by my lady."

Margery grunted.

"Shall we have you at Ashlydyat again, Margery?"

"Now don't you bother your head about me, Jean, woman. Is it a time to cast one's thoughts about and lay out plans? Let the future take care of itself."

Jean remained silent after this rebuff and attended to her tea, which she could not get sufficiently cool to drink comfortably. She had been an inferior servant to Margery at Ashlydyat, in a measure under her control; and she still deferred to her in manner. Presently she began again.

"It's a curious complaint that your mistress has died of, Margery. Leastways it has a curious name. I made bold to ask Dr. Beale to-night what it was, when I went to open the gate for him, and he called it—what was it?—-atrophy. Atrophy: that was it. They could not at all class the disease of which Mrs. George Godolphin had died, he said, and were content to call it atrophy for want of a better name. I took leave to say that I didn't understand the word, and he explained that it meant a gradual wasting away of the system without apparent cause."

Margery did not reply for the moment: she was swelling with displeasure.

"Margery, what *is* atrophy, for I don't understand it a bit?"

"It's rubbish," flashed Margery—" as applied to my poor dear mistress. She has died of the trouble—that she couldn't speak of—that has eaten into her heart and cankered there—and broke it at the last. Atrophy! but those doctors must put a name to everything. Jean, woman, I have been with her all through it, and I tell you that it's the *trouble* that has killed her. She has had it on all sides, has felt it in more ways than the world gives her credit for. She never opened her lips to me about a thing—and perhaps it had been better if she had—but I have my eyes in my head, and I could see what it was doing for her. As I lay down in my clothes on this very sofa last night, for it wasn't up to my bed I went, with her so ill, I couldn't help thinking to myself, that if she could but have broken the ice and talked of her sorrows they might have worn off in time. It is burying the grief within people's own breasts that kills them."

Jean was silent. Margery began turning the grounds in her empty tea-cup round and round, staring dreamily at the forms they assumed.

"Hark!" cried Jean.

A sound was heard in the next room. Margery started from her chair and softly opened the door. But it was only her master, who had gone round the bed and was leaning over Meta. Margery closed the door again.

George had come to the conclusion that the child would be best in bed. Meta was lying perfectly still, looking earnestly at her mamma's face, so soon, so soon to be lost to her. He drew the hair from her brow as he spoke.

"You will be very tired, Meta. I think you must go to bed."

For answer Meta broke into a passionate storm of sobs. They roused Maria from her passive silence.

"Meta—darling," came forth the isolated words in the difficulty of her laboured breath—"I am going away, but you will come to me. You will be sure to come to me, for God has promised. I seem to have had the promise given to me, to hold it, now, and I shall carry it away with me. I am going to heaven. When the blind was drawn up yesterday morning and I saw the snow, it made me shiver, but I said there will be no snow in heaven. Meta, there will be only spring there; no sultry heat of summer, no keen winter's cold. Oh, my child! try to come to me, try always! I shall keep a place for you."

The minutes went on: the spirit fleeting, George watching with his aching heart. Soon she spoke again.

"Has it struck twelve?"

"Ten minutes ago."

"Then it is my birthday. I am twenty-eight to-day. It is young to die!"

Young to die! Yes, it was young to die: but there are some who can count time by sorrow, not by years.

"Don't grieve, George. It will pass so very soon, and you will come to me. Clad in our white robes, we shall rise at the Last Day to eternal life, and be together for ever and for ever."

The tears were dropping from his eyes. The grief of the present, the anguish of the parting, the remorse for the irrevocable past, in which he might have cherished her more tenderly had he foreseen this, and did not, were all too present to him. He laid his face on hers with a bitter cry.

"Forgive me before you go! Oh, my darling, forgive me all!"

There was no answering response, nothing but the feeble pressure of her hand as it held him there, and he started up to look at her. Ah no: there could never more be any response from those fading lips, never more, never more.

Had the hour come? George Godolphin's heart beat quicker, and he wildly kissed her with passionate kisses—as if that would keep within her the life that was ebbing. The loving eyes gazed at him still—it was he who had the last lingering look, not Meta.

But she was not to die just then : life was longer in finally departing. George—greedily watching her every breath, praying (who knows?) wild and unavailing prayers to Heaven that even yet a miracle might be wrought and she spared to him—supported her head on his arm. And the minutes went on and on.

Meta was very still. Her sobs had first subsided into a sudden catching of the breath now and then, but that was no longer heard. Maria moved uneasily, or strove to move, and looked up at George in distress; dying though she was, almost past feeling, the weight of the child's head had grown heavy on her side. He understood and went round to move Meta.

She had fallen asleep. Weary with the hour, the excitement, the still watching, the sobs, sleep had stolen unconsciously upon her: her wet eyelashes were closed, her breathing was regular, her hot cheeks were crimson. " Shall I take her to Margery?" he whispered.

Maria seemed to look approval, but her eyes followed the child as George raised her in his arms. It was impossible to mistake their yearning wish.

He carried the child round, he gently held her sleeping face to that of his wife, and the dying mother pressed her last feeble kiss upon the unanswering and unconscious lips. Then he took her and gave her to Margery.

The tears were in Maria's eyes when he returned to her, and he bent his face to catch the words that were evidently striving to be spoken.

" Love her always, George."

" Oh, my darling, there is no need to tell it me ! "

The answer seemed to have burst from him in anguish. There is no doubt that those few last hours had been of the bitterest anguish to George Godolphin: he had never gone through such before—he never would go through such again. It is well, it is well that these moments can come but once in a lifetime.

He hung over her, suppressing his emotion as he best could for her sake; he wiped the death-dews from her brow, fast gathering there. Her eyes never moved from him, her fingers to the last sought to entwine themselves with his. But soon the loving expression of those eyes faded into unconsciousness: they were open still, looking, as it may be, afar off: the recognition of him, her husband, the recollection of earthly things had passed away.

Suddenly there was a movement of the lips, a renewal in a faint degree of strength and energy; and George strove to catch the words. Her voice was dreamy; her eyes looked dreamily at him whom she would never more recognize until they should both have put on immortality.

" And the city has no need of the sun, neither of the moon, to shine in it : for the glory of God lightens it, and the Lamb is the light—— "

Even as she was speaking, the last words of her voice dropped, and was still. There was no sigh, there was no struggle; had Meta been looking on, the child's pulses would not have been stirred. Very, very gently had the spirit taken its flight.

George Godolphin let his head fall upon the pillow beside her. In his overwhelming grief for her? or in repentant prayer for himself? He alone knew. Let us leave it with him!

Once more, once more—I cannot help it, if you blame me for relating these things—the death-knell of All Souls' boomed out over Prior's Ash. People were rising in the morning when it struck upon their ear, and they held their breath to listen: three times *two*, and then the quick sharp strokes rang for the recently departed. Then it was for her who was known the previous night to be at the point of death! and they went out of their houses in the bleak winter's morning, and said to each other, as they took down their shutters, that poor Mrs. George Godolphin had really gone at last.

Poor Mrs. George Godolphin! Ay, they could speak of her considerately, kindly, regretfully now, but did they remember how they had once spoken of her? She had gone to the grave with her pain and sorrow—she had gone with the remembrance of their severe judgment, their harsh words, which had eaten into her too-sensitive heart: she had gone away from them, to be judged by One who would be more merciful than they had been.

Oh, if we could but be less harsh in judging our fellow-pilgrims! I have told you no idle tale, no false story conjured up by a plausible imagination. Prior's Ash lamented her in a startled sort of manner: their consciences pricked them sorely; and they would have given something to recall her back to life, now it was too late.

They stared at each other, shutters in hand, stunned as it were, with blank faces and repentant hearts. Somehow they had never believed she would really die; even the day before, when it had been talked of as all too probable, they had not fully believed it: she was young and beautiful, and it is not common for such to go. They recalled her in the several stages of her life: their Rector's daughter, the pretty child who had been born and reared among them, the graceful girl who had given her love to George Godolphin, the most attractive man in Prior's Ash; the faithful, modest wife, against whose fair fame never a breath of scandal had dared to come. It was all over now: she and her broken heart, her wrongs and her sorrows had been taken from their tender mercies to a land where neither wrongs nor sorrows can penetrate—where the hearts broken here by unkindness are made whole.

When Meta woke in the morning it was considerably beyond her usual hour, the result probably of her late vigil. Jean was in the room, not Margery. A moment's surprised stare, and then recollection flashed over her. She darted out of bed, her flushed cheeks and her bright eyes raised to Jean.

"I want mamma."

"Yes, dear," said Jean evasively. "I'll dress you, and then you shall go down."

"Where's Margery?"

"She has just stepped out on an errand."

"Is mamma in her room? Is she in her bed?"

"We'll go and see presently, dear," repeated Jean with the same evasion.

The worst way that any one can take is to attempt to deceive a thoughtful, sensitive child, whose fears may be already awakened: it is certain to defeat its own ends. Meta knew as well as Jean did that she was being purposely deceived, that there was something to tell which was not being told. She had no very defined idea of death, but a dread came over Meta that her mamma was in some manner gone out of the house, that she should never see her again: she backed from Jean's hand, dashed the door open, and flew down the stairs. Jean flew after her, crying and calling.

The noise surprised George Godolphin. He was in the parlour at the breakfast-table; sitting at the meal but not touching it. The consternation of Prior's Ash was great, but that was as nothing in comparison with his. George Godolphin was as a man bewildered. He could not realize the fact. Only four and twenty hours since he had received intimation of the danger, and now she was—there. He could not realize it. Though all yesterday afternoon, since his arrival, he had known there was no hope—though he had seen her die—though he had passed the hours since, lamenting her as much as he could do so in his first stunned state, yet he could not realize it. He was not casting much blame to himself: he was thinking how circumstances had worked against him and against Maria. His mind was yet in a chaos, and it was from this confused state that the noise outside disturbed him. Opening the door, the sight came full upon his view. The child flying down in her white night-dress, her naked feet scarcely touching the stairs, her eyes wild, her hot cheeks flaming, her golden hair entangled as she had slept.

"I want mamma," she cried, literally springing into his arms, as if for refuge. "Papa, I want mamma."

She burst into a storm of sobs distressing to hear; she clung to him, her little arms, her whole frame trembling. George, half unmanned, sat down before the fire, and pressed her to him in his strong arms.

"Bring a shawl," he said to Jean.

A warm grey shawl of chenille which Maria had often lately worn upon her shoulders was found by Jean, and George wrapped it round Meta as she lay in his arms, and he kept her there. Had Margery been present, she would probably have taken the young lady away by force, and dressed her, with a reprimand: but there was only Jean: and George had it all his own way.

He tried to comfort the grieved spirit; the little sobbing bosom that beat against his; but his efforts seemed useless, and the child's cry never ceased.

"I want mamma; I want to see mamma."

"Hush, Meta! Mamma"—George had to pause, himself—"mamma's gone. She——".

The words confirmed all her fears, and she strove to get off his lap in her excitement, interrupting his words. "Let me go and see her, papa! Is she in the grave with Uncle Thomas? Oh, let me go and see it! Grandpapa will show it to me."

How long it took to soothe her even to comparative calmness, George scarcely knew. He learnt more of Meta's true nature in that one interview than he had learnt in all her life before : and he saw that he must, in that solemn hour, speak to her as he would to a girl of twice her years.

" Mamma's gone to heaven, child; she is gone to be an angel with the great God. She would have stayed with us if she could, Meta, but death came and took her. She kissed you; she kissed you, Meta, with her last breath. You were fast asleep: you fell asleep by her side, and I held you to mamma for her last kiss, and soon after that she died."

Meta had kept still, listening: but now the sobs broke out again.

"Why didn't they wake me and let me see her? why did they take her away first? Oh, papa, though she is dead, I want to see her; I want to see mamma."

He felt inclined to take her into the room. Maria was looking very much like herself; far more so than she had looked in the last days of life : there was nothing ghastly, nothing repulsive, as is too often the case with the dead ; the sweet face of life looked scarcely less sweet now.

" Mamma *that was* is there still, Meta," he said, indicating the next room. " The spirit is gone to heaven; you know that : the body, that which you used to call mamma, will be here yet a little while, and then it will be laid by Uncle Thomas, to wait for the resurrection of the Last Day. Meta, if I should live to come home from India; that is, if I am in my native land when my time comes to die, they will lay me beside her——"

He stopped abruptly. Meta had lifted her head and was looking at him with a wild, questioning expression ; as if she could not at first understand or believe his words. " Mamma is there?"

"Yes. But she is dead now, Meta; she is not living."

"Oh, take me to her! Papa, take me to her!"

" Listen, Meta. Mamma is changed; she looks cold and white, and her eyes are shut, and she does not stir. I would take you in: but I fear—I don't know whether you would like to look at her."

But there might be no denial now that the hope had been given; the child would have broken her heart over it. George Godolphin rose; he pressed the little head upon his shoulder, and carried her to the door, the shawl well wound round her body, her warm feet hanging down. Once in the room, he laid his hand upon the golden curls, to insure that the face was not raised until he saw fit that it should be, and bore her straight to the head of the bed. Then, holding her in his arms very tightly that she might feel sensibly his protection, he suffered her to look full upon the white face lying there.

One glance, and Meta turned and buried her head upon him; he could feel her trembling; and he began to question his own wisdom in bringing her in. Another minute, and she looked back and took a longer gaze.

" That's not mamma," she said, bursting into tears.

George sat down on a chair close by, and laid her wet cheek against his, and hid his eyes amidst her curls. His emotion had spent itself in the long night, and he thought he could control it now.

"That is mamma, Meta; your mother and my dear wife. It is all that is left of her. Oh, Meta! if we had only known earlier that she was going to die!"

"It does not look like mamma."

"The moment death comes, the change begins. It has begun in mamma. Do you understand me, Meta? In a few days I shall hear read over her by your grandpapa——" George stopped: it suddenly occurred to him that the Reverend Mr. Hastings would not officiate this time; and he amended his sentence. "I shall hear read over her the words she has I know often read to you; how the corruptible body must die, and be buried in the earth as a grain of wheat is, ere it can be changed and put on immortality."

"Will she never come again?" sobbed Meta.

"Never here, never again. We shall go to her."

Meta sobbed on. "I want mamma! I want mamma, who talked to me and nursed me. Mamma loved us."

"Yes, she loved us," he said, his heart wrung with the recollection of the past: "we shall never find any one else to love us as she loved. Meta, child, listen! Mamma lives still; she is looking down from heaven now, and sees and hears us; she loves us, and will love us for ever. And when our turn shall come to die, I hope—I hope— we shall have learnt all that she has learnt, so that God may take us to her."

It was of no use prolonging the scene: George still questioned his judgment in allowing Meta to enter upon it. But as he rose to carry her away, the child turned her head with a sharp eager motion to take a last look. A last look at the still form, the dead face of her who yesterday only had been as they were.

Margery had that instant come in, and was standing in her bonnet in the sitting-room. To describe her face of surprised consternation when she saw Meta carried out of the chamber, would take time and trouble. "You can dress her, Margery," George said, giving the child into her arms.

But for his subdued tones, and the evident emotion which lay upon him all too palpably in spite of his efforts to suppress it, Margery might have given her private opinion of the existing state of things. As it was, she confined her anger to dumb-show. Jerking Meta to her, with a half fond, half fierce gesture, she lifted her hand in dismay at sight of the naked feet, turned her own gown up, and flung it over them.

CHAPTER VIII.

A SAD PARTING.

AGAIN another funeral in All Souls' Church, another opening of the vault of the Godolphins! But it was not All Souls' Rector to officiate this time; he stood at the grave with George. Isaac Hastings had come down from London, Harry had come from his tutorship; Lord Averil was again there, and Mr. Crosse had asked to attend. Prior's Ash looked out on the funeral with regretful eyes, saying one to another, what a sad thing it was for her, only twenty-eight, to die.

George Godolphin, contriving to maintain an outward calmness, turned away when it was over. Not yet to the mourning-coach that waited for him, but through the little gate leading to the Rectory. He was about to leave Prior's Ash for good that night, and common courtesy demanded that he should say a word of farewell to Mrs. Hastings.

In the darkened drawing-room with Grace and Rose, in their new mourning attire, sat Mrs. Hastings: George Godolphin half started back as they rose to greet him. He did not stay to sit: he stood by the fireplace, his hat in his hand, its flowing crape almost touching the ground.

"I will say good-bye to you, now, Mrs. Hastings."

"You really leave to-night?"

"By the seven o'clock train. Will you permit me to express my hope that a brighter time may yet dawn for you; to assure you that no effort on my part shall be spared to conduce to it?"

He spoke in a low, quiet, meaning tone, and he held her hand between his. Mrs. Hastings could not misunderstand him—that he was hinting at a hope of reimbursing somewhat of their pecuniary loss.

"Thank you for your good wishes," she said, keeping down the tears. "You will allow me—you will speak to Lady Averil to allow me to have the child here for a day sometimes?"

"Need you ask it?" he answered, a generous warmth in his tone. "Cecil, I am quite sure, recognizes your right in the child at least in an equal degree with her own, and is glad to recognize it. Fare you well; fare you well, dear Mrs. Hastings."

He went out, shaking hands with Grace and Rose as he passed, thinking how much he had always liked Mrs. Hastings, with her courteous manners and gentle voice, so like those of his lost wife. The Rector met him in the passage, and George held out his hand.

"I shall not see you again, sir. I leave to-night."

The Rector took the hand. "I wish you a safe voyage!" he said. "I hope things will be more prosperous with you in India than they have been latterly here!"

"We have all need to wish that," was George's answer. "Mr. Hastings, promises from me might be regarded as valueless, but this much I wish to say ere we part : that I carry the weight of my debt to you about me, and I will lessen it should it be in my power. You will "—dropping his voice—" you will see that the inscription is properly placed on the tombstone ? "

" I will. Have you given orders for it ? "

" Oh yes. Farewell, sir. Farewell, Harry," he added, as the two sons came in. " Isaac, I shall see you in London."

He passed swiftly out to the mourning-coach, and was driven home. Above everything on earth, George hated this leave-taking : but there were two or three to whom it had to be spoken.

Not until dusk did he go up to Ashlydyat. He called in at Lady Godolphin's Folly as he passed it : she was his father's widow, and Bessy was there. My lady was very cool. My lady told him that it was his place to give the refusal of Meta to her : and she should never forgive the slight. From the very moment she heard that Maria's life was in danger, she made up her mind to break through her rules of keeping children at a distance, and to take the child. She should have reared her in every luxury as Miss Godolphin of Ashlydyat, and have left her a handsome fortune : as it was, she washed her hands of her. George thanked her for her good intention as a matter of course ; but his heart leaped within him at the thought that Meta was safe and secure with Cecil : he would have taken her and Margery out to make acquaintance with the elephants, rather than have left Meta to Lady Godolphin.

" She'll get over the smart, George," whispered Bessy, as she came out to bid him God-speed. " I shall be having the child here some-times, you know. My lady's ail talk : she never cherishes resentment long."

He entered the old home, Ashlydyat, and was left alone with Meta at his own request. She was in the deepest black : crape tucks on her short frock ; not a bit of white to be seen about her, except her socks and the tips of her drawers ; and Cecil had bought her a jet necklace of round beads, with a little black cross hanging from it on her neck. George sat down and took her on his knee. What with the drawn blinds and the growing twilight, the room was almost dark, and he had to look closely at the little face turned to him. She was very quiet, rather pale, as if she had grieved a good deal in the last few days.

" Meta," he began, and then he stopped to clear his husky voice— " Meta, I am going away."

She made no answer. She buried her face upon him and began to cry softly. It was no news to her, for Cecil had talked to her the pre-vious night. But she clasped her arms tightly round him as if she could not let him go, and began to tremble.

" Meta !—my child ! "

" I want mamma ! " burst from the little full heart. " I want mamma to be with me again. Is she gone away for ever ? Is she put down in the grave with Uncle Thomas ? Oh, papa ! I want to see her ! "

A moment's struggle with himself, and then George Godolphin gave way to the emotion which he had so successfully restrained in the churchyard. They sobbed together, the father and child : her face against his, the sobs bursting freely from his bosom. He let them come; loud, passionate, bitter sobs; unchecked, unsubdued. Do not despise him for it! they are not the worst men who can thus give way to the vehemence of our common nature.

It spent itself after a time; such emotion must spend itself; but it could not wholly pass yet. Meta was the first to speak: the same vain wish breaking from her, the same cry.

"I want mamma! Why did she go away for ever?"

"Not for ever, Meta. Only for a time. Oh, child, we shall go to her: we shall go to her in a little while. Mamma's gone to be an angel; to keep a place for us in heaven."

"How long will it be?"

"Not a moment of our lives but it will draw nearer and nearer. Meta, it may be well for us that those we love should go on first, or we might never care to go thither ourselves."

She lay more quietly. George laid his hand upon her head, unconsciously playing with her golden hair, his tears dropping on it.

"You must think of mamma always, Meta. Think that she is looking down at you, on all you do, and try and please her. She was very good: and you must be good, making ready to go to her."

A renewed burst of sobs came from the child. George waited, and then resumed.

"When I come back—if I live to come back; or when you come to me in India; at any rate when I see you again, Meta, you will probably be grown up; no longer a child, but a young lady. If I shall only find you like mamma was in all things, I shall be happy. Do you understand, darling?"

"Yes," she sobbed.

"Good, and gentle, and kind, and lady-like,—and remembering always that there's another world, and that mamma has gone on to it. I should like to have kept you with me, Meta, but it cannot be: I must go out alone. You will not quite forget me, will you?"

She put up her hand and her face to his, and moaned in her pain. George laid his aching brow on hers. He knew that it might be the last time they should meet on earth.

"I shall write to you by every mail, Meta, and you must write to me. You can put great capital letters together now, and that will do to begin with. And," his voice faltered, "when you walk by mamma's grave on Sundays—and see her name there—you will remember her—and me. You will think how we are separated: mamma in heaven; I, in a far-off land; you here: but you know the separation will not be for ever, and each week will bring us nearer to its close—its close in some way. If—if we never meet again on earth, Meta——"

"Oh don't, papa! I want you to come back to me."

He choked down his emotion. He took the little face in his hands and kissed it fervently: in that moment, in his wrung feelings, he almost wished he had no beloved child to abandon.

"You must be called by your own name now. I should wish it. Meta was all very well," he continued, half to himself, "when *she* was here; that the names should not interfere with each other. Be a good child, my darling. Be very obedient to Aunt Cecil, as you used to be to mamma.

"Aunt Cecil is not mamma," said Meta, her little heart swelling.

"No, my darling, but she will be to you as mamma, and she and Lord Averil will love you very much. I wish—I wish I could have kept you with me, Meta!"

She wished it also. If ever a child knew what an aching heart was, she knew it then.

"And now I must go," he added—for indeed he did not care to prolong the pain. "I shall write to you from London, Meta, and I shall write you quite a packet when I am on board ship. You must get on well with your writing, so as to be able soon to read my letters yourself. Farewell, farewell, my darling child!"

How long she clung to him; how long he kept her clinging, he gave no heed. When the emotion on both sides was spent, he took her by the right hand and led her to the next room. Lady Averil came forward.

"Cecil," he said, his voice quiet and subdued, "she must be called Maria now—in remembrance of her mother."

"Yes," said Cecil eagerly. "We should all like it. Sit down, George. Lord Averil has stepped out somewhere, but he will not be long."

"I cannot stay. I shall see him outside, I dare say. If not, he will come to the station. Will you say to him——"

A low burst of tears from the child interrupted the sentence. George, in speaking to Cecil, had loosed her hand, and she laid her head down on a sofa to cry. He took her up in his arms, and she clung to him tightly: it was only the old scene over again, and George felt that they were not alone now. He imprinted a last kiss upon her face, and gave her to his sister.

"She had better be taken away, Cecil."

Lady Averil, with many loving words, carried her outside the door, sobbing as she was, and called to her maid. "Be very kind to her," she whispered. "It is a sad parting. And—Harriet—henceforth she is to be called by her proper name—Maria."

"She will get over it in a day or two, George," said Lady Averil, returning.

"Yes, I know that," he answered, his face turned from Cecil. "Cherish the remembrance of her mother within her as much as you possibly can, Cecil: I should wish her to grow up like Maria."

"If you would only stay a last hour with us!"

"I can't; I can't: it is best that I should go. I do not know what the future may bring forth," he lingered to say. "Whether I shall come home—or live to come home; or she, when she is older, come out to me: it is all uncertain."

"Were I you, George, I would not indulge the thought of the latter. She will be better here—as it seems to me."

"Yes—there's no doubt of it. But the separation is a cruel one. However—the future must be left. God bless you, Cecil! and thank you ever for your kindness."

The tears rolled down her cheeks as he bent to kiss her. "George," she whispered timidly—"if I might only ask you one question."

"Ask me anything."

"Is—have you any intention—shall you be likely to think of—of replacing Maria by Charlotte Pain—of making her your wife?"

"Replacing *Maria by her!*" he echoed, his face flushing. "Heaven forgive you for thinking it!"

The question cured George's present emotion more effectually than anything else could have done. But his haughty anger against Cecil was unreasonable, and he felt that it was so.

"Forgive me, my dear: but it sounded so like an insult to my dear wife. Be easy: *she* will never replace Maria."

In the porch, as George went out, he met Lord Averil hastening in. Lord Averil would have put his arm within George's to walk with him through the grounds, but George drew back.

"No, not to-night: let me go alone. I am not fit for companionship. Good-night. Good-bye," he added, his voice hoarse. "I thought to say a word of gratitude to you, for the past, for the present, but I cannot. If I live——"

"Don't say 'if,' George: go away with a good heart, and take my best wishes with you. A new land and a new life! you may yet live down the past."

Their hands lingered together in a firm pressure, and George turned away from Ashlydyat for the last time. Ashlydyat that might have been his.

CHAPTER IX.

A SAFE VOYAGE TO HIM!

WAS it ever your fate or fortune to be on board an Indian vessel when it was just about to start? If so, there's no doubt you retain a more vivid than agreeable reminiscence of the reigning confusion. Passengers coming on at the last moment and going frantic over their luggage or the discovered inconveniences of their cabins; cords and ropes creaking and coiling; sailors shouting, officers commanding; boxes shooting up from the boats to the deck, and to your feet, only in turn to be shot down again to the hold!—it is Bedlam gone frantic, and nothing less.

On a fine ship, anchored off Gravesend, this scene was taking place on a crisp day early in January. A bright, inspiriting, sunny day, giving earnest—if there's anything in the popular belief—of a bright voyage. One gentleman stood aloof from the general *mêlée*. He had been on board half an hour or more; had seen to his cabin, his berth, his baggage—as much of the latter as he could see to; and now stood alone watching the turmoil. Others, passengers, had come on board in groups, surrounded by hosts of friends; he came alone: a tall and very distinguished-looking man, attired in the deepest mourning, with a grey plaid crossed on his shoulder.

As if jealous that the ship should have all the confusion to itself, the shore was getting up a little on its own account. Amidst the drays, the trucks, the carts . amidst the cases and packages, which were heaped on the bank, not all, it was to be hoped, for that ship, or she would never get off to-day; amidst the numerous crowds of living beings, idlers and workers, that such a scene brings together, there came something into the very throng of them, scattering everything that could be scattered right and left.

An exceedingly remarkable carriage, of the style that may be called "dashing," especially if height be any criterion, its wheels red and green, its horses of high mettle, and a couple of fierce dogs barking and leaping round it. The scattered people looked up in astonishment to see a lady guiding those horses, and deemed at first that the sun, shining right into their eyes, had deceived them: pawing, snorting, prancing, fiery animals; which, far from being spent by their ten or twelve miles journey, looked as if they were eager to start upon another, The lady managed them admirably. A very handsome lady was she, of the same style as the carriage; dashing, with jet-black eyes, large and free, and a scarlet feather in her hat that might have been found nearly thirty-six inches long, had it been measured from top to tip. A quiet little gentleman, slight and fair, sat beside her, and a groom lounged grandly with folded arms in the back seat. She, on her high cushions, was almost a yard above either of them : the little gentleman in fact was completely eclipsed : and she held the reins in her white gauntleted hands and played gallantly with the whip, perfectly at ease, conscious that she was those foaming steeds' master Suddenly, without the least warning, she drew them back on their haunches.

"There she is ! in the middle of the stream. Can't you read it, Dolf ? *The Indus*. How stupid of the people to tell us she was lying lower down ! "

Jumping from the carriage without waiting to be assisted, she left the groom in charge and made her way to the pier, condescendingly taking the gentleman's arm as she hastened up it, and hissing off the dogs as a hint that they were to remain behind. I am sure you cannot need an introduction to either of these people, but you shall have it for all that; Mr and Mrs. Rodolf Pain.

She, Charlotte, did all the acting, and the talking too. Her husband had always been retiring in manner, as you may remember; and he had grown far more retiring than he used to be. Charlotte bargained for a boat : and they were pulled to the ship's side.

For a few moments they had to take their chance : they made only two more in the general confusion : but Charlotte seized upon a handsome young man with a gold band upon his cap, who was shouting out orders.

"Can you tell me whether Mr. George Godolphin has come on board yet ? "

"Mr. George Godolphin," repeated the young officer, cutting short some directions midway, and looking half-bewildered in the general disorder.

"Bound for Calcutta," explained Charlotte.

"I can inquire. Tymms," beckoning to him one of the middies,

" go and ask the steward whether a gentleman of the name of Godolphin has come down."

But there was no need of further search. Charlotte's restless eyes had caught sight of George—the solitary passenger in mourning whom you saw standing alone. She and Mr. Pain made the best of their way to him, over the impediments blocking up the deck.

He did not see their approach. He was leaning over the vessel on the side opposite to that facing the shore, and Charlotte gave him a smart rap on the arm with her gauntlet-glove.

" Now, Mr. George Godolphin! what do you say for your manners !"

He turned quickly, his face flushing slightly with surprise when he saw them standing there : and he shook hands with them both.

" I ask what you have to say for your manners, Mr. George? The very idea of your leaving England for good, and never calling to say good-bye to us ! "

" I met Mr. Pain a day or two ago," said George. " He——"

" Met Mr. Pain ! what on earth if you did ! " interrupted Charlotte. " Mr. Pain's not me. You might have found time to dine with us. I have a great mind to quarrel with you, George Godolphin, by way of leave-taking."

Something like a smile crossed George's lips. " The fact is, I thought I might have seen you at the Verralls', Mrs. Pain. I went there for half an hour yesterday. I charged Mrs. Verrall——"

" Rubbish ! " retorted Charlotte. " When you must have known we had moved into a house at Shooter's Hill, you could not suppose we were still at the Verralls'. Our catching you this morning here was a mere chance. We stayed late in town yesterday afternoon at the furniture warehouse, and, in driving back down the Strand, saw Isaac Hastings, so I pulled up to ask what had become of you, and whether you were dead or alive. He informed us you were to sail to-day from Gravesend, and I told Dolf I should drive down. But it *is* ill-mannered of you, Mr. George."

" You will readily understand, that since my last return from Prior's Ash, I have not felt inclined for visiting," he said in a low grave tone, unconsciously glancing at his black attire. " I intended you no discourtesy, Mrs. Pain : but, for one thing, I did not know where you might be met with."

" And couldn't find out ! " retorted Charlotte. " Dolf could have given you the address, I suppose, the other day, had you asked. He's too great a fool to think to give it of his own accord."

George looked at " Dolf," whom his wife seemed so completely to ignore ; looked at him with a pleasant smile, as if he would atone for Charlotte's rudeness. " We were not together a minute, were we, Mr. Pain ? I was in a hurry, and you seemed in one also."

" Don't say any more about it, Mr. Godolphin," spoke Dolf, as resentfully as he dared. " That's just like her ! Making a fuss over nothing ! Of course you could not be expected to visit at such a time : and any one but Charlotte would have the good feeling to see it. I am pleased to be able to see you here, and wish you a pleasant voyage ; but I remonstrated with her this morning, that it was scarcely the right thing to intrude upon you. But she never listens, you know."

" *You* needn't have come," snapped Charlotte.

"And then you would have gone on at me about my bad manners, as you have to Mr. Godolphin! One never knows how to please you, Charlotte."

George resumed: to break the silence possibly, more than from any other motive. "Have you settled at Shooter's Hill?"

"Settled!" shrieked Charlotte; "settled at Shooter's Hill! Where it's ten miles, good, from a theatre or any other place of amusement! No, thank you. A friend of Verrall's had this place to let for a few weeks, and Dolf was idiot enough to take it——"

"You consented first, Charlotte," interrupted poor Dolf.

"Which I never should have done had I reflected on the bother of getting up to town," said Charlotte equably. "Settled at Shooter's Hill! I'd as soon do as you are going to do, Mr. George—bury myself alive in Calcutta. We have taken on lease a charming house in Belgravia, and shall enter on a succession of dinner-parties: one a week we think of giving during the season. We shall not get into it much before February: it takes some time to choose furniture."

"I hate dinner-parties," said Dolf ruefully.

"You are not obliged to appear at them," said Charlotte with much graciousness. "I can get your place filled up at table, I dare say. What *is* that noise and scuffling?"

"They are weighing anchor," replied George. "We shall soon be on the move."

"I hear that great alterations are being made at Ashlydyat," remarked Charlotte.

"Only on the spot called the Dark Plain. The archway is taken down, and a summer-house is being built on the site. An elaborate sort of summer-house, for it is to contain three or four rooms, I believe. It will have a fine view."

"And what of those ugly gorse-bushes?"

"They will be cleared away, and the place laid out as a garden."

"Is my lady starring it at the Folly?"

"Scarcely: just now," quietly answered George.

"Miss Godolphin has gone to Scotland, I hear."

"Yes. Bessy will reside with Lady Godolphin."

"And tart Margery? What has become of her?"

"She remains with Maria at Ashlydyat."

Charlotte opened her eyes—Charlotte had a habit of opening them when puzzled or surprised. "Maria! Who is Maria?"

"The child. We call her by her proper name now."

"Oh, by the way, I had nearly forgotten it," returned Charlotte in the old good-natured tone: for it may be remarked, that during the interview her tone had been what she had just called Margery—tart. "I should like to have the child up on a visit when we get into our house, and astonish her mind with the wonders of London. I suppose Lady Averil will make no objection?"

A very perceptible flush, red and haughty, dyed the face of George Godolphin. "You are very kind to think of it, Mrs. Pain; but I fear Lady Averil would not consent. Indeed, I have desired that the child may not visit, except amidst her immediate relatives."

"As you please," said Charlotte resentfully. "Dolf, I think we may as well be moving. I only meant it as a kindness to the child."

"And I thank you for it," said George warmly. "For all the kindness you have shown her, Mrs. Pain, I thank you, sincerely and heartily. Take care!"

He interposed to prevent a rope, that was being borne along, from touching her. Charlotte began in earnest to think it was time to move, unless she would be carried down the river in the ship.

"When shall you come back?" she asked him.

He shook his head. He could not tell any more than she could. The future was all uncertain and indistinct.

"Well, you won't forget to find us out whenever you do come?" returned Charlotte.

"Certainly not. Thank you."

"Do you know," cried Charlotte impulsively, "you are strangely different in manner, George Godolphin! You have grown as cold and formal as a block of ice. Hasn't he, Dolf?"

"If he has, it's your fault," was the satisfactory answer of Dolf. "You keep firing off such a heap of personal questions, Charlotte. I see no difference in Mr. Godolphin: but he has had a good deal of trouble, you know."

"Shall we ever hear of you?" continued Charlotte, pushing back Dolf with her elbow, and completely eclipsing his meek face with her sweeping scarlet feather.

"No doubt you will, Mrs. Pain, from one source or another. Not that I shall be a voluminous correspondent with England, I expect: except, perhaps, with Ashlydyat."

"Well, fare you well, George," she said, holding out both her gauntleted hands. "You seem rather cranky this morning, but I forgive you: it *is* trying to the spirits to leave one's native place for good and all. I wish you all good luck with my best heart!"

"Thank you," he said, taking the hands within his own and shaking them: "thank you always. Good-bye. Good-bye, Mr. Pain."

Mr. Pain shook hands less demonstratively than his wife, and his leave-taking, if quiet, was not less sincere. George piloted them to the gangway, and saw them pulled ashore in the little boat.

They ascended to the carriage, which to all appearance had been keeping up a perpetual commotion since they left it, the fault probably of its horses and dogs; and Charlotte, taking her high seat, dashed away in style; her whip flourishing, the dogs barking, her red feather tossing and gleaming. What she will do when these feathers go out of fashion it's hard to say: Charlotte could hardly stir out without one.

And by-and-by, the anchor up, the tug attached, the good ship *Indus* was fairly on her way, being towed smoothly down the river under command of her pilot. The passengers were tormenting themselves still: the sailors seemed to be perpetually hurrying hither and thither, the steward was in a tumult: but George Godolphin, wrapped in his grey plaid, remained in his place, quiet and still, gazing out over the bows of the vessel. What were his reflections, as his native land began to recede from his eyes? Did he regret it? Did he regret the position he had lost; the ruin he had wrought; the death of his wife? Did he, finally, regret the inevitable PAST, with all its mistakes and sins?—and think that if it could only come over again, he would act differently? Possibly so. Once he lifted his hat, and pushed the golden hair further from his brow, from his handsome face, not less bright or handsome than of yore—except in its expression. In that, there was an unmistakable look of weary sadness, never before seen on the features of gay George Godolphin.

And when, hours after, the rest of the cabin passengers were summoned to dinner, he never stirred, but kept his place there, looking far into the dusky night, glancing up at the stars that came glittering out in the blue canopy of heaven.

A safe landing to him on the shores of Calcutta! A safe and sure landing on a different shore that must come after it!

And Mr. and Mrs. Pain's dinner-parties in Belgravia are a great success.

THE END.